THE SHADOW OF TYBURN TREE

DENNIS WHEATLEY

DENNIS WHEATLEY

THE SHADOW OF TYBURN TREE

Frontispiece Portrait by
MARK GERSON

Original Illustrations by
JOHN HOLDER

Distributed by
HERON BOOKS

Published by arrangement with
Hutchinson and Co. (Publishers) Ltd.

© *Brook-Richleau Ltd.*
© 1972, *Illustrations, Edito-Service S.A., Geneva*

3933

CONTENTS

I	The Best of Friends	1
II	A Losing Battle	13
III	A Desperate Gamble	23
IV	A Night in a Life-Time	41
V	A Bid for Life	55
VI	The Parting of the Ways	73
VII	Young Mr. Pitt	93
VIII	The *Bal Masqué*	112
IX	The Uncrowned Queen	131
X	The Two Tests of Natalia Andreovna	148
XI	The Inexperienced Spy	160
XII	Unmasked Again	179
XIII	Hell's Kitchen	194
XIV	The Order of Death	209
XV	The Plot	222
XVI	The Ambush	235
XVII	Penalty for Murder	245
XVIII	Her Majesty's Pleasure	263
XIX	Like a Sheep to the Slaughter	276
XX	For the Honour of England	293
XXI	In Baulk	318
XXII	The Fate of the Nation	333
XXIII	The Shadow of Tyburn Tree	345

CHAPTER I

THE BEST OF FRIENDS

GEORGINA ETHEREDGE'S limpid black eyes looked even larger than usual as, distended in a semi-hypnotic trance, they gazed unwinkingly into a crystal goblet full of water. It stood in the centre of a small buhl table, at the far side of which sat Roger Brook. His firm, well-shaped hands were thrust out from elegant lace ruffles to clasp her beringed fingers on either side of the goblet while, in a low, rich voice, she foretold something of what the future held in store.

She was twenty-one and of a ripe, luscious beauty. Her hair was black, and the dark ringlets that fell in casual artistry about the strong column of her throat shimmered with those warm lights that testify to abounding health; her skin was flawless, her full cheeks were tinted with a naturally high colour; her brow was broad and her chin determined. She was wearing a dress of dark red velvet, the wide sleeves and hem of which were trimmed with bands of sable, and although it was not yet midday the jewels she was wearing would have been counted by most other women sufficient for a presentation at Court.

He was some fifteen months younger, but fully grown and just over six feet tall. His white silk stockings set off well-modelled calves; his hips were narrow, his shoulders broad and his back muscular. There was nothing effeminate about his good looks except the eyes, which were a deep, vivid blue with dark, curling lashes, and they had been the envy of many a woman. His brown hair was brushed in a high roll back from his forehead and tied with a cherry-coloured ribbon at the nape of his neck. His coat, too, was cherry-coloured, with a high double collar edged with gold galloon, and open at the neck displaying the filmy lace of his cravat. His teeth were good; his expression frank and friendly.

They were in Georgina's boudoir at her country home; and, having breakfasted together at eleven o'clock, were passing away the time until the arrival of the guests that she was expecting for the week-end.

So far, the things she had seen in the water-filled goblet had been a little vague and far from satisfactory. For him a heavy loss at cards; concerning her a letter by a foreign hand in which she suspected treachery; for both of them journeys across water, but in two different ships that passed one another in the night.

For a moment she was silent, then she said, "Why, Roger, I see a wedding ring. How prodigious strange. 'Tis the last thing I would have expected. Alack, alack! It fades before I can tell for which of us 'tis intended. But wait; another picture forms. Mayhap we'll learn. . . . Nay; this has no connection with the last. 'Tis a court of justice. I see a judge upon a bench. He wears a red robe trimmed with ermine and a great, full-bottomed wig. 'Tis a serious matter that he tries. We are both there in the court and we are both afraid—afraid for one another. But which of us is on trial I cannot tell. The court is fading—fading. Now something else is forming, where before was the stern face of the judge. It begins to solidify. It—it. . . ."

Suddenly Roger felt her fingers stiffen. Next second she had torn them from his grasp and her terrified cry rang through the richly-furnished room.

"No, no! Oh, God; it can't be true! I'll not believe it!"

With a violent gesture she swept the goblet from the table; the water fountained across the flowered Aubusson carpet and the crystal goblet shattered against the leg of a lacquer cabinet. Her eyes staring, her full red lips drawn back displaying her strong white teeth in a Medusa-like grimace, Georgina gave a moan, lurched forward, and buried her face in her hands.

Roger had started to his feet at her first cry. Swiftly he slipped round the table and placed his hands firmly on her bowed shoulders.

"Georgina! Darling!" he cried anxiously. "What ails thee? In Heaven's name, what dids't thou see?"

As she made no reply he shook her gently; then, parting her dark ringlets he kissed her on the nape of the neck, and murmured, "Come, my precious. Tell me, I beg! What devil's vision was it that has upset thee so?"

" 'Twas—'twas a gallows, Roger; a gallows-tree," she stammered, bursting into a flood of tears.

Roger's firm mouth tightened and his blue eyes narrowed in swift resistance to so terrible an omen; but his face paled slightly. Georgina had inherited the gift of second-sight from her Gipsy mother, and he had known too many of her prophecies come true to take her sooth-saying lightly. Yet he managed to keep his voice steady as he said, "Oh come, m'dear. On this occasion your imagination has played you a scurvy trick. You've told me many times that you often see things but for an instant. Like as not it was a signpost that you glimpsed, yet not clearly enough to read the lettering on it."

"Nay!" she exclaimed, choking back her sobs. " 'Twas a gibbet, I tell thee! I saw it so plainly that I could draw the very graining of the wood; and—and from it there dangled a noose of rope all ready for a hanging."

A fresh outburst of weeping seized her, so Roger slipped one arm under her knees and the other round her waist, then picked her up from her chair. She was a little above medium height and possessed the bounteous curves considered the high-spot of beauty in the female figure of the eighteenth century, so she was no light weight. But his muscles were hardened with riding and fencing. Without apparent effort he carried her to the leopard-headed, gilt day-bed in the centre of the room, and laid her gently upon its button-spotted yellow satin cushioning.

It was here, in her exotic boudoir reclining gracefully on her day-bed, a vision of warm, self-possessed loveliness, that the rich and fashionable Lady Etheredge was wont to receive her most favoured visitors and enchant them with her daring wit. But now, she was neither self-possessed nor in a state to bandy trivialities with anyone. Having implicit belief in her uncanny gift, she was still suffering from severe shock, and had become again a very frightened little girl.

Roger fetched her the smelling-salts that she affected, but rarely used in earnest, from a nearby table; then ran into her big bedroom next door, soused his handkerchief from a cut-glass decanter of Eau de Cologne and, running back, spread it as a bandage over her fore-head. For a few moments he patted her hands and murmured endear-ments; then, realising that he could bring her no further comfort till the storm was over, he left her to dab at those heart-wrecking eyes that always seemed to have a faint blue smudge under them, with a wisp of cambric, and walked over to one of the tall windows.

It was a Saturday, and the last day of March in the year 1788. George III, now in the twenty-seventh year of his reign, was King of England, and the younger Pitt, now twenty-eight years of age, had already been his Prime Minister for four and a quarter years. The Opposition, representing the vested interests of the powerful Whig nobles, and led by Charles James Fox, was still formidable; but the formerly almost autocratic King and the brilliant, idealistic, yet hard-headed son of the Great Commoner, with a little give and take on both sides, between them now controlled the destinies of Britain.

The American colonies had been lost to the Mother country just before the younger Pitt came to power. Between the years '78 and '83 Britain had stood alone against a hostile world; striving to retain her fairest possessions in the distant Americas while menaced at home, locked in bitter conflict upon every sea with the united power of France, Spain and the Dutch, and further hampered by the armed neutrality of Russia, Prussia, Denmark, Sweden and Austria also arrayed against her.

From this desperate struggle Britain had emerged still proud and defiant, having given her continental enemies harder knocks than she sustained; but so exhausted by the effort that the great majority of her people believed that she was ruined for good and, still isolated as she was, must now sink to the station of a second-class power.

Yet, in four short years the colossal industry and ability of young Billy Pitt, both in the sphere of commerce and foreign relations, had lifted his country once again to first place among the nations. His financial genius had restored her prosperity and his broad vision had gained her friends. In '86 he had struck at the roots of England's most cancerous, wasting sore—her centuries-old feud with the French—by a commercial treaty which was now rapidly bringing about a better understanding between the two countries. And in recent months he had successfully negotiated defensive treaties with both the Dutch

3

and the King of Prussia; thus forming the Triple Alliance as an insurance against future aggression. Since the Peace of Versailles in '83 his wise policies had done more than those of any other statesman to stabilise a shaken world, and it seemed that Europe might now look forward to a long period of tranquillity.

Roger Brook was justly proud that, young as he was, he had, in some small measure, secretly contributed to the new Alliance[1]; and, during the past five months, he had put all thought of work from him, to enjoy to the full the almost forgotten feeling of well-being and security that Mr. Pitt had re-won for the people of England.

Several of these care-free weeks Roger had spent with his parents, Rear-Admiral and Lady Marie Brook, at his home on the outskirts of Lymington, in Hampshire; others he had passed in London; frequently going to the gallery of the House to hear the learned, well-reasoned but tedious orations of Edmund Burke, the melodious, forceful eloquence of Fox, and the swift, incisive logic of the young Prime Minister; but he had devoted the greater part of his time to the tomboy companion of his early adolescence, who had since become the beautiful Lady Etheredge.

Meeting again after a separation of four years they had seen one another with new eyes. During most of November they had danced, laughed and supped together in the first throes of a hectic love affair; and since then he had been a frequent guest here at "Stillwaters," the magnificent setting she had secured for her flamboyant personality down in the heart of the Surrey woods, near Ripley.

The stately mansion had been designed by William Kent, some half a century earlier, and was a perfect specimen of Palladian architecture. Forty-foot columns supported its domed, semi-circular, central portico; from each side of which broad flights of stone steps curved down to a quarter-mile-long balustraded terrace with pairs of ornamental vases set along it at intervals; and between these, other flights of steps gave onto a wide lawn, sloping gently to the natural lake from which the house took its name. Kent, the father of English gardens, had also laid out the flower-borders and shady walks at each end of the terrace; and nature's setting had been worthy of his genius, since the house and lake lay in the bottom of a shallow valley; a secret, sylvan paradise enclosed on every side by woods of pine and silver birch.

Now that spring had come blue and yellow crocus gaily starred the grass beneath the ornamental trees, and the daffodils were beginning to blossom on the fringe of the woods, which feathered away above them in a sea of delicate emerald green. The scene was utterly still, and not even marred by the presence of a gardener; for it was her Ladyship's standing order that none of the thirty men employed to keep the grounds should ever be visible from her windows after she rose at ten o'clock.

Indeed, the prospect on which Roger looked down was one of such peace, dignity and beauty as only England has to show; but there was

[1] *The Launching of Roger Brook* (His story in the years 1783-87).

4

no peace in his heart. He loved Georgina dearly. They were both only children, and his fondness for her was even deeper from having filled to her the role of brother, than that of a lover. But she had been aggravatingly temperamental of late, and now this dread foreboding, that one or both of them would fall under the shadow of the gallows, had shaken him much more than he cared to admit.

After some moments he turned and, seeing that her weeping had ceased, went over and kissed her on her still damp cheek; then he said with as much conviction as he could muster:

"My love, I beg you to use your utmost endeavours to put this horrid vision from your mind. You know as well as I that all such glimpses of the unknown are only possibilities—not certainties. They are but random scenes from several paths which circumstances make it possible that one may tread; yet, having free-will, we are not bound to any, and may, by a brave decision taken opportunely, evade such evil pitfalls as fate seems to have strewn in our way. You have oft predicted things that have come true for both of us, but there are times when you have been at fault; and others when you have seen the ill but not its context, so that in the event it proved harmless after all, or a blessing in disguise. With God's Mercy, this will prove such a case."

Georgina was far too strong a personality to give way to panic for long, and having by an effort regained her composure, she replied firmly, "Thou art right in that, dear heart, and we must take such comfort from it as we may. Yet, I confess, the vision scared me mightily; for I once before saw a gibbet in the glass when telling poor Captain Coignham's fortune, and he was swinging from one on Setley Heath within the year."

"Egad!" exclaimed Roger, with a look of shocked surprise. "Coignham was the highwayman you once told me of. The same that held you up in the New Forest when you were scarce seventeen, and robbed you of your virginity as ransom for your rings. Dost mean to tell me that you took to meeting the rogue afterwards? Damme, you must have! No occasion could have arisen for you to tell his fortune otherwise."

She smiled. "I'll not deny it. Dick Coignham was near as handsome as you are, Roger darling; and 'twould be more fair to say that he persuaded me to give, rather than robbed me, of what he took. It never cost me a moment's regret, and 'twas a fine, romantic way to lose one's maidenhead."

"That I'll allow, as an unpremeditated act committed in hot blood —but to deliberately enter on an affair with a notorious felon. How could you bring yourself to that?"

"And why not, Sir?" she countered, with a swift lift of her eyebrows. "You may recall that 'twas soon after my first meeting with him that I went to Court for my presentation, and during that season I threw my slippers over the moon with the handsomest buck of the day. On my return to Highcliffe there came yourself; but only that once, then you went to France. You'll not have forgotten how Papa's having taken a Gipsy for his wife had estranged him from the county, and the almost solitary existence that I led down there in consequence. After a little, with not even a local beau to buy me a ribbon, I became prodigious bored. So when out riding one day I encountered Dick Coignham again, what could be more natural than that I should become his secret moll. More than once I slipped out at night to watch him waylay a coach in the moonlight, and afterwards we made love with the stolen guineas clinking in his pockets. He was a bold, merry fellow, and I vow there were times when he caused me to near die of excitement."

"Georgina, you are incorrigible!" murmured Roger, with a sad shake of his head.

She gave a low, rich laugh. "And you, m'dear, are the veriest snob. Why should you be so shocked to learn that I took a tobyman for my lover? Since that day long ago, when I turned you from a schoolboy into a man, I've made no secret of the fact that I was born a wanton and will always take my pleasure where I list. 'Tis naught to me how a man gets his living, provided he be clean, gay and good to look upon. Think you poor Dick was more to blame because he paid for the gold lace upon his coats by robbing travellers of their trinkets, than all the fine gentlemen at Westminster who take the King's bribes to vote against their consciences?"

"Nay, I'd not say that. I meant only that there are times when I fear your reckless disregard for all convention may one day bring you into grievous trouble."

"Should that occur I'll count it a great injustice. Men are allowed to pleasure themselves where they will, so why not a woman? When you were in France. . . ."

With a smile, he held up his hand to check her. " 'Tis true enough. I tumbled quite a few pretty darlings whose lineage did not entitle them to make their curtsy at Versailles, and I know, of old, your contention that what is sauce for the gander is sauce for the goose in such matters. But the world does not view things that way. And—well, should aught occur to part us I do beg you, my pet, to harness your future impulses with some degree of caution."

One of those swift changes of mood to which she was frequently subject caused her tapering eyebrows to draw together in a sudden frown. "You were thinking of the horrid thing that I saw but now in the glass?"

"Nay," he protested quickly, cursing himself for having brought her thoughts back to it.

"Indeed you were, Roger. To me your mind is an open book. But have no fears on that score. 'Tis all Lombard Street to a China Orange against my ever again becoming a cut-purse's doxey, and getting a hanging from being involved in his crimes. Dick Coignham was an exception to the breed, and I was a young, romantic thing, in those days. For the most part they are a race of scurvy, unlettered, stinking knaves, that no female so fastidious as myself would lay a finger on. 'Tis you who must now take caution as your watchword.

'Tis far more likely that, as a man, your temper may lead you into some unpremeditated killing than that I, as a woman, should shed human blood."

"I'll have a care," he agreed. "But from what you said it did appear that should rashness or stupidity bring us to this evil pass we'll both be concerned in it."

"Dear Roger," she laid a hand on his. "How could it be otherwise when our destinies are so entwined? Would not either of us hasten from the ends of the earth to aid the other in such an hour of trial? Physical passion between all lovers must always wax and wane, and in that we can be no exception. Yet, in our case, passion is but a small part of the link that binds us, and we shall love one another till we die."

He raised her hand to his lips. "Thou art right in that; and neither temporary disagreements nor long separations will ever sever this sweet bond, that I value more than life itself. But tell me. When you saw the wedding ring, had you no inkling at all for which of us it was intended?"

"None. And that, m'dear, comes from thy foolishness in proposing that I should seek to tell the future for us both at the same time. 'Tis a thing that I have never before attempted and it created a sad confusion in my telling. Seeing that I am married already, though, the odds are clearly against it being for me."

"Not necessarily. Humphrey may break his neck any day in the hunting-field, or die any night from an apoplexy brought on by his excessive punishing of the port."

She sighed. "I wish him no harm; but each time I've seen him of late he's been more plaguey difficult. We liked one another well enough to begin with, but now we have not even friendship left, or mutual respect."

Roger made a comic little grimace. "Your main reason for choosing him rather than one of your many other suitors was because you had set your heart on Stillwaters. You have it; and he leaves you free to lead the life you choose, so it does not seem to me that you have much cause to complain."

"After the first year we agreed to go our separate ways, and until last autumn he gave me very little trouble. But since then he has developed sporadic fits of prying into my affairs, and 'tis a thing that I resent intensely."

"You've never told me of this."

"There was no point in doing so. 'Tis not normal jealousy that causes him to make me these scenes when we meet. 'Tis resentment that I should continue to enjoy life to the full while he is no longer capable of deriving pleasure from aught but horseflesh and the bottle; and, something quite new in him, a morbid fear that he may become a laughing-stock should my infidelities to him be noised abroad. I've a notion that the liquor is beginning to effect his brain. Should I be right in that a time may come when he will have to be put under restraint; and if that occurs he may live to be a hundred. So you see all the chances

7

are that you will marry long before there is any prospect of my being led to the altar as a widow."

"I've no mind to marry," Roger declared. "I would hate to be shackled for life to any woman; that is, unless I could marry you. But perhaps the ring was an omen of the future meant for both of us. Would you marry me, Georgina, if in a few years time you became free?"

"Lud no!" she exclaimed with a sudden widening of her eyes. "I thank thee mightily for the compliment, but 'twould be the height of folly. Marriage is the one and only thing which might sap away the true love which otherwise will last us a life-time. Once we were tied I vow we'd be hating one another within a year."

"Nay. I'll not believe it. We have so many interests in common, and never know a single dull moment when in one another's company. Even when passion faded we'd have a wealth of joyous things to do together."

"Be truthful, Roger," she chided him gently. "Although I have been your mistress only for some five months you have already come to take me for granted, and there are now times when you are just a little bored with me."

"I deny it," he cried hotly.

" 'Tis so, m'dear. Why did you ask me to invite your friend Lord Edward Fitz-Deverel down this week-end, if not because I am no longer capable of retaining your whole attention, and you are beginning to feel the need for other interests?"

"Oh, come! That is nonsense. Whenever you entertain you must, perforce, give much of your time to your other guests, and I have never taken the slightest umbrage over that. I simply wished Droopy Ned to see your lovely home; and to have someone to talk to, other than your father and the Duke, in order to lessen the chance of my being rude to Mr. Fox."

She laughed. "How you dislike poor Charles, don't you? Yet he is the kindest and most genial of men."

"He is amusing enough and generous to a fault. 'Tis not his company I hate, but his politics. Not a bill goes before the House but he uses his brilliant gifts and mastery of intrigue to get it thrown out—entirely regardless as to the degree of good its passage might do the country."

"That is but natural in a leader of the Opposition."

"There are times when the Government has the right to expect the co-operation of the Opposition for the well-being of the State," Roger replied warmly. "But Fox would not restrain his venomous animosity to the Ministers of the Crown even if the Cinque Ports were in jeopardy. He is the bond-slave of an ungovernable ambition and would stick at nothing to obtain office. His unholy pact with my Lord North in '83 was proof enough of that. 'Twas the most despicable manœuvre that has ever disgraced British politics, and why you should elect to make a friend of such a man passes my comprehension."

Georgina shrugged her ample shoulders. "I have three perfectly

8

good reasons. Firstly, I like Charles for himself. Secondly, your idol Mr. Pitt is a boorish, uncouth recluse, who despises society; and since I cannot have the Prime Minister at my table, the next best thing is the leader of the Opposition. Thirdly, Mr. Pitt's reign cannot last indefinitely, and when he falls Charles will become the occupant of Number Ten. Then, Roger, my love, I'll be able to make you Paymaster of the Forces—as I promised I would when you were fifteen."

"You are wrong about Mr. Pitt," Roger smiled, his good humour restored. "He is very shy, but neither boorish nor uncouth; and while your Mr. Fox is making pretty speeches to the ladies at Carlton House, or gambling thousands a night away at Brook's, Mr. Pitt is at his desk, working into the small hours for the good of the nation. As for your offer of the most lucrative post in the Kingdom, I am mightily obliged; but rather than accept it from the hands of Charles James Fox I would prefer to starve in the gutter."

"Hoity-toity!" Georgina mocked him. "What high principles we have, to be sure. But as your patron, Mr. Pitt, has the King's purse to play with no doubt you can count on his keeping you from beggary."

Roger ignored the gibe, and asked, "Is Mr. Fox bringing Mrs. Armistead with him?"

"Yes. His 'dear Betty' has become an institution rather than a mistress these days. He rarely leaves London now without her, and makes her place at Chertsey his home whenever the House is not sitting. She has some education and is not a bad creature, even if she did graduate by somewhat dubious ways from being a serving wench."

"How will his Grace of Bridgewater and his sister take her presence here? If Lady Amelia Egerton is as straightlaced as her brother I foresee noses in the air."

"There will be no awkwardness," Georgina replied easily. "They are old friends and I know their tastes well. His Grace will be perfectly happy talking of canals and coalmines with Papa, and Lady Amelia, like many another old spinster, finds the breath of life in scandal. 'Tis for her that I asked that delightful old rake George Selwyn. He will keep her amused for hours."

Roger laughed. "I had temporarily forgotten your artistry in mixing the most diverse types successfully."

"I owe much of my success as a hostess to it; yet 'tis easy enough. One has only to give a little thought to seeing that each guest is paired by love or interest to another and, their own happiness being assured, none of them will give a fig who else is in the party."

"All the same thou art a witch, my pet, in more ways than looking bewitching. Few other women would dare to brew the politics of both parties, the demi-monde and the aristocracy, industry and vested interests, a puritan Duke and an ex-member of the Hell-Fire Club, all in one week-end cauldron, without fear of its boiling over."

"You may add diplomacy," Georgina told him with a smile. "Methinks I had forgot to tell you that Count Sergius Vorontzoff, the Russian Ambassador, is also coming."

"And where does he fit into your scheme of pairs?" Roger asked with the lift of an eyebrow.

Georgina's smile became seraphic. "Why, I have asked him to amuse myself, of course; while you are playing backgammon with your crony, Droopy Ned."

"Seeing that Droopy is not a woman that hardly seems a *quid pro quo*."

"Indeed it is. The conversation of your friend will entertain you admirably twixt now and Monday; whereas I have yet to meet the female who could engage my attention pleasurably for more than an hour or two at a stretch."

"What sort of a man is this Muscovite?"

"He comes of one of the great families of his country. His father was Grand Chancellor to the Empress Elizabeth. One of his sisters was the mistress of her nephew, the ill-fated Emperor Peter III; while another, the Princess Dashkoff, entered the other camp, and played a leading part in the conspiracy by which the present Empress Catherine unseated her husband and usurped his throne."

"I had meant, what is he like personally?"

"He is a dark man, not yet past the prime of life, with a clever, forceful face; and, I should hazard, is quite unscrupulous by nature. Underneath his culture there is a touch of barbarism which must give him a strong appeal to women. I met him at the Duchess of Devonshire's several times this winter, and on the very first occasion he showed the good taste to express the most ardent desire to become my lover."

Roger frowned. " 'Tis my belief that you have asked him down with the deliberate intent to make me jealous."

"Lud no, dear man!" she replied airily. "We are both, thank God, far too sophisticated to fall a prey to such a sordid emotion. Did we not agree when first we became lovers that if either of us should choose to be unfaithful to the other no word of reproach should mar our friendship?"

"I know it!" Roger stood up and walked over to the window. The dark blue eyes that he had inherited from his Highland mother had become a shade darker, as he went on a little sullenly. "Yet I am not of the temperament to stand idly by and watch another man making a play for your favours."

Georgina stretched and yawned. "Then m'dear, you are about to become a plaguey bore, and will be going back upon our clear understanding. We agreed that we would remain free to indulge in casual amours if we wished, and tell or not tell of them as we felt inclined; to ignore such frailties in one another or, if in the case of either such a matter developed into a *grande affaire*, to separate without ill-will. 'Tis the only condition upon which I have ever entered on a liaison, or ever will; and you entirely agreed with me that, only so could two people live together and be certain of escaping sordid, wearing scenes of futile recrimination."

10

Turning back from the window Roger said quietly, "That was our pact, and I will honour it. But tell me, frankly. Is it your intention to start an affair with the Russian this week-end?"

She shrugged. "You know better than anyone how varied are my moods, and how unpredictable. How can I tell in advance what my feelings may be towards him upon closer acquaintance."

He scowled at her for a moment, then said reproachfully. "I've felt for the past week or two that you were becoming restless, and that we were no longer in perfect accord; but I had not thought that our parting was to come so soon."

"Dear Roger," she murmured, with a sudden return to gentleness. "I confess that my heart no longer leaps at the sound of your footfall coming to my room. But you too have lost something of your first fine rapture in me; and if you are honest you will admit it. A time always comes when even the best of friends should part for a season; and wise lovers always do so while there is still an edge upon their passion, instead of waiting for it to become entirely blunted. Only by so doing can they preserve a hope of coming together again with renewed zest sometime in the future."

"So be it then; but at least let our relationship remain unchanged throughout the week-end. Then I will take my *congé* with a good grace, and leave with your other guests on Monday."

She hesitated a second, then she said. "I am most loath to do anything which would give you pain. And think not, I beg, that I am wearied of you to a point where I would have you make so hurried a departure. Stillwaters is so lovely in the Spring, and there is no one with whom I would rather gather daffodils in the woods than your dear self. Stay on for a further week or two, and bear me company while you make your future plans. But for this evening and to-morrow I crave your indulgence to try my wiles on Sergius Vorontzoff."

Roger had too much pride to accept the proffered olive branch at the price. Instead, he snapped sarcastically. "From what you've already said 'twill need but little trying on your part to rouse the cave-man in this northern barbarian; and you must forgive me if I say that you seem in a positively indecent hurry to begin."

"Nay. 'Tis not that," she murmured, her tone still mild. "I'll admit the man intrigues me, but I would have been well content to wait until our affair was ended, had not circumstances forced my hand. The truth is Charles knows that the Russian has a fancy for me and wrote asking permission to bring him down. It seems that the Opposition are particularly anxious to gain his interest, and, naturally, if I decide to take him in hand I shall be in a position to exert a certain influence over him."

"May the devil take Charles Fox!" cried Roger angrily. "Damn him and his filthy political intrigues."

"Oh, be sensible, m'dear. 'Twill prove well worth my while to render him this service, should I find that my own inclinations coincide with his interests."

"Surely you would lose nothing by postponing the issue for a while?"

"There lies the rub. I fear one might lose everything. 'Tis said that these Russians are as proud as they are bold. After the avowals he has already made me he will come with high expectations. Should I not give him some encouragement he may think that I have deliberately made a fool of him, and the strength of his resentment might rob me of any future chance to develop his acquaintance."

Roger's face hardened. "You must have known he was coming days ago, yet you told me nothing of it. 'Tis clear that you were already considering him as a possible successor to myself yet lacked the frankness to tell me what was in your mind."

"I thought of doing so but refrained, from an instinct that you would take it ill and behave towards me like a jealous husband; and rightly, so it seems."

"On the contrary, Madam, I should have packed my bags and relieved you of my presence; as I would this very afternoon were it not that Droopy is coming here at my behest. Since that renders my immediate departure impossible I feel that I have the right to ask that, whatever assignations you may choose to make with Vorontzoff for the near future, you will spare me the humiliation of allowing him to make love to you till I have left your house."

Georgina sighed. "Roger you weary me a little. I have been entirely faithful to you for these past five months; but now I invoke our pact. Before Athenaïs de Rochambeau gave you her heart you already loved her desperately; yet, as you have told me, you did not scruple to take mistresses for your amusement. Why then should you cavil so now if I elect to give something of myself to another, which will not detract one iota from my deep, abiding love for you. Besides, as I have already said, I may give the Russian no more than a few kisses."

"If you'll promise that I'll say no more."

Slowly Georgina stood up, shook out the folds of her voluminous red velvet gown and drew herself up to her full height. They faced one another only a yard apart; two splendid, strong-willed, passionate young people. Then she said firmly:

"I have already told you, Sir, all will depend upon how much or how little he attracts me on closer acquaintance. I refuse to be dictated to, and I will promise nothing."

At that moment a coach-horn sounded in the distance, and she added, "There! That will be some of my guests arriving. I must hurry down to join Papa for their reception."

As she was about to turn away he seized her by the arm, and cried furiously: "I'm damned if I'll let you *tromper* me under my very nose."

"About that we'll see!" she snapped back, her dark eyes blazing. "But please to understand that from this instant I forbid you the *entrée* to my private apartments; and that I'll do as I damn well please!"

Then, wrenching her arm from his grasp, she sailed regally from the room.

12

CHAPTER II

A LOSING BATTLE

A s Georgina reached the top of the main staircase Roger caught her up. Below them her father, Colonel Thursby, who adored, spoilt and lived with her almost permanently, although he had two houses of his own, had just come out of one of the four splendid reception rooms that gave onto the spacious entrance hall of the mansion.

On catching sight of him Roger made Georgina a formal bow and offered her his arm. Laying her hand lightly on it she gathered up her billowing skirts with the other, and they walked down the broad, shallow stairs. By the time they reached the bottom not a trace of ill temper was to be seen on the face of either, although both their hearts were still beating with unnatural swiftness as a result of their quarrel.

The front door was already open and a squad of liveried footmen were relieving the first arrivals of their wraps. These proved to be Lord Edward Fitz-Deverel and Mr. Selwyn. Both were members of White's Club and it transpired that the former, learning that the latter was also going to Stillwaters for the week-end, had carried him from London in his curricle.

Roger's friend was some three years older than himself; an extremely thin but rather tall young man with pale blue eyes and a beaky nose. He had derived his nickname of Droopy Ned from his chronic stoop, but he was a great dandy; and under his lazy manner he concealed a quick, well-balanced and unusually profound mind.

George Selwyn was nearly seventy, although he did not look it; and from his mild, benign face no one would ever have guessed that in his youth he had been one of the most notorious rakes in London. He possessed an enchanting wit, a most kindly disposition and friends without number, being equally popular with Queen Charlotte and Betty the flower woman of St. James's Street.

With the courtly manners of the day both the new arrivals made a gallant leg to Georgina, who curtseyed deeply in response; then, with hands on their hearts, they exchanged bows with Colonel Thursby and Roger, while the well-bred greetings echoed round the hall.

"Your ladyship's most humble."

"And yours, m'Lord."

"Your Servant, Sir."

"My duty, Sir, to you."

They were still uttering polite platitudes about the journey and the fortunate state of the weather when another coach-horn sounded, so they all remained in the hall until the next vehicle drew up.

It contained Mr. Fox and Mrs. Armistead, and close on their heels came the Russian Ambassador. He had taken breakfast with them at her house, St. Anne's Hill, on Fox's suggestion that afterwards his coach could follow theirs and thus more easily find the way.

The famous leader of the Opposition was then in his fortieth year. His big frame was still vigorous, but his swarthy countenance showed the marks of the dissipation in which he had indulged ever since his cynical father had taken him from Eton to Paris, and encouraged him to indulge in vice at the age of fourteen. In his youth he had been a dandy and the leader of the young macaronis, who startled the town with their exaggerated toilettes; but now he had become slovenly in his dress. His black hair, streaked with grey, was ill-brushed, and he took no measures to restrain the great, ugly paunch that seemed every moment to threaten to burst his silk breeches.

Mrs. Armistead, a lady of uncertain age, still possessed a certain coarse beauty, but she showed an admirable restraint in both her dress and manners; evidently being well content to play the moon to her distinguished lover's sun.

Roger greeted them both with the utmost politeness, but he had no eyes for either. The second he had made his bows his gaze fastened on Count Vorontzoff, and he felt that Georgina had given him a very fair description of the Russian.

The Count, Roger judged, was not less than forty, but his face, figure and movements all bespoke a forceful, virile personality. He was of medium height, well-made and very dark. His rather flat face, high cheekbones and jet black eyes suggested Tartar blood, and the last had all the inscrutability of an Oriental's. His clothes were evidently London made, but his wig and the rich jewels he was wearing at his throat and on his hands added to the foreignness of his appearance.

He stood for a moment quietly smiling at Georgina before he bowed to her. The smile lit up his rather sombre features, giving them a strange attraction; but there was something more than greeting or frank admiration in his glance; something insolent, cocksure, possessive, that made Roger itch to slap his face.

When the Russian spoke it was in French, and with the greatest fluency. Two of his servitors, rough hairy men, had entered behind him carrying a small, leather, round-lidded trunk. Having reached out, taken both Georgina's hands with the greatest assurance, kissed them, and murmured some most lavish compliments, he went on to say that he begged to be permitted to offer her a trifling present— a bagatelle quite unworthy of her but in which she might care to dress up one of her servants for her amusement. Then he beckoned his men forward.

Roger, having spent four years in France, and speaking French like a native himself, had understood every word of this; so he was not surprised when the two *moujiks* went down on their knees before Georgina and, opening the trunk, took from it a costume. But he and everyone else present were filled with admiration at its richness.

It was the gala skirt and bodice of a Russian peasant girl, the rainbow-hued embroideries of which had been stitched with infinite care; and with it were the filmy white petticoats, a pair of soft, red leather boots and a splendid headdress tinkling with gold coins, to complete the costume.

As Georgina exclaimed with delight at this exciting gift Vorontzoff bowed again, and said in his slightly husky voice: "Should my Lady take a fancy to try on these poor rags before casting them to her maid, she will, I trust, find that they fit her exquisite figure perfectly."

"But *Monsieur le Comte!* How can you possibly be sure of that?" smiled Georgina, her eyes widening.

The Russian's strong white teeth gleamed for a second in a confident grin. "If they do not, my steward's back shall make acquaintance with the knout; since the rogue was given ample funds to secure the correct measurements from your dressmaker."

"Indeed, Sir; I am prodigious grateful to you for your forethought," Georgina replied a trifle breathlessly. Then, beckoning over one of her footmen she added, "Here, Thomas! Take these lovely things to Jenny. Tell her that I desire her to press them at once and place them in my wardrobe."

As the footman took the costume from the *moujiks* Georgina placed her hand upon the Ambassador's arm and led him across the hall towards the drawing-room. The others followed, Droopy Ned and Roger bringing up the rear.

The latter, unheeding of his friend's casual chatter, was cursing the Russian beneath his breath. His sole source of income was the £300 a year which his father allowed him. Having no establishment of his own to keep up, that was normally ample for his needs; but his extravagant taste in clothes left him little over, and during the past few months he had strained his resources to buy Georgina presents. Yet, even so, to a wealthy woman of fashion, his gifts had been no more than knick-knacks; whereas this confounded foreigner could produce a present of greater value than them all, by a mere wave of his hand. Moreover, as Georgina loved dressing up, few gifts could have been better calculated to appeal to her.

After passing through a long suite of reception rooms the party arrived at the Orangery, in the south-western extremity of the house. It was something more than a conservatory for the cultivation of semi-tropical plants such as citrus fruits, banana-palms, mimosas and camellias; since Georgina spent much of her time there, and had had sofas, chairs and tables set in alcoves formed by pyramidal arrangements of exotic greenery.

The tables now carried an assortment of wines and spirits for the refreshment of the male travellers, and hot chocolate for the ladies. It was as yet only a little past mid-day, but the custom of the times was to breakfast late, making it a full dress meal, and to dine at four o'clock, or shortly after.

As Colonel Thursby poured Selwyn a glass of Madeira he inquired: "Have you been to any executions lately, George?"

The question was a perfectly natural one; as, although there was nothing the least ghoulish in Selwyn's appearance or morbid in his manner, he was well known to have an insatiable interest in hangings, exhumations and everything connected with death. It was even said that when the body of Martha Ray, Lord Sandwich's mistress, had been exhibited after her murder by an unsuccessful suitor, he had bribed the undertaker to be allowed to sit at the head of the corpse dressed in the flowing weeds of a professional mourner.

"Nay, Newgate has been plaguey unproductive of recent months," Selwyn replied; then added with a smiling glance at Fox: " 'Tis my belief that all our most desperate criminals must have taken refuge in the House."

"Oh, come, George!" Fox exclaimed with his ready laugh. "How can you pass so harsh a judgment on those amongst whom you sat for twenty-six years as Member for Ludgershall?"

"In my day they were of a different metal, Charles. My Lord Chatham would never have allowed the impeachment of so great a servant of the Crown as Mr. Warren Hastings; or this miserable trial which still agitates the nation and threatens to drag on interminably."

" 'Twas the only way to bring the natives of India some measure of protection from the rapine of the Company's servants. Pitt, himself, admitted that, when condemning Hastings' action in mulcting the Zamindar of Benares of half a million sterling; and made it clear that the case was not a party issue, but one upon which members should vote according to their consciences."

"Yet, Sir," broke in Droopy Ned, "The Prime Minister stated on more than one occasion that Mr. Hastings is placed at a grave disadvantage; in that many State papers which would show good reason for his acts cannot be made public without disclosing the secret understandings that we have with certain of the native Princes."

"In the government of an Empire, my Lord, 'tis not particulars which should concern us so much as general principles."

Droopy waved a scented lace handkerchief airily beneath his long nose. "Perhaps, Sir, you can tell us then what principle it was that governed His Highness of Wales when, before the India debate early this month, he filled Mr. Erskine so full of brandy that his language to the Prime Minister would have made a Billingsgate fishwife blush?"

Fox laughed again. "If you would have us all set a limit on our potations before entering the House, my Lord, you should start with the Prime Minister. 'Twas but two nights later he was so indisposed as to be unable to answer me; and that from having been drinking through the whole of the previous night at My Lord of Buckingham's with Harry Dundas and the Duchess of Gordon."

"Yet, Sir," interposed Roger. "I'll wager that he never forgot his manners."

"Nay. I'll give you that, young Sir. And I will admit that the language Erskine held in his personal attack passed all bounds of decency. But, as Lord Edward says, the Prince had primed him before he spoke, and we all know His Royal Highness's irresponsibility."

16

Fox spoke with restraint; yet he had ample reason to have used a far stronger term. The unnatural hatred that the Heir Apparent bore to his father had caused him, from his first entry upon manhood, to become the most ardent supporter of the Opposition. Fox being the King's *bête noire*, the young Prince had deliberately cultivated his friendship, and in return, that generous-hearted statesman had obtained from Parliament grants totalling many score thousands of pounds to enable His Highness both to set up an establishment of his own at Carlton House and to indulge his wildly extravagant tastes.

More, when the Prince had fallen desperately in love with Mrs. Fitzherbert it was Fox and Mrs. Armistead who had, night after night, consoled him in his tearful fits of despair because the lady would have none of him. Apart from the undesirability of any official union of the Heir Apparent and a commoner, on account of it being morganatic, Parliament viewed such a prospect with particularly grave alarm in the case of Maria Fitzherbert because she was a Roman Catholic; but she made no secret of the fact that her price was marriage.

In consequence, on his publicly establishing her in a larger residence, members demanded a plain answer, if he were married to her or no, and made a further grant of funds to pay his mountainous debts dependent on the answer. Faced with this impasse in the previous April, the despicable young man had allowed Fox to issue a categorical denial on his behalf. Thus he had secured the supplies he needed by causing his bosom friend to appear a most barefaced liar; for Mrs. Fitzherbert, refusing to remain longer in what she considered an intolerable position, had forced the Prince to admit two days later, to Earl Grey, that he had been married to her on 15th December, '85—over sixteen months earlier—and it seemed impossible to everyone that Fox should not have been a party to their secret.

On learning the truth of the matter from Sir James Harris, Fox had felt so ashamed that he had absented himself from the House for several days, and his resentment against the Prince was such that he had refused to speak to him for the best part of a year. But rumour had it that they had recently become reconciled; since should any misfortune befall the King, it was certain that the Prince would call upon the Whigs to form a Ministry, and Charles James Fox was far too ambitious a man to allow a personal treachery to deprive him indefinitely of the chance of becoming Prime Minister.

Among the men grouped round the table in the Orangery there was a momentary silence, as all of them were thinking of the unsavoury episode that Fox's words had recalled, but Colonel Thursby swiftly filled the breach, by remarking:

"A more narrow-minded and pig-headed man than our present Monarch it would be hard to find; but for all his selfishness 'tis difficult to believe that he deserved two such sons."

"You are right in that, Sir," agreed Droopy Ned. "And the Duke of York even outdoes the Prince in the besotted, boorish way he takes his pleasures. So plebeian are his tastes, and so little faith is to be placed in his word, that the nobility of my own generation have now abjured his Grace entirely, and count his company *mauvais ton.*"

"In that, Charles, we have the advantage of you at White's," smiled Selwyn. "I must say that I pity you at Brook's, across the way, in having to support the frequent presence of these two uncouth young rakehells."

" 'Tis so no longer, George," Fox countered swiftly. "Had you not heard that on H.R.H. proposing that fellow Tarleton, and Jack Payne, for membership we blackballed both of them, and that, in consequence, the two Royal sons have left us in a dudgeon? With some of their cronies they have started a new club of their own called Welzie's, at the Dover House, where General "Hyder Ali" Smith and Admiral Pigot are said to be rooking them of from two to three thousand guineas nightly."

The conversation was interrupted by the arrival of the Duke of Bridgewater and his sister, Lady Amelia Egerton. He was a man of just over fifty, ill-dressed and of a somewhat unprepossessing countenance. In his childhood he had been so shamefully neglected by his stepfather, and so sickly, that his mind had almost entirely failed to develop; so that, at the age of twelve, when his elder brother died, his exclusion from the dukedom on the gounds of feeble intellect had been seriously contemplated. The grand tour had done little to improve either his perceptions or his graces, and after an unhappy love-affair with one of the 'beautiful Miss Gunnings' he had, at the age of twenty-three, abandoned society to settle on his estates at Worsley, near Manchester.

It was there that his latent genius for all matters to do with commerce, and particularly coal-mining, had developed. At times the financing of his vast canal schemes had reduced him almost to beggary, but now he was regarded as the uncrowned King of Manchester, and his industrial ventures alone were bringing him in an income of eighty thousand a year.

His sister, a pale spinster, kept house for him at Ashridge in Hertfordshire, his southern seat; and she was the only woman that he could endure for any length of time, for he was so confirmed a misogynist that he would not even allow a woman to wait on him.

Lady Amelia had been brought by him at the special request of Georgina, who felt deeply sorry for the poor woman on account of the exceptionally circumscribed life she was compelled to lead; while his Grace had come solely because he wished to talk about steam-engines with Colonel Thursby.

Georgina's father was about the same age as the Duke but a thin-faced, delicate-looking man, and of very different personality. He was widely travelled, extremely well-read and a distinguished connoisseur of the arts. It was due to his loving fashioning of his daughter's mind that she possessed, in addition to her beauty, the ability to hold her own with most men in conversation on a great variety of subjects. Yet the Colonel, although a dilettante by nature, had once been an officer in the Corps of Engineers, and a streak of shrewdness had enabled him to foresee the financial possibilities of many of those new inventions which were already in the process of ushering in a new age. It was this which had led to his association with the Duke, Josiah Wedgewood, Sir James Arkwright and others; by participating in whose ventures he had, while still comparatively young, converted a modest patrimony into a fine fortune, thereby making Georgina a great heiress in her own right.

When the company had been presented to his Grace and Lady Amelia, Georgina suggested that they should take a turn round the gardens. The majority of her guests agreed to the proposal with alacrity, but the Duke gave her a lowering glance and shook his head.

Taking a huge snuff box from his pocket he helped himself to a lavish pinch, the bulk of which scattered down the already snuff-stained lapels of his coat, and declared.

"Flowers! I hate 'em! Some fool planted some at Worsley once. I struck their heads off with my cane and ordered 'em to be dug up. Waste of time and money! I'll stay here and talk to your father."

Colonel Thursby knew of old both the story and his friend's fanatical absorption in the useful to the complete exclusion of the beautiful. Himself a keen gardener, he had done much to add enchantment to the gardens at Stillwaters, and would have liked to go round them with the rest; but, concealing his disappointment with a politeness which was natural to him, he resigned himself to listen to a discourse by His Grace on experiments with steam-pumps in coal-mines, while the others followed Georgina out onto the terrace.

The sun had been shining all the morning in a serene, pale blue sky, and it was now the hottest hour of the afternoon; so that in this well-sheltered valley, although it was only the last day of March, it was as warm as if it had been early May. To the west of the house there was a Botticelli garden, which had been planted three years before by Colonel Thursby when Georgina came to live there. In it the young almond trees were already in blossom, and the cherries, crab-apples, mays and standard lilacs showing their buds. Beneath them small neat clusters of crocus and primroses starred the grass, and larger clumps of green spikes showed where narcissus, hyacinths and tulips would presently flower; so that in another month it would be an earthly Paradise.

As they stood admiring the prospect Georgina turned to Vorontzoff, who since his arrival had never left her side, and asked: "Is your Excellency fond of the country?"

"So much so, Madam, that I live in it," he replied at once.

"But surely your embassy is in London."

"Near London, but not in it. We occupy a pleasant old mansion in the St. John's Wood, a mile or so below the village of Hampstead. My staff insisted on calling the place after me, but your London cockneys find some difficulty in pronouncing my name, so it has become known as Woronzow House. I hope that you will allow me to entertain you there when you are next in London?"

"You are most kind," Georgina said with just a suggestion of primness. "But embassies are foreign soil, and we still have an old-fashioned law in England that a woman may not venture abroad without the consent of her husband."

"Then I shall beg you to break this foolish law," smiled the Count. He had already found out from Fox that Georgina's husband played a very small part in her life, but her reference to him implied that she was not a woman who would allow herself to be thought of as easy game. Without pressing the point he went on lightly, "At least I can promise you, Madam, that even if my house is part of my Imperial Mistress's dominions, you will never meet within it a temperature which will cause you to think yourself in Siberia."

She was secretly amused at the innuendo, but did not show it as she said: "Unfortunately it is not a matter of temperature but of convention, Monsieur, and there are times when I feel it proper to consult the wishes of my husband."

They had been conversing in French, but Fox, who had come up on Georgina's other side, now said in English: "I ran into Humphrey on Thursday. He was coming out of the family mansion in St. James's Square."

"Then thank God I was not in London," she remarked tartly. " 'Tis our only common meeting ground these days, and he seldom comes up for more than a few nights; but even that I find too much. I vow he bores me to distraction."

"He seemed mightily interested in you, all the same. When he learned that I was coming here he plied me with a host of questions; wanting to know who else would be in the party, who was here on my last visit, and whose houses you now most frequent when in the Metropolis."

Georgina frowned. "Damn the man's impertinence; prying into my affairs. I would to Heaven that I were rid of him."

"You may be soon," Fox laughed. "That is if he continues to drink and ride at such a furious pace. He was going down to stay at Goodwood this week-end, and spoke with enthusiasm of a most fractious gelding on which he vows he will win the point-to-point that is being held there to-day."

"Goodwood," Vorontzoff, suddenly broke in. "I believe I have been there. Is that not the name of the Duke of Richmond's seat in Sussex?"

"Why, yes, your Excellency," Georgina replied, a little taken aback. She had never heard the Ambassador speak in any language other than French, so had assumed that he knew very little English; but he had evidently understood her asides to Fox, and she was considerably disconcerted at the thought that he should have so soon discovered her true attitude towards her husband. Roger's attempt to dictate to her had driven her to defy him at the time, but she fully appreciated his feelings, and was most loath to do anything to hurt him; so she had intended to plead an old-fashioned loyalty to her spouse as a first-line of defence if the wooing of the Russian became too impetuous over the week-end, and now she had stupidly cut that ground from under her own feet.

As they moved on towards the glass-houses Vorontzoff launched into an amusing account of how, soon after his arrival in England, he had been invited down to Portsmouth to see something of the British Fleet, and his coachman, having taken a wrong turning, had got hopelessly lost. Neither he nor his retainers being then able to speak a word of English, it was not until they had come out of some woods upon the Duke of Richmond's great house on the downs that they had found anyone who spoke French sufficiently fluently to set them on their way again.

For another hour or more the party continued to saunter round the gardens, then made the circuit of the great lake and returned to the house. Georgina took Lady Amelia and Mrs. Armistead up to their rooms, and her father performed a like office for the men guests, so that they might all change out of their travelling clothes and powder themselves for dinner.

On Roger's first coming to Stillwaters Georgina had put him in her husband's old room. As it lay on the far side of her boudoir the proprieties were reasonably preserved, yet the arrangement had the advantage that he could come in to her at any time without being seen entering or leaving her room by the main corridor.

Having pulled off his coat and thrown it on the bed he cast a look of uncertainty at the boudoir door. He was in half a mind to ignore her prohibition and go in to her now, in the hope of patching up their quarrel. Their love-affair had been such splendid fun, and even if they had been getting on one another's nerves a little lately, it seemed tragic that it should end like this.

As he looked at the door and recalled the joyous hours of love and laughter that he had spent on the far side of it during the past months, he knew that he was very far from being tired of Georgina, and he did not believe that she was tired of him. Perhaps she was right in her contention that mutual passion could not endure for any great length of time in two such volatile natures as theirs, when given full rein, and that their only hope of a second innings lay in parting for a season before their desire for one another had burnt right out. But he felt certain that the break need not have come yet, or with such lack of grace, had it not been for the machinations of the unscrupulous Mr. Fox.

With his hands thrust deep in his breeches-pockets Roger began to pace gloomily up and down. He had little doubt that Fox knew, as well as he knew himself, Georgina's boundless ambition. She loved to rule and to influence important people; and had often vowed to him that she would be a Duchess before her hair turned grey. In spite of her temporary pessimism that she might be tied to her present husband for some years to come, he considered the odds to be all against that; and once Sir Humphrey Etheredge was dead she would be free to take her pick from a score of Earls and Marquesses. Then, if she had rendered valuable assistance to Fox and he came to power, as she clearly expected him to do, she might reasonably count on his forcing the King to elevate her second husband to a Dukedom. That, Roger felt, was the essence of some, probably unspoken, pact that lay between them; and Fox, needing the Russian influence for some dirty piece of business the Opposition were plotting against the Government, was now pressing for her immediate aid in securing the goodwill of Vorontzoff.

Against such pressure could be set the fact that, although Georgina's gipsy blood made her as amoral as the average man, nothing would induce her to take a lover whom she did not fancy. But, here again, Fox had played his cards with his usual shrewdness; since he must be aware that one of the weaknesses in Georgina's otherwise strong character was her love of the bizarre. It was as good as certain that when he selected her, as the best bait with which he could attempt the snaring of Vorontzoff, he had also counted on the streak of barbarism that underlay the Muscovite's cosmopolitan polish, as the very thing most calculated to appeal to her tastes.

While they had all been walking round the grounds Roger had purposely refrained from forcing himself on Georgina, but his eyes never left her for long, and he was so well acquainted with every line of her expressive face that he felt certain the Russian had succeeded in both amusing and intriguing her. From his own experience he knew that if a man could do that with a woman who already regarded him as a potential lover, he had more than half-won his battle; its victorious conclusion was then seldom more than a question of time and opportunity.

The full weakness of his own position was suddenly borne home to Roger on a wave of distress. In the course of an unofficial honeymoon lasting nearly half a year he had given himself with all the joyous vigour of youth, both in body and mind, to Georgina; and now he had nothing fresh left to offer.

There seemed no alternative but for him to swallow the bitter pill and resign himself to the triumph of his rival, of whose appearance on the scene he had had so little warning. The only question now remaining was, would the beautiful Georgina present him with a pair of horns over the week-end, or not?

Left to her own inclinations he felt sure that, out of consideration for him, she would refrain. But he had no means of judging how pressing was Fox's need of Vorontzoff's co-operation, and feared that if it was urgent, since Georgina obviously regarded herself as perfectly free, she might precipitate matters on that account.

Roger was a typical product of his age. He was bold, resourceful, and, while setting a high value on his personal honour, could be quite unscrupulous in serving what he considered to be justifiable ends. He had developed into a man of the world while still in his teens, and his excellent education in the classics, coupled with his personal experience of eighteenth-century life, had led him to regard all sex-relationships with detached cynicism. Yet, in addition to his dark blue eyes, he had inherited from his Highland mother a romantic streak, and it was this which entered into his long relationship with Georgina.

Had she been any other woman he would either have let her go with a shrug or wept, prayed, cursed and threatened suicide in a desperate endeavour to keep her faithful. But, for him, Georgina was neither a light-of-love nor a grand passion. She was something apart which had grown up with him out of his boyhood, and while he was now quite prepared to kiss and leave her for a season, all his romantic feelings cried out against their parting being marred by her being unfaithful to him before he had even left the house.

Again he glanced uncertainly at the boudoir-door. If he told her that it would really hurt him he knew that she would place his feelings before all else. But he suddenly realised that he had left it too late. Her maid, Jenny, would be with her by this time, helping her to dress, and as Jenny had to clear up afterwards she would not leave the room again until after her mistress had gone down to dinner. Georgina had no secrets from Jenny, but this was not a matter that could be discussed before a maid.

Taking off his frilled shirt he slowly began to change; his sense of injury and frustration steadily mounting while he dressed. As the Daniel Quare clock on the marble mantelpiece of his room chimed four o'clock, powdered, pomarded and most elegantly clad in a suit of lavender blue silk, he went downstairs; now obsessed with a cold, angry determination to resort to desperate measures to spike the Russian's guns.

CHAPTER III

A DESPERATE GAMBLE

ALTHOUGH the usual hour for dinner among the gentry of England was still four o'clock, a tendency had already started in the fashionable world to dine somewhat later, and Georgina had recently put the meal on to half-past; so Roger had ample time to prepare the scheme that he had hatched while dressing, for the discomfiture of the Russian Ambassador.

Going into the big drawing-room that was always used when Georgina had company, he opened a walnut bureau in which, he knew, a morocco-leather case was kept containing a special set of cards for playing Pharo. It held six packs, all having the same backs, but no cards of a lesser value than the tens. Four of the packs, making eighty cards in all, were used in play; the other two packs were spares for the lay out. From the latter he removed two Aces, two Kings and two Queens, which he secreted about his person, placing the Aces and Kings under his cuffs and the Queens in an inside pocket of his coat which was low down on a level with his left hip.

23

It was a foregone conclusion that in a party such as this there would be cards after dinner, for those who wished to play, and an almost equal certainty that the game chosen would be Pharo, as that was both fashionable and Georgina's favourite gamble. Roger had never cheated at cards in his life, but he meant to do so on this occasion, for a particular purpose, and about his intention he did not feel the least scruple.

For some ten minutes he remained alone, standing straddle-legged in front of the big log-fire, then Colonel Thursby joined him and shortly afterwards the other guests began to trickle down. Georgina arrived last, with a flutter of entirely insincere apologies to the other ladies, for she dearly loved to make an entrance, and had never been known to appear for dinner until the whole company was assembled.

She was dressed to-night entirely in white, her full bare shoulders rising like those of some dark Venus from a sea of thin silk; but, splendid as she looked, Roger thought that certain colours suited her voluptuous beauty better. To himself he hazarded a guess that she had selected this virginal costume to intrigue the sophisticated Russian.

Immediately on Georgina's arrival, the butler threw open the double doors and announced that Her Ladyship was served; upon which, they went in to dinner.

Colonel Thursby, as host, gave his arm to Lady Amelia, and Count Vorontzoff followed with Mrs. Armistead. Droopy Ned then bowed to Mr. Fox, who in turn bowed to George Selwyn as the eldest among them, but having returned the bow, he stepped back a pace, insisting that the younger son of the Marquis of Amesbury was the proper person to lead in the unattached males. Georgina then brought up the rear with her principal guest, the ponderous Duke.

Nearly everyone at the table had been brought up to regard good talk as of as much importance as good clothes. From their youth they had cultivated repartee as an art, and quite naturally vied with each other in capping one another's sallies. In deference to Vorontzoff much of the conversation was in French, but even had he not been there French expressions would have found frequent utterance, as it was considered fashionable to use them; and Latin tags were bandied about without the least suggestion of priggishness, since everyone present knew their meaning.

For the best part of two hours oysters, lobsters, trout, salmon, a sucking pig, a saddle of lamb, capons, ducks, pies, pasties, meringues, jellies and hot-house fruit, were devastated by the gargantuan appetites with which a life-time of habit had equipped the men and women of those times; each item being washed down with a glass of Chablis, Rhenish, Sillery, Claret or Champagne. At length Georgina caught Lady Amelia's eye, upon which the ladies left the men to belch at their ease and settle down to a little really serious drinking.

Fox was soon launched on a series of bawdy stories that set the table in a roar; Selwyn, Vorontzoff, Droopy Ned and Roger all contributed a few. Colonel Thursby, like a good host, kept the port circulating, and encouraged them with a quip here and there. Only the lugubrious Duke remained silent. He seemed to have neither humour nor humanity, but possibly he was moderately contented in his own queer way; as, immediately the ladies left the room he had fetched a long churchwarden pipe, and ever since he had been puffing at it like a suction engine, so that he was now surrounded by a cloud of smoke as dense as that issuing from one of his new factory chimneys. The others had given up all attempts to draw him into their merriment, and for them laughter and jest caused three-quarters of an hour to vanish in what seemed only the twinkling of an eye.

During the gale of mirth that followed some witty French verses with which Droopy Ned had delighted the company, Vorontzoff stood up, and, bowing slightly to Colonel Thursby, left the room by its main door, which gave on to the hall. The Colonel had already turned his attention to Selwyn, who had just started on some equally amusing couplets, so he caught Roger's eye and made a faint sign to him.

Roger guessed at once what was in the Colonel's mind. Through another door, at the opposite end of the room, one of those new innovations, a water-closet, had been installed, and they had all used it within the past hour, so it could not be for that reason that the Ambassador had left them. The Colonel feared that he might be feeling ill, and since he could not without rudeness break away from Selwyn, he wished Roger, as the guest who was best acquainted with the house, to follow Vorontzoff and ascertain what ailed him.

Getting to his feet, Roger hurried after the Russian, and caught up with him on the far side of the hall. With a quick bow he said politely: "Colonel Thursby sent me after your Excellency to inquire your reason for leaving us. I trust that you are not indisposed?"

The Ambassador smiled, and replied with equal courtesy: "Why, no, I thank you. But in the country from which I come a lady occupies the throne. With us, too, the men like to sit over their wine after dinner, but my Imperial mistress is apt to become a trifle bored if left too long in the company of her women. So it has become customary for one of us to leave our companions and place ourselves at her disposal. 'Tis a pleasant courtesy, I think, and in pursuance of it I am about to seek the Lady Georgina."

"Indeed!" said Roger, stiffly. "In that case pray do not let me detain your Excellency."

Whether the Russian was telling the truth or had just thought up the story, he had no idea; but to leave one's host prematurely for the purpose of getting in first with the ladies, was according to English standards, an abominable piece of rudeness. As Roger bowed again and turned away, he realised to his chagrin that by this skilful move Vorontzoff had secured himself a good hour, in virtually a free field, to develop his pursuit of Georgina. However, there seemed no way in which he could have prevented it, and, angrily consigning all foreigners to the devil, he went back to the dining-room.

During his short absence the atmosphere had undergone a sudden change and they were now talking politics. In his languid voice Droopy Ned was putting up an extremely able advocacy of Pitt's contention that the East India Company, and not the nation, was liable for the cost of the transport of four additional regiments of troops that had been sent out to India during the war-scare of the previous summer.

The question had recently been fought most bitterly in the House; not so much on its own account but as a fresh battle-ground on which to deploy those divergent views about the reconstruction of the Government of India, which had occupied so much of Parliament's time in the past few years.

With grandiloquent gestures and melodious voice Fox reiterated several of the most telling arguments that he had employed against the Government; but he failed to shake the stooping, short-sighted young nobleman, and at length he said good-humorously: "When may we welcome you to a seat in the House, my Lord? 'Tis the natural habitat of the younger sons of peers, as witness both Mr. Pitt and myself. Your logic and tenacity would do you credit there."

"I vow you flatter me, Sir." Droopy bowed across the table. "But even were I competent to play such a part, I should be loath to sacrifice the pursuits that already occupy a great part of my time."

"And what may they be?" inquired the Duke, suddenly emerging from his long silence.

"I, er—experiment on myself with rare drugs, and collect antique jewellery."

"Antiques, eh!" the Duke grunted. "Waste of time and money. When I was taken to Rome as a young man my fool of a tutor argued me into buying some marbles. Feller called Wood, I remember. They're still in their packing-cases somewhere. I've never had time to open the damn things, and don't suppose I ever shall."

Droopy raised his quizzing-glass and remarked a trifle acidly: "Among such marbles 'tis a fair bet that there are certain of the Roman gods. Since your Grace has elected to keep them hidden from mortal eyes for some thirty eyes, 'tis clear that you can have little sympathy with my third interest—the study of ancient religions."

"No, none whatever," replied the Duke, with the bluntness of a Dr. Johnson; to whom in fact some people considered that he had a certain resemblance. "Not only are such studies futile, but they may even become dangerous; for all Pagan religions were the invention of the Devil."

Roger had not been taking much interest in the conversation, as his mind was on Vorontzoff and Georgina; and he was wondering if by this time the Russian had managed to separate her from the other two ladies on some pretext, such as showing him her collection of silver toys, in the far drawing-room, so that he could whisper sweet nothings to her at his leisure. But he now came to the rescue of his friend, by saying:

26

"Surely your Grace would not lump the religion of the Greeks and Romans with the Devil-worship of more primitive peoples?"

"Sir, I would indeed!" came the prompt response. "For the former developed directly from the latter."

"Permit me to disagree," declared Droopy quickly. "And I have spent much time investigating the origins of both."

"If the rituals of Satanism interest you, my Lord, you should consult George Selwyn on that subject," Fox cut in with a laugh. "Ask him to tell you how he once raised the Devil."

All eyes were immediately turned on the benign, bishop-like face of the elderly wit, who said with rueful smile: "It seems that I shall never live down my association with the Hell-Fire Club, although 'tis so long ago. Its heyday was in the late '50s, and in '62, the year that Dashwood both succeeded to his Barony and became Chancellor of the Exchequer, 'twas disbanded. That is before some of you were born, so I pray you let it rest."

"Nay, nay!" cried Colonel Thursby. "Everyone knows that you were a leading member of it, and I've often meant to inquire of you what really went on there. Tell us, I beg?"

Except by the Duke, who had retired once more into his smoke screen, Selwyn was pressed on all sides, so after a moment, he said:

"Since you insist, I'll give you the gist of it. The idea originated with Sir Francis Dashwood one night at White's. My Lord Sandwich, Charles Churchill, Bubb-Dodington, Paul Whitehead, Robert Lloyd and myself, were other moving spirits in the affair. We had all become *un peu blasé* with the easy favours of society women and the ladies of the Italian Opera, so we were seeking a new outlet for our amorous propensities. Dashwood urged the claims of a masquerade with its dual attraction of dressing-up and the amusement of laying siege to an unknown partner. He proposed that we should form a new order of St. Francis, but differing from the old in that Venus should be the object of our worship; and that the rites and ceremonies to be performed should culminate in a Bacchic orgy.

"For the scene of this frolic, and it started as no more, Dashwood selected the half-ruined Abbey of Medmenham. 'Tis on an island in the Thames 'twixt Marlow and Henley, and is a most lovely spot. Later we took to gathering for a fortnight there each summer. Part of the place was made habitable, the larder and the cellar amply stocked, and a well-known bawd in Southwark brought down a score of well-chosen nymphs. We were all clad as monks, and the women, all heavily veiled, were habited as nuns. When we had dined in the old refectory, we repaired to the ruined church, and later, danced in it. As you can imagine the wine flowed freely, and on many a moonlight night we created merry Hell there."

"Oh, come, George!" protested Droopy Ned, "there must have been more to it than ordinary debauchery if, as Mr. Fox tells us, you succeeded in raising the Devil."

Selwyn looked a trifle sheepish. " 'Tis true that an element crept

27

into those meetings which had no connection with our original intentions. Once in our cups the atmosphere of the place and the garments that we wore led us into all sorts of senseless follies. All of us were staunch Protestants, and though I confess it was in bad taste, there were times when we thought it something of a jest to parody the Roman Catholic rituals."

Everyone present guessed that Selwyn was referring to the celebration of the Black Mass, but no one liked to question him about it, and Droopy said: "There is nothing new in that, either. I have oft' read accounts of such practices; but 'twould be a genuine novelty to talk with a man who has actually seen His Satanic Majesty. Did he in truth ever appear at your bidding?"

"Not at mine, but at another's."

"You saw him, though?"

"Yes, once. At least, if not himself 'twas the very image of him."

"What looked he like?"

"He was not as tall as myself but with broad shoulders and most powerfully built. He was black and hairy, with a flattened skull and red eyes gleaming from it like live coals."

"Odds blood!" exclaimed the Colonel. "I marvel that you did not all die of fright."

"We near did. My scalp still prickles at the recalling of it. Half our company fled into the night and did not stop running till they reached Marlow. The braver of us remained from a natural impulse to protect the women, the greater part of whom had fainted. But after suffering a few moments of stark terror, our courage was well rewarded."

"How so?" asked Droopy.

Selwyn smiled. "By the discovery that our visitor was quite a friendly fellow and asked no more than to take supper with us."

"George, you are romancing," Droopy laughed. "I'll not believe it."

" 'Tis true. I pledge you my word. On closer acquaintance he proved to be a tame chimpanzee hired from a circus. That irrepressible joker John Wilkes was one of our company. He had brought the ape down earlier in the day and hidden him in a box beneath the altar. Then, just as Dashwood in the role of High Priest was about to make the offering to Venus upon it, Wilkes pressed a spring and the creature jumped out."

Fox's corpulent body rocked and the tears came into his eyes with mirth, as he chortled: "Stap me! But I'd have given as much as I won at Newmarket last year for a sight of poor Dashwood's face."

"Aye, one can laugh over it after all these years," said Selwyn soberly. "But it taught us a lesson we never forgot; and 'twas the end of the Hell-Fire Club. Wilkes's ape was too like the real thing for us ever again to play at being monks and nuns, by night, in the ruins of Medmenham Abbey."

"What a character Wilkes is!" exclaimed the Colonel. "He must have caused more commotions in the past half-century than any man in England."

28

"Than any ten," cried Fox. "The controversy over that article of his in the *North Briton*, his suspension as a Member of Parliament and arrest, near caused a revolution. For twelve years the electors of Middlesex refused to be represented by any other candidate and repeatedly brought actions aimed at forcing the House to re-accept him. More of our time was spent in losing our tempers over John Wilkes than we gave in succeeding sessions to debating the American war."

"I wonder you don't blush to recall it, Charles," Selwyn smiled, "seeing that the part you played in hounding him, and battling to restrict the liberties of the press, was so contrary to your present principles."

The wily politician shrugged. "Times change, George. I was then a young, full-blooded aristocrat with little understanding of what is due to the common people. 'Tis strange to think, though, that I was once a King's man, hot to defend all privilege, whereas now Farmer George has not a subject in his whole realm that he hates more bitterly than myself."

"In that you have changed places with Wilkes, Sir," Roger laughed. "For time was when the King counted him his worst enemy; yet I have heard it said that more recently, when Wilkes had to present a petition as Lord Mayor of London, his Majesty said that he had never met a more civil man in all his life."

"'Tis true," Fox acknowledged. "And there again, see how time's magic brings the most amazing changes in the affairs of men. For who would have thought that after the publication of Wilkes' licentious '*Essay on Women*,' the straight-laced City Fathers could ever have brought themselves to elect him their Chief Magistrate; or that as a sometime member of the Hell-Fire Club he should now be spending his declining years in the grave role of City Chancellor."

"The public memory is ever plaguey short," remarked Colonel Thursby. "His private immoralities have long been submerged in most men's minds by his vast popularity, and no man of his generation has done more for the preservation of the people's liberties."

Fox nodded. "*Wilkes and Liberty!* For a score of years anyone could raise a mob at a moment's notice by that cry. I'll not forget how, after one of my speeches against him in the House, they attacked my coach and rolled me in the mud; or the cheering thousands who drew him in triumph up Ludgate Hill after he was at last released from prison. Yet, to the detriment of my own hopes of reform, a sad apathy seems to have seized upon the public mind of recent years; and there is no longer that stalwart spirit of resistance to the abuses of the Ministerial power that there was when Wilkes defied the King."

"The reason for that is not far to seek, Sir," said Droopy Ned. " 'Twas the excesses committed by the mob during the Gordon riots that put a check upon its power. That hydra-headed monster seized upon the project of extending toleration to the Roman Catholic faith as a pretext for glutting its carnal appetites. All those who saw large parts of London ablaze have since had a feeling of acute distrust

29

for popular movements. The King alone kept his head in the crisis, and insisted on calling out the troops for the rounding up of those hordes of drunken looters; so 'tis but natural that all law-abiding people should have come to look on him as the saviour of society."

Roger was still thinking fitfully of Georgina and waiting with some anxiety for the time to pass until they would join the ladies, so that he could put into operation his plan for the discomfiture of the Russian; but he now remarked: "It may well be that the brief reign of terror that so horrified everyone in June '80 will save the country from something far worse in the next decade. Discontent against the old order of things is rife in every country on the continent, particularly France, from whence I returned last autumn after a residence of four years. The middle-classes there are now leagued solidly with the masses in their demand for an end of privilege, and even the nobility themselves have come to regard a revolution as inevitable."

Droopy nodded. "Thou art right about the people of London, Roger. Having seen for themselves the horrid violence of which the mob is capable they will be mighty chary of letting it get loose again."

"That sounds good sense," Fox agreed. "And, as far as France is concerned, I would be the last to gainsay Mr. Brook's contention that we may soon see grave disorders there. The oppression and abuses under which the people of that great nation groan have detached the sympathy of all decent men from its Government; and Louis XVI is far too weak and vacillating a Monarch to succeed in maintaining his authority much longer. The sweeping away of the parasites who batten on the throne is generations overdue, and I'll be the first to acclaim it. Through its blindness and extravagance the Monarchy itself has long been riding for a fall, and should it be shaken to its foundations, so much the better. The humbling of that pair of wastrels at Versailles may well have excellent repercussions at Windsor."

"Nay, nay, Sir," cried Colonel Thursby. "I do protest that there you have allowed your feelings to run away with your sense of comparison. Whatever may be the faults of King George and Queen Charlotte no one could accuse them of being wastrels. Why, all the world knows that they entertain but once a week, and keep so poor a table that even the most spartan Ministers shun an invitation to it."

" 'Tis the fact," laughed Droopy. "Have you not heard the latest of the Queen's economies. 'Tis said that throughout the week she saves every crust from the Royal table; then has them stuck like a fence round a mess of cooked apple and served at her Saturday parties under the name of Charlotte Russe."

So, for another half-hour, the talk ran on, alternating between the grave and gay and covering another score of subjects, till the Colonel glanced at his watch and said: "Gentlemen, 'tis after eight and I am sure some of you must be eager to get to the card-table, so I suggest that we join the ladies."

In the drawing-room matters were just as Roger had suspected. Lady Amelia had brought down her needlework, and seated by the fire, was explaining various intricate stitches to the tactful and self-effacing Mrs. Armistead; while, well out of earshot at the far end of the long room, Georgina was lending an attentive ear to the Ambassador.

As the men entered, and she stood up to curtsy in response to their bows, they all exclaimed in surprise and admiration. She was no longer dressed in her creation of white silk, but in the gay Russian peasant costume that Vorontzoff had brought her, having, as she told them, changed into it with the help of the other two ladies immediately on leaving the dining-room.

The rich colouring of the embroideries and the horse-shoe shaped headdress suited her dark beauty to perfection, and although men were used to seeing women in riding-boots, there seemed to them something terrifically daring in their combination with knee-high petticoats. Raising their quizzing-glasses they crowded round her like bees about a honey-pot, and even his Grace of Bridgewater was heard to declare: " 'Tis a demmed sensible costume, and for the life of me I can't think why women don't wear such short skirts habitually."

When the sensation had subsided Georgina rang for the footmen to bring in a large card-table and began to count heads as to who wished to play. The Colonel and his Grace excused themselves on the plea of wanting to talk business and repaired to the library. Lady Amelia said that she never touched a card but would be quite happy to continue with her needlework. Fox, Selwyn, Vorontzoff, Droopy and Mrs. Armistead all declared themselves enchanted to join Georgina in a game of Pharo, then she looked interrogatively at Roger.

She knew that he could not afford to play, even for stakes which would be considered quite modest by the others; and, knowing that Lady Amelia would not play, she had counted on being able to spare him the embarrassment of a refusal, by indicating that politeness enjoined that someone should keep Lady Amelia company.

Her glance, moving with apparent casualness to the spinster by the fire, clearly suggested the line of retreat that she expected him to take; but, to her surprise, he ignored it and said: "Your servant, Madam, I will take a hand with pleasure."

The seven of them then settled themselves round the big card-table and began to share out the engraved mother-of-pearl counters, which were of several different shapes. After some discussion it was agreed that the rounds should represent crowns, the squares half-guineas, the oblongs guineas and the octagonals five-pound pieces; that five pounds should be the maximum for any initial bet and that no player should be allowed to leave his stake on to double up more than five times. Roger having elected to play, Georgina had deliberately kept the stakes down as low as she reasonably could, but she was conscious that the limit must now appear pettifogging to a man like Fox who on many occasions had won or lost upwards of ten thousand pounds in a night at Brook's or Almack's; so she smiled at him and said:

"With so low a maximum, Charles, this makes but a baby game

for you. I trust you'll bear with our modest habits when in the country."

"M'dear," he laughed good-humorously. " 'Tis a favour you do me; since nine times out of every ten that I play I finish up a loser."

On the cards being dealt round the first bank fell to Vorontzoff, who at once proceeded to make the lay-out from one of the spare packs.

The game required no skill, and was the simplest form of straight gamble. The banker merely laid out in a row in front of him an Ace, King, Queen, Knave and Ten, upon which the players placed their bets. He then dealt through the four-pack deck from which all the lower cards had been eliminated, laying each card face up, as he turned it over, to his right and left alternatively. At the beginning of each hand he declared whether he would pay out on the cards which fell to his right or to his left, and on the opposite pile he drew in. As each card was exposed he either won or lost on its equivalent Ace, King, Queen, Knave or Ten, until he had run through the deck, upon which the bank passed to the player on his left and the process was repeated.

Since only the banker handled the cards it was impossible for anyone to cheat at the game until the bank came to them; but, given the bank, an expert could so manipulate the pack as to ensure that certain of the cards equivalent to those on the table carrying the most money should fall upon the winning side. Roger was no expert, and the last thing he wished to do was to win money by cheating Georgina or any of her friends. When the bank came to him he meant to play one of his hidden cards against the card Vorontzoff had put his money on, and deliberately allow the Russian to catch him cheating.

While dressing he had racked his brains in vain for a legitimate method of heading the Russian off from his quarry, and the only means he had been able to think of was to force a duel upon him. However pressing his rival's attentions might be, he felt confident that Georgina set too high a value on herself to succumb to him on the night of his arrival. But given the Saturday afternoon and evening, and all Sunday, for gentle dalliance, if her inclinations tended that way and Fox stressed the urgency of winning the Russian to the interests of the Opposition, it was quite on the cards that she might grant him the opportunity for which he was obviously so eager before the week-end was out. Having already met him several times in London, that, according to the lax standards of the day, would not be unduly to cheapen herself.

Therefore, Roger had argued to himself, his object would be achieved if he could render the Russian *hors de combat* during the next twelve hours. The prospect of a duel had no terrors for him, since he had fought three already, and knew himself to be an extremely accomplished swordsman. The fact that duels were forbidden in England also gave him few qualms, as the penalties were rarely pressed unless one of the combatants was killed, and he had no intention of doing more than disabling his potential adversary. The problem that remained

32

was how to force a quarrel on Vorontzoff that night so that he would
be compelled to fight first thing the following morning.

At this point in his deliberations Roger had found himself badly
stuck. To pick a quarrel with a man was easy enough, but while he was
Georgina's guest he could not possibly openly insult the Russian. He
might by so doing achieve his object, but at too high a price. Georgina
would be so disgusted with his behaviour that it might make a permanent breach between them, and that he was not prepared to risk
on any account. It had then occurred to him that this difficulty could
be got over if he could so arrange matters that the Russian insulted
him. Cheating at cards was by no means unusual, even in private
houses, but if the person cheated was a man of spirit he would naturally
denounce the cheat; upon which the cheat would either attempt to
laugh it off and pay up or declare himself insulted and demand satisfaction. Roger knew that as he was not a habitual gambler, if he handled
matters skilfully, no one except Vorontzoff would believe that he had
cheated and it would be considered perfectly natural for him to call the
Russian out.

In view of his intentions Roger was anxious that he should finish
up a loser rather than a winner on the evening's game; but on the other
hand he could ill-afford to lose any considerable sum, so during the first
round of banks he confined himself to punting in five-shilling chips
and on most occasions when he won leaving his money on so that when
the cards turned against him at his second, third or fourth double
he appeared to be losing quite a lot, although, in fact, he had only lost
his original stake. Normally the steady drain of such a policy would
have cost him five or six pounds, but it seemed that his luck was in
as on two occasions his stake doubled up to the agreed limit of five
times and he had to take it off, in each case his five shillings having
become eight pounds; so when the bank came round to him he was
thirteen pounds in hand.

As each player could limit his bets at will the only chance of any
individual losing really heavily was when they took a bank, since they
were then pitted against the whole table and had to accept the heaviest
bets as well as smaller ones. In this case, five pounds being the limit,
if such a bet was left on and doubled up five times, the banker might
go down one hundred and sixty pounds against a single player. All
the odds were that he would get a considerable part of it back from the
others, but it was a risk that had to be faced and a heavy one for Roger.
Normally, he would either have passed his bank or sold it, as he had
a right to do. Mrs. Armistead had just sold hers to Fox for twenty
pounds and Georgina had passed hers. Knowing Roger's financial
circumstances she naturally expected him to do the same, so she was
surprised and a little worried when she saw him making the cards
with the obvious intention of taking it.

After a moment she said: "I think 'twould pleasure me to take
the bank after all; will you sell me yours, Sir? I'll bid you twenty
pounds for it."

Roger was touched by her offer. She was, he guessed, assuming that as he had won money on the round he felt that he ought to give the other players a chance to win it back, and had made the offer solely with the idea of enabling him to avoid the risk of losing more than he could afford. But he smiled at her and shook his head. "I thank you, Madam, but I've a feeling that my luck is in to-night, so I will take it myself."

As they had been playing for the best part of an hour he felt that he might quite well take advantage of his first bank to develop his plot, instead of waiting for it to come round to him again. Fox and Vorontzoff were both playing the maximum all the time; Selwyn, Droopy and Georgina were playing in guineas or occasionally more when they felt that they were due for a win, and Mrs. Armistead, like Roger, confined herself to the lowest stake. Up to about half-way through the deck the bank ran about even, then Fox doubled up three times and knocked Roger down for forty pounds. Soon afterwards Vorontzoff's stake upon the Ace also doubled up to forty pounds, and he still left it on.

It was the chance for which Roger had been waiting. He put down the cards for a moment to take out his handkerchief and blow his nose. While putting his handkerchief back he took an Ace out of his cuff and palmed it onto the top of the pack as he picked the cards up again. He then turned it up on the winning pile and scooped Vorontzoff's forty pounds off the ace.

As he was not a card-sharper the task he had set himself was no easy one. The last thing he wanted was for anyone other than the Russian to accuse him of cheating, so he dared not do so openly. He was counting on the fact that habitual players only take particular notice of their own losses, so that if Vorontzoff had more than average ill-luck while his neighbour was banker he would begin to watch the turning of the cards with additional care, and thus spot the cheating while it passed unnoticed by the others.

Towards the end of his bank Roger again blew his nose and, during the process, managed to get a King out of his other cuff. The Russian had doubled up twice on the King and by playing the card Roger took a further twenty pounds off him. Vorontzoff made no remark as Roger raked in the counters, but gave him a rather searching look, so he felt satisfied that during his first bank he had succeeded in arousing his enemy's suspicions.

Fox's forty pound win had hit the bank badly and without the Russian's money it would have shown a loss of twenty-six. As it was, including Roger's original gain of thirteen, he was now forty-eight up. However, he regarded Vorontzoff's sixty pounds as a liability since, had there been no cheating, the Russian might equally well have won double that or lost the lot; so Roger felt that when he had put his rival out of the running for Georgina he was under a moral obligation to return his stakes to him. In consequence, he regarded himself on balance, as now being twelve pounds down.

During the second round of the bank he once more staked only single crowns, but luck being with him in the main he made up eight pounds of his nett loss. To all appearances he was doing excellently, as when the bank came to him again he had over sixty pounds worth of chips in front of him; so Georgina, knowing nothing of his secret liability, made no further attempt to protect him from the chances he seemed perfectly content to take.

His bank opened well for him and within five minutes he had taken a profit of over thirty pounds. Selwyn then scooped sixteen off him and Georgina twelve, so two-thirds of the way through the deck he was running more or less even. But the thing which perturbed him was that Vorontzoff was now betting consistently on the Ten, and, not having thought it wise to take too many cards from the spare packs, Roger had no hidden ten to play against him. Having played the ten for some time without any marked success the Russian suddenly changed to the King and his stake began to double up. When it had reached forty pounds Roger casually inquired what the time was. Everybody glanced towards the clock upon the mantelpiece, except Vorontzoff, and as Roger slipped his second King out of his cuff, several of the players murmured: " 'Tis just on ten."

Roger played the King, feeling certain that his victim must have seen him fluff the card on to the top of the pack. As he stretched out his hand to take the stake he expected every instant that Vorontzoff would denounce him, but to his amazement, the Russian let him rake in the counters without making any protest; yet, as he glanced at him he caught a faint, hard smile of understanding in his dark Tartar eyes.

Momentarily, Roger was a further forty up, but his bank ended with a run of ill-luck. Droopy suddenly doubled up on three successive Aces and took thirty-two pounds, Selwyn had also been on the Ace and took ten, and on the very last card, a Queen, Fox took twenty. Roger still had a fair pile of chips in front of him, but on checking up he found to his considerable alarm that he was now over sixty pounds out of pocket in addition to his moral obligation of a further hundred to Vorontzoff.

He realised now that he had been incredibly foolish to choose cards as a means of getting at the Russian Ambassador; as his plan necessitated his taking the bank, and he had overlooked the fact that, quite apart from any sum which he might feel in honour bound to make good to his enemy, he would be laying himself open to much greater losses than he could afford to the other players.

His only consolation was a confident belief that at his next bank he would achieve his object. The glimpse he had caught of the Russian's eyes had convinced him that his victim now knew positively that he was being rooked; and there seemed little doubt that he was only waiting for a chance to pounce when there was a better prospect that someone else at the table might also see what was going on. Roger knew that to avoid such a calamity he would need all the skill he could muster, as Vorontzoff was now watching him like a lynx, and might, if he could catch him taking the next card from his cuff, expose him in front of the whole company before he could get it on to the table.

As the bank went round again Roger became more and more miserable and depressed; and the fact that he was winning small sums fairly consistently did little to cheer him. He felt that he must have been absolutely crazy to embark on this wild-cat scheme and would never have done so had he given the matter proper thought. Just before he had come down to dinner it had seemed so simple, but he knew now that his jealousy and resentment had temporarily obscured his judgment, and led him to act on an inspiration which was not only fundamentally dishonest but needed the abilities of a professional card-sharper to carry through. Yet, having once made up his mind to a course it was against his whole nature to abandon it, and the very fact that he was now so heavily committed made him more determined than ever to play the game out to its end.

Georgina, having seen how heavily he had gone down on his last bank, made a further attempt to rescue him while he appeared to have some of his earlier winnings in hand. While the bank was still two away from him she yawned and said: " 'Tis getting quite late for a country bumpkin, like myself. What say you to ceasing play after the next hand?"

"But 'tis barely eleven o'clock," remarked Fox in some surprise, and Vorontzoff added with a gallant little bow:

"Only a clod, Madam, would seek to rob so lovely a lady of her beauty sleep; yet if a further twenty minutes will not cause a dimming of your eyes to-morrow, I pray you let the bank complete its third round, as Mr. Brook has taken a hundred or so off me, and I would fain have a chance to get it back."

To that there could be only one answer, so play went on, and in due course the cards were shuffled for Roger's third bank. He had now only two Queens and an Ace, left so his opportunities for cheating were limited to two out of the five cards on the table, and to his annoyance, Vorontzoff once more favoured the Ten. Since it was the last hand all the players, except Georgina and Mrs. Armistead, were putting on the limit, but for a third of the deck their bets practically cancelled each other's out; then Fox and Droopy entered on a run of bad luck, both losing five pounds a time on the Ace for two runs of six and four respectively, but Vorontzoff won a *coup* of forty pounds on the Ten, thus reducing Roger's hundred pound gain from the other two to sixty and making him, apart from his moral liability to the Russian, all square within a few pounds.

Having gathered up his winnings Vorontzoff began to bet again, this time on the Queen. There were only some twenty odd cards to go, yet in the next eight cards played three Queens came up on Roger's losing side.

He knew that it was now or never. If he could get one of his hidden Queens on to the top of the pack without anyone except the Russian seeing him do it all the odds were that he would, after all, pull off his stupid, hair-brained scheme. But he realised that, with the additional excitement which always accompanies the close of a game, all eyes were now upon him; and he could not pause; he had to go on turning up the cards at the same pace and with apparent unconcern.

The next losing card again proved to be a Queen. As he added counters to Vorontzoff's stake, turning it from forty pounds into eighty, his throat was dry and little beads of perspiration broke out on his forehead.

He expected the counters to be swept away, but, with mixed feelings, saw that the Russian made no move towards them. The accumulated stake being left on gave Roger one more chance to either win it back fairly or to endeavour to palm one of his Queens and carry out his plan. But if he failed to do one or the other, instead of eighty pounds he would go down for one hundred and sixty, and, as five times were the limit for doubling up, the rule would then compel Vorontzoff to remove it, so that all further chance for Roger to recover his losses would be gone for good.

Six pairs of eyes were now riveted upon him so he positively dared not attempt to cheat. Moistening his lips he turned the next card, a King and an Ace, then the next pair, an Ace and a Ten, then the next a Jack and a Queen.

A faint tremor of indrawn breaths went round the table. Roger had lost yet again. He gave the shrug of well-bred indifference that was expected of a good loser, but his palms were moist as he drew from the pool of counters in reserve a further sixteen five-pound octagonal plaques to pay up the Ambassador.

Still the Russian did not take up his winnings, now piled high upon the Queen. Instead he said quietly: "It may be that there is yet another Queen among the remaining cards. If Monsieur Brook has the courage to extend the limit, I will give him a further opportunity to test his fortune."

Georgina's eyes were on Roger, begging him to refuse the offer, but he ignored her glance. If he left things as they were he had already lost far more than he had the means to pay, and the Russian had challenged him to make it double or quits. Since he had let himself in for the nightmare folly, it seemed to him that he might just as well be hung for a sheep as a lamb. With a pale smile at Vorontzoff he replied:

"With pleasure, Excellency."

All thought of endeavouring to cheat had now left his mind, but as he made to turn up the next card the moisture of his fingers caused it to stick for a second; instead of falling on to the right-hand pile it hit the table-edge, hovered, and fluttered to the floor. As he stooped to recover it, the thought flashed upon him that fate was giving him a last moment opportunity to carry out his plan. With a quick movement he palmed one of the Queens from his inside pocket under cover of his lace ruffle.

With a murmured apology for his clumsiness he passed the few cards left in the pack to Fox, and said: "I pray you reshuffle for me, Sir."

Fox did as he was asked and returned the cards. As Roger took them back he covered them with his lace frilled hand and slid the Queen on top. Since five out of the six people against him had not the least suspicion that he had been cheating, none of them had any reason to suppose that his having dropped one of the cards had been anything but an accident, or gave a second thought to his rather clumsy way of taking them back from Fox. But to anyone who suspected him already the movement must have been transparent.

To Roger, for a few seconds, time seemed to stand still. Every instant he expected the Russian to lurch forward, grab his wrist and accuse him. The revelation that a Queen was on top of the pack would give point to his accusation, but be no proof. Roger would then be entirely within his rights to challenge him. It darted through his mind that he would still be morally liable to his enemy for a sum which he would have very considerable difficulty in raising. But that was beside the point. As he waited, tense and expectant a little glow of triumph warmed his heart; for he felt that he had succeeded, after all, in what a few minutes before had seemed utterly impossible.

Gradually the sudden wave of elation ebbed away. Vorontzoff did nothing; said nothing. The silence seemed to Roger to become unbearable until Fox said: "Go on, Sir. For what are you waiting?"

With a strained smile Roger picked up the cards. He was within a hair's breadth of turning up the Queen on to the winning pile, when, with a swift movement, Vorontzoff checked him.

Roger's heart leapt. He was no longer thinking of the money, but longing for the accusation which would enable him to issue a challenge. "God be thanked," he thought. "Here it comes, at last."

But the Russian said, almost casually, "Seeing that we are now playing outside the limit, have you any objection, *Monsieur*, to my giving the cards a final shuffle?"

The blood drained from Roger's face, but he could only bow and reply: "I have no objection whatever, your Excellency."

With the deft fingers of an expert card-player Vorontzoff shuffled the now slender deck and replaced them with a slap in front of Roger.

Picking them up he began grimly to turn them over, knowing that his Queen was now lost somewhere in the centre of the little pack. As he laid them down, first to one side then the other, he paid out or took in on the smaller bets that remained on the table. He came to the last two cards; the first was a Ten, the second a Queen.

He knew then that he had been hoist with his own petard. Instead of accusing him of cheating, Vorontzoff had chosen to await his opportunity, and under the eyes of the whole table, being a really skilful cheat, had, during his swift shuffle, transferred the Queen from the top to the bottom of the pack.

There was nothing that Roger could do about it; nothing at all.

His supply of chips had enabled him to pay out everybody else, leaving him with thirty shillings in excess of his original allocation; and Vorontzoff's own act had cancelled out any moral liability to pay him later the sums of which he had been rooked earlier in the game. But the appalling fact remained that he owed the Russian three hundred and twenty pounds—which was more than he received as a whole year's income.

Roger knew that he deserved the stroke of nemesis that had overtaken him, but that did not make him feel less sick at heart. With commendable *savoir faire* in the circumstances he bowed to the Ambassador and said: "I congratulate your Excellency. As I have not this sum with me I trust that you will accept my I.O.U."

"With pleasure, *Monsieur*," Vorontzoff bowed back, smiling sardonically; and, while the other losers settled their smaller losses in cash, Roger went over to a Dutch bureau that stood between two of the windows and wrote out a promissory note for three hundred and twenty pounds.

On the game breaking up Georgina pulled the bell by the fire place. A few minutes later a servant wheeled in a two-tiered wagon with a tea-set on top and dishes of pastries and stuffed *brioches* below. He was an elderly man who walked with a limp, and in strange contrast to the scarlet and gold liveries and powdered hair of the footmen who had waited at dinner, he wore a simple blue blouse and baize apron.

Those of the guests who had been there before showed no surprise, but Vorontzoff looked so taken aback that Georgina laughed, and said: "I have a strange whim concerning my maids and men, and will not allow them to be kept up till all hours. From nine o'clock they are free to do as they will, and old Barney, here, looks after our requirements. His days are his own, but at night he occupies a chair in the hall, tends the fires and amuses himself polishing my riding-boots. He taught me to ride as a child and has a marvellous touch with leather."

With a smile she added in English to the old groom. "How go that new pair of boots of mine from Lobb, Barney?"

"Fine, m'Lady," he beamed back. "I need but another week on they an' ye'll be able to see your pretty face in 'em better 'n in any mirror."

As the old man limped away, Vorontzoff said: " 'Tis a most strange innovation to dismiss one's servants after dinner. I fear mine would think me gone mad did I attempt to do so; but it speaks a volume for your graciousness as a mistress."

"I thank you, Sir. And now, while the tea-kettle boils, I would have you give me your opinion of a painting by Canaletto that I bought last year whilst in Italy. 'Tis in the small drawing-room yonder, if you would give me your arm so far."

Roger had been brought up in the tradition that whatever personal emotion or distress a gentleman may be feeling he never shows it in company; so he was making a great effort to appear quite normal as he chatted with the others, and not show by the least sign how seriously his heavy loss had affected him. Out of the corner of his eye he saw Georgina and Vorontzoff move off together, and it was clear to him that the twelve hours they had now spent in one another's company had been quite sufficient for them to have got on most excellent terms; but he endeavoured to force both that and his debt into the back of his mind.

The pair were absent for only a few minutes and on her return Georgina infused the fine Bohea. Meanwhile old Barney had wheeled in another trolley carrying an array of wines and spirits, and everyone partook of either a dish of tea or some stronger night-cap.

After ten minutes or so Georgina walked over to one of the windows, and, drawing back the heavy brocaded curtain a little, looked out. It was a clear, starry night, and returning to the group by the fire she said to Roger: "I've a mind to take a breath of air on the terrace before I retire. You know the closet in the hall where I keep my cloak. I pray you get it for me and we will take a turn together."

Wondering what this forboded he accompanied her to the door, fetched her cloak and rejoined her on the top of the terrace steps. As they walked down them she said at once: "What in the world came over you to-night, Roger, to behave with such consummate folly?"

He shrugged. "Need we go into that, m'dear. I'll admit that I behaved like a fool; but the damage is done, and no good can come of holding an inquest on it."

"But, damn it man, you cannot afford such losses! Your pocket is no match for those of men like Fox, Selwyn and the Ambassador; and common sense should have warned you to eschew playing with them in the first instance."

"I know it; but I little thought then that I would go down so heavily."

" 'Twas your own fault," she countered angrily. "And 'twas not like you, Roger. In all our lives I have never known you to lose your head before. You are no gambler either, normally, and rarely touch a card. What possessed you I cannot think. Again, and again I sought to check your rashness, yet you ignored my signals and deliberately plunged deeper as the game progressed."

" 'Tis true. But I beg you spare me your reproaches. 'Tis punishment enough that through an ill-conceived impulse I should have sunk myself for more than I receive from my father in a year."

"And how do you intend to raise this money?"

"I have the best part of two hundred in the funds. For the rest, I shall sell my mare and some of the more extravagant items of my wardrobe that I have bought since my return from France. Then I shall go abroad again, and once more seek to support myself as best I can."

Georgina paused in her walk and laid a hand on his. She felt that she had punished him enough for his strange lapse into reckless folly, and her voice was warm again as she said: "Poor Roger! Be not down-cast. Such desperate remedies will not be necessary. Thy debt is paid, or very soon will be."

"What mean you?" he exclaimed, swinging round towards her.

She drew a crumpled half sheet of notepaper from her bosom and pressed it into his hand. "Here is your I.O.U. Destroy it, m'dear; and think no more of your three-hour fit of madness."

"How—how did you get this?" Roger stammered, with a sudden feeling of apprehension.

Georgina laughed. "Why, I asked Vorontzoff for it, of course; while I was showing him the Canaletto. He gave it to me in exchange for the privilege of carrying my candle when we go up, and lighting me to bed."

CHAPTER IV

A NIGHT IN A LIFE-TIME

R O G E R was three-quarters of a head taller than Georgina and for a moment he stood staring down into her upturned face, a prey to the most wildly conflicting emotions. After his almost suicidal feelings of the past half-hour, the thought that he would not, after all, have to part with his small nest-egg and most of his treasured possessions in order to raise three hundred and twenty pounds, came as an immense relief. Also he knew that he should be deeply grateful to Georgina, and that she was standing there expecting him to burble out his heartfelt thanks for having saved him from the results of his folly.

Yet he was not grateful to her. Or, at least, while he was far from lacking in appreciation of the swiftness with which she had come to his rescue, he was also bitterly resentful of the means she had adopted to that end. He guessed that, as so often was the case with her, she must have acted on a generous impulse; but, in so doing, had pre-cipitated the very situation which, even to the point of reckless folly, he had been seeking to postpone until after their parting.

Striving to control the emotion in his voice, he said:

" 'Twas mightily good of you, Georgina; but, by taking my debt over in this fashion you have unwittingly put a humiliation upon me that I find it monstrous hard to bear."

"Stuff and nonsense," she replied sharply. "I simply told his Excellency that since 'tis our custom to let the servants seek their beds at a reasonable hour we have a row of candles left for us in the hall, and that when you are staying here 'tis your privilege, as my oldest friend, to light me to my room. He rose to the bait like a trout at a mayfly, and hazarded that if you would sell him that privilege for to-night he would gladly accept it in cancellation of your debt; where-upon I closed the deal. What, pray, do you find humiliating in that?"

41

"I find it humiliating that you should have to barter your favours to pay my debts."

"I promised him no favours."

"By inference you certainly did."

She shrugged. "That I'll admit; but they will be only what I choose to give."

"Think you so? Once you present that Russian with a fair field to set about you, I'd give little for your chances of receiving quarter."

"Oh, Roger, why must you dramatise the matter so? You are acting like a romantic schoolboy and talking to me as if I were a girl in her first season. I'll pay your debt in my own fashion, but there will be no sordidness about the transaction, as you suggest."

"Yet you would not have offered him an opening so soon; had it not been for my predicament."

"Perhaps not; but since you press the point, your own conduct has brought matters to a head more speedily than I expected."

"If you admit that, 'tis as good as admitting that you are selling yourself to pay my debt, and therein lies my humiliation."

Georgina drew herself up. "How dare you suggest that I would sell myself for a paltry three hundred pounds!"

" 'Tis not the money but the principle of the thing. You know as well as I that you have made an unspoken bargain with the man and are by nature too honest to go back upon it."

"I tell you that I have made no bargain! The Russian has taken a gamble on my good-will, no more. He may count himself lucky if I allow him to kiss me good-night."

Roger's laugh rang with angry scorn. "Is it likely that he will be content with that?"

"I do not know, and I do not care," Georgina flared. "I told you this morning that what I had seen of him in London had predisposed me in his favour. On closer acquaintance I find him both intelligent and amusing. Therefore I pray you disabuse yourself of this notion that anything I may choose to do will be done on account of your own folly. Both political interest and my own inclination conspire in urging me to favour his suit. In the circumstances, it seemed to me that if by accelerating matters a little I could also cancel out this wretched debt of yours, I should be doing you a service. Now, Sir, I pray you take me within doors again."

Roger bowed stiffly. "Since those are your sentiments, Madam, no more remains to be said." Then he offered her his arm, and in stony silence escorted her back to the drawing-room.

It was now close on midnight, and within a few moments of their reappearance the company declared for bed. Going out into the hall they lit their respective candles, and having mounted the broad staircase in a body, separated on the landing with a chorus of "good nights."

Georgina and Vorontzoff turned to the right. Roger, following a few paces behind, saw them pass the door of her bedroom and enter the next one to it, which led into her boudoir. As he passed it the door closed behind them. Biting his lip, he walked on down the corridor to the third door in the row, that of Sir Humphrey Etheredge's room, which he was occupying; and, going in slammed it behind him with a loud bang.

In the boudoir Vorontzoff had just completed the lighting of a three-branched candelabra that stood on an occasional table at the head of the golden day-bed. As the slam reverberated through the room he shot a quick look at the communicating door, then smiled at Georgina. " 'Twas young Mr. Brook behind us just now, was it not? He seems to have sought his bed in something of a temper."

She made a little face. "Poor fellow! He sets considerable store on his privilege of lighting me to bed and was most loath to surrender it, even for the cancellation of his debt."

"That I can well understand, *Madame*. And lest it trouble him so much as to cause him to walk in his sleep we will take due precaution that he should not disturb you."

As he spoke the Russian took three swift steps towards the communicating door and shot its bolt; then he turned to face her again and gave her a long steady look.

He was not as tall as Roger but broader in the shoulders, and all his movements denoted a quick, determined mind. His flattish face was saved from ugliness by its strength, and the upward slope of his dark eyebrows at their outer ends gave him a faint resemblance to a satyr.

Georgina, faintly smiling, returned his look. She was intensely curious to know what line he would take with her. In such a situation the usual technique of the day was for the gallant to pour out a stream of wildly exaggerated compliments, beseech the fair to take pity on him, and falling on his knees before her, vow that he would commit suicide unless she salved the sweet but deadly wound that Cupid's arrow had made in his heart. If the lady actively disliked him, or wished to prolong his torment, she firmly rejected all his pleas. Otherwise she pretended an exaggerated virtue and alarm, gradually appeared to become affected by her lover's emotion and finally, apparently quite distraught, half-fainting and with languorous sighs, succumbed to his attack.

Having been the object of a score of such attempts during the past five years Georgina had come to find them a little boring, and the Russian's only real attraction for her lay in the fact that she believed his love-making would prove quite different from anything that she had so far experienced.

As their long look broke, he picked up the candle again and moved with resolute steps towards her bedroom.

"Monsieur!" she exclaimed. "Whither are you going?"

"Why, to light the candles you will need for your night-toilette, Madame," he replied airily. "Surely you do not think that I am a man

43

who would leave anything half done. I pray you come with me and show me which lights you will require."

She wondered if he meant to pounce upon her immediately he had got her inside, and she was by no means prepared to let him do so as yet. But the casualness of his tone suggested that he intended no more than to complete his service with the candle; so, a little uncertainly she followed him through the door. Then, keeping well away from him, she said: "If you will light the candles on my dressing-table and the night-light beside my bed, those will serve."

He complied without giving her a glance, set down the candle he was carrying next to the night-light on the far side of the big four-poster, and, stepping into the centre of the room looked round it with the eye of a connoisseur.

" 'Tis a lovely apartment," he declared, "and well-suited to be Hymen's playground for the loveliest lady in all England."

"Fie, Monsieur!" she rebuked him. "I am not used to hear such outspoken thoughts from a new acquaintance."

"Indeed!" His eyebrows lifted in faint mockery. "Then English-men must be even poorer champions in the lists of love than they are reputed. In my country even acquaintanceship is accounted redundant when two pairs of eyes have met and kindled the Divine spark."

"Then it must be a plaguey dangerous place for the poor females," Georgina smiled. "But come, Monsieur, let us return to my boudoir and you shall tell me something of your country before I send you to your rest."

She had already turned to go through the doorway. Suddenly he took two swift strides forward and seized her from behind. One of his arms shot round her waist and caught her to him, the other encircled her breast with the hand raised to grasp her chin. Catching it firmly between his fingers and thumb, he jerked round her head and, thrust-ing his own face over her shoulder he kissed her full upon the mouth.

For a moment she let him have his way, then she made a violent effort to free herself; but his grip held her like a vice, and he kept his mouth pressed against hers until they were both breathless.

At last he jerked back his head, smiled down into her eyes, and panted: "A demonstration of how a Russian can love is better than any tales I could tell." Then, shifting his grip, he picked her up, carried her across the room and threw her down upon the bed.

As she made no attempt to cry out, or even to protest, he felt that his triumph was assured; but he had reckoned without Georgina's agility and resourse. Within a second of his having thrown her face upward on the bed she had jerked herself over, squirmed off it and stood facing him on its far side.

"Enough of this!" she panted. "Your Excellency is much mistaken if you think that I am to be taken so."

He laughed, his dark eyes boring into hers, his white teeth flashing. "If you prefer the French style to the Russian, Madame, you have but to say so. I am accounted a tolerably good lady's maid and would be charmed to assist at your unrobing. I ask only that you should spare me the pretended vapourings, faints and tears, which most English ladies seem to regard as an essential accompaniment to their surrender."

"I will spare you both that and all other exertions," Georgina said regally. "The favours you have received elsewhere have led you to count your chickens before they are hatched on this occasion. 'Tis my pleasure that you should now leave my room."

"Nay. That is too much to ask," he shot back. "You are a woman in a million, and I have set my heart upon you. I mean you no disrespect when I say that you have long lived apart from your husband and taken other lovers in his place. And you openly encouraged me to hope. Choose for yourself, then, if we are to play Cupid's game with the leisurely refinement of the French, or if you would have me leap this bed and catch you as I can."

Georgina's heart was hammering in her breast. The novelty of the Russian's forthright love-making had already surpassed her expectations. She found it wildly exciting; and now the time had clearly come when she must either give in to him or take some drastic action to cut matters short.

The thought of Roger crossed her mind. She still felt that he had behaved boorishly in seeking to put a restraint upon her contrary to their original pact; yet she knew that she had hurt his pride by breaking away from him so abruptly; and had wanted to be able to salve it the following morning by telling him that she had dismissed Vorontzoff after letting him take only a couple of kisses.

Suddenly she decided that she had had enough excitement for one night, and that the present game would lose nothing from keeping; so she took refuge in a clever lie.

"Monsieur," she said. "I have ordered you to leave my room. I now beg you to do so in order to avoid a most unseemly incident. My father and I are much attached and 'tis his invariable custom to come in and wish me goodnight after I have retired. He will be here at any moment now and I should be mightily shamed if he found you with me."

Vorontzoff had no means of telling if she was speaking the truth, yet he could not decently refuse such a request. It seemed that she had completely foiled him, but after thinking furiously for a moment, he said: "So be it, Madame. At what hour shall I return?"

"I—I fail to understand . . . " she faltered.

" 'Tis quite simple," he said with sudden gravity. "While we were admiring your Canaletto we made an unspoken bargain. Under pretext of my lighting you to your room you invited me here. Men and women such as you and I do not make assignations for such an hour and place to tell one another nursery-rhymes. Besides: you cannot have so soon forgotten the clothes that you are wearing."

Georgina gave a swift glance down at her embroidered bodice and short skirts. "Why no!" she said, with a puzzled frown. " 'Tis the Russian peasant costume, you gave me. But, what of it?"

"Surely, Madame, you realised that it is a wedding-dress; and that I should naturally take your having donned it so promptly as a clear sign that you were willing to grant me a husband's place to-night."

She shook her head. "I donned it in your honour, Monsieur, but with no thought that the garment had any special significance."

"Then let that pass," he shrugged. "There still remains our un-spoken bargain."

"Do you dare to infer that I am to be bought for three hundred pounds," she cried hotly.

"Nay," he protested. "You are unfair. The matter hinged upon your desire to save that young man from an embarrassment. The money itself is a mere bagatelle, and I crave permission to place at your feet jewels of ten times that value. But of more worth still are the services that I can render you. I am no fool, Madame, and I know both your love of power and the value that Mr. Fox sets upon the Russian interest. If you will honour the inference upon which you brought me here, and the significance of the dress you wear to-night, I will place all my influence unreservedly at your disposal to-morrow."

Georgina hesitated. She had believed that while this hard-headed diplomat might prove a novel and amusing lover, she would probably find it extremely difficult to sway him politically; yet he was now offering her that power to exercise a secret influence on great events which was her most cherished ambition.

"I must think," she murmured. "Give me a little time, I beg."

"Madame! You are playing with me!" His voice held a sudden note of anger. "We Russians are not accustomed to such finesse, and when we want a thing we want it badly. You are old enough to know your mind on such a matter. Have done with these delays and give me your answer."

She gave him a half smile and pleaded: "To-morrow. Surely, you can wait till to-morrow for it."

While they had been talking he had imperceptibly edged round the corner of the bed. Suddenly he moved again and, with one bound was on its far side; but he made no attempt to seize her. Falling on his knees he reached up, and grasping her hands he began to smother them with kisses, as he cried.

"To-morrow! Why to-morrow when to-night can be ours! Oh, my beautiful Georgina, I beg you to take pity on me. I am no pretty, strutting youth, but a strong man worthy of your love. All these winter months since I first saw you in Devonshire House I have adored you with the adoration that we Russians reserve for the Saints. I cannot live unless you will grant me what I ask. I am your slave to do with as you will, but let me return in half an hour to renew my worship at the loveliest of shrines. Let me come back I implore—I entreat you."

Georgina's heart was now beating fast again. Had she been in any state to think clearly she would have realised that the Russian's love-making was no more than a reversal of the usual procedure; yet his having attacked her first and reserved his impassioned pleas for later had proved more effective, and her brain was in a whirl. As she bent above him she felt all the thrill of having, after all, reduced this strong, virile representative of a great nation to a suppliant at her feet, and emotion now combined with interest to incline her to be merciful.

"What I would not do for jewels I might do from kindness," she whispered. "For your passion moves me much. Yet I will make no promises."

He suddenly released her hands and stood up to renew his anguished pleading. "Madame, how can you have the heart to torment me further? Be plain with me or I shall be forced to think you the hardest-hearted of coquettes."

"Nay, I will not be rushed into yielding on a wave of emotion," she declared with sudden firmness. "You must grant me, Monsieur, the next half hour to make up my mind while I undress. You may return then if you wish to put out the lights and learn my decision."

His flushed face broke into a smile and, stepping back, he made her a low bow. "With that, Madame, I rest content. Unless your heart is made of stone, April the first will now prove to be the happiest dawn that I have ever known."

Her nerves were still taut, and as he turned away, she gave a little semi-hysterical laugh. " 'Twould be unwise to count on anything on such a date; for 'tis All Fools' Day."

Evidently he guessed that she had made the silly joke in an effort to recover her normal poise, since he did not reply but crossed the boudoir without even a glance over his shoulder; and a moment later she heard the door click as he let himself out into the corridor.

With a breathless sigh she sat down at her dressing-table and began to unpin the golden headdress. Standing up again she stripped off the gay wedding costume and slipped on her filmy night robe; then she settled herself before her mirror once more.

For a moment she remained quite still, regarding the lovely image of herself. She was still in the first flush of her beauty; not even the suggestion of a wrinkle marred her skin, and with her abounding health, she saw no reason why they should do so for many years to come. Slowly she gave her face the few touches that it needed with the hare's foot and the powder-puff; then she combed through her lustrous black hair, and very conscious that this was no night to do it up in curl-papers, re-arranged it with a blue satin bow to gather her curls in a cluster at the back of her neck.

Dousing the candles on the dressing-table, she walked through to the boudoir and put the lights out there. On her way back she left the door ajar, then removed the big copper warming pan from the bed and wriggled down into its soft, warm depths.

The room was lit now only by the glow of the dying fire and the fat, shaded night-light beside the bed.

Georgina turned on her back and stretched luxuriously, then she relaxed and lay staring up at the draped canopy of the great four-poster.

Her thoughts were still a little chaotic. She was somehow more certain than ever now that she had never really intended to commit herself to-night, and she realised that it was only Roger's stupidity at the card-table that had led her into doing so. Yet she could not find it in her heart to blame him. Such a loss of his normally well-balanced head could only have been caused by some secret disturbance that was going on inside it, and for that there could be only one explanation—her own jilting of him without adequate preparation.

It occurred to her now that she ought to have sent him away a few days ago and said nothing of Vorontzoff's projected visit. He would have gone quite cheerfully then, knowing well enough that in due course she would take another lover, yet still retaining his romantic feelings for her. It grieved her now to think that she had hurt and offended him quite unnecessarily.

This was not the first time that she had had to reproach herself with the results of her besetting sin, which was demanding too much of life. That was the trouble; she always wanted to eat her cake and keep it too. In her heart of hearts she had known perfectly well that Roger would take the Russian's overtures to her badly, yet she had not been sufficiently strong-minded either to send him away or refuse Fox's request that she should invite the Ambassador down for this week-end. She knew too that the reason for that was not far to seek. In spite of the occasional tiffs that had crept into her intimacy with Roger, she was still physically in love with him and wanted him to stay on at Stillwaters with her through the spring.

She was already wishing that it was he who would be coming to her in a few moments now. She loved to gaze her fill into those deep blue eyes and feel his strong arms hold her close. He was such a marvellous lover too, because he had such a happy nature. When roused his passion matched her own, but at times he could be very gentle, and he teased her deliciously. She had never known another man who could bring such an element of merriment to his love-making.

But in a fit of temper she had forbidden Roger her room, and the evening's events had made it quite certain that he would not risk a fresh humiliation by ignoring her prohibition. By now he was either asleep or tossing restlessly in his bed, a prey to bitter, angry thoughts about her. For a moment she thought of getting up and going in to him, but she dismissed the idea almost as soon as it arose. To do so now might result in a most appalling scene culminating in a duel. It was too late now to undo the web of her own spinning in which she had entangled herself. She must stop thinking about Roger and think about the strange, dark, violent man who was coming to her instead.

She had forced him to give her half an hour's respite and insisted that her mind was not yet made up; but she knew full well that on his return that would count for nothing. There was no escape now from the grasp of those strong, square-fingered hands, and the avid mouth that had crushed itself against hers so fiercely. He was considerably older than any lover that she had previously taken but she felt certain that he did not lack virility. Perhaps, just as she had first thought, his very strangeness would prove terribly exciting. She had not relished his hot flat face being pressed against her own, yet she had given way before to men who had attracted her less, in order to satisfy her curiosity. In any case she had made her bed and must now lie upon it. She wondered then how long he would remain with her, and with a sinking heart recalled his mentioning the dawn. In vain she sought to fight off the conviction that she would hate him before the morning.

A soft footfall caught her ear, followed by the gentle closing of a door. She gave a start, then quickly shut her eyes and stilled her breathing as though she had fallen asleep. It was a last poor little effort at defence on the slender chance that, finding her so, he would grant her a reprieve and refrain from waking her. Yet she knew all the time that it was childish to think for an instant that such a scruple would induce him to forego his victory.

The footsteps drew nearer. They crossed the soft carpet and halted beside the bed. For a moment that seemed to her of almost unendurable length nothing happened. She could hear her heart thumping wildly; a lump was rising in her throat. She felt that unless the tension ended in another instant she would scream.

Then a quiet voice said: " 'Tis a pleasant change to find you without your hair done up in curl papers."

"Roger!" She started up on her elbow; her eyes wide, the blood draining from her face, as she gasped. "What brings you here?"

"To see that you were well, happy, and to wish you a good night," he replied lightly.

"But I forbade you to come!"

"As a lover, perhaps; but you have not withdrawn from me the privilege of a brother."

" 'Tis no time for splitting straws," she said in a fierce whisper. "You must go—go instantly."

"Why this perturbation?" he smiled. "And your prodigious eagerness to be rid of me?"

"Because—because Vorontzoff's coming back, and will be here at any moment. If he finds you here . . ." her voice trailed away on a note of panic.

"And what if he did?"

"Oh, are you mad?" She sat up and wrung her hands. "Spare me, I beg, a brawl in my own room! Or worse! He may challenge you to a duel in which one of you might be killed."

"Nothing would please me better than the chance to spit him like the conceited turkey-cock he is. It made my gall rise till it near choked me to see the way in which he treated you as if already you were his, this evening."

"Oh, Roger, please!" she begged. "I have been at fault, I know. I

49

did not originally intend to bring matters to a head this week-end. I swear it! If I have hurt you 'tis I who am paying for it now. I would with all my heart that I could stop his coming. But 'tis too late. Add not to my distress by creating some dreadful scene that may end in tragedy."

"So you would stop his coming if you could?"

"Yes, yes. But that is of little moment. 'Twill be no more than *un mauvais quart d'heure*; then I'll get rid of him. What matters is that he should not find you here. Leave me, I implore you!"

He smiled down at her. "Then it seems that I have been able to render you a service. You may set your mind at rest m'dear, regarding this meeting that you now find distasteful. Count Vorontzoff will not be returning to you to-night."

"Roger!" she cried, starting forward in fresh panic. "What have you done?"

"I left him but five minutes back; having delivered a message purporting to come from you."

"From me?"

"Yes. I had the door of my room open a crack and saw him leave your boudoir after a bare ten minutes. 'Twas a sack of peas to a million pounds that he would not count so short a conversation adequate payment for my I.O.U.; and by the smile upon his conceited face I guessed that you must have given him permission to return. So I went to him and paid my debt. Then I told him that, since you were no longer under an obligation to him, you had exercised a lady's privilege of changing her mind, and had desired me to inform him that you would dispense with his attendance."

"You paid your debt! But how?"

"I went first to Droopy; who gave me a draft on sight at Coutts for the money. The Russian could not refuse to accept it."

"But—but your debt was not the only thing which caused me to commit myself," she stammered. "I could easily have found three hundred for you next week. I had made a bargain with him to give Charles Fox his political support. I do confess it. Oh, Roger, he may yet come back on that account."

"Nay, he will not. I guessed that you would do that, and 'tis for me now to confess that I took drastic measures to ensure against it. When I handed him the draft I drew his attention to the date."

"What!" Georgina gasped. "And 'tis April the first."

"You have it, sweet!" Roger began to titter. "I told him that you and I had been leading him on the whole evening, and that we had made of him our this year's first April Fool."

"Roger, you didn't!" Suddenly her sense of humour got the better of her, and throwing up her hands she began to rock with laughter.

For over a minute they chortled with childish glee. Then, as she wiped the tears from her eyes, she exclaimed:

"Oh, darling, you'll be the death of me. But how did the poor man take it?"

"Badly, I fear," Roger admitted. "He went as white as a sheet, and I hoped that he would call me out. But he refrained, and merely remarked sarcastically that, in time, no doubt, he would learn how to adapt himself to our English sense of humour."

"You were right to term it a drastic measure," Georgina said more soberly. " 'Tis an injury that he will not forget, and I'll swear to it that he has a vengeful nature. Henceforth we must beware of him and take all measures possible to guard against his enmity."

Roger shrugged. "I can take good care of myself, and you have no cause to worry. To-morrow you can be huffy with him and avoid a *tête-à-tête*. On Monday morning, before he leaves, give him an opening for an explanation. Ask him why he failed to return here to-night, and when he tells you be wide-eyed with pretended ignorance. Throw the whole thing on me, and vow that I alone was the cause of this *contretemps*. 'Tis no departure from the truth. Then you can give him an assignation for later in London, or not, just as you please."

"That will not serve," she shook her head. "To-night, as so often is the case, our minds must have been *en rapport*, or 'twas by the merest fluke. But the very last remark I made to him before he left this room was to the effect that it being after midnight, we were in All Fools' Day. He'll not have forgotten that, and nothing will ever persuade him now that I was not a party to your plot."

"It seems that I have caused you to lose him for good, then. For that I ask your pardon; and I hope that it will give you no serious regret."

"Nay. I fear that poor Charles Fox will be gravely disappointed; but he knew to begin with that he could count on me only if I found that my inclinations marched with his interests. As for myself, you were right in contending that I might scratch a Russian and find a Tartar. Russian women may like such violent handling by their lovers, but I find that I have a preference for quieter ways. I am not easily scared, but, I'll confess now, that I was more than a little frightened by the thought of his coming back to me to-night."

"God be thanked, then, that it occurred to me to go to Droopy."

Georgina suddenly sat forward from her pillows. "Roger! I had forgotten! By doing so you have made yourself liable for this wretched debt again."

" 'Tis true," he answered, with a rueful smile. "But I shall repay Droopy just as I had intended to pay the Russian. I can still collect my money from the funds, and sell my mare and other things."

A look of great tenderness came over her face, as she said: "Oh, Roger, darling! You make me feel monstrous mean in having treated you so. I have but this moment realised that, though we have been lovers for five long months, you have given a whole year's income to spend another night with me. Never in my life have I been paid so great a compliment, and never shall again."

His blue eyes twinkled. "Am I then restored to favour, and about to spend the night with you?"

"How can you ask?" Her glowing smile was in itself an embrace.

"You have been such a wicked baggage that I'm not sure I want to," he teased her.

"Beast!" she cried. "When I have you here I'll pay you out for that."

"I have not decided yet if I've a mind to play proxy to your earlier visitor."

"Enough, Sir! Thou knowest full well that thou art the only man that I have ever truly loved, or ever shall. Come to my arms this instant."

Slowly he took off the blue silk robe that he was wearing and laid it over a chair. For a moment he bent above her, then her soft arms closed round his neck. He was twenty and she was twenty-one. Both of them could look forward to ten thousand to-morrows without a care, and this night was theirs.

The hours sped all too swiftly. It was as though the healing of this, their first serious difference in all their lives, had knit them together more closely than ever before. They dozed a little now and then, his arm about her shoulders, her dark head pillowed on his chest; but in the main, between caresses, they talked and whispered a thousand absurdities while the world around them slept.

At last he roused from a timeless interval of semi-conscious bliss, and murmured: " 'Tis time for me to leave you, sweet, to get a few hours sleep. The dawn is on us. Look, the light is now quite strong where it creeps in between the curtains."

"Nay, stay and love me yet a while," she whispered drowsily. "I could never have enough of you."

"That ill consorts with your opinion of yesterday," he rallied her.

She got up on one elbow, and leaned across him, smiling down into his face. "I must have been a little crazy then, and we were both quite so last night. Our kisses have cured our affliction since, and we are sane again. You'll not leave here on Monday, as you threatened; will you, Roger?"

He was silent for a moment, then he said: "I had no thought of doing so until our discussion on ourselves arose. But your contention then, that if we had the strength of mind to part while our passion was still unblunted, we might later cheat the Gods into giving us a second honeymoon, impressed me mightily."

" 'Twas sound reasoning I'll admit. But this past night has given our passion a new lease of life; so there is now no point in our precipitating the parting. Stay with me these next two months at least; for Stillwaters is a veritable lovers' paradise in the spring."

"Hark!" he said suddenly; and in the stillness of the early morning they both caught the faint clatter of a horse's hoofs on stone.

"Who would be going out riding at this early hour?" he asked, with a puzzled frown.

She shrugged. "I know not, neither do I care. One of the grooms most probably, taking a horse to exercise."

"Nay. 'Tis Sunday, and no good groom would gallop a horse across the flagstones of the yard."

"What boots it, anyway?" She gave him an impatient shake. "Attend to me, Sir; and tell me if you will stay and love me through the spring."

"Aye," he smiled. "Since 'tis your wish, dear witch, I will. None but the Gods can tell what may have befallen us by this time next year. So let us suck our golden orange till 'tis dry. We'll still have the rind, and in that lies the essential essence of the fruit; its quality of greatest value, like our sweet companionship."

Georgina gave him a long kiss, and murmured: "Well said, dear love. I am now content; and when thou hast left my side I shall fall asleep only to enjoy sweet dreams of thee."

"Then I will leave thee now to my most fortunate dream image."

As he made to rise she pushed him back, on a sudden thought occurring to her. "That horse. Think you it could have been Vorontzoff leaving for London in a dudgeon?"

Roger shook his head. "Nay. He came in a coach with outriders. He would not set out to return alone."

"I would to God it was," she sighed. "How I'll face him when we next meet, I cannot think."

"Then think not of it, angel. I'll stick by your side throughout the day; so that he has no chance to corner you alone."

"The sight of you beside me will infuriate him the more. After your visit to him last night 'tis a hundred to one that he guessed you to be my lover."

"Were the odds a thousand to one I would not take them," Roger laughed. "I would wager any money that he slipped along the corridor after I left him to make certain that you were not alone. And discretion is not your major virtue, my pet. A score of times I have begged you to lower your voice when we are in here together, but you persistently ignore my counsel; so he is bound to have heard us.

"Oh, drat the man! the thought of him has now robbed me of all wish to sleep. Keep me company a while longer, dear one. Nibble my ear for a little, you know how I love that."

"Thou art a veritable child," he smiled. "Turn over, then; and I'll indulge thee."

For a few moments they lay quietly side by side while he gently teased the lobe of her right ear, then she said with a happy sigh: "Oh, darling, 'tis the most lovely feeling; and I adore thee so. Thou hast but one single shortcoming."

Stopping, he raised his head and asked in mock indignation. "And what may that be, pray?"

She giggled. "That thou hast not two mouths with which to nibble both my ears at the same time."

It was at that instant both of them caught the sound of heavy footsteps pounding along the corridor at a run. Jerking apart they sa up in bed. Georgina snatched at her nightdress. Roger stretched out a hand in an endeavour to reach his gown.

The crashing footfalls came to an abrupt halt outside the door. Suddenly it was thrown open, and a tall figure burst into the room.

The intruder paused just inside the doorway. He was a man of about thirty; fair-haired, red-faced, broad-shouldered. He was booted and spurred and his clothes were covered with dust. In his right hand he held a heavy riding crop that trailed a long lash; in his left a handkerchief with which he began to mop his perspiring face.

Roger had never seen him before, but he guessed instantly that this must be Georgina's husband.

Confirming his thought came her swift cry: "Humphrey! What brings you here? How dare you invade my privacy in this barbarous fashion!"

Slamming the door behind him Sir Humphrey Etheredge strode forward to the foot of the bed. "And you, Madam!" he bellowed like an angry bull. "How dare you commit your whoredoms in my house?"

"'Tis not your house," she retorted, her black eyes flashing. "Stillwaters is mine for life under our marriage contract."

"I care not!" he roared. "I told you when last we met in London that you must be more circumspect in your affairs. I warned you that I would no longer tolerate being made an open mock of. I'll not submit to being pointed at as a figure of fun to pleasure you or any other harlot!"

Georgina had covered herself by jerking the bedclothes up to her chin. Roger had seized the chance while they were storming at one another to slip out of bed and pull on his robe. Now, stepping forward, he said firmly:

"Sir Humphrey. My name is Roger Brook. I am prepared to give you full satisfaction whenever it may suit you. Let us curtail this undignified scene and behave like gentlemen. Be good enough to leave the room with me and give me the names of your seconds."

The irate husband swung upon him. "My quarrel is not with you, Sir! That Frenchman, whoever he may be, said in the note he sent to Goodwood that if I immediately took horse and got here by dawn I should find a young cockscomb warming my wife's bed for me. But whether 'twas yourself or another I do not give a damn. 'Tis her I have ridden twenty-five miles to catch. And now I've caught her I intend to give her a damn good flogging, for 'tis the only language she will understand."

As he ceased his tirade he stepped swiftly round the side of the bed and, raising his whip, struck at Georgina.

Roger threw himself across the bed in an effort to shield her and grabbed at the lash as it descended. Missing her face by an inch it caught him across the back of his left hand, but he failed to grasp it. Realising the futility of such half-measures he slid off the bed and squared up to Sir Humphrey.

Ignoring him, the purple-faced Baronet struck at Georgina a

second time. She had stretched out her hand to snatch up a heavy cut-glass scent bottle that stood on her bedside table. Just as she grasped it the lash came down again, cutting her across the neck and down the upper part of her naked back.

Out of the corner of his eye Roger saw the lash fall, and heard her give a swift whimper. Head down, fists clenched and half-mad with rage he sailed into Sir Humphrey, striking out with all his force. His right caught the Baronet a terrific blow just below the heart. At the same instant Georgina flung the scent-bottle and it caught her husband on the temple. He gave a grunt, lurched, and fell to the floor.

For a moment he lay silent and they stared at him in horror; then he began to groan. Georgina jumped out of bed and made to kneel down beside him; but Roger thrust her aside.

"Leave this to me," he muttered. "And in heaven's name get some clothes on before the commotion we have raised brings the household upon us."

As she hurried into her nightdress and pulled a chamber-robe over it, he swiftly loosed Sir Humphrey's cravat to ease his breathing. The Baronet continued to groan and rolled his head painfully from side to side a little; but he showed no signs of returning consciousness.

Georgina ran to her washstand, picked up a jug of cold water and, running back with it, sluiced its contents over his head and shoulders.

Roger had already examined the side of the injured man's head where the scent-bottle had struck it. There was only a small cut from which a few drops of blood were oozing; but the scent had sprayed all over him and the whole room now reeked of the heady perfume.

Kneeling down opposite Roger, Georgina wiped the few drops of blood from her husband's head with a handkerchief. She had hardly done so when the movements of his neck ceased, his mouth fell open, and a horrible rattling noise began to issue from his throat.

It continued for a full minute while they knelt there petrified. Suddenly it ceased. Both of them looked up at the same moment and their terrified glances met across the body.

CHAPTER V

A BID FOR LIFE

R O G E R was kneeling on the left side of the corpse; Georgina on its right. Neither of them moved. White-faced and stunned they continued to stare at one another across it.

Suddenly Georgina broke the silence in a frightened whisper.

"Roger—in the crystal yesterday! Your—your heavy loss at cards!"

He nodded. "And for you—the treachery through a letter writ in a foreign hand!"

Again there flashed into both their minds the third picture she had conjured up from the depths of the water-filled goblet; the court-room scene—the judge in his red robe—the gallows tree.

Georgina's mouth opened wide to give forth a terrified scream. At the sight something clicked in Roger's brain. From a scared youngster with a mind numbed by shock and fright, he became in an instant a clear-headed man of action. Reaching out he slapped her smartly across the face.

Her scream was cut short in her throat. She blinked her eyes and tears welled up into them; but her nerves steadied as she felt Roger's hand grasp hers and heard him speaking in a swift low voice.

"If we would save our necks 'tis imperative that you should quell your hysteria, and disregard that ugly portent. To count it a glimpse of a future definitely ordained is to admit defeat and invite conviction. 'Twould be as sensible to surrender ourselves to the sheriff's officers within the hour, and confess to murder. If God grants us a little time we may yet concoct a story; and save ourselves by con-vincing the authorities that he died by an accident."

As she did not reply, he added urgently: "Speak, Georgina; speak! Say you understand me!"

She nodded dumbly, then threw an anxious glance over her shoulder towards the door, and muttered, "After the noise he made 'tis a wonder that the household is not already upon us."

Roger too, had feared that the dead man's shouting would have brought guests and servants running; but as the early morning quiet of the house remained unbroken he said softly: "I've a feeling now that God has granted us a respite. The walls of the house are thick and the rooms on either side of this unoccupied. Across the corridor lie only your clothes-closets; and the servants would not yet be moving about this part of the house. Our worst danger is that old Barney may have seen him come upstairs, and followed. He may be listening outside the door, there."

Georgina shook her head. "Even were that so, he would allow him-self to be cut in pieces rather than say aught hurtful to me. But, 'tis most unlikely. At this hour he will be tending to the fires."

As her glance fell again upon her husband's body, fresh tears started to her eyes, and she exclaimed: "Oh, poor Humphrey! To think that he was once a fine handsome fellow; see the ruin he has made of himself these past few years. And worse! To meet so sudden and terrible an end all through my wickedness."

"Cease talking nonsense!" said Roger, with sudden brutality. He knew that at all costs he must prevent her from breaking down, and went on ruthlessly. " 'Twas no fault of yours that excessive drink first coarsened all his appetites, then robbed him of the power to enjoy the wives of stable-hands, and the like, that he took for his mistresses. He condoned your infidelities and laughed at them until recent months, when the liquor began to affect his brain. His behaviour but five minutes since was that of a lunatic, and he is better dead. I've no regrets at having rid you of him."

"Thou did'st not do so, Roger. 'Twas the scent-bottle I flung catching him on the temple that killed him."

"Nay, 'twas my blow upon his heart. Had I not been half-crazed myself from seeing him strike you I should have remembered the type of life he led, and had the sense to pull my punch."

"You seek to take the blame upon yourself. 'Tis like your chivalry; but, whatever the rights of it, I'll not allow you to say that the blow upon his head was also yours. I'd sooner be driven to Tyburn in a cart."

"My brave Georgina," he squeezed her hand as they stood up. "Maintain that spirit for an hour or two and we will cheat the gallows yet. But all will depend on the first account given as to how he met his death. No jury could fail to be prejudiced against you from the outset if 'tis known that your husband came upon you *in flagrante delicto*. Therefore I must leave the revealing of his death to you. 'Twill be your worst ordeal. But once 'tis over I shall be by your side again; and, should things go ill, nothing you can say will stop me from coming forward to reveal that 'twas my blow that caused him to be seized with an apoplexy. Now, thinkest thou that thy courage is equal to telling convincingly the story we will invent?"

"Aye!" she agreed, passing her tongue over her dry lips. "I'll not fail thee in a gamble that may mean the saving of both our lives. And thou art right that I must play this first scene of it out alone. Any other course would spell disaster. But what story shall I tell? How account for his unheralded arrival here at such a godless hour; his sudden attack, and the cut upon his head?"

"The last is simple, you can say that as he fell he struck his head on the corner post of the bed. As for his stroke, that might have been brought on from his riding twenty-five miles at topmost speed. Such an arduous feat demands considerable fitness. 'Twould prove a far greater strain than riding in a single race or the hunting to which he is accustomed, for in a day out there are always frequent checks and pauses.

"He raved about having ridden twenty-five miles, but how can you be certain that he did so at topmost speed? If he left Goodwood after dinner, or even after midnight, 'twould have been mere hacking to reach here by dawn."

"Damme! Do you not realise whom we have to thank for bringing us to this evil pass?"

"Humphrey spoke of a note from some Frenchman, with whom he did not appear to be acquainted. But what Frenchman has the ill-will to denounce me, or could possibly know. . . ."

" 'Twas not a Frenchman, but a man who habitually uses French. Vorontzoff, and no other. 'Tis thus he has avenged himself on us for our treatment of him last night."

"Oh, the dastard!" Georgina breathed. "How could any man bring himself to play so mean a trick?"

"You told me that you judged him to be a man of few scruples; and his provocation was considerable. I've not a doubt now but that he listened at the door to our laughing together over his discomfiture. He must then have gambled on my remaining with you till morning, and despatched one of his outriders post haste to Goodwood."

She nodded. "My mind has been so mazed since Humphrey's discovery of us that I have lacked the wits to put two and two together; but it must be so. The Russian understands more English than he pretends. He heard Charles Fox both speak with me yesterday of Humphrey s morbid spying upon me, and say that after the point-to-point at Goodwood he would be lying there to-night."

"I know it. I was standing but a yard behind you at the time. Vorontzoff then remarked that he had once been at Goodwood. He knew where it lay and would have had no difficulty in giving his messenger directions how to find it."

"But how could the man have done the journey and Humphrey returned here in so short a time?"

"You make my very point. 'Twas near a quarter to one before I joined you. The Russian would then have had to scribble his note, get old Barney to rout out one of his servants, and give the fellow his instructions. The courier could not have left much before half-past one; thus leaving no more than five hours for the double journey, including the rousing of Sir Humphrey from his bed and his dressing to set out. Nine-tenths of the way lies along the Portsmouth Road, where remounts are readily obtainable. Even so, he must have ridden hell for leather the whole distance to get here by dawn; and in his condition placing so great a tax upon himself might well have proved too much for him."

"I will say then that the strain resulted in a fit soon after he arrived. But what reason can I give for his coming to me through the night at such a breakneck pace?"

"Aye, there lies our worst conundrum. To give the real one will lead people to suppose that you were not alone, and any such suggestion would vastly increase our danger."

"We dare not count on evading that. The Russian's courier may talk of the midnight mission on which he was despatched."

"He would know nothing of the contents of the note."

"Humphrey may have left it in his room, and if 'tis found there we would be undone."

" 'Tis more likely that he has it on him," Roger muttered, and stooping down, he began to hunt swiftly through the dead man's pockets.

After a moment he pulled out a paper and held it to the light that was now coming strongly between the still drawn curtains. Then he gave a cry of relief. "God be thanked! I have it here! 'Tis anonymous, and brief but to the point. Sir Humphrey quoted it practically verbatim. Well, we are safe on that score."

Georgina shook her head. "Nay! On reaching Goodwood Vorontzoff's man would have had to rouse some of the household in order to gain access to Humphrey. 'Tis no every-day occurrence for a guest to call for his horse at three in the morning and gallop off in a flaming temper. In his state of mind he was quite capable of blurting out the fact that he meant to surprise me with a lover. I tell you we dare not count on the reason for his coming remaining secret."

Roger now found himself faced by a most appalling dilemma. He could not deny that there were grounds for her fear. There could be no concealing that fact that Vorontzoff's messenger had caused Sir Humphrey to leave Goodwood for Stillwaters in the middle of the night. If he had disclosed the contents of the note before setting out, any explanation that Georgina might offer to account for his arrival, which did not tally with it, would be proved a lie. Her story as to the way in which he had died would then inevitably become suspect. And *everything* hung on its acceptance without question.

For these few moments Roger had it in his power to destroy the note.

If he did, and its contents were already known to someone at Goodwood, the very fact of its disappearance would jeopardise Georgina's position still further. It would be believed that she, or whoever had been with her, had searched her husband's body after his death and made away with the incriminating paper in an attempt to conceal their guilt.

On the other hand if he returned the note to the dead man's pocket it was certain to be found there; then suspicion would immediately be aroused that her husband *had* actually caught her *in flagrante delicto*, and had been killed in a brawl either by her hand or that of her lover. In that case, if her fears were groundless, it would be by his own act that he would have robbed them of their best chance of escaping the gallows.

A clock ticked on, seeming unnaturally loud. Barely five minutes had yet elapsed since Sir Humphrey had breathed his last, but every moment that Georgina now delayed in rousing the house made it more improbable that her story would be believed. Her husband's last effort in mounting the stairs at a run might have caused him to collapse within a few moments of entering her room, but given an interval for recovery such an attack was far less likely; and she could not say that he had been lying there for any length of time without her calling for help. Terribly conscious of the dreadful urgency of reaching some decision Roger stood staring at the floor; but it seemed that whichever course he chose the risk was equally appalling.

"Vorontzoff has revenged himself upon us far more terribly than he can ever have thought to do," Georgina said with sudden bitterness. "His denunciation of me to Humphrey was vicious enough in all conscience but inspired, I've not a doubt, by a grim humour. He meant to return our compliment of last night with interest, and make of us both this morning *his* April Fools."

Instantly Roger's glance lifted, and he exclaimed: "Damme! I believe we can yet turn that vicious jest to our own advantage."

"How so?"

"To divert suspicion from you of having had a lover here. How could one better make an April Fool of a man than to cause him to ride twenty-five miles in the middle of the night for no reason. Just think on it! The jealous husband roused from his bed by false intelligence and galloping up the Portsmouth road as though all the furies were after him, only to find his wife sleeping the sleep of innocence. But for its tragic ending 'twould have been the joke of the century."

Georgina's eyes lit up. "And if Humphrey had found himself so fooled, his choler might have been the final straw that led to his apoplexy."

"If rage can kill that might have done it."

"But wait! Why should Vorontzoff have played so bitter a jest on Humphrey, with whom he was not even acquainted?"

" 'Tis common knowledge that there was no love lost between you and your husband. You can say that he had been plaguing you recently with his jealousy; and that to teach him a lesson you put the Russian up to it."

"He may deny that."

"Nay! Why should he? I am convinced that you have hit upon the truth in thinking that Vorontzoff meant to make us April Fools. So 'tis but a modification of the truth to suggest that Sir Humphrey was his intended victim. What better explanation could he offer for the sending of his note?"

"The true one."

"He dare not. As a diplomat he must regard his standing with society as a matter of importance; and he would be despised by everyone if he admitted to having taken so base a revenge upon a woman merely because she preferred another to himself."

"Aye, we have him in a cleft stick there."

Roger knelt down and slipped the note back into Sir Humphrey's pocket. Then, as he stood up he said: "Put a bold face on things, sweet, and all will be well. From the moment the Russian learns what has occurred he will be puzzling his wits for a way out of his own dilemma. 'Twill be no small relief to him when he hears of your having given out that 'twas an ill-starred jest, plotted between him and you, which was responsible for Sir Humphrey's sudden appearance. He will back your story to the limit; I am prepared to stake my life on that."

"We shall both be doing so," said Georgina grimly.

"Be not despondent, dear one, I beg." Roger seized her hand and pressed it. "Strive to believe that it happened as you mean to say and others will believe you."

"Others may, but not Vorontzoff."

"Why so? He cannot have known that I was still with you when

Sir Humphrey burst into the room. He gambled on that being so, but I might have left you earlier."

"He is bound to wonder how I learned that he sent the message."

"He will assume that Sir Humphrey must have told you of it; as was in fact the case."

"He knows for a certainty though, that I did not enter into any plot with him to send it, and that 'twas not inspired by me."

"He will assume that your motive for saying so was to protect yourself from the scandal which would result from the truth. That it should save him at the same time from the mortification of having to confess the meanness of his intentions is incidental, but he will count it monstrous fortunate."

"I pray you may be right; but I fear that if he knows me to have lied in one thing he may suspect me with regard to others."

"Oh, come! Even if his interests did not march with yours, in the suppression of the true reason for sending the note, I can scarce believe that his rancour against you is so strong that he would wish to see you sent to the gallows."

"Nay. I trust not. Yet I count it a doubly dire misfortune that he, of all people, should know any part of my story to be false."

"In the worst event 'twould be only his word against yours! He has no proof; not an iota! Courage, Georgina, courage! I tell you there is nought to fear, if you can but tell your story convincingly."

She drew in a sharp breath. "So be it then. I'll say that Humphrey burst in upon me at dawn owing to a message sent him by the Russian at my instigation. 'Twas a joke, albeit a malicious one, intended as a lesson to him on account of his recent persecution of me. He took it monstrous ill and the *dénouement* coming on top of his gruelling ride, caused him to have a seizure. Is there aught else that I should add?"

"Yes, one thing more," said Roger swiftly. "That weal upon your neck, my poor sweet; where the brute lashed you. 'Tis showing red now, and 'twill be difficult to conceal. You must tell of that blow and, yes—'twill help account for the time we have spent in talking—say that you fainted upon receiving it. When you came to he had already fallen at the foot of the bed, there. You ran to him, unloosed his cravat, and called for help."

"And you? How soon will you reappear to give me the support of your presence?"

" 'Twould ruin all if I returned too soon and was the first to reach you; for Vorontzoff would then regard it as a certainty that I had been here all the time. I'll not delay a second longer than prudence dictates, but must wait until I hear other feet running along the corridor."

"Roger!" she said suddenly, staring at him with wide eyes. "Make me a vow, I beg."

"Willingly, if it be within my power to fulfil."

"It is. Swear to me that if things go ill you will not make yourself a party to the crime. If the fates are adamant, one of our lives should still be enough to appease them for such a life as his. 'Twas I who killed him, and the debt is mine."

"Nay. 'Twas from my blow upon the heart he died; so you ask a thing beyond my power to grant. I'd liefer die from hanging than from shame, and by confessing I might save you at a pinch."

"Then give me strength to fight for both of us. Take me for one moment in your arms before you go."

Stepping up to her, he jerked her to him with unaccustomed violence. They did not kiss, but stood crushed together, straining their muscles to the utmost; so that her arms held his neck as in a vice, and his her body so tightly that it seemed as if her ribs must crack.

With a sudden gasp, as though by mutual consent, they relaxed. He smiled deep into her eyes, took her hand and kissed it, then turned away.

As the door of the boudoir closed behind him she forced herself to kneel again beside her husband's body. She no longer felt afraid but terribly excited; yet her brain was clear and she knew exactly what she had to do. She could feel her heart beating but had no sense of breathlessness. She deliberately counted fifty of its beats in order to give Roger ample time to get back to his room. Then she opened her mouth wide and began to scream.

Her piercing cries echoed through the lofty room. For what seemed to her an age they were the only sound that broke the stillness. Fear surged up in her once more. What had happened? Was the house empty or everybody dead, that they did not come? The dead man's face stared up at hers, bloated and unhealthy.

Suddenly, to her stark horror, she thought she saw his eyelids move. Seizing him by the lapels of his coat, she began to shake him violently, screaming in a hoarse voice: "Humphrey! Humphrey! Humphrey!"

It was at that moment that Vorontzoff entered the room. She did not hear his approach until he was right upon her. Placing a hand upon her shoulder, he pulled her back as he exclaimed: "*Madame! Madame!* What in God's name has happened?"

For a second she stared at him without replying. Then she took in the fact that his being the first person to reach her could mean only one thing. He must have been up and waiting in his room, in the hope of witnessing the *dénouement* of his plot to revenge himself upon her.

Flinging wide her arms she cried. "He's dead! He's dead! He told me of the note that brought him here from Goodwood, and it could only have been from you. See what you have done!"

Vorontzoff's dark face flushed. His grip upon her shoulder tightened and he gave her a quick shake. "Say nothing of that; for your sake as well as mine. 'Twould embroil us all in a most unsavoury scandal."

"I have no wish to tell anything but the truth," she flared, now on her mettle. "He entered my room dead-beat from his ride, and finding me alone thought that I had played a trick upon him. His rage was such that he lashed me with his whip and then was taken with an apoplexy. 'Tis you who are responsible."

"He thought you sent the note, eh?" Vorontzoff's dark eyes held hers and she could almost see the thoughts racing behind them as he muttered. "I meant but to repay you and Mr. Brook adequately for the slight you put upon me last night. But if your husband thought 'twas *you* who had made of *him* an April Fool I see a way that may save us all from grave embarrassment."

Both of them caught the sound of running footsteps outside as he went on hurriedly. "You have an English proverb, Madame. Where there is smoke there is also fire. If I tell the truth you must realise what everyone will infer from it. Yet if I say that I sent that note at your behest, intending only to make an April Fool of your husband, 'twill save your name as well as mine!"

Georgina felt hysteria surging up in her. The Russian's attitude was so exactly what Roger had predicted it would be; and his arrival on the scene before anyone else now seemed the dispensation of a Merciful Providence. Fighting down her hysteria she dumbly nodded an acceptance of his suggestion, and next moment found herself the centre of a little crowd. Her father, Roger, Selwyn and old Barney had all come running into the room in various states of attire, and the rest of the household was arriving hard upon their heels.

Colonel Thursby gave one look at the prostrate figure of his son-in-law, then took charge of the situation.

"Quick Barney!" he said. "Send one of the grooms to fetch the doctor; and two of the men to get Sir Humphrey to a bed."

"He is already dead," remarked George Selwyn, who was eyeing the corpse with the morbid curiosity that everything to do with death always aroused in him.

"I judged as much," replied the Colonel, "but 'tis fitting that a doctor should be called without delay."

"He died of a stroke," Selwyn went on. "The suffusion of his face may be largely due to his habits; but he shows all the signs of a seizure brought on either by over exertion or a mental shock."

"Or a fit of rage," added Vorontzoff. "I fear this tragedy is to be attributed to a practical joke plotted between Lady Etheredge and myself, last night."

Georgina was still crouching by the body, her face buried in her hands. As her father took her arm and drew her towards a chair, he raised his voice and said: "I beg that everyone will now leave the room, with the exception of his Excellency."

Concealing their disappointment at being deprived of a first-hand account of this grim occurrence, the guests and several scared-looking housemaids ebbed away. George Selwyn alone ignored the request and closed the door behind the others. The men had all hurried from their rooms wigless, and his bald, polished skull gave him some resemblance to a rather benign-looking vulture.

"And now, your Excellency," said the Colonel. "Perhaps you will tell us what you meant a moment back, when you said that Sir Humphrey's death came about through some ill-considered jest?"

The Russian shrugged and spread out his hands. "I am not well acquainted with your English ways; but I understand that to-day is the Feast of Fools, and that it is your national custom to play pranks upon each other, most of which are taken in good part."

" 'Tis true," the Colonel nodded, "although nowadays such practices are mostly confined to the rude country folk who still dance round the Maypole and jump the November bonfires. Did you and my daughter seek then to make an April Fool of Sir Humphrey?"

"Alas, Sir; I fear we did," Vorontzoff admitted; and he then went on to give a brief account of his note and how he had despatched one of his outriders with it to Goodwood.

When he had done the Colonel turned to Georgina. She was sitting hunched up in an elbow chair with her back to the light, a wisp of handkerchief pressed against her eyes. Her father touched her gently on the shoulder, and said: "Can you make an effort, m'dear, and tell us what happened on Humphrey's coming in to you?"

"There is little to tell," she replied, choking back a sob. "I was asleep when he burst in upon me. He was panting like a grampus from the strain he had put upon himself to get here by dawn. He blurted out the contents of the note he'd had and demanded from me the name of my lover. I told him I had none; and that to teach him a lesson for his ill suspicions of me, had made of him an April Fool. On that his anger suddenly mounted to a monstrous rage and he struck at me with his whip. Look! It caught me here on the neck and seemed to sear half-way through my back. I fainted from the pain and shock. When I regained my senses the room was still, but on sitting up I saw Humphrey lying there on the floor. I jumped out of bed and sought to bring him to by loosening his cravat and throwing a jug of water over him; but 'twas no good. Then the sight of his face sent me into hysterics and my screams brought you all running."

"So that was the way of it," the Colonel murmured. "I pity the poor fellow for having met such an end; but he was always of a hot temper and is not the first man to have died from a fit of rage."

Georgina heaved an inward sigh of relief. She recalled Roger saying that everything would depend on the unquestioning acceptance of her story, and it seemed that matters could not possibly have gone better.

Selwyn had been standing staring at the body. He now pointed to it and remarked. "There is a small wound upon his head; see, the skin is broken just above the left temple. 'Tis a vulnerable spot, and 'tis possible that while he might have recovered from a stroke the blow that made the wound may have been the actual cause of death."

Covering her face again with her hand and handkerchief, Georgina bit her lip. It seemed an interminable time before anyone said anything, and she had a sudden desperate fear that, after all, the truth was now about to come out. But, at last, her father replied, "He must have struck his head against something as he fell."

There was a discreet knock at the door, and on the Colonel's calling

"Come in," two footmen entered. At his directions they carried Sir Humphrey's body away to one of the spare bedrooms.

On the door closing behind them Vorontzoff suddenly stooped and picked up the cut-glass scent-bottle which, having rolled just under the valance of the bed, had been hidden until a moment before by the dead man's leg. With a sharp glance at Georgina he asked: "How did this bottle come to be on the floor, Madame?"

Her mouth seemed to go dry and she swallowed quickly, before replying with a shrug. "I do not know, Monsieur. He must have knocked it off the dressing-table—perhaps when he made to strike me with his whip."

"That accounts for the room being so heavy with your scent," remarked her father. "But you should go back to bed now, m'dear, and get some rest after this dreadful shock. I'll send Jenny up to you. Come, gentlemen; there is no more to be done here."

To her immense relief each of them made her a courtly bow and a moment later she was alone. Up till then, although she had been dabbing at her eyes for appearance sake, she had been too wrought up to weep; but now the tears came and when Jenny arrived she found her mistress crying quietly.

Jenny was not only the soul of loyalty but an extremely kind-hearted and competent girl. She had maided Georgina ever since her first going to Court and had a deep affection for her. With soothing words and little comforting noises she sponged her mistress's face and brushed her hair, then she remade the bed and tucked her up in it. Having lit the fire she took another look at Georgina and, seeing that she was lying quite still with her eyes shut, went off to make a soothing tizane of lime-flowers.

On her return with the steaming brew she said: "Now drink this Milady; 'twill do you good." Then she pointed at two large white pills in the saucer and added. "I met with my Lord Edward Fitz-Deverel in the passage, and his Lordship says, his compliments to you Milady, and please to pleasure him by taking these, for they'll send you to sleep and prevent you having the headache."

"Thank you, Jenny," Georgina smiled a little wanly. "Mr. Brook tells me that Lord Edward is something of an expert upon strange drugs; so thank him for me please and tell him that I took his medicine gladly. Did you perchance see Mr. Brook when you were fetching this dish of tisane for me?"

"I did, indeed Milady," Jenny smiled back. "He took me aside to inquire for you, and I was please to tell you that he thinks it more discreet not to come to your boudoir to-day unless you send a message by me desiring him to wait upon you. I was to tell you, too, that he loves you dearly."

"I know it Jenny, and I love him with an equal fondness; but not a word of that except between us two."

Jenny bridled. "I'd liefer have my tongue cut out, and you should know better than to suggest otherwise. Take your pills now, and get to sleep. I'll stay and do some mending by the fire, so as to be here should you need me."

"Bless you, Jenny. You're a dear, and I'd be lost without you," Georgina murmured; then she swallowed the pills, finished the tisane and settled down in her big comfortable bed.

She began to think of Humphrey and cried a little at the remembrance of their early days together. As the beautiful Georgina Thursby she had not only been the reigning toast of the town but a rich heiress to boot. Half a hundred suitors had striven to win her hand; old men and young ones, some with coronets, others with great fortunes, and some with nothing but good looks and a load of debts. Humphrey had been only one out of half-a-dozen that she had seriously considered as a husband. Mentally he was an overgrown child, and the only topic upon which he could talk with fluency was horses; but he had been handsome in a fair, bold way, was well-made, easy to get on with and he owned Stillwaters. It was the last which had made her take him in preference to a good-looking young Earl.

To begin with, their marriage had been successful, as such eighteenth-century marriages went. She recalled the fun that they had had during their first winter's hunting together, when she had been so proud of him as the finest and most daring rider in the field. Then she remembered with nausea his bouts of drunkenness, and the way in which he seduced every maid that she took into the house. It was not his unfaithfulness that she had minded but his lack of taste, and the squalidness of his indulging in those casual amours in the attics under their own roof. But she knew that she too had been to blame. She had soon become impatient of his stupidity and began to amuse herself with more intelligent men.

And now it was all over. Poor, weak, stupid Humphrey was dead; and would never blow a hunting-horn till he got red in the face, any more. She thought of his hearty laugh and the tears came into her eyes again; then she suddenly realised that she was not in the least sorry about his death, but only that they had not been able to remain good friends. Her mind wandered to a dinner service of three hundred pieces with the Etheredge crest that she had ordered to be made in China soon after their marriage. The merchant in the City had said that he could promise delivery in from three to four years, so it might arrive at any time now.

Then she fell into a dreamless sleep.

When she awoke it was well on in the afternoon. She felt rested and her mind was clear; but the events of the early morning flooded back into it with a terrible reality that precluded any possibility of their having been a nightmare.

Jenny heard her stir and came over to her, carrying a tray with some cold chicken breast in aspic and fruit upon it. As she set it down on the bed-table to tempt her mistress she said: "You're looking better already, Milady. Your sleep has done you good. Now eat this up and you'll be as fit as a trivet."

"Thank you, Jenny." Georgina sat up and, while the girl re-arranged her pillows, asked with an anxiety which she could not conceal. "What—what is happening downstairs?"

" 'Tis that gloomy with all the blinds pulled down that we're better off up here, Milady. None of them went to church this morning, and all the guests have gone back to London. That is, excepting Mr. Brook, whom you may say is one of the family, and the Russian gentleman. 'Tis said below stairs that as he was the first to find you with Sir Humphrey, the Colonel asked him to stay on to attend the inquest."

"Inquest!" Georgina dropped her fork.

"Why, yes, Milady. Seeing Sir Humphrey died so sudden there has to be an inquest. 'Tis to be held at ten o'clock to-morrow in the library, so I'm told."

"Will they—will they wish me to attend it?"

"That's more than I can say, Milady. But don't look so worried, now. If they do 'twill not be for more than a few minutes to tell how Sir Humphrey died."

Jenny produced a small folded note from her apron pocket and went on. "The Russian gentleman asked me to give you this, Milady; and Mr. Brook and the Colonel both inquired after you again."

Georgina took the note and opened it. As she read the fine French writing she compressed her lips, then pushed it aside with apparent casualness; but she was considerably disturbed. It ran:

My Lady,
At ten o'clock to-morrow morning there is to be an inquiry into the manner in which your Ladyship's husband came by his death. Colonel Thursby has requested me stay on and make a formal deposition of such particulars regarding it as are known to me. I understand from him that your Ladyship will be called on to do the same. While I should be the last to suggest that your Ladyship, any more than myself, has the least desire to conceal any essential portion of the truth my feeling is that no good purpose could be served in disclosing irrelevant details to the idle curiosity of the vulgar. Should your Ladyship be of the same mind, you will realise the importance of our agreeing upon the lines that our respective statements should take, before attending the inquiry. Unless, therefore, your maid brings me a message to the contrary, I propose to do myself the honour of waiting upon your Ladyship in your boudoir this evening at eight o'clock.

> *Your Ladyship's*
> *Most obliged, obedient and humble servant.*

While she ate her chicken Georgina considered the implications of the new development. Instinctively she shrank from granting the Russian the *tête-à-tête* that he requested. She knew that she had behaved like a fool and treated him badly the previous night; but he had sought to revenge himself in such a despicable manner, and brought such grievous trouble upon her, that she felt they were more than quits over that. She had counted on his departing without her having to see him again, and was determined to avoid his society in the future.

On the other hand, since this wretched inquest had to be faced, there was sound sense in his suggestion. Unless their statements about the sending of the note tallied, certain facts that they both wished to conceal might yet emerge. If that happened further probing might bring to light other, far more damning, matters. Georgina shuddered, and decided to see the Russian.

At seven o'clock she told Jenny that she meant to get up for a few hours, and set about making her toilette. Feeling that dead black would be overdoing matters for an interview with a man who knew that she had been on far from good terms with her husband, she put on a dove grey gown relieved only by a cross-over fichu of white muslin at the breast and frills of the same at the wrists.

She thought it unlikely that, in the circumstances, the Russian would try any tricks, but as a precaution, she told Jenny to remain in the bedroom to be within call; then, shortly before eight o'clock, she settled herself with a book in her boudoir.

Vorontzoff was punctual to the minute. He was dressed with his usual richness, but, appropriately, in a coat and breeches of sombre purple satin. His dark eyes gave her a quick, searching look, but his glance remained inscrutable. Having curtseyed to his bow, she waved him to a chair and, forcing herself to smile, said as lightly as she could:

"I am obliged to you, Monsieur, for waiting on me. 'Twas a most sensible suggestion of yours that we should meet before attending this plaguey inquiry. 'Tis an ordeal that I would gladly be spared but I take it my presence is considered essential?"

"I fear so, Madame," he smiled back. "And I appreciate that any public appearance must naturally be distressing to you at such a time. But I pray you do not concern yourself about it unduly. 'Tis merely a formality, and providing we agree as to what each of us should say 'twill call for no more than a repetition of what was said this morning."

"Concerning last night . . ." she hesitated, and then went on boldly. "It had been my intention to make you a sincere apology; but I think you will agree that the steps you took to repay my disappointing you have cancelled out any obligation of that kind upon my part. I will only say now that matters did not transpire altogether as you have been led to suppose, and that to some extent unforeseen events governed my actions."

He nodded. "I had an idea that might be the case. 'Twas clear to me from early in the evening that Mr. Brook was the victim of an acute jealousy. For my part, while I do not seek to excuse my act, I can assure you that it was carried out only on an impulse engendered by what I considered to be extreme provocation. Yet, even so, 'twas aimed at Mr. Brook rather than at yourself."

Georgina gave an inward sigh of relief. That difficult hurdle had been got over with a fair degree of face-saving on both sides.

The interview was not going to be as difficult as she had expected, and it seemed that owing to her tact she could now rely on the good-will of the Russian. After a moment, she said: "Perhaps you would acquaint me now, Monsieur, with what you have in mind regarding to-morrow?"

"Merely, Madame, since we are good friends again, to do all in my power to spare you embarrassment."

" 'Twould reflect upon us equally if the true reason for your sending your messenger to Goodwood became common property; and I am no less willing to spare you embarrassment with regard to that."

He shrugged his broad shoulders. "I pray you take no thought for me, Madame. 'Tis no longer necessary."

"How mean you?"

"Since you find the position obscure, you must forgive me if I put the matter with some bluntness. After your admission of this morning that you inspired my act, should you retract 'twould be only your word against mine. Moreover, your original statement will receive the greater credence, and the case against you will only become the more damning should you begin to contradict yourself."

She was quick to see his point and realise that she had already let him out. He was no longer dependent on her; whereas if he chose to retract, and declare that he had instinctively sought to protect her from scandal that morning but could no longer bring himself to do so when placed on oath, her whole position would be jeopardised. Yet it was clearly to his own interest to maintain the fiction, so she was not particularly disturbed, and said: "We are agreed then that we should continue to explain your note as a plot between us, inspired by me with the intention of making a fool of my husband?"

"Why, yes. If you, Madame, can provide an adequate reason for wishing to play so aggravating a trick on him."

"There would have been reason enough in the way he has plagued me during recent months by prying into my affairs. Charles Fox and numerous other people could substantiate that."

" 'Tis well, then." Vorontzoff stood up, apparently to go, and Georgina was greatly relieved to think that this trying interview had passed off so smoothly. But, instead of making her a leg, he stood for a moment regarding her with a faintly sardonic smile. Then he said: "It remains only for me to offer you my felicitations."

She kept her tone light and raised an eyebrow. "I cannot think, Monsieur, of any matter upon which felicitations are called for."

He pretended amused surprise. "Your memory is short, then. 'Twas but yesterday you declared in the presence of Mr. Fox and myself that you wished to Heaven you were rid of your husband."

Georgina did not at all like the turn that the conversation had so suddenly taken, and she replied with marked coldness. "Given grounds for annoyance people oft make such thoughtless statements without meaning aught by them. And I count it in ill-taste, Monsieur, that you should remind me of my words."

Vorontzoff bowed. "I take it, however, that they are one of the things which you would prefer that I should not mention at the inquest."

She looked quickly away. "Naturally, Monsieur; since an entirely false construction might be put upon them."

"In that, Madame, permit me to disagree. And at the risk of incurring your further displeasure I offer you my congratulations. 'Twas neatly done. I much admire the manner in which you handled a situation calling for great resource and courage."

"What mean you, Monsieur?" she frowned, endeavouring to hide her rising apprehension.

"I refer to the little secret that we share. Fortunately, I am reasonably confident that no one else suspects the truth."

"You were speaking of the real reason which prompted you to send that message?"

"Oh, no, Madame. That is quite a minor matter. Since you have already saved my face while saving your own I have scarce given the note another thought. The secret that I have in mind has no connection with the bringing of Sir Humphrey here; 'tis what befell him when he reached your chamber."

Georgina paled. Her thoughts were racing. What did the Russian suspect? What could he possibly know? Perhaps he was only trying to draw her out on the off chance that she might have concealed some details of the fatality. In any case she must say as little as possible and choose her words with the utmost caution.

"I—I fail to understand . . ." she began.

"You understand very well, Madame," he cut her short, and went on with cynical gallantry. "Again I congratulate you on your resolution. His was a useless life, and I admire you all the more, in that, finding yourself cornered, you seized the opportunity to take it."

"Monsieur!" She sprang to her feet. "How dare you make so infamous an accusation?"

Vorontzoff shrugged. "If 'twas not you who actually struck the blow, then 'twas Mr. Brook. The two of you killed Sir Humphrey Etheredge between you."

" 'Tis a lie!"

"Calm yourself, Madame, I beg. Your secret is safe with me. But 'tis essential that we should understand one another on certain matters if 'tis to be kept from others."

"I have no secret!" Georgina cried; but she was frightened now and she could not keep the huskiness out of her voice as she hurried on. "Mr. Brook played no part in the affair. He left me earlier. To that I swear!"

"Indeed!" The Russian laughed. "You admit then that he spent most of the night with you, to my discomfiture?"

"To you I'll not deny it; though I'll call you a liar to your face if you repeat me."

" 'Twill be a case of the pot and the kettle, then. For I call you one now, in maintaining that Mr. Brook had left you."

"He had, I tell you! As to the rest, matters befell exactly as I reported. Sir Humphrey arrived in a state bordering on exhaustion. On learning that he had been fooled his rage became uncontrollable. He struck me with his whip, then fell in a fit on the floor after I had fainted."

"Pardon one slight correction, Madame." Vorontzoff bowed. "You should have said: 'After I flung my scent bottle at his head'."

Georgina stared at him with distended eyes as he went on quite casually. " 'Twas the finding of that bottle which gave me the clue to all that had taken place. You said that he must have knocked it from your dressing-table. I am prepared to state on oath that last night it was beside your bed. Moreover, the shoulders of his coat and his cravat were saturated with its contents. How could that have come about had he knocked it from the table with his whip. No, Madame. You threw it at him and it hit him on the temple. He fell and, perhaps, had some sort of fit. Having reduced him to a helpless state you saw your opportunity. I have little doubt but that you played Lady Macbeth and gave the word. Then Mr. Brook took steps to ensure that your victim should not recover."

"I tell you Mr. Brook had left me earlier!" Georgina almost screamed.

The dark Tartar eyes of the Russian held hers as those of a snake holds those of a bird, and he slowly shook his head. "You fatigue yourself unnecessarily, Madame, by, yes—as the English say—attempting to pull the wool over my eyes. Mr. Brook sought to protect you from your husband's whip. He has since kept his hand concealed in a scarf on the pretence of having hurt it; but this morning the weal from the lash showed plain across its back. That mark is a fair match for the one upon your neck. 'Tis the proof that he was with you, and that a brawl occurred before Sir Humphrey had his seizure."

"I deny it! You are inventing all this for some wicked purpose of your own."

"Since you disbelieve me, when I am gone, send for Mr. Brook and ask him to show you his hand."

Georgina recalled the way in which Roger had flung himself across the bed in front of her. With an awful sinking feeling in the pit of her stomach she realised that the Russian could not have made up his last assertion. What he had said about the scent-bottle could be no more than a shrewd guess, but if Roger's hand was marked with a weal such a damning piece of evidence could send them both to the gallows.

"Do you—do you intend to disclose this at the inquest?" she faltered.

"Why no, Madame!" he reassured her quickly. "How could you ever suppose such a thing? Did we not agree but a while back to bear no further malice to one another on account of last night's events?

Now that we are again good friends my only desire is to be of service to you."

"I thank you, Monsieur." She moistened her dry lips, and, realising the necessity of playing up to him, went on after a moment. "I am most sensible of the service you propose to render me; and for the future you may indeed count on my friendship."

Taking the hand that she extended to him, he kissed it. Then he said quietly. "Be assured 'tis a friendship that I shall treasure beyond rubies. It remains only for us to cement it."

She gave him a quick, sideways look. "What mean you?"

He caught her glance and smiled. "Have I not already made it plain, Madame, that I count the qualities required to participate in such a deed, and to carry it off, an addition to your attractions?"

" 'Tis a strange form of flattery, Monsieur."

"Not from a man such as myself. A bold and violent woman touches a responsive chord in my own nature; more especially when such qualities are enshrined in one so superbly beautiful as yourself. At what hour shall I wait upon you to-night?"

"To-night!"

"Why, yes. For the cementing of our friendship."

Her eyes were wide and frightened again, but she knew how vitally important it was to keep his goodwill, so she said hurriedly. "Monsieur; you must surely see that it is impossible for me to receive you to-night. Bold and violent I may be in some things; but I am not without a sense of decency. My husband died only this morning and his body still lies unburied in the house. 'Twould not only be unfitting but a most shameful act."

"I'll not believe that you are seriously troubled by such squeamishness," he smiled. "A woman of your metal must know that love tastes at its best when 'tis salted with death. For myself, were any added incentive needed, the thought of the part you played this morning would provide it."

She shrank away from him, exclaiming: "Nay! Nay! I will lie with no man to-night."

"You mock me still, then," he said with sudden harshness. "Do you accept my friendship or reject it? Answer."

"I—I accept it," she stammered, now terrified at the thought of what he might do if she made him her enemy. "But you ask too much of me. Perhaps when I come to London. . . ."

"Do you take me for a fool, Madame! What value can you expect me to place upon any promise you may make after your treatment of me last night. Think you I'll give you rope to send your Mr. Brook to put a further slight upon me at some future date? No, no! The inquest is to-morrow, and after it my trump-card will have lost its value. You will pleasure me to-night or never."

"You cannot—you cannot mean that you would tell all you know—all you suspect, unless I consent?"

He bowed ironically. "Madame; you have summed up the situation perfectly. Events have placed you completely in my power; and for having so lightly given Mr. Brook the preference over myself, after having raised my hopes, I mean to make you pay to the last farthing. By eleven o'clock you will see to it that you are alone and that the door of your chamber is unbolted."

Something snapped in Georgina's brain. White to the lips and with her eyes blazing, she cried: "I'll do no such thing! I will not lie with you to-night or at any other time. Nay, never! Not if you were the last man on earth. I will hang rather! Now, get you from my sight! Be gone this instant, or I will ring for my servants to throw you from the house."

"Such a show of spirit makes you more desirable than ever," he mocked her; but he moved quietly to the door. At it he turned and delivered a final ultimatum. "You still have two hours in which to think matters over, Madame. No doubt time will restore your calm and reflection bring you wisdom. You can send me a message by your maid. But remember; only your kisses to-night can seal my lips at the inquest to-morrow."

CHAPTER VI

THE PARTING OF THE WAYS

W H E N the door had closed behind Vorontzoff, Georgina did not give way to either tears or panic. Her rage was white-hot but she knew that this was no time to allow hysteria to overcome her. She had to think, and use her brain calmly and logically in order to decide which she should take of two horrible alternatives.

The Russian's threat to make her pay to the last farthing was ample evidence of the intensity of the bitterness she had aroused in him the night before. She had sensed the barbarian streak in him and now knew that it lay more than skin deep. He was vicious, brutal and unscrupulous to the last degree. She felt certain that if he could not have her he was quite capable of destroying her.

Had she alone been concerned she would have stuck to her guns and taken a desperate gamble on the Russian being disbelieved; but she had Roger to think of. His swiftly made plan to save them both had proved sound in all essentials. Vorontzoff alone had seen through it; and that only on account of the special knowledge he had of the previous night's events. He alone had had reason from the start to suppose that Roger had been with her, thus making it easy for him to connect the weal on Roger's hand with the mark on her neck. He alone had known that she kept the scent-bottle not on her dressing-table, but by her bed. Everyone else had accepted the story she had told in its entirety. And there was every reason now to suppose that, subjec to the Russian keeping his mouth shut, it would also be believed at the official inquiry.

She knew that any chance she had, so far, of escaping the terrible penalty which must follow discovery, she owed to Roger's quick wits and sure handling of her during those moments of crisis. Now it was her turn. She had it in her power to save the situation; could she do less for him? He would not wish her to, at the price; of that she was certain. But his life was in her hands. Her conviction would mean his too. There was no escaping that; and she could not let him die. She loved him with a greater, deeper, more constant love than she would ever feel for any husband. Whatever it cost her she must save him by her surrender.

She thought then of what that would mean, and a little shudder ran through her. Somehow, last night the same prospect had seemed at first intriguing, then vaguely distasteful and rather frightening, but no worse than that. Now it was horrible—repulsive. She recalled again Vorontzoff saying that he would make her pay to the last farthing, and wondered what he had meant. She had a fairly shrewd idea. To revenge himself the more fully he intended to treat her with unbridled viciousness and brutality. It had been her sensing of his desire to do that during their first encounter which had frightened her. And now there would be no reason why he should put any restraint upon himself. Last night, if he had handled her roughly, she could have got rid of him by threatening to call for help, and saying that he had forced his way into her room against her will. But she would not be able to do that to-night. He would continue to hold his blackmail over her and force her to submit to his every wish for seven long hours, until dawn at last set her free.

Little beads of perspiration broke out on her broad forehead and her hands were damp. She wondered with a sick feeling, that made her near to vomiting, whether she could go through with it, even to save Roger's life and her own. As in a nightmare, ghastly scenes with the Russian and herself as the actors seethed in her brain. Grimly a thought came to her. She had always loved weapons, and in the drawer of her bedside table she kept a beautifully chased Italian stiletto. If the Russian drove her too far she would use it on him.

If she killed him they would hang her for that. But no; if she swore that he had crept into her room while she was asleep and had tried to rape her, they would let her off. Her eyes glittered dangerously. That was the solution to this dreadful business. The stiletto was sharp as a razor and no wider than her thumb at its broadest part. One swift blow and it would be all over. Then, whatever might happen to her, Count Vorontzoff would have got his just deserts and, with the closing of his mouth for good, Roger, at least, would be safe.

At that last thought another struck her. It was going to prove difficult, if not impossible, to keep Roger out of this new development. She never went to sleep before midnight, and whenever she and Roger spent the night apart it was his habit to come to her room and give her a good-night kiss before retiring to his own. It was certain that he would do so to-night, and as Vorontzoff proposed to come to her at eleven Roger would find the Russian with her. That could now result in only one thing; another killing in her bedchamber.

She began to consider how she could prevent Roger coming to her, but could see no way to do so. Not having seen her all day he must be consumed with anxiety about her state of mind and desperately anxious to prime her further for to-morrow's inquest.

It occurred to her that she could send a note to Vorontzoff putting him off till after midnight, but she feared that if she made the assignation for later than one o'clock he would rebel, and send a reply insisting that she should give him full value for his money. And even a two-hour postponement was no certain guarantee against a clash. Roger would have so much to talk over with her that he might easily remain until long after one, and if she tried to get rid of him prematurely it was certain that he would suspect something.

It dawned on her then that, as their minds were so well attuned, he would suspect something in any case. It was useless to attempt to deceive him. They could both lie convincingly to other people, when the need arose, but they were not good liars to one another. She knew that before he had been with her for ten minutes the whole miserable story would come out.

There was only one thing for it. She must send for Roger and tell him the truth. She need not tell him her worst fears. She could spare him those, at least, and she would say nothing of her intentions if driven to desperation; then, hate the thought as he might, he would assume that she was paying no higher price for their safety than she had been apparently quite willing to pay for the Russian's political influence on the previous night. She must hear anything that he had to say about the inquiry to-morrow, now; and positively forbid him to come in to her later.

Having made up her mind she scribbled a note, asking Roger to come to her boudoir as soon as he could find an opportunity, and sent it down by Jenny.

For a quarter of an hour she paced her room consumed with impatience. Then Roger appeared. They exchanged a single look, and without a word, flew to one another's arms.

"My love," he murmured. "I have been driven near crazy from the thought of you here alone and uncomforted all day."

"And I for you," she whispered back. "Our separation at such a time has proved nigh insupportable to me; yet I knew 'twas wise that we should remain apart."

He held her away from him and smiled. "Yet all goes well! You need fear nothing from this inquest which is being held to-morrow. The court will consist only of local farmers and shopkeepers from the village; mostly tenants of your own; so naturally subservient from their station. They will accept your father's version of what occurred before you appear. All you will be called on to do is to confront them dressed in black and give the bare outline of your story. They'll ask no questions but simply offer you their sympathy."

She let him finish, then slowly shook her head. "All does not go well, dear Roger. Let me see your hand."

With a sudden frown he held it up, bound round with a silk handkerchief. "What of it? There is a red weal across the back where 'twas caught by Sir Humphrey's whip. But no one suspects that. I have given out. . . ."

"Someone not only suspects, but knows it," she interrupted.

"Who?" he gasped.

"Vorontzoff! He was here but half an hour back, and he has guessed the truth." She then gave Roger a brief résumé of her interview with the Russian.

When she had done, he said abruptly. "You cannot do this. I will not have it."

"Why not?" she countered. " 'Tis my affair and a small enough price to pay for both our necks."

"It would have gone against the grain with you last night. You admitted that."

"Upon your coming I felt the contrast, I'll agree. Yet earlier I had thought it might be quite amusing. I feel that way about it again to-night."

"Georgina, you are lying. I can see it in your eyes."

She sighed. "Roger, dear heart, I beg you not to make things more difficult for me. I did not count my blessings when I had them, and like a fool was led on by curiosity to play with fire. This morning it threatened to consume us both in an inferno, but your wit and courage has saved us from that. Now, at worst, it can but scorch me a little, and to-morrow you will be here to kiss me well again. Do not be stubborn and oppose me in this. To-night will be even harder for you to bear than for me. That, I now realise, and am shamed that I set so little store on what your feelings might be before. But now I have no choice, and you must support this burden with such fortitude as you can muster. I would not even have told you of it, had it not been imperative that I should warn you that in no circumstances must you come to my room. To-morrow we'll start life anew. But to-night I am determined to see this matter through. There is no other course."

During her outburst Roger had been holding her by the arms and looking straight into her face. He now released her, and, thrusting his hands into his breeches pockets, began to walk angrily up and down.

"There *is* another course," he muttered. "That is for me to send Vorontzoff a challenge."

" 'Tis useless. He would simply laugh at you. Since he has both of us in his clutches he would be crazy to accept it. And even if he was fool enough to do so you could not fight until to-morrow morning."

"I could waylay him in his room to-night before he comes to you, force him to fight there, and kill him."

"You'll attempt no such thing!" she declared firmly. " 'Twould be counted murder and they would hang you for it. If you do I'll announce the reason for your act and confess the whole affair from the beginning. That I swear, by my love for you. So you would have gained nothing and have my blood upon your hands as well."

He knew from her tone that she meant it and that it would be futile to argue with her; yet his whole nature cried out in protest against tamely accepting the present situation. With a scowl upon his face he continued to pace to and fro, vainly seeking a way out of the snare in which they had been caught.

She watched him narrowly, praying that her ultimatum would prove a sufficient deterrent to prevent him from risking his life afresh, in a desperate attempt to relieve her of the hateful thing to which she was committed.

For a long time neither of them spoke. She could almost see his brain seething with revolt, as he thought up idea after idea only to reject each in turn as either useless or impractical; but she dared not break in upon his deliberations for fear of precipitating a decision on his part to adopt some desperate course. She was hoping, that given a little time, he would become calmer and accept the inevitable.

At last he spoke. "So be it, then. You shall give the Russian the assignation he demands; but not in your chamber. There are pens and paper in your secretaire. I pray you sit down there and write as I shall dictate."

"Roger, what have you in mind?" she asked nervously.

"Oblige me by doing as I say," he replied with a hard note in his voice; and when she had seated herself he went on. "No superscription is necessary. Simply write as follows:

"Privacy is essential to our meeting, and any interruption of it would prove most dangerous to you as well as to myself. For reasons which you will guess, it is beyond my power to ensure our remaining undisturbed together in my apartments. Therefore, I pray you, be in the Orangery at midnight, and when all is quiet I will join you there."

In a bold, flowing hand Georgina wrote as she was bid. When she had done Roger said, with a thoughtful narrowing of his eyes. "You need say no more. On reading that he will assume that you have not dared to tell me of the demand he has made upon you, and can think of no means to guard with certainty against my coming to you myself sometime during the night. He will have the sense to see that in such a case bloody murder would result; so, albeit somewhat reluctantly, he will accept the rendezvous you offer him in the Orangery instead of coming to your room."

"How will that serve us, apart from the postponement of the meeting shortening by an hour the time that I must spend in his company?"

A sudden smile lit up Roger's face. "If he reacts as I have forecast,

77

my pet, you will not be called on to spend a single moment in his company. 'Tis I, not you, who will keep this midnight rendezvous."

She started up from her desk. "I have already vowed that if you kill him. . . ."

"Nay, I seek but an opportunity to converse with him secure from interruption."

"Why waste your breath? Neither prayers nor threats will move him from his purpose; and your intervention will serve only to irritate him further."

"That we shall see. If Jenny is still up I pray you send him the note by her."

Georgina hesitated. "I—I can scarce believe that you intend no more than to talk with the Russian. I'll not send this note unless you pledge me your honour that you meditate no attempt upon his life."

"I give you my word that at this interview I will not seek to draw him into a fight, or by any other means shed one drop of his pestiferous blood. Is that enough?"

She smiled, rather wanly. "I know the clever brain that lies behind those seemingly innocent blue eyes of yours too well, not to suspect that it has formulated some audacious scheme. Yet I must take your word, lest I drive you to some more desperate measure. When may I hope to learn the outcome of the meeting?"

"Persuading him to see reason may take some time, and I should be loath to rouse you from your sleep."

She gave a bitter little laugh. "How can you think I'd find it possible to sleep, until I know what to expect?"

"Then I will look in upon you on my way to bed. But be not anxious for me if the hour grows late before my coming."

"No matter the hour, I'll thank God on my knees if it be you who comes at all. I'll not believe that I've escaped him till I see you."

Roger took her hand. "Be not so despondent, sweet; but send the note, and put your trust in me."

"I will. I beg you, though, to have a care for your dear self. He is a monstrous tricky beast and may seek to do you some injury if you detain him overlong."

"I'll keep good watch against that," he promised. Then, after a single kiss, he left her.

She had only just given the note to Jenny when her father came in. As he stooped to kiss her cheek his lean face broke into a smile, and he said:

" 'Tis good to learn that you are already sufficiently recovered to receive visitors, m'dear; as I had felt that in any case this evening 'twould be as well for us to have a talk." Then he made himself comfortable in an armchair opposite her.

Father and daughter were so close in heart and mind that he was fully aware how matters had lain between her and her late husband, so she felt no restraint in talking to him about her marriage, and made no secret of the fact that she was thoroughly glad to be rid of Sir Humphrey.

The Colonel added his assurances to those Roger had already given her, that the inquest would be no more than a formality; then they dropped the subject and talked for a while of interesting places that they might visit when next they went abroad together.

His easy manner and charming humour did much to soothe her nerves and take her mind off her anxieties. He had not been with her for ten minutes before she mentally blessed his coming, and it was not until nearly two hours later, when he stood up to go, that she realised how the time had flown.

Just as he was about to kiss her good-night he paused, and said with unwonted gravity. "Georgina. If there is anything else about this morning's events which you think I ought to know, now is your opportunity to tell me of it."

She looked him straight in the eyes and shook her head. "No, papa. I have nought to add to what I have already said."

He took a pinch of snuff and nodded. "You are old enough now to use your own judgment, m'dear. But no one knows better than myself the impulsiveness of your nature, and the sort of trouble into which it may lead you. I have every confidence in Roger's level-headedness and you have no doubt had the benefit of his guidance. Do nothing contrary to that, I beg, and say as little as possible to-morrow. Good-night, my love, and may God have you in his keeping."

As he left her she wondered just how much he suspected. He knew, of course, that Roger was her lover, since she had never sought to conceal such matters from him; but the way he had looked at her suggested that he believed her to be concealing something concerning her husband's death. She thought that he had been silently inviting her to tell him the truth, and that perhaps she ought to have done so; but she had instinctively acted on his own teaching—that one must bear one's own burdens in life, and that it was a mark of cowardice to seek to unload them onto other people.

"Man-made laws," he had once told her, "are but a rough guide to conduct, for the general protection of society. They should be disregarded when they are no longer in keeping with one's sense of right. Do what you will, provided that you can square it with your own conscience. But even if you fail in that you must endeavour to regain your own integrity by finding the courage to face the consequence of your act without whimpering about your lot to others, and involving them in your troubles."

She had lived by that philosophy and felt that now was no time to go back upon it. If her father suspected anything it was because he believed that Roger had been with her. Had he had it in his power to help her, that would have been different. It was legitimate to ask a friend for any concrete aid that he could render. That was the essence of friendship and a high compliment to the friend concerned; but it was not right to confess one's sins merely for the squalid luxury of weeping on a friend's shoulder.

Convinced that she had acted rightly Georgina sought her bed. It was now just on eleven o'clock, the hour that Vorontzoff had intended to come to her; but she felt fairly certain now that Roger had been right in asserting that the Russian would prefer to accept a later assignation rather than risk being surprised in her room.

She took her time undressing and doing her hair so that it was midnight before she doused the candles on her dressing-table and got into bed.

With a little shudder she thought of all that had happened since she had lain there, so secure and happy, snugly curled in Roger's arms. She wondered if he and the Russian had yet met in the Orangery and what would be the outcome of the meeting. She had no great hopes for it as regards herself; as she could not believe that Vorontzoff would pay the least regard to any appeal Roger might make to his better nature; neither could she imagine any way in which Roger could strike a bargain with the Russian, or coerce him, short of using force.

Vorontzoff, she felt certain, would merely laugh at him and, within a few moments openly declare his intention of coming up to her. That would be the crucial point upon which everything hung. Would Roger stand aside and let him? Would his promise to her weigh sufficiently with him to restrain him from some act of violence? Her life as well as his would depend upon it, and, ruthless as he might be once he let himself go, she had never known him lose his head in a crisis.

Among other things her father had taught her was, that one can pray every bit as effectually either standing up or lying down as one can when kneeling; and also that prayer is far more potent when offered up for another than for oneself. So she began to pray; silently, fervently, not that she should be spared the ordeal that she now dreaded so terribly, but that Roger be given sagacity, restraint and wisdom.

After a time her prayers gave place to a conscious effort to coordinate the power of her will with his. She did not seek to dominate him, but to strengthen all his best qualities by letting her own flow out of her towards him. Suddenly it came to her as clearly as a light in the darkness that they were *en rapport*, and she knew without a shadow of doubt that Roger was laughing.

It was so. Despite the grimness of the task upon which he was engaged, Roger found something irresistibly comic in the sight of the Russian Ambassador's limp body spreadeagled in a wheelbarrow. Probably it was the absurd, puppet-like way in which his enemy's legs and arms dangled helplessly over the sides of the barrow, and waggled at its every movement; but he could not help chuckling to himself as he wheeled his unconscious human load along a shadowy path through the shrubberies of the moonlit garden.

The Orangery had also been lit only by the moon, and ten minutes earlier Vorontzoff had swaggered into it exuding his usual self-complaisance. He had been annoyed by the postponing of his anticipated triumph, even for an hour; although conceding that there appeared to be an adequate reason for the alteration of the rendezvous. But he was in no mood to let Georgina get away with a brief encounter among the ill-lit semi-tropical greenery. He was an epicure in women and wanted to gaze his fill at her, in comfort and at his leisure; so he had determined to insist that, since in her own room they might be liable to interruption, she should accompany him to his.

Instead, he had been standing there awaiting her coming for barely a minute when Roger stepped softly from behind a banana-palm, and slugged him heavily on the back of the head with a small bag containing four pounds of wet sand.

It was over two hours since Roger had left Georgina, so he had had ample time to make his preparations; and, so far, his plan had gone with the smoothness of clockwork. As the sandbag hit Vorontzoff he had given a single grunt, his knees collapsed and he slumped unconscious onto the mosaic pavement. Picking him up, Roger carried him outside to the wheelbarrow which he had placed there for the purpose. In it there was already a small portmanteau containing various things that he might require. Bracing his muscles he had lifted the shafts and set off cheerfully down a garden path that led away from the back of the house.

On emerging from the shrubberies he followed the east side of the walled fruit garden, then, with no small effort, pulled the barrow over a steeply curved Chinese bridge that spanned a small stream. On its far side the garden ended, but the path continued, winding its way through semi-cultivated woodlands that had been planted with many thousands of bulbs and clumps of rhododendrons. A quarter of a mile farther on, the tops of a group of tall Scotch pines, rising high above the other trees, stood out clearly against the night sky. Their prominence was due to the fact that they had been planted on a great artificial mound several hundred yards in circumference. In its interior, under many feet of earth, lay a large, low, circular chamber, to which access could be gained by a short passage, ending at a stout wooden door set in one side of the mound.

Nearly all large country houses of the period had in their grounds similar man-made wooded knolls with a subterranean chamber underneath. Many of them were of great antiquity, as they were an ingenious Roman device for ensuring a supply of ice right through the summer. When the lakes froze in winter hundreds of big blocks of ice were cut from them and stored, after which the change of temperature above ground affected them hardly at all, as even in the height of summer, the shade of the trees kept cool the thick layer of earth beneath which they were stacked.

Having visited the mound during one of his walks with Georgina a few days before, Roger knew that the door of the chamber was not kept locked. Halting the wheelbarrow at the bottom of the slope he pulled the Russian across his shoulders, carried him to the entrance

81

opened the door, from which there issued a blast of cold air, and pushed him inside. He then returned for the portmanteau, rejoined his victim and, producing a dark lantern, lit it from his tinder-box.

Vorontzoff was still lying comatose. Shining the light upon his face Roger leaned forward and gave it a couple of hard slaps. The Russian began to roll his head about slightly and make a low moan. Roger repeated the tonic and his enemy's eyes flickered open. Pulling him roughly to his feet Roger half led, half pushed him along the short passage as far as the opening into the chamber and let him drop to the floor there. Then he fetched his portmanteau, got out four candles, stood them up and lit them. Their light struck rainbow colours from the nearby ice blocks, giving the weird scene a resemblance to Dante's frozen seventh Hell.

It was as silent as the grave there; until the Russian scrabbled his feet in wriggling into a sitting position from which he stared malevolently up at his captor.

Roger grinned down at him, and said suavely. " 'Tis not quite the type of entertainment to which you were no doubt looking forward, Excellency, but I advise you to accept it with as good a grace as you can muster, or 'twill be the worse for you."

His victim muttered something in his own language, then swore at him. Stooping, Roger grabbed him by his lace jabot, shook him violently and cursed him with great fluency for a solid two minutes. He then opened his case again, took from it two lengths of whipcord and holding them up addressed the Russian.

"Listen, you rat. Heed carefully what I am about to say, for your life hangs upon it. No doubt you have places such as this in your own country. You can judge for yourself that the temperature here is below freezing point. I have but to tie your hands and feet, gag you, and thrust you out of sight behind one of the ice-stacks at the far end of the chamber for you to die here. How like you the idea?"

The Russian's wits had now returned to him, and he muttered: "You are already in jeopardy of a hanging. To murder me would make it a certainty."

"On the contrary, Monsieur. To do as I suggest is the one method by which I can make positive beyond all doubt that your mouth will remain closed at to-morrow's inquest; and, believe me, I am much inclined to adopt it."

"You may thus escape a charge of having aided the Lady Georgina to murder her husband, but they will get you later on one of having murdered myself."

"You are wrong there, Monsieur rat. And 'tis the very essence of my plan that no one will suspect me of having had any hand in your death. Should I do as I say, you will be dead before morning, but with not a mark upon you. The gardeners come here from time to time to fetch supplies of ice for the house, but if I conceal your miserable carcass with some care 'twould remain undiscovered for many months. I plan, however, to leave Stillwaters after the inquest to-morrow, then to return here secretly four or five nights hence, carry your corpse into the woods and cast it into some ravine. 'Twould thaw out there during the night and when, at length, someone chances upon it there will not be a thing to show how you died. 'Twill be assumed that you decided to-night to go upon a moonlight ramble, were of a sudden taken ill, attempted a short cut back to the house, fell into a gully and there expired before your calls for help could attract attention."

Vorontzoff shivered, partly from the intense cold, partly from fear; because he knew now that he was at the mercy of a man as ruthless as himself and one who's wits had outmatched his own.

"You'll not do it, Monsieur!" he declared, but he could not keep the uncertainty out of his voice as he hurried on. " 'Twould prove your undoing if you did. When 'tis discovered in the morning that I have disappeared the investigation into Sir Humphrey's death will be affected to your detriment. It may be thought that I have voluntarily absented myself because I am unwilling to give evidence, or even that someone has made away with me to prevent my doing so. Remember, I alone can confirm the reason that the Lady Georgina intends to give for the sending of the note. Without the support of my testimony she may be disbelieved; and, once she becomes suspect, shrewd questioning could easily send you both to the scaffold."

"There is something in what you say," Roger admitted, with hidden satisfaction. He was prepared to kill the Russian if he must, but the thought of committing murder in cold blood was most repellant to him; and it now appeared that his enemy was already thinking on the lines he wished; so he asked: "You are, then, prepared to buy your life?"

"It seems I must," Vorontzoff shivered again. "Tell me the price you demand quickly, so that we can get out of this accursed cold."

"I require you to write a letter to Colonel Thursby. You will begin by saying that, until to-night, to-day's tragic events had put out of your mind a meeting of the first importance which you must attend in London at midday to-morrow; therefore you cannot, after all, remain on to attend the inquest. You will go on to suggest that, instead, he should produce this letter at it; then give a full account of how Lady Etheredge and yourself planned to make an April Fool of Sir Humphrey. You will conclude by offering your apologies to the Colonel and Lady Etheredge for the early hour of your departure preventing you making your adieus to them." Roger paused for a moment, then added. "The production of that letter will support Lady Etheredge's testimony as effectively as if you had given it yourself. Do you agree to write it?"

Vorontzoff gave him a crafty look. "Do you attach any other conditions to restoring my complete freedom?"

"Only that you should also give me a chit for your coachman, ordering him to be ready to take you back to London at seven o'clock to-morrow morning; and an undertaking that you will set out at that hour without leaving any message behind you or having spoken to anyone at Stillwaters on the subject of Sir Humphrey's death."

"In the circumstances, Monsieur, you flatter me by placing any value on such an undertaking."

The chill of the icy atmosphere was getting into Roger's bones and he replied quickly. "Of that we will talk later; if you accept my terms?"

"I see no alternative," Vorontzoff muttered, with chattering teeth. "For God's sake let us get from this place."

"Take two of the candles in each of your hands, then," Roger told him, "and precede me down the passage. Think not of attempting to escape by dropping the lights and running off into the woods; for my legs are longer than yours and I should catch you before you had taken a dozen paces. Any trick of that kind will merely provide me with the excuse I would gladly have to give you a good thrashing."

Picking up his bag he followed the Russian to the entrance of the mound, then told him to halt there and sit down on the ground. The candles were set up out of the draught, just inside the doorway; and Roger having taken a pen, inkhorn and paper from his portmanteau, Vorontzoff used its top as a desk on which to write. In ten minutes the business was concluded. As Roger put the letter to the Colonel and the note to the coachman in his pocket he smiled to himself; the whole matter had gone much more smoothly than he had expected.

Having collected his things he shut the door of the ice-house and walked down the slope with his prisoner to the wheelbarrow. On reaching it he said. "This might well have proved your Excellency's funeral coach. As it has not, you will be good enough to push it back to the shed from whence it came, which I will show you."

For a moment the Russian looked like rebelling, but on Roger giving him a vigorous push he picked up the handles of the barrow and set off with it along the path.

After they had covered a hundred yards in silence Roger remarked: "We will now talk a little about the undertaking which you have given me. As you have pointed out yourself, I have no means of preventing you from leaving a completely different written testimony for the chairman of to-morrow's inquiry, to the one you have just inscribed; or taking some other steps to repudiate your letter and betray Lady Etheredge and myself. Should you do so, have you considered what the result of your act would be?"

"It would result in the Lady Georgina and yourself providing a grim spectacle for the mob at Tyburn, one fine morning," replied Vorontzoff with an ugly laugh.

"Indeed, I think you right," agreed Roger, placidly. "At least all the odds favour such an outcome. You realise, then, that should you repudiate your letter to Colonel Thursby I must count my chance of life exceedingly slender?"

"So slender, Monsieur, that I mean to take an early opportunity of booking a window in a nearby house to see you hung."

" 'Twould be waste of money, since you will not be there to occupy it. We have an English proverb which fits the case to a nicety. It runs: 'Tis as well to be hung for a sheep as a lamb. Do you now perceive my meaning?"

Vorontzoff gave him a quick sideways glance. "You infer that if hang one must, it makes little difference if 'tis for one murder or for two."

"I am happy that your Excellency should have put so exact an interpretation on my thought. Should aught go awry at to-morrow's inquiry I shall hold you responsible. I shall have ample warning of any dangerous trend that it may take before I become suspect myself. Temporarily I may have to deprive myself of the privilege of doing what I can to protect my Lady Etheredge, but 'twill be easy for me to slip away, and get to horse without it even occurring to the sheriff's officers to detain me. Later, no doubt, the Bow Street runners will be asked to undertake my capture. There are some good men among them and they usually get their quarry in the end, I'm told. But I flatter myself that I shall be able to evade them for quite a while; and I now make you a promise. During that time, wherever you may be, I will seek you out and kill you."

The Russian knew that he was caught again. He enjoyed his life; and the prospect of having it menaced by an assassin who might spring out upon him from behind any bush or doorway for weeks, or perhaps months, to come, did not appeal to him at all. After a moment he said. "It seems that you hold all the cards, to-night, Monsieur. You may place full reliance on my undertaking and if aught goes ill in the matter of Sir Humphrey's death 'twill be through no act of mine."

"I felt sure that I had only to put the position to you frankly for you to see reason," replied Roger smoothly.

A few minutes later they reached the rambling outbuildings behind the house. Having replaced the wheelbarrow in its shed they went in by the Orangery and through the now dark suite of reception-rooms to the hall. Old Barney was sitting there polishing Georgina's new riding-boots to a mirror-like sheen. Roger slipped the chit that Vorontzoff had written for his coachman back into his hand. The Russian gave it to Barney for delivery first thing in the morning; then victor and vanquished in this midnight interview went upstairs side by side, to part with a curt "good-night" on the landing.

It was now getting on for two in the morning, but when Roger peeped into Georgina's room he saw her by her nightlight that she was not yet properly asleep. She was propped against her pillows with her eyes only half shut, so obviously dozing. The second she heard the faint noise of the door opening she started up, and after one swift look, exclaimed, " 'Tis you! Oh, God be thanked!"

"Surely you were not expecting anyone else to visit you at this hour," he smiled. "If 'tis so, to spare your blushes, I will withdraw at once."

"Oh, Roger, 'tis no time for teasing," she said reproachfully. "Tell me without delay. You—you have not killed him?"

"Nay. I have but this moment left the fellow sound in wind and limb, and on his way to bed. 'Tis all arranged, and we need fear nothing from him either to-morrow or in the future."

She sighed. "How did you work this miracle? Come; tell me all. I can scarce yet believe it possible."

Roger perched himself on the side of her bed and gave a laughing résumé of his doings since midnight. When he had done, she suddenly hid her face in her hands, and a moment later he saw that she was crying.

"What ails thee, sweetheart?" he asked her with swift concern. "Think not from the lightness of my tone that I would belittle the danger we were in. But, knowing that we had no intent to shed innocent blood, God has extended His protection to us; and given us both courage and sagacity wherewith to shield ourselves. I do assure thee that thou needest have no further fears. The worst is over, and within a few hours now thou wilt not be called on to give another thought to this tragic business."

"Nay," she murmured. " 'Tis no longer from fear that I am crying, but solely because I love thee so."

Gently he drew her hands away from her face, then smiled into her tear-dimmed eyes. "Thou hast no cause to weep on that account; for if love be a willingness to give one's life for another, thou knowest that I would gladly give mine for thine."

"I know it; and 'tis not sorrow, but my very joy and pride in thee that brings the tears to my eyes. Thou art the most splendid champion that any woman ever had. Dost thou remember how things were with me when I was but a little girl? How all those stupid fools of county people, whom I despise to-day, sent me to Coventry on account of my gipsy blood. Not a boy nor girl of their oafish progeny would so much as give me a 'good-morrow' when I rode past them in a lane. Thou alone hadst the spirit to ignore the ban and cheer my solitude with thy dear companionship. And now thou art grown into an audacious, determined man; and so monstrous handsome that thou couldst have any woman for the asking; yet it seems that thou still preferst me to all others, and would stick at nought to protect me from the results of my own follies. I weep from humility, to think that I am so fortunate."

He kissed her hands and smiled again. "Then weep no more, dear love; for is not my debt to thee the greater? When I was but a scared schoolboy fearful of what road to take, didst thou not make of me a man, point out the way, and give me resolution? And now; what am I but a near-penniless fellow, trained to nothing and of no position; yet thou, the loveliest lady of all England, rich, powerful, and courted by all, hast taken me for thy lover. 'Tis I who should be humble, as I am, that thou givest me, rather than another the right to protect thine happiness by all means in my power."

Like sunshine after an April shower, a smile came to her eyes.

"Oh, Roger, we are a sad pair; and no one will ever truly understand either of us, except the other. Dost realise that I am free to marry again now? 'Twas but yesterday that thou asked me, would I marry thee if I could? And I said nay; being then too scatter-witted to count my blessings. Ask me again and I'll give thee a different answer; for I will never know another man whom I will always honour, and at least have the desire to obey."

He shook his head. " 'Twas you who had sound sense on your side in that discussion. It arose, you will recall, while you were preparing the ground to *tromper* me with Vorontzoff. Before the summer is out a similar situation would arise, if not on your side then on mine. Agreements to disregard such things are well enough in theory; but when it comes to the point 'twill always prove that one party only has developed a craving for pastures new, so the other is bound to be hurt in consequence. Had matters gone as you originally planned for this weekend, we would still have parted good friends; but had we been married 'twould have resulted in a most bitter quarrel. And if one decides to marry one should at least set about the business without doubts as to its lasting out the year."

"You had none of these doubts concerning Athenaïs de Rochambeau last summer; and would have married her out of hand, had it not been for the difference in your religions."

"Aye, I admit it. But I was younger then and somewhat moonstruck."

"You are not, then, moonstruck with myself?"

"Nay, Georgina, and I never shall be. Yet, had I any mind to marry at all, which I have not, 'tis the one fact that would induce me to sue for your hand. For, did you grant it me, I would know that I was espousing no figment of my imagination, which might later prove an empty shell; but a woman whose best qualities will always far outweigh her very human shortcomings."

"It seems, Sir, that you are become illogical," she quizzed him. "If you would have me on that count, while yet a moment back arguing that you would not, from fear that any lapse from virtue on my part would prove too great a strain on your affection!

"*Au contraire, Madame*," he smiled. "I am being logical for us both. You know that in your heart of hearts; confess it now!"

She stretched and yawned, then gave a little laugh. " 'Tis so, dearest Roger. For if we did marry, and I caught you cocking your hat at a wench, I vow I'd claw her eyes out. But you'll stay on and love me through the spring, will you not? I insist upon it."

His smile became mischievous. "I'll stay on until those wicked, roving eyes of yours look favourably upon another beau—or until my own light upon some toothsome morsel of femininity."

"Beast that thou art! I do believe thou meanest to pay me back in mine own coin."

"Nay. I was but joking. My whole object will be to make thee forget this terrible affair as soon as possible." He leaned forward and kissed her lightly on the cheek. "And now, sweet, 'tis time that I should leave thee to get some sleep."

For a moment her fingers gently caressed his hair. "Thou art right. I am near exhausted by the day's events. I only pray that all will go well in the morning."

"It will, dear heart. Have no fear of that." And with this last reassurance Roger left her.

His prophecy was proved correct. Vorontzoff took his departure promptly at seven o'clock. Half an hour later Roger sent the letter that he had extracted from the Russian up to Colonel Thursby by a footman. A little before ten the coroner's court assembled in the library. It was composed of honest but simple folk who asked few questions and acted with all the discretion that they felt was due to the persons of quality who were concerned.

Having decorously viewed the body, they listened respectfully to Colonel Thursby's statement, and a translation that he gave them of Vorontzoff's letter. Georgina was called on to make only a brief appearance. She was dressed in black and veiled, but not so heavily that they were unable to see her lovely face. After a few tactful questions and her low-voiced replies, they offered her their deepest sympathy and she withdrew. The doctor then gave it as his opinion that Sir Humphrey had died from a seizure, brought on by intense cerebral excitement following immediately upon the abnormal exertions of his long ride; and a verdict was brought in to that effect.

Afterwards the members of the court were taken to the dining-room, where an abundance of refreshments had been provided for them, and relaxing into a restrained cheerfulness ate and drank their fill. By two o'clock, well loaded with good liquor they rode away, their somewhat bemused minds now again centred on their individual concerns.

Roger had not appeared at any part of the proceedings. So that he should not be observed hanging anxiously about he had gone out for a ride, returning only at eleven-thirty. Shortly before midday the butler had informed him of the verdict and he had then settled down to read a book in the Orangery. Soon after the last of the visitors had clattered away a footman found him there and said: "The Colonel's compliments, Sir, and he'd be glad if you would join him in the library."

On obeying the summons, Roger found Colonel Thursby sitting behind a big mahogany desk-table, sipping a glass of Madeira. His longish, intellectual face appeared grave but showed no sign of undue worry. Motioning to the decanter and a clean glass that stood beside it, he said: "You'll have heard, no doubt, that all went smoothly and that the matter is now officially closed; but I think it well that I should put certain facts before you. Pour yourself a glass of wine, my boy, and make yourself comfortable."

With a word of thanks, Roger did as he was bid, wondering what the devil was coming now.

"As you may be aware," the Colonel began, "Sir Humphrey having died without issue, his heir is his eldest uncle, who now becomes Sir Isaiah Etheredge. I despatched a courier to him yesterday to inform him of his nephew's death, and I suggested that the funeral should take place on Wednesday. We may therefore expect him here tomorrow, or even, possibly, to-night, if curiosity moves him to seek a detailed account of the tragedy before the rest of the family arrive. He will benefit to some extent on coming into the baronetcy, but not to the degree that he would have done had Humphrey not married Georgina."

"Under her marriage settlement she retains Stillwaters for life, does she not, Sir?" Roger put in.

The Colonel nodded. "And a sufficient capital to keep it up. That will absorb the greater part of the Etheredge fortune as long as she lives; and since Sir Isaiah is a man of well over fifty 'tis unlikely that he will ever enjoy the house or the income that goes with it. The marriage settlement was exceptionally rigorous; and, by it, Georgina has secured very much more than the average widow's portion. I do not blame her for insisting on such terms, as she could have married a much richer man had she wished. On the other hand one can hardly blame Sir Isaiah and the rest of the Etheredge clan from bearing her considerable ill-will in consequence. I trust I have made the situation clear to you?"

"You have, Sir," Roger replied, much relieved to think that the Colonel had nothing more serious on his mind than some slight unpleasantness over money matters with Georgina's in-laws.

"Then you will realise that Sir Isaiah has a very special reason for interesting himself in Georgina's affairs."

Roger looked a little puzzled. "I do not see how anything she may do can alter the situation to his advantage?"

The Colonel gave him a quick, sideways glance. "Should she announce it as her intention to re-marry quite shortly, that might do so."

"I was under the impression that she would continue to enjoy Stillwaters whether she re-married or not."

"Those are the terms of the settlement; but it was not that which I had in mind. I see that I must ask you a leading question. Are you contemplating asking Georgina for her hand?"

Roger coloured slightly. "I waited on her after dinner last night, Sir, and we discussed the question then. The conclusion we reached was that, fond as we are of one another, to embark on marriage was to risk the wrecking of our long friendship; and as we count that very precious we should be wiser to remain only friends."

"I am much relieved to hear it," said the Colonel. "Not, let me hasten to add, that I should have anything against you as a son-in-law. Far from it, I am extremely fond of you, and have a high opinion of your abilities. Georgina has ample money for you both and I am well aware of your devotion to one another; so in normal circumstances I should give the match my blessing most willingly."

"I thank you, Sir, for your good opinion of me. But if those are your sentiments, may I ask why you should be so relieved that Georgina and I have decided against marriage?"

"Because I consider that your association with her has become highly dangerous to you both; and any announcement of your intention to marry would draw Sir Isaiah's attention to it."

"I fear I don't quite follow you, Sir."

"Then it seems that I shall have to go into matters which I would have preferred to avoid." The Colonel looked at Roger squarely. "I tell you nothing that you do not already know, when I say that while Georgina is a most lovable young woman, her morals, by orthodox standards, leave much to be desired. For that, the passionate nature she inherited with her mother's blood is partly accountable, but I am also much to blame. I emancipated her mind from the narrow outlook to which those of girls are usually confined, and brought her up to think as a man. As a man of honour, I trust, but one with a sense of values quite different from those of most of her sex. My intention in so doing was to enable her to stand on her own feet, and get the best out of life by fighting men with their own weapons, as well as those natural to her, whenever the need should arise. I do not regret it; but I cannot disguise from myself that while my policy has, in the main, helped to create a remarkably fine personality, it has, in some respects, exposed its subject to the over-hasty judgment of others."

Having paused to take a pinch of snuff, the Colonel went on: "Since Georgina thinks like a man where her amours are concerned, she also acts like one. She goes gaily about such matters and takes little trouble to conceal them. In consequence, many people consider her to be quite unprincipled. You and I know that is not the case. Yet there are some who believe that she would stick at nothing to gain her ends; even, yes—even the murder of her husband."

Roger sat deathly still for a moment; then he said in a low voice: "Perhaps, Sir, you would care to—er—elucidate."

"Again I regret the necessity," said the Colonel, quietly. "But 'tis imperative that you should know where you stand. I ask you neither to admit or deny anything that I may suggest, but the following are certain points which could hardly help occurring to anyone in my position. Count Vorontzoff's note has been satisfactorily explained; but did he really send it at Georgina's instigation? We knew that she had grown to dislike her husband, but 'tis entirely out of character for her to play stupid practical jokes on anyone; and the last thing she would have embarked upon deliberately was any project to bring Sir Humphrey here. If she did not inspire the note why did Vorontzoff send it? And why did they both say yesterday that they had planned this Fool Day joke between them? Was that collusion, brought about through a mutual urge to prevent certain unpalatable facts emerging at the inquiry? In any case there is no getting away from the contents of the note. Its gist was that if Sir Humphrey at once got to horse he would catch Georgina with a lover in her room. If she did inspire that note she was expecting her husband in the early hours of Sunday morning, so would certainly have seen to it that she had no lover with her then. But was she really alone when Sir Humphrey burst in upon her? I do not think so; and I will tell you why. I was present when his body was examined by the doctor. It had a large purple bruise just below the heart."

With his eyes fixed on the carpet, Roger strove to fight down the agitation he was feeling, as the level voice continued.

"The bruise was just such a one as might have been made by a fist striking a hard blow—a harder blow than any Georgina could have struck. But if it came to light that such a blow was delivered in her presence, the fact that she has concealed this attack upon her husband, which doubtless contributed to his death, would be taken as proof that she was concerned in it—and she will be judged equally guilty with his attacker."

White to the lips, Roger suddenly looked up. "I beg you, Sir, inform me of the worst? Does anyone else suspect. . . ."

The Colonel shook his head. "I trust not. Fortunately I was able to provide a plausible theory to account for the bruise. I remarked that it was probably the result of a fall; and that Sir Humphrey might easily have had one the previous afternoon, as he was known to have ridden a dangerous horse in the Goodwood point-to-point. The doctor's mind being entirely free from suspicion, he accepted that explanation and made no reference to it in his evidence."

Knowing that the Colonel would never betray Georgina, Roger gave a great sigh of relief. "You comfort me mightily, Sir; for it seems that all is well."

"Nay. I fear we cannot consider ourselves out of the wood, as yet. From ancient times motive and opportunity have oft alone been enough to cause suspicious minds to probe, unearth the truth and exact a fatal penalty. That you have been, and are, Georgina's lover, she has never sought to conceal from me; and, unfortunately, owing to her casual disregard of the most elementary precautions, at least half-a-dozen of the servants here must have good reason to suspect it. If it comes to Sir Isaiah's knowledge that Georgina *did* have a lover staying in the house, he *might* begin to play with the idea that she had encompassed her husband's death because she wished to share Stillwaters openly with her paramour."

Roger paled again. "You mean, Sir, that if Sir Isaiah once becomes suspicious he will leave no stone unturned which might lead to Georgina's conviction; since, could he but bring about her death, he would, after all, come into Stillwaters and the bulk of the Etheredge money?"

The Colonel finished his wine. "That is the nightmare possibility which has haunted me for the past twenty-four hours. Yet by a simple precaution it can be reduced to an unlikely chance. I refer to the elimination of the motive. If you do not share Stillwaters with Georgina, either as her husband or her lover, why should anyone suspect that Sir Humphrey was the victim of a crime?"

"You feel then, Sir, that I should leave at once?"

"I do; now that the inquest is over. I would have suggested your leaving before, had I not thought your presence in the house essential to support Georgina through her recent ordeal. But if you are not gone before Sir Isaiah makes his appearance, he will naturally wonder why you should have remained on after the other guests departed. He would start questioning the servants about you, and that might prove the beginning of the end."

"I see the sense in what you say, Sir," Roger said slowly, "and will act upon it without delay. But I fear Georgina may take my going hard."

"I've not a doubt of that. So I will break the matter to her while you make your preparations for departure. I need hardly add that the less you see of one another for the next twelve months the better."

Roger nodded. " 'Twould be best if I sought some employment abroad."

"That would be wise. I also plan to take Georgina out of England until talk concerning her husband's death has died down. She has often expressed a wish to see Constantinople, so I may take her there, and on a tour through the Balkan lands. Business affairs will prevent my setting out for some six or seven weeks to come; but the less you are seen about the less people will talk of your having been so much in Georgina's company this past winter, and the fact that you made one of the house-party here the weekend that the tragedy occurred. So I hope that you will arrange to make your exit from the scene as soon as possible."

"I will expedite my departure by every means in my power, Sir," said Roger, standing up. "Should aught occur in the next few days I beg you let me know. I shall be staying with Lord Edward at Amesbury House. In the last event the responsibility is mine, and I am prepared to face it."

"If need be I will come to town and call upon you; but I trust that will not prove necessary." A kindly smile lit the Colonel's lean face, as he added: "Had I been in your situation I should have done as you did, my boy; so let it not lie too heavy on your conscience."

An hour later Roger was with Georgina in her boudoir. She had changed back into the grey dress that she had worn the night before, but she was looking very mournful. For the past ten minutes they had been discussing the recent conversations that they had each had with her father. Both agreed that, reluctant as they were to part, Colonel Thursby's reasons for their doing so brooked no argument.

"Let us not prolong the agony, dear heart," Roger smiled, after they had said all there was to say. "Wish me luck with one of your long kisses, then I'll go seek my fortune once again."

"Bide but a moment," she replied. "I have something here that I wish to show you."

Going over to a lacquer cabinet she unlocked it, produced a large morocco-leather box, and opening that upon a table displayed a magnificent diamond tiara; then she asked him: "What think you this would fetch?"

"I have no idea," he shrugged. "But at a guess I would say that it must have cost not less than two thousand pounds."

" 'Twas Humphrey's wedding-present to me; so 'tis not an heirloom, and mine to do with as I wish. If it cost so much it will easily pay your debt to Droopy Ned, and furnish you with a few hundreds over for your journey. Take it, I beg."

"Nay, I'll not rob thee . . ." he began, but Georgina placed a soft hand over his mouth.

"Dearest Roger," she reasoned gently. "Thou knowest well enough that I have many jewels and will scarce miss this bauble. Doest thou not remember on thy going away as a boy, how, to finance thee, I parted with the half of my girlish trinkets. I am offering thee far less than half, to-day. That debt must be paid, and thou hast beggared thyself in buying gifts for me. Add not to my present burden the misery of knowing thee to be in sore straits for money. Give me, instead, at least the joy of sponsoring thy departure as I did before; so that I may count it an omen that thou wilt come back to me safe and sound a second time."

"So be it, sweet," he murmured. "I've no words to thank thee, but thou knowest what is in my heart."

"Aye! Keep it faithful to me, dear one."

"I will do better; for the heart is fickle; but no woman can usurp the throne thou wilt ever occupy in my mind."

"And thou in mine, dear Roger. Indeed, I meant it so. We may take our pleasure where we list, but neither time nor distance nor other loves, can tarnish the sweet mental bond that unites us two."

For over a minute they were locked in a tight embrace, each vying with the other to give all that they could of themselves in a last lingering kiss. Then he left her; and as the door closed behind him he wondered miserably if another four long years must pass before he would know the joy of holding her in his arms again.

CHAPTER VII

YOUNG MR. PITT

W H E N Roger reached London he went straight to the Marquess of Amesbury's mansion in Arlington Street. In those times most of the great nobles still kept open house for their family and friends, who were expected to stay a few nights or a few weeks, just as it suited them. As Roger had no *pied-à-terre* of his own in London Droopy Ned had insisted on his accepting the freedom of the house, and had instructed his father's major-domo that Roger was always to be given accommodation.

On this occasion, having come up from Stillwaters only the day before, Droopy was still in residence; and Roger found him upstairs in his own suite, amusing himself by re-arranging some of his collection of antique jewellery in a shallow, glass-topped miniature table.

After admiring his friend's most recent purchases Roger produced Georgina's tiara and asked him what he thought it would fetch. Droopy peered at it with his short-sighted pale-blue eyes, then examined the larger stones through a jeweller's lens, and said: " 'Tis the type of thing on which the trade makes a good profit, since its worth lies rather in its decorative effect than its intrinsic value. I doubt if a goldsmith would give *you* a thousand for it, but I think I could place it in Hatton Garden for twelve-fifty."

"I'd be mightily obliged if you would," Roger said. "I plan to go abroad again, and the balance of nine-hundred, or so, will keep me in funds for quite a while."

Droopy knew all about Roger's hectic love affair with Georgina, but he was much too tactful to inquire the reason for this sudden decision. Instead he asked: "To what part of the continent do you intend to travel?"

"I've no idea as yet," Roger admitted. "But you'll remember that last November, Mr. Pitt offered me employment in some form of foreign service. I mean to write and remind him of his promise, and see if he can suggest something for me."

They supped together and talked afterwards for an hour or so on the tragedy at Stillwaters and other matters; then Roger went to his room and wrote the letter. In it he begged for an early interview, making it plain that he wished to leave England as soon as possible; and the letter was despatched by hand to Downing Street first thing the following morning.

Two days elapsed without his receiving any reply, so on Thursday afternoon he wrote again; but by Saturday evening he had still not received even an acknowledgment of either of his letters.

As he was now becoming worried at the delay he consulted Droopy, who said: "If you wish a swift decision your best plan would be to beard Mr. Pitt in his den. Why not ride down to Holwood Hill, his place near Hayes, in Kent, to-morrow. 'Tis certain you'll find him there, as 'tis a Sunday."

On Roger demurring at the idea of breaking in on the great man Droopy shrugged his narrow shoulders. "Be not so modest, my friend. Since you served him by going to Holland on his behalf in a confidential capacity, I'll warrant that he'll afford you a courteous reception."

So after breakfast next day Roger mounted his horse and set off. It took him some time to ride through the narrow, crowded streets of London, thick with swarms of church-goers dressed in their Sunday best; but the going was easier after the first mile of the Old Kent

Road. At New Cross he turned south, through the pleasant suburb of Lewisham, and so out into the open country. A few miles south of the village of Bromley he inquired for the Prime Minister's house, and ten minutes later was riding up the drive.

This small estate of Holwood Hill was, as Pitt had remarked himself, "a most beautiful spot, wanting nothing but a house fit to live in," but, even so, it possessed quite a sizeable mansion. He had bought it three years before, mainly on account of its gardens, the improvement of which gave him much delight; and because he had a special fondness for the country round about, having been born and brought up on another property nearby.

At the door Roger inquired for Mr. Pitt, stating that his business was confidential. The footman asked him to wait in the hall, and after a few minutes, returned to say that Mr. Pitt would see him; then took him through the house and out into the garden.

The young Prime Minister was in his shirtsleeves, planting a small magnolia, and seated near him in a wicker chair was an exceptionally delicate-looking man of about the same age. At Roger's approach Pitt looked up, and his long, austere face broke into a smile as he said: "Why, Mr. Brook, 'tis a pleasure to see you again. I thought you had quite forgotten me."

"On the contrary, Sir," Roger bowed. "I have written you twice in the past week, and receiving no reply made so bold as to break in upon your privacy; for which I do most humbly apologise."

"Ah, me!" Pitt shook his head drolly. "I fear I am the laziest of men where dealing with my correspondence is concerned. To my shame I confess that few who write me ever get an answer. In fact, as most of my letters are bills, I've long since given up even opening the demmed things." With a wave of his hand towards his companion, he added: "You know William Wilberforce, of course."

Roger bowed again, to the frail man, whose fine eyes and head made such a contrast to his puny frame.

Wilberforce had been Pitt's contemporary at Cambridge, and had later become his closest personal friend. As the member for Hull, Wilberforce had been one of the staunchest supporters of Pitt's first administration, and during those difficult times the two had been almost inseparable; spending most of their evenings at Goostree's Club, which had been founded by Pitt's friends in opposition to Brooks, and their week-ends at Wilberforce's house on Wimbledon Common, where Pitt had a room always kept ready for him. In '84-'85 Wilberforce had made a long tour abroad, and returned from it with a resolution to lead henceforth a strictly religious life, so in recent years he had withdrawn somewhat from party politics to give more of his time to social reform. His first efforts had been in the direction of amending the criminal law and the suppression of blasphemous and indecent publications; but, only a few months earlier, while seated meditating one day under an oak in Holwood Park, he had come to a definite decision; to devote the rest of his life to the abolition of the Slave Trade.

Although only twenty-eight he had, like his illustrious friend, long been a national figure, so, as Roger bowed, he said: "Mr. Wilberforce's moving eloquence and good works are alike well known to me."

"I thank you, Sir." Wilberforce inclined his head. "I pray you forgive my rising, but since January I have been the victim of a most vicious illness; and am here to-day only to make my adieus to Mr. Pitt before leaving for Bath in the hope of deriving some benefit from its waters."

Pitt gave him an anxious look. "I trust that the fatigue you have sustained in coming here will not affect you adversely."

"Nay. I had to come; and your assurance that you will bring the first measure forward during the next session, should I be unable to do so, are better medicine than any with which a doctor could provide me."

Feeling that he might have interrupted a discussion on political business, Roger said: "Gentlemen, I fear my arrival is inopportune. Permit me to retire and walk a while in these lovely grounds, until a more appropriate moment."

With a wave of his slender hand Pitt dismissed the suggestion. "Our business is finished, and alas, Mr. Wilberforce is only awaiting his carriage to carry him back to Wimbledon." Then turning to his sick friend he added: "Since 'twas I who first persuaded you that parliamentary action would be far more efficacious against the slave traders than any appeal to the sentiment of the nation, 'tis but fair that I should champion the cause in your absence."

" 'Twill add to your difficulties, and bring much odium on you from certain quarters," Wilberforce said frankly.

"I know it. The City of London has never cared for aught save to keep its purse well lined. The merchants of Bristol and Liverpool will raise the devil; and the planters in the sugar-isles will allege that such measures must bring ruin to the nation. But the cause is just; so be of good cheer. I count our first measure as good as already carried."

"Ah, Billy." Wilberforce shook his head a little dubiously. "You were always an optimist. You said the very same in eighty-five, before you brought forward your Bill for winning the friendship of the Irish, and once and for all eliminating the grounds for their centuries-old grievances against us. And you were up against the same thing there; the inherent greed of the British merchants and the middle-classes, mobilised against you by such news sheets as the *Morning Chronicle*."

Pitt shrugged. " 'Twas, I suppose, too much to expect that such folk could yet have absorbed Adam Smith's great doctrine, that States which throw down their customs barriers become effectually part of the same body, and both benefit in consequence. Look at the admirable effect our recent Commercial Treaty with France is already having. Yet Ireland is nearer, and should be dearer to us. 'Twas my fondest ambition to make the two countries one, and it rankles with me still that my plan was brought to nought by the greed and self-interest of a small minority in our midst."

"Were not the Irish much to blame themselves, Sir?" Roger hazarded. "As I recall it, your generous offer to open our markets freely to their goods would have assured them a great increase of wealth, from the fact that their labour is so much cheaper than ours; yet they boggled over your one condition, that they should assist in their own defence by making a modest annual contribution to the up-keep of the Royal Navy."

"You are right, Mr. Brook, in that certain meaner spirits fastened upon the point; and that the Bill was thrown out in the Dublin Parliament after having passed its first reading at Westminster. Grattan and Flood there, and Burke and Sheridan here, all most shortsightedly opposed these measures which I so earnestly desired to bring about for the benefit of their own country. Yet the real cause of my defeat, was the determination of powerful factions in both Kingdoms to wreck my proposals, by representing each concession made to the sister-island as an injury or insult to the other."

" 'Tis true," Wilberforce agreed. " 'Twas Fox and his friends who whipped up the commercial interests against you, by a campaign of slander and misrepresentation, waged in both countries with a vigour worthy of a better cause. I pray that the same may not be the case. . . ."

He broke off as he caught sight of a servant approaching from the house to announce that his carriage was now in readiness.

"Have no fears on that score; and think only of getting well again," Pitt admonished him, as he tenderly helped him to his feet. "The question of Abolition is solely a humanitarian one, and we know already that on this great issue Fox and Burke are both with us."

"Aye; and The Lord!" cried Wilberforce, with shining eyes."For are not the poor negroes His children every wit as much as ourselves? May His blessing be upon you in all things, Billy; and on you, Mr. Brook."

With a word of thanks Roger offered his arm and assisted Pitt to support the invalid to his carriage. When he was settled comfortably in it the farewells were said, and at an easy pace it drove away. As the other two stood looking after it, Pitt said:

"Now there goes a true Saint; for so great-hearted is he that even the worst of sinners feels no awkwardness in his company. But come, Mr. Brook, let us return to the garden. I crave your indulgence to finish planting my tree; but, if, meanwhile, you will tell me to what I owe the pleasure of this visit, I vow to you that I shall not lose a single word of your discourse."

" 'Tis soon told, Sir. Last November, after my return from Holland, you were good enough to say that you might be able to find me some employment of a confidential nature, which would necessitate travelling abroad."

"I remember the occasion perfectly; and, you were then so eager for it, I find it surprising that you have not applied to me before."

The statement implied a question; and Roger had already learned that to win and hold the Prime Minister's esteem one must be frank, brief and to the point; so he said: "I had meant to approach you sooner, but I got caught up in a love-affair."

Pitt looked at him curiously. "The early twenties are the years when the foundations of great careers are laid. I had judged you too ambitious to sacrifice six months at this period of your life to such a purpose, however bright the lady's eyes."

" 'Twas worth it," said Roger simply.

"Since you can say that with such conviction you must be right, and I'll confess to envying you." Pitt smiled. "You see, I have never had a love-affair. 'Tis not that the fair sex lacks attraction for me, but that, somehow, on such occasions as I have felt the inclination, I have never been able to give the time to following the matter up."

"Your loss has been the nation's gain, Sir."

"You are kind to put it so, rather than to chide me with sacrificing the humanities to my ambitions. But reverting to yourself. I recall the details of our conversation now, and realise that your half-year's cessation from worldly striving is not out of keeping with your character. You are intolerant of discipline, and have no desire for public office or to make a career for yourself in one of the Services. Your ambition is rather to indulge your tastes for travel and the society of cultured people; but to do that in comfort you need a greater income than the three hundred a year your father gives you. The assets you have to offer are a good presence, a ready tongue and pen, fluent Latin and French, some Greek and a smattering of German; a specialised knowledge of French foreign policy and the affairs of the Dutch Netherlands; sufficient industry to have held an arduous secretarial post and sufficient courage to wield a pretty blade effectively. Am I right?"

"Apart from the fact that in some respects you flatter me, Sir, I marvel at the excellence of your memory."

They had reached the little tree, and Roger held it steady while Pitt completed the filling-in of the earth about its roots, as he went on thoughtfully: "The thing I had in mind for you was a somewhat nebulous post as my personal agent on the continent. Her Majesty's diplomatic representatives are, on the whole, a very able body of men; but their facilities for obtaining information are limited to what they can pick up themselves and what their paid spies can obtain for them. In the first case they are at a natural disadvantage from their obvious connection with the Court of St. James, and in the second, the type of person they employ, while well enough for counting the number of ships ready for war in a potential enemy's dockyard, are rarely of the social status to probe out diplomatic secrets at a foreign court."

"You propose that I should become a professional spy," Roger said bluntly.

"Yes. Does the idea offend you?"

Roger considered for a moment. The idea of a gentleman soiling his hands with such work was entirely against the canons of the age. On the other hand the offer would enable him to lead the type of life he desired, unfettered by any routine drudgery or subservience to a possibly uncongenial master.

Seeing his hesitation, Pitt added: "After our last interview I made inquiries about you, and learned that, quite apart from your spectacular *coup* concerning French intentions in the United Provinces, your father had already placed you in touch with our collator of secret information, Mr. Gilbert Maxwell; and that you had sent him valuable data regarding both the new fortifications at Cherbourg and Monsieur de la Peyrouse's expedition to New Zealand. Since you did so without instructions from anybody, why should you not continue such activities, but to a far more useful tune from receiving guidance as to the matters about which it is most urgent that we should know?"

"I acted spontaneously in the first instance, and later refused all payment for my small services; whereas your proposal, Sir, would place me on a very different footing."

"True. Yet it is clear that you possess both the ability and temperament to serve your country in this manner. If you were a young man of fortune I would ask you to do so out of patriotism, and I've little doubt but that you would agree. As you are not, I merely propose to make good the deficiency to an extent which would enable you to cut a decent figure at the foreign Courts; since unless you can do that, you are likely to be of little value to me."

Roger smiled. "Your arguments are well designed to dissipate my scruples, Sir."

"Let me clinch the matter then, by saying that, can you but uncover to us once every few years secrets as valuable as that which you brought home last autumn, I shall count you no less an asset to the nation than a regiment of foot or a ninety-four gun ship."

"Then I am your man, and will do my damnedest to deserve your good opinion of me."

The tree was planted and the earth around it well stamped down. Pitt was perspiring slightly, for he was far from strong and any physical exertion soon took its toll of him. As he mopped his high forehead he said: "Let us return to the house and take a glass of Shrub after our exertions. Then I will outline to you my views on the foreign policy that Britain should pursue. You'll stay to dinner, of course?"

"You are most kind, Sir," Roger replied, and as they walked back across the grass he marvelled that anyone could regard the tall, thin Prime Minister as cold, aloof and boorish.

It was true that, being a born aristocrat, he counted the applause or scorn of the mob as of so little moment that when he drove through the streets he kept his head held superciliously high, and would not even vouchsafe a nod to his most ardent supporters. It was also true that, as a child and youth, his extreme precocity had debarred him from enjoying the society of young people of his own age, so that he had never succeeded in overcoming a certain awkwardness of manner in mixed company. His major fault, if fault it was, but also his greatest strength, lay in his unquestioning belief that he alone was capable of guiding Britain's destinies to her best advantage. At the early age of seven, on learning that his great father had been raised to the Peerage, he had declared that "he was glad that he was not the eldest son, but that he would still be able to serve his country in the House of Commons like papa"; and this superb self-confidence, mistaken by lesser men for vanity, had earned him many enemies. But he was by nature kindly, tolerant and generous; and in the scant leisure that he allowed himself for relaxation he made a charming host and most stimulating companion.

Over the spiral-stemmed glasses of their orange-flavoured cordial Pitt made his beliefs and ambitions clear.

"Mr. Brook," he said. "I have never subscribed to the doctrine that wars are a necessary evil. In every age they have brought famine, desolation, pestilence and death to the common people, whose only desire is to be left to till their land and go about their usual avocations in peace. That the rulers and nobility of the stronger nations have, in the past, profited by waging war upon their weaker neighbours, I will admit. To them has gone the captured lands and the loot of despoiled cities; but the era in which war offered, even to the upper classes, something of the mixed attractions of a bloody gamble and a glorified hunt, has gone for ever.

"With the passage of time each succeeding European convulsion has resulted in a more thorough mobilisation of the resources of the countries involved. In medieval times the feudal lords went out to battle taking only their personal retainers and a modest percentage of their serfs; agriculture and commerce were able to continue almost undisturbed. To-day matters are very different. A nation at war soon becomes affected in all its parts and the strain of conflict eats so deeply into its vitals that whether it emerge as victor or vanquished it is still a loser. With the growth of industrialism, and our dependence on foreign markets for raw materials and supplies, this tendency must continue to increase; until a war of only a few years' duration between two great nations will suffice to bring starvation and bankruptcy to both. Therefore, we must seek by every means in our power, short of bowing our necks to a foreign yoke, to avoid wars in the future. And more; wherever we can, by offers of mediation or threats of intervention, seek to prevent hostilities breaking out between other nations."

" 'Tis a great conception, Sir; and no one could dispute the soundness of your reasoning," Roger agreed.

"Time," Pitt went on, "is the governing factor in all diplomacy designed to prevent war. 'Tis sudden, unexpected moves, leading to ill-considered counter moves, that inflame the tempers of nations and result in armed hostilities. Given early intelligence of the secret intentions of a foreign power there is time to consider matters calmly, and exercise a restraining influence before the potential aggressor feels that he has gone so far that he cannot turn back without loss of face. 'Tis the province of the Foreign Department to procure for us that information, but as it oft lies hid in the cabinets of Kings 'tis far from easy to come by. Your province, then, will be to supplement their efforts in special cases. But I pray you, from this moment on, to carry engraved upon your heart the prime object which will apply to all your journeyings. Information upon military matters, internal affairs, the dispositions of high personages, and Court intrigues, will always be of value; but you should not expose yourself to risk in order to obtain any of these things. Your task is to ferret out for me such secret ambitions of the sovereigns and their advisors, as might jeopardise the peace of Europe; and, wherever you are able, to advise me on such measures as you feel would assist in the preservation of a balance of power, so that steps can be taken in time to prevent these ambitions leading to an outbreak of hostilities."

Roger made a little grimace. "I am most sensible of the compliment you pay me, Sir, in charging me with so great an undertaking; but I fear you rate my powers over-high."

"Nay, Mr. Brook, I am the best judge of that. Last summer you made no small contribution to saving us from a war, on this same principle that a stitch in time saves nine. The country is still in your debt on that account; so if our Secret Service funds become the poorer by a thousand guineas, from maintaining you for some months in St. Petersburg without result, you'll have no cause to blame yourself but may count it as a holiday already earned."

"St. Petersburg!"

"Yes. 'Tis there that I have it in mind to send you; for Russia now provides the greatest enigma in the European scene. Let us briefly review it, and you will see why I should choose the Court of the Czarina Catherine, rather than another, for your first foray."

Pitt refilled the glasses and went on quietly. "When I first took office Britain was entirely isolated. Every power in Europe that counted had been but recently either in active war or armed neutrality against us. The major threat to our survival still seemed to come from France and she, through the strong influence of Queen Marie Antoinette, was firmly allied to Austria. In view of Frederick the Great's inherent animus against Austria it seemed that Prussia should be our natural ally, so I made appropriate overtures to 'old sour mug,' as his own Berliners termed him. He was already half-senile, and he allowed his secret hatred of England to weigh more with him than his best interests, so he flouted me; but time has removed him from my path."

"And his successor has proved more amenable," Roger interjected.

"Yes. Some wit once remarked that Frederick the Great had the wisdom of Solomon and that his nephew resembled that potentate only in respect to his overflowing harem; but, be that as it may, Frederick Wilhelm II has at least had the sense to allow himself to be persuaded by his far-seeing minister Count Hertzberg, and our own minister Mr. Ewart, of the value of an alliance with us. So we may eliminate Prussia from our anxieties."

"The Dutch also, since the events of last autumn."

Pitt nodded. "The United Provinces were within an ace of becoming provinces of France, but our timely intervention has re-established the Stadtholder firmly in control of his subjects; and both he and his Prussian wife are staunch friends to England. So we need have no fears of a Dutch fleet burning our shipping in the Medway. As for France, she was forced to eat humble-pie as a result of that affair, and, in my view, has not only shot her bolt for the moment, but is now well on the way to becoming our good friend."

"You really think so, Sir?"

"I do. The growth of resistance to the Royal authority, during the past half-year, has been such that I believe France incapable of waging another war until some radical change has taken place in her form of Government. But, even then, I see no reason why our age old enmity should be resumed. The Commercial Treaty is working wondrous well. You must have seen for yourself how French fashions, French foods and French literature have been all the rage here this past winter; and I'm told that in France, to be in the mode these days one must have everything 'A l'Anglaise'."

Roger shook his head. " 'Tis not for me to gainsay you, Sir; but I'd attach little weight to such superficial matters. As I see it the crux of the matter lies in the fact that the population of France is more than double ours; yet 'tis we who have now secured to ourselves Canada and India, and, by our control of the seas, first footing in the great new lands that Captain Cook discovered in the Southern Hemisphere. The French maintain that they must have living-room to expand, and Colonial markets for their goods, or perish. 'Tis on that count I fear that we shall yet be called on to face another bloody war with them."

"Mayhap I am over optimistic," Pitt smiled. " 'Tis certain that our Foreign Secretary, my Lord Carmarthen, would agree with you. He vows that I will never succeed in my ambitions to make our new friendship with the French a permanency. But in that he is much influenced by Sir James Harris, whose hatred of the French is near a mania."

"He has reason enough for that, seeing the years he spent fighting their intrigues while Minister at the Hague," Roger remarked. "But for his determination and fine fearless handling of the Dutch our cause would have been lost; and during my brief time there I formed a great admiration for him."

"Then it will please you to hear that he should be joining us within the hour. Sir James, Harry Dundas and my Lord Carmarthen are all driving down from town to dine here to-day."

"Indeed!" Roger exclaimed; and he could not keep a faint note of surprise out of his voice, as it was public knowledge that the Prime Minister and Sir James Harris were on far from good terms.

"I read your thought, Mr. Brook," Pitt laughed. "You are wondering why I should receive Sir James privately when, as member for Christchurch, he has so often and so bitterly opposed me in the House. But I do not count that against him. It arises, I am convinced, not from hatred of myself, but from a great personal loyalty that he feels towards Mr. Fox, born of their youthful friendship. Fox, Harris and William Eden formed a brilliant trio at Merton in their Oxford days, and ever since have stood firmly together in their politics. Yet I would think shame of myself did I neglect to employ the two latter on that account, seeing that they are both outstanding among our diplomats. 'Twas Eden, you will recall, that I sent to Paris to arrange the Commercial Treaty; and although it was the Rockingham ministry that nominated Harris for the Hague I confirmed him in the appointment as soon as I came to office. But let us return to our survey of Europe. We were speaking of France, were we not?"

"You were saying, Sir, that you had no fears of war with that country."

"Not for some years to come, at all events. Nor do I fear it with Spain, since she is now reduced to dependence on France, and would not act alone. Nor Austria. The sweeping reforms that the Emperor Joseph II has carried out in his wide-spread dominions have well earned him the title of 'the crowned revolutionist,' but he is paying a heavy price for them. The Magyars, Belgians, and various others of his subject-peoples are in constant revolt against his innovations; so, having now entered the war against the Turks as the ally of Russia, his hands are overfull already. Russia remains then at the present time the only country having the power, and possibly the will, to be plotting a new war of aggression which might set all Europe ablaze."

"As you have just remarked, she is already at war with the Grand Turk."

"And we are supporting him in secret with supplies and money."

"Yet not so long ago we allowed the Russian fleet to refit and victual in our British ports, on its way to attack him in the Mediterranean."

"That was agreed to in the hope of securing Catherine's friendship. But it proved a mistaken policy, since she still withholds it and it resulted in the Russians securing bases for themselves in the Greek Islands. They are, too, now firmly established in Genoa, owing to the complaisancy of the Grand Duke of Tuscany. 'Tis these footholds they have secured in the Mediterranean that are one of my causes for alarm, and I wish you to attempt to ascertain how far it is their intention to extend them."

"In the event of war the Russian Fleet would prove no match for the British, so we should be able to cut them off there."

"True; but no fleet can have its major strength in two places at the same time, and in a crisis it might be necessary to retain the bulk of ours in northern waters. Moreover, it is the Czarina's possible ambitions in northern Europe which fill me with far graver concern. We are now supporting the Turk in the hope of keeping her fully occupied against him; but her resources are so vast that one cannot rule out the possibility of her launching another campaign, perhaps against the remnant that is left of Poland, perhaps against the Swedes in their Finnish territories. 'Tis of such designs as she may harbour in secret for further expanding her empire westward that I am anxious to learn; and how we might dissuade her from them, or in the last event, take steps to check the aggrandisement of Russia before she becomes a serious menace to the whole European family."

Roger nodded. "I take your meaning, Sir; and will do my utmost to procure you a few useful pointers, if no more. Is it your wish that I should report to you direct or send such data as I can gather to Mr. Gilbert Maxwell?"

"I prefer that you should write direct. Take your letters to Mr. Alleyne Fitzherbert at the British Embassy, and he will arrange for their safe despatch; but see to it that you give them to the Ambassador personally, as it is undesirable that any members of his staff should know that you are in correspondence with me."

"There are certain objections to such a procedure if I carry out a plan which is already forming in my mind. It seems that I should have a better prospect of becoming privy to the Empress's intentions if I appear at her court as a subject of that nation she so much admires, and term myself *Monsieur le Chevalier de Breuc.* I passed as a native of the half-German province of Alsace while I was in France, so I should have no difficulty in doing so in Russia. But the British Ambassador would be unlikely to cultivate the acquaintance of a Frenchman of no particular distinction, and in my case it would bring most unwelcome suspicion on me if he did; so I'd prefer to have no dealings with him."

Pitt's long face broke into a grin. " 'Tis clear, *Monsieur le Chevalier,* that you have a natural flair for this work, and that I was right to count upon you. As regards our method of communication we will consult Sir James Harris. Previous to his appointment to the Hague he was our representative at the Czarina's court for some five years, so he should be able to suggest a way out of our difficulty. We'll discuss it over dinner."

"May I submit that the fewer people who are made aware that I am to act as your secret agent, the better," said Roger earnestly.

"I'll not gainsay you there, Mr. Brook. But you may rely on the discretion of the men who are to dine with us, and I have a personal reason for wishing them to be informed of the work you are about to undertake. From my childhood I have been of a frail constitution, and I fear that my life will not be a long one. When I went to Cambridge, at the age of fourteen, my doctors recommended me to fortify myself with port. A brace of tumblers of that generous wine, taken before addressing the House, undoubtedly stimulates my powers of oratory; yet I can hardly think that it will add to my longevity. If I am fated to die before my ambitions for this great nation come to fruition, others, thank God, will now carry on my policies; Dundas and Carmarthen among them; so 'tis as well that they should be aware of your activities in order that they may continue to employ you should a sudden illness remove me from the scene."

"I sincerely trust that no such dire event will rob the country of your leadership," Roger said in quick concern.

The Prime Minister shrugged his narrow shoulders. "With God's grace I'll have a few years yet, and I pray you put the matter from your mind."

He then went on to talk about the ambitions of the Czarina and the numerous wars she had already launched in her reign; the leading part she had played in the partitioning of Poland in 1771, her annexation of the Crimea, and the new war that she had launched against Turkey the preceding August. That February Austria had come in with Russia, and it was believed that Gustavus III of Sweden had signed a secret treaty promising to support the Turks. Pitt was speculating whether the Swedish King would really dare to take up the cudgels against his powerful neighbour, when Lord Carmarthen and Sir James Harris were announced.

The two friends were a good-looking pair. The Marquis was still only in his late thirties and the younger by some five years; he was also slimmer in build and dressed in quieter taste. He was an amiable person with pleasing manners, but inclined to be capricious and vain. As the eldest son of the Duke of Leeds and Lady Mary Godolphin, he was able to exert considerable political influence, but it was not this alone which had decided Pitt to offer him the Foreign Secretaryship in his first administration. The young Prime Minister had been attracted to him by his honesty and the way in which he had lost no opportunity of attacking corruption and waste on the part of the previous Governments.

Sir James Harris, with his brilliant eyes and bold, handsome face, was a much more flamboyant personality. On entering the Diplomatic service he had been sent as secretary to the Embassy in Madrid. In the summer of 1770, his seniors having all gone on leave during the great heats, he found himself temporarily acting in the role of *Chargé d'Affaires*. At this juncture he learned that the Spaniards were secretly fitting out an expedition in Buenos Aires for the capture of the Falkland Islands. Although only aged twenty-four he took so high a tone with the Spanish Prime Minister that the attempt was abandoned. This spirited act had gained him swift promotion; at twenty-six he was sent as Minister to Berlin, at thirty-one as Ambassador to St. Petersburg, and at thirty-seven, having retired to amuse himself with politics, he had been persuaded to re-enter the diplomatic arena at the Hague, then the danger-spot of Europe; and there, with his audacity, courage and genius for intrigue, had created and matured a counter-revolution in the interests of Britain.

Lord Carmarthen was a stranger to Roger, but Harris hardly waited for them to be introduced before clapping him on the shoulder, and recalling the festivities in which they had shared the previous October when Prince William V of Orange was happily restored to authority in his own capital.

Roger inquired after the Princess, who had treated him with special kindness, and Harris gave a jovial laugh. "So you fell a victim to her, too, eh! Well, I don't wonder. She's a monstrous fine woman, and those gay blue eyes of hers near made me forget her exalted station more than once. And where we'd have been without her high courage I know not. I left her in good health, but chafing as ever at being tied to that miserable weakling of a husband who makes so plaguey poor a showing as Stadtholder."

" 'Tis a strange coincidence," remarked Carmarthen, "that there should be so close a similarity between the rulers of the Dutch Netherlands and those of France. In both cases the men are poor vacillating creatures, while the women are not only beautiful and high-spirited but possess the forceful personalities fitted to the wearing of a crown."

"Is there aught fresh out of France?" Pitt inquired.

"Nay, nothing of moment. The Parliament of Paris is still striving to force the King to surrender his right of issuing *Lettres de Cachet;* and the Provincial Parliaments are, as usual, at loggerheads with the Royal authorities on a score of matters. His Grace of Dorset has just gone on leave, but Mr. Hailes wrote me this week, that notwithstanding the very extraordinary advantages with which the last loan was offered it is now below par, so confidence in the Government is clearly declining still further."

For a time they talked of the troubles of the French monarchy, then Henry Dundas joined them.

He was a big raw-boned Scot, who possessed little refinement or literary taste, but had enormous political sagacity and was indefatigably industrious. Coming from a well-known Scottish legal family, he had rapidly made his way up in that profession to become solicitor-general for Scotland at the age of twenty-four. As a speaker, although steady and logical, he was rated poor; but he was a tower of strength at Westminster, since he not only ruled the *bloc* of Scottish members with a rod of iron, but also controlled the election of the Scottish representative Peers. This was in part due to the fact he had pushed a Bill through Parliament by which Scottish estates forfeited after the Jacobite rising of '45 had been restored to their owners. So powerful was he north of the Tweed that he was known as Harry the Ninth of Scotland. In Pitt's administration he still occupied the comparatively minor post of Treasurer of the Navy, but in recent years the Prime Minister had tended more and more to treat him as his principal lieutenant; and by having made him a member of the new Board of Control for India, had opened the way for him to dominate it, so that he had soon become, in all but name, the ruler of that great country. He was now forty-six years of age; he drank like a fish and swore like a trooper.

Shortly after his arrival, dinner was announced, and over it their quick minds led them to comment on and dismiss a vast variety of subjects. Roger, with becoming modesty, said little, except when directly addressed, until towards the end of the meal. Harris brought up the subject of Sir Humphrey Etheredge's tragic death as the result of an All Fools' Day joke, which had been the talk of the town during the proceeding week. He had had the story from his friend Charles Fox and, glancing at Roger, said: "If my memory serves me, Mr. Brook, Charles mentioned that you were of the company at Stillwaters when the fatality occurred."

Roger was at once pressed by the others to give a first-hand account of the affair; and he did so as casually as he could. When he had done, Dundas remarked in his rich Scots accent: "Weel! 'Tis an ill wind that blows nae man any guid. By this Isaiah Etheredge becomes a bonny Baronet; though he'll no be aware of it for many a week yet to come."

"Why say you that, Sir?" asked Roger.

"Because, Sir, I know him ta ha' taken ship for Jamaica a se'n-night before the tragedy," came the prompt answer. "He has a wee bit of a plantation there, and was of the opeenion that by a visit he might screw a few more bawbees out of his factor."

To Roger these were the most excellent tidings. During the past week he had heard nothing from Stillwaters, and although he had endeavoured to take comfort from the old adage that "no news is good news," he had felt a constant anxiety lest Sir Isaiah should nose out something during his visit. Now it was clear that the new Baronet could not have attended his nephew's funeral, and better still, would not be back in England for several months to come, by which time the whole business would be ancient history. It was a minute or more before Roger realised to the full the strain that he had been living under and the magnitude of the relief that Dundas's casual words had brought him. By keeping their heads he and Georgina had escaped the awful fate that had threatened them. The affair could now be considered as closed, and he could go abroad free of all worry that she might yet be overtaken by Nemesis.

As Roger brought his thoughts back to his present surroundings he realised that the port had been put on the table, the servants had left the room, and that Pitt was telling his friends of his project for endeavouring to ascertain the Czarina's secret intentions.

Harry Dundas swigged back his first glass of port and grinned at Roger. "If ye're the man ye look, Mr. Brook, ye'll no regret this enterprise. The Russian men are fine hard drinkers, and the women as free with their charms as any young laird could wish, so I'm told."

Carmarthen offered Roger his snuff-box and said: "Indeed, Sir, I wish you all the pleasures that Mr. Dundas implies, but also a more

107

solid success. From the very nature of their position our diplomatic representatives are often prevented from learning facts not meant for their ears, which are yet almost common talk at the courts to which they are accredited. With so pleasing a presence and address as you possess, if you convey the impression that you are but an idle fellow travelling for pleasure you may well secure for us information of considerable value."

"You have taken my very thought, Francis," nodded Pitt, as Roger murmured his thanks for the compliment paid him, and the Foreign Secretary went on:

"As the Prime Minister may have told you, he does not share my belief that the French continue to bear us malice for the past, and out of jealousy will, when they have found a solution to their internal troubles, become a serious menace to us again. His optimism may be justified, but I feel that we should at least leave nothing undone to guard ourselves against such a contingency."

"Hear! Hear!" exclaimed Harris heartily.

" 'Tis for that reason," Carmarthen continued, "that I am most anxious to regain Russia's friendship, and that of Austria as well. England was Russia's first friend when she emerged from her own borders, and until quite recent times we enjoyed the traditional good-will of the Court of Vienna. Yet, during the late war we lost both, and instead they now look to France as the protector of their interests in Western Europe. By the new Triple Alliance we have bound Prussia and the United Provinces to us, and are in a fair way to add Sweden and the Turk to our *bloc*. Yet I would willingly sacrifice the two latter, could we but regain Russia and Austria, and thus isolate France."

"I too would welcome a *rapprochement* with the two Imperial powers," declared Pitt, "but not from the project of isolating France, and thus driving her into renewed suspicion and enmity. Rather we should strive to win the goodwill of all. 'Tis not by secret pacts aimed at individual nations that we shall ever secure a lasting peace, but by sound commercial treaties which need cause fear to none."

"You agree though, Billy, that Mr. Brook should send us such data as he can which might assist in our gaining Russia as an ally?"

"I do. Yet seeing that James Harris, here, and Alleyne Fitzherbert have both failed in that, I see little hope that Mr. Brook will be able to furnish us with anything to act upon. 'Twould be unreasonable to ask him to seek for a goodwill in the existence of which none of us have the least cause to believe. His function, rather, as I see it, will be to inform us as far as he can regarding Russia's intentions in the north, in order that we may take such steps as we can to put a check on her further aggrandisement."

Carmarthen then took the opportunity to press Pitt into agreeing that, as a gesture of goodwill to Russia, her fleet, which was fitting out in the Gulf of Finland, should again be allowed the freedom of the British ports on its voyage round to the Ionian Sea; and this led to a discussion on the role of Austria, as Russia's ally in her war against the Turks. Dundas joined in with his usual vigour, leaving Harris and Roger, who were seated side by side, temporarily out of the conversation.

The thoughts of both the latter were still on St. Petersburg and, after a few minutes the ex-ambassador said: "I wish you better fortune in your mission to the Venice of the North, than I had in mine. 'Tis a fine city and the Russians, although crafty and unreliable, are a gay and hospitable folk. I soon took their measure and would I think, in time, have succeeded in pinning them down; but I confess that the Czarina bested me. She is as slippery as an eel, and never seemed to tire of lending a favourable ear to my arguments, while all the time she was secretly planning to embarrass us in our war with the French, by forming the League of Armed Neutrality and leading it against us. I take it you are acquainted with her history?"

Roger shook his head. "I fear I know little very about her except that she was the daughter of a petty German Prince, and, having married the heir apparent to the Russian throne, deposed him by a successful conspiracy some six months after he had ascended it as Peter III. That was before I was born, and for the past quarter of a century she has continued to occupy the throne herself, apparently illegally, as her son is long past his majority and should be seated on it as the Emperor Paul."

"That is so. She was the daughter of Prince Christian of Anhalt-Zerbst-Dornburg; and her husband was also a German Princeling. His father was only a Duke of Holstein-Gottorp, but his mother, Anne, was the elder daughter of Peter the Great. It was her younger sister who became the Empress Elizabeth. She had many lovers but never married, so in due course, she selected her nephew, the little Holstein-Gottorp, as her heir, and had him brought to Petersburg at the age of fourteen. Three years later she picked Catherine, who was then sixteen, for him as a wife. He had the ill-luck to contract the smallpox just before the wedding, and it left him hideously disfigured. Added to which his parts were tied, and since he funked a small operation it was several years before he was able to consummate the marriage."

"How prodigious strange," remarked Roger, "that Marie Antoinette should have found herself in exactly the same case with Louis XVI. 'Twas eight years, I'm told, before he would bring himself to face a nick with a knife so that they could lie together."

" 'Twas a year or so more than that for Katinka."

"Such a situation must have been a sore trial for both Princesses."

"Mightily so," Harris agreed, "since through no fault of their own they became the mock of their courts from failing to produce heirs; and one could scarce blame either for consoling themselves with a lover. 'Tis averred that the fair Austrian kept her virtue; but the beautiful little German succumbed to the blandishments of her husband's Chamberlain, a fellow named Soltikof, about a year before her spouse succeeded in co-habiting with her. By that time she had long since lost any affection she may ever have had for the boorish, pock-marked

Peter, but his having shared her bed at least saved her from any question being raised as to the legitimacy of her only son, Paul Petrovitch, who was born in October '54."

"The man who should be Czar is now thirty-four, then?"

"He is. But I'd give long odds against his ever ascending the throne while his mother is alive."

"How old is she now?"

"Nearly sixty; and for the past twenty-six years she has been the most powerful woman in the world. The Empress Elizabeth, after a long illness during which she was drunk the greater part of the time, died early in '62. Peter succeeded her but reigned only six months, then Catherine deposed him and he died in mysterious circumstances a week or so later. Technically she assumed power as regent for her infant son, but she soon forgot that convenient fiction. Meanwhile, Soltikof had become only a memory of the past. Poniatowski, whom she afterwards made King of Poland, succeeded him in her affections; then Gregory Orlof, who arrested her husband for her during the *coup d'état*. Since then she has taken scores of lovers, so she is well named the Semiramis of the North. In her youth and prime she was a great beauty and of a most lively disposition, so must have proved a fine bedfellow for many a lusty young gallant, but I pity the poor devils whose duty it is to tumble her now."

"What! She has lovers still!"

"Aye," Harris nodded. "Though she be fat, grey and toothless, I'm told she shows no decline in that respect. And an invitation from the Empress is a command."

" 'Tis unnatural," Roger declared.

"Unusual, would be the more suitable word," commented Harris quietly. "And, believe me, little Katinka is an unusual—nay, a remarkable—woman. So arbitrary, violent and licentious has been her private life that she may well go down to history as a second Messalina; yet she is far more highly cultured and intelligent than any other monarch of our age. She is not merely absolute in theory but makes her autocratic power felt in every department of the State. In her own hand she recodified and modernised the whole of Russia's laws. She has colonised great empty spaces of her Empire with poor but hardworking Teutons, and has founded innumerable schools. She selects her own military commanders and lays down their objectives for each campaign. Her Foreign Minister is merely a cipher, for 'tis she who furnishes all her diplomats with their instructions. Despite these herculean labours she finds ample time to indulge her love of pleasure, and to carry on a vast correspondence concerning art and literature with such men as Voltaire, Diderot and d'Alembert. In her private relationships she is as capricious as a flighty minx of eighteen; yet her mind as so well balanced when it turns to affairs of State that she never allows her personal prejudices to interfere with her judgment. In her love for Russia she has become more Russian than the Russians; and at her order the most powerful army in the world will march east, south or west as she may choose to direct it."

Harris paused for a moment, then added: "I trust that what I have said may have given you some conception of the real greatness of the wicked little old woman whose hand you may soon be privileged to kiss."

"It has indeed," Roger said thoughtfully. "And you would make me still further your debtor if, before I leave, I might consult you on various aspects of my mission."

"I had been about to suggest placing my small experience of life at the Court of Petersburg at your disposal. Would it suit you to dine with me at Brook's on Tuesday?"

"I'd be honoured, Sir; and more than grateful to you for your guidance."

Seeing that they had finished their semi-private conversation, Pitt leaned forward and said to Roger: "Have you spoken to Sir James with regard to some method of sending me your despatches privately?"

Before Roger could reply Harris did so for him. "We are meeting again next week, Sir, and I already have in mind a sound channel for that. There is, however, the, er—question of funds. My mission to Russia cost me twenty thousand pounds of my private fortune over and above my emoluments as Ambassador, and I should not like to think that Mr. Brook is to be out of pocket to even a twentieth of that amount."

"Nor I," laughed Pitt, and Carmarthen smiled affably across the table, as he said: "If you will be good enough to wait upon me at the Foreign Office, Mr. Brook, I will arrange both funds and passage for you."

The conversation then again became general until, at half-past eight, they left the table and the guests prepared to go back to London.

As Roger, now full of good port and inward excitement at the new prospects which the day had opened to him, was about to mount his horse, Pitt and Dundas warmly wished him every good fortune. Carmarthen and Harris he was to see again, so as they got into their carriage they only waved him a cheerful "good-night."

The carriage bowled swiftly down the drive, and as it passed out of the gates with Roger a hundred yards ahead, Carmarthen asked his friend: "What think you are the prospects of that young man's mission having profitable results?"

"None," answered Harris bluntly.

"Why so, Jimmy?" yawned his Lordship. "I thought him a likeable fellow; modest yet not slow to answer when addressed, and of good intelligence."

"He is all of that, and a man to mark; for he will, I believe, go far. But not in this."

"What reason have you for your pessimism?"

"The venu of the mission he has been given; and Billy Pitt is at fault in that. Having ever lived aloof from the world himself he still remains completely oblivious to the fact that other human beings are made of flesh and blood. Had it been otherwise he would have had more sense than to send this lad to Petersburg. We must afford him all the help we can, but he will fail there for a certainty."

"Why should he have a greater chance of success in any other capital?"

Harris gave a short, hard laugh. "Because, my friend, I will eat my Order of the Bath if, after one look at his fine figure and bonny blue eyes, that old bitch of an Empress does not order him to her bed. And I do not think young Mr. Brook will stand for that."

CHAPTER VIII

THE BAL MASQUÉ

O N April the 17th Roger landed at Copenhagen. It had been Sir James Harris's idea that an oblique approach to St. Petersburg would offer advantages not to be obtained by a direct descent upon it. The wily diplomat had pointed out that while Roger's plan of passing himself off as a Frenchman in the Russian capital was basically sound, he would be greatly handicapped if he arrived there with neither background nor introductions; whereas if he spent a few weeks in Denmark and Sweden on his way, he should be able to establish his new personality while in those countries, and later enter Russia adequately sponsored by friends that he had made while in the Scandinavian capitals.

It had transpired that the first available ship was sailing from Edinburgh about the 20th of the month, so Roger had had ample time to go down to Lymington and spend a few days with his mother before taking coach for the north. This visit to his home had also enabled him to have several additional conferences with Sir James, as the diplomat was about to be elevated to the peerage under the title of Baron Malmesbury for his part in bringing about the Triple Alliance; and, as member for Christchurch, he wished to secure the support of his constituents in the coming bye-election for his party's nominee. In consequence, two days after their dinner at Brook's, they travelled down into Hampshire together, and Roger had benefitted by much sage advice about his mission.

Quite apart from Sir James's great prestige in his own service he had most valuable personal relationships with other leading figures in it. His wife had been a Miss Amyand, and her sister had married Sir Gilbert Elliot, whose youngest sister was the wife of William Eden, the negotiator of the recent commercial treaty with France, and whose younger brother, Hugh, was now minister at Copenhagen. It had therefore been decided that no one could be better fitted to launch Roger into the Baltic scene than Mr. Hugh Elliot, and Sir James had furnished him with a letter for that purpose. He had also given him a letter for the Reverend William Tooke, the chaplain to the trading factory in St. Petersburg, where all cargoes of British goods shipped to the port were warehoused before being distributed. Sir James had described the clergyman as a shrewd, discreet fellow, long resident in Russia and possessing an encyclopædic knowledge of Russian affairs. It was to him that Roger was to give his despatches, as he was admirably situated to pass them on to Mr. Alleyne Fitzherbert for transmission by Embassy bag to London.

While sailing up the Sound towards Copenhagen, through waters alive with shipping, Roger had been pleasantly impressed with the fertile, undulating country, studded with fine private houses set in well-wooded picturesque parks; and on landing he was similarly impressed by the Danish capital. Sixty years before it had been almost totally destroyed by a great fire, so all its principal buildings were comparatively modern, and it had a much more spacious air than any other city that he had so far visited.

Roger had travelled from Edinburgh as Monsieur le Chevalier de Breuc, and The Silver Hart having been recommended to him as the best inn at which to put up, he went straight to it and took rooms there in that name. As soon as he was settled into them he wrote a note in French to Mr. Elliot, simply saying that he had a letter for him from Sir James Harris and would be glad to know when it would be convenient to deliver it. The same evening a reply came back that the Minister would be happy to receive him at eleven o'clock the following morning.

Next day therefore he hired a horse and rode out to Christiansholm, the residential suburb in which the British Legation was situated, and found it to be a small but very beautiful villa. Immediately he was alone with Mr. Elliot he disclosed the fact that he was an Englishman and presented his credentials. Then, as the Minister gave him a quiet smile and settled down to peruse them, Roger had ample opportunity to study him at leisure and think over the outline of his history, which had been supplied by Sir James.

Hugh Elliot hailed from Minto in Roxburghshire and was the second son of a Scottish Baronet. He was educated for the Army but, owing to his father's friendship with Lord Suffolk, the Foreign Secretary of the day, had, without being consulted by either, been appointed His Brittanic Majesty's Minister to the Elector of Bavaria, at the age of twenty-one. After a tour of duty in the charming and easy-going city of Munich he had been transferred at twenty-five to the much less agreeable but far more important post of Berlin. Here he fell in love with and married the beautiful Fraulein von Krauth, only to learn a few years later that she was deceiving him. At this juncture he had just been transferred to Copenhagen, and his romance ended by his secretly returning to Berlin to kidnap his own little daughter in the middle of the night, fighting a successful duel with his young wife's lover, and then divorcing her.

He was a rather frail-looking, fair-haired, blue-eyed Scot, now thirty-six years of age. Roger thought he looked considerably older, but attributed that to the tragic failure of his marriage.

Having finished reading the letter Hugh Elliot said: "I will willingly serve you in any way I can, Mr. Brook, but your having appeared here in the guise of a Frenchman makes it somewhat difficult for me to do so openly. For example, it would not be *de rigueur* for me to present anyone not having British nationality, at the Danish Court."

Roger bowed. "I am aware of that, Sir, and the last thing I would wish to do is to prove an embarrassment to you. However, Sir James suggested that you might perhaps be able to arrange an occasion when I could meet the French Minister here, casually. My story is that I am a native of Strasbourg, but have been living with relatives in England for the past six months; so that while I am lacking in introductions from my own countrymen, friends in London were good enough to give me a letter of introduction to yourself."

"That sounds like a typical James Harris ruse," smiled Elliot. "He would reason that once I have brought you into contact with Monsieur le Baron la Houze, you will only have to make yourself pleasant to him, for him to offer, quite spontaneously, to present you himself; then you will be launched every bit as much under the French ægis in Denmark as though you had arrived here with your pockets stuffed full of letters from Versailles."

"That was the idea, Sir," Roger grinned back.

"Regard the matter as arranged then. I'll not ask Monsieur le Baron here to meet you, as that might appear a shade too pointed. But he is certain to be at Count Bernstorff's *soirée* next Tuesday so you shall accompany me to that. Now, in what other way can I be of assistance to you?"

"If I did not fear to trespass on your good nature I would ask if you could spare an evening to put me *au courant* with the politics of the Scandinavian Kingdoms *vis-à-vis* Russia."

"I will do so with pleasure. As I lead a bachelor existance 'tis my custom to spend most Sundays with my good friends the Reventlows; but I can easily excuse myself to-morrow, and if you will dine with me we can have a long talk afterwards."

"Please don't let me interfere . . ." Roger began.

The Minister waved the polite hesitation aside. "Believe me, Mr. Brook, 'tis mere selfishness out of my eagerness to hear the latest gossip from London, that makes me seek so early an opportunity to talk with you at leisure. I'll be your debtor for giving me your company to-morrow. How long do you plan to remain with us in Copenhagen?"

"In that, Sir, I should value your guidance. My mission is of so nebulous a character that any reasonable delay in my reaching the Russian capital may well be compensated for, if during it, I acquire a better knowledge of how to interpret such allusions to future policy as I may pick up when I am once established there. Yet I am naturally eager to reach my destination and set about the business on which I have been sent."

"I agree that a good understanding of the background against which you are to work should prove of great value to you; and I will give you a verbal survey of the Danish court to-morrow. I think too, that either through Monsieur la Houze or some other agency we must arrange for your presentation, so that you can see the leading personages here for yourself. But once you have made your bow there will be little point in your lingering here. Denmark now pursues a policy of strict neutrality, so Copenhagen has become something of a backwater and you would be more likely to learn of matters to your advantage in Stockholm."

A servant now appeared with a pot of hot chocolate, and over it they talked of lighter matters for a quarter of an hour, then Roger took his leave.

He spent the rest of the day wandering about the Danish capital, and found to his relief that language presented no barriers to his enjoyment. All the better class of people whom he addressed, as also the shopkeepers and hackney-coachmen, spoke either fluent French or German; and he soon learned that few of the nobility even understood Danish, as it was then considered by them to be only the barbarous tongue of churls.

The Royal Palace of Christiansborg appeared to him vast in comparison with the smallness of the city, but such churches as he visited proved disappointing. Since the Reformation the Danes had adopted the strictest form of Calvinism, so their places of worship were bleakly puritanical. Such people of quality as he saw were richly dressed in the French fashion, but the bulk of the citizens wore sober black, and the tattered garments of the poorer people led him to judge that, as in France, the wealth of the country was most unevenly distributed. The food that was served to him at his own Inn he found excellent, as, although plain, it was beautifully fresh and included a greater number of fish-dishes than he had seen before on one table.

On the Sunday the entire city assumed an air of intense sobriety. Every shop was shuttered, the cries of the street-vendors were stilled, and amusements of every kind were strictly prohibited. In consequence, he was glad when the time came for him to ride out again to Christiansholm. The air was crisp, but now that May had almost come a brave sun heightened the tender green of the gardens that he passed, and brought out the rich colours of their flowers.

At the Legation the tall, blue-eyed Scot received him kindly and they sat down to dinner *à deux*. Once more Roger noted the profusion of fish-dishes, including a delicious cold salmon; and, on his commenting on it, his host told him that, as Norway formed part of the Danish dominions, such salmon were to be had all through the season in Copenhagen for a few pence.

After they had dined, instead of remaining at table, they took their wine into the library and settled themselves comfortably at a table in a bay-window which had a lovely view across the garden to the Sound, where an armada of small yachts was rocking gently at anchor in Sabbath quiet.

Having filled Roger's glass, Hugh Elliot said: "Now to business. To give you a picture of the people who control the destinies of Denmark I must go some way back. You will, no doubt, have noted the strictness with which Sunday is kept here. Well, 'tis a feast-day now to what it was when King Frederick V ascended the throne in 1746. Before his time the Court lived in almost unrelieved gloom, on week-days as well as on the Sabbath, but he altered that, for the nobility at least. He was one of the most dissolute monarchs that ever lived, and was hardly surpassed in his excesses by his contemporary Louis XV. The Reformed Church here naturally regarded him as its worst enemy, but the Danish Kings are absolute. They have no Parliament, and neither the nobility nor the clergy has any legal means of opposing their wishes—so their word is law. In consequence King Frederick emancipated his upper-classes from their hair-shirts; and ever since his time the court has been to some extent lax in its morals, whereas the bulk of the people have continued to lead outwardly the most puritanical lives. Apart from his debaucheries he was by no means a bad King, and with the aid of his very able Prime Minister, Count Bernstorff, he brought a moderate prosperity to Denmark."

"That would be the uncle of the present Prime Minister, would it not?" Roger asked.

"Yes. And the nephew is as gifted as the uncle. Frederick V married twice. His first wife was Louisa the daughter of our King George II, and by her he had two children, Christian VII, the present ruler of Denmark, and Sophia Magdalena, who is now the wife of King Gustavus III of Sweden. For his second wife Frederick, in an evil hour, took Juliana Maria, the daughter of the Duke of Brunswick-Wolfenbüttel. He died in 1776, and from that time this cunning, ambitious and ruthless German Princess has been the curse of the Royal House of Denmark."

" 'Tis she who is known as the Queen-Dowager, I take it."

Elliot nodded. "The root of the trouble lies in the fact that she also had a son, Prince Frederick, and has never ceased her scheming to place him on the throne instead of his elder half-brother, Christian. She is, to the life, the wicked step-mother of fiction, and during Christian's minority treated him with the utmost brutality. 'Tis said that she attempted to poison him, but, be that as it may, she certainly starved and beat him; denied him all proper education, and instead, by surrounding him with the most dissolute companions at an early age completely debauched him. In fact, she took every step she could devise to wreck his health so that he should die, or, failing that, grow up totally unfitted to be a ruler."

" 'Tis to her treatment that his madness can be attributed, then?"

"Undoubtedly. And she endeavoured to have him set aside on that account, in order that her own, stupid, deformed, horse-faced son, Frederick, could mount the throne. But in that she failed, since opposing interests in the Royal Council maintained that Christian was not mad enough to be deposed."

"What form does his madness take?"

"The type of senseless and often violent pranks that one would expect from a warped and undeveloped brain. He is totally lacking in all dignity, or even cleanliness; guzzles his food like a pig and gives way to ungovernable tempers. He can converse with some degree of sly sense, but uses the most disgusting language, and his moods are entirely unpredictable. In the middle of a royal banquet he is quite liable suddenly to begin amusing himself by throwing the crockery at one of his guests, and 'tis no joke to be so picked upon, for his aim is uncannily accurate. He has defaced every statue and painting in the palace by throwing things at them, and often of a morning breaks two or three dozen panes of glass in the windows by casting the same number of pebbles at them from fifty paces."

"So 'twas to such a creature that King George's youngest sister was sent as a bride!" Roger interjected with disgust.

"Yes. Poor little Caroline Matilda was scarce fifteen when she arrived here from England to be his Queen, but she soon grew to be a very lovely woman. She was unusually tall with the fairest of fair hair, a complexion of milk and roses, fine white teeth and large, expressive blue eyes. All Denmark fell in love with her, except, of course, Juliana Maria; whose hatred of the young sovereigns was intensified to fever pitch when Caroline Matilda gave Christian an heir—the present Crown Prince Frederick—thus forming a second obstacle to his step-uncle Frederick ever ascending the throne. As that ill-favoured youth was cordially disliked, Caroline Matilda's popularity knew no bounds for a year or two after the birth of her son; but it then began to suffer a sharp decline."

Roger smiled. "Is this where the famous—or perhaps I should say infamous—Dr. Struensee enters upon the scene?"

"You know the story?" Elliot asked.

"Only vaguely, as these events occurred some eighteen or nineteen years ago. I pray you continue the narrative."

"Struensee, then, was not only a bold, handsome fellow, and a devil with the women, but an extremely able German doctor and a political thinker of no small merit. After Christian's son was born it was decided that the monarch should go abroad to see something of foreign courts. With him he took Count Holcke the most vicious of his favourites, and Dr. Struensee. They visited the Hague, London and Paris, spending some months in each; and in each the King indulged in the lowest forms of depravity. Holcke encouraged him in that and often took him straight from official receptions to sailors' brothels in Amsterdam or down to the stews in Wapping. Struensee was too shrewd a man to interfere with the King's pleasures, but it seems that he possessed the power of calming him during his fits of violence, and making him behave with reasonable restraint when in decent company. Moreover by the use of drugs he relieved the King's headaches and eased his insomnia. By these means he made himself indispensable to his royal patient, so by the time they returned to Denmark Struensee had replaced Count Holcke and become prime favourite.

"From that point Struensee's rise to power was meteoric. You must remember that here the King is absolute, with no check of any kind upon his authority. He has but to sign a paper to alter the law, increase taxation, double or disband his army, and cause any of his subjects either to receive the highest honour, or to be tortured and put to death without trial. For Struensee, providing he kept the King amused with bawdy books and semi-drugged, it was easy to get the royal signature to any measure he desired. In the space of a few months he had banished all the old ministers and become himself the absolute ruler of Denmark."

"And the Queen's lover," added Roger.

"Yes. Although in fairness it must be said that she went more than halfway to meet him. But, with such a husband, who can blame her? Christian's excesses on his tour had completed what those of his youth had began, and rendered him practically impotent; in addition he had given the unfortunate young woman a clap. The *Herr Doktor* cured her of it and took her husband's place. Their liaison might have continued for years, bringing prolonged happiness to them both, had not Struensee's political reforms earned him many enemies, and the open flaunting of the fact that they were living together provided the Queen Dowager with a lever for their undoing."

"What type of political reforms did he initiate?"

"Many of them were excellent. He abolished torture in the prisons, gave freedom to the press, and ordained that whenever it was sought to inflict the penalties on a woman for loose living, her seducer must be named in court and share her punishment if she was found guilty. You can imagine how this last aroused against him the hatred of the many mealy-mouthed hypocrites among the Calvinist burghers and clergy. 'Twas no longer safe for them to force their poor little serving-wenches in a corner, then later, when they were found to be with child, turn them on to the streets while lifting their own hands to Heaven in pious horror.

"But the measure which brought him the greatest degree of unpopularity was the freeing of the serfs from their bondage. Up to Struensee's time the peasants were the property of the nobles on whose estates they were born, and bound by law to remain on those estates as vassals from birth to death. He gave them their freedom, but the result proved almost disastrous for Denmark. These wretched, uncouth, brutalised creatures left the land and swarmed into the towns by the thousand. The fields remained uncultivated, which led to a severe famine, and the towns became subject to riots and rapine at the hands of starving mobs."

"Yet his reforms seem to have been in keeping with the spirit of the age."

"They were. His mistake was in pushing them through too quickly, and without due preparation or thought for their possible consequences. In the meantime Caroline Matilda had taken the bit between her teeth. She was still only twenty-two and with all the headstrong folly of youth gloried in her adultery. She encouraged the ladies of her court to follow her example in taking a lover, and turned the Palace into a haunt of Bacchanalian revelry. Still worse, as far as her public reputation was concerned, she took to painting her face, and when she went out hunting, wore leather small-clothes and rode astride like a man."

"I see no great wickedness in the last."

Elliot laughed. "If you think of Denmark as England in Oliver Cromwell's time you would, my friend. The townsfolk knew little of what went on inside the Palace, but when they saw her in such guise, they straightway were filled with righteous indignation, and abjured her as the Great Whore of Babylon. Unfortunately too, the chase was her passion; and for each of her three hunts, stag, hare and hawk, she made her courtiers wear a different uniform; light blue and silver for the first, green and bronze for the second, and crimson and gold for the third. Imagine the effect of parading such gay extravagance four or five days a week before the sober Danish burghers. Christian squandered a quarter of à million pounds on drink and women during his year abroad, but his subjects remained unaware of that; whereas they could see Matilda enjoying herself, and hated her for it."

"What of the King, though? Since he is not entirely mad, did he make no protest at having both his wife and his Kingdom taken from him?"

"They let him continue to attend all the Court entertainments and used to take him out to hunt with them, but no one was allowed to speak to him without permission; and Struensee employed a Count Brandt to sleep in the King's anti-chamber and act as his keeper. At least, I should have said the anti-chamber of Struensee's old room, for he had taken over the King's apartments for himself and put Christian into his on the excuse of preventing him from having access to Matilda, so that she should not be subject to his fits of violence. That was Struensee's crowning folly; since when the young Queen gave birth to a daughter in the summer of '71 everybody knew that he must be the child's father."

"Did the end come swiftly, then?"

"Nay, not for another six months. In secret Juliana Maria had been gathering all Struensee's most bitter enemies about her, and she selected Count Rantzau to take the lead in a conspiracy, the theoretical object of which was to restore the King's liberty. Actually, of course, seeing that Struensee had been able to rule through him she meant to keep him captive and replace the Doctor by her son, Frederick, in the role of Regent. On the 16th of January '72 there was a court ball. Brandt was lured away from his post to spend the night with his mistress. In his absence Count Rantzau succeeded in penetrating to

Christian's chamber and persuading him to sign an order for the arrest of Struensee and the Queen. In the early hours of the morning both were apprehended. Struensee was taken to the town-citadel and Matilda was sent to the castle of Cronenburg. They never saw one another again."

Roger sighed. "Despite their guilt I cannot but feel sorry for them."

"I have more sympathy for her than him," Elliot rejoined slowly. "She behaved with splendid courage throughout and defied her enemies to the end, whereas he played the part of a poltroon. 'Tis true that they put him to the rack, but even so, his confession gave many salacious details of his intercourse with the Queen such as could not have been invented by his examiners, and showed by its tone that he had done his utmost to obtain leniency for himself by sacrificing her. Of course, it availed him nothing and he was executed with Count Brandt, who made a courageous end, whereas Struensee had to be dragged to the block."

"And the Queen?"

"She was divorced, and Juliana exerted all the influence she could command to have her executed for treason; but my predecessor here, Colonel Sir Robert Murray Keith, threatened the Danes that Britain would go to war if she were harmed, and His Majesty rewarded his firmness by conferring on him the red ribbon of the Bath. Three English men-of-war were dispatched to convey her to King George's Hanoverian dominions, and she lived in retirement in the castle of Zell there until her death three years later."

"So the Queen Dowager triumphed in the end?"

Elliot smiled. "For twelve years she realised her ambitions. At the time of Matilda's divorce the Crown Prince was barely four years of age. During his minority Juliana Maria ruled through her loutish son, with her creature Guldberg as Prime Minister; but a just fate has dispossessed her of power in the end. The little Crown Prince Frederick grew up to loathe his uncle and step-grandmother, and he developed into a boy of great promise and resolution. While still quite young he entered into a secret correspondence with the exiled Count Bernstorff and between them they plotted a *coup d'état*. Juliana Maria delayed his confirmation as long as possible, but when it had taken place he could no longer be denied a seat in the Privy Council. On his first appearance there, although only fifteen, he forced his imbecile father to sign a document empowering him to act as Regent, and to the effect that the King's signature should no longer be valid unless counter-signed by himself. His uncle and Guldberg were completely taken by surprise and found their power snatched from them before they could do a thing to prevent it."

Roger smiled. "What an amazing feat, for a boy of that age to have carried through a bloodless revolution."

"It was indeed; but 'twas touch and go for a few days. I had been *en poste* here for two years then. I immediately offered the young Prince my support, and as there were several English ships in the harbour at the time nothing would have pleased me better than to lead their crews into action against the supporters of the Queen Dowager. But 'twas unnecessary. Juliana Maria and her son were so stunned that they lost all power of initiative. Count Bernstorff was recalled and the Crown Prince became King in all but name. That was four years ago this month, and poor Caroline Matilda's son shows every sign of continuing to be a wise and talented ruler."

" 'Tis a fascinating story," Roger declared. "And I shall look forward now with even greater interest to seeing some of the actors in it."

For the rest of the evening they talked of other matters, and when Roger left it was arranged that Hugh Elliot should call for him at his inn on Tuesday evening, to take him to the Prime Minister's *soirée*.

At the *soirée* everything went according to plan. *Monsieur le Chevalier de Breuc* was duly presented to Monsieur le Baron la Houze, a charming and polished diplomat. They talked of Paris at some length and Roger said that he had spent a year there after completing his education at Strasbourg. He was able to speak with truth of his friendship with the Abbé de Talleyrand-Périgord, the Vicomte de la Tour d'Auvergne, and the Comte de Choiseul-Gouffier, whom he knew to be still the French Ambassador at Constantinople, and he inferred that he had more than an acquaintance with the Baron de Breteuil, the Duc de Polignac, and other members of Queen Marie Antoinette's intimate circle. La Houze was as favourably impressed by Roger's delightful manners as by his admirable connections, and within ten minutes of their having met, offered to present him at the Saturday evening drawing-room.

Four evenings later Roger accompanied his new friend to the Christiansborg Palace. It seemed even vaster inside than out, and the few score of courtiers and ladies present appeared almost lost in the huge reception-hall; but several great wood-fires gave the place a cheerful atmosphere, and the etiquette of the small court was not so rigidly formal as to prevent the Danes from obviously taking pleasure in the function.

The French Minister duly presented Roger to the half-mad King, who was now thirty-eight years of age but looked considerably older. He was a puny, sly-eyed creature and much embarrassed Roger by digging him in the ribs and asking him several extremely indecent personal questions; but Count Bernstorff drew His Majesty's attention away from the visitor and the King spent most of the remainder of the evening sitting on the floor playing with his dog.

His son, the young Crown Prince, proved a most pleasing contrast and held Roger for some twenty minutes in intelligent conversation. He was then presented to the sinister Queen Dowager, her awkward, horse-faced son, and several other notabilities. Hugh Elliot was there and introduced him to the Count and Countess Reventlow, who invited him to accompany the British Minister to their house next day; and a number of other people he met asked him to call upon them.

121

Having achieved his first objective of establishing himself as a young French nobleman, travelling for pleasure through the northern capitals, he returned to his inn highly satisfied. Then the following morning he once more rode through the sabbath quiet of the city streets to the wooded parks of Christiansholm, and spent some very pleasant hours at the Reventlow mansion, as one of a charming family circle of about a dozen people.

When the party broke up it was still light, as the long evenings of the northern summer were already beginning; and Elliot suggested that Roger should ride back with him as far as the Legation. After going at an easy canter through the park, on the grass of which the big trees were now casting fantastically elongated shadows, the diplomat reined his horse in to a walk, and as Roger followed suit, said to him:

"I took this opportunity for a word with you, because it is unlikely that my interest in a young Frenchman would normally lead me to entertain him privately more than once; and now that you are known to la Houze I shall not invite you again, for fear of arousing his suspicions that you are not, after all, quite what you seem. Tell me, now, is there any further way in which I can be of service to you, or do you feel that you have got what you can from Denmark?"

"I could doubtless learn many things of interest from a prolonged stay, Sir, but little of moment by remaining for a fortnight," Roger replied. "So I feel that I ought to go on my way as soon as I can decently do so. Numerous persons of the court were kind enough last night to ask me to call upon them, and la Houze has bidden me to sup with him on Wednesday. I therefore plan to busy myself socially these next few days, and, in the meantime, see if I can find a ship which will carry me to Sweden towards the end of the week."

"That should not be difficult, as there is a large and constant traffic between Copenhagen and Stockholm."

Roger acknowledged the information with a nod, and went on. "As to your other question; although I am now *au fait* with the domestic scene I still know next to nothing of Denmark's foreign policy, and I'd be still more your debtor if you would give me a few pointers on that."

"Most willingly," Elliot smiled. "Denmark is still a maritime power of some consequence, but in other respects she is a poor country and seeks to keep herself free of entanglements. For many years her policy was governed by her anxieties over the Duchies of Schleswig-Holstein; since, as you may know, the Czarina's late husband, Peter III, was a Holstein-Gottorp and inherited the Duchies from his father. Peter's claim to them was undoubtedly legal, and the idea of having a Russian army established on their border was, not unnaturally, viewed with the gravest apprehension by the Danes. However, in '73 they succeeded in persuading Catherine to forego her claim to the Duchies in exchange for those of Oldenberg and Delmenhorst."

"That would appear to have been but a poor swop as far as the Russians are concerned," Roger commented.

" 'Twas indeed. And for that reason I have always suspected that there was something fishy about the deal—some secret clause in the treaty that has never been disclosed."

" 'Tis certainly unlike all one hears of the Empress to give much for little."

Elliot nodded. "Mayhap the real price was that Denmark should remain neutral in the event of Russia going to war with Sweden. Some years ago Denmark feared that Gustavus III harboured designs against her Norwegian territories, so it seems that her interest lies in a pact with Sweden which would secure them from his aggression. Yet now that more recently he has endeavoured to win Denmark to him his efforts have proved unsuccessful. Last year, soon after the outbreak of the Russian war against the Turks, King Gustavus came here on a visit to his nephew, the Prince Regent, and did his utmost to persuade the Danes to enter into an alliance with him against Russia; but although the Prince and Count Bernstorff showed him much politeness, they firmly rejected all his overtures."

"That admittedly gives grounds for supposing that they are already bound to neutrality, as you suggest. If so, there can be little prospect of gaining their support for the Triple Alliance."

"None, I fear. Our only hope of counteracting Catherine's designs in the north lies in Gustavus. He is an able and forceful monarch, with a strong ambition to revive Sweden's ancient glories. 'Tis secretly reported that he is already receiving subsidies from the Turk and plans a campaign against Russia this summer. 'Twas that which made me feel that you would do well to make an early remove to the Swedish capital."

"I hope to obtain a letter of introduction from Baron la Houze to the French Minister in Stockholm," Roger remarked. "But it might be helpful, Sir, if you would also be good enough to furnish me with one for the British representative."

The diplomat laughed a shade bitterly. "Had we one I would willingly do so; but for reasons best known to our Foreign Secretary the post has been vacant for some time; and I have no intelligence that it is likely to be filled in the near future, although it is now the key point of the north. In the meantime I am charged with a watching brief, but there is little I can do at such a distance."

For a moment Roger was silent, then he asked: "What think you of Sweden's chances against Russia should Gustavus decide to attack her?"

" 'Tis hard to say," Elliot shrugged. "While Russia remains fully extended against the Turks Gustavus will have her at a grave disadvantage. On the other hand he will, I think, be fighting with a half-blunted sword."

"How mean you, Sir?"

"He is popular with his people but much disliked by his nobility; since he has deprived them of the power they had held in earlier reigns. Therefore his officers will not follow him to war with any

123

great enthusiasm. Moreover, he has not a single good General, whereas Russia is well-found in that way; and both her officers and men will show the most desperate valour against any foe that their Empress may order them to attack. Having fought in the Russian army myself I can vouch for its metal."

Roger looked his surprise. "Sir James told me that as a youth you had military ambitions, Sir; but how came it that you saw service with the Russians?"

"Simply because the British would not have me," came the smiling reply. "When I was ten a friend of my father's exercised his right as Colonel of a newly-raised regiment to present me with a Lieutenant's commission in it. Naturally my parents would not allow me to take it up until I had completed my education, but from that day I looked upon myself as a soldier. I spent two years at a military school in Paris before going to Oxford and afterwards resumed my military studies at Metz and Strasbourg. Only then did I learn that the War Secretary, Lord Barrington, had refused to ratify my commission with the seniority technically due to me."

"What a wretched stroke of fortune."

"Yes. I was most bitterly disappointed; because by that time I was nineteen, and I had no fancy to go in as junior to a dozen lads several years younger than myself. Instead I got the authorities to grant me the honorary rank of Captain with permission to serve in a foreign army. Austria seemed to offer the best prospects, as there were over five hundred British officers serving with the Austrian army at that time. But fortune proved against me in Vienna, and later in both Warsaw and Constantinople. I was in Bucharest, and almost in despair, when I learned that Russia was about to open a new campaign against the Turks, and that Marshal Romantzof was forming his headquarters at Jassy. I had scarce heard the news when I received a letter from my father, ordering me home; but I ignored it and offered myself to the Marshal. Under him I was present at Giurgevo, where we were surprised and outnumbered by the Turks. Quite a tale was made of the manner in which I jumped over the heads and scimitars of a line of fierce-looking Janissaries right into the Danube, and swam across to the other bank; though the fact is that my only thought was to escape with my life, and that for more than half the distance I was clinging to the tail of a Cossack's horse."

"I vow you're being over-modest, Sir."

"Nay, 'tis the fact," Elliot laughed. "But 'twas a stroke of luck for me that the Russians should have taken it for a feat of valour. The Marshal gave me a most handsome mention in despatches and that, reaching my irate father's ears, pacified him for my having run half-round Europe when I was supposed to be gone only for a sojourn in Vienna."

"How liked you the Russians?"

"As soldiers and boon companions they left nothing to be desired; yet if I were ordered to Petersburg as Ambassador I confess that I'd set out with considerable misgivings. I recall, even now, a passage from a letter Sir James Harris wrote me during his Embassy; he said: 'The monarch is an arrant woman—a vain, spoilt woman—with more masculine than manly virtues, and more female vices than weaknesses. The men in high life, monkeys grafted on bears, and those in lower, bears not inoculated. Religion, virtue and morality nowhere to be found; honour cannot be expressed in this language'."

They had reached the gate of the British Legation, and as Elliot brought his mount to a halt he added: "But soon now, you will be able to form your own judgment of Semiramis and her people. When you reach Stockholm I suggest that you should endeavour to cultivate the acquaintance of the Russian Ambassador there, Count Andrew Razumofsky. 'Twill give you a foretaste of their style and character."

Roger smiled. "I've already had that in certain dealings with Count Vorontzoff, their Ambassador in London."

"Even so, 'twould repay you to become *persona grata* with Razumofsky, if you can. That will not be easy. Like most of Catherine's representatives he is as proud as a peacock, and considers no one less than a prince fitted to consort with him on equal terms. Yet he is high in the Empress's confidence, and if you can flatter him into giving you the *entrée* to his circle, 'tis just possible that he might speak before you as a Frenchman with a freedom he would never use in the presence of English ears."

"I will bear your advice in mind, Sir," Roger promised. Then he thanked the British Minister for all his help and kindness, and rode off through the gathering dusk back to the city.

He was, however, to see Hugh Elliot once more before leaving Copenhagen. Having found a four-masted barque that was sailing from the Oster Port for Stockholm on the afternoon tide of Saturday, the 12th of May, he gave a farewell breakfast that morning at a French restaurant he had discovered in the Reverentz Gaarten on Kongens Nytorv. The place was run by a Parisian named Mareschal, and he provided a most excellent meal at which Elliot, la Houze, Count Reventlow, and several other gentlemen who had entertained Roger during the past week, met to wish him a good journey.

At two o'clock in the afternoon Monsieur le Chevalier de Breue went on board carrying a heavy cargo of good French Claret and a letter in his pocket from Monsieur le Baron la Houze to Monsieur le Marquis de Pons, the French Minister in Stockholm; and he did not feel that his fortnight in Copenhagen had been by any means wasted. The weather was moderately good and three mornings later the barque carried him through the lovely waterways that grace the entrance to the beautiful Swedish capital.

On going ashore he had his baggage carried to the Vasa inn; and after taking his midday meal there, sent a note to Monsieur de Pons asking when it would be convenient to present a letter from Monsieur la Houze. He then went out for a walk round the town.

When he got back he found to his surprise and pleasure that the French Ambassador had already sent a reply, which ran:

The annual entertainment which I give to celebrate the ascension of our gracious sovereigns to the throne should have been held on Thursday the tenth last; but has been postponed until to-night in the hope that H.M. King Gustavus will have returned to his capital and be able to honour us with his presence.

I pray you therefore, my dear fellow-countryman, to dispense with formality, and give me the pleasure of welcoming you to Sweden this evening.

I have the honour, etc., etc.

Enclosed was a large crested card showing the entertainment to be a *Bal Masqué*, for which guests were bidden to assemble at eight o'clock. So Roger promptly made arrangements at the inn for a coach to take him to the French Embassy, and hurried out again to get himself a domino.

In Stockholm, as in Copenhagen, he found that the shopkeepers as well as the upper classes all spoke either French or German, and at a big mercer's in Paul's Gatan he secured a pale blue domino and mask. Back at the inn he had a barber dress his hair in the prevailing French fashion; with side curls, *toupet* and turned up behind, and, for such an occasion, heavily powdered. The domino, like the loose, light costume of a pierrot, entirely concealed his long scarlet coat, gold-laced waistcoat and frilled shirt, but his quizzing-glass hung outside it on a black moiré ribbon. To complete his toilette he scented himself and put a beauty patch on the lower part of his left cheek. Then, at a little after seven-thirty, he went down to the waiting coach.

He had already ascertained that the French Embassy was a country mansion situated a little way outside the city on one of the many promontories that fringed the fiord, so he was not surprised when his coach left the cobbled ways and entered a belt of sweet-scented pine woods. About half-a-mile further on it turned a sharp corner, then suddenly swerved to one side of the track.

Recovering his balance Roger saw at once the reason for his coachman's sudden swerve. Just ahead of them was another coach, a huge gilded vehicle with six horses, postillions and outriders; one of its wheels had come off and it was lying at an angle half in and half out of the ditch. Beside it, among the richly-liveried servants, stood a big broad-shouldered man and a girl with flowers and feathers in her high-dressed hair. Both of them were masked and wearing dominoes.

Roger at once called on his own coachman to halt and got out. In spite of the presence of the girl the owner of the broken-down vehicle was cursing his servants in French with language which would have made a fishwife blush. As Roger came up the angry man hit his coachman with his clenched fist and sent the poor wretch sprawling into the ditch.

After a loud cough to draw his attention, Roger said: "I see, Sir, that you are the victim of an unfortunate accident, and from your domino it appears that you were on your way to the French Embassy. Pray allow me to offer you and your lady seats in my coach."

With a visible effort to swallow his rage, the man replied: "I thank you, Sir. We are mightily obliged."

Turning to the girl Roger made her a gallant leg, and said: "Your servant, Mademoiselle. Permit me to introduce myself. . . ."

But with a quick gesture of her fan she stopped him and laughed behind her mask. "Nay, Monsieur. I beg you to do no such thing. 'Tis quite romantic to be rescued from our predicament by a strange cavalier; and the whole object of our dominoes is to preserve the secret of our identity until midnight. Let us all retain our incognito until then."

"Willingly, Mademoiselle," smiled Roger, and he bowed his new acquaintances into his coach; then, getting in himself, swiftly took more careful stock of them.

The man was not particularly tall but immensely broad across the shoulders. His forehead was low and sloping, his hair, under the powder, black; as were also his eyes. Below the mask his lips showed full and red, and his heavy chin was thrust forward aggressively. The girl was a little above medium height, and her hair was only lightly powdered, as it was so fair as to be almost silver. Her eyes, which held a merry sparkle, were green; and although the domino concealed the details of her figure, Roger judged her to be slim. He naturally assumed them to be Swedes, and having remarked that he had arrived in Stockholm only that morning, began to praise the beauty of their capital.

Both of them agreed about its attractions, and the girl spoke of society there as both gay and civilised; but they had been talking for only a few moments when the coach pulled up behind a line of others and, shortly afterwards, set them down.

The French Embassy was a miniature palace with a fine entrance hall, now thronged with dominoes slowly making their way up a broad, shallow staircase towards a landing where the Marquis and Marquise de Pons were receiving their guests. They were masked and made no attempt to probe the identity of the men and women with whom they formally exchanged bows and curtseys at the stair-head; so Roger passed on with his new friends into the ballroom.

The fiddles were just striking up for the second dance, and Roger seized the opportunity to lead the girl out to a gavotte, during which, from politeness more than interest, he at once began to flirt with her. He soon found that she was an adept at the art and her green eyes gave him ample encouragement as he whispered pretty nothings in her ear each time they came together in the movements of the dance.

When it was over he led her into the next salon and endeavoured to find out who she was; but she would not give him a hint and said that he must wait until after midnight to find out. He begged her to give him the first dance following the removal of masks, but she told him that it was already promised and that, much as she would have liked to oblige him, she was already committed to a score of beaux from midnight onwards. On his pretending the most bitter disappointment she laughingly consoled him by saying that Stockholm was such a small place that he would be certain to have many opportunities of seeing her in the future if he wished.

A tall domino then came up and asked her for the next dance. As the newcomer offered his arm to lead her away Roger noticed that his left hand was encased in a black kid glove, suggesting that it was either malformed or injured in some way.

Left to his own devices Roger amused himself for a little by making a tour of the fine run of reception rooms. Then he asked half-a-dozen ladies to dance; but none of them particularly intrigued him. He had as yet had no opportunity to judge if the green-eyed girl was really good-looking, but all that her mask left revealed of her features suggested that she was, and the fact that she had refused him a dance for after midnight because she was already promised to a string of beaux gave strong support to the assumption. Looks apart, she certainly had personality and wit, as was borne in upon him more sharply from contrast with the comparative insipidity of the other young women that he led out on to the floor.

As the evening wore on he realised that she had possessed a certain subtle attraction, of which he had not been fully conscious until he began to think about her after she left him; so he decided to try to find her again. But it proved no easy matter to pick her out among the scores of women, all of whom were masked and most of whom had flowers and feathers in their high-dressed powdered hair. All the dominoes were of plain colours and the fact that she had been wearing one of lilac was of no great help, since all the ladies were in pastel shades of blue, pink or mauve.

Once, he felt certain he had identified her, but she was taking part in a minuet at the far end of the ballroom, and as the crowd of dancers left the floor he lost sight of her again. It was now nearing midnight so he gave up the attempt and consoled himself with the thought that she had definitely encouraged him to develop their acquaintance during his stay in Stockholm. No doubt she had refused to commit herself later that night only for the purpose of leading him on; her tantalizing smile had certainly conveyed that impression.

Roger decided that this must be his lucky night. Within a bare twelve hours of his landing in Sweden he had been received at the French Embassy, and by a fortunate accident, had the prospect of developing an affaire with an unusually intriguing young woman. He was not of a type to take no for an answer, and made up his mind that as soon as the company removed their masks he would find her again, and by hook or by crook, persuade her to give him another dance.

The pre-midnight dance ended and the throng swarmed out to shed its dominoes in the ante-chambers, returning still masked but in all the splendour of silk, velvet, satin and brocade, to line the sides of the ballroom four deep. A file of footmen entered carrying silver salvers loaded with glasses of champagne, which they handed to the guests. The Ambassador and his wife emerged from the crowd at one end of the room, leading deferentially between them a regal-looking woman; a little cortège of older men and women wearing the stars and sashes of orders formed up behind them, someone called for silence and in a high, precise voice their host made a short speech.

He said how greatly they all regretted that His Majesty King Gustavus was still detained by his labours at Carlscrona, but how highly they were honoured by having his august consort, Queen Sophia Magdalena, in their midst. At this point, the regal-looking lady unmasked, disclosing the handsome but rather sad features of a woman in her late thirties. Everyone else then unmasked and made her a deep obeisance.

She smiled graciously round on them and gave the Ambassador her hand to kiss; after which he continued his speech, asking them to drink long life and happiness to his sovereigns, King Louis XVI and Queen Marie Antoinette, in this, the opening of the fifteenth year of their reign.

When the health had been drunk and the cheers subsided the Queen was led to a canopied chair on a low dais; and on her having signified that the merriment should continue the richly dressed crowd began to mingle, friends greeting one another gaily and the men who had met attractive partners while masked endeavoured to identify them again.

As soon as Roger could get near enough to do so he made himself known to the Marquis de Pons, and thanked him for having so kindly invited him to the ball. The Ambassador was a dapper, alert-eyed little man of about forty. He inquired after la Houze, asked Roger to come to breakfast two days later to give him the news from Copenhagen, then presented him to the Marquise.

She was considerably younger than her husband, not strictly beautiful, but extraordinarily *soigné*, and possessed a rather roguish mouth and eyes. Roger was keeping a sharp look-out for his charmer of the coach but he knew that he was now on duty, and although his rank was hardly sufficient to warrant it, he boldly asked his hostess for the dance that was just starting.

Taking her lower lip between her pretty teeth she gave one swift look at the elderly group surrounding the Queen, then smiled into Roger's deep blue eyes, and whispered: "I shall lose my reputation by treading a measure with a handsome young gallant instead of devoting myself to those stupid old Generals."

He returned her smile. "Rather, Madame, will your reputation be enhanced, from your charity in taking pity on a fellow-countryman who is a stranger in a strange land."

"Ah, yes; we are both exiles," she sighed. "And what would I not give to be back at Versailles! Lead me out then, Monsieur; talking to you will remind me of its gaieties, and make me forget this poor unhappy Queen."

During the dance Roger whispered the same sweet nothings into the ear of the Ambassador's wife that he had in that of the green-eyed girl some hours earlier, and she responded with even greater finesse. When the music stopped he sought to lead her away to one of the sitting-out places, but she shook her head. "Alas, Monsieur, I must return to my duties; but 'twas a pleasant interlude. I pray you come often to see us while you are in Stockholm and lighten the *ennui* of my lot here by talk of our fair France."

"Madame; to be with you is to lose all regret that I ever left it," he replied gallantly; thinking once more what a lucky evening it was for him; since the friendship of the charming woman at his side might prove not only delightful in itself but of considerable value in his mission.

As they were moving back towards the end of the room where the Queen sat surrounded by a little court, Roger suddenly caught sight of the green-eyed girl. She was, as he had supposed, very slim, and definitely good-looking in a queer, unusual way.

"Can you tell me, Madame?" he asked quickly. "Who the tall fair lady is, over there? The one wearing the splendid emeralds and in a primrose dress covered with little silver stars."

The Marquise shot him a sideways glance from her china-blue eyes and asked in a slightly piqued voice: "Are you attracted by her?"

"Nay, Madame," he lied. "I could not be attracted by anyone while in your company. 'Tis only that on the way here her coach broke down, and I carried her and her elderly cavalier here in mine."

"You are forgiven," smiled the Marquise. "But even had you been, I would have been charitable enough to warn you to beware of her. She is a young widow with a curiously malicious turn of humour. 'Tis said that her favours can be won, but when she tires of her beaux she has a most unpleasant trick of making fools of them afterwards. Her name is Natalia Andreovna Stroganof and she is the daughter of the Russian Ambassador, Count Razumofsky."

Roger saw that the green-eyed lady had also recognised him, and was now regarding him with a seductive little smile. As he smiled back he could hardly believe his good fortune in having so swiftly and effortlessly acquired an *entrée* into the heart of both the French and Russian camps. It seemed indeed a lucky evening; but had he been able to foresee the future he would have fled the ballroom there and then.

CHAPTER IX

THE UNCROWNED QUEEN

W H E N they reached the outer fringe of the Queen's circle, Madame de Pons told Roger to remain where he was, and went forward herself to speak to her Royal guest. After a moment she returned to say that she had obtained permission to present him, then led him forward to make his bow.

The Queen smiled wistfully at him and beckoned to him with her fan. As he advanced, bowing again with each step, he wondered why she looked so sad and had been referred to by the Marquise as "this poor, unhappy Queen." He knew nothing about her except that she was the sister of Christian VII, the mad King of Denmark, and had been married to Gustavus of Sweden for some twenty years.

On learning that he had just arrived from Copenhagen she inquired after her brother and her nephew the Prince Regent, then, after a few minutes of not very inspiring conversation she said she hoped that Roger would enjoy his stay in Sweden, and gave him her hand to kiss as a sign that the audience was over.

As soon as he was free Roger went in search of the green-eyed lady, now more determined than ever to pursue his acquaintance with her, not only from pleasure but as the best possible line for gaining information which would be useful to him in his task.

He found that she was dancing with a tall fair man of about thirty, and after a moment, noticed that his left hand was encased in a black kid glove; so he was evidently the masked gallant who had claimed her earlier in the evening. Roger waited patiently for the dance to end, then followed the couple as they left the ballroom with the intention of learning where they meant to sit out, and giving them ten minutes or so together before making another attempt to persuade the young widow to give him a dance.

Green-eyes and her escort went down the grand staircase and entered a salon on its right, where a handful of people were partaking of refreshments from a long buffet. As Roger followed he saw a fat elderly man, who was standing by himself, set down his glass of wine, bow to the girl and say something to her cavalier; upon which both men bowed to her, evidently asking her permission to have a word apart; she nodded to them and went on alone through a doorway into a further room.

Seeing his opportunity Roger hastened his pace, passed the two men, who were now conversing earnestly together, and followed his quarry into the next room. In one glance he saw that it was a small library and empty except for the girl, who had advanced to the window and was standing with her back towards him. With a wicked little smile he softly closed the door behind him and shot the bolt.

On hearing his footfall she turned and gave an exclamation of surprise at seeing Roger instead of her cavalier.

As he stood there smiling at her he had his first opportunity of really taking in her features. Natalia Andreovna was twenty-five years of age. Her bust was small, almost flat for that period when abundant curves were the fashion, and this gave the impression that she was even thinner than was in fact the case. Above her green eyes, narrow, darkish eyebrows slanted upwards towards her temples in strange contrast to her ash-blonde hair. Her cheekbones were high; her face a long oval. Her nose was short and her mouth thin, but her head was beautifully set on a long swan-like neck. Her physical charms were unusual but strongly compelling.

Raising the tapering eyebrows she said with feigned hauteur: "What means this, Monsieur?"

Roger retained his impudent grin and bowed. "Merely the claiming of the promise you made me, Madame."

"I made you no promise."

"By inference you did. 'Twas at your suggestion that we retained our incognito until midnight. And the reason you gave for that was that it would be more romantic to do so. No romance could flourish in a crowd, so I assumed that I had your permission to seek you out alone."

Her eyes held no anger but a faint amusement as they ran over his tall, muscular figure, his healthily-bronzed face, strong white teeth and long, well-made hands.

"Permit me to make myself known to you," he went on. "I am the Chevalier de Breuc, of Strasbourg, and your most humble servant. Nay, more. If you would have it so, I am already your adoring slave."

She smiled. "And I am the Baroness Stroganof, but. . . ."

The door handle rattled sharply; then there came a swift knock on the door.

" 'Tis my partner, Count Yagerhorn!" she exclaimed.

Roger put his finger to his lips to enjoin silence, tiptoed quickly forward, took her by the hand and turning her about pulled her gently towards the window.

"Monsieur!" she whispered. "What—what are you about to do?"

"Why, carry you off," he whispered back with a low laugh. "Is not climbing in and out of windows the very essence of romance?"

The knocking came again, louder and more imperative.

"But Count Yagerhorn!" she protested quickly. "I cannot leave him thus. And your having locked the door compromises me sadly. Unless you let him in at once and make him an apology he may challenge you to fight."

Roger had thrust up the lower half of the window. It was only a four foot drop to the broad stone terrace that overlooked the bay.

" 'Tis against my religion to apologise to any man," he declared gaily. "But if the Count wishes to fight let me at least rob him

132

of more than two minutes' converse with you as a cause for shedding his blood. Come, I will go first, and catch you as you jump."

Suiting the action to the word he scrambled out on to the terrace and, turning, held up his arms to her.

She leaned forward, her green eyes narrowed in a speculative look. "You seem mightily cocksure of a victory, Monsieur. I wonder are you truly as bold as your words imply?"

"Try me, and see," he laughed, stretching up to take her hand. "I'd fight half-a-dozen men for a kiss from you."

"If I've ever a mind to test you as a champion I'll take you up on that," she smiled. Then, suddenly deciding that this tempestuous new beau offered more prospect of amusement than her recent partner, she stepped up onto the low sill and jumped lightly down.

As Roger caught her in his arms he drew her body swiftly against his own and kissed her firmly on the mouth. She made no attempt to stop him and for a full minute they clung together mouth pressed to mouth.

"La! Monsieur," she exclaimed breathlessly as they drew apart. "I had no idea that any man other than a Russian could make so bold with a woman on so short an acquaintance."

"Nor I," he countered, "that any woman not of French blood had the temperament to lend her lips so well to a first kiss."

She smiled at him. "Then you have never visited my country, Monsieur. Russian men have no opinion of a woman who pretends to get the vapours at a peck."

"'Tis most fitting that our countries should now be allies, then, for our minds on that are of a kind." As he spoke he threw his right arm round her waist and gave her another, even longer, kiss.

"Enough!" she gasped. "Enough! And now, Monsieur; having got me out here what is it your intention to do with me?"

"Were it high summer I could suggest a score of things," he said lightly, "but I fear for you the chill of the night air in that thin dress. Having separated you from the Count my first objective is achieved; so I can but take you indoors again by another route, and hope to find a secluded corner where I can tell you how ravishing I find you."

She shrugged. "I vow you say that to every woman that you meet."

"Nay, Madame. Only to those who make my heart beat faster, and if you have a single doubt that you do that, I pray you give me your hand that I may place it on my pulse."

"Maybe I'll apply the test on some other occasion," she laughed. "But you are right about it being too cold to dally here to-night. Take me within and you shall tell me all about yourself."

With their arms round one another's waists they strolled along the terrace, and reaching some shrubberies at the side of the house embraced again in their deep shadow. For a few moments she let him caress her then, with an eel-like movement wriggled away, exclaiming: "Nay, nay! 'Tis not the time or place for such familiarities. Nor am I the woman to permit them."

Her last statement was so much at variance with her first that Roger had difficulty in preventing himself from laughing; but the darkness enabled him to conceal his amusement. The slim Russian's temporary complaisance had given ample promise that she held fire enough to melt one of her native icebergs, and he was well content to have made such swift progress with her. So soothing her pretended indignation with appropriate phrases of contrition he led her back into the house by a side door.

The salon on the right of the grand staircase had also been turned into a refreshment room, so they had a glass of champagne and a helping of lobster mousse apiece there, then carried two more glasses of wine through to a conservatory that lay beyond it.

Immediately they had settled themselves she began to catechise him with a directness that some men might have found embarrassing; but Roger did not mind it in the least. He had played the part of Monsieur le Chevalier de Breuc so long in France that he could give all that suited him of that gentleman's fictitious history as easily as he could of his own; and he found a peculiar delight in watching the varied emotions aroused by his answers chase each other across his companion's exceptionally expressive face. Moreover, when she at length began to hesitate over fresh questions to put to him he was able, without impertinence, to catechise her with equal thoroughness.

It emerged that she was the only daughter of Count Razumofsky; that she had lost her mother at the age of ten, and married Baron Stroganof when she was twenty. The Baron's father had been the Empress's Chamberlain during the brief reign of her husband, Peter III, and also, for a short time, her lover. The Baron himself had been one of General Suvarof's aides-de-camp and with him in the Russian-held fortress of Kimburne, on the Black Sea when, in the previous year, five thousand Turks crossed the river from the neighbouring town of Otchakof and attempted to take the Russian garrison by surprise. The plan had miscarried and the Russians, sallying out, had driven the Turks back to their boats; many of which had been sunk by cannon balls and others, during the ensuing confusion, gone aground on mud-banks. An appalling massacre had ensued, for General Suvarof, with ruthless brutality, had refused the Turks quarter; but he was seriously wounded himself, and the young Baron had died on the field from the stroke of a Turkish scimitar.

Natalia Andreovna had then left St. Petersburg to act as hostess for her father in the Embassy at Stockholm. She had one child, a daughter, now four years old; but she did not like children, and had left her own in Russia to be brought up on her late husband's estate near Vologda, by one of his aunts. She was very rich, owning in her own right over twelve thousand serfs; and was, she declared, enjoying her freedom too much to contemplate marrying again for a long time to come. In fact, fear that the Empress, whose word was law, might marry her off to one of her own ex-lovers whom she wished to enrich had been Natalia Andreovna's principal reason for settling in Stockholm; since she much preferred life at the Russian court, and despised the Swedes as a soft, cold-blooded, degenerate people.

They had got thus far when Roger heard a rustling of the palms behind him and turned to see that Count Yagerhorn had invaded their corner of the conservatory. The tall fair-haired man was standing there glaring at him, his fresh-complexioned face flushed and his pale blue eyes positively popping with anger.

Roger could be more coldly insolent than most people when he chose, and as he was perfectly prepared to fight, he decided to make the most of the situation in order to impress Natalia. Not yet having been introduced to the Count he was not strictly called upon to stand up; so after eyeing him through his quizzing-glass from head to foot he turned his back and lolled again lazily in his chair.

"Madame, your pardon!" said the Count in a voice half-choked with rage. "Monsieur, I require a word with you."

Turning again Roger got slowly to his feet, and murmured: "Are you addressing me, Monsieur? I don't recall you as a person of my acquaintance."

Natalia Andreovna's voice came from behind him. "Messieurs, allow me to introduce you. Monsieur le Chevalier de Breuc—Count Erik Yagerhorn." Then she went on with a hint of amusement in her tone. "You seem annoyed about something, Erik. Mayhap 'tis because I shut you out of the library; but 'tis you who were at fault for leaving me in order to talk with Colonel Fricke."

" 'Twas but for a moment; and I had your permission to do so," the Count protested quickly. "I can scarce believe that you deliberately chose to compromise yourself by locking that door, and. . . ."

"What!" snapped Roger. "You dare to cast doubt upon this lady's word?"

The Count went as red as a lobster. "That is between her and me. My quarrel with you, Monsieur, is that you have deprived me of her company; and I demand an explanation."

Roger shrugged. "The time and place are ill-chosen. But I am lying at the Vasa Inn. Send your friends to me there at whatever hour you choose after dawn and nothing would please me better than to take a walk with you."

"Erik! You will do nothing of the kind," said Natalia Andreovna sharply. "I forbid you to fight with Monsieur le Chevalier."

"But, Madame . . ." he began in protest.

"You heard what I said," she interrupted him. "Later, an it so please me, I'll afford you an opportunity to settle your difference with Monsieur de Breuc. But for the time being I'll not have you risk a wound that may place you *hors de combat.*"

To Roger's surprise the Count calmed down at once. He even smiled as he said: "Later then, Madame. I shall take that as a promise," and, having made a formal bow, he walked away.

135

The more Roger thought about it the more extraordinary this de-nouement of the affair appeared. He had often known cases in which women had intervened to stop a duel, from a natural desire to prevent two men whom they liked or respected injuring one another, but apparently Natalia Andreovna had not been moved by any such humane motive. She had as good as said that she would have not the the least objection to their slitting one another's throats at some later date, but that it did not suit her that they should do so for the present. Her attitude could be explained by the opinion he had already formed, that she was a hard-hearted, bloodthirsty little piece; but what puzzled him more was that she should have the power to make any man take a step so compromising to his honour as to withdraw a challenge, at her bare order.

"I hardly know," he said, after a moment, "if I should thank you for having ensured my keeping a whole skin for a week or two, or reproach you with having deprived me of the chance of bringing you a handkerchief dipped in Count Yagerhorn's blood tomorrow. But I pray you satisfy my curiosity as to why he should have instantly withdrawn his challenge at your bidding?"

She shrugged. " 'Tis one of the prerogatives of royalty to forbid a duel."

Seeing his puzzled look she smiled, and went on. "Surely you realise that 'tis not the unhappy woman upstairs but myself who is the real Queen of Sweden."

"In beauty, without question," he said gallantly.

"Ah, and in power, too." Her voice took on a haughty note, and her green eyes narrowed. "There is not a Finnish noble in the land, and scarce a Swede, who would dare to disregard my wishes. How think you it comes about, otherwise, that we have been sitting here for over an hour, yet not one of the men to whom I promised a dance after midnight has had the temerity to claim me?"

"I had wondered at my good fortune in retaining you so long," remarked Roger, still considerably mystified.

She shrugged again. "With your back to the passageway between the palms you would not have noticed the people who have passed or approached us. Had Erik Yagerhorn not been a special pet of mine he would never have had the self-assurance to break in upon us in the way he did. But half-a-dozen others have discovered us here, and one glance from me has been enough to inform them that I did not wish our *tête-à-tête* interrupted, so they have withdrawn discreetly without a word."

Roger bowed. "Then, fairest of Queens, I am more favoured than I knew, and humbly thank you for it. Yet I am still at a loss to appre-hend whence comes your Royal status."

Her dark, tapering eyebrows lifted in surprise. "La! Monsieur! Even your having landed in Sweden but this morning is hardly excuse enough for such ignorance. Have I not told you that I am the daughter of the Russian Ambassador?"

This sounded to Roger as if the girl was suffering from *la folie des grandeurs*; yet he could not help but be impressed by the deference that her partners had shown in taking a mere glance as an order not to disturb her, and he felt that if he led her on there might be something worth knowing at the bottom of her strange pretensions, so he said with a smile: "Forgive me, your Majesty; but I still fail to understand why your father should consider himself as of more importance than—er—let us say, Monsieur de Pons, or yourself than Madame la Marquise?"

"Then you are more stupid than I thought, Monsieur. The Empress Catherine being the greatest sovereign in the world, it follows that her Imperial Majesty's representatives are regarded as the equals of Prime Ministers, wherever they may be, and of a rank hardly less than those Sovereigns to whose courts they are accredited."

"'Tis not so in France, England or Holland," Roger averred. "Nor in any country in Southern Europe, as far as I am aware."

Natalia Andreovna's green eyes went a little sullen, but she said stubbornly: "Well, 'tis so in the North. When my uncle, Count Stackelberg, was Ambassador at Warsaw, he always treated the Polish King, Stanislas Augustus, as an inferior and would not even stand up when he came into the room. Here too, although my father shows King Gustavus a reasonable politeness, he stands no nonsense from him; and does not hesitate to hammer the King's table with his fist when he is presenting a demand on behalf of her Imperial Majesty."

"You intrigue me greatly, Madame; but I must confess my surprise that King Gustavus should submit to such treatment. If I were he I should be tempted to send your father home."

"No doubt he would like to, but he dare not," she sneered. "And 'tis clear you know little of Swedish politics to suggest it."

"I know nothing," Roger admitted, "and would be grateful for enlightenment."

"You will know at least that for the half-century preceding Gustavus's ascension of the throne, the Kings of Sweden were but puppets, entirely under the control of an oligarchy; and that in 1772, just a year after he became King, he carried out a *coup d'état* by which he put a curb upon their power and became in theory an autocratic monarch?"

"Yes, I have heard tell of that swift and bloodless revolution. For a young Prince of twenty-six, he appears to have carried it through with remarkable skill and resolution; but I thought that he had made himself abolute in fact."

She shook her head. "He has all the appearance of a despot without the actual power. His mistake lay in the new Constitution he gave Sweden, which he wrote himself. He gave his pledge that he would never alter it, and although, by it, he reassumed many of the prerogatives of the ancient monarchy, he also bound himself not to do certain things without the consent of his *Riksdag*. For example, he not only allowed them to retain the purse-strings of the nation but solemnly undertook not to engage in an offensive war without their agreement. To Russia the knowledge that her north-west frontier cannot be attacked without the consent of the Swedish parliament is worth an Army Corps."

"You mean because the obtaining of such an assent would give her ample warning of Sweden's hostile intentions?"

"Not only that. Russia controls the *Riksdag* and so could ensure its veto."

"How so, Madame?"

"You will have heard of the Caps and the Hats?"

"They were the two great political parties of Sweden, were they not? But I had thought that King Gustavus abolished both on his seizure of power."

"He forbade the use of the terms, but the parties still exist. The nicknames arose, I am told, from Old Count Horn, who was Prime Minister of Sweden some sixty years ago, being dubbed a 'Night-cap' from the sleepy, unambitious policy that he pursued. His opponents, a group of vigorous, warlike young nobles, then adopted the *soubriquet* 'Hats' from the tricornes that they wore. In due course the Hats got the upper hand, and financed by France, made war on Russia. The war proved disastrous for Sweden and gradually the power of the Hats declined. In the meantime Russia had begun to finance the nobles of the Cap party in secret and they in turn came to power. The pendulum has oscillated a little since; but the Caps still take their orders from Petersburg, and the leading Hats are still the pensioners of France. And France, having in recent years become Russia's ally, no longer disputes her policies in the Baltic, but instructs her Swedish bondmen to dance to Russia's tune. So you see now why nine-tenths of the Swedish nobility look, not to their King, but to my father, as their suzerain."

Roger "saw" in no unmistakable fashion, and was appalled to learn that Sweden, the only possible bulwark in the north of the new Triple Alliance, was so riddled with venal treachery.

Without waiting for an answer Natalia Andreovna added: "As for the Finns, they have long been bitterly resentful of Swedish despotism. In the event of war, Gustavus would find himself hard put to it to prevent his Finnish levies from going over to Russia, and offering to liberate their country in order that they might lay it at the feet of the Empress. Therefore, whatever ambitions Gustavus may cherish in secret, he can do little to further them at the expense of Russia, unless he is prepared to defy his *Riksdag* and jeopardise his crown."

It was just such intelligence of the way the Russians saw things, garnered from the highest sources, that Mr. Pitt had foreseen that Roger, in his character of a well-bred, wealthy, young idler, might be able to pick up; and as Natalia Andreovna clearly knew what she was talking about he would have liked to continue the conversation for much longer. But, rising to her feet and shaking out her wide, star-spangled skirts, she said with a smile: "And now, Monsieur, for one evening I have given you a more than fair measure of my time; so you may take me back to the ballroom, that I may dance with a few of my beaux before I go home."

Roger was too tactful to seek to detain her; but, as he escorted her upstairs he pressed her to give him an early opportunity of seeing her again, and she said that he might present himself at her *salon* on Thursday evening. They had hardly reached the ballroom before half-a-dozen men came up and formed a little court round her, so with one last, meaning look straight into her green eyes, he bowed himself away.

It was now past two o'clock. Queen Sophia Magdalena had already left and many of the older guests were leaving. As the party no longer held any interest for Roger he decided to go too, and, having made his adieu to his pretty hostess, he went downstairs again and had his hired coach called up to the door.

As it rumbled back towards the city he felt that he had ample cause to congratulate himself on the fruits of his first night in Sweden. In it he had accomplished more than during the whole of the fifteen days he had spent in Denmark; as the good relations he had established with the French Ambassador's wife and the Russian Ambassador's daughter could not possibly have been bettered for his purpose.

He smiled to himself a little as he thought of the familiarities he had so boldly taken with Natalia, and wondered if he would have dared to do so had he then known that she was regarded as a semi-royalty. All unknowing he had taken a big risk, for had she been of a different temperament she might have held it against him and seriously queered his pitch, but it seemed that he could hardly have played his cards better.

She had not the faintest resemblance to any other girl that he had ever met, and he could not make up his mind if he liked her or not. She had a great opinion of herself, but not without reason, as she was unusually intelligent as well as beautiful in a strange way that was all her own. He recalled the Marquise's warning that the slim, green-eyed Russian was reputed to have a most malicious sense of humour, and his own experience of her led him to believe that when her passions were aroused she would prove extremely vicious; but he knew that he was already strongly attracted, and decided that it was, perhaps, just as well that his inclination coincided with his duty, since it was so clearly in the interests of his mission to develop his budding affaire with her.

The whole of the next day he spent in exploring the city and entering into conversation with everyone with whom he came in contact; and the opinions of the townsfolk gave him cause to moderate the view that Natalia Andreovna had given him of King Gustavus, as a monarch with little real power or prestige.

He gathered that before Gustavus's reign Sweden had been reduced to abject poverty by the misrule of several generations of rapacious nobles who had preyed upon her mercilessly; whereas during the past sixteen years the King had brought her people both freedom and prosperity. With the aid of the banker Liljencrantz he had straightened out the appalling mess in which he found the country's finances; and with the aid of the jurist Liliestrale he had restored both justice and the dignity of the church. He had himself impeached the two Supreme Courts before the Senate, disbenched five of the eight judges, and dismissed scores of lesser magistrates convicted of taking bribes. He had redistributed the clergy's livings and compelled the venal priests among them to live in their parishes and serve their parishioners, instead of taking their fees for doing nothing. He had reorganised the army, abolished the sale of commissions, and made merit the only road to promotion.

The latter step was one of the causes of the hostility with which the nobles regarded him, but their main grievance was that, having robbed their Estate of much of its former power, they could no longer sell their votes on domestic matters to the highest bidder, which venality had previously been one of their main sources of income.

The King, it emerged, was a great lover of the spectacular and also of the theatre. Some people resented the large sums he spent on display, and his purchase of a magnificent collection of art treasures from all parts of Europe; but most were of the opinion that the former was compensated for by the resulting free entertainments and that the latter redounded to the glory of their country.

The only matter in which Gustavus had seriously jeopardised his popularity with the masses was in the taxation of spirits. Formerly it had been an age-old right for everyone to distil whatever they required for their own consumption, and the bare idea of taxing liquor raised a most frightful outcry. Troops had to be employed to collect the tax, and, on even this proving ineffective, the King had sought to turn the manufacture into a royal monopoly by ordering the destruction of all private stills and erecting large distilleries of his own. Riots had ensued, and the indignant mob burnt down several of the royal distilleries, so the King had endeavoured to sell the monopoly to the Government, but without success, and the struggle still continued.

Apart from this grievance, Roger formed the opinion that the great mass of the people was solidly behind their King. Moreover, they both hated and feared the Russians, and since they still regarded the Baltic provinces as the rightful property of the Swedish crown, were quite prepared to support Gustavus in a war aimed at retrieving this portion of their old empire.

Next morning Roger drove out to the French Embassy, and at breakfast there was introduced by the Ambassador to several gentlemen, most of whom were Swedes. Among them was Count Hans Axel af Fersan, a great Francophile, who openly avowed that when he had been a visitor at the Court of Versailles he had fallen in love with Queen Marie Antoinette. He and Roger took an immediate liking to one another and on Roger's side, although he was in no situation to acknowledge it, the bond was strengthened by the discovery that they were both partially of Scots descent; since his mother had been a McElfic and the daughter of the Earl of Kildonan, while the af Fersans were a branch of the Macpherson clan which had settled in Sweden many years before.

The name of Count Axel af Fersan was already known to Roger, from his talks with various people on the previous day, as that of a prominent Swedish statesman who was the leader of the Hat party and one of the King's most bitter opponents in the *Riksdag;* but he felt that his new acquaintance could hardly be old enough to have played a leading part in Swedish politics for any length of time, and on his tactful inquiry the Count burst out laughing.

"Nay, nay, my friend!" he declared with a shake of his head. "You are confusing me with my revered senior Count Fredrik, who was already a great figure in Sweden before I was born. And, being of a younger generation, I do not share the prejudices against the King which still rankle among the older nobility. In fact I think that many of the reforms he has introduced were long overdue, and in some ways I have a considerable admiration for him."

Roger smiled. "I notice, Count, that you qualify your last statement. Would it be indiscreet to inquire the traits that you admire in him and those you do not?"

"Since he has given us a free press and the right of free speech I will do so willingly," Count Hans smiled back. "Being a normal man myself, to whom the vices of the Greeks have never made any appeal, I regard his private life as most unsavoury; and his character leaves much to be desired. Mayhap 'tis due to the manner in which he was brought up, with his person surrounded by people whom he could only regard as spies and enemies, that is to blame; but he is so secretive and deceitful that it would be difficult to find his equal as a liar. On the other hand he is a man of great attainments, high courage and prodigious brain. As a lad he was extraordinarily precocious, with a vivid imagination and most retentive memory. He had only to see a play to absorb the whole content of it; and his attendants declare that on dressing the following day he would solemnly declaim the longest speeches to which he had listened, without fault. Before he was twenty-five he had read every important book of which French literature can boast, and among others, acquired a mastery of the barbarous Swedish tongue. He was the first monarch capable of addressing his people in their own language that we have had for generations; and, even in the age when oratory has again become a great art, he is among the finest orators in all Europe. He is an arch-plotter but capable, resolute and brave. His greatest merit, to my mind, is his intense love of his country, and 'tis that which attaches me to him more than anything else."

To Roger's annoyance their host interrupted the conversation at that moment to inquire as to the length of his stay in Sweden. He returned an evasive answer, and then became involved in general talk; as several of the gentlemen present, including Count Hans, asked him to call upon them and offered to show him some of the beauties of their country.

When he was about to leave, the black-clad major-domo came up to him and said that Madame la Marquise hoped that his engagements were not so pressing that he would fail to wait upon her in her boudoir before returning to the city; so he willingly allowed himself to be conducted upstairs.

During his short stay in Sweden Roger had already been struck with the individuality of the house furniture. It was nearly all of natural unpolished wood or else painted white and decorated with scrolls of flowers in the gayest colours; but Madame de Pons' boudoir was a little oasis of Versailles set down in this far-northern country. Its cabinets, chairs and occasional tables, were of highly polished and elaborately inlaid satin-wood, a Buhl clock adorned the mantel and pictures by Boucher and Fragonard hung in the satin-covered panels of the walls. It was the perfect setting for its elegant owner.

She made Roger sit down and tell her all about himself, then she discoursed a little plaintively on the hard lot of a diplomat's wife, separated for years on end from her family and friends. Roger learned that her name was Angélique, which he thought very pretty; and that before coming to Sweden she and her husband had been stationed in Berlin. She greatly preferred Stockholm to the Prussian capital, as there were many more entertainments at King Gustavus's court than there had been at that of the mean, cantankerous Frederick the Great, who had ruled from his bleak, barrack-like town of Potsdam until his death twenty-one months ago. But, even so, she hankered sadly after the super-civilised delights of her own country.

Roger sought to console her and by gentle stages introduced a flirtatious note into his conversation; then he moved swiftly over to the tapestry-covered sofa on which she sat, took her hand, and lightly kissed her cheek.

She let her hand remain in his but drew her head away with a laugh. "You silly boy. What made you think I wanted you to do that?"

" 'Twas mere selfishness," he declared. "And for my own gratification. You are the most charming person in all Sweden and my thoughts have been full of you ever since we danced together."

"Then you had best find some other image to enshrine in your mind; for I warn you that you will derive little profit from thinking of me other than as a friend."

"I'll not believe it," he cried, pressing his attack; but she pushed him firmly from her and said seriously.

"I mean it, Monsieur. Your ardour is a charming compliment, but if you were older you would realise that appearances are often deceptive. I hope I do not look it, but I am near old enough to be your mother."

"Nay, 'tis impossible," Roger protested. "I'll vow you're not a day over twenty-six."

142

"I am thirty-one," she told him with a little grimace.

"Well, what of it? 'Tis truly said that a woman is as old as she looks and a man is as old as he feels. I rate you as twenty-six and, if you'll let me, I'll show you that I have as much experience as most men of thirty."

"You delightful child," she rallied him. "If I were ten years younger I'd be tempted to make trial of you; but the question of age apart; I, like the Queen, feel that any woman who holds a public position owes it to France to set a standard; so I am faithful to my husband."

Roger felt certain from her tone and glance that she was not seeking to set a higher value on surrendering to him later, but really meant what she said; and as deliberate virtue was so rarely to be found in a woman of her class at that time, he admired her for it.

After a moment he said: "I would that you were ten years younger, then; or at least not the wife of France's representative. But from what you say Queen Sophia Magdalena must be a puritan indeed, for if any woman had good cause to take a lover, it seems, from what I hear, that 'tis she."

"Nay, I was speaking of Queen Marie Antoinette," replied the Marquise quickly. "As for the other, her case is very different; and from my heart I pity any woman who is forced to take a lover against her will."

"What mean you, Madame!" exclaimed Roger in surprise.

Angélique de Pons' blue eyes were grave as she said: "Since you appear not to know her situation 'tis well that I should put you *au fait* with it; for knowledge of it may prevent you from making some unfortunate *faux pas* when in Swedish society. There is good reason to suppose that King Gustavus has never co-habited with his Queen."

"I had heard that he was no constant votary to the goddess Venus," Roger remarked, "but had supposed. . . . Surely you do not mean that the young Crown Prince, and the Queen's little daughter, born more recently. . . ?"

The Marquise shrugged her plump shoulders. "Alas, 'tis the fact. Quite soon after their marriage Gustavus endeavoured to persuade his wretched bride to take one of his friends as a lover, in order that she might provide him with an heir; but he met with a most indignant refusal. He ceased then from his vile proposals and for eleven years they lived apart. But it seems that a time came when he realised that if he allowed many more years to pass she might not be able to give him an heir at all, and he again attempted to persuade her to take a lover. She still resisted but, finding that her scruples were mainly of a religious nature, he finally gained her consent to an arrangement whereby he divorced her in secret and with equal secrecy she was remarried to his friend Major Muncke."

"Then the heir to the Swedish throne has no legal title to it."

"None; but there is every reason to suppose that he will succeed; since Gustavus disguised the whole affair from the common people with his usual cunning. Everyone knew that he and his Queen had been estranged for many years, so he stage-managed a grand reconciliation in '77, the year before the Crown Prince was born. But all the nobility saw through the imposture and the old Dowager-Queen, Louisa Ulrica, publicly refused to acknowledge the child as her grandson."

"She was Frederick the Great's sister, was she not?"

"Yes; and a finer woman than he was a man. I know little of politics and care about them less; but I have many times heard it said that had it not been for the weakness of her husband, the old King Frederick, in allowing the *Riksdag* to ride rough-shod over the Royal authority, she would have done great things for Sweden. As it was, all she could do was to instil her own courage, good taste and love of learning into her son; but Gustavus has ill-repaid his mother for her care. So disgusted was she by his depravity, and his having foisted another man's child upon the nation as his heir, that she retired from court; and her death, six years ago, was hastened by her revulsion at the news of Sophia Magdalena's second unnatural pregnancy."

As they talked on Roger soon found that the Marquise's statement, that she knew little of politics and cared about them less, was indeed the case. Her interest lay in people, entertainments and the arts, and of these she would talk with the greatest animation; but whenever he touched on international affairs she displayed either ignorance or boredom.

From the point of view of his task this was a disappointment; but the one thing which had given him some concern since undertaking it was that he might be called on to betray confidences made to him as a friend, and it consoled him somewhat to think that such a circumstance was unlikely to arise in the case of Angélique de Pons.

On thinking the matter over later in the day Roger was surprised to find that, whereas he would have greatly disliked having to abuse Angélique's confidence, he would have felt not the least scruple about betraying that of Natalia Andreovna. This difference in his mental attitude towards the two women brought home to him the fact that the slim Russian's attraction for him was entirely physical, whereas he really liked the French woman as a person.

They had parted with the most friendly feelings; as she had told him frankly that if she had led him on a little it was simply in order to reach a quick understanding with him, and to make it clear that she was not a prude but a woman with whom he could talk freely on any subject. She had added that if he would not regard her as a mother he must certainly do so as a sister, since she made the happiness of all young Frenchmen who came to Sweden her especial care. He had thanked her with genuine gratitude and promised to call upon her at least twice a week to keep her informed of his doings.

That night Roger drove to the Russian Embassy to attend Natalia Andreovna's *salon*. He found it to be a great mansion standing in its own grounds in the most fashionable suburb of the city, and from the many liveried servants in evidence it was clear that it was maintained in a degree of state which would have done credit to a minor palace.

Although he arrived early a small crowd was already assembled in Natalia's green and yellow drawing-room, so, obviously, there was no hope of any private conversation with her; but Roger had come prepared to find that the case, and had spent the best part of the afternoon composing a love-letter, in which, having raved about her beauty and attainments, he begged for an assignation.

She greeted him with her thin-lipped smile then turned to her father, who was standing beside her settee, and informed him that it was Roger who had rescued them two evenings before, when their coach had broken down.

Count Razumofsky, evidently to show his contempt of accepted custom, was wearing, instead of the silk tail-coat suit and patterned waistcoat usual for such receptions, a Russian costume consisting of a black velvet blouse trimmed with sable, black cloth breeches, and instead of silk stockings, high Hessian boots. Over his left shoulder he wore the broad, deep-red, watered ribbon and eight-pointed golden star that was the insignia of the Order of St. Alexander Nevsky, the second highest in Russia; so despite his unconventional dress, he made a most striking figure.

To-night he was in a very different mood from that in which Roger had first seen him. With a hearty guffaw over the accident and many jovial expressions of thanks, he slapped his rescuer on the shoulder, and abruptly leaving the people to whom he had been talking, led him away into the next room where there was a buffet with food and drink. Bawling loudly for vodka and caviare the broad-shouldered bull-necked Russian pressed Roger to take his fill, swallowed three vodkas in quick succession himself, then introduced him to some other gentlemen who had come in, told him that he would be welcome at the Embassy at any time, and left him.

Natalia Andreovna's drawing-room and two smaller rooms leading out of it were soon filled to overflowing; and Roger began to wonder how he could possibly give her his letter without attracting undue attention. He had been talking to various people for over an hour before he hit upon a plan, but once having thought it out he took the letter from his pocket, and without making any attempt to conceal it, went up to her.

As soon as he caught her eye he bowed and said: "Madame, there is a poor stricken fellow lying at my inn. Knowing your charity he begged me to give you this letter, which sets forth the particulars of his desperate situation, in the hope that you will be so touched as to succour him."

The words Roger used applied perfectly well to his own case, but he felt certain that her great wealth must cause her to receive frequent appeals to her benevolence, and that the people about her would take what he had said in that sense. As they did not show the faintest sign of interest it seemed that his stratagem was entirely successful; and the sudden flicker of curiosity which showed in Natalia's green eyes added to his satisfaction. She was not of the type to be the least intrigued by a begging-letter; yet she opened it at once, glanced at its beginning and end, then said with an amused little smile: "Be sure the matter shall have my most sympathetic consideration, Monsieur."

After bowing himself away he ran into two of the men he had met that morning at Monsieur de Pons' breakfast-party, and they, in turn, introduced him to their ladies and others of the company; so he spent a further two hours in light, amusing conversation; then, finding that the crowd was thinning he went up to Natalia Andreovna to take his leave. As he bowed over her hand she said softly: "To-morrow evening, if you will, Monsieur, you may call for me and give me your escort to my box at the Opera."

"Madame," he murmured. "Though I shall have no eyes for it 'twill be for me the most memorable spectacle I have ever had the good fortune to attend."

Their eyes met and held one another's for a second; then, with the happy feeling that his evening had been very far from wasted he left the Embassy and returned to his inn.

The following morning Count Hans Axel af Fersan called upon him, and took him to the Guild House of the Society of Toxophilists, in the garden of which an archery contest was being held to the accompaniment of the drinking of much lager-beer and considerable betting. When it was over Count Hans carried him off to dine with a company of gay young men, all of whom pressed Roger to accept their services, so by the evening of his fourth day in Sweden he found himself already well-established to pass his time in most agreeable society.

Excusing himself when the meal was over he returned to his inn, dressed himself in his best and presented himself at the Russian Embassy. A few minutes later Natalia Andreovna, looking truly regal in white satin, great clusters of diamonds, and an ermine cape, came down the stairs, and he led her out to the big gilded coach.

In it, on their way to the Opera House, he had too much good sense to attempt to make love to her, but he told her in no unmeasured terms how lovely he thought both herself and her toilette. On their arrival he found to his great satisfaction that she had not invited any-one else to share the roomy private box, so he could count on having her to himself for the best part of three hours.

When they had settled themselves she exchanged greetings with several people in the nearby boxes and waved her fan to some of the young gallants in the pit, meanwhile keeping Roger amused with a running commentary on who they were and their idiosyncrasies. As befitted the Russian Ambassador's power in the land, he retained the permanent use of a box in the first tier next to the Royal box. The latter was so far empty and Roger, knowing the King's partiality to the theatre and that this was a first night, asked his companion if she thought it likely that his Majesty would attend the performance.

She shook her head. "Nay, he still dallies at Karlskrona."

Recalling that the King had been expected back in Stockholm for the party at the French Embassy four nights before, Roger inquired: "What is it that detains him there?"

"I would that we knew for certain," she replied, thoughtfully. "He is said to be inspecting his fleet, but certain intelligence suggests that he may be supervising its preparations for putting to sea."

Roger pricked up his ears. "Is Karlskrona his principal fleet base, then?"

"Why, yes. 'Tis the largest harbour and naval arsenal in the world."

"Oh, come!" he protested. "Surely 'tis not bigger than Toulon, or the great new base that King Louis is constructing at Cherbourg?"

"Indeed it is," she assured him. "And virtually impregnable; for 'tis situated in the heart of a great island of rock that can only be reached from the mainland by way of two other islands. The Swedes have been working on it for many years, constructing the most ingenious hydraulic works, and hewing dry-docks, underground canals and storehouses out of the solid mountain side. The port itself is very deep and capable of holding a hundred ships of the line."

"King Gustavus can have nothing near that number."

"True, but for the past six years he has been building at the rate of four a year, and there are now thirty-seven ships of the line lying there, as well as numerous frigates. Then there must be others at Trollhätta and Sveaborg; so he now has a fleet quite formidable enough to cause Russia considerable anxiety in the Baltic."

"Do you fear then that he contemplates an attack against your country?"

Her tapering eyebrows drew together in a frown. " 'Tis hard to say. We know that he has been receiving subsidies from the Turks, and it may be he feels that he should at least make some demonstration to justify them. Yet I cannot believe that he would be such a presumptious fool as to defy the Empress. 'Twould be suicidal to invite a revolution in his own country with Russia, Austria and France all leagued against him."

The lights had been put out, and at that moment, the curtain went up. Roger drew his chair up beside Natalia's and a little behind it, and took her hand; then, after they had watched the scene for a while he began to whisper in her ear. The Grand Opera season was over, so only a light musical with no great stars appearing in it was being played; and the plot was of such an airy nature that they could almost ignore the stage without losing its thread.

Knowing that much as most women enjoyed a meed of flattery, the majority greatly preferred a man who could make them laugh, to one who confined himself to solemnly praising their beauty, he ventured on a slightly *risqué* joke. Natalia's quiet chuckle showed him that he was on the right track, and soon they were swopping stories which, had the lights been up, should have made even a young widow blush.

During the long interval she received a little court of callers in the box, and most of them did not hide the fact that they envied Roger his good fortune in being her escort for the evening. When they had retired he drew his chair up to hers once more, but he bided his time until half-way through the second act before giving their conversation a serious turn and begging her to give him a proper assignation.

For a time she listened to his pleading in silence, then she said: " 'Twould be idle for me to pretend a virtue in which, after our first meeting, you would not believe; and I'll not deny that I have had a number of lovers; but I am mightily particular as to the men I choose for such a role. 'Tis, in fact, my custom to test such gallants as attract me both for their courage and sensibility before granting them my favours."

"I pray you then, even if I only attract you a very little, allow me to essay these tests," said Roger, quickly.

She gave a low laugh. "I confess to just the suspicion of a hankering for you, so it shall be as you wish."

The scent of Attar of Roses that she favoured was strong in Roger's nostrils. Her head was now so close to his that he could feel her warm breath on his cheek. She was leaning very lightly against his shoulder, and she seemed to him now unutterably desirable. His heart began to hammer in his chest.

CHAPTER X

THE TWO TESTS OF NATALIA ANDREOVNA

THE dim light in the box was just sufficient for Roger to catch the fleeting smile of promise that flickered over Natalia's lovely face, then she went on. "But if you fail me in either test I'll be adamant. Moreover I warn you now that should I take you for my lover I'll expect complete faithfulness. On that I insist, and if I catch you deceiving me I'll give you cause to rue it."

He kissed her hand, and his voice trembled with eagerness as he said: "Your conditions are mine, Madame. May I know the tests?"

"Nay, that is my secret," she replied with a note of amusement in her voice. "But from to-night you may call me Natalia Andreovna, and, if you will tell it me, I will call you by your given name; for in Russia these formal 'Messieurs' and 'Mesdames' are never used between friends."

"My name is *Rojé*, and that of my father *Christophe*," he said, pronouncing both as was customary in France. "So I suppose that in Russia I should be called Rojé Christorovitch."

"Then, Rojé Christorovitch, you may take me riding to-morrow morning at ten o'clock. 'Tis unnecessary for you to hire a horse, as I can provide you with a good mount from the Embassy stables. The pine-woods outside the city now smell delicious, and as we ride through them we can talk and laugh to our hearts' content."

"I'll scarce sleep from savouring the pleasure of it in advance, dear Natalia Andreovna," he said gallantly. Then, seeing that the singers on the stage had massed for the final chorus, he drew her to her feet and to the back of the box, where they exchanged a few long kisses before the flambeaux-men ran in to light the theatre up.

On the way home she was very firm with him, and when they reached the Embassy she would not let him come in, but insisted on sending him home in her coach. Nevertheless he felt that he had made excellent progress. The thought of the tests she demanded did not worry him. They seemed to add to the romance of the affair, making her still more desirable; and he reasoned that no woman who wanted a man would make such tests unduly hard. Their long evening together had given him good grounds for believing that she wanted him, and he now felt that she was a much nicer person than he had at first supposed. In fact he was rapidly falling under the beautiful young widow's spell.

When he awoke next morning he found to his delight that the day was fine; and well before ten o'clock he was striding up the steps of the Russian Embassy. A quarter of an hour later Natalia Andreovna came down to him, and the sight of her was enough to make any gallant's heart beat faster. With that same disregard of convention which characterised her father, she was dressed as a man. Her outfit consisted of a dove-coloured beaver tricorne hat with a deep gold band and tassels; a long scarlet coat faced with gold brocade; a buff, gold-laced waistcoat, frilled shirt and man's neckerchief; buckskin small-clothes, jack-boots, gold spurs and a diamond-studded riding-switch. This male attire suited her boyish figure to perfection, and chin in air, she walked with a swagger that made her quite irresistible.

Somewhat to Roger's surprise no horses were being walked up and down in readiness for them outside, but she told him that she had thought that he might like to try one or two mounts and choose which he preferred before setting out; then she led him round to the stable yard.

A little group of grooms were waiting for them with a small white, long-tailed Arab, and a big black mare measuring a good sixteen hands. The men were Russians, with shaggy hair and flat, dark, peasant faces. One of them led the Arab to a mounting block for Natalia and another held the black for Roger. The moment he was in the saddle the *moujik* sprang away, gave a loud hiss and clapped his hands. Instantly the mare reared wildly and tried to throw her rider.

The next few minutes were hectic. Fortunately Roger was an excellent horseman, and his long legs enabled him to keep a good grip of his mount, otherwise he might easily have had his brains dashed out on the cobbles of the yard. Round and round went the mare, bucking, prancing and kicking, while he hung grimly on and strove to quieten the half-crazy animal.

For a second he caught a glimpse of Natalia; she was smiling broadly and the squat, ugly peasants were grouped round her loudly guffawing at his discomfiture. He realised then that she must **have** deliberately mounted him on this vicious brute and instructed the *moujik* beforehand to frighten it. The thought filled him with rage but made him more determined than ever not to afford her the satisfaction of seeing him thrown off.

Jerking round the mare's head he gave her both his spurs and sent her careering through a gate at the back of the yard that led into the Embassy garden. In a flash, he had crossed the lawn with its neatly patterned flower-beds, and was heading down a path between some plots of early vegetables. Beyond them lay a wooden fence and a paddock. Another touch of the spurs and the mare sailed over the fence. She was a splendid animal, and once he had her in the field, he began to enjoy himself. For ten minutes he rode her round and round it, towards the end forcing her pace to teach her a lesson. Then he found a gap in the fence, put her through it and trotted her back across the garden to the stable-yard.

The wicked little Russian, now mounted astride the Arab, was still there laughing among her varlets. Pulling up the foam-flecked and quivering black in front of her, Roger swept off his tricorne and said with a smile: "My apologies for having delayed your setting out, Natalia Andreovna; but having tested the mount you selected for me I find your choice admirable."

Her green eyes danced with amusement and just a hint of admiration, as she cried: "Let us away, then, Rojé Christorovitch"; and turning her white steed she cantered out of the gate beside him.

They soon left houses and gardens behind, and were riding through woods of larch and pine. After an hour they came out of the forest onto a high promontory from which there was a magnificent view of the slate-blue fjord. Reining in her Arab, Natalia suggested that they should pause there for a while, so they both dismounted and Roger tied the reins of the horses to a tree stump.

Although he had not shown it he was still seething inwardly at the dangerous trick she had played him; and as he tied up the horses it occurred to him that it would serve her right if he took the Arab and left her to ride home on the temperamental black. But he dismissed the thought almost as soon as it came to him, as, quite apart from the physical attraction she had for him, he knew that it was of the utmost importance for his work that he should keep on good terms with her.

She had seated herself on a fallen tree. As he sat down beside her she took his hand, and said seriously: "Rojé Christorovitch, I am pleased with you. Not many men could ride that black devil as you did, and I am well satisfied with your courage. You have passed the first test with honour."

"So it was a test, eh?" he laughed. "I wondered if it could be. Yet, if you have a liking for a man, and you say you like me, to put him in the way of breaking his neck is a strange way to show it."

"But it gives me pleasure to see a brave man face danger," she replied, quite unabashed. "I would that I had been born a Roman

Empress; in all time there can have been no sport to compare with watching the gladiators contend in the circus."

"And what of the wretched Christians? Would you have enjoyed seeing them herded defenceless into the arena to be savaged by wild beasts?"

She shrugged. "The Christians of those days were like the Masons of our own time; a secret society, propagating among the slaves the criminal doctrine that they were the equals of their masters, and plotting against the safety of the state. For such treason they were with justice condemned to death; so what odds does it make if they were strangled in their dungeons or given to the lions?"

Her callousness repelled him, yet it in no way detracted from her striking good looks, and putting his arm round her waist he said: "What a bloodthirsty little person you are, Natalia Andreovna; but let us talk of pleasanter things. When may I undergo your second test and be proved as to my sensibility?"

"There is ample time for that," she told him with a smile. "For a little you must be content to attend upon me, so that I can come to know you better." But for the next half-hour she allowed him to kiss and caress her; then they remounted their horses and rode back to the city.

When they rode into the yard the grooms were waiting to take their horses, but just as he was about to dismount she cried: "One moment, Rojé Christorovitch. Did you find the black, after all, a good ride?"

"Why, yes," he replied. "She is a fine animal, powerful and with an easy pace. She needs but the firm hand of a practised rider."

"Take her then, as a gift from me. You have proved yourself worthy of her, and will need a mount during your stay in Stockholm. Ride her away and have her stabled at your inn."

Roger knew that the mare was as fine a mount as he had ever ridden and a most valuable animal, so he thanked her effusively for her generosity and, as he rode away, found himself more puzzled than ever as to whether he liked or disliked her. Those green eyes and that slim figure were playing the very devil with his emotions and he decided that he must not let her cruel streak weigh too much against her; since it was no doubt largely due to her nationality and upbringing.

During the week that followed he called twice on Angélique de Pons, developed his friendship with Count Hans Axel af Fersan, and found himself well-established as a popular member of the younger set in Stockholm. But between dinners, routs and other entertainments he danced constant attendance on Natalia. He became a familiar figure at the Russian Embassy, and the bull-necked Count Razumofsky now treated him as one of his immediate circle. He learned nothing of importance, but sensed that there was a definite tension in the air, and that the Ambassador regarded the doings of the still-absent King Gustavus with considerable suspicion.

In the course of the week Roger several times came into collision with Count Yagerhorn, as he too was a frequent visitor at the Embassy. Their mutual dislike increased upon a closer acquaintance, and Natalia Andreovna obviously derived considerable amusement from stimulating their rivalry; but as she maintained her prohibition on the tall, fair pink-faced Finn issuing a challenge, and Roger felt that in the circumstances it was unfair to provoke him, they continued to treat one another with frigid courtesy.

Whenever occasion offered Roger pressed Natalia to give him an assignation, or at least proceed with her second test; but she would not be hurried, and his affair with her progressed no further until an afternoon nine days after he had first taken her riding.

By that time they had got to know one another well, and quite apart from her beauty, he ranked her as the most interesting and amusing young woman in Stockholm; so he was more eager than ever to bring matters to a head.

They were walking in the garden, and in the hope of forcing a decision he told her that, so desperate had she made him, unless she was prepared to take pity on him soon he would be driven to the conclusion that she was only playing with him, and, in an endeavour to tear her image from his heart, he would seriously consider leaving Sweden.

She softened at once, telling him that she liked him greatly, and had come to count upon his society, so she would seek to prove him no further. Then she nodded towards a window on the first-floor at the back of the house, and said: "That is my room; do you think you could climb up there?"

He gave one glance at the balcony below it, which was supported by the scrolled iron-work of the ground-floor verandah, and laughed. "Indeed I could. Let me do so this very night, my sweet, I beg."

"So be it," she smiled. "Come to me at midnight, but not a moment before. As to your entry to the grounds, you see that postern-door in the wall over there? I will give you the key of it before you leave."

On that side of the house the garden-wall ran within twelve feet of the building, and the door, although at right angles to her balcony, was almost beneath it. He saw that once through the door he would have only a dozen paces to take to reach the verandah. It was an admirable arrangement, as he could not possibly lose his way in the darkness, and the risk of running into anyone during so short a passage from the street to her room was infinitesimal. An hour later, on his way back to the inn with the key in his pocket, his senses almost reeled at the thought of the promised delights of the night to come.

It was not until he was considering what clothes he should wear for his expedition that it suddenly occurred to him that Natalia Andreovna had, after his long siege of her, surrendered at the last somewhat precipitously and only on his threatening to abandon his pursuit of her. Could it be that she did not really mean to receive him after all, but intended instead to play him some scurvy trick, like mounting him on the black horse? Perhaps she would rouse the house pretending to mistake him for a burglar, for the fun of seeing him chased and perhaps beaten by her servants.

On thinking matters over he decided that his suspicions of her were both unjust and unreasonable. She could be very sweet at times and recently had shown in a dozen small ways that she was fond of him. Moreover she had admitted to having had lovers and, just before he left her, had gone up to her room to fetch the key of the postern gate, suggesting pretty clearly that she had made use of it before for a similar purpose. If she had let others come to her that way in the night, why should she not let him?

Nevertheless his lingering distrust of her vicious sense of humour led him to take special precautions. He decided to wear loose, dark easy clothes, as they would not only render him as inconspicuous as possible and facilitate his climb up the verandah, but they would also give him a much better chance of getting away and disappearing in the darkness, if she was base enough to have him ambushed for her amusement. Moreover, a long sword being an awkward weapon to take to such a rendezvous, he would normally have gone unarmed; but on this occasion he decided to carry a hanger and, going out, bought himself a short, thick-bladed seaman's cutlass, which would not get in his way but prove a good, handy weapon if he were attacked.

As he buckled it on he was inclined to laugh at his fears, and his optimism recovered, waited with the greatest impatience for midnight. When it came he was outside the postern door with its key in his hand, yet he deliberately waited for another five minutes before inserting it in the lock. It turned easily and without a sound, showing that the mechanism was well-oiled. He smiled to himself, feeling certain now that others before him had trodden this road to a night of bliss in the young widow's arms, and he would have betted his valuable black mare against a tabby cat that Count Yagerhorn had been among them.

The night was warm and it was the dark phase of the moon. As he opened the door and slipped through it he was only a blacker patch in the shadow of the wall. Nothing stirred, and he found that the door closed behind him noiselessly, its hinges being as well-oiled as its lock. For a moment he paused with his back against it, looking cautiously round. There was just enough light to discern the outlines of the house and the trees in the garden. Reassured by the utter stillness he tiptoed forward.

The latticed iron-work of the verandah was, as he had expected, easy to climb. Barely a minute after leaving the ground he swung himself over the low balcony. In the faint light he could now see that one of the two French windows which gave onto it was standing ajar. Quickly pulling off the gloves he had used to keep his hands free from the dirt on the iron, he thrust them in one of his pockets, and gently pushed the window open.

"Natalia Andreovna," he whispered.

As no reply came he stepped inside. The room was almost pitch-dark. A faint light came from its far end outlining a curtained doorway, and this was sufficient to show him the position of a big four-poster bed. As his eyes grew accustomed to the darkness he could just make out her head upon the white pillow.

Tiptoeing forward he whispered her name again. She moved slightly, showing that she was awake, but still made no reply.

It struck him then that perhaps she was much shyer than he had thought her, or wished to make a pretence at the last moment that she was being taken against her will. Smiling to himself he swiftly slipped out of his loose clothes, stepped up to the bed and, stooping above it, kissed her.

Her lips responded warmly and her arms closed round his neck. Pulling the sheets back he slipped into bed beside her, and began to murmur little phrases of endearment.

Without a word she pulled him to her and kissed him again; but with her movement there suddenly came to him a wild, almost incredible notion. Something told him that the woman he was embracing was not Natalia Andreovna.

Her perfume was that which Natalia affected, and she seemed about the right height; but her breasts were larger and her waist thicker than he had imagined could possibly be the case with the lithe Russian.

Putting up one hand to caress her hair, he felt it. Natalia's ash-blonde tresses were as smooth and as fine-spun as the sheerest silk; this was much coarser and slightly crinkled.

Pushing the woman from him, he sat up with a jerk, exclaiming angrily: "What is the meaning of this trick? You are not Natalia Andreovna! Where is she?"

There came a low laugh from behind the curtain and it was pulled aside, allowing a dim light to seep into the room. Natalia stood framed in the doorway. She was wearing a satin night-robe and her long ash-blonde hair, now parted in the middle, fell like a smooth cascade of silver about her shoulders.

"Here I am, Rojé Christorovitch," she smiled. "Waiting to make you welcome. Had you had my maid you would never have had me. But you have passed my test for sensibility with as much honour as you did that for courage."

As Roger gaped at her she spoke in Russian to the woman beside him. He saw now that she was a dark-haired merry-eyed girl of about twenty. At her mistress's order she jumped out of bed, flashed her white teeth at him in a wide grin, and ran giggling past Natalia Andreovna into the next room, which, from what he could see, was a clothes-closet.

With an enigmatic smile on her thin lips, the uncrowned Queen of Sweden drew the curtain behind her, plunging the room again into near darkness. Then she ran forward with outstretched arms and, as he caught her, buried her face in his neck.

In the hours that followed he had no reason for complaint. Having finally made up her mind to give herself the slim Russian did so in no half-hearted manner. All the promise of her strange exotic beauty and the slumberous fires of passion that he had sensed in her were fulfilled. When, as the first streaks of dawn came through the window, he at last rose to leave her, he knew that this was one of the nights of his life that he would always remember.

Having dressed he bent above her for a last kiss and murmured: "Tell me, my miracle of love, when may I come to thee again?"

"Be outside the postern gate each night at midnight," she whispered. "If there is a pale light showing from the window of my closet next door, thou mayest take it that I shall be willing to receive thee. If there are full lights in my apartments, or darkness, thou wilt know that I am not in a mood for love. But I warn thee, once again, that even if twenty nights pass without a welcoming signal I still require thee to be faithful to me. And if I have cause to believe that thou art otherwise, I'll give thee good reason to regret thine infidelity."

"Heaven having sent me the most wondrous mistress in all Stockholm why should I be fool enough to dally with any woman of lesser calibre?" he replied; and he meant it, too, as he added with a laugh: "For my part, should I suspect thee of favouring another gallant I'll slit his gizzard as surely as a cook would spit a capon for the roast."

"I like thee the more for that," she laughed back. "Go then; and for what remains of the night sleep well, that thou mayest love me the better when darkness falls once more."

Roger descended to the garden, reached the street and locked the door behind him, without incident. On his mile walk back to his inn he felt as though he was treading on air. The city was still silent and deserted, seeming almost unreal in the pale dawn light. A gentle breeze from the sea was wafting away the cobwebs of the night and its cool freshness tasted to him as good as champagne.

He thought of Georgina. It was almost two months since he had parted from her and he wondered if she and her father had gone abroad yet. Not for the first time he thanked her in his heart for having caused him while still a boy to set an extremely high standard for his loves, so that he had not frittered away his manhood in casual, sordid little amours, but always chose his women carefully and took time and trouble to win the very best. He did not think that she would like Natalia Andreovna as a person, but he knew that she would applaud his having won the uncrowned Queen of Sweden for his mistress.

June came in with glorious weather and Roger's only regret now was that the nights were all too short; particularly as Natalia would not let him come to her every night. After three visits in succession she had told him on the 30th of May that she thought they ought to be content with three or four clandestine meetings a week in future; but that he was to come just the same each night to see if the dim light was in the window of her dress-closet, as she had no wish to make up her mind in advance which nights she would receive him.

As society in Stockholm did not keep late hours the tie of going every midnight to see if the dim light was offering him a welcome did not seriously interfere with his other enjoyments; and although he had an engagement every evening, during the first half of June he had to slip away early from parties to keep his appointment only on three occasions.

He had no qualms at all about lingering in the Swedish capital instead of going on to St. Petersburg, where lay the vortex of his mission; since, having become one of Count Razumofsky's circle, he was now admirably placed for acquiring the latest information on international relations between the courts of northern Europe.

The Count, as Roger soon found, was not of the school of diplomats who believed in finesse. He scorned such tactics, and relied instead on the immense power and prestige of his position as the representative of Her Imperial Majesty, the Czarina of All the Russias. He was a loud-mouthed, blatant bully, who took delight in boasting openly that if King Gustavus had the insolence to play any tricks he would have him off his throne.

Yet, that the Swedish King was planning something, there could no longer be any doubt. The Russian Ambassador's spies kept him constantly informed of Gustavus's activities and Roger, in his role of a Frenchman and pro-Russian, had only to ask the most casual leading questions on his daily visits to the Embassy, to be given the latest intelligence.

Early in June he learned that great quantities of barrels containing salt-meat and fish, and other stores, were being secretly despatched from Stockholm to the Fleet base at Karlskrona; but that the King had left there and was now engaged in a tour of inspection of his principal military depôts.

Roger also learned that there was considerable activity in the other camp; particularly among the Finnish nobility. Count Erik Yagerhorn continued to be a daily visitor to the Russian Embassy; and, although he spent much of the time dancing attendance on Natalia, he was frequently closeted with her father, often bringing other Finnish nobles and discontented Swedes with him to these conferences.

It was soon clear to Roger that the tall, fair Finn was in the pay of Russia, and a prime mover in organising the powerful party in the *Riksdag* which could be counted to oppose the King and veto any measure he might introduce for Sweden to honour her obligation to her Turkish allies.

Roger's one regret in this connection was that having supplanted Yagerhorn in Natalia Andreovna's affections rendered it impossible for him to cultivate the Finn's acquaintance and thus learn something more concrete of his designs. As it was, whenever they met they either glowered at one another or endeavoured to provoke the fair Russian's amusement by being witty at one another's expense. Roger's tongue being considerably sharper than that of the bovine-looking Count he usually came off best in these encounters, but he knew by the looks he received from the man's hard, pale-blue eyes that he had made of him a most deadly enemy.

On the 15th of June, intelligence came in that King Gustavus was expected back in his capital on the 18th, and Count Razumofsky announced his intention of calling him to account. The Ambassador was still fully persuaded that the King positively dared not go to war with Russia, and was convinced that his military preparations were designed, not with a view to active operations, but as a threat intended to force Russia to withdraw troops from the Crimea in order to reinforce her northern frontier.

As that frontier had been almost entirely denuded of its garrisons for the war against the Turks, it was of the first importance that Russia should know if Gustavus was about to launch a colossal bluff or a real attack, and Razumofsky meant to force him to declare himself.

On learning that matters had reached such a critical stage Roger thought that the time had come to make his first report to Mr. Pitt. Much of the knowledge he had gained while in the Scandinavian capitals could be of no interest to the Prime Minister, since the personal intrigues of the royal families of Denmark and Sweden must be known in Whitehall already; but if he could get to England an account of the present crisis and, above all, the result of Count Razumofsky's coming interview with King Gustavus, before it reached there through any other source, he felt that he would have earned his keep.

Since the post of British Minister in Stockholm was vacant there seemed an excellent chance of being first with the news, and his only problem was how to send it. Inquiries at the port disclosed that there was no ship sailing for England until the 26th, but there was a British ship outward bound for Copenhagen on the 20th, so he decided to send his letter by it to Hugh Elliot, who would ensure it being forwarded to London by the quickest available means.

In consequence he devoted a good part of that evening to writing at considerable length to Elliot, regarding Gustavus's military preparations, the machinations of the Finnish nobility, and Count Razumofsky's view that the King did not really mean to fight. He then hid the letter in a jack boot at the bottom of his trunk, intending to add a postscript at the last moment immediately he had learned the outcome of Razumofsky's *démarche* on the 18th.

He had scarcely relocked his trunk when a note was brought up to him which proved to be from the Marquise de Pons. In it she said that Sunday the 17th was her birthday, and that Monsieur le Marquis had to be present as the guest of honour at the annual dinner of the French Literary Society in Gothenbörg, so she was inviting a few young people to a small, intimate party starting at eight o'clock. She hoped that she might count on Roger to make one of their number.

As he had kept on excellent terms with Angélique de Pons he at once accepted the invitation, and thought no more of it; but he had not been at the French Embassy on the Sunday evening for long before

157

he realised that the party might have unforeseen and unfortunate repercussions.

It consisted only of the Marquise, three other young married women, himself and three other young men. All Angélique's friends were French, and the idea seemed to be that for her birthday celebration they should forget that they were exiles in a land where early hours were the rule and consider themselves as back in France with youth at the prow and pleasure at the helm.

Roger knew at once that meant supper at midnight and carriages at three in the morning, and he was considerably perturbed at the idea that he would not be able to keep his usual rendezvous with Natalia Andreovna. In such a carefully chosen little company it would be out of the question for him to excuse himself at eleven-thirty, short of feigning illness and that, as it would spoil Angélique's party, he felt most disinclined to do. However, as his welcoming dim light had been in evidence on both the last two nights he thought that the odds were all against it being there a third night in succession; so he decided to take a chance on that, and gave himself up to enjoyment.

They played King Louis XVI's favourite game of blindman's-buff, dumb-crambo, forfeits, and at all sorts of other simple, laughter-raising pastimes which had become the mode at the Court of France when Marie Antoinette had arrived there as a very young Princess, and had remained fashionable ever since. The chef surpassed himself in the collation served for his mistress's birthday-supper, the wines were from the finest vineyards of Vouvray, Champagne, Burgundy and Sauterne, and the kisses, taken as forfeits behind a screen after midnight, had enough spice in them for all the women to feel that they had been deliciously wicked, but not enough so to cause later regrets. Roger got to bed at four in the morning having enjoyed every moment of it, and without giving another thought to Natalia.

Six hours later he called at the Russian Embassy to take her out riding. She was in excellent spirits and made no mention at all of the previous night, so he was much relieved to think that his assumption that she would go to bed early had been right, and that she had no suspicion of his having failed to keep his rendezvous. As he always entertained her with an account of his doings he told her that he had been out to the French Embassy to Madame de Pons' birthday party, but he said nothing of its intimate nature, of the Marquis's absence or of his own belated return to his inn.

Her only comment was that she supposed that Madame de Pons had given herself out to be twenty-five, but she must be twenty-eight if she was a day; which made Roger laugh inwardly, as he knew Angélique to be thirty-one; but he would not have dreamed of giving his friend away and simply replied that her age had not been mentioned.

At midnight he was at his usual post outside the postern door. The dim light of welcome was showing, so in he went, and up the iron-trellis work to his twelfth clandestine meeting with Natalia. It was three weeks exactly since he had first tiptoed into her room yet neither had reason to complain of any falling off in the other's ardour. But it was nearing the longest day of the year, and the dawn came very early now, so at half-past three he kissed her farewell and climbed over her balcony down into the garden.

The place was as utterly still as usual and for a moment he stood there drawing the cool night air deep into his lungs, while admiring a clear half-moon that was now low on the horizon; then he opened the postern door, stepped out into the street and put his hand in his pocket for the key to lock it.

Suddenly a group of figures detached themselves from the deep shadow cast by the wall and ran at him. In a second he saw that he was opposed to four ragged ruffians armed with cudgels and a tall, masked man who wore a sword. Blessing the habit he had fallen into of carrying his cutlass on these midnight expeditions he sprang back and drew it.

The tall man was urging the others on. His figure and voice gave away the fact that he was Count Erik Yagerhorn. Roger knew then that this was no chance hold-up by a gang of robbers who would let him go if he gave up his purse. He had been ambushed by an enemy who meant him grievous injury; and five to one were too heavy odds for him to have much prospect of fighting his way out of the ring that had so swiftly formed about him. His only chance of escape lay in using all his wits without an instant's delay.

As he side-stepped his nearest attacker the thought came to him that if he could get back through the postern Natalia would rouse the Embassy servants to come to his assistance. He could say that he had been attacked in the street, and finding the door open, had taken refuge there. She would know that he was clever enough to think of some such excuse to save her from being compromised. But on his dodging the first rush one of the rogues had slipped behind him, and now stood between him and the door. Ducking one blow he parried another; then ran at the man who barred his path to the postern and the safety that he hoped lay behind it.

On running forward his glance was caught for a second by something white ten feet above the wall. It was the moonlight glinting on a pale face. Up on the balcony, wrapped in a dark cloak and leaning forward in an intent attitude, silently watching the fracas below, stood Natalia Andreovna.

Instantly it flashed into Roger's mind that she must, after all, have known that he had failed to keep his rendezvous the previous night, and had assumed that his failure to do so meant that he had been unfaithful to her. In the same second he realised that Count Yagerhorn would never have dared to ambush him beneath her window without her consent. She must have deliberately invited the Finn to take his revenge.

Roger's cutlass bit into the shoulder of the man in front of the door. He let out a yell of pain. Like a distorted echo there came from the balcony above a low laugh.

Filled with rage and revulsion Roger realised that the beautiful green-eyed Russian was thinking of herself as a Roman Empress who, believing that her lover had deceived her, had had him thrown to the lions and was now deriving a vicious excitement from the prospect of seeing him torn to pieces.

Three of the men closed in on him. Grimly he realised now, that there was no escape. Striking out right and left he began to fight for his life.

CHAPTER XI

THE INEXPERIENCED SPY

R O G E R had never before used a cutlass in earnest, and at the many fencing-schools he had attended he had always disdained the sabre; but he found that in his present emergency the short, thick-bladed weapon was likely to serve him better than a sword. Had it been a case of steel to steel he would have chosen a rapier every time, but a blow from a heavy cudgel might easily snap a thin blade; moreover, if driven home by a thrust of any force into the muscle of an antagonist it was liable to become gripped there and prove difficult to pull out.

As he recovered from the stroke with which he had wounded the man in front of the door, a big fellow in a leather jerkin made a swing at his head. He ducked, and struck sideways at the man's body. The blow was a glancing one, and the leather turned it, but the man backed away with a grunt.

Swivelling round, Roger was only just in time to parry a swipe from a thick-set ruffian, and using the agility which was one of his principal assets in a fight, landed him a sharp kick on the knee. But he was too late to avoid the fourth man's cudgel. It descended with a dull thud on the back of his left shoulder-blade, knocking him forward, so that he stumbled and nearly fell.

His sudden lurch saved him from the big fellow's second stroke. It missed his head by a bare inch, cleaving the empty air behind him. Regaining his balance he struck upward at the tall man's chin. The blade cut into it, crunching on the jaw bone. With a moan the man dropped his cudgel and staggered back, his hands pressed to his bleeding face.

For a moment Roger thought that his prospects looked a little brighter. He had put two of his five attackers out of the game, temporarily at least. If only he could deal equally effectively with their leader the others might lose heart and take to their heels. But Count Yagerhorn was behaving warily, and stood well out of reach behind his men.

It seemed, too, that the Count was still quite confident of the outcome of the affair. He had not even bothered to draw his sword, and was standing there smacking his boot impatiently with a riding-crop from the end of which snaked a long lash.

As Roger glimpsed it his gorge almost choked him with rage. Evidently Natalia Andreovna had ordered him a whipping. The gutter-carls had been hired to disarm and overcome him, then the Finn meant to give him a thrashing in front of her. Rage, disgust and hatred seethed in Roger's brain, but the desire to be revenged only flickered in and out of it; he was far too hard-pressed to give more than an instant's thought to anything other than avoiding and dealing blows.

The man who had struck him on the back and the thickset ruffian rushed at him simultaneously. The first, a thin, lanky fellow, was coming in on his right. Roger sliced at his long arm as it came down, hoping to sever it at the wrist; but the other man got in first. His cudgel took Roger on the upper part of the left arm. The pain was so intense that for a moment he thought it had been broken. The blow swung him half round and his cutlass, instead of meeting flesh, buried itself in the lanky man's cudgel.

For a moment the two of them swayed violently back and forth in a nightmare tug-of-war, as each tried to wrench free his weapon. The thickset man brought down his cudgel again, but Roger dodged the blow and kicked him in the stomach. With a gasp of agony he fell backwards, doubled up and rolled in the gutter. But, as Roger delivered the kick, his other antagonist jerked him sideways. In his endeavour to keep a hold on his cutlass he lost his balance and pitched forward on to his knees. Cutlass and cudgel were still locked together. The lanky rough pulled with all his weight on the latter, dragging Roger a few yards along the roadway.

Suddenly Count Yagerhorn came into action. His whip hissed through the air, striking Roger full across the shoulders and curling round his body. With a cry of pain he let go the hilt of his cutlass. Throwing up his arms to protect his head he attempted to stagger to his feet. But the man in the doorway, who had been crouching there staunching the blood from the wound in his shoulder, now ran forward and kicked him in the ribs. The kick sent him sprawling on his hands and knees. The Count's lash bit deep into his flesh a second time.

Except for the swift shuffling of feet and an occasional curse or cry of pain, the fight was being waged with silent ferocity. Beyond the little circle of swaying, lunging figures the stillness of the pre-dawn hour had, up to that moment, remained unbroken, but now the ring of horses' hoofs came with sudden clearness on the crisp, cool air.

Instantly Roger began to shout for help. During the past two months the use of French had become so habitual to him that he instinctively used that language, calling out at the top of his voice: "À moi! À moi!"

The hoof-beats grew rapidly louder, and by the direction from which they came he knew that a coach must be driving along the main road, past the front of the Russian Embassy, only fifty yards away.

Lurching to his feet he began to run towards it, redoubling his cries as he went. Count Yagerhorn lashed him again; the lanky man kicked him on the thigh; but he staggered on yelling with all the power of his lungs.

In the moonlight he could now see the leaders of the team that drew the coach. To his infinite relief they swerved round the corner into the bylane, drawing the vehicle swiftly towards him. But the Count and his bullies were determined that their prey should not escape. The Finn was only two yards behind him and striking at him again and again as he ran. Heavy footfalls told that at least two of the others had recovered sufficiently from their hurts to assist in the pursuit.

The champing horses of the coach team were reined in to a halt. It had hardly stopped before a thin man of medium height jumped from it into the roadway.

At that second the thick-set man threw his cudgel. It struck Roger a violent blow on the back of the head. Pitching forward he fell at the feet of the newcomer. Aching in every limb, dazed and exhausted he was conscious for a moment that, in a high-pitched voice, the man from the coach was shouting short, imperative phrases in Swedish, and that Yagerhorn and his roughs had halted, turned, and were fleeing; then he fainted.

When he came to, he found himself being lifted from the coach. Supported by two men he was half-pulled, half-carried through the doorway of a house and up several flights of steep stairs. The effort to help rather than hinder his progress proved too much for him, and, as they reached an attic-room at the top of the house, he lost consciousness again.

On his regaining his senses for the second time, he saw that he was now in bed in the attic-room and that a middle-aged man with thick fair hair cut *en brosse*, who wore a severe dark cloth suit but did not look like a servant, was bending over him. His hurts had had salves put on them and been bandaged while he was unconscious. They smarted considerably less than they had when he had been helped upstairs, but his head was aching vilely.

On seeing his eyes open the soberly-clad man asked in French: "How feel you now?"

"Better, I thank you; but for my head," Roger replied with an effort. "Pardon me if I fail to recognise you; but surely 'twas not you who rescued me from that crew of villains?"

"Nay, it was my master," came the quick answer, "and he has charged me to care for you. But, tell me, Monsieur; what is your name and where is your abode? I ask that I may send to let your friends know that you are here, lest they be anxious for you."

Roger smiled gratefully up into the aesthetic face of his questioner. "I am fortunate in having quite a number of friends in Stockholm; but none who would be concerned for me at the moment. I am the Chevalier de Breuc, a visitor to Sweden, and for the past five weeks have been lying at the Vasa Inn."

The man's eyes narrowed slightly, then he nodded. "In that case no such measures as I had envisaged are required. But 'tis dawn already, and you had best sleep for a few hours."

Not only had Roger been up all night, but his beating had taken a good deal out of him; so, within a few minutes of the man having left him, he fell into a deep sleep from which he did not wake until well on in the afternoon.

His left arm and shoulder-blade pained him sharply as he moved and his head was still aching dully. Cautiously, he lifted his arm and felt it all over; to his relief no bones seemed to be broken. He noticed that his clothes had been brushed and lay neatly folded on a nearby chair, but he felt no inclination to get up and was quite content to lie there dozing for another hour or so; until the door opened softly and his dark-clad host came in carrying a tray of food for him.

Roger expressed his thanks, then added: "I have no wish to trespass on your kindness unduly, Monsieur, and I find myself now sufficiently recovered to get up; so when I have eaten I will dress and return to my inn."

The other shook his fair, close-cropped head. "It is better that you should bide here for the night. I am sure, too, that my master will wish to see you before you leave, and 'tis unlikely that he will come in until midnight. If you feel well enough to dress then, so much the better, as he would be able to talk to you in greater comfort downstairs."

It struck Roger as somewhat strange that his rescuer should require him, while still a semi-invalid, to wait upon him at so late an hour; but both gratitude and politeness forbade him commenting on the fact, so he said: "As you wish, Monsieur. May I know the name of the gentleman to whom I am indebted for my safety; and your name too?"

"My master is the Count Haga," came the quiet reply. "As for myself, I am usually known as the Prebendary."

Alone once more Roger pondered this slender information. The name Count Haga had a vaguely familiar ring, but somehow he could not place it, and assumed that the Count must be one of the many Swedish nobleman whom he had met casually at some reception during the past five weeks, or had heard mentioned in conversation. The designation of Prebendary conveyed nothing, except that its bearer was a clergyman, and Roger concluded that the fair man must be Count Haga's private chaplain.

When he had finished his meal he slept again. On waking he felt much better and found that the room was almost in darkness. His watch had been placed on a table beside his bed and wound up for him; a glance at it showed that it was half-past nine, so he decided to get up. Having lit the candles on the dressing table he set about his toilette. It was a slow and painful process, but by half-past ten he had made himself as presentable as was possible without a change of linen.

To kick his heels in the attic for an hour and a half seemed an uninspiring way of passing the time, so he thought he would go down-stairs and talk to the Prebendary until Count Haga put in an appear-ance. But, on going to the door, he found to his great surprise that it was locked. He remembered then having noticed earlier in the day that the single, sloping skylight in the steep roof of the attic was heavily barred.

As it dawned upon him that he was a prisoner he recalled having already thought it a little queer that, being obviously a person of quality himself, he should have been put in an attic; when, in a noble-man's house, there were nearly always a number of spare bedrooms. Puzzle his wits as he would, he could think of no possible reason why the mysterious Count Haga should wish to detain him there against his will; but there had been no indication that any harm was intended him, so he sat down to await a solution to the mystery with such patience as he could muster.

Soon after midnight the Prebendary came for him, and refraining from comment on the locked door, he followed his guide downstairs to a comfortable book-lined room on the first floor.

A richly-dressed man whom Roger judged to be a little over forty was standing with his back to the empty grate smoking a long pipe. His features were sharp; a big, slightly-curved nose jutting out from his somewhat receding chin and forehead. But his brow was broad, his eyes large and intelligent, and his mouth firm.

He returned Roger's bow only by a slight inclination of the head but courteously waved him to a chair; then said briskly in such ex-cellent French that his Swedish accent was hardly perceptible.

"I am happy to see, Monsieur, that you have sustained no serious injury. Tell me, please; what were you about outside the side-door of the Russian Embassy in the early hours of the morning?"

Strong as was Roger's cause for resentment against Natalia Andreovna, he had been brought up in the tradition that a gentleman does not "kiss and tell," so his immediate instinct was to protect her reputation. He was about to reply that, finding the summer-dawns in Stockholm irresistible, he had been taking an early morning walk, when Count Haga forestalled him, by adding:

"If you had been lying with that vicious Russian slut you are not called upon to protect her name from any mistaken sense of chivalry. 'Twould not be the first time that having quarrelled with one of her gallants she has had him whipped beneath her window."

Roger recalled Angélique de Pons' warning to him on his first night in Stockholm, that Natalia had a reputation for playing malicious tricks upon her discarded beaux. Having never thought of himself as on the point of being discarded it had not recurred to him since; but it now appeared that the little Russian's sadistic manner of ter-minating her love-affairs was a habit, and comparatively well-known, so there seemed no point in lying about the matter.

"Then, Monsieur, I'll confess to having been her latest victim," he said with a rueful smile.

"I have found little time for women," remarked Count Haga, puffing out a cloud of smoke, "and from such results am glad of it."

"And I," Roger retorted crisply to this uncalled-for rudeness, "none at all for smoking a pipe. But mayhap we are both missing something."

The Prebendary had seated himself behind a desk at the end of the room and was studying some papers. He suddenly looked up and Roger, catching his startled glance, read in it an obvious fear that such a caustic comment might have given offence to his master. But the Count only laughed and cried: "*Touché!* You are a bold-spoken young man, and I like you for it."

In spite of the locked door of his room Roger felt now that he had spoken somewhat abruptly for a guest, so he replied: "Your pardon, Monsieur le Comte. Having been made such a fool of rankles with me still; but I should not have shown resentment at your remarking on the cause of my undoing, particularly as I have not yet expressed my deep gratitude to you for having saved me from those villains."

The Count waved his thanks aside. "Think no more of it, Monsieur. By a fortunate chance I happened to be coming here from my—my house across the bay, and I heard your cries. However, seeing that my intervention saved you from serious chastisement I think that, on balance, you may still consider yourself as the gainer from your commerce with the Baroness Stroganof."

"I had no reason to complain of the lady's ardour," Roger admitted, as that seemed the obvious reply.

"I meant not that," said the Count quickly. "The Baroness' temperament has not the least interest for me. I referred to all that you learned, owing to your intimacy with her, of her father's affairs."

Roger's heart missed a beat, but he managed to keep his face quite blank as he murmured: "I fear that I fail to understand you, Monsieur."

"You understand me well enough!" The Count's tone now held a threatening note. "And you had best be honest in your replies to me; for I have not yet made up my mind how I shall deal with you."

Wondering what the devil was coming next, Roger replied coldly: "You speak in riddles, Monsieur; and I resent your tone."

"You will have something more solid to complain of unless you answer my questions promptly," came the swift retort. "To start with you will admit that you are a secret agent—a spy."

"Forsooth!" cried Roger feigning intense indignation. "There are bounds even to gratitude, and the fact that you saved me from a worse beating than I got does not give you the right to bring such a charge against me. I am a simple traveller here; and, did my debt to you not forbid me, for such an insult I'd call you out."

He could not conceive any possible way in which this suspicion of his real reason for being in Sweden had arisen, but he knew that to allow it to be pinned upon him might spell ruin to his mission. Rather than submit to an interrogation he determined to make an attempt to break out. The Count and the Prebendary were both more than twice his age and neither appeared to be armed. Even incommoded as he was by his recent injuries he believed that in a free fight he would prove more than a match for the two of them. He realised that he would not be able to prevent them raising an alarm, and it was certain that there would be servants below stairs who would endeavour to prevent his escape; but with luck he might succeed in reaching the street; and once free he must now do his best to disappear from Stockholm before he could be caught, or knowledge of his activities become more general.

"Cease this pretence!" snapped the Count. "I know you for what you are! 'Tis fourteen years since I abolished torture in Sweden, but spies are without the law. Admit the reason for your being in my capital or I'll have the public executioner use the rack upon you until you do."

Aghast Roger stared at him. The connection in which he had heard the name Count Haga before now flashed into his mind. It was the incognito under which the King of Sweden had made his long tour of Italy and France four years earlier. At the thought that his fist had already been tight-clenched for the purpose of knocking Gustavus III out by a straight right to the jaw, the blood drained from his face. As befitted the revelation he sank slowly onto one knee.

"Rise, Monsieur," said the King abruptly. "Whilst in this house I prefer to be known as Count Haga. But remember; if you seek to deceive me further you do so at your peril."

"Sire!" murmured Roger, remaining on bended knee. "I beg you to forgive my temerity. Your Majesty has been absent from your capital ever since my arrival in it, and I swear that I did not know your face. I am shamed beyond words that in your august presence I should have been guilty of such rudeness."

"That has the ring of honesty, at least," Gustavus remarked, a shade less angrily. "Rise now, and tell me of yourself. That you are not French, but an Englishman, I already know."

As Roger stood up his blue eyes were wide with amazement, and he gasped: "I pray you, Sire, at least enlighten me as to how you discovered that? I had believed my French near perfect."

"It is. In fact there's little 'twixt it and my own. But when I carried you here unconscious in my coach you muttered certain English phrases. Then, on your coming round, as you were helped into the house, you changed to French and gave out that you were a Frenchman. My curiosity being aroused I told Prebendary Nordin to lock you up and take steps to ascertain the truth."

Roger had been long enough in Sweden to become familiar with the names of the King's principal advisers. During his frequent absences abroad the country was virtually ruled by a secret council of four: Johan Kristoffer Toll, a great administrator who held the post of War Minister; General Baron Armfeldt, a handsome pervert, but a man of great courage and absolute devotion to his royal master; and two clergy-men of widely differing characters. The first, Olaf Wallqvist, Bishop of Wexiö, was a masterful and eloquent prelate, whom Gustavus used to defend the royal measures in public; the second was Carl Gustaf Nordin, who at his own wish remained a simple Prebendary. The last was feared and hated by the others, since the King regarded his advice as indispensable, and always took it in secret before consulting his council.

It seemed strange that Gustavus, whose attitude towards religion was so cynical, that while he played the part of a devout Lutheran in Stockholm, he had also acted as though he was a devout Catholic when in Rome, should confide so much of his most important business to two clerics; but it was rumoured that the deeply religious, self-effacing Nordin was the only man who had the power to put a check upon the rasher schemes of the impulsive King.

It was clear to Roger now that this was Nordin's house, and that he owed his rescue to the fact that Gustavus had been on his way to visit it in the middle of the night, no doubt for the purpose of discussing the present crisis with the man who acted to him in the role of a "Grey Eminence."

As these thoughts flashed through Roger's mind the King began to speak again.

"On learning the name by which you are passing here, the Pre-bendary had your baggage collected from the Vasa Inn. Hidden in a boot in the bottom of one of your trunks he found a letter, all ready for despatch, addressed to the British Minister in Copenhagen. I read it but ten minutes since, and it gives a most lucid account of your activities here; enough, at least, to land you in a dungeon."

"In that case, Sire, there remains little of interest that I can tell you," Roger said a shade nervously. "If I have in any way contravened your laws I can only cast myself upon your mercy."

As he spoke he was berating himself for a careless fool, and felt that he must have been quite crazy to leave such a document where any determined thief might have come upon it. He decided there and then that if he managed to get out of his present scrape the experience should prove a sharp lesson to him. Never again would he pen so damn-ing a letter in advance; or, if he did, he would keep it nowhere but on his person.

But was he going to get out of his present scrape? That was the now extremely perturbing question. The usual punishment for spies con-victed during a war was death, and in peace to be locked up in a fortress for an indefinite period. The King was all-powerful and had caught him out red-handed. In the face of his own letter he could not possibly deny that he was Mr. Pitt's secret emissary. At the thought he flushed with shame. This was indeed a sorry ending to his first mission; to have given himself away through his own crass carelessness before he had even reached the focal point of his inquiry.

"As far as I am aware you have not contravened my laws," remarked Gustavus coldly. "But persons of your calling automatically make themselves outlaws when they adopt it; and, as a potential danger to any State in which they may be found, are liable to be dealt with summarily. As for your letter, it tells me much but not all that I wish to know. With what instructions did you set out from England?"

Since the King knew so much already and Roger's instructions had in no way been aimed at Sweden it seemed to him that he could do no harm by filling in the gap, so he replied: "May it please your Majesty, I was on my way to Petersburg. My visits to Copenhagen and Stockholm were for no other purpose than to provide myself with a background as to the personalities of the northern courts before appearing on the scene of my endeavours. Mr. Pitt's dearest wish is to prevent, or at least limit, future wars; and to that end he is prepared to use all means within his power. He has great hopes for his pact with France and for the new Triple Alliance which has just been brought into being; but he does not consider that those treaties should exclude his making additional ones of a similar nature with other countries. My task in Petersburg was to discover if it is still possible to revive Russia's ancient goodwill towards England, with a view to a new understanding by which the Empress Catherine would bind herself to assist in preserving the peace of northern and central Europe. And, if I found that she was adamant in her resolution to pursue her ambitious projects, to seek ways by which her aggressions might be forestalled, or the power of Russia curbed."

For the first time King Gustavus smiled. "I fear Mr. Pitt is somewhat of a visionary if he hopes to make an end to wars; and, for my part, I would not have it so, as 'twould also be the end of glory. But in this last endeavour that you speak of we are at one."

Swift to take advantage of his captor's change of mood, Roger went down on one knee again, exclaiming: "Dare I hope then, Sire, for your Majesty's clemency?"

"About that we'll see," was the non-committal reply. "Had you been of any other nationality I would have had you clapped in a dungeon ere this, and left you there to rot; but the contents of your letter and what you tell me now cause me to wonder if I cannot find a use for you."

Suddenly he swung round on the Prebendary, and asked: "What think you, Nordin?"

"If you feel that you can trust him, Majesty," answered the cleric quietly.

Gustavus looked at Roger. "Are you prepared to buy your freedom by taking service with me?"

Roger felt little beads of perspiration breaking out on his forehead. He knew that his fate lay in the balance, and that to this impatient, impulsive monarch he must make an immediate answer. At any age the thought of being cast into a dungeon, with no guarantee of ever being released, holds all the horror of a nightmare, and at the age of twenty even a violent and painful death seemed preferable. Yet he knew that there were some things he could not do if he was ever to have any respect for himself again. Rallying all the firmness he could muster, and desperately seeking the most tactful way to phrase his reply he said: "I would count it a high honour to serve so wise and gallant a King as your Majesty, were I not already committed to my own. I beg you to believe, Sire, that during my stay in Stockholm I have heard so much in praise of you from the common people, that in this I speak the honest truth."

"Well said, Monsieur!" exclaimed the King; and with a pleased glance at Nordin, he added: "See you, he is trustworthy; and I judged as much."

Turning swiftly back to Roger, he went on: "In the matter that I have in mind you can serve your own master and myself at the same time. But to start with you must disabuse yourself of the idea that you or anyone else can hope to change the nature of that she-devil Catherine. She is a born thief, and had she been bred in the gutter would have delighted even more in picking her clients' pockets than practising the monstrous whoredoms that are her very breath. As it is she has become a robber on the grand scale. She covets land and subject peoples, and will grab them at every opportunity that offers until the day of her death. You may take my royal word for that, and I am in a far better position to judge her than Mr. Pitt can ever hope to be. I have talked to her for hours at a stretch, and after my last visit to her court, in '83, I came away with the conviction that war between Sweden and Russia was inevitable. I have been planning for it and strengthening my forces ever since; by playing the part of David to Goliath is the only way we Swedes can hope to keep our independence."

There was something infectious in Gustavus's obvious conviction that he must risk everything by going to war with a far greater power in order to save his people from a foreign yoke, and Roger, realising with immense relief that he was no longer threatened with life-long incarceration in a dungeon, caught it. Forgetting for a moment that he was addressing a King, and should have waited until his opinion was asked, he cried impulsively:

"From all that I have learned while in the north I judge you right, Sire. But what of your nobility? I gravely doubt if one-tenth of them see the matter with the same clarity as yourself. They are blinded by their own petty interests, and I beg you not to count on their support."

" 'Tis true enough," declared the King. "Their mean and narrow outlook is the gravest danger that I have to face. For their own aggrandizement they would pull me down to-morrow if they had the chance. They prate of patriotism yet have not an ounce of it between the lot of them, and would rather see the Russians masters here than lift a finger to help me save the country. For nigh on seventy years the stiff-necked hide-bound aristocracy has been the curse of Sweden. Yet I

169

made myself their master when little more than a boy and I am their master still."

Gustavus's eyes were gleaming and in his excitement he began to pace up and down. Suddenly he swung round on Roger. "Did you ever hear tell, Monsieur, how I put a period to their rapacity which was bleeding the country to death, and brought them to heel?"

Roger bowed. "I have heard, Sire, that with great courage you defied your *Riksdag* in 1772 and assumed the reins of Government yourself; but never the details of how you accomplished that great feat."

"I will tell you, then," said the King, evidently delighted to have a new audience for his favourite story. "You'd scarce credit the humiliation to which the monarchy was subjected when I was a boy. My father, Adolphus Frederick, was nearer to being a figurehead of the nobles while lacking the freedom they enjoyed, than a King. He had but two votes in the Senate, no power to make peace or war, levy taxes or raise recruits; and he could not even grant new patents of nobility except on the occasion of his Coronation. His ministers were chosen for him and he was not allowed a say in the filling of any of the principal appointments of the State. My tutors were selected by the Senate; not for their learning but on account of their subservience to it, and they were changed regardless of my education each time the Caps outed the Hats or vice versa. The Palace was so full of spies that we dared not talk of our private concerns above a whisper; and my father and mother were not even allowed a voice in the choice of a wife for me. Would you believe it, Monsieur, that odious oligarchy actually picked on the sister of the mad King of Denmark as my bride; and did so out of pure malice, well knowing the hatred the two royal houses had long borne one another."

Roger made an appropriately sympathetic face. He had not known the circumstances leading up to Gustavus's marriage, and while they could not possibly excuse his abominable treatment of the unfortunate Sophia Magdalena, they certainly gave grounds for his initial prejudice against her.

"Yet the protests of all my family were of no avail," Gustavus hurried on. "I was forced to marry her whether I would or no; and, year by year we became more obviously naught but prisoners in a gilded cage. The insolence of the Senate grew to be insupportable. They took to nominating their creatures as our chaplains, ordered our clothes and decided what we should have to eat. The final limit was reached when they announced that in future they meant to dispense with the King's signature on documents of State and, instead, use a name-stamp."

Gustavus's handsome but slightly foxy face had gone a bright pink, and his prominent eyes were popping with anger as he repeated indignantly: "A name-stamp! Just think of it; a name-stamp!

"But that was too much, even for my father. He was a studious and kindly man, but a poor weak creature. I doubt if he would have jibbed even then had it not been for myself and my mother. Louisa Ulrica was a worthy sister of Frederick the Great. For her wisdom, taste and learning she well deserved the appellation of 'the Minerva of the North.' And she had courage, too; abundant courage. That rabble of a Senate feared her, and endeavoured to bring discredit on her by an accusation of sending to Berlin some of the jewels which had rightfully been presented to her from the Royal Treasury. She flung the lot back in their faces and told them to keep their trash. When the crisis arose she and I, between us, forced my father to threaten to abdicate unless they abandoned their project of the name-stamp. For a few days he feared that he would share the fate of your Charles the First; but we kept him firm, for once, and I made a personal tour of every department of State, forbidding them to act on any order that did not bear the King's written signature. The Senate found that it could not govern without even the shadow of a King, and collapsed like a pricked bubble."

Abruptly the speaker relapsed into silence, evidently becoming absorbed in his memories; so Roger, thinking it to be the end of the tale and that some comment was called for, said: "That was indeed a most satisfactory outcome to your Majesty's fine display of initiative."

"Nay, nay!" cried the King, looking up. "That was but the beginning; the testing time which taught me that when called to book the Senate were no more than a pack of craven fools. The affair of the name-stamp occurred over two years before I came to the throne. While still Crown Prince I had to bide my time, but I began to make my preparations for a *coup d'état* in secret. When my father died I was in France. The Estates busied themselves against my return by wrangling over the terms of an even more stringent coronation oath than any that had been forced upon my predecessors; those stupid babblers little knew that I was already taking measures for their overthrow. For my project I needed an ample supply of money wherewith to bribe key-men and suborn my own troops. I managed to persuade old Louis XV to subsidise me to the tune of six million *livres;* though what that cost me by way of a *pourboire* to the Du Barry, I shudder to recall."

Gustavus gave a sudden laugh. "Still, 'twas worth it; even though the Comte de Vergennes arrived as the new French Ambassador to my Court having failed to bring the first instalment with him, and I had to borrow on the promise of it from the Dutch. But I anticipate. On my return I found the Four Estates at loggerheads among themselves. Those of the Peasants, Burgesses, and Clergy were entirely dominated by the Caps, and so controlled by my enemy Catherine, who was prepared to spend a fortune as long as by so doing she could keep me in chains. Only the First Estate still showed some spark of independence; yet even in that the nobles were thinking not of the monarchy, but of themselves. Things were in the very devil of a mess, and that firebrand Count Pechlin caused me endless trouble. He was

171

an extraordinarily astute political intriguer; as dangerous, self-seeking and unscrupulous as your Charles James Fox. Do you know Mr. Fox?"

"I know him slightly, Sire," Roger bowed in answer to the abrupt question. "He has great personal charm but I consider his political machinations utterly despicable. 'Tis clear that your majesty had the most appalling difficulties to contend against."

"I had indeed. The people knew nothing then of the reforms I intended for their benefit; so the whole country was against me: except for a few nobles who had the sense to see that we were on the verge of a revolution. Yet even they thought me too young and inexperienced to handle the situation myself, and relegated me to a minor part in the *coup d'état* we planned to save the situation. However, they soon learned their mistake."

The King was silent for a minute, then he ceased his excited pacing. "Johan Kristoffer Toll and Baron Sprengtporten, Colonel of the Nyland Dragoons, were the ringleaders. The first has since become my faithful Minister; the other has turned against me. He and Count Yagerhorn are the leaders of the Finnish nobility, who wish to hand their country over to Russia."

" 'Twas Count Yagerhorn who set those rogues upon me, Sire," Roger interjected. "Despite his mask I recognised him plainly."

"That surprises me not at all, seeing that he is Russia's best-paid lackey, and tied both by interest and love, if you can call it that, to Razumofsky's daughter."

"I crave your pardon for interrupting," said Roger after a moment. "Your Majesty was saying. . . ."

"Ah, yes. The plan was that Sprengtporten should proceed to Finland, seize the fortress of Sveaborg and muster an army there. Meanwhile Toll was to secure Christianstadt as a rendezvous for our supporters in Sweden. When both had accomplished their tasks the two armies were to advance from east and south on Stockholm. Then, as Sprengtporten had the impudence to put it to his colleagues, 'we must thrust a weapon into the young King's hand and trust him to use it'."

Gustavus sniffed indignantly. "They had yet to learn that I have two weapons of my own; my sword and my tongue, and that I can use both better than most men. As so often happens with conspiracies, the affair went wrong at the last moment. Contrary winds prevented Sprengtporten from sailing, and before Toll could assemble an army at Christianstadt news of their activities leaked out to the Senate. I was left high and dry in the capital, surrounded by my enemies and with scarcely a man I could count on. On the evening of the 18th of August I learned that on the following day the Senate intended to arrest me."

For a moment the King paused dramatically; then, throwing himself into his role of hero like a born actor, he cried: "That night and the day that followed were the most exciting of my life. 'Twas my wits against those of the whole governing class of Sweden. If I won, Sweden would have a real King for the first time in seventy years; if I lost, my life would be the forfeit. But my years of secret preparation stood me in good stead. I had taken the trouble to cultivate the goodwill of a number of Army officers. While darkness lasted I sent messages requesting them to meet me the following morning in the great square facing the arsenal. Some two hundred obeyed the summons. I led them to the guardroom of the barracks and there addressed the soldiery. I spoke to them in Swedish, which no monarch had done within living memory. I made the speech of my life, painting in vivid colours the sad state into which our dear country had fallen. I ended by crying 'If you will follow me as your forefathers followed Gustavus Vasa and Gustavus Adolphus, I will venture my lifeblood for the safety and honour of my country'."

Again Gustavus paused, then he threw up his right hand. "On that they cheered me to the echo. The Senate was in secret session debating the question of my arrest. I sent a picket to lock them in, dictated a new oath of allegiance binding the troops to my person, and took possession of the artillery-yard for my headquarters. Then I tied a white handkerchief round my left arm as a mark of recognition and bade all my adherents do the same. Within the hour the whole city had donned my symbol. The gates of the capital were closed at my order, the fleet, which was lying off the Skepperholm, was secured, and I returned to my palace absolute master of the situation."

"What a triumph!" Roger could not help exclaiming in genuine admiration.

The King's eyes gleamed. "Ah, but my crowning triumph took place two days later. On the 20th I sent out heralds to proclaim that the Four Estates should meet in the *Riksaal* at four o'clock the following afternoon. On the 21st I had my troops line the streets of the city and one hundred cannon trained on the *Riksaal* with a grenadier behind each holding ready a lighted match. My terrified enemies crept to the meeting place in twos and threes. When they had assembled I appeared before them in my full regalia and from the throne trounced them for their lack of patriotism. Then I read to them the new Constitution, which I had already prepared with my own hand. Not one of those loud-tongued bullies who, all my life, had treated me with such insolence, had the courage to say a single word in protest. To a man they swore to keep the new Constitution inviolable, and at last there was a real King in Sweden once more."

With that tact which was one of Roger's greatest assets he again went down on one knee, as the most suitable way in which he could express his admiration for the royal actor.

Nothing could have pleased Gustavus more, and this time he gave Roger a friendly pat on the shoulder, as he said: "Rise, Chevalier; or perhaps I should say Mr. Brook, since it was in that name you signed your letter. We still have much to discuss before morning, and the night advances."

As Roger obeyed he said with feeling: "Your story, Sire, has but

173

added to the high admiration I had already conceived for your Majesty's courage and abilities. This detailed knowledge of your brave handling of the discontented nobility in '72 also gives me more confidence that if the need arises you will again succeed in circumventing their evil machinations. And in that was my greatest fear for you should it be your royal will to go to war with Russia."

"It is my royal will," declared the King proudly. "The die is cast, and I sail for Finland on the 24th."

Prebendary Nordin gave a deferential but warning cough.

Gustavus swung round towards him. "Be easy, my friend. We know from this young man's letter to Mr. Elliot that his interests march with our own. If he is to be of any value to us he must trust him, or he will not know how to serve us best."

Roger bowed. "I thank you, Sire, and vow that I will never abuse any confidence which you may do me the honour to make me. May I be permitted to inquire if Count Razumofsky has yet been officially informed of your intention to go to war with his country?"

A crafty smile flickered over Gustavus's thin lips. "The Count made his *démarche* to-day. He demanded to know the reason for our military preparations and seemed mightily perturbed about them. He has good cause for his anxiety, seeing that the Empress has entirely denuded her Finnish frontier in order to reinforce her armies on the Black Sea. She knows my hatred of her and of my alliance with the Turks; but she counts upon my not daring to declare openly against her without the sanction of my Estates, and relies upon her paid hirelings in them to thwart me. 'Twas clear to me that Razumofsky counts upon that too, and believes that I intend only a gigantic bluff for the purpose of drawing pressure off my allies. I gave him fresh grounds for continuing to think it."

A little shocked at such duplicity, Roger murmured: "Then your Majesty has no intention of sending the Czarina an ultimatum; and intends to attack her without warning?"

The King nodded. " 'Tis a chance in a lifetime, and I am not the man to miss it. With the Finnish frontier virtually undefended I'll be at the gates of Petersburg within a month; and that proud, evil woman will have no option but to submit to such terms as I'll dictate— unless she wants her capital burned about her ears. But I told Razumofsky that I intended only to journey to Finland to make further inspections of my troops, and that I had no mind to offer any fuller explanation until I arrived there."

Roger smiled, which brought the swift question: "What matter do you see for merriment in that, Monsieur?"

"Knowing the Russian, Sire, I was thinking how baffled and angry he must have been at receiving so ambiguous an answer."

"Aye, he was angry as a bull before which a matador waves a red cloak." Gustavus gave an abrupt laugh. "But I gave him more reason for that than I have so far said. For once I allowed myself the pleasure of carrying the war into the enemy's camp. I accused him of fomenting internal treachery here, and aiming at sowing discord between my people and myself. Then I ordered him to leave my Kingdom."

"If I may be permitted to say so, Sire, 'twas a bold step; for is not the dismissal of an Ambassador without asking for him to be recalled by his own Court almost tantamount to a declaration of war? Will not the Empress read your intention in it?"

"Nay, I made it a personal matter; and by the time he reached Petersburg 'twould be too late for anything that the Empress might deduce from his return to be of value to her. I was anxious to have him out of the way before I left Stockholm myself. But, unfortunately he foiled me in that. He declared that he would accept his dismissal from his post only on receiving a direct order signed by his Imperial mistress. 'Twould bring discredit on my Crown to seize the person of an Ambassador and forcibly put him aboard a ship; so he remains. But to some extent I have curbed his power to do mischief in my absence. I insisted that, apart from his personal servants, all his staff should go, and his daughter too, since she is one of his principal links with those of my subjects who conspire against me. For the purpose I have placed a ship at their disposal, and she will sail on the afternoon tide to-morrow."

"Have I your leave, Sire, to add a postscript, reporting these latest moves, to my letter to Mr. Elliot?"

"*Mort dieu*, Monsieur! You lack not for boldness," exclaimed the King, pausing in his stride. "You should consider yourself plaguey fortunate to have escaped a prison, and I am amazed at your effrontery in even thinking that I would permit you to despatch your letter."

Roger put on his most disarming smile. "I beg your Majesty to reconsider this matter. We are agreed, I think, that while serving you I should not cease to serve my own Sovereign. But, apart from that, there is the question of a long-term policy, to which I humbly draw your attention. This war that you plan with Russia should result in curbing her power in the North, and that well suits the interests of Britain. Therefore, it seems to me, that, in an emergency, your Majesty would have a good case to claim my country's support. Should such an emergency arise I feel sure, Sire, that your chances of obtaining aid from Britain will be far greater if you have, from the beginning, allowed me to keep Mr. Pitt informed as to your projects and your prospects."

Obviously struck with the idea, the King turned to Nordin and asked abruptly: "What think you, Prebendary?"

"I think, Sire, that this young man has a good head on his shoulders," replied the cleric. "I have his letter here; and should you decide to accede to his request, when he has added a postscript under my supervision, I will see that the document is sent to Copenhagen by a safe hand."

"So be it then," Gustavus nodded to Roger. "And now for your instructions. You will proceed to Petersburg with the minimum of delay, using your French identity, and find out all you can which may prove to my advantage. The Russian capital is within two days' ride of the Finnish frontier, and no regular guards are maintained for the interception of travellers passing between the two countries. When you have aught of interest to report go over into Finland. On arriving there, and not before, set your news down on paper. Sign such notes only with an initial—E for Englishman will serve; superscribe them to me and mark them as of the utmost urgency. Seal them carefully and hand them to the first Swedish officer you may come upon for immediate transmission to my headquarters. Have I made myself clear?"

"You have, Sire," Roger bowed. "But surely once hostilities commence the frontier will be closed and pickets posted along it?"

"They will not interfere with the passage of a neutral. Moreover, I do not desire you to make the journey often; only when you have something to convey which you consider to be of prime importance, so there should be no grounds for them becoming suspicious of you through your crossing with any frequency."

"One other point, Sire," Roger said a trifle hesitantly. "If I set out instantly, as your Majesty commands, I must leave Stockholm without such letters of introduction from the French Ambassador, and others, as I would normally have carried with me. Lack of them will almost certainly delay my securing a foothold in Petersburg society, and thus swiftly becoming well-placed for being of service to you."

The King pinched his slightly receding chin between his fingers and thumb, and remained thoughtful for a moment; then he replied: " 'Tis something of a quandary. I would have you there as soon as possible, and you could have sailed to-morrow in one of the sloops that is to act as escort to the ship which is transporting the personnel from the Russian Embassy. Yet I think your contention sound. On balance 'twould be worth your dallying in Stockholm for a few days to arrive in Petersburg well accredited."

"It is most unfortunate that Mr. Brooks should have quarrelled with the Baroness Stroganof," remarked the Prebendary, glancing up from his papers. "For she could have launched him in Petersburg society with greater *réclame* than any number of letters could do."

Roger snapped his fingers. "I have it, Sire! Why should I not sail in the same ship as the Baroness?"

"I fail to see how that could serve you," Gustavus said, with a frown. "In view of her recent treatment of you 'tis clear that she has no further use for your attentions. Did you do as you suggest it would result only in her making of you a figure of public mockery when you reach Petersburg, with a tale of having had you whipped."

"Unless I take some steps to prevent it, she may do that on my arrival, in any case," Roger argued. "Let me make the voyage with her, Sire, and I vow I'll find a way, not only to stop her tongue but to make her serve our ends."

The King shot him a suspicious look. "I believe you are still in love with the wench, and are prepared to swallow your humiliation for the sake of a chance to plead your cause anew?"

"Nay, Sire. I pledge your Majesty my word that I am not. On the contrary I've an itch to be revenged upon her; and how could I be so better than by making her my catspaw?"

"As you will, then. The Prebendary will make the necessary arrangements for your accommodation in the ship."

"I thank your Majesty." Roger bowed and turned to the cleric. "I am anxious, Monsieur, that neither the Baroness nor any of her people should be aware of my presence on board until the ship is well out at sea. Could you ensure that for me?"

The Prebendary nodded his close-cropped head. "The Captain is discreet and will accept my orders; but it will mean your going aboard very early in the morning and lying hid in a cabin all day."

"I'll count that no hardship; and trust it will not cause you serious inconvenience to make arrangements for me at such an hour."

"Best use my coach and take him down to the port now," the King remarked to Nordin. "We'll have the matter done with then, and on your return can proceed with our private business."

Nordin rose to his feet and bowed. "A wise decision, Sire; for while darkness lasts there is even less likelihood of anyone seeing us board the ship, and talking of it afterwards, than there would be at break of day. The letter for Mr. Elliot is here. Perhaps Mr. Brook would like to write his postscript to it while I have his baggage carried down in readiness for his departure."

On the King signifying his approval, Roger took the Prebendary's place at the desk and added the final lines to his letter. Gustavus looked over his shoulder as he wrote and, when he had done, murmured: "I've no objection to that. Nordin shall send your missive by special courier, so it should be in Copenhagen within forty-eight hours."

A few minutes later the Prebendary returned to announce that all was in readiness. King Gustavus was smiling now and, exerting all the charm which he could command when he wished, he held out his hand to Roger, but would not allow him to kneel and kiss it.

"Nay," he said gently. "I feel that I have made a good friend to-night. Let us shake hands, Mr. Brook, in your English fashion."

Roger smiled frankly in response, took the royal hand and bowed over it as he murmured: "I thank your Majesty for the clemency and honour you have shown me. You may rest assured, Sire, that I will do my utmost to merit it."

Five minutes later he was with Nordin in the plain closed carriage, arranging for his reckoning at the Vasa Inn to be settled and to have his black mare stabled there until his return. Within half an hour they were being rowed out to a full-rigged ship that lay at anchor in the bay.

On their going aboard, the night-watchman roused the Captain from his bunk. He proved to be a taciturn, thick-set Swede, whose second language was German; but he accepted Prebendary Nordin's instructions with deference and quick understanding, after which the

Prebendary and Roger took leave of one another with discreet good wishes on both sides.

Roger then held a halting conversation in German with the Captain, who took him down to a small cabin, where they superintended his baggage being stowed away, and afterwards on a short tour of the ship's passenger accommodation. In the principal stateroom, which had naturally been allocated to Natalia Andreovna, Roger observed a roomy hanging-cupboard, that he felt would serve for the plan he had already formed. He also learned that she would take her meals with the Captain; then, having apologised to that worthy for having roused him from his bed, he wished him good night.

It was not until he was undressing that he suddenly realised that he had had no supper, and now felt hungry; but he was loath to disturb the Captain again, and endeavouring to comfort himself with the old adage that 'he who sleeps, dines,' he crawled into his bunk.

On thinking over the events of the past few hours he decided that he was extremely lucky to be where he was instead of in a prison-cell. Once more he told himself that in this new career of his he must exercise far more caution if he was to avoid coming to grief, and being cut off from all the joys of life while still in the flower of his youth.

He felt sure that King Gustavus would not have dealt so leniently with him had it not been in his interests to do so, and it was very certain that if the Empress Catherine caught him out she would show him no mercy.

The thought brought home to him the fact that he was now as good as on the last lap of his journey to Russia, and he wondered what the fates held in store for him in that strange, exotic, semi-barbarous country.

He wondered too, just what Natalia Andreovna would have to say to him when he disclosed himself to her. She would almost certainly regard his presence in the ship as a most unwelcome surprise. So long as they remained at sea she could do him little harm, but once they landed in Russia she would be complete mistress of the situation. If she cared to pursue the vindictive policy she had recently adopted, owing, as it appeared, to her belief that he had been unfaithful to her, no doubt her influence in her own country was quite sufficient to have him thrown into prison on some trumped-up charge.

A little belatedly he realised that, in having acted on a sudden impulse to inflict himself on her as a fellow-passenger during her voyage home, he had given himself as a hostage to fortune. He had gambled, without due thought, on his wits being sharper than hers. If he could succeed in fooling or beguiling her, all would be well; but if he failed it seemed now that he might well be called on to pay a high price for his rashness.

With this perturbing thought he fell into an uneasy sleep.

CHAPTER XII

UNMASKED AGAIN

WHEN Roger woke it was a little before midday. For a second he wondered how in the world he came to be in a ship's cabin; then his arrival on board with Prebendary Nordin in the early hours of the morning and the events which had followed the attack beneath Natalia Andreovna's balcony, rushed back to him.

Again he was seized with apprehension at the thought that he had placed himself in the power of the slim, green-eyed Russian for whom he felt at the same time such a strong attraction and repulsion. He was like a man who, in a tropical jungle, comes upon a gloriously-hued flower which he knows perfectly well exudes a deadly miasma, yet finds the temptation to examine it closely almost irresistible. He had toyed with this poisonous blossom for a time with complete impunity, only to receive a sudden violent reminder of its toxic emanations, and now he had deliberately put himself in a situation where there was no escape from the proximity of this fascinating but evil flower.

His first spontaneous idea had been to get aboard the ship in which she was being expelled from Sweden and tell her that, learning of her expulsion, his love for her was so great that he could not bear to part with her; and so had bribed his way aboard to accompany her to Russia.

On the other hand, he now felt, such an abject admission of her power over him might satiate her vanity to a point where she would despise him. If so, instead of assisting him when they reached Russia, she might find fresh grounds for malicious amusement in persecuting him.

Suddenly he became conscious that he was ravenously hungry, and remembered that he had not eaten for close on twenty hours. Jumping from his narrow bunk he pulled on his clothes, then cautiously opened the cabin-door.

The ship was still riding at anchor and no sound suggesting the arrival of passengers came from above decks. Stepping out into the passage he mounted the first companionway he came upon, and, gaining the upper deck saw the Captain leaning idly on the rail of the poop.

As Roger approached, the Captain straightened and greeted him with a slow smile. After the usual courtesies had been exchanged, Roger said: "'Tis many hours, Sir, since I have eaten, so I should be grateful for a meal. Moreover, as Prebendary Nordin informed you, there are certain duties I am called upon to perform whilst in your ship. Should it meet with your convenience I'd be glad of the opportunity to have a word with you about them while I regale myself on such fare as your cook can offer me."

The Captain nodded. "The hour of your rising is well chosen, Chevalier. In ten minutes my own meal is due, and a second cover is easily laid. May it please you to accompany me to the stateroom."

They descended to the main cabin beneath the poop and were soon seated opposite one another at the single long, narrow table. When the cabin boy had served the first dish Roger said in carefully thought-out German:

"I am, as you know, in the service of King Gustavus. My mission is a somewhat delicate one. I am already acquainted with the Baroness Stroganof but have quarrelled with her. 'Tis necessary that I should regain her confidence. To that end I plan to take strong measures. While she is at supper I intend to conceal myself in her cabin, and later surprise her there. There will be a scene and she may shout for help to have me turned out. I give you my word that I will do your passenger no harm, but 'tis essential that we should not be interrupted. Can you arrange to ensure that for me?"

The Captain considered for a moment, then he replied: "As you are already aware I am giving her my own cabin, which lies behind this. All the other Russians will be accommodated below decks, so 'tis unlikely that they would hear her shouts. The officer of the watch, the helmsman, and any other members of the crew who happen to be about might do so; but I could place a sentry on the passage leading to her stateroom, with orders that no one is to be allowed to pass."

"Excellent," smiled Roger. "Please do so; but not until her maid and all the other Russians have retired to bed; then, late to-night, when we are well at sea, I'll venture on my attempt to make her see reason. In the meantime it is important that none of the Russians should know of my presence on board. So I shall remain in my own cabin, and should be grateful if you would send me down some supper."

Matters having been thus satisfactorily arranged they talked for a little of affairs in Sweden, then Roger borrowed a few books from the Captain, with a view to improving his German, and retired to his self-imposed confinement.

Soon after four o'clock the sounds of shouting overhead told him that the boats bringing off the party from the Russian Embassy had come alongside. Then half an hour later there came the clanking of chains as the anchor was weighed, and a slight rolling of the ship as her unfurled sails were caught by the wind. Gradually the bustle subsided and at a steady pace the ship ploughed her way out to sea.

Eight bells, terminating the second dog watch, had only just sounded when the Captain poked his head through the door of Roger's cabin, and said to him:

"Your meal will be coming down in a few minutes now, Chevalier, and the Baroness will be leaving her stateroom to sup with me. Her maid feeds below decks in a mess that I have arranged for the Russian servants; so for the next hour or so your way will be clear."

Roger smiled his thanks and soon after the Captain had left him he was despatching a hearty meal washed down with a bottle of toler-

ably good Bordeaux. Immediately he had finished he went up on deck, loitered under the break of the poop for a few moments with apparent casualness, then stepped into the narrow passage and tiptoed along it to Natalia's stateroom. It was a low but large apartment shaped like a bow, with six small-paned windows in its curved extremity looking out onto the foaming wake of the ship. Beneath the sloping windows there ran a long curved plush-covered settee with lockers under it, and instead of the usual bunk there was a large, low, box-like bed screwed to the deck. A table occupied the middle of the room and a commodious desk was fixed to one of the walls; a Turkey carpet on the floor, and the red patterned curtains framing the windows, gave the place a comfortable air, which was now the greater from having Natalia's belongings scattered about it.

Roger made straight for the big cupboard that he had noticed the previous night. The four hours since they had sailed had evidently been sufficient for Natalia's unpacking, as hanging from hooks in it there were now a score or more of her dresses. But behind them there was still ample room for him to conceal himself, and appreciatively sniffing the heady scent she used, he squeezed his way through the silken screen; then he drew the door to after him and settled himself as comfortably as he could on the floor.

Some half-hour later he heard the cabin-door open and light footsteps moving about the room. He thought it a fair bet that Natalia had returned from her supper, but he made no move to leave his hiding-place, as it might have been her maid.

After another ten minutes the door opened again and two voices came so clearly to him that he could have caught every word they said had he understood Russian; but he knew the tones of both so well that he recognised them at once as those of Natalia Andreovna and the girl who had been in her bed on his first midnight visit to the Russian Embassy.

For over an hour, he sat in the close, hot darkness, while they continued a desultory conversation and moved about, evidently arranging the stateroom to Natalia's liking. Then he heard them exchange two of the Russian sentences that he had picked up on his visits to the Embassy: "Good night; good rest," said one; and the other replied: "May St. Nicholas guard you while sleeping." The door closed behind the maid with a sharp clack, and a sudden silence ensued which led him to judge that Natalia must now be in bed.

He could not see his watch but thought it to be about a quarter past ten, so that most of the ship's company, apart from the duty-watch, would have turned in; but he decided to wait a further quarter of an hour, as the fewer people who heard any commotion the little Russian might make on his appearance, the better.

This last wait seemed interminable, but at length he decided that the time had come to act, so he cautiously stood up and flexed his cramped limbs. The slight noise he made in pushing his way through the dresses and opening the door of the cupboard a crack was covered

181

by the hissing of the sea, as it rushed past the stern of the ship, and the creaking of her timbers.

By pushing the door open a little further he could see across the cabin. It was still broad daylight outside, but the red curtains had been drawn, giving the room a warm subdued twilight. Natalia Andreovna was lying on her back in the broad box-like bed with her eyes shut.

As Roger looked across at her he wondered with grim humour if he would share it with her for the rest of the night or if she would prove adamant and drive him from her. On that, or rather, on the next half hour everything depended. He knew that he would have to fight a battle-royal with her which would require all his wits and courage if he was to emerge victorious. He had had ample time to make up his mind on the policy he meant to pursue, and intended to burn his boats by not only charging her with her perfidy but punishing her for it. Such a grasping of the nettle, he felt, offered the only chance of gaining a mental ascendancy over her; but if it failed she would have real cause to vent her spite on him, and he would find himself in the very devil of a mess when they landed in Russia.

Thrusting the door wide he stepped out into the room. Natalia was not asleep. She sat up with a start, and failing to recognise him for a moment in the dim light, cried sharply in German: "Who are you? How did you get into my room?"

" 'Tis I, Rojé Christorovitch!" he replied harshly, advancing towards the bed. "Surely you did not think to throw off a man of my metal with impunity?"

She stared at him, her eyes widening with sudden fear; but her voice was steady as she demanded: "How did you come to be aboard this ship?"

" 'Twas the talk of the town this noon that King Gustavus had ordered you and the staff of the Russian Embassy out of his country. I had no sooner heard it than I came off to the frigate and persuaded the Captain to give me a passage in her."

"With what intent? What do you want with me?"

His laugh was tinged with bitterness. "That should not be hard for you to guess."

"Your face is hard and cold, Rojé Christorovitch." Her voice faltered a little. "I have never seen you so before. Can it—can it be that your love for me has turned to hate; and that you have sought me out to be revenged upon me for that which occurred after our last meeting? If so, I swear to you that it was none of my fault."

"You lie," he said tersely.

"Nay," she protested, her long fingers clutching nervously at the sheets. "The commotion in the street below fetched me out onto my balcony, and I saw that you were attacked. But 'twas all over in a few moments, and I saw you rescued by the stranger in the coach. Otherwise I would have roused the Embassy and brought you aid."

"You lie," he repeated. "You stood there laughing at the vile sport you had planned for your own diversion. I both saw and heard you whilst I fought. And the leader of my attackers was Count Yager-horn. I knew him by his voice. Believing me to have been unfaithful to you with Angélique de Pons you deliberately set your ex-lover on to give me a whipping before your eyes."

Seeing that he knew too much for there to be any sense in deny-ing it further, she flared with sudden anger: "Well, what if I did? I warned you when I took you for my lover that I'd give you cause to rue it if you betrayed me with another. From your first night in Stock-holm you had a fancy for that French bitch. You admitted that you had been to her birthday-party, and you failed to keep our midnight tryst. In Sweden only big functions are kept up so late; 'twas proof enough that you had remained on, or gone back afterwards. I know the Marquis to have been in Gothenbörg, and 'twas too good a chance for the pair of you not to take a tumble in her bed."

He shook his head. "In that you wrong both myself and Angélique. 'Tis true I was unable to keep my midnight tryst with you, since the party was on the French model and a late one; yet in that lies the very proof of my innocence. We kept it up till past four o'clock, and I then returned to the city in company with the six other guests, who would vouch for dropping me at my inn. 'Twas full daylight already and, even had I left my inn again to return to the French Embassy, by the time I had got there the servants would have been up and about, so there was nought of the night left to make love in."

"I care not," she muttered sullenly. " 'Tis my opinion that my suspicions were fully justified by your having failed to be at my disposal at the usual place and time. I warned you that I should take it ill should you ever fail in that."

"I've not forgotten it," he snapped. "But at least you should have had the decency to first accuse me to my face, and seek to verify your suspicions before setting your bullies on to me. To conceal your evil thoughts beneath false smiles, and let me lie with you after you had already planned to have me treated worse than a dog, was a most shameful thing to do."

"Nay," she protested with an outrageous frankness that quite took him aback. "How otherwise could I have ensured your being out-side the postern-gate at dawn and getting the beating I believed you to deserve?"

"But, damn it!" Roger gasped. "Have you no understanding of the baseness of such an act?"

She shook her head. "I know only that I had wanted you the night before and believing you to be in the arms of another was rendered half-mad from jealousy. At two o'clock, since you had not come, and I could not beat you, I pulled my maid from her bed and beat her instead. But I vowed that I'd make you pay for the misery you had caused me before another night was past, and laid my plans accord-ingly."

Roger scowled at her thin, sullen face below him, and the thought that the wretched maid had been beaten for no fault of her own added fresh fuel to his anger.

" 'Tis over-time that someone put a check upon your vicious habits," he stormed. "Have you never a thought but for yourself? Did it not occur to you that in such an ambush as you planned someone might have lost his life? You knew that I carried a cutlass and would be certain to use it; but with five of those rogues against me I might well have received a mortal wound myself."

She shrugged her slim shoulders. "I loved you passionately and thought that you loved me no longer; so had you been killed I should have suffered less than in believing that you had cast me off and that another was the recipient of your caresses."

"Love!" he snarled. "You do not even begin to know the meaning of the word!" And he slapped her hard with the flat of his hand across the face.

He had wrought himself up into a temper, yet his anger was nothing near so great as it appeared; and the blow was not delivered spontaneously, but as a set-piece in an act that he had worked out with great care several hours before. He meant to break her spirit if he could, and had decided that in offering her violence lay his only real chance of making her his submissive puppet by the time they reached Russia.

White and shaken she recoiled from the blow with a little gasp. Then her mouth opened to let out a scream. With a second slap he checked it, so that her cry was half-strangled in her throat.

Squirming away from him she choked out a torrent of abuse mingled with the most terrifying threats. "You filthy Frenchman! By the death of God you shall pay for this. Son of a whore, how dare you strike me in the face! Wait only until we reach Russia, you gutter-bred parvenu, and I'll have the Empress's Cossacks ply their knouts upon you till you're flayed alive!"

"We are not in Russia yet," he said curtly. "And before we get there I mean to teach you how a decent woman should behave herself."

"You'll teach me nothing!" she screamed. "You'll not have the chance. I'll rouse the ship and have the Captain put you in irons for making an assault upon me."

Swift as an eel she slid out of bed. He grabbed at her shoulder and caught her night-robe, but it ripped right down to the waist, and half-naked, she dashed towards the door with Roger in hot pursuit.

Before she could get it open he was upon her. Grasping her wrist he gave it a violent jerk, which swung her round and sent her crashing to the floor. Swiftly he shot the bolt, then turned again towards her.

She was already on her feet and had kicked herself free of her trailing night-robe. Agile as a panther, she bounded across the room towards the heavy desk, wrenched open one of its upper drawers and grabbed a long, curved knife. Before he could get within two yards of her she had whipped round and flashed the glittering blade before his eyes.

Roger halted abruptly in his tracks. For a moment they both

remained motionless, glaring at one another. Even in that moment of crisis he could not but catch his breath at the violent beauty of the figure she made. She had not a stitch of clothing on her slim, lissome body but her long, silvery-blonde hair hung like a cloak about her shoulders and half-way down her back. Her small breasts heaved violently with stress and emotion, and her green eyes blazed at him with the fury of a trapped animal.

He felt certain that she meant to kill him if she could, yet he dared not back down now. To have shown a trace of fear or attempted to temporise would have spelled certain disaster. Even if it meant an ugly wound he had got to get the knife from her; otherwise there could be no reconciliation, and within a week she would carry out her threat to have him knouted to death. She was not the woman to forget an injury. Immunity from her vengeance could be secured only by subduing her completely. He had gambled on being able to do that, and now he must go through with it or pay the forfeit.

Suddenly it came to him that, for these next few moments, he must forget that she was a woman, and deal with her as he would a drunken sailor who attempted to knife him in a brawl. So far he had merely slapped her; but now he must hit her in good earnest as the only means of preventing her from giving him an ugly wound.

As he clenched his fists and raised them her eyes widened with astonished dismay. His left shot out straight for her face and she flung herself back against the desk in an attempt to escape the blow. But it was only a feint and did not even touch her. Before she could recover her balance his right landed with a thud in the middle of her stomach.

Her mouth gaped open as the breath was driven from her body. A spasm of pain shot across her features, and dropping the knife, she clutched wildly at the place where his blow had landed, doubled up, then slid gasping to the floor.

Roger kicked the knife away well out of her reach, picked her up and threw her on the bed. For a minute he stood watching her as she writhed there, but he knew that he had only winded her and the moment she got her breath back she would be cursing and threatening him again; so he decided that now was the time to go through with the distasteful task he had set himself.

Striding across the room to a cloak-rack near the door he took from it the stoutest of Natalia Andreovna's three long parasols. By the time he got back to the bed her writhing had ceased; she was lying there panting heavily and staring up at him with a strange expression in her eyes. Ignoring her glance he grabbed the hair on the top of her head with his left hand. Instantly she clawed at it with her long nails in an effort to free herself, but she could do no more than scratch him, and twisting her head round sideways he forced her over onto her face. Then he set about belabouring her bottom with the parasol in no half-hearted manner.

For a few moments she bore her beating stoically, alternatively gritting her teeth and snarling curses at him. Then she began to shout

185

for help, but he forced her face down into the pillow, half-muffling her cries. Next she started to beg for mercy, but he ignored her pleas and continued to belabour her. At last she ceased to curse, struggle and plead, went suddenly limp beneath his grip and burst into a flood of tears.

Only then did he stop, and, throwing the parasol on the floor, stood back from her, panting as a result of his exertions.

She did not move but continued to lie there with her face buried in the pillows, sobbing as though her heart would break. When he had recovered his breath he slowly began to undress, intent now on completing his plan for her subjugation.

He hated the thought of taking her against her will, but not from any moral scruple. He had had her first, and many times since, with her eager consent; so this would have no semblance to a violation. But he disliked the thought of forcing a woman in any circumstances, and, moreover, believed that he had now come to far the most difficult part of the battle that he was waging; since, should she prove really stubborn, and refuse to respond to his passion by finally melting in his arms, all that had gone before would count for nothing. They would part still unreconciled and himself inevitably become the victim of her unappeasable hatred.

Yet in this his fears were groundless. Had he lived in Russia for years and been an expert on Russian character and customs he could not have dealt more effectively with her than he had already done. As he laid his hand upon her shoulder she turned over of her own accord, smiled up at him from tear-dimmed eyes and, choking back her sobs, murmured:

"Oh, Rojé Christorovitch, how deeply you must love me, to beat me so."

"Indeed I love you," he replied; and looking down on her thus he almost believed he meant it as he went on: "Surely you do not think that I would have left Sweden at a moment's notice for the sole purpose of paying you out by giving you a beating. You are a wicked child, and it seems that like a fond parent I needs must be stern with you for your own betterment. But I determined at once to sail in this ship because I could not bear to be parted from you."

"Yet you have found the way to my heart," she sighed contentedly. "All that you needed to be a perfect lover was the violence of a Russian. You were too soft, too considerate, too woman-like before. You allowed me to bully you unmercifully without complaint, and that is wrong. No woman of my country ever believes that her man truly loves her unless he beats her now and then. Even the Empress Catherine has taken her beatings from the Orlofs' Potemkin and other favourites, and loved them for it all the more. Rojé Christorovitch, you are now my master and I your slave. Lie down here while I kneel at your feet and you, my lord, shall tell me how best I may pleasure you this night."

Roger knew then that he had achieved a victory beyond his wildest dreams. Their reconciliation was in keeping with the violence of their previous feelings and when, at last, their emotions were spent Natalia Andreovna wept again; but this time from sheer joy, and in the small hours she sobbed herself happily to sleep in Roger's arms.

From then on everything about the four-day voyage went as merry as a marriage-bell. Roger came out into the open as Natalia's cavalier, and henceforth took his meals with her, the Captain, and two Secretaries of the Embassy, whom King Gustavus had compelled Count Razumofsky to send home. One, Vladimir Paulovitch Lepekhin, was a tall, dark, amusing young man and the other, Dr. Drenke, was a fat, kindly, blue-eyed German of middle age, who had spent many years in the Russian service. Roger had, of course, already met both of them on numerous occasions, and together they formed a merry party.

The weather was excellent and the sea like a mill-pond. On the evening of Sunday, the 24th of June, they ploughed their way steadily up the Gulf of Finland, and late that night, dropped anchor in Crondstadt Bay. The following morning the Russian authorities came aboard and gave the Swedish frigate permission to proceed up the channel to St. Petersburg for greater convenience in landing Natalia Andreovna and her party. As a member of it Roger went ashore with the others, and by eleven o'clock, found himself at last in the Imperial city where lay the focus of his secret mission.

Natalia was in duty bound to take up her residence in the palace of her grandfather, Count Cyril Razumofsky. The Empress Elizabeth, whose lover he had been, had made him Hetman of the Cossacks, and later he had played a leading part in the *coup d'état* that had placed Catherine on the throne. But he was now old, crotchety and abhorred strangers; so, although it had at first been mooted that Roger should be her guest there, they decided that it would be wiser for him to take lodgings in the city.

Naturally he refrained from saying so, but this suited him much better, as he was far from wishing to place himself in a situation where he would have to account to his beautiful mistress for all his comings and goings.

In the matter of a suitable lodging Dr. Drenke offered his assistance. He retained two rooms on the third floor of a house in a turning off the Nevsky, and thought that his landlord would be able to find Roger accommodation either in the same house or nearby. In consequence, having arranged with Natalia that she should let him hear from her through the Doctor, he took affectionate leave of her, and set off from the wharf in a *droshky* with the amiable German.

Roger knew that St. Petersburg was still less than a hundred years old; that it had been built with immense labour, and at the cost of thousands of lives, on countless piles driven deep into the boggy marshes at the mouth of the Neva; and that this extraordinarily unsuitable site had been chosen for the city solely because Peter the Great had desired a capital in which he could supervise the building

187

of his beloved Navy. He was, therefore, all the more astounded at its size and magnificence.

The only remaining traces of the marshes were the numerous canals and rivulets intersecting the city, and these were spanned at frequent intervals by stout wooden bridges gaily painted in different colours. Such narrow, twisting streets and noisome alleys as composed almost the whole of London, Paris and Stockholm were entirely absent, and even the open modern Danish capital was a mere model village compared to this splendid metropolis.

The main thoroughfares had been laid out with a prodigal disregard of space and were grand boulevards on a scale that he had never even imagined. On either side of them were raised footways, so that pedestrians could traverse the town dry-shod during the autumn floods. The majority of the smaller houses were made of the native timber, but on every side there arose vast palaces of stone which housed the Government departments and the families of the aristocracy.

When they arrived at the doctor's lodging they found that the first-floor suite, consisting of a bedroom and sitting-room, was free, and the landlord, a Courlander named Ostermann, agreed to let it to Roger for three roubles a week, which, as the rouble was then the equivalent of four shillings, he considered very cheap; but he was soon to learn that living in St. Petersburg was far less expensive than in London or Paris. He could have his meals sent in from a nearby pastrycook's and would provide his own servant, but Ostermann undertook to find one for him by that evening.

Roger knew that German was the language most frequently spoken in St. Petersburg, and he had already mastered it sufficiently to understand beyond chance of mistake when Ostermann asked him: "By what military rank shall I address your nobleness?"

He was about to reply "None," when Dr. Drenke intervened, and explained. "Since Russia is an autocracy every Russian is given a military grade. For example, the Empress's chief cook and chief coachman are both colonels. Since you are of noble birth you will automatically be classed as an officer, and you must get yourself an officer's cockade to wear in your hat, as you will find that all the common people pay great respect to that symbol. The usual practice with foreigners is to grade them on their income; so, tell me please, how much you are worth a year?"

Since it was essential to his mission to cut a good figure at the court, Roger thought it well to rate himself as a thousand-a-year man; so he replied, "Five thousand roubles."

"You are wealthy then," the doctor smiled, "and with such an income cannot be ranked as less than a Major-General." While Ostermann, obviously much impressed, made his new lodger a deep obeisance, then hurried away to carry up his baggage.

The doctor then invited Roger to dine with him, and they adjourned to the pastrycook's along the street. Roger had eaten caviare on a few occasions with Georgina, as a rare delicacy, but only the pressed variety which, packed in ice, was the kind then exported; but now he was given a plateful of the large grained grey *ikra* which comes from the Ural river, and he tucked into it most heartily. This rich *hors d'œuvre* was followed by a hare, baked whole. While they made a skeleton of it the Doctor sent out to have some money changed for him, and when it came back, explained the values of the Russian currency.

A gold Imperial, their two-pound piece, was worth ten roubles, and a half-Imperial, five. The silver consisted of roubles, half-roubles, quarter roubles and twenty, fifteen and ten cent coins; the copper of five, two, one, a half, and even a quarter, kopecks; so there seemed to be a coin suitable to every possible requirement.

Doctor Drenke then went on to speak of the Russians and some of their customs. "So great a respect have they for St. Nicholas," he remarked, "that they never pray to God except through him; and in the living-room of every house there is an *ikon* of the Saint, to which visitors are always expected to bow before greeting their host. On the other hand they are far from being a religious people in the western sense. They observe the celebrations of their church with much pomp, but do not give to their clergy, except for the higher dignitaries, the status of gentry. In the main they are drunken, untrustworthy, and extremely immoral. You will find a certain attraction about their childish, inconsequent gaiety, and they will tell you the most barefaced falsehoods in their eagerness to make a good impression on you; yet they will cheat you at every turn if they possibly can. The only way to earn their respect is by curses, kicks and blows, lavishly administered to men and women alike."

"I have already gathered that," Roger nodded. "I am told that Peter the Great used even to beat his Generals."

The Doctor laughed. " 'Tis true enough. And the Generals beat the Colonels, the Colonels the Majors, and so on down the line. The whole nation expects such treatment, and given it willingly work long hours for small reward. Thus, if properly disciplined, they make excellent servants; and, despite the fundamental dishonesty of the Russian character, they are not given to thieving where money is concerned. It is to get something for nothing by the exercise of their wits that delights them, and they would leave a drawer of silver untouched while going to great pains to swindle you out of a few coppers."

As a great pancake bursting with cherry jam was placed on the table, the Doctor went on: "One thing greatly to their credit is the efficiency with which the police keep law and order here. You will neither be pestered by swarms of mendicants, such as infest all other large cities, nor be in danger of having your pocket picked. There is a *Ukase* forbidding begging, which is enforced most rigorously, and acts of robbery are almost unknown. The 'Residence' as the city is termed, is divided into ten districts, each of which has a police-president who is answerable for the safety and well-being of everyone living within it. By law, the doors of his house may not be locked either night or day, so that anyone who has suffered an injury may have immediate access to him, and he can send his assistants to apprehend the wrongdoer without delay. Moreover, five hundred night-watchmen are always on duty in watch-houses placed at the junctions of all the main thoroughfares, so you may walk the streets unarmed at any hour with perfect safety, as a single shout would be enough to bring one or more of them running to your assistance."

" 'Tis truly most admirably ordered," Roger remarked. "And far in advance of any measures taken to protect the lives and property of the citizens in the great capitals of the west."

The Doctor made a slight grimace. "Against it one must set the debit that, as the price of such security, the citizens of Petersburg have lost the freedom that most men count so dear. The vigilance of the police is so thorough that they know everybody's business. In fact it is the duty of the police-president of each district to be fully informed of the life and circumstances of every household, and for the purpose enormous numbers of police-spies are employed. Every innkeeper, and private person too, must give the police full particulars of all who come to lodge with them, and if a lodger stays out all night they must inform the police of it, at the latest on the third day of his absence, so that he can be traced up and come under police surveillance again."

"But that is monstrous," protested Roger. "Provided one keeps within the law, what right has the Government to pry into one's private comings and goings?"

" 'Tis the law," shrugged the Doctor, "and one must submit to it. The Empress is an autocrat in a sense which makes all other, so-called, autocratic monarchs mere puppets of their people. She is the legal owner of the entire country and everything in it. Even the greatest nobles only hold their lands, serfs and wealth by virtue of her pleasure. And she regards every one of her people as hers to dispose of as she sees fit; therefore she considers it not only her right but her duty, as the mother of them all, to have available at any time she may require it a full account of their most intimate affairs."

"Does this also apply to foreigners while they are in her country?"

"Most certainly; and before you leave Petersburg you must insert in the news-sheets three weeks running your name, quality and abode, advertising your intention to depart; since until you have done so you will not be granted a passport permitting you to quit the country. The measure is designed to prevent strangers slipping away with their debts unpaid, and so has much to recommend it."

Roger nodded, thinking to himself that, while it had proved easy enough to get into Russia, it might not be quite so simple to get out again.

When they had finished their meal they left the pastrycook's, and the Doctor having affairs of his own to attend to, Roger declared it his intention to hire a *droshky* and go for a drive round the city. The Doctor found him a driver who understood German, and after genially offering his services at any time Roger required them, saw him off.

For the best part of an hour Roger let his driver carry him at random along the broad streets and point out to him the principal objects of interest; among them, the Church of Kazan, the great bridge over the Neva, the Taurian Palace of Prince Potemkin, who had long since ceased to be the Empress's lover, but was still the most powerful man in Russia, and the gigantic equestrian statue of Peter the Great that Catherine had erected in front of the Admiralty. This amazing monument had been cut from the solid rock of a single meteorite—measuring twenty-one feet in height, thirty-four in breadth and forty-two in length—which had been found in the marshes outside the city, and, despite its immense weight, dragged eight miles to the place of its erection. The particulars of the almost insurmountable difficulties which had been overcome to achieve this extraordinary undertaking made a deeper impression on Roger of the powers commanded by Russia's remarkable ruler than had anything else in her magnificent capital.

At length, feeling that he had allowed sufficient time to elapse to disguise his true intention, he told his driver that he had had enough of sight-seeing for one day, and wished to be driven to the English Factory.

A quarter of an hour later he paid the man off outside the entrance to a great jumble of buildings down by the docks. The factory consisted mainly of a series of spacious warehouses in which all merchandise arriving from Britain was stored pending its distribution to various parts of Russia; but three sides of its principal courtyard were occupied by offices and living-quarters, and the fourth by a small stone church. On inquiring for the Reverend William Tooke, Roger was directed to a pleasant little house adjoining the church. There, in the broken English suitable to a Frenchman, he asked the servant who answered the door if her master was at home, and on giving his name as Monsieur le Chevalier de Breuc, he was shown into a comfortable library on the ground floor.

Five minutes later the Reverend Mr. Tooke appeared. He was a robust man in the middle forties with a genial expression and rather studious air. During his wait Roger's eye had lit upon "The Loves of Othniel and Achsah," published in 1769, and several other handsomely bound volumes of which Mr. Tooke was the author; so he was prepared to find him of the intellectual rather than the hunting type of parson.

In excellent French the clergyman asked his visitor's business; upon which Roger apologised in English for having presented himself as a Frenchman, and produced Sir James Harris's letter.

Having read it Mr. Tooke smiled and said: "I am happy to make your acquaintance, Mr. Brook; and, within certain limits, I will willingly be of service to you. However, I have now lived in Russia for some seventeen years; my three children have all been born and brought up here, and innumerable Russians, the Empress among them, have shown me much kindness. Therefore, I should be most loath to become involved in anything to the detriment of my adopted country."

"That, I can well understand, Sir," Roger agreed. "And 'tis far from my intent to burden you with any of my business. The sole request I have to make is that from time to time you will be kind enough to pass on to Mr. Alleyne Fitzherbert any letters that I may give you, so that I should not be seen entering the British Embassy."

"If that is all you require I will do it with pleasure. Now sit down and join me in a glass of wine," replied his host, moving over to a row of decanters. "Is your preference for Sack, Madeira or Canary?"

Roger chose Madeira and, handing him a glass, the clergyman went on: "How long have you been in Russia, and what think you of the country?"

"I landed only this morning, Sir; so I have had little time to judge. The fine streets and buildings of the capital fill me with admiration; but, at first sight, the majority of its inhabitants strike me as exceedingly uncouth, and more like bears than men."

Mr. Tooke laughed. "Indeed, the lower orders here are not far removed from animals, and even their betters oft display a violence which we would regard as most reprehensible at home. Yet the Russians have their good points and one is their complete freedom from all bigotry. That has made my work here both pleasant and easy, which I well might not have found it had I taken a post as chaplain in some of the, so-called, more enlightened countries."

"Do they place no restrictions at all then on the practice of the Protestant faith?"

"None whatever, nor upon any other. And, in fact, the Russian Government's toleration has had such a beneficial effect that, instead of being at daggers drawn as we should be in any other country, the clergy of all sects work together here in the greatest harmony. I count many friends among the pastors of other denominations, and those of us who are of the Reformed religions meet together once a week to discuss how we may better the lot of our respective congregations. I have often preached by invitation in the Calvinist church; and, strange as it may seem to you, I once even stood sponsor at the christening of a Roman Catholic child, the priest very civilly omitting those questions from the service which he knew that my conscience would not allow me to answer in the affirmative."

"Indeed I find that most remarkable," Roger smiled, "when at home we still debar the Papists from entering any form of public life, and in many Catholic countries Protestants are still frequently the victims of persecution."

" 'Tis very different here. All men may hold such religious beliefs as they choose, and although the Empress herself is a strict follower of the Orthodox Greek Church she has recently appointed an Archbishop for her Catholic subjects, and established a seminary of Jesuits at Mohilef. This spirit of goodwill is even carried to the extent of Her Majesty's confessor, Ivan Pamphilief, giving a 'Dinner of Toleration' each year on the 6th of January. At it the Metropolitan Gabriel presides, and the principal clergy of all religions are invited. On one occasion when, before the dinner, wines of various kinds were handed round on a salver, our host made a charming allusion to the widely divergent creeds of the assembled company, by remarking: 'These wines are all good; they differ only in colour and taste.' And that is the happy spirit which animates religion in this land which the western nations stigmatise as barbarous."

Roger nodded. " 'Tis certainly a much nearer approach to a true interpretation of the teaching of Our Lord than anything so far achieved elsewhere in Europe. Yet in other respects the Russians appear to be still only half-civilised. Their brutality is a by-word; and I gather that for quite insignificant faults they inflict punishments on their servants which we should consider ferocious."

"That I admit; yet a death-sentence is a rarer thing here than in most other countries."

"What though, Sir, of exile to Siberia? 'Tis said that thousands of hapless folk are despatched every year to drag out a miserable existence in those icy wastes?"

Mr. Tooke made a deprecating gesture. "News of general conditions in such a distant country as Russia travels but slowly to the outer world. No doubt in England people still believe the state of things here to be much as they were in the days of Her Majesty's predecessor, the Empress Elizabeth. She was as great a tyrant as her father, Peter the First, yet lacking his originality and abilities. On her ascension to the throne in 1741, she took a vow never to resort to capital punishment, but since she was mean, cruel and suspicious by nature she allowed countless judicial atrocities to be committed in her name.

"In cases of suspected treason even inferior magistrates were empowered to have prisoners' hands tied behind them to a rope by which they were then hoisted to the ceiling, let down with a jerk so that their arms were wrenched from their sockets, then knouted in that position to extract a confession. Quite frequently, too, innocent people were dragged from their beds in the middle of the night by her secret police and, without any form of trial, carried off into exile. 'Tis said that during the twenty years of her reign she banished over twenty thousand of her subjects to Siberia. But things are very different to-day. On coming to the throne the Empress Catherine forbade the use of all forms of torture, and although she sometimes sends those who have displeased her into exile, 'tis only on comparatively rare occasions. Her private life leaves much to be desired, but she is of a kindly disposition and rules with great humanity."

Roger was about to ask Mr. Tooke's personal impression of the Empress when heavy footfalls sounded in the passage outside, the door opened, and a rugged face surmounted by crisp, iron-grey hair was thrust round it.

"Your pardon, William!" the newcomer exclaimed on seeing Roger. "I was not aware that you had a visitor; and having delivered a parcel from my wife to your good lady, had thought that I would look in on you for a word before making my way home.

"Come in, Samuel, come in," cried Mr. Tooke; then, turning to Roger, he added in French. "Allow me to present you, Monsieur, to one of Her Majesty's most distinguished and devoted servants; Admiral Sir Samuel Greig, of the Imperial Russian Navy. Samuel, permit me to introduce Monsieur le Chevalier de Breuc, a young Frenchman newly arrived in Petersburg."

The Admiral had advanced into the room. He was a stalwart, thick-set man in his early fifties. His weatherbeaten face was lit by a pair of impatient, flashing eyes. He looked a rough diamond, and when he spoke it was with abrupt forcefulness. Instead of returning Roger's bow he stared at him truculently for a moment, then bellowed with a heavy Scots accent.

"Young Frenchman, eh? Tell that to the Marines! I'll swallow my own anchor if he's not as much an Englishman as yourself. And you, young man! Tell me this instant what criminal intent leads you to come to Russia deceiving honest men into believing you a Frenchie?"

CHAPTER XIII

HELL'S KITCHEN

TAKEN completely off his guard, Roger remained tongue-tied for a moment. He had not the faintest idea what had led to this swift penetration of his incognito. He knew only that if the Admiral's loyalty to his Imperial Mistress proved greater than any sentimental ties he retained for the land of his origin, the game was up. He, Roger, could count himself lucky if no worse befell than for his mission to end before it had properly begun, by his ignominious and immediate expulsion from Russia. That was, unless he could somehow manage to bluff his way out of the extraordinarily unfortunate encounter.

He had often heard of Admiral Greig. Indeed, the intrepid sailor was regarded as almost as much of a hero in the country of his birth as in that of his adoption. He had commanded a division of the first Russian Fleet ever to enter the Mediterranean; and, although the Supreme Command had been vested in Count Alexis Orlof, the brother of the Empress's first great favourite, there were good grounds for believing that Greig and his fellow Scot, Rear-Admiral Elphinstone, were the real authors of the signal victory by which the Russians had annihilated the entire Turkish Fleet in the Bay of Chesme.

Since then, he had distinguished himself by leading numerous spectacular actions, and, between wars, had become, in all but name, Commander-in-Chief of the Russian Navy. His rise was all the more spectacular in that he had started his sea-career in merchant ships, then served before the mast in the British Navy for six years before being allowed to accept a Lieutenant's commission in the Russian service.

He now held the rank of Grand Admiral; and the five great jewelled stars blazing upon his breast—denoting him to be a Knight of the Orders of St. Andrew, St. George, St. Vladimir, St. Anne and St. Alexander Nevski—were more than enough to show the unlimited faith that the Empress placed in him. To Roger, it seemed in the highest degree improbable that such a man would be prepared to abuse his mistress's confidence to the extent of allowing a spy to remain at large in her country.

His only course seemed to be to lie like a trooper, and pray that Mr. Tooke would not give him away; so, drawing himself up to his full six feet, he said haughtily: "You are under a sad misapprehension, Sir, and obviously mistake me for another. I have lived in England long enough to speak your language with some fluency, but my name is de Breuc, and I am a native of Strasbourg."

"Enough of such lying, boy!" snapped the Admiral. "I know you for what you are."

Hopelessly puzzled as to the reason for this unshakeable assurance, Roger could only stand his ground and take refuge in assumed anger.

"Since you give me the lie, Sir," he said sharply, "although you are my senior by many years, you leave me no alternative but to call you out."

The Admiral gave a great bellow of laughter, then shook his head with a humorous grin. "'Tis easy to see that you have not been long in Petersburg, my young fire-eater. The Russians may be a backward people in many ways, but at least they realise the idiocy of settling differences of opinion by jabbing at each other with their swords. Should you slap a Russian's face he will hit you back or break his cane over your head; but you will not find one fool enough to submit himself to a contest in which justice has no part, and the best swordsman, be he right or wrong, comes off victorious."

"Then, Sir," snapped Roger. "Should you persist in giving me the lie, my palm will itch so that it will inevitably make contact with your face."

With a slight cough the Reverend Mr. Tooke intervened.

"Gentlemen, this matter has gone far enough. Why you should imagine, Admiral, that the Chevalier is an Englishman I have no idea; but I trust you will be satisfied that he is a person of good standing when I tell you that he has brought me a letter of introduction from our old friend Sir James Harris."

Roger was filled with admiration for the extraordinarily tactful way in which the learned churchman had provided a bridge while skilfully evading the point at issue. Mr. Tooke had made no admission that his visitor was not, to the best of his belief, a Frenchman, neither had he vouched for his integrity; but he had, by naming him a protégé of the ex-Ambassador, placed him at once on a respectable footing.

"Ah! Then I'll say no more," cried the Admiral with ready good humour, but he added with a broad wink at Roger: "Except to ask the Chevalier to remember me most kindly to Admiral and Lady Brook, should his travels ever take him to a little town called Lymington."

With a friendly grin Roger hid his confusion at being so completely bowled out. Then, feeling that in the circumstances it would now be both churlish and stupid to persist in denying his true identity, he said. "I pray you pardon me, Sir, for my extreme rudeness, but I had good grounds for striving to preserve my incognito. Tell me now, I beg, how it comes about that you knew me the second you set eyes on me?"

The Admiral laughed. "You'd not remember me, but I've known you ever since you were a toddler, and I've a long memory for faces."

"I must confess I don't recall our meeting, Sir, though I've often heard my father speak of you with friendship and admiration. You served under him at the reduction of Havana, did you not?"

"Aye, that was way back in '62 and long before you were born, boy. Your father and I were much of an age and became firm friends despite the deck that lay between us. 'Twas he who persuaded our captain to recommend me as suitable for a commission when the Russians asked for a few British seamen to help train their fleet. Years later, when my squadron re-victualled in England on our way round to Greece, he came aboard to see me, bringing both your mother and yourself. You were no more than a child of two then, but I saw you again at Lymington when you were about eight. You've altered little since then, except that you've grown into a fine figure of a man."

"I still marvel that you should have recognised me so instantly, Sir."

" 'Twas the similarity of the name coupled with those dark blue eyes of yours, lad. They are your mother's very own, and I fell in love with her for them the first second I saw her. But tell that to Lady Greig and I'll have you keel-hauled out in Cronstadt Bay. I still see your father on the rare occasions when I get leave to spend a few weeks in the old country, and it chances that he is not at sea himself. Can you tell me how fares it with him?"

"Why, yes, Sir. When I sailed from England towards the end of April I left him mightily well and in the best of spirits."

"Ah! The two of you are reconciled, then. I'm monstrous glad to hear it; for your defiance of him and running away to France near broke his heart."

Roger flushed. "So you knew of that, then?"

"He told me of it when I was last in England, two summers back; and I had not heard that you had since made your peace. 'Twas that which made me at first suspicious of your intentions here. I thought mayhap that you were still living by your wits, and had come to Russia in the guise of a Frenchman as a precaution against disgracing your own name, should you be caught while up to some nefarious business. But since you come sponsored by our good Sir James that puts a very different complexion on the matter. I trust that you left that handsome rascal also in good health?"

"In the very best, Sir. And, I am happy to report, about to be raised to the peerage as Baron Malmesbury, in recompense for his great services to the Crown."

"He well deserves the honour. 'Twould in fact have been earned alone by the splendid fight he put up while here against Frederick the Great's malign influence over the Empress."

"Let us then drink a glass of wine to his long enjoyment of his new title," put in Mr. Tooke.

"I thank you, William," the Admiral smiled. "I'd not say nay to a glass of your good dry Sack."

When they had drunk the toast, they all sat down, and the Admiral gave Roger a shrewd glance, as he said: "I'll ask no questions as to your purpose here, and thereby invite no lies. But your posing as a Frenchman while bringing a secret introduction from Sir James to my old friend, suggests certain possibilities which, in my position, it is difficult to ignore."

"I appreciate that, Sir," Roger replied seriously, and the Admiral went on:

" 'Tis said that no man can serve two masters; yet we British—and there are quite a number of us here now that I have leavened the whole Russian Fleet with British officers—have, in effect, achieved an honourable compromise. Technically we are no more than loaned to the Russian Government and can be recalled at any time; but our recall could not be enforced, and many of us have made our homes here. Therefore, most of us feel that our first loyalty should be to the hand that feeds us and the land in which our fortunes lie; yet out of natural sentiment we have pledged ourselves never to take any action which would be definitely to the detriment of the land of our fathers.

"For example, during the last war the Empress was persuaded by her Minister, Count Panin, to form the League of Armed Neutrality, by which Russia, Sweden, Denmark, Austria and Prussia bound themselves to defend their merchantmen from search for contraband of war being carried to Britain's enemies. Since Russia was the initiator of this pact she would normally have taken the foremost part in these anti-British activities; but whenever a Russian ship-o'war commanded by a British officer appeared liable to be involved he put a blind eye to his telescope and sailed off in the opposite direction; thus rendering Russia's part in the Armed Neutrality a nullity."

"Tell Mr. Brook what came about from the arrival of Paul Jones, Samuel," put in their host, "for that is a more recent example of our compatriots' feelings."

"Aye," the Admiral nodded. "You'll have heard of the English renegade who turned pirate and played the very devil with our merchantmen, in the American interest, during our war with the Colonies. When the fighting was over he found that persons of quality in the

197

United States had little time for such a rapscallion and traitor as himself. So, greatly disgruntled, on learning of the outbreak of the new war 'twixt the Russians and the Turks, he came here to offer his services to the Empress. He is a bold enough rascal, but ignorant, and never having directed the operations of more than one ship at a time, completely unfitted for high command. However, misled by tales of his courageous exploits Her Majesty was sufficiently ill-advised to offer him a high appointment in the Grand Fleet, which has been equipping these few months past at Cronstadt.

"Immediately I was informed of this I called a meeting of the senior British officers in the Fleet. Their opinion was unanimous. Not one of us were prepared to serve either with or under an ex-pirate and a man who had played traitor to his country. Some thirty of us went to the Empress in a body and resigned our commissions."

"Well done, Sir," murmured Roger.

The Admiral chuckled. "That put the poor lady in a pretty fix; for such a step being utterly impossible to her own officers it had never entered her mind that we might undertake it. To accept our resignations would have immobilised the Grand Fleet, which is soon due to sail again under Count Orlof for Turkish waters; while to give way to our demand that the man Jones should be dismissed from her service would have created a precedent which might have had most serious repercussions among her own countrymen. She solved this unique challenge to her authority with her usual ability, by sending Jones as second-in-command to the small fleet in the Black Sea. But this little passage of arms is enough to show you that, although far from home and the servants of an autocrat, we British still reserve our right to use our own judgment in all that we feel concerns us."

Roger smiled his most winning smile. "I've never doubted that, Sir, and I trust that in my own case, whatever you may suspect to be the object of my visit here, you will not disclose your thoughts to others."

"Not so fast, young man," the Admiral frowned. "If I catch you seeking information regarding the Fleet and its objectives in next winter's campaign against the Turks, I'll regard it as no less than my duty to the Empress to hang you from a yard-arm."

"You may be at rest on that score," Roger volunteered. "My mission is political and diplomatic rather than military. Indeed, I am charged to do no more than assess the feelings of the Court on various international problems."

"Stick to such matters and I'll regard it as no affair of mine," said the Admiral gruffly. "But please to understand that the Fleet and the port of Cronstadt are barred to you."

" 'Tis a limit that I will willingly observe; and I thank you, Sir, for placing no other restriction upon me."

The Admiral shrugged. " 'Tis no part of my duty to prevent Court gossip finding its way to Whitehall; but, if I may advise you, I would suggest that you should seek to learn something of the Russian character before endeavouring to assess the value of such rumours as you may pick up. Your ignorance of it was clearly demonstrated by your demanding satisfaction of me a while back; and you will find many other traits in them which will appear fantastic to your English mind."

"In that I'd be prodigious grateful for any guidance you may care to give me," Roger said quickly.

"To start with then, there is no such thing as honour among the Russians. Neither man's nor woman's word is to be relied upon; so put your trust in no one. They lie more often than they tell the truth, and not from any sense of malice, but partly from habit and partly from the amusement it affords them. There is a law against gambling, yet it remains the principal national pastime, and rich and poor indulge their passion for it alike. Their improvidence is only equalled by their hospitality, and within a week you will find a dozen well-served tables at every one of which you will be welcome by merely appearing at meal-times every day. In fact the rich nobles measure their prestige by the number of hangers-on they can collect and feed gratis at their tables."

"Surely that robs their hospitality of much of its merit?" Roger remarked.

"You are right there, lad. 'Tis mere childish vanity and ostentation which prompts the majority of them to it. And worse, in many cases, since some of them expect their guests to take a hand at cards with them after supper every night, and seek to recoup themselves for the price of the meal by playing on credit."

Roger gave the Admiral a puzzled look. "I fail to see, Sir, how that can benefit them; since, if they are losers, they must settle up just the same in the long run."

"Not a bit of it," laughed the Admiral. "I tell you that the word 'honour' has no equivalent in the Russian tongue. If you indulge in gambling and are fool enough to let one of your opponents play on credit, should he lose, it is entirely at his option whether he pays you his debt later, or not. Should he decline and you complain of it, every-one else will simply laugh at you, and he will go up in their estimation as a clever fellow. What is more, they boast openly of their ability at cheating, and are always on the look out for gullible strangers from whom they may make a picking."

"I would that I had known this a few months back," Roger said, with a rueful grin. "I lost three hundred guineas one night to Count Vorontzoff, the Russian Ambassador to the Court of St. James. Had I but been aware that I could have so lightly laughed off the debt the following morning, it would have saved myself and others a multitude of complications."

"That would be Count Sergius Vorontzoff," remarked Mr. Tooke. "His father was the last Grand Chancellor. No other has been appointed since his death and the powers of the post are more or less shared by Prince Potemkin and Count Bezborodko, who succeeded Count Panin as the Empress's principal adviser on Foreign affairs. The latter is a connection of the Vorontzoff's, and the family's influence is still very great. One of the old man's daughters is the celebrated Princess Dashkof. At the age of eighteen she played a leading part in the conspiracy which placed Catherine on the throne. Her sister, Elizeveta Romanovna, was Peter the Third's mistress while he was Grand Duke, and during his short reign; and the other brother, Count Alexander, is the head of the College of Commerce."

"It seems strange to think that so violent a man as Count Sergius has a brother who is a Professor," Roger remarked, "and stranger still that a country so backward as Russia should have a college devoted to training young men to enter trade."

"Nay," Mr. Tooke smiled. "You are mistaken on both counts. Here, when one speaks of the College of Commerce, or War or Justice, one means the Government department, and the head of each is the responsible Minister. Yet the present Empress, herself a woman of quite exceptional culture, has performed prodigies in improving educational facilities. In addition to greatly increasing the number of military, naval and agricultural schools, she has instituted academies of Medicine, Mines, Teaching, Art and the Theatre, and even founded a seminary for young ladies of the nobility. So that nearly seven thousand pupils now receive their education at the expense of the Imperial purse; as once nominated to these institutions there are no fees to pay, the whole cost being borne by the Empress."

"Russia certainly seems a land of extraordinary contrasts," said Roger, thoughtfully.

"You will indeed find it so," nodded the Admiral. "Nine out of ten of the acquaintances you make will entertain you most hospitably one day, yet not scruple to steal your snuff-box the next. So light-fingered are they by habit that after eating your food they will think nothing of pocketing your table-silver the minute your back is turned. My wife and I found ourselves at such loss through this that we took an early opportunity to have made in Leith several dozen spoons and forks of base metal, especially for use when entertaining Russians."

"They are even more inveterate cheats than they are thieves, opined Mr. Tooke. " 'Tis the common practice among merchants to ask foreigners five times the proper price for any article, in the hope that the buyer will think it a good bargain if he can secure it by offering half that sum, and only later discover that he has paid more than double its real value. Worst of all are the *rasnoshchiks*, as the street-vendors are called. They will offer you a box of tea, which on being carried home will be found to have only a sprinkling of tea-leaves on the surface, the rest of the box being filled with sand and wood-shavings. They are adepts at pumping air into chickens so that the eye is tempted by what appears to be a fat capon, when in reality 'tis but a scraggy old hen wasted to near nothing from rearing her last brood of chicks. In my early days here I even had a bundle of asparagus sold to me, which, at a casual glance, looked in prime condition for the table.

'Twas not till my wife was about to put it to boil that we discovered the edible tips to have already been removed, and the woody stumps repointed and painted."

Roger threw up his hands with a laugh. "Tell me no more, Gentlemen, I beg; for it seems I am come to a veritable sink of iniquity. Yet I thank you for your warnings, and will endeavour to buy my own experience as cheaply as possible."

"I must be on my way," declared the Admiral, getting to his feet. "Mr. Brook, my barouche is at the door, can I carry you in it to the centre of the city, or have you further business to discuss with our good friend?"

"Nay, Sir," Roger replied. "I have already importuned Mr. Tooke for over-long, and gladly accept your offer."

Mr. Tooke smiled at him. "I would have liked to bid you sup with us and meet my wife; but the fewer people who know you to be an Englishman, the better, and 'twould be somewhat embarrassing for both of us did I introduce you as aught else. Therefore I will confine myself to wishing you good fortune, and assuring you that I will perform the small service you have requested of me whenever called upon to do so."

Roger thanked the friendly clergyman and leaving the house with the Admiral was swiftly conveyed by him back to the Nevski, where they parted with expressions of mutual goodwill. He then walked the last hundred yards to his lodging.

Upstairs in his sitting-room he found three people patiently awaiting his return; Ostermann, a bearded, middle-aged peasant in a clean white blouse, and a pretty little girl of about fourteen decked out in a gaily embroidered costume.

As he entered they all stood up and bowed almost to the ground; then Ostermann indicated the girl and said:

"Subject to your approval, most noble General, Zaria Feodorovna begs leave to become your servant."

Roger looked at her with interest. Her face was a trifle flat and her black eyes were no more than medium size, but they were full of liveliness. Her brow was broad, her teeth were white and even, her lips cherry-red and her complexion that of a sun-ripened apple. Crisply curling dark hair framed her piquant features and the delicate curves of her figure showed that she was already approaching womanhood. She looked an attractive little thing, but struck Roger as hardly strong enough to carry heavy trays upstairs and perform other such services as he would require. Moreover, he had, not unnaturally, expected Ostermann to find a man to wait upon him.

On his voicing his doubts as to little Zaria's suitability, the Courlander broke into vigorous protest. "Small she may be, noble General, but she is as strong as an ox. These peasant girls are brought up to labour long hours and carry heavy burdens. Feel her muscles for yourself, I beg; behold the sturdiness of her calves. She is capable of doing all the work of your apartment, cleaning your clothes, running your errands, carrying up the wood for the stove, and will still greet you with a smiling freshness when you return in the evenings."

Roger was tired after his long day and did not wish to argue; so he shrugged. "Very well, then. I will give her a trial. How much is she asking?"

"Her father is willing to let you have her for one hundred roubles."

Recalling Mr. Tooke's dictum that Russians always asked five times the proper price from all foreigners, Roger swiftly worked it out that twenty roubles, or four pounds, was near enough the correct wage; but even that seemed high for a quarter—the minimum term for which servants were then hired in western Europe—so he asked the period that such a sum would cover.

Ostermann looked at him in surprise. "Why, as long as it pleases you to retain her, noble General. Once the payment is made she will be yours to do what you like with, short of killing her. You must give her enough to eat and drink, let her go to the public baths on Saturdays and to church on Sundays. You must not take her out of the country without first having obtained permission to do so; as although she becomes your slave by this payment to her father she still remains the property of the Empress. But you may beat her to your heart's content and have her arrested if she attempts to run away from you—unless she can return the hundred roubles that you gave for her."

Roger had no intention of ill-treating the pretty little creature, but, seeing that slave-owning was the custom of the country, the idea of having one of his own rather amused him. He expected to be in Russia for several months at least, and twenty pounds did not seem excessive for the outright purchase of a human being. Yet he felt that he would be regarded as easy game, and in future be constantly cheated by his landlord over other matters, if he did not make a show of driving a bargain. So he declared that the price was outrageous.

"Indeed it is not!" Ostermann spread out his hands. "The noble General has no doubt heard tales that we are all cheats here; but in this case he need have no fears. If, Sir, you had not been brought here by Doctor Drenke I should consider it my right to ask a far higher sum, but I dare not; for if the Doctor learned that I had robbed his friend he would beat me black and blue."

This naive confession both amused and somewhat reassured Roger, but he still shook his head; upon which Ostermann cried: "A hundred roubles is a great deal of money, I know, but she is worth every *denushka* of it! I would rather break my own neck than be the means of installing here some slut who might give the noble General a loathe-some disease, and I defy anyone to find for him at a lesser sum a girl of such looks who is still a virgin."

Such an aspect of the deal had not even entered Roger's head, and his surprised laugh was taken by Ostermann as a sign of disbelief so the Courlander hurried on: "I beg you, noble General, to examine the girl for yourself. Her father is an honest man and will wish you to

202

do so before the money is paid over. She will wish it too, that she may have the pleasure of proving to her father that she has led a chaste life."

Roger shook his head. "I thank you, but I asked you to provide me with a servant, not a child to sleep with."

Ostermann shrugged. "She is fully ready to become a woman as soon as the noble General chooses to make her one. Naturally so handsome a gentleman will have many ladies to visit him, and at such times Zaria Feodorovna can sleep in one of the attics. At other times she will always be at your disposal; and if on coming home drunk late at night her presence annoys you, 'twill prove easy enough for you to kick her out of bed. When the cold weather comes 'tis essential that you should have someone to warm your bed for you; everyone does here. Look at it which way you will, noble General, the offer is a genuine bargain."

Feeling it futile to raise further objections Roger unlocked the brass-bound coffer in which he kept his funds, produced some Swedish gold pieces equivalent in value to one hundred roubles, and somewhat to his embarrassment, completed the formalities of Zaria's purchase. The hitherto silent peasant kissed him on the shoulder and, through Ostermann, expressed his happiness at having found for his daughter such a rich and handsome young master; then the girl snatched awkwardly at Roger's hands and falling on her knees kissed them, showing by her eagerness that she was a willing partner to the deal.

Roger told Ostermann that he wished her to go out and fetch him a light supper of cold chicken and a bottle of red wine; and after much bowing and scraping they left him, all breaking into an excited chatter in Russian the second they were outside his door.

As their voices faded down the stairs he began to pull off his clothes. Then, while he changed into a light silk chamber-robe, he considered a trifle dubiously how he could best disembarrass himself of the more private services which Zaria Feodorovna evidently expected to render him. She would, he thought, in due course make somebody an admirable wife or mistress, but he had no desire whatever for a child-concubine, and he wondered now if he had not been a little rash in allowing himself to be persuaded into buying a female slave. He had gone through with the deal mainly because he was tired out and it had seemed easier to acquiesce, and acquire a willing little maidservant than wait until the next day to find a man whom he would have to beat and bully. It occurred to him somewhat belatedly that Zaria Feodorovna might prove hurt and resentful at his indifference; so he could only hope that she would see the sense of keeping her virginity until he dispensed with her services, as an additional asset with which to catch a husband.

A quarter of an hour later she returned with his supper, and Ostermann accompanied her to act as translator for any orders that Roger might wish to give on initiating her into his service. Having shown her where he kept his things and stated his requirements about brushing his clothes and cleaning his boots, he asked Ostermann to explain to her that he thought her too young, as yet, to be any man's bed-fellow, and that he wished her to sleep in the attic until she grew a little older.

The result was a sudden crimsoning of the apple-hued cheeks, followed by a deluge of tears and heartrending lamentations. Ostermann translated her sobbing protests as despair at having failed to find favour in her master's eyes. She had, it seemed, fallen in love with him on sight and believed herself to be the luckiest girl in all Russia, whereas, at his words, he had made her the most miserable.

Roger saw that there was only one thing for it. Taking the bundle of noisy woe in his arms, he drew her onto his knees, where he petted her like the child she was and kissed the tears away. Then he made her a present of a rich silk scarf, which delighted her beyond measure, and packed her off, greatly consoled, with Ostermann, to her attic.

Just as they were leaving the room the loud boom of a cannon reverberated through the city, and thinking that it might be an alarm signal of some kind, Roger called after Ostermann, asking him if he knew its cause.

" 'Tis nought but the night-gun, noble General," replied the Courlander. "Few of the common people in Petersburg are rich enough to own a watch and many are so ignorant that they cannot read the public clocks even when they can see them; so at this season of the year when there are no hours of darkness a gun is fired from the fortress each evening to let them know that the night has begun."

It was still broad daylight but Roger had been up since half-past five that morning, and his experiences of the day had been so new and varied that he felt more than ready for bed. After despatching a wing of the chicken and a glass of wine he locked the door and went into the bedroom. Almost half of it was occupied by a broad divan; it had no sheets but was covered with innumerable layers of rugs. Pulling the heavy curtains across the window he settled himself on the divan, drew its topmost rug over him, and was almost instantly asleep.

But not for very long. He woke with a start and the instinctive feeling that it was still early in the night. He knew already that a movement beside him had been the cause of his waking, and the faint light percolating between the chinks of the curtains was sufficient to show him a hump under the rug, from the edge of which protruded a tumble of crisp black curls that could only belong to Zaria Feodorovna.

How she had got in he could not imagine, and it was not until the following morning that he learned that she had climbed up to the fanlight of the door that gave onto the landing, then succeeded in squeezing herself through. Evidently terrified that he might send her packing again if she so much as showed her face, she lay as still as a mouse buried in the rugs. Daunted at the idea of starting a fresh argument in a language that he did not understand, Roger took the path of least resistance, turned over on his other side, and went to sleep again.

When he awoke in the morning she was no longer beside him, but subdued sounds from the sitting-room told him that he had not dreamed her midnight appearance, and, shortly afterwards, she brought him in his breakfast.

Her down-cast eyes and trembling hands were clear evidence of her shyness, but she now showed no servility, and he soon found that she possessed the natural tact and good manners which grace most of the peasantry of Europe. As he had now landed himself with her it seemed to him that the sooner he could teach her to understand him the better; so, on getting up, he amused himself for an hour pointing at various things and giving her a first French lesson by making her repeat their names in that language after him.

The lesson was terminated only by the arrival of Doctor Drenke, who brought Roger a note from Natalia Andreovna, in which she said that she proposed to visit him at two o'clock that afternoon. While Roger read the note the Doctor addressed a few casual sentences in Russian to Zaria after which he congratulated her master on acquiring her. He then carried Roger off to the morning levée of Count Bezborodko, the head of the College of Foreign Affairs.

At the levée, as well as presenting Roger to the Count, who talked to him for a few moments on Sweden, the Doctor also introduced him to several members of the *Corps Diplomatique;* all of whom asked him to breakfast, dine or sup, so by the time he left the reception he found himself already launched in Petersburg society.

That afternoon, Natalia appeared at his lodgings cloaked, hooded and wearing a little lace mask, as was then the custom of ladies who wished to preserve their incognito when visiting their gallants. Unfortunately she arrived a good quarter of an hour before she was expected so he had not yet dismissed Zaria, who was seated in a corner of the sitting-room diligently polishing the silver buttons of one of his coats.

No sooner did the green eyes of Roger's aristocratic mistress light upon his pretty little slave than their expression changed from joyous anticipation to indignant anger. Instantly assuming the worst she advanced on him with a spate of curses and soundly boxed his ears; then, vowing in both French and Russian that she would kill the girl if she ever found her there again, she grabbed up Roger's cane and drove the unfortunate Zaria screaming from the room.

Roger swiftly endeavoured to disabuse Natalia of her black suspicions, but she knew the ways of her country better than he did; his denials of having slept with Zaria the previous night were so lacking in conviction that she obviously did not believe him, and it took him a considerable time to pacify her.

In the past week she had come as near to loving Roger as she was capable of feeling that passion for any man, and this had resulted in redoubling her natural tendency to jealousy; but so true is it that, given mutual attraction, to start with, love will almost inevitably beget love, the effect of their voyage from Sweden on Roger had been to make him excuse her worst characteristics to himself and come near to loving her in return. In consequence, the genuine concern he displayed at having upset her, and the undiminished warmth of his amorous feelings, were such, that the subject of Zaria Feodorovna was at length allowed to lapse by mutual consent, and a passionate reconciliation ensued.

When Natalia had departed, after having promised to come again the following afternoon, Roger began to wonder if his little maid would return to him, or had abandoned him for good from fear of being beaten to death by his virago of a mistress. But he need not have concerned himself; Zaria's courage was equal to her swiftly-acquired devotion to him, and on his returning from keeping a supper-engagement made that morning, he found her curled up sound asleep in his bed.

Having more or less promised Natalia Andreovna that he would dismiss the child, he made a half-hearted attempt to do so next day. But, with Ostermann as interpreter, she declared that rather than face the shame of returning to her father she would drown herself in the Neva. Roger, not having the heart to drive her away, told her that she might remain, provided she was never visible in his apartments between midday and midnight except when sent for; and salved his conscience for the lies he would have to tell Natalia with the thought that she would equally readily have lied to him. Within a few hours he had dismissed the matter from his mind and settled down to enjoy life in St. Petersburg.

For this he was given ample opportunity, as half a dozen invitations reached him on his second day in the capital from Doctor Drenke's friends in the College of Foreign Affairs, and each party he attended produced a shower of others. True, many of them were from adventurers and scallywags whose only object was to lighten his purse, but forewarned by Mr. Tooke and Admiral Greig, he succeeded in protecting himself from all but minor losses and, in the meantime, ate freely and well in the best taverns, several of the Embassies, and the houses of nobles and rich merchants.

In his role of a Frenchman he naturally took an early opportunity of paying his respects at the French Embassy. He had already learned that the Ambassador was the Comte de Ségur and the son of the old Marshal of that name whom he had known as Minister of War during his time in Paris. The acquaintance, slight as it was, but backed up by his more recent ones with the Baron la Houze and the Marquis de Pons, would, he felt sure, be sufficient to secure the Comte's agreement to presenting him at the Russian Court. But here he met with a disappointment as de Ségur was temporarily absent from St. Petersburg on a fishing expedition to Lake Ladoga.

Natalia Andreovna came masked to his lodging every afternoon, and towards the end of the week, announced that the Empress had appointed her one of her ladies-in-waiting. Roger was delighted at this news as, despite his physical attachment to her, he had no intention of allowing any scruples to prevent him from using her to further his mission; and since she was to be situated so close to the Empress he hoped to learn from her all the inner gossip of the Court. Moreover, in view of the French Ambassador's absence, it offered another avenue to a speedy presentation; so he asked her if she could arrange some means by which he could make his bow to the Empress.

"Oh, nothing could be easier," Natalia replied, stretching out a supple arm to reach for a bon-bon from a box that lay beside the divan. "She prides herself on being accessible to all, and takes especial delight in receiving foreigners. You must come to the entertainment that Alexis Orlof is giving for her on Monday evening, and I will present you to her myself."

"Can you get me an invitation?" Roger asked.

"Indeed I can. You could walk in if you wished, as half the town will be there and the more people that attend the better pleased the High Admiral will be. But as you are a stranger I will ask him to send you a card. He is an old friend of mine. In fact, I am inclined to believe that he is the father of my daughter, for the child is growing monstrous like him."

Roger turned over and stared at her in surprise. She was lying on her back contentedly munching the large, sticky sweet, and evidently did not consider that there was anything particularly startling about her announcement, as she went on quite casually: "Since One-Eye is at the wars Alexis is back in favour again; though I doubt whether he cares much one way or the other these days, and he leaves it to Bezborodko to advise the Empress on most affairs of State."

"Whom do you mean by One-eye?" Roger asked.

It was she who now looked surprised. "You are monstrous slow not to recognise it as the nickname of Prince Potemkin."

"How should I, when I have never seen him?"

"Ah, forgive me, dear one! I had forgot that your arrival here is so recent and that it is quite a while since he left the Residence to command the armies that are fighting the Turk. He lost his eye when the Empress first took him into favour. Until then Gregory Orlof had the ordering of everything and remained Catherine's chief confidant, as those who succeeded him in her bed were little more than handsome puppets. But so puffed up with pride did Potemkin become that, one night while playing a game of billiards, he boasted of his power to dispose of all offices about the Court. Gregory's brother, Alexis, was present and promptly put out the new favourite's eye with a billiard cue. That was fourteen years ago, and 'tis the reason why he has ever since carried his head on one side with the look of a knowing parrot."

"He has performed no small feat in retaining for so long his influence over so fickle a woman as the Empress."

"The Orlofs have retained theirs for near double that time. 'Tis all but twenty-six years since by the *coup d'état* they raised her to the throne."

"But Gregory is dead now, is he not?"

"Yes. He died some four years ago. 'Twas a curious coincidence that Catherine should have lost both him and Count Panin, the other ringleader in the conspiracy, who was her principal minister for so long, within a month of one another. Prince Gregory spent much of his later life travelling in great magnificence, and towards the end he became near unhinged from the premature death in Switzerland of his beautiful young niece."

"Was he so devoted to her?"

"He positively worshipped her, and had married her but a short time previously."

Roger raised his eyebrows. It was borne in upon him more strongly every day that these Russians were, beyond all prediction, unprincipled; and that his lot was now cast in a veritable hell's kitchen. But Natalia was going on with complete unconcern. "Yet the family influence never waned, as Count Alexis had been Catherine's lover, like his brother, and he is still a power to be reckoned with."

"Have none of the other favourites been men of mark?" Roger inquired.

Natalia considered for a moment. "Nay, none of them; except perhaps Lanskoi. Now he was a true Prince Charming; so good-looking that as a girl I lost my heart to him completely, and of so sweet a disposition that, having not a single enemy of his own, he would even go out of his way to render services to those of his patron, Prince Potemkin. Eighty-four was a bad year for Her Majesty; since, in it, she lost not only Gregory Orlof and Nikita Panin, but Lanskoi also. She utterly adored him, and so distraught with grief was she that she refused all food for several days and remained for three months shut up in her palace at Tzarskoi-selo refusing all consolation."

" 'Tis quite a revelation that the modern Messalina is, after all, possessed of a heart and capable of such deep feeling," smiled Roger cynically.

Jerking herself up Natalia clapped a hand over his mouth and cast a frightened glance towards the door.

"Speak not so of the Empress, Rojé Christorovitch, I implore you," she whispered. "By comparison with her predecessors, she is an angel of clemency; yet, outside the circle of her intimates, she will not tolerate the faintest disrespect. Were the appellation you have given her to reach her ears she would despatch you straight-way to Siberia."

With a muffled laugh Roger playfully bit the slim fingers that were pressing on his lips; then taking his beautiful mistress in his arms he soothed her fears and made love to her again.

He was too young, confident and carefree, to take the warning seriously. He did not know his Russia yet.

CHAPTER XIV

THE ORDER OF DEATH

O N the evening of Monday, the 2nd of July, Roger duly attended the reception at the Orlof Palace. It was not quite as vast as the Tavritscheskoï Palace, which the Empress had built for Prince Potemkin, but equally richly furnished, and was now the scene of a magnificent spectacle. From every window hung rich oriental rugs, and in front of it a huge carpet had been spread half-way across the street, so that the Empress might not soil her shoes when she stepped from her coach.

A great concourse of people entirely blocked the roadway; guests were constantly arriving in every type of vehicle, including great numbers of sedan-chairs; footmen in liveries of every hue were making way for them, and on the broad steps sweeping up to the front entrance a solid jam of people elbowed their way towards the door.

Entering the crush Roger was carried by it inside the tall doorway. There the pressure eased owing to the spaciousness of the long suite of marble-floored reception rooms. Semi-circular archways gave easy access for the streams of people passing from one into another and the whole of the suite was double-tiered, the windows in the upper story lighting the jasper columns and fine pieces of statuary that adorned the walls of the lower. Along the sides of all the rooms there were long tables bearing innumerable dishes and bottles. A good half of the guests stood three deep already guzzling at them, but the supplies appeared inexhaustible, as scores of servants were constantly shouldering their way through the press with big cauldrons of food and silver coolers the size of small bath-tubs packed with bottles of iced wine.

Roger began to wonder how he would ever find Natalia Andreovna in such a multitude, but comforted himself with the thought that she would be somewhere near the Empress, which should help him to locate her when the sovereign arrived. For an hour he wandered about, occasionally running into someone he had met during the past week and pausing to talk to them for a while. Then a sudden hush falling upon the throng announced the approach of the Czarina of All the Russias.

The crowd immediately divided, forming a broad lane through the middle of each apartment, and a few minutes later Roger set eyes for the first time on the remarkable woman of whom he had heard so much.

She was much smaller than he had imagined and very fat, but extraordinarily regal-looking. A small crown, scintillating with precious gems and supported by a wreath of gold bay leaves, was set firmly on her grey hair, two curls of which fell from a rather severe coiffure down the front of her left shoulder. Her eyes were bright blue and extremely lively as they surveyed the ranks of her bowing subjects. Her nose was small but high-bridged and wide-nostriled; her mouth was tight-lipped and determined; her rounded chin jutted out despite the fleshiness of her neck.

Any other woman of her height would have been completely dwarfed by Alexis Orlof, on whose arm her hand rested, for the High Admiral was a rugged giant six feet six inches tall. But such was the strength of personality radiated by the plump little Empress that her gigantic escort seemed only a proper adjunct to her.

At first sight, in spite of the grossness of her figure, Roger found it difficult to believe that she was in her sixtieth year, for her cheeks were unlined and she appeared to have the milk and roses complexion of a girl of twenty. But, as she passed near him, he detected a certain brittle hardness about her face, and realised that the whole of it had been so heavily painted as to virtually constitute an enamel. It was only with difficulty that he suppressed a laugh, as the sudden idea came to him that if she tripped and fell her face would suffer the fate of a piece of precious porcelain and break into a hundred pieces.

To his dismay Natalia Andreovna was not among the little galaxy of bejewelled courtiers who made up the entourage of the Empress; so he followed at a distance, hoping that if he kept in her vicinity his lady-love would sooner or later appear to pay her respects to her Imperial mistress.

On reaching the end of the galleries the Empress was led into a huge octagonal ballroom, a large part of which was railed off. Only members of the aristocracy were allowed beyond the rail, and Roger stood by it for a few moments. He had just watched the Empress seat herself under a canopy when he received a sharp rap on the arm with a fan, and turned to see Natalia smiling at him.

"Ah, there you are!" he exclaimed. "I was near fearing that I should miss you altogether in such a multitude. Never before have I seen so great a concourse of people assembled under one roof."

She raised an eyebrow. "Methinks that Versailles can be but a paltry palace, then; or perhaps it is that your King Louis is too close-fisted to entertain with the lavishness becoming to a sovereign. I doubt if Alexis has more than three thousand people here to-night, and that is no great number compared to the eight or ten thousand who attend the masked-balls that the Empress gives in winter at the Peterhof."

"It amazes me to hear that there are ten thousand gentry all to be found in this one city," he replied, as he gave her his arm.

"Oh, they are not all persons of quality," she shrugged. "Merchants, small landowners, professional men, and foreigners staying in the Residence, are all admitted on the production of a card; and cards are obtainable on request from anyone about the court."

"I should have thought that the Empress would have been greatly averse to lending her countenance to such motley assemblies."

"On the contrary. The earth is hers and all that is upon it; and it gives her pleasure to lavish something of its bounties as frequently as occasion offers on all classes of her subjects."

"Why were you not in her train when she made her entrance, just now?" Roger inquired.

Natalia smiled up at him. "Because I am not in attendance on her this evening. I thought you would enjoy our spending it together, so I begged her to excuse me and she readily agreed."

Roger squeezed her hand. "That was sweet of you. I vow I'll derive a thousand times more pleasure from this party than I could otherwise have done."

As they talked they had gradually moved forward to within a few yards of the Empress. No western Court could conceivably have rivalled the semi-oriental magnificence of the costumes of the men grouped about her; yet there was a refreshing lack of restraint about their attitude in her presence. They spoke to her with respect but without servility, and she laughed good-naturedly at the jokes they cracked.

The band had struck up a gavotte, and she was just sending her ladies out to dance, when Natalia Andreovna caught the royal glance. Floating into a graceful curtsey she said: "Katerina Alexeyevna, may I present to your gracious Majesty Rojé Christorovitch, Chevalier de Breuc, the young French gentleman of whom I spoke to you; he who escorted me back from Sweden."

Catherine smiled and nodded, upon which Roger stepped forward and made a deep obeisance. As he straightened himself, she beckoned him to her and gave him her plump hand to kiss; then she held him in conversation for several minutes. She asked him how long it was since he had left Paris, the latest gossip of the French Court, if he was interested in literature and painting, who his favourite authors were, and a dozen other questions; to all of which he gave swift, concise answers, his usual quick inventiveness coming to his aid in cases where he was compelled to make them up.

She appeared much pleased with his prompt replies, as she concluded the interview by saying: " 'Tis common knowledge that I have a great fondness and admiration for the genius of your country, and I count you a true representative of it. 'Tis my wish that you should carry away a good impression of Russia; so should you find yourself incommoded in any way while you are here, or lack for money, do not hesitate to apply to me through your Ambassador. Now take that little bag of bones, the Baroness Stroganof, away and dance with her."

Murmuring his thanks, Roger kissed the plump, heavily beringed hand again, and bowed his way back into the crowd. Natalia Andreovna congratulated him on the excellent reception with which he had been favoured, and added with a slight touch of spite: "Katinka does not usually converse with strangers who are of no special importance for so long. Momonof will have to look to his laurels, or he will find himself supplanted by you."

"God forbid!" laughed Roger. "I take it that Momonof was the tall, sulky-looking fellow, seated on a *tabouret* to the Empress's left. He has been the reigning favourite for some time, has he not?"

She nodded. "Yes, for well over a year. He was another of Potemkin's protégés; but he is a vain, stupid oaf and now seeks to bite the hand that elevated him. His reign may be abruptly terminated at any time, as he is not even faithful to the Empress. He is also the lover of the Princess Scherbatof, and everyone except Katinka knows it. So it needs but a word in her ear from someone who bears him malice to secure his dismissal."

After dancing for a little they made a leisurely progress through the other apartments. Five orchestras were now playing a variety of French, Russian and German dance music, so dancing as well as feasting was in full swing in most of the rooms. Natalia pointed out various high dignitaries of the Court to Roger and introduced him to a number of her friends. From time to time they joined in a dance themselves, and between dances ate and drank of the lavish refreshments.

The Empress had arrived at six o'clock and at about nine they drifted back to the main ballroom, to find the centre of the floor occupied by a troupe of tumblers, who were essaying the most amazing feats for her amusement. Three performing elephants were then led in, and after them an Italian prima donna sang most gloriously. The entertainment was concluded by a grand parade representing the might of Catherine's realm. For it Orlof had mobilised large detachments of warriors from all over the empire, and resplendent in their native costumes, Kalmucks, Tartars, Laplanders, Yakuts, Kazbecks, Circassians and Don Cossacks all streamed past the throne, shouting their wild war-cries and excitedly firing bullets off into the ceiling.

When the pandemonium had died down dancing was resumed; then, at a little before eleven, a sudden hush fell again on the whole brilliant gathering while the Empress was escorted back to the doors of the palace by Orlof, and took her departure. But the party showed no signs of breaking up; the sweating fiddlers, boosted with generous wine, sawed more vigorously at their violins, often joining in the dances themselves; the dancing became faster and more abandoned; the drinking and shouting of healths more unrestrained.

It was almost midnight when Roger and Natalia came upon their giant host sitting moodily on the lower steps of a side staircase with an empty, gem-encrusted tankard dangling from his great hand.

"Why do you look so glum, Alexi?" Natalia Andreovna inquired. "Was not Katinka pleased with this fine entertainment you have given her?"

"Aye, the old bitch was pleased enough," he mumbled ungraciously. "But I am bored. Time was when I enjoyed this sort of thing, but now it seems to me nought but foolishness."

"That is because you are getting old," she mocked him.

It was obvious that he was three-parts drunk, but a sudden gleam came into his dull eye, and he stood up.

"I'm not too old to give you a good tumble still, my pretty. Come upstairs and join me in a cup of wine."

She shook her head and indicated Roger. "Nay, I thank you. I am pledged for this evening to Monsieur le Chevalier de Breuc."

The High Admiral returned Roger's bow with a morose stare. A few years earlier it would have been typical of him to knock his young guest down with one blow of his great fist and carry Natalia Andreovna upstairs on his back. To do so did occur to him, but he felt too tired to bother, so he grunted: "As you will. Bring him upstairs too, then. I am sick of the sight of all these stupid people."

They followed him up to a landing and across it to a suite of rooms on the first floor at the back of the house. The one they entered could best be described as a study, and an open door led to a bedroom beyond it. Both rooms were in a state of chaotic disorder. They did not look as though they had been cleaned for a decade, and smelt abominably; yet their contents were worth a fortune. About them were scattered sable cloaks, weapons of all kinds encrusted with precious gems, jewelled ikons, gold baldrics, top-boots, pictures of ships and naval charts. In one corner a chained ape was quietly chattering to itself, and another was occupied by a great pile of empty bottles.

"What'll you drink?" asked their host, thickly, as he pulled open a cabinet; "Tokay, Malmsey, Vodka, Champagne, French Brandy?"

Natalia Andreovna chose champagne and Roger said he would join her. Orlof handed him a bottle and, while he opened it, swept a mass of documents mixed up with gaming chips from the table to the floor, then produced three crystal goblets. All of them were dirty, but he took no heed of that. Knocking the head off a bottle of cognac with one swift, practised, blow against the table edge, he slopped half its contents into one of the goblets for himself, and slumped into a high-backed chair.

Roger poured the champagne, and lifting their glasses to each other, they drank. After a couple of big gulps of the brandy Orlof set down his glass and declared: "That's better! That's a real man's drink. I wouldn't insult my stomach with that fizzy muck you're drinking, Chevalier. But young men are all the same, these days. They're girls, not men as they were in my time."

Seizing on this golden opportunity to win so important a man's regard and confidence, Roger replied with a laugh. "That may be so in Russia, Excellency, but 'tis not so in France. I may not have your capacity, but I'll drink bottle for bottle with you any time till one of us is under the table."

"Well said," exclaimed the Count, clapping him on the shoulder with sudden affability. "I'd see you under the table seven times out of seven; but 'tis good to meet a youngster for once who is not afraid to drink man's liquor. Pour that filth you're drinking into the monkey's pot and fetch yourself a bottle of brandy."

Roger did as he was bid, and as he settled himself down again Orlof continued with a sad shake of his leonine head. "The youth of France may still be virile; but in Russia 'tis now pestiferous. For a decade or more the Empress has surrounded herself with a riffraff of weaklings who are capable of nought but scribbling poetry or painting pictures. When my brother and I raised her to the throne 'twas vastly different. She was dependent then on us rough soldiers, but we gave her an empire and made her the mightiest sovereign in the world. Aye, we fought, and drank, and leched like men in those days, and stood no nonsense from Katinka either. To see her now you'd never realise what a monstrous handsome baggage she was as a young woman, and 'twas a joy to smack her bottom when she got foolish ideas into her pretty head."

"I would that I had been a girl then," Natalia Andreovna remarked. "Life at the time of the *coup d'état* must have been prodigious exciting. Tell us about it, Alexi?"

"You've heard the story often enough," he grumbled; but evidently he enjoyed recalling the bold stroke that had lifted him from a poor soldier to great fortune, as after very little pressing from Natalia he started off reminiscently.

"I doubt if the conspiracy would ever have taken place had not Peter the Third been a fool, a weakling and a traitor. With all her faults, the Empress Elizabeth was a true Russian, but her nephew was born a German and remained a German all his life. Bringing him here at the age of fourteen and changing his name from Karl Peter Ulric to Peter Feodorovitch did not have the same effect as changing Katinka's name did on her, when she was brought here three years later to marry him. As he grew up he developed a passionate admiration for Frederick the Great. Well, I've nothing against youngsters playing at soldiers, but the men of his bodyguard didn't like it when he put them into Prussian uniforms. They liked it even less during the last years of Elizabeth's reign, when we were at war with Prussia. Yet worse, as Grand Duke and Heir-Apparent he was a member of the Royal Council, and time and again he used his position to betray our plans."

Orlof spat on the floor in disgust. "In spite of that we had old martinet Frederick rocking on his pins and our armies were on the very point of taking Berlin. Then the Empress died. Without even having the decency to inform his allies in Vienna and Versailles of his intentions, Peter Feodorovitch made peace; and a shameful peace at that. He bartered the fruits of all the victories won by Russian lives and blood for the Prussian Order of the Black Eagle, and went about proud as a peacock, flaunting it on his chest."

"What a monstrous thing to do," Roger remarked feelingly.

" 'Twas indeed," Orlof nodded. "And he disgusted us further by his affair with Elizaveta Romanovna Vorontzoff. It seems that while she was his mistress as Grand Duke, he had promised her that when he came to the throne he would put away Katinka and make her Czarina instead. Katinka had been slipping out of one of the palace-windows

214

at night for years past, to go in disguise to Yelaguin's house in order to keep assignations there with Poniatowsky—the fellow she afterwards made King of Poland—so Peter had ample grounds for divorcing her, but he hadn't got the guts. His failure to carry out his promise resulted in some frightful scenes. He and the Vorontzoff used to get drunk together every night, then she used to beat him, and boast about having done so in public afterwards. Well, no one can respect a man who lets his woman beat him, can they?"

"No," agreed Roger, with an amused glance at Natalia Andreovna. "They certainly cannot."

"So naturally all our sympathies gravitated towards Katinka. My brother Gregory had been A.D.C. to Count Peter Schuvalof. While Katinka was still only Grand Duchess the fates decreed that the Count should catch him in bed with the Princess Kurakin; and as she was Schuvalof's mistress he threatened Gregory with Siberia. Katinka got to hear of it, and her curiosity being aroused, she arranged to get a sight of him without his knowledge. One look at his handsome face was enough, and his destination was changed from Siberia to a much warmer spot."

The High Admiral guffawed at his own joke; then went on. "Mark you, Katinka was remarkably circumspect about her amours in those days. She had wearied of Poniatowsky for quite a while and only continued to visit him in order to divert suspicion from her other pranks. Whenever she saw a likely-looking young officer of the Guards she used to tell her woman, Katarina Ivanovna, to arrange matters for her. On some pretext the fellow was persuaded to allow himself to be blindfolded, then he was secretly introduced into her chamber at night. Often enough, if the young man was a stranger to the Court, he went away next morning with a purse full of gold but not the faintest idea whom he had slept with.

"Gregory knew well enough, but he had the sense to keep his mouth shut. In fact, when the Princess Dashkof sounded him, as just the type of bold bravo who would be required if any sword-play was needed to carry through the conspiracy, she was unaware that Katinka had ever set eyes on him. Actually he had been her favourite lover in secret for some months, and he was shrewd enough to see that if she did not get rid of her husband he would eventually screw up the courage to get rid of her."

"Moreover," Natalia put in, "Gregory also knew that once Peter was out of the way he would be able to come out into the open. And you Orlofs have never been slow at seeing where your best interests lay."

"True enough!" cried the Count. "But the little Dashkof was the prime mover in the affair, inspired by the virulent hatred she bore her own sister, Elizaveta Romanovna. The Dashkof was no more than eighteen then, yet so great was her talent for intrigue that she won over to her project, in turn, the Hetman Cyril Razumofsky, Count Nikita Panin and Prince Volkonsky, the major-general commanding the Brigade of Guards. Katinka pretended afterwards that she knew nothing of all this, and 'tis certain that none of these folk were fully aware of the game the others were playing; but 'tis my opinion that she directed the whole business through the Dashkof and, towards the end, my brother."

"Towards the end, too, the conspirators surely met," Natalia interposed again, "and in the presence of the Empress. Have I not heard that there was a violent altercation in which the Dashkof and Gregory vowed that once Peter was deposed Katinka must be enthroned as supreme ruler; whereas Nikita Panin stood firmly by his contention that she should act only as Regent for her son, Paul Petrovitch; believing that his post as governor to the boy would then assure him first place in the Empire?"

Orlof tipped the other half of the bottle of brandy into his goblet, and nodded. "Aye, and it looked as if a deadlock had been reached; but the Dashkoff was persuaded to save the situation by her confidential secretary, an ambitious Piedmontese named Odart, whom she used as her go-between in the affair. By the grace of St. Nicholas, Panin had fallen in love with her during these secret negotiations. As he had been her mother's lover she believed herself his own daughter; so she was, at first, loath to give way to him. But Odart overcame her scruples, and on Katinka promising that Panin should be her principal Minister, between them, the two women brought him to heel."

Roger was no puritan himself and accepted the low morality of the age as natural; but even he was shocked by these disclosures which make it ever more apparent that, compared with the licence that reigned in London and Paris, the Court of St. Petersburg was a positive sink of iniquity.

"Yet the time wasted over this wrangle was near our undoing," Orlof continued. "Peter had succeeded to the throne on the 5th of January, 1762, and it was now the first week in July. The breach between the royal couple had reached such dimensions that Peter had banished Katinka from the city with orders to live at Peterhof until his further pleasure; and we feared that any day Elizaveta Romanovna might prevail upon him to have her cast into a fortress. My brother, myself, our friend Bibekof and a Lieutenant Passick had steadily been gaining adherents to the plot in the regiments of Guards; but not all of them were trustworthy. So many people were now involved that talk became inevitable. Frederick of Prussia got to hear that there was something in the wind and sent Peter a warning by Baron Göltz. Fortunately Peter was too drunk or lazy to bother about it; but another warning reached him through a French architect named Valois. As a result, Teplof, the Councillor of State, who was one of our number, was arrested."

Orlof paused dramatically, then he gave a great guffaw of laughter. "Would you believe it, that fool of a Czar had not the sense to put Teplof, to the question, so our necks were saved. But we were near undone again. This time by a soldier, one of Passick's people, who inadvertently gave away our intentions to his Captain. It was nine o'clock at night. Passick was arrested and thrown into a cell; but, realising the desperateness of the situation he managed to get a message out which reached Princess Dashkoff, urging us to act before morning."

Again Orlof paused, then went on more quickly. "Panin came in to keep an assignation with her just as she received the message. His courage did not prove equal to the occasion and he begged her to await events. Scorning his counsels she changed into man's attire, sent a message to my brother and met him at the Green Bridge over the Moika. Gregory returned to the barracks to prepare the soldiers and to myself allotted the perilous task of going to fetch the Empress.

"She was then living retired in a small summer house called Monplaisir on the shore of the Gulf of Finland, at the extremity of the Peterhof gardens. As her lover, Gregory, had the key to it, and on his giving it to me with directions how to find the place, I took two soldiers and we set off hell-for-leather.

"It was two o'clock in the morning before we reached the Peterhof, and I had the devil's own ado to find Katinka's retreat. Knowing nothing of what had passed in the capital, she had long since retired and was sound asleep. Shaking her awake I told her that if she valued her life she had not a moment to lose and must follow me.

"Katinka never lacked for courage, and although she had never set eyes on me before, within five minutes she was up and dressed. Meanwhile my two men had harnessed horses to a coach that the far-sighted little Dashkof had stabled in an outhouse nearby for just such an emergency. No sooner was Katinka in it than I climbed on the box and took the reins myself.

"Stomach of St. Nicholas! How I drove those horses! Everything depended on Katinka arriving in the Residence and being acclaimed by the guards before our intentions were discovered. But we had twenty-five *versts* to cover and I overdid the part of Jehu. While we still had a good part of the way to go, the poor beasts foundered and died in their tracks.

"There was nought for it but to walk, and being this season of the year it was as light as day. Poor Katinka feared that at any moment some of Peter's officers might come galloping up on their way to arrest her at Peterhof, and recognising her there upon the road, seize her person. Then, after a while, we met a market-cart. Dispossessing the peasant of it, I put her in it, and on we went again. As we neared the city we suddenly saw a carriage approaching us at full gallop. For a few moments our hearts were in our mouths; but it was Gregory, who had set out to discover what had caused the delay in Katinka's arrival. He paused to shout to her that they only awaited her coming, then turned about and galloped off to prepare for her reception. At last, near dead with suspense and excitement, at seven o'clock in the morning, we entered the city.

"I drove Katinka straight to the quarters of the Ismailofsky guards, and she earned her crown that day—the 9th of July of glorious memory. Despite her exhausting experiences of the night she addressed the half-clad men with splendid fire and courage; telling them that being in peril of her life she cast herself on their protection. The sight of her beauty and distress melted the hearts of those rough soldiers as nought else could have done. The Chaplain of the regiment fetched the crucifix from the altar of the chapel and everyone of them swore to die in her defence.

"By that time the Simeonofsky and Prébaginsky guards had heard the news and also declared for her; while Razumofsky, Volkonsky, Stroganof and others had arrived to form a brilliant company about her person. We all proceeded to the church of Kazan. The Archbishop of Novgorod had already been warned and came out with all his priests to receive her. At the high altar he placed the Imperial crown upon her head and proclaimed her Sovereign of All the Russias.

"She then repaired to the old Palace of the Empress Elizabeth. There Panin brought her son to her, for 'twas on the excuse of assuring the succession to little Paul Petrovitch that the revolution had been carried through. She took him out on to the balcony and showed him to the people, whose plaudits redoubled in the belief that they were acclaiming their future Emperor. We had put it about the city that Peter had planned to put them both to death that very day, and 'twas that which raised so great an indignation among the populace as to counteract all thoughts of resistance. By nightfall of that glorious day we had fifteen thousand picked troops sworn to obey Katinka and the whole city was in our hands with not one drop of blood spilled."

As Orlof paused, at last, and took another gulp of brandy, Roger asked: "What part did Prince Potemkin play in these stirring events?"

The High Admiral shrugged his massive shoulders. "None, worth the telling. He was but an ensign in the horseguards at the time, and if you have heard his name mentioned in connection with the *coup d'état* 'twas but as the result of an incident that has been made too much of since. When we had made certain of the city Katinka dressed herself in the uniform of a guards officer and rode out to review the troops. One-eye was sharp enough to notice that she had no plume in her hat, so he galloped up and offered her his; but for the next eight years she scarce looked at him again."

"And what of the Czar Peter, all this time?"

"He and his mistress had been drinking themselves stupid for some weeks at the palace of Oranienbaum, which lies some distance further along the Gulf than Peterhof. On the morning of the *coup d'état* they set out to return to the latter place, as Peter was expected to participate in the celebration of the feast of St. Peter and St. Paul there on the following day. As they were approaching their destination they were met by a Chamberlain on his way to inform the Czar that the Czarina had escaped during the night. Peter was alarmed, but lacked the will to take any action.

"In the afternoon tidings of what was occurring in the city reached him from a French barber, who had sent his servant with a message.

218

Peter was urged by Gudovitch his A.D.C. and the veteran Marshal Munich to call up his three thousand Holsteiners from Oranienbaum and advance upon the Residence; but he was too frightened to take their advice.

"They then advised him to throw himself into the fortress of Cronstadt and secure the fleet, with which he might yet have reduced Petersburg. Again, he vacillated, but at length was persuaded to put off for the island in his yacht. Fortunately for us he arrived half an hour too late. Admiral Taliezin had just landed there and secured the place for Katinka; and the Admiral threatened to sink the yacht if Peter attempted to come ashore.

"Marshal Munich then urged him to sail down the coast to Reval, take ship for Pomerania and put himself at the head of the army that he had assembled there for the reconquest of his native province of Holstein; then return with it and subdue his rebellious subjects. Once more he could not bring himself to act like a man. Instead, he took refuge in the cabin of the yacht and mingled his tears with those of the Vorontzoff and other women who were in the party. With his tail between his legs, he put back for Oranienbaum.

"At six o'clock that evening Katinka again mounted her horse. With a drawn sword in her hand and a wreath of oak leaves about her brow, she led us out of Petersburg to defeat and subjugate her husband. But we were not called upon to fight. At the news of her approach, twice in the space of a few hours Peter wrote to her; in the first case offering to rule jointly with her, in the second begging her to let him retire peaceably to Holstein and grant him a pension. She disdained to reply to either missive.

"Even at the eleventh hour old Marshal Munich urged him again to fight or fly, but he was too irresolute to do either. Katinka sent the Chamberlain Ismailof to him. Ismailof persuaded him to get into a carriage, drive to Peterhof, and there make an abject surrender. He was stripped of his Orders and Panin made him sign an act of abdication. Then, on the evening of the second day, he was taken under guard some twenty *versts* to the royal villa at Ropcha; and that was the end of the matter."

"No, no!" cried Natalia Andreovna. "Tell us the rest of the story. Tell us how he died!"

Orlof belched, loudly. "There is nought to tell. He died of a bloody flux six days later, on the 17th of July, 1762."

"Fiddlesticks!" she retorted with a sneer. "The official account of his death declared it due to piles, but no one ever believed that."

"It served well enough, and I've nought to add to it," he said sullenly.

"You were there when he died," she insisted. "Come now! Tell the truth and shame the Devil."

It was now well past one in the morning. Since six o'clock Natalia had indulged her taste for heady wines at frequent intervals, and in the past hour she had put away the best part of a bottle of champagne.

From the glitter of her green eyes and the flush on her thin cheeks Roger knew that she was three-parts drunk. Orlof, now lurching across the table, was very drunk indeed; and Roger himself felt far from sober. But he was sober enough to fear that the other two were about to enter on a violent quarrel, and made an effort to prevent it.

"I give not a damn how Czar Peter died," he declared roundly. "But I'm mightily obliged to your Excellency for your first-hand account of so enthralling a piece of history."

Natalia ignored him and leaning forward focussed her eyes on Orlof. "Go on, Alexi," she muttered. "You told me about it once before. Tell me again how you and Teplof strangled him."

Orlof jerked himself back and, his muscles tensed, snatched up his heavy goblet. Roger half rose, from the conviction that the drunken giant meant to hurl it in her face; but suddenly Orlof relaxed, set the goblet down, and gave a low laugh:

"Since you know how things went already, what's the odds? Katinka appointed the brothers Baratinsky to be his gaolers out at Ropcha. She had meant to keep him a prisoner, but the excitement of July the 9th had swept the troops off their feet, and a few days later a reaction set in. It was clear that if Peter Feodorovitch were dead no counter revolution could be launched in his favour. So Katinka sent Teplof and myself out there to see him."

"And then?" whispered Natalia Andreovna, eagerly.

"We asked permission to dine with him. Poison was put in the wine that he was offered before dinner. He drank it and was almost instantly seized with an acute colic. We urged him to drink some more of the wine and thus make a quick finish. But, a coward to the end, he refused. I threw him to the floor and Teplof twisted a table-napkin round his neck. We pulled it tight. Thus died a weakling and a traitor."

"May God have mercy on your soul!" muttered Roger, shocked into the exclamation by this barefaced confession to most brutal murder.

Orlof swung upon him. "Keep your prayers for those who need them, boy! I was but a soldier executing orders. If pray you must, pray for the Empress, who sent me to do her husband's business."

"I'll not believe it!" cried Natalia Andreovna. "Katinka has too mild a nature to initiate such a crime. 'Twas Gregory and you others who decreed in secret that Pater Feodorovitch must die, from knowing that as long as he lived your own necks would be in jeopardy."

"Aye, he had to die!" shouted Orlof. "But 'twas the Empress who gave the order!"

"You're lying."

"I am not. 'Tis as I tell you."

As they glared at one another across the table Roger felt certain that next second they would fly at one another's throats. But once again he was mistaken. Orlof suddenly kicked his chair from under him, lurched to his feet, and staggered across his room.

"I'll prove it!" he cried, pressing his great thumbs against **two** carved rosettes in a heavy oak bureau. "May St. Nicholas strike me dead, if I don't prove to you that Teplof and I did no more than play the part of executioners."

The hidden locks of the bureau sprang back under the pressure and it opened. Roger saw him jab his thumb again against an interior panel low down on the right, and a door slid back disclosing a secret cavity. For a few moments Orlof rummaged in it muttering angrily. "Where is the accursed thing? I've not set eyes on it these ten years past; but I'll swear 'tis here somewhere. Aye! This is it!"

Turning he slammed a piece of yellowed parchment down on the table in front of Natalia Andreovna. Roger peered over her shoulder and saw that it was a brief letter signed "Katerina Alexeyevna." The note was addressed to Prince Baratinsky, the text was in German, and it ran:

A new crisis menaces our authority and life. Therefore we have this day determined on sending Alexi Orlof and Teplof to have speech with the person whom you have in keeping. They have orders not to return until they can hail us with the cry "Live long, Czarina."

For a moment Roger was puzzled by the last sentence; then he recalled having heard that on the death of a Russian sovereign it was customary for those who brought the news to his successor to break it by using those words in salutation.

He had hardly grasped the full significance of the note when he caught the sound of running feet outside on the landing. Next second a dishevelled officer burst into the room. Flinging himself on his knees before the High Admiral the breathless intruder panted:

" 'Tis war, Excellency! 'Tis war! Gustavus of Sweden has landed at Helsingfors with an army of forty-thousand men, and is advancing on Petersburg."

"Ten thousand devils!" bellowed Orlof.

Natalia Andreovna sprang to her feet, and cried: "I feared as much, although my father would not listen to me! With our armies dispersed all over Southern Russia what hope have we of saving the Residence from that treacherous toad!"

Orlof seemed to have suddenly sobered up. Snatching the parchment from the table, he threw it among the jumble of papers in the bureau and snapped down the lid. With his heavily-pouched eyes showing something of their old fire he turned upon her. "We still have the Fleet. St. Nicholas be praised that its sailing for the Mediterranean was delayed. It may prove our salvation yet!"

Next moment he had grabbed up a great jewelled scimitar and brandishing it above his head ran from the room shouting at the top of his voice in a jumble of French, German and Russian. "To arms! To arms! Find me Admiral Greig! Every man to his post! To arms! To arms! We are attacked!"

The officer who had brought the news, Natalia and Roger all followed him at the run. Halfway across the landing Roger halted in his tracks and shouted to his mistress. "I left my snuff-box on the table. Don't wait for me. I'll get it and be with you again in one moment."

Swinging round he dashed back into the High Admiral's foul-smelling den, went straight to the bureau and pressed the two rosettes, just as Orlof had done. The lid flew open. In frantic haste he searched among the papers. Suddenly his eye fell upon the note that Orlof had produced. Thrusting it into his pocket, he snapped down the lid again and ran to join the others.

The impulse to steal the document had come to him on the spur of the moment. It had suddenly flashed upon him that it was probably the only existing proof in the world that Catherine II was a murderess; and had deliberately ordered the assassination of her husband. As such it was a State paper of incalculable value. Yet he also knew that if the theft were discovered and the paper found in his possession death under the knout would be his portion.

CHAPTER XV

THE PLOT

A T the bottom of the staircase Roger caught up with Natalia. The scene had changed since they had come upon Orlof sitting there an hour and a half earlier. The long rooms were less crowded, the more respectable guests having gone home, but hundreds of people were still dancing and feasting, the great majority of them now obviously the worse for liquor. The veneer of civilisation symbolised by the minuets, gavottes and quadrilles, danced while the Empress had been present, had been replaced by *Tsardas*, *mazurkas* and wild Russian country-dances; here and there men lying dead-drunk on the floor and couples were embracing openly in nearly every corner.

Towering head and shoulders above the crowd, the giant High Admiral was running through it, bellowing for the bands to stop and beating the drunks he came upon into some sensibility with blows from the flat of his scimitar. Within five minutes the revelry had ceased only to be replaced by panic, as the drunken mob, believing the Swedes to be at the very gates of the city, began to fight its way towards the doors.

Roger kept Natalia well back out of the press. After some twenty minutes it eased; a number of fainting women were carried back into the palace, and they were able to get out into the street. Having found her coach he took her home and it then carried him on to his lodging. He was now feeling cold and stale-tight from the amount of neat brandy he had drunk on top of a wide variety of wines; but little

Zaria was, as usual, warming his bed for him, and, tumbling into it, he soon drifted off into a troubled sleep.

When he got up and went out the following morning he found the city in a tumult. Everyone knew that North Russia was entirely denuded of troops, except for a few battalions of the Imperial Guard, and it seemed that short of an abject surrender by the Empress to any terms that Gustavus might dictate there was no way of preventing his army from taking and sacking St. Petersburg.

It occurred to Roger that, since he was posing as a Frenchman, it might be thought odd if, at such a time of crisis, he did not place himself at the disposal of the French Embassy. On calling there he found a crowd of excited Frenchmen gathered round their Ambassador, who, it transpired, had returned from his fishing trip only the day before. The Comte de Ségur proved to be a young man still in his twenties. He received Roger very affably and they discoursed for a little on their mutual acquaintances, then he remarked: "In the present emergency, Chevalier, you are no doubt anxious to place your sword at the disposal of the Empress?"

Actually there were few things that Roger was less anxious to do than get himself sent to the front just when his introduction to the Court had opened a good prospect of getting to grips with his mission; but in those days, when all armies had large numbers of foreign officers in them, it was as natural to expect visitors who happened to be in a threatened city to participate in its defence as it is now for a house-holder to expect his male guests to assist him in catching a burglar.

Faced with this dilemma Roger swiftly evaded the issue by replying: "It so happened, Comte, that I was with Admiral Orlof last night when the news of the invasion reached him, and I am in hopes that he may find some employment for me."

"I am delighted to hear it," replied the young Ambassador. "And, since you tell me that you have already been presented, you will doubt-less now frequent the Court until you hear further from him."

Roger readily agreed to the suggestion, although not for the reason it was given; and offered to make one of Monsieur de Ségur's suite should he be going there that evening. The Comte accepted the offer, so later that day Roger found himself one of a company of some dozen Frenchmen who set out in a small cavalcade of coaches for the Imperial Palace at Peterhof.

The Empress, perhaps feeling the need of her most intimate possessions round her, had moved on that day of crisis to her quarters in the Hermitage, and had announced the holding of a special court there for that night. This suite of so-called private apartments was in fact little less than a palace itself, as it consisted of a splendid pavilion containing many reception as well as living-rooms, an art-gallery, a library, various cabinets for the display of her collections of porcelain and coins, and a spacious winter-garden; the whole being connected with the main palace by a covered passage over an archway.

As Natalia Andreovna had, for the first time, failed to visit Roger that afternoon, he was all the more eager to see her; and he had hardly entered the main salon in company with de Ségur when his desire was gratified by catching sight of her among a bevy of beauties behind Catherine's armchair.

A master of ceremonies having announced the Ambassador, the crowd gave way and he advanced to make his bow. The Empress gave him her hand to kiss and asked at once: 'Since you are just arrived from the Residence, Monsieur, tell us what the people there are talking?"

"They say that your Majesty is preparing to seek refuge in Moscow," he returned at once.

Her fat little body bridled and her blue eyes flashed. "I trust then that you did not believe it. 'Tis true that we have ordered great numbers of post-horses to be kept in readiness, but only for the purpose of bringing up soldiers and cannon."

The Empress's words, Roger soon found, were the keynote of the evening. Gustavus's unprovoked aggression had caught her napping. There were plenty of defeatists round her who counselled a flight to the ancient capital of Russia, but she would not listen to a word of such talk. She had given orders for the mobilisation of every man available, even the convalescents in the hospitals, and the police. Couriers had been sent post-haste in every direction to summon such skeleton garrisons as had been left within five hundred miles of St. Petersburg; and she meant to remain, to fight the invader on the frontier with every resource she could command.

Roger quickly made his way to Natalia, and, as the room grew ever more crowded with people arriving to proclaim their devotion to the throne, she pointed out many of the most interesting.

Among them, Count Cobentzel, the immensely rich and very able Ambassador of Catherine's ally, Joseph II of Austria; old General Sprengtporten, the Finnish nationalist leader who had aided Gustavus III to become an autocratic monarch, then quarrelled with him and come to Russia in the hope of persuading the Empress to champion the discontented Finns against their Swedish sovereign; and another exile, Prince Alexander Mauro-Cordato, Hospidar of Moldavia, who had sided with the Russians in their quarrel with the Turks as the most likely means of securing independence for his Rumanians.

Roger talked for some while with the last in Latin, and as a result of it formed an entirely new view of the then little-known Balkan country from which the Prince came. He had believed it to be even more barbarous than Russia, but learned that the Prince claimed direct descent from a Roman Emperor, and that in spite of three centuries of Ottoman oppression the Rumanian nobility still maintained the culture and traditions of the Grœco-Roman civilisation. Mauro-Cordato told him that his library contained many ancient works of the greatest interest that had never reached the western world, and said that when he was restored to his capital of Jassy he would be delighted if Roger would pay him a visit there.

By contrast with this charming Balkan potentate Roger found Bobrinsky, Catherine's natural son by Gregory Orlof, uncouth and barbarous. So too, were her legitimate grandsons, Alexander and Constantine. The latter had been so named, and received a Greek education, owing to her ambition to revive the ancient empire of Byzantium and place him on its throne; but both the boys were insufferably conceited and ill-mannered, having been abominably spoiled by her and ruined by bad tutors pandering to their vices.

Their father, the Grand Duke Paul Petrovitch, struck Roger as being of a much quieter and more amiable disposition. The heir to the Imperial throne was now thirty-four years of age, but his mother still kept him very much in the background and he lived in semi-retirement. Only the invasion crisis had brought him and his wife to court on this occasion, and Natalia Andreovna said of him:

"He takes after his father in that he is a great admirer of the Prussians, and spends much of his time training his regiment in their barrack-square evolutions. He and his wife are very devoted to one another, and I should think, the only couple in the whole court who have remained faithful to their marriage-vows. She was a Princess of Württemberg, and is of a very different nature from her predecessor. His first wife was Wilhelmina, the youngest of the three Hesse-Darmstadt girls, and she had a great taste for gallantry. My father became her lover. The Empress found them out and packed him off as her Minister to the two Sicilys; but the Queen of Naples then became his mistress, so he lost nothing by the exchange."

Suddenly rapping Roger's arm with her fan, she went on: "Hist! I have just caught the Grand Duke's eye, and will present you to him."

Neither the Grand Duke's features nor his manner were impressive. Above a long upper-lip he had a silly little retrousse nose and a pair of rather prominent brown eyes; he spoke with the jerkiness of a shy man who is called upon to display an air of authority for which he is quite unsuited. After asking Roger a few questions about himself, he said:

"I have just obtained Her Majesty's permission to take my regiment to the front. If you are not already engaged elsewhere I should be happy to number you among my military household."

Caught properly this time, there was nothing that Roger could do but bow and render thanks for the honour done him. Later that evening he learned its cause. Catherine, true to her policy of never taking any step which might bring her son into the public eye, had refused him the command of the emergency army that was being got together for the defence of St. Petersburg. Instead, all her great Captains, Romantzof, Repnin, Suvarof, Kamenskoi and Soltikof, being away at the Turkish war serving under Prince Potemkin, she had given the command to a comparatively inexperienced general named Mouschin-Pouskin. Smarting under the humiliation of being made to play second fiddle to this almost untried commander, the Grand Duke had determined to outshine him by the size and brilliance of his personal entourage; so he was recruiting everyone he could to it as swiftly as possible.

Roger was intensely annoyed at the turn affairs had taken, but the following morning he looked to his weapons and duly presented himself at Paul Petrovitch's temporary headquarters. There, he soon saw, from the number of gentlemen assembled, that his duties would be entirely nominal and consist of no more than making one of a showy cavalcade whenever the Grand Duke chose to ride forth to battle.

For a while they all stood about watching the military-minded Prince bark orders at his troops like a Prussian drill-sergeant, then the majority of them dispersed to go about their own business.

That afternoon Natalia Andreovna brought the news that Alexis Orlof, feeling old and tired, had had the good sense voluntarily to surrender his right to command the Fleet so that the Empress might vest it in Admiral Greig; and that at that moment the gallant Scotsman was preparing to take it to sea. It sailed that evening, to the great relief of the citizens of St. Petersburg, who felt that in it lay their only real chance of protection.

For the next few days Roger danced attendance on the Grand Duke, while a vast amount of baggage was being got together, and exercised a fine bay mare which Natalia had presented to him to carry him in the campaign. Then on the 8th of July, he was warned to be ready to set out the following day. He had a last hectic meeting with his green-eyed mistress, and did his best to comfort little Zaria, by telling her that he hoped to return soon so he was keeping on his rooms, and that she could remain there in the care of Dr. Drenke. On Monday, the 9th, to much blowing of trumpets and banging of drums, he made one of the brave company which rode out with Paul Petrovitch to the war.

They had no great distance to cover, and on the third day pitched an elaborate camp, from which it was proposed to operate against the Swedes. So far there had been no pitched-battle, only a number of skirmishes to secure frontier defiles, in most of which the Swedes had had the best of it. The people on both sides of the frontier were pro-Russian, so fairly reliable reports were constantly coming in about the invading army.

It appeared that Gustavus had arrived at Sveaborg with sixteen ships of the line, five large frigates and a great fleet of war-galleys specially designed for operating in the shallow waters among the coastal islands. Rumour had it that he had intended to march direct upon the considerable town of Frederikshamn, but had been delayed by difficulty in landing his artillery. In consequence, having now lost the chance of taking the place by surprise, he proposed to attack it from both sides simultaneously, and was waiting for his fleet to come up to seaward of it.

Roger had never yet participated in any military campaign so, annoyed as he was at having to leave the Court within a few days of securing the entrée to it, he felt that he would at least be compensated by the excitement of seeing his first battle; but his hopes were doomed to disappointment. The nervy, narrow-minded little Grand Duke proved to be no more than a parade-ground soldier. Instead of seeking out the enemy he spent his days playing the petty martinet, inspecting and drilling his troops, and inflicting savage punishments on them for such slight misdemeanours as appearing with dirty buttons. Roger soon became extremely bored, but as he was technically on active service he could think of no possible excuse which would justify him in asking leave to return to St. Petersburg.

On the 18th of July news came through that a great sea-battle had taken place the previous evening. At five o'clock in the afternoon while cruising off the island of Hogland, Admiral Greig had come across the Swedish fleet half-hidden by a fog-bank. A most bloody encounter ensued, which for a time had to be broken off from mutual exhaustion; but at eight o'clock Admiral Greig received reinforcements and attacked again. The fog had increased to such a degree that few of the ship's companies were aware of what was going on except in their immediate vicinity, and the deadly carnage continued with groups of two or three ships fighting isolated duels to a finish.

Both sides claimed a victory, but in the course of a few days it emerged that Admiral Greig had scored a great triumph, as he succeeded in driving the remains of the Swedish fleet into Sveaborg, and declared himself confident of being able to keep them bottled up there for the remainder of the campaign.

Meanwhile it became clear that, having taken a few small towns, Gustavus had no intention of advancing further until he had reduced Frederikshamn. The immediate threat to St. Petersburg having been removed, General Mouschin-Pouskin showed no inclination to give battle, and informed the Grand Duke that he was not to risk his troops for the time being. Paul Petrovitch regarded this as a fresh insult, and, evidently having no stomach for the more active part that he might be called on to play later, seized on it as an excuse to resign his little command. To Roger's great delight, on the 28th of the month the camp was packed up, and on the 30th, he accompanied the Grand Duke ingloriously back to St. Petersburg.

The only thing he had gained from his three weeks of abortive campaigning was the somewhat disquieting knowledge that, should he have the good luck to gain any special intelligence which might prove of value to King Gustavus, it would be no easy matter for him to get through with it to the Swedish lines. On numerous occasions he had ridden out with reconnaissance parties, and each time they had approached one of the comparatively few ways of ingress through the exceptionally marshy and difficult country into Swedish Finland, they had found it guarded by a strong outpost with orders to turn everyone back. In addition the woods and fens were patrolled by *sotnias* of wild Cossacks, who were apt to give short shrift to anyone they suspected of attempting to go over to the Swedes.

That these precautions were well justified Roger learned on his return to St. Petersburg. Apparently Gustavus was having considerable trouble with his army. It was said that, to justify his unconstitutional act in going to war without having first obtained the consent of his *Riksdag*, he had dressed up a lot of Finnish peasants in Russian uniforms, caused them to fire upon his troops, then fired upon them in return; afterwards declaring that Russia had attacked Finland and he was within his rights in waging a defensive war.

This measure of the crafty King had not fooled his own officers, and many of the nobility among them were reported to have expressed their disapproval of the war in the strongest terms; while others, particularly from the Finnish regiments, had deserted and come over to the Russians.

On the other hand many of the Russians also displayed little inclination to fight; and after his successful action off Sveaborg Admiral Greig had sent three of his Russian captains back to Cronstadt in irons, charged with deliberately mishandling their ships in order to evade coming to action. Thus, cowardice and treachery being feared by the commanders on both sides, special measures were being taken to prevent traitors communicating with the enemy.

The only land-route from Helsingfors to Stockholm being well over a thousand miles, and a great part of it through almost trackless mountains, Gustavus was now completely cut off from his base. This new development provided a good reason for him to offer the Empress an accommodation, and he did so, but not with any desire for peace. He was clever enough to see that in whatever terms he made it the fact of its rejection would serve to strengthen his hand with his discontented officers, and he took care that its conditions should be entirely unacceptable, even demanding that Russia should disarm until the conclusion of the treaty.

Natalia Andreovna told Roger that the Empress was so furious when she received it that she had exclaimed: "What language! If the King of Sweden were already at Moscow I should even then show him what a woman is able to do, standing on the ruins of a mighty empire."

Her only reply was to replace the inept Mouschin-Pouskin with the more active General Mikhelson, who promptly attacked a strong Swedish post at Savolax and won a somewhat costly victory.

Gustavus, feeling that he had already lingered over-long at Frederikshamn now determined to take the town by assault. Embarking some half of his troops into galleys, he sent them to the far side of the bay under General Siegeroth with orders that when they had landed and were ready to attack, the General should fire a cannon, upon which both forces would hurl themselves upon the enemy.

After some difficulty with contrary winds Siegeroth carried out the manœuvre and fired his cannon. It proved a signal for the most bitter humiliation of the unfortunate King. He had already placed himself at the head of his troops and was about to give the order to charge when a Colonel Hesteko and a number of other officers rode up to him.

The Colonel declared firmly that it was wrong for His Majesty to expose his own life and that of his subjects for such an unjustifiable cause, and that he and his friends refused to be a party to it.

In vain the King upbraided the group as cowards. Then, turning to the troops he appealed to them in Swedish to follow him without their officers. Not a man would budge, and it was only with the greatest difficulty that he prevailed upon them not to lay down their arms there and then.

Gustavus, far from home, the major part of his fine fleet destroyed, his lines of communication cut and his army in a state of sullen mutiny, now seemed in a desperate situation; and as tidings of the parlous state to which he had so swiftly been reduced drifted through to St. Petersburg, Roger became extremely worried.

It was not that he felt any particular attachment to the Swedish King, although he had a considerable admiration for his courage. Moreover his personal sympathies naturally inclined towards the Russians, both because they had been attacked without justification or warning and owing to their ready acceptance of him in their midst as a friend and comrade. Yet he knew well enough that far deeper issues were involved. However unprincipled Gustavus might be, he was fighting Britain's battle. He alone among the Princes of the North had had the insight to see that unless a check could be put upon Catherine's lust for power, she would subjugate the whole of Scandinavia. Mr. Pitt had foreseen that the rise of the mighty Russian Empire now constituted a new menace to all Europe and had specifically laid it down that, unless Catherine could be induced to enter into a pact for the maintenance of lasting peace, no effort must be spared to assist those who were prepared to challenge Russian aggrandisement.

Apart from the Grand Turk, who was merely endeavouring to defend himself, Gustavus was the only monarch who had dared to defy the growing might of the unscrupulous Muscovites, and Roger knew that it was his duty to aid him if it were in any way possible to do so. The trouble was that he could think of no means by which anyone in his position could conceivably lessen the plight in which the Swedish King had landed himself.

In due proportion to the decline in Gustavus's fortunes, Catherine's elation soared. She had now succeeded in mustering twenty thousand men, and in view of the semi-mutinous state of the Swedish army, could consider St. Petersburg safe from attack by land as well as by sea. Moreover, with the truly maternal desire not to hazard the lives of her soldiers needlessly, and the brilliant generalship which was one of her many gifts, she had been swift to seize upon the possibility of rendering further fighting redundant by causing Gustavus's own subjects to bring about his final destruction. To this end she sent secret agents to put certain proposals before her enemy's rebellious officers, and issued fresh orders that deserters from the Swedish army were now to be encouraged and allowed to pass through the Russian lines.

The result was that in mid-August a deputation of Finns, representing a considerable body of Gustavus's mutinous troops, arrived in St. Petersburg.

Since his return from the front Roger had assiduously attended all Court functions and exercised his social talents to cultivate the acquaintance of as many influential people as possible; so he was now *au courant* with all the general gossip of the day. But he still relied mainly on Natalia Andreovna to supply him with the more intimate tid-bits which were let drop by the Empress when she was alone with her ladies. It was, therefore, from Natalia that he learned of the arrival of the Finnish deputation and that it was headed by Count Yagerhorn.

As it was not always easy for Natalia to drive as far as St. Petersburg in the afternoons to visit Roger at his lodgings, they sometimes met at the *Krasnoë-Kabac*, some eight *versts* outside the city. The place was a small red-painted inn with a pleasant garden, where tables were set in creeper-covered arbours giving a welcome seclusion to couples who wished to dine in private and afterwards linger there in amorous dalliance. It was a favourite haunt of the rich bourgeois of the city on Sundays, but on weekdays was usually almost deserted. They had dined there off sturgeon and a well-hung reindeer-steak, and were well into their second bottle of wine when Natalia told Roger about the Finns.

He said nothing for a moment, but his mind instantly quickened with the most lively emotions. He was far from having forgotten his last meeting with Count Yagerhorn, and had sworn to himself that sooner or later he would get even with him.

At first sight, the Count's arrival in St. Petersburg seemed to present a most welcome opportunity, but on turning the matter over in his mind, Roger realised that as duelling was contrary to custom in Russia, it was unlikely that his enemy would accept a challenge, and that, owing to the vigilance of the night-watch, it would be highly perilous to waylay him in the street and force a fight upon him.

Natalia broke in upon his thoughts. "Will you give me an extra long kiss if I tell you what you are thinking? 'Tis how you can revenge yourself on Erik Yagerhorn for the beating that he gave you."

He laughed. " 'Twas easy to guess, but you shall have your kiss and more like it as soon as we have finished this dish of creamed rowanberries. Tell me, what are your feelings now towards the Count?"

"I have none," she shrugged. "You know as well as I that you have made me love you to distraction. There is no place in my heart for other lovers, old or new. Should it be your wish I will aid you to settle your score with him. But you must have a care how you set about it, for as a semi-official Ambassador he will be under the special protection of the Empress."

Knowing Natalia to be an habitual liar, Roger took most of her statements with a grain of salt, but for once he thought she was giving true expression to her feelings. He knew that since he had adopted Russian methods with her he now represented in her eyes the best combined qualities of east and west, which it would have been difficult for her to find in another lover; and he was as certain as any man could be that she was faithful to him. Moreover, any project of revenge was calculated to appeal to the vicious streak in her nature.

"You are an enchantress," he said, after a moment. "And since you could offer me no better proof of your love, I accept it. 'Tis certain that you will see the Count, so I would have you renew your old friendship with him. Mark you, 'tis far from my mind that you should once more become his mistress, and did I catch you out as having pleasured him I would beat you till you are black and blue. But make it appear that you have pleasant memories of your former intercourse, and lead him on to hope that you will give him an assignation."

Her green eyes brightened with amusement. "I take your thought; and when I eventually grant it to him 'twill be you that he will find tucked up in bed, instead of myself. So be it then; I make only one stipulation. I must be there hid behind a curtain to see the fun."

Roger readily agreed and they both laughed heartily at the thought of the Count's discomfiture.

In the ten days that followed Natalia kept him informed both of the progress of this intrigue and the Empress's negotiations with the Finns. It seemed that a deadlock had been reached, as the deputation was divided into two factions. Both were prepared to turn their arms against Gustavus if Catherine would give them her support by prosecuting the war more vigorously; but one group demanded complete independence for Finland as the price of their treachery, while the other, led by Count Yagerhorn, was willing to see their country a Russian province provided only that she would assist them to expel the Swedes. Meanwhile Natalia had found it easy to enmesh Yagerhorn in her toils again, and he was pressing her ardently for a private meeting.

On the afternoon of Monday, the 27th of August, while she was visiting Roger at his lodgings, she said to him: "The plum is ripe for the picking when you have a mind to it. No sooner did I show him that I was not averse to his attentions than he naturally assumed that I would be willing to resume our old relations. He has taken my excuses in good part so far, but it will soon become difficult for me to find adequate ones with which to fob him off much longer."

Roger grinned. "I should have realised how swiftly your charms would madden any man who had once known you, and have prepared a plan already. As it is I pray you keep him dangling for a day or two yet, while I work out the details."

"So be it then, Rojé Christorovitch, but delay not too long, for the affair of the Finns will shortly reach a crisis; and once a decision is taken they may hasten back to their own country."

He looked up quickly. "How so? What new development has taken place to precipitate their reaching an agreement?"

" 'Tis the Danes," she said softly. "But I beg you speak of it to no one, for 'tis still a State secret of the highest order. I learned it only because the Empress must have forgotten that she had left me in a closet adjacent to her room last night, while she received Bezborodko. She had set me to read through some papers concerning the hospital she established a few years back to which women of all classes can go in secret for the treatment of certain diseases. I was to report to her upon them, but I heard every word that was said. It seems that when she ceded her deceased husband's patrimony of Holstein to the Danes in exchange for the little duchies of Oldenburg and Delmenhorst, in '73, there was a secret clause in the treaty by which Denmark bound herself to come to Russia's assistance should she be attacked by Sweden."

Roger's mind flashed back to his talks with Mr. Hugh Elliot the previous April in Copenhagen. This was the very thing that shrewd diplomat had suspected; but for something of the sort, Catherine appeared to have made such a poor bargain.

Leaning towards him, Natalia Andreovna went on in a whisper: "Last month the Empress called on the Danes to honour their bond, and they have now agreed to do so. As soon as their preparations are completed they intend to declare war on Sweden."

With a swift glance at the thin, clever face so near to his own, Roger took her up. "And your conclusion is, that now the Empress knows that she can count upon the Danes she can tell these Finnish rebels that she no longer requires their aid; or will accept it only on her own terms of Finland becoming a Russian province?"

Natalia nodded. "You have it. So they will be forced to say yea or nay within the next few days. But Her Majesty and Bezborodko agreed that not even the Finns should be told what lies behind the ultimatum; so that the Danish attack on Sweden may come as a complete surprise, and prove the more deadly. I entreat you, therefore, not even to hint it to another soul."

"Be easy; no one in Petersburg shall learn of it from me," he assured her with swift duplicity. His mind was now working fast and furiously. It was just such advance information of coming events that Mr. Pitt had sent him to Russia to get. He must send a despatch that night via Mr. Tooke and the British Embassy, although the chances were against it reaching Whitehall before the Danes had acted, or their intention of doing so was an open secret. But, far more important, King Gustavus must be warned, because he was so intimately concerned in it. These tidings could hardly be less welcome to a man already in such a difficult situation, and Roger did not see what the Swedish King could do to counter this new threat. Still, that was beside the point. Good or ill, the news must be got to him with the least possible delay.

As Roger wondered how he could get a message to Gustavus, he recalled Natalia having told him some days earlier that, in order to win the confidence of the Finnish deputation and show them how strong she was, the Empress had ordered that all its members should be given *laisser passer,* which would allow them to pass all military posts at will. It then occurred to him that Count Yagerhorn would be carrying such a pass, and that if he could entrap the Count he could not only give him a good beating, but also take it off him, thus killing two birds with one stone. Armed with the pass he should find no difficulty in getting through the Russian lines, and once in Swedish-held territory, he could himself carry the vital news to Gustavus.

"You are right about Yagerhorn," he murmured. "If we delay further he may slip through our fingers. Think you that to-morrow evening you could get leave of absence?"

Natalia smiled. "I am in personal attendance only every fourth night, so that should not be difficult."

"Then I suggest that you do so, and give the Count his assignation. Tell him that a discreet friend has lent you a lodging off the Nevski, and that you intend to pass the night there under the name of—let us say—Madame Zabof. The apartment, of course, will be my own. You can come there at any hour you wish and I will warn the landlord that a stranger will inquire for you, and that he is to say nothing of my presence but show the fellow up."

"I could get leave for the evening but not for the night," replied Natalia. "I have told you oft enough that the Empress insists on all her ladies-in-waiting sleeping at Peterhof."

·"I have had frequent cause to curse the rule for depriving me of your company," he agreed, "yet hoped that for once you might get a dispensation from it."

"Nay, 'tis impossible. But no matter; I can gain admission by the side door of the palace at any hour up to midnight. There will be ample time to settle Erik Yagerhorn's business before I have to leave you."

Roger was still thinking quickly, and said: "I am all the more sorry that you will be unable to spend the night with me; in that, after to-morrow evening, I shall not see you for a few days. I have accepted an invitation to go fishing on Lake Ladoga."

"With whom?" she asked sharply.

"Monsieur de Ste. Croix," he lied, naming an elderly Frenchman who rarely came to Court. "The trip is but for three days. I leave on Wednesday morning, and expect to be back by Friday night."

"Why did you not tell me of this before?"

"Because the invitation was offered to me only this morning!"

Her green eyes narrowed. "I believe you intend to deceive me and have invented this expedition in order to be free of me for a while, so that you can amuse yourself with another woman."

For a second he was on the point of conforming to the Russian code that he had adopted towards her since they left Sweden, by giving her a good slap and telling her to mind her own business; but he thought better of it. To do so would quell her complaints but leave her still suspicious, and he did not want her to start inquiring into his movements while he was away. So he brushed her accusation aside with a laugh, and said:

"I pray you use that good brain of yours, my beautiful Natalia Andreovna. Since you must perforce always occupy your bed in the palace, I could sleep with a different woman every night and you know nothing of it. But, having you for a mistress, none but a fool would waste himself in such infidelities, and I trust that there are as yet no signs that I am wanting in my wits."

She smiled and kissed him. "You are right, my handsome one. I've enough experience of men to tell when they have begun to cheat me, from a falling-off of their ardour. Go then to your fishing, and may you have good sport. To-morrow I will be at your lodging by four o'clock, so order a good dinner to be sent up, and I'll bid Eric Yagerhorn to rendezvous with me there at seven. His discomfiture will provide us with a most diverting dessert."

Immediately Roger got back to his apartment he wrote a lengthy despatch, giving his impressions of the Russian Court and ending with the news that the Danes were preparing to intervene in the Russo-Swedish war.

The following morning he carried it round to the Reverend William Tooke, who promised to arrange for its transmission to London with the minimum of delay.

He then set about his preparations for the culmination of his plot against Count Yagerhorn and his projected journey into Finland. At the pastrycook's he ordered an excellent meal to send to his lodgings that afternoon. He also bought some cold food and a couple of bottles of wine, which he carried round to the livery-stable where he kept the mare that Natalia had given him. Having assured himself that she was in good fettle to take the road, he packed the provisions into her saddle-bags, and gave orders that she was to be saddled and ready for him at ten o'clock that night.

Returning to his lodgings he arranged with Ostermann to serve dinner and gave him his other instructions. Lastly he saw Zaria. First he impressed upon her that in no circumstances was she to come down from her attic that evening until he came up to fetch her; then he told her that she was to go to bed and sleep that afternoon, as he had a special task for her which would mean her staying up from ten o'clock till dawn.

Having thought the matter over with considerable care he had decided that whether he succeeded in securing Count Yagerhorn's *laisser-passer*, or not, he would set out that night. Natalia would have to start back for the Peterhof soon after ten. If all went well, Yagerhorn would by then have been *hors de combat* for some hours; so it should not be difficult to keep him captive until the following morning, in order to prevent him from going straight to the police, reporting that he had been attacked, and raising an immediate hue and cry. By the time the Count was free Roger hoped to have put many miles between himself and any possible pursuit. Natalia, Ostermann and Zaria would believe that he had gone off on his fishing-expedition, and the Finn would be baffled by his disappearance. If Yagerhorn did then go to the police Roger thought it unlikely that, the first excitement being over, they would interest themselves much in a fight between two foreigners; and that, although he might be called on to answer their questions on his return to St. Petersburg, providing he had not done the Count any serious injury, nothing would come of the matter.

By the time he had completed his arrangements it was near midday, so he lay down on his divan and put in a few hours' rest against the long night-journey that lay ahead of him.

At three o'clock he woke from a light doze and flexed his muscles thoughtfully, as he wondered what the outcome of his encounter with his enemy would be.

CHAPTER XVI

THE AMBUSH

NATALIA ANDREOVNA arrived a little before four, smirking like an exceptionally pretty vixen who has just robbed the hen-roost, with the news that Erik Yagerhorn had swallowed the bait without a qualm, and, short of an earthquake, could be counted on to arrive at seven o'clock. Then they sat down to dine.

The excitement they were both feeling detracted somewhat from their appetites, but they drank fairly copiously; although Roger was careful not to overdo it to an extent which might put him to a disadvantage when he came face to face with his intended victim. By a quarter to seven he had had enough to make him just ripe for a fight, and he was becoming impatient for the Count's arrival.

Since there could be no hiding Natalia's part in the plot, she had decided against concealing herself; so they cleared the middle of the room and drew the table across the embrasure of the window, arranging it so that when seated behind it she was as well installed for the coming spectacle as if in a Royal box. Roger took up his position behind the door, so that he could not be seen by anyone on first entering the room; then, sinking their voices to a whisper, they began to count the moments to the springing of their ambush.

At length there came footfalls on the stairs, the door was opened and Ostermann showed Count Yagerhorn in. His glance immediately lit on Natalia Andreovna at the far side of the room, and, his florid face wreathed in smiles, he hastened forward to greet her. As Ostermann closed the door Roger stepped from behind it and exclaimed: "Turn, Sir! 'Tis I who will provide your entertainment this evening."

The tall Finn spun round, his mouth gaping open, as Roger went on sternly: "You recall me, do you not? And the last time we met? 'Tis your turn now to take a beating."

"I recall you well enough, Monsieur," snapped the Count. Then swinging about, he cried to Natalia: "And so Madame, you have led

235

me into a trap! Are you not ashamed to sit smiling there at your own perfidy?"

"Nay, Count," she laughed lightly. "It is but tid-for-tat. Some two months past you pressed me to afford you an opportunity for an explanation with Monsieur de Breuc, and I obliged you. Now that he has made a similar request, how could I refuse him?"

"Yet there is a difference," Roger intervened. "You were not man enough to cross your sword with mine, so brought four bullies with cudgels to aid you. I am content to make do without such hired ruffians and grant you at least an even chance to defend yourself from chastisement."

"Your complaint on that score should be addressed to the Baroness Stroganof," sneered the Count, "for she it was who ordered me to make certain you should not escape the penalty of her displeasure."

"For shame!" cried Roger. "Is it not enough that you are a coward, and a traitor to your King, without seeking to father your craven conduct on a woman?" And, raising the riding-switch with which he had armed himself, he struck the Finn full across the face.

As Yagerhorn recoiled with a sharp cry, Natalia Andreovna gave a gasp of thrilled excitement; but the Count was quick to recover from the blow. Before Roger could get in another he had sidestepped and came charging in upon him.

Roger was equally agile and, springing away, slashed at the Count's head. He winced under the cut, but, swerving, managed to grasp Roger's arm. A second later they had clinched and stood swaying together in the centre of the room.

They were of about equal height, but the Finn was of a broader build and much the heavier of the two. His left hand was still encased in a black kid glove, but whatever unsightliness the glove was worn to cover did not incommode him in the full use of it. He got the gloved hand on Roger's throat and his grip was as tenacious as that of a bulldog.

Locked together as they were, Roger's whip was no longer an asset to him but an encumbrance. Dropping it, he jabbed the Count sharply in the face; but the Finn's grip on his throat did not relax. Roger felt himself forced back; there was a sharp pain in his lungs from the lack of air and his head was singing. He knew that if he could not break the hold upon his windpipe within another minute he would be forced to the ground and ignominiously receive the beating that he had intended to give his enemy.

Desperate measures were necessary and, he considered, justified. Bringing his knee up sharply, he jabbed it into his adversary's groin.

The sudden move had the desired effect. With a gulp Yagerhorn loosened his hold. Roger jerked his head back, pushed him off and sprang away. He was not a skilled pugilist, having devoted himself by preference to fencing and pistol practice, but he had picked up enough of the noble art at Sherborne to be much more adept at it than the majority of Continental noblemen, who despised fisticuffs

236

as the sport of churls. As the black-gloved hand darted out to renew its grip, Roger struck it up with his right and landed a heavy left on the Count's eye.

The Finn staggered back, recovered and came in again, throwing out both hands to catch Roger in a bear-like hug. But Roger was wary now. He had experienced the great strength that lay in his opponent's massive arms and knew that he could not match it. Darting aside he struck Yagerhorn hard, first in the ribs, then on the side of the face.

Panting harshly, the heavier man swerved and made another bull-like rush. Again Roger checked it with a body-blow, and another that glanced across his red, perspiring cheek. It seemed now that the more agile Englishman had the Finn's measure. Circling round him he got in blow after blow till Yagerhorn was reeling and it seemed that he must succumb.

But suddenly the Count dashed to the side of the room, seized a chair by its back, and swinging it aloft, struck with its legs at Roger's head. His jump to save himself was a second too late; one leg caught his head a glancing blow, another crashed upon his shoulder. With a gasp of pain he fell half-stunned to the floor. Next moment the Count flung himself on top of him, driving the breath out of his body.

Natalia Andreovna leapt to her feet. Her green eyes were flashing like those of a wild animal who smells blood. Leaning right across the table to see the better, she let out a shrill screech of intense excitement; but she made no move to come to her champion's aid.

Breathless, his wits befuddled, his left shoulder half dislocated from the blow and the arm below it numb, Roger writhed impotently beneath the weighty body of the Count. As in a nightmare he felt the black-gloved hand grasp his throat once more, and knew himself now to be at his enemy's mercy.

Suddenly it flickered through his mind that Yagerhorn, driven to a frenzy by the blows he had received, might kill him. The thought had no sooner entered his head that it became a conviction. The frightful clutch upon his neck and the agonising pains that pierced his chest were the last sensations he would ever know. This then was death.

The thought appalled him. His life was so full and gay, and there were so many joys in it that he had not yet experienced. Yet he could neither shout to Natalia for help, nor even beg for mercy had he wished. Only a faint hissing sound escaped his purple lips, and as through a reddish mist, he could see the Finn's blue eyes, glaring with implaccable hatred, boring down into his own.

The instinctive urge to escape death, rather than any remaining strength in Roger's limbs, still kept him jerking frenziedly in abortive efforts to throw the Count off. His clawing right hand stabbed ineffectively at the livid features above him, but was smashed aside and fell limply to the floor. By the will of Providence it struck the handle of the riding-switch that he had dropped some minutes earlier. His fingers closed avidly upon it, and with the butt-end foremost, he struck savagely at the murderous face leering down into his own.

The metal butt thudded dully against Yagerhorn's eye. He gave a bellow of pain, his grip on Roger's throat tightened convulsively, then eased a fraction. Blindly, frantically, with the maniacal strength of despair, Roger struck again and again.

The Finn's eyes became suffused and swimming; his nose was broken and began to drip great splashes of blood; his cheeks and forehead were lacerated where the metal had torn the flesh, yet he still hung on. But his aching fingers no longer had the power to check Roger's gasps for breath. Suddenly the metal whip-butt caught the Count on the temple, and half-stunned, he lurched sideways. Roger jerked free his neck but remained where he lay, still pounding with all his remaining strength on his enemy's face and head.

For a moment the Count struggled up into a sitting position, astride Roger's body, and swayed there, thrusting out his arms in an effort to protect himself; then he gave a moan and rolled over onto the floor.

Panting, gasping, dripping with sweat, Roger pulled his legs from beneath those of his enemy, and supporting himself with one hand got up onto his knees. He could not yet believe that he had escaped with his life, and still felt that it was in imminent peril as long as Yagerhorn had a kick left in him. Filled with mingled fear and rage he rained blow after blow with his whip upon the Count's head and shoulders until they ceased to writhe and he lay insensible.

Not till then did Roger slowly regain full possession of his own senses. For a few moments he remained kneeling there staring at the blood-spattered mass beside him. Then he slowly got to his feet, lurched across to the couch and fell upon it, still fighting for breath, and utterly exhausted.

Natalia had come out from behind the table and, running to him, began to smother his bloodstained face with kisses, as she exclaimed:

" 'Twas a truly marvellous fight. Never have I seen a finer. I would not have missed it for the world; nay, not even for a promise from the Empress of a ribbon of her Order. There came a time in it when I was quite fearful for you, but I knew full well that in the end my brave Rojé Christorovitch must emerge victorious."

Knowing that she had stood by watching with fascinated enjoyment while his life was being choked from him, Roger made a feeble attempt to push her away. Yet, as she rattled on, praising his dexterity and courage, he found it difficult to maintain his belief that she had failed to attempt his rescue solely on account of the sadistic delight she was deriving from the hideous conflict. Her inner mind was still an unfathomable deep to him, and he could not feel positive that she had not, in fact, refrained from aiding him owing to a complete faith in his ability to get the better of this enemy. In consequence, he sighed; and, when she had fetched water to bathe his hurts, submitted to her ministrations without further protest.

By the time he had revived a little he saw that Yagerhorn was coming round; so he got to his feet and, fetching some lengths of cord that he had placed handy for the purpose, he tied the Count's wrists and ankles, and stuffed a handkerchief into his mouth; then lay down again.

For the best part of an hour he remained sprawled upon the settee, while Natalia sat beside him gently stroking his hair and whispering endearments. At last, when he felt more like himself, he got up once more and, with Natalia's help, dragged the Count into the bedroom. When they had levered his body on to the divan Roger sent her back into the sitting-room to fetch a cloth for use as a proper gag, as Yagerhorn too had now more or less recovered and was growling and biting like a savage animal.

While she was absent Roger swiftly searched the Count's inner pocket. From it he pulled a batch of papers, and to his great satisfaction, found among them a *laisser-passer*. One glance was enough to show that it was what he sought, as the Russian text was translated below in both French and German. Without further examination he stuffed the whole lot inside his shirt. A minute or two later Natalia rejoined him. Together they re-gagged the Finn more efficiently, made certain that his bonds were secure, then returned to the sitting-room.

Not having eaten much dinner Roger now felt hungry; so, at his suggestion, they sat down to demolish the remains of a venison-pasty and some fruit. They were almost silent during their meal, and towards the end of it Natalia amused herself by spitting cherry-stones with commendable accuracy right across the room into the wood-basket beside the stove. When she had run out of ammunition she said: "Tell me, Rojé Christorovitch, what have you in mind to do with that miserable Yagerhorn?"

"Keep him here for the night in uncertainty as to his fate," Roger replied casually, "then let him go in the morning."

"The villain deserves worse," she remarked with a shrug. "But you are magnanimous by nature; and wise too, for the Empress might inquire into the matter with serious results to yourself should any permanent harm befall him. Otherwise I would suggest that you should mark him in some way, so that he should never forget this night of your triumph over him."

Roger gave her a side-long glance. Her harshness towards a man whom she had once taken with glad laughter as her lover was quite incomprehensible to him. During these past weeks her beauty had never failed to rouse his passion or her intellect to stimulate his mind. Yet he knew that in his heart he hated and despised her, and would have broken with her long since had it not been for her usefulness to him in securing the type of information he had come to Russia to obtain. Now that he was again in full possession of his senses the vicious delight that she had displayed, when he caught glimpses of her while he and Yagerhorn were locked in mortal combat, sickened and revolted him. He thanked his stars that their liaison depended only on his own convenience, and that as soon as he was better established at the Court he would be able to break it. He felt that he would not have married her for a million, and that there could be few more frightful fates than to find oneself tied to such a woman for life.

As he did not reply she stood up, came round to him, and perched herself upon his knee. "My poor Rojé Christorovitch," she murmured. "What a gruelling experience you have been through; but it is past, and your victory should serve to incite you to triumphs of another kind. I am the spoil of victory and yours to do what you will with. Yet I have none too much time to reward you as you deserve, for it's near half after nine already, so in less than an hour I must be gone."

Suddenly he realised that at some point of time within the past few hours his passion for her had died. Apart from a slight soreness in his throat and a dull ache in his left shoulder he was feeling perfectly fit again; yet he had not the least desire to make love to her, and doubted now if he would ever feel the urge again. On the other hand he knew that he could not yet afford to dispense with her. So, although he shook his head, he smiled at her and said diplomatically:

"Nay, my beautiful Natalia Andreovna. For once I fear that I must disappoint you. I still feel sick and heady from the recent brawl, and am not equal to challenging you in love's lists to-night. I pray you excuse me and allow me to rest again, while you solace my sadly frail and aching body by the very fact of lying quiescent by my side."

Immediately she was all concern, and on his pretending a renewed attack of vertigo, she helped him to the settee; then lay beside him with one arm about his neck. They remained so, hardly speaking, until, at ten o'clock, Ostermann knocked upon the door and announced that the lady's carriage awaited her below. She poured a final glass of wine, and while they drank it, he assured her that he would send her a message asking for a rendezvous immediately on his return from Lake Ladoga.

This night of strife and blood seemed to have had exactly contrary effects on them. Never before had her farewells been so lingering and so loving; and she swore that if any ill befell him she would die of grief on account of it. Her declarations were so fervid that he found it difficult to doubt their sincerity, and he had to admit to himself that, in her own extraordinary way, she must certainly have a very deep and genuine feeling for him.

At a quarter past ten, she put on her hooded cloak and mask, and despite her protests, he saw her down to her carriage. She had allowed an ample safety margin of time for her return and she would have lingered, had he not insisted that she must run no risk of some unforeseen misadventure upon the road causing a delay which might result in her finding herself locked out.

As her carriage clattered away Roger drew a deep breath of the fresh night-air into his lungs, and his apparent tiredness fell from him. Re-entering the house he called to Ostermann to fetch his horse round immediately, then ran upstairs to find Zaria Feodorovna.

She was sitting in her attic fully dressed and waiting for him. At the sound of his footsteps she jumped to her feet and threw open her door. He had only to beckon and she hurried after him down to his apartment.

In the two months that she had been with him she had picked up quite a lot of French, and although she could speak it only in a garbled fashion she now had no difficulty in understanding everything he said to her.

When they reached the sitting-room he told her briefly that an enemy of his had attempted to kill him, but had been overcome, and was now lying tied up in the bedroom. To punish the fellow he meant to keep him there all night; but as he had to set out at once on a journey himself he wished her to act as wardress.

Taking Zaria into the bedroom he gave her a hunting-knife, pointed to the prostrate Count and said: "I want you to sit here with him till morning. If he starts to struggle go over and look at the knots which secure him. Should they appear to be slackening prick him with the knife until he stops wriggling. But also examine the gag over his mouth. If you find that he shows signs of suffocation, and is struggling on that account, loosen it a little, so that he gets more air. At six o'clock you are to cut the cord that ties his wrists, then leave him to untie his ankles himself. He will be too stiff to grab you and do you any harm. As soon as you have freed his hands you are to leave the house and take a holiday with your parents for the next three days. I expect to be back on Friday, so you can return here that night. If, in the meantime, anyone seeks you out and questions you about this man, you will simply say that I told you that he was a villain who had attempted to assassinate me, and that you did no more than carry out my orders."

Zaria felt the point of the knife with her finger and grinned at him. "You may leave all to me, lord, and know that I shall do exactly as you bid me. May St. Nicholas protect you on your journey."

He was troubled with no scruples at having involved her in an illegal act, since, as his serf, she was bound by law to obey him in all things, and could not be called to account for carrying out any orders he might give her. Having kissed her on the forehead and chucked her under the chin, he hurried back to the sitting-room to collect his cloak, sword and pistols.

As he was doing so his eye fell upon three rings, lying on a low table near the settee. They were Natalia's; she had taken them off before bathing his face and had evidently forgotten to put them on again. Snatching them up he unlocked the brass-bound coffer in which he kept his money, threw them inside, re-locked it and ran downstairs.

Ostermann was outside walking the mare up and down. With a word of thanks to him Roger mounted her and trotted off down the street. He had Yagerhorn's *laisser passer* in his pocket, and was well satisfied with the eventual outcome of the night's events. His arrangements had worked so smoothly that barely eight minutes had elapsed between Natalia Andreovna's leaving and his being on his way to Finland.

Once clear of the city the road led north-west across the Karelian isthmus. Unlike the splendid highways to the south of the Gulf which led to Peterhof and Tzarskoe-selo, it had no fine columns of marble, jasper and granite to mark the *versts*, or the eleven hundred globular lamps which were always kept burning at night to light the way for courtiers and couriers hastening to or from the Imperial Palaces; but fortunately the moon was nearly at the full and shining in an almost cloudless sky.

Without forcing the pace, so as to save his mare, and dismounting every hour to give her a good breather, Roger steadily ate up the miles. He had the best part of a hundred and fifty miles to go, and shortly before three in the morning he entered the little town of Kyrolä, having covered a good third of the distance.

Knowing that the inn would be certain to prove squalid and verminous, he watered his mare at the village-trough, tethered her to a nearby tree, and gave her a feed from her nose-bag; then he wrapped himself in his heavy cloak and lay down in a dry, grassy ditch to get some sleep. It was Wednesday, the 29th of August, and the chill of autumn was already in the air, but he was warmly clad and felt no discomfort from it.

The nights were lengthening now, but it was full daylight when he woke at seven to see a group of peasant-women regarding him with mild curiosity as they filled their buckets at the well. After watering and feeding his mount he made breakfast off some of his provisions. Then he mounted again and set out to do the twenty miles to Viibörg.

The ancient Finnish city offered much better accommodation; so he had a second breakfast at the hostelry there at ten o'clock and, leaving his mare in its stable, continued his journey on a post-horse.

He had been passing through a desolate land of lakes and marshes, interspersed with dark forests of larch and pine; but, for the greater part of the way the road now ran along the coast, where small villages inhabited by primitive fishing-communities were comparatively numerous. Having twice more changed his mount at post-houses, and taken a good rest at midday, he entered the area of military operations about five in the afternoon. Leaving the road he proceeded with some caution for a further two miles, avoiding all camps as he came in sight of them; then, the terrain forced him to return to the highway, and shortly afterwards he was halted by a Russian outpost.

The sergeant in charge was unable to read and regarded him with considerable suspicion; but Roger could now speak a few words of Russian and he demanded to be taken before an officer. After some twenty minutes delay a young lieutenant examined his *laisser-passer*, pronounced it to be in order, and gave him permission to proceed.

On reaching the first Swedish post he asked the whereabouts of Gustavus, and learned, as he had hoped, that the King was still in his camp outside Frederikshamn. Two dragoons were detained to escort him there, with orders to see that he did not escape; but he had no desire to do so and shortly before seven o'clock he reached the Swedish headquarters.

When he gave his name and said that he had come from St. Petersburg with urgent news for the King, he was taken to the pavilion of General Baron Armfeldt. Gustavus's handsome favourite at once announced that he was the proper channel through which all news should reach the King, but Roger politely declined the offer of his services and insisted that he must speak personally and in private with His Majesty.

Upon this he was shown to a smaller tent, where he waited for well over an hour. Then an officer led him in the failing light across the grass to a large marquee. In it Gustavus was sitting at a table strewn with maps. His foxy face looked drawn and a little older, but his slightly protuberant eyes still shone with energy and courage. Roger bowed and stood silent, waiting to be addressed.

"Well, Mr. Brook," Gustavus smiled slightly. "We had almost come to believe that you had forgotten us; yet always had a feeling that sooner or later you would honour your obligation, and that when you did you would bring us intelligence of more worth than a dozen of our paid spies. Stand not on ceremony, but earn our eternal gratitude by telling us that Admiral Greig has hung himself from his own yardarm, or that Catherine the harlot has died from taking an overdose of some new aphrodisiac."

Roger mutely shook his head and, as befitted the bearer of bad news, fell on one knee as he replied: "Alas, Sire, I fear that I bring you ill-tidings. In fact they could scarce be worse."

"No matter," the King's voice was firm. "God knows, fortune has dealt us blows enough these past few months; yet, despite all calamities our shoulders are not become so weak that we cannot bear more, and still face the future with becoming fortitude."

"Sire," Roger said sadly, "in a treaty made some years back, by which the Empress surrendered the Holstein territories to the Danes in exchange for two small duchies, there was a secret clause. By it the Danes bound themselves to aid Russia should she ever be attacked by Sweden. They have agreed to honour it, and are at this moment arming with intent to stab your Majesty in the back."

Gustavus leapt to his feet. "Is this the truth? Are you certain of it?"

"I had it, Sire, not more than sixty hours ago, from an impeccable source."

"Then God be praised!" The King ran forward, raised Roger to his feet, and embraced him. " 'Tis the best news we have had since we landed in this accursed province. And for the bringing of it we will make you a Chevalier of our Order of the Sword of Sweden."

Roger stared at him in dumbfounded amazement as he began to pace up and down, and breaking into the first person went on excitedly: "Do you not see how this apparently disastrous development may be turned to my advantage? All the world knows that I led my army into Finland. What they do not know is that it is three parts composed of poltroons and traitors. Owing to the disaster sustained by my fleet the army is cut off here; and even could my personal eloquence persuade the men to a renewed sense of their duty their efforts would be rendered abortive through an acute shortage of warlike stores. My forces are completely moribund and can effect nothing, so their state must go from bad to worse. The only hope for them lies in my own return to Stockholm, where I could raise a new fleet, challenge Admiral Greig's temporary supremacy in the Gulf, and bring them succour. Yet how could I abandon my own troops in their present plight without being branded as a coward in their eyes and those of all Europe alike? This news you bring me provides the one excuse by which the army's situation and my personal honour may be saved. Since our homeland is to be attacked the Monarch's proper place is in his capital. To gain it I needs must run the hazard of the blockade; yet even capture in the attempt would be better than to remain here until things reach such a pass that I may risk the indignity of being arrested by my own officers. Mr. Brook, you have brought me new life, and I am your eternal debtor for it."

For Roger this outburst threw an entirely new light on the situation, and from having anticipated an ill-reception on account of the gloomy duty he had undertaken, he found himself instead a welcome and honoured guest. He spent over an hour with Gustavus, giving him the latest particulars of affairs at the Russian Court, and left the marquee with the Star of his first Order of Chivalry glittering upon his chest. That night he supped with the King and slept in reasonable comfort in the camp.

Next morning he set off back to St. Petersburg, reaching Viibörg that night; and on the Friday he completed his journey, arriving at his lodging soon after four in the afternoon.

He had taken the last stage slowly, and during it, thought out the line of conduct he should adopt if Count Yagerhorn had laid a complaint against him with the police. It seemed best to state frankly that, on account of a love-affair that he had had while in Stockholm, the Count had waylaid him and given him a beating; and that on learning that the Count had come to St. Petersburg he had availed himself of the opportunity to lure him to his lodging and repay the compliment. The Russian mentality was such as to consider his act fully justified. He hoped that the Count would not drag Natalia Andreovna into the matter, as she might incur the Empress's displeasure for the part she had played; but if that did occur it could not be helped.

The only point that bothered him a little was how to explain away his having stolen Yagerhorn's *laisser-passer* but he decided that here a lie would serve him best. He could say that after the affray in Stockholm the Count had taken the papers from his pocket and maliciously destroyed them with the object of causing him inconvenience; and that he had returned tid-for-tat without even noticing that the *laisser passer* was among them.

On arriving at his lodging he met Ostermann in the hallway. The Courlander gave him good-day with a somewhat shifty, surprised look, but refrained from saying anything further. Running upstairs to his apartment Roger threw open the door; grouped round the table there were three men playing a game of dice. They were wearing the uniform of the Russian police.

At his entrance they all jumped to their feet. The tallest of the three stepped forward, gave a curt bow and said in German: "You are the Chevalier de Breuc are you not? Since you left all your money here we were in hopes that you might return for it before attempting to leave the country, and our patience is well rewarded."

Roger returned the bow politely. "I had no intention of leaving the country, Sir. I have been absent on a fishing-expedition for the past few days; but this being my lodging I naturally intended to return to it. May I inquire the reason for your desiring to see me?"

The officer coughed, brushed up his flowing moustache and said firmly: "It is my duty to arrest you, Chevalier, for the murder of Count Erik Yagerhorn."

CHAPTER XVII

PENALTY FOR MURDER

"MURDER!" gasped Roger, his blue eyes opening wide with shock and sudden apprehension. "Is the Count then dead? I left him. . . ."

He broke off half-way through his sentence from a swift realisation that, for the moment, the less he said the better. He had already committed himself to one lie, by saying that he had been on a fishing-expedition, and if found out in that it might throw discredit on all else he said. What had gone wrong in his absence he could not even remotely guess; but it was clear that some fatal accident had now placed his own life in the direst peril.

The officer relieved him of his sword; one of the men left the room for a few minutes, and on his return, Roger was taken downstairs. Outside in the street there now stood a plain carriage with iron shutters instead of windows. They all got in and drove off.

Suddenly Roger's benumbed wits began to work again and he had an inspiration. His companions were not police-officers at all but men hired and disguised in police uniforms by Yagerhorn. The Count evidently meant to make a vendetta of their quarrel and had thought up this clever ruse for a double purpose; firstly to inflict a terrible fright upon him and secondly in order that he might be conveyed unresisting to some lonely spot where full vengeance could be exacted.

Five minutes later this illusion was abruptly dissipated. The carriage halted, and as Roger got out he recognised the police-office of his district. He was led inside and immediately taken before the local police-president.

The official asked him his name, rank and nationality. Roger gave them as "Rojé Christorovitch de Breuc; Major-General, and Chevalier; native of Strasbourg, France."

When these had been noted down, and his age, his address and the date of his arrival in Russia had been taken, the next question was: "When did you last see Count Erik Yagerhorn?"

To this Roger refused to reply, and added that he would make no statement of any kind until he was given full particulars as to why they should suppose that he had killed the Count; and had also been allowed to see the French Ambassador.

The police-president shrugged, and said that given a little time in a dungeon to think matters over the prisoner would, no doubt, see the advisability of answering straightforward questions. In view of his rank he could not be put into the ordinary criminal prison, so would be taken to the Fortress of Schlüsselburg.

Roger had never seen the fortress but knew that it lay some twenty miles to the east of St. Petersburg, on a small island in the mouth of the Neva where it enters Lake Ladoga; and he had heard of it in connection with the tragic life and death of the Czar Ivan IV.

This unfortunate prince, although the legitimate heir to the throne, had been deposed while still a babe in arms in favour of his aunt Elizabeth. From fear of his being used as the focus of a conspiracy against her she had kept him a solitary prisoner during the whole of his childhood and youth. At the time of her death he was twenty-two, and, report had it, a personable young man of agreeable manners, who, considering that he had spent his whole life behind prison-walls, showed every sign of good mental abilities. For a few months his prospects had then brightened as Peter III, owing to his hatred of his wife Catherine, had during his short reign, contemplated putting aside both Catherine and his son by her and making the poor captive his heir. He had even visited the prisoner at Schlüsselburg and given orders for more comfortable accommodation to be provided for him. But the *coup d'état* had put an end to any hopes of poor Ivan ever knowing the joys of freedom. Worse, after Peter's death all those who had a grudge against the new Empress began to contemplate another *coup d'état* which would place Ivan on the throne. The conspiracy misfired and during an abortive attempt to rescue him he had been brutally murdered by his guards. Some people whispered that Catherine had known of the conspiracy and deliberately allowed it to develop to a point at which she could use it as an excuse to rid herself of this inoffensive yet potentially dangerous rival to her power.

While Roger was on the way to Schlüsselburg, in the closed carriage, he recalled all that he had heard of this melancholy tragedy, and particularly the rumours, though they were no more, which inferred the the complicity of the Empress in young Ivan's untimely death. With fresh trepidation he remembered that no more than rumour accused her of having ordered her husband's death, yet he carried the written proof of her guilt upon him.

That damning piece of evidence against the autocrat was carefully sewn up in the stiff buckram lining to the collar of his coat; but he knew that when he reached the fortress his clothes as well as his person might possibly be searched. Alexis Orlof had, apparently, never missed the document and still believed it to be where it had lain untouched for years, safely in his secretaire; but Roger knew that, whether it could be proved that he was responsible for Yagerhorn's death or not, he could expect no mercy if the paper was discovered.

His fears for himself were further augmented by the fact that he still had both Yagerhorn's *laisser-passer* and King Gustavus's gift, the Order of the Sword of Sweden, in his pocket. If they were found upon him it should not be difficult to put two and two together and, since Russia was in a state of war with Sweden, he would be shot as a spy. Yet he could not possibly rid himself of the *laisser-passer* or the Star and its yellow ribbon while in an iron-shuttered carriage with his guards watching him.

With such concrete grounds for apprehension on three separate counts, any one of which might result in his speedy death, Roger felt that his chances of leaving the fortress alive were almost non-existent; and by the time they reached it his very natural fears had caused him to break out in a muck sweat.

On arrival, his particulars were entered by a sour-faced clerk into a heavy ledger, and the police then handed him over to two hefty, ill-favoured gaolers. They lit their lamps, took him to a gloomy stone-floored room, and waited there with him for some twenty minutes until a senior warder joined them. The newcomer beckoned, and Roger was taken along seemingly endless, low-vaulted corridors. At length they halted in front of a heavy iron-studded door. It was unbolted; Roger was thrust in and it clanged dismally behind him.

There was no light or heat and the place smelt dank and foul. His heart sinking to his boots Roger stood still for a moment, listening to the eerie echo of the warders' retreating footsteps. Then there fell complete and utter silence.

Nerving himself against the unexpected, he shuffled forward a few paces, his hands outstretched before him. His feet made a softly-padding sound, so he judged the floor to be covered with a layer of sodden straw. At about twelve paces from the door his fingers suddenly came in contact with damp, rough-hewn stone. Feeling about with his hands, in places he touched slime, and as he continued his investigation, he discovered that he was in an underground cell which measured about four paces by three, and had at one side of it a solid stone slab raised some eighteen inches from the floor which could be used as a seat or for lying down.

Seating himself upon it he cupped his chin in his hands and began afresh to contemplate his hopeless situation. After a few moments a faint sound from the far corner of the cell caught his attention. A second later he jumped to his feet and cowered back against the wall. He could not see them but he knew that there were rats there, perhaps swarms of them; and he had heard stories of the feet of living prisoners, in just such circumstances as he now found himself, being gnawed away by packs of rodents made desperate by hunger.

Roger was no coward. Before he reached the age of twenty he had challenged, fought and killed one of the finest swordsmen in all France; with a weapon in his hands he was prepared, if need be, to prove his metal against heavy odds; but the thought of his clothes and flesh being torn from him in small pieces by scores of sharp little teeth utterly unnerved him. The sweat of terror broke out upon his face and he began to shout for help with all the power of his lungs.

No answer came to his frantic cries, and after a while, he fell silent. The sounds from the corner of the cell told him that there was a number of rats there, but they came no nearer. Gradually calmness returned to him, and with the perspiration now cold upon his forehead, he sat down again.

For some time his mind was too numb with misery for him to think coherently; then he remembered that in one thing at least he had been granted a reprieve; he had not so far been searched.

Taking the papers from his inner pocket he fumbled among them in the darkness until, by his sense of touch he had decided which of them must be the *laisser-passer*. He then got out his tinder-box, and with some difficulty succeeded in igniting it. When at last the paper burst into a flame, he heaved a sigh of relief. At least he had succeeded in destroying one damning piece of evidence against him.

Yet, as he looked up he cowered back again. The flame was reflected in the corner of the cell by a galaxy of little starlike lights, the eyes of the rats who were watching him, and there could not be less than a score of them.

When he had recovered from that unnerving turn he took from his pocket the Swedish Order. Since it was his first decoration, and a great honour for so young a man, he was most loath to part with it, but he knew that it would cost him his life if it was found upon him. The sodden straw was a good six inches deep, since one layer had been thrown down upon another and it seemed improbable that the cell had been cleaned out for years. Digging the toe of his boot into the soggy mess, he scooped a hole until he reached the floor, laid the much prized jewel and ribbon on the exposed stone, and trampled the decaying straw well down over it.

He heaved another sigh; partly of regret but partly also of relief. He had enjoyed the possession of it for barely forty-eight hours, but it could not now convict him of being in league with Russia's enemies; since it was most unlikely that it would be found for months to come; and, even if it were, no proof could be brought that it was he who had hidden it there.

With a little gleam of humour it occurred to him how admirable it would be if only he could lay Count Yagerhorn's ghost as easily as he had disposed of the other two more material objects which had threatened to bring him to an untimely grave.

There remained, too, Orlof's letter; but, lacking a knife or scissors, he knew that it would be extremely difficult to get it from its hiding-place, and influenced partly by the unlikelihood of its being discovered there and partly by his belief in its immense potential value, he decided not to attempt its destruction.

Puzzle his wits as he would he could not even hazard a theory as to how the Count had met his death. It could not possibly have been a heart-attack, as had he been liable to such a seizure it would have taken him while he was being flogged into insensibility. It could not have been suffocation either, since he distinctly recalled giving Zaria implicit instructions to ease the Count's gag if that became necessary; and he did not believe for an instant that Zaria would have failed to carry out his orders. The flogging with a riding switch across the head and shoulders could not possibly have been the cause of his death, seeing that he had survived for the best part of three hours afterwards.

At length Roger gave up the riddle and his thoughts drifted to the strange fate which had carried him so far from home. He thought of his dear, wicked Georgina, and wondered if she had returned yet to her beloved Stillwaters or was somewhere in the distant Mediterranean, travelling with her father. He thought, too, of his sweet-faced mother with her circumscribed yet active existence, bounded by her charities and her Hampshire garden; and of his father, that rampaging, forth-right, jolly sea-dog of an Admiral. His small but stately home in Lymington was in fact several thousand miles away, but in mental distance it seemed a million.

Roger began to feel very tired, but he knew that he dared not sleep. As long as he kept awake the rats would keep their distance, but if he once allowed himself to drop off, the foul creatures would sneak up and begin to nibble at his extremities.

Now and again he stood up and, for a little, paced the narrow cell to keep himself awake and warm; yet, despite these periods of exercise, towards morning the deathly chill of the place began to make him shiver.

Time stood still. It was a place of eternal night where months might pass without its occupant ever being aware that the sun he once had known had passed across the sky. The stomach of the prisoner was his only clock, and but for the lack of craving in his, Roger would have thought that several days had passed, before at last, he caught faint footfalls coming down the corridor.

The footfalls grew louder; they halted, and the heavy door grated open. By the dim light of a lantern Roger saw the head-gaoler and another. The senior called to him and he stumbled from his cell. They took him through endless vaulted corridors again, up several flights of stone steps to the blessed daylight once more, and showed him into a room where an oldish man, dressed in a handsome uniform, was seated behind a desk.

To Roger's amazement this obviously important person not only offered him a chair, but proceeded to apologise to him for the unpleasant hours that he had passed since his arrival. Apparently, unless special instructions were received to the contrary, all new prisoners were put in one of the lower dungeons for their first night, in order that they might form some impression of what a month of such confinement would be like; and thus be persuaded of the folly of bringing such a penalty upon themselves by attempting to escape.

The elderly officer introduced himself as Colonel Tschevaridef; then told Roger with bluff heartiness that he was very pleased to see him, would endeavour to make him as comfortable as possible, and hoped that his stay in the fortress would be a long one. So did Roger, providing it was not in the dungeon—as even a lengthy imprisonment seemed better than the short shrift he had been envisaging for himself since four o'clock the previous afternoon—but all the same he thought the greeting a little queer.

However, it soon emerged that the old soldier was the Governor of the fortress, and he admitted quite frankly that the amount of his income depended on the number and quality of the prisoners in his keeping. He received so much a day for each and the higher their rank the higher the rate he was paid. He was responsible for feeding them out of the money, and the more he got for them the better they fared. Roger, ranking as a Major-General, would be classed as of the second grade, at two roubles a day, and feed almost as well as if he were eating at the Governor's table. The Colonel concluded this reference to his organisation by remarking that he prided himself on giving all grades of his prisoners better fare than was the case in other fortresses, and that when Roger was released he would be doing both him and any friend of his who might be a prisoner elsewhere a good service by urging them to use such influence as they might have to get themselves transferred to Schlüsselburg.

The idea of a prison-governor canvassing for captives made Roger smile for the first time in seventeen hours, and he said quickly: "I only pray that I may have the opportunity to do so, Sir; but I may be hard put to it to escape being executed on this charge of murder."

"So you are charged with killing someone, eh?" the Governor raised a white eyebrow. "That is a pity, since it may be the cause of my losing you in a day or two; but otherwise it is no affair of mine. A magistrate will visit your cell to question you on that. In the meantime your treatment will be no different to that of other prisoners of your grade, and I have received no order that you are not to be allowed visitors." With a grin which showed several decayed teeth he added: "A young man of such handsome parts, as yourself, General, will no doubt know a number of pretty women who will be delighted to solace you during your captivity."

Roger grinned amiably back at the old rascal and said: "At the moment, Sir, I am more concerned with the question of my defence;

and I should be deeply grateful if you would send a message to the French Ambassador, asking him to come and see me."

The Governor promised to do so, then summoned the warders and told them to take Roger to cell twenty-four. When he reached it he found it to be a spacious room with a heavily-barred window giving a view of the lake. It was furnished with an old, but fairly comfortable-looking bed, an oak chest, a wash-basin and commode, an elbow-chair and two others, and a stout table on which there were pens, sand and an inkhorn. The head-warder told him that on payment he could have extra wine, brandy, paper, books and other small luxuries brought in; then he was left to his still far from sanguine reflections.

But not for long. Five minutes later one of the warders returned to show in a dark hatchet-faced little man in a wig much too big for him, and a lanky fellow carrying a portfolio. They proved to be the magistrate and his clerk; but, when Roger said that he was not prepared to answer any questions until he had seen his Ambassador, they withdrew.

It now occurred to him that it was many hours since he had eaten, and that he was very hungry; but evidently his gaolers had not been unmindful of the fact that he had not had any breakfast, for soon after the Magistrate's departure, one of them brought him some cold meat, an apple-turnover and a jug of beer.

He was still eating when the door opened again, and, to his surprise and delight Dr. Drenke was shown in. After his first day or two in St. Petersburg Roger had not seen very much of the middle-aged German diplomat, but they sometimes passed one another on the stairs and had remained on a friendly footing. In his misery of the previous night he had not once thought of the Doctor, but now he welcomed him with open arms, as he was the one person to whom he could talk with complete frankness about the Yagerhorn affair, as it was unnecessary to conceal from him the part that Natalia Andreovna had played in it.

"Well, my poor Chevalier," said the Doctor, when he was seated. "I am much relieved to see that you appear to be in your right mind, for I doubted finding you so. What in the world possessed you to murder Count Yagerhorn in so barbarous a manner, and then throw the unfortunate little Zaria downstairs?"

Roger gaped at him, then exclaimed: " 'Tis the first I have heard of Zaria's mishap! As for the other matter I know nothing of what occurred after I left the house at ten o'clock on Tuesday night. I beg you to enlighten me."

" 'Tis soon told," the Doctor replied gravely. "At about half-past ten Ostermann came up from his basement to lock the street-door. At the bottom of the stairs he found Zaria lying in a crumpled heap, unconscious. Later, when she was taken to the hospital it was found that she had broken a leg and that her skull was fractured. Ostermann had seen you off on your fishing-expedition at ten o'clock, so he thought at first that a thief must have stolen into the house, and that Zaria had surprised him. He ran up to your sitting-room, and on seeing that nothing had been taken, hurried up to mine. I was there reading, and some twenty minutes before I had heard the sounds of a quarrel below me in your room; so we assumed that, having forgotten something you had returned for it, and catching Zaria in the act of making free with your property you had exercised your right to knock her senseless. We gave you the credit for not realising how seriously you had injured the poor girl, in fact that you thought she had only fainted; and supposed that being already late in your setting out you had jumped on your horse again and ridden away, believing that the sturdy little peasant would be fully recovered from her lesson by morning."

The Doctor paused a moment, then went on: "When Ostermann visited your apartment he took only a hurried look round and did not enter the bedroom. The following day he gave the usual notice to the police that you were absent, but they were quite satisfied by his explanation that you had gone fishing on Lake Ladoga, and would be back on Friday. When Friday morning came, since Zaria was in hospital with a broken leg and severe concussion, Ostermann felt that it was for him to tidy up your apartment against your return. On entering your bedroom he found Count Yagerhorn lying gagged and bound upon the bed. When he fetched the police, they said that the Count had died of suffocation."

"So that was the way of it," nodded Roger. Everything was plain to him now except the attack on Zaria; but, perhaps after all, Ostermann's first theory had been right, and she had been the victim of a thief. She should have been in the bedroom watching Yagerhorn, but if she had heard a noise in the sitting-room she would have come out to see who was there. She might have come upon the thief before he had had time to take anything, and the cries that the Doctor had heard were her efforts to rouse the house; but the thief had overcome her, thrown her down the stairs, and fearing that someone else might come on the scene, hurriedly made his escape. With Zaria suffering from concussion the wretched Count had been left to his fate, and died horribly in consequence.

"I should like to tell you the truth of the matter," Roger said, after a moment. "But only if I may rely on you regarding what I say as in the strictest confidence; for another person is involved in this."

"You may rely on my discretion, Chevalier," the Doctor bowed. "And you refer, I take it, to the Baroness Stroganof?"

Roger gave him a swift glance. "Is it generally known that 'twas she who preceded Yagerhorn to my apartment?"

The Doctor shook his head. "Nay, only that a woman of quality who often came to visit you, dined with you there before the Count's arrival. I guessed that it must be she from knowing of your association with her in the ship that brought us from Sweden, and from having more recently met her once or twice on the stairs."

"That relieves me mightily. For the sake of her reputation I have been at some pains to conceal her identity; so although Ostermann knows her well by sight I doubt if he knows her name. Her only part in this was giving the Count a rendezvous in my apartment; and that she did at my most earnest solicitation and without previous knowledge of what I meant to do to him. She left before myself and can have had no more idea than I of what befell him later. So you see what a terrible thing it would be if she were charged with me in having assisted at his murder?"

"I do not think there is any great fear of that, Chevalier, unless you deny that it was you who killed him. The police of Petersburg are argus-eyed but very discreet. The odds are that they have known for a long time past about the Baroness's visits to you; but they will not drag her into this unless compelled to it. She has many powerful relatives, and moreover, the Empress does not like scandals in connection with her ladies, so they will not stir up trouble for themselves unless it proves unavoidable."

"You mean that if I take full responsibility they will be satisfied with that; but should I protest my innocence they will then be forced to turn their attention to the Baroness in the hope of getting a statement from her that will convict me?"

"Exactly. The present assumption is that the lady who dined with you was an innocent party to the affair. 'Tis thought that the Count was also in love with her and having traced her to your rooms surprised you together. What followed is, therefore, put to your account. But why, in the name of reason, did you choose so barbarous a method of killing the wretched man?"

"I did not," Roger assured the Doctor, earnestly. Then he told him the whole story as he knew it.

When he had done the Doctor shook his head. "I willingly accept your word for it, Chevalier, that you had no intention of killing the Count; but that does not affect the fact that you are responsible for his death and will be held to account for it. And even if the Baroness came forward I do not see how anything that she could say would lessen your responsibility."

"I know it," agreed Roger. "So I am all the more anxious that her part in the matter should not become public. Would you be good enough to see her for me, and assure her that should she become involved it will be through no word of mine?"

The Doctor agreed to do so; and to Roger's further request, that little Zaria should be allowed to lack for nothing; then, with renewed expressions of friendship, he took his departure.

When he had gone Roger paced restlessly up and down his room. He at least knew now the way in which his plan had miscarried, but that did not lessen the acute danger of his situation. For a time he thought miserably of the terrible death that Yagerhorn had suffered, yet he felt that he was not wholly to blame for that. The Count would be alive and free had it not been for the dastardly attack on poor little Zaria.

At three o'clock the key of the heavy door grated in the lock.

253

Roger stood up hoping that the Comte de Ségur had arrived to see him, but a woman in black with a heavy hood over her face was shown in. The second they were alone she threw it back and ran to him.

"Natalia Andreovna!" he exclaimed, as her arms closed round his neck. "You should not have come! 'Tis madness to proclaim your association with me in this way."

"I had to come!" she cried, bursting into tears. " 'Tis my fault that you are here; but I did not learn the awful result of my impetuous act until this morning."

"Act?" He held her firmly from him. "What mean you?"

"On Tuesday night I left my rings behind," she sobbed. "My carriage had carried me but half a mile when I remembered them. As I had ample time I returned to your apartment. I was looking for them in the sitting-room when the bedroom door opened, and out of it came that little baggage that you bought for a hundred roubles on your first arrival in Petersburg."

In a flash Roger saw the whole thing. To appease Natalia's jealousy he had told her that he had got rid of Zaria and that Ostermann was looking after him. On finding the girl in his room again two months later Natalia, had, not unnaturally, believed the worst.

" 'Twas you, then, who beat her and threw her downstairs!" he muttered angrily. "Did you not have the sense to realise that I had left her there to watch over Yagerhorn and release him in the morning?"

"How should I?" she wailed. "You told me that you were not setting out for your fishing until the morning. As you were nowhere about I thought that you had merely gone down to the privy in the backyard, or to fetch another bottle of wine from the cellar, and would be back at any moment. You had lied to me about that pretty child and I was furious. I thought that finding her on your return with her looks spoiled would teach you a lesson."

"You broke her leg and devilish near killed her."

"I care not for that. I love you, Rojé Christorovitch, and was half-mad with jealousy from the thought that you had deceived me; and kept her with you for a full two months without my knowledge."

"You wrong me by these base suspicions. She was a virgin when I bought her and is one still. I kept her only out of compassion, because she would have been so shamed had I sent her back to her father."

Natalia ceased her crying. "You do love me then! Oh, St. Nicholas be praised for that! But I could not know that you had already set out and charged her to act gaoler to Erik Yagerhorn. I guessed that only on learning last night how he had been found dead in your room. Then came the news of your arrest this morning. Oh, Rojé Christorovitch, I'll never forgive myself, and I'll die of grief if—if. . . ." Again she burst into a fit of weeping.

Roger did not love her any more. His passion for her had died utterly; but it was clear that she now loved him madly, and in common decency, he strove to comfort her. For over an hour they talked round and round his plight, but saw no way by which he might evade responsibility for the Count's death.

The best line which seemed to offer was for him to admit to having left the Count bound and gagged, but plead that he had died only because the arrangements for his release had miscarried. If the court still judged Roger guilty of murder, Natalia would then use all her personal influence to get the sentence commuted from death to imprisonment. They agreed that if she could be kept out of the affair her hand would be strengthened in that. And, as he did not wish to be placed in a situation where he would have to make love to her again, he persuaded her that it would be wisest to refrain from making further visits to the fortress unless she had definite news to bring him. After a last tearful embrace they summoned the warder, and she departed.

The French Ambassador did not arrive until seven o'clock, and his visit was a comparatively brief one. The shrewd-eyed young Count was evidently far from pleased that one of his nationals should stand accused of such a brutal crime; but, after having listened to Roger's story, he became much more sympathetic.

He said gravely that he did not see how a court could fail to convict, but hoped the sentence might carry a recommendation to mercy. An appeal to the Empress was useless at the moment, as, although at a word she could stop any legal proceedings, there was nothing whatever about the present case which might induce her to do so. However, as the representative of the Court of Versailles he was in a position to draw Her Majesty's attention to any verdict pronounced on one of his countrymen, and could do so the more easily in this case as the Empress had told Roger on his presentation that if he found himself in any difficulty, he was to apply to her. So, when the time came, he would use his best endeavours to persuade her that death was too harsh a punishment for a crime that had only been in part premeditated.

Within twenty minutes of the Comte de Ségur's departure, the thin-faced magistrate and his clerk again appeared. Roger now agreed to make a statement, and after he had done so, answered most of the questions put to him with complete frankness. When he declined to give the name of the lady who had supped with him before Yagerhorn's arrival the magistrate refrained from pressing him to do so, and even volunteered the opinion that, since Roger had admitted his guilt, it would probably be considered unnecessary to seek out witnesses for the purpose of securing evidence against him.

When Roger was left to sort out his impressions of the day he felt considerably more cheerful than he had twenty-four hours earlier. His immediate circumstances were improved out of all recognition and he now thought it unlikely that he would be called on to pay with his life for Yagerhorn's death. There was also the immensely comforting thought that nobody appeared to be the least interested in his movements during his absence from St. Petersburg, or be aware that he had stolen Yagerhorn's *laisser-passer;* and even Natalia apparently saw no reason to doubt his statement that he had been fishing on Lake Ladoga.

Two mornings later the Comte de Ségur appeared again. His news was that at the previous night's Sunday Court the Empress had raised the question of Roger's affair on her own initiative, and said that she had given orders for proceedings to be temporarily suspended, as she had formed the desire to go into the matter herself.

It immediately occurred to Roger that Natalia Andreovna had seized upon some suitable opening to get to work on his behalf; but the Ambassador's next words destroyed this comforting theory.

He said, "I find myself quite unable to express an opinion whether this new development is likely to have a favourable or adverse effect on your prospects; and I should be serving you ill if I did not warn you that this signal honour is due to no more than curiosity." Smiling a little wryly he added: "The truth is that in Petersburg you are now accounted a monster, and Her Majesty, ever eager for new sensations, is desirous of having another look at you."

With this cold comfort Roger had to be content till afternoon, when Dr. Drenke came to see him, bringing more cheerful tidings. Zaria was now pronounced out of danger and had made a statement to the police. She confirmed all that Roger had said of his instructions to her, and had disclosed that her attacker had been a lady of quality whom she had seen once before but whom she did not know by name.

Roger was much relieved to hear that his little serf was on the way to recovery; but he rather doubted if, in Russia, any great weight would be attached to the testimony of a young girl-slave who was known to be devoted to him. However, her corroboration of his statement was very much better than nothing, and once again, Natalia Andreovna had escaped implication, which was a mercy, as any charge against her would have seriously impaired her influence when the time came for her to make her plea for him to the Empress.

During the forty-eight hours that followed he received no fresh news at all of his affair, and hardly knew whether to count that a misfortune or a blessing. The food he was given, while by no means luxurious, was plentiful and varied, and he had been allowed to send in to St. Petersburg for his clothes and money, so he was living in quite reasonable comfort. Yet, while he realised that any change in his situation might prove very much for the worse, uncertainty as to his eventual fate kept him in a state of nervous tension, and he was beginning to be afraid that the Empress had forgotten him.

That she had not, became apparent on the afternoon of Wednesday, the 5th of September, when two handsome young men of her Chevalier Guard were shown in to his room. After greeting him civilly they asked him to prepare himself to be taken before Her Majesty. He changed into his best suit, scented and powdered himself as if he were going to a ball, then accompanied them down to the echoing entrance-hall of the fortress. A shuttered carriage similar to that in which he had been brought to Schlüsselburg was waiting outside. The two young men mounted their horses, Roger, his heart beating considerably faster than usual, was locked into the carriage, and it started on its long drive via St. Petersburg to the Peterhof.

They had set out at three o'clock, and with halts for changing horses, it was nearly eight by the time they arrived at the Imperial Palace. Roger was conducted to the inner guard-room and left to wait there for over an hour; then the two officers returned, drew their swords, and placing themselves one on either side of him, marched him across the vast hall and up a great marble staircase. Some way down a corridor six more glittering members of the Chevalier Guard were drawn up before a pair of tall, ornate double doors. A chamberlain tapped upon the doors with an ivory-headed staff, two footmen threw them open, and drawing himself up, Roger walked forward into the presence of the Empress.

Seated behind a great carved desk she seemed even smaller than he had first thought her, but no less regal. As he advanced he saw that the dark, sly-faced old Katerina Ivanovna, who was both the Empress's personal confidant and the head of her household, was seated just behind her, that her favourite, Momonof, looking very bored, was in one corner of the room playing with a spaniel, and that two young ladies-in-waiting working on some embroidery, occupied another.

As the guards halted, six paces from the table, Roger went down on one knee.

"Stand up," commanded the Empress sharply. "And give us your account of this heinous crime, which brands you the most abominable of murderers."

"August Majesty," he began. "With your own fine mind, great heart and able hand, you gave a new code of laws to Russia. Throughout all the world you are revered for your sense of justice. I pray you, therefore, suspend judgment as to the degree of my guilt until you have heard the stroke of ill-fortune which renders me now a suppliant for mercy at your feet."

Her blue eyes were hard and her little curved nose imperious, as she replied: "You sound a plausible rogue; but think not to curry favour with us by idle flattery. The governance of an Empire leaves us little time for such as you; so be brief and to the point."

Roger had intended to give a full description of the affair from his first meeting with Yagerhorn in Stockholm, but he now promptly changed his tactics. In a few brief sentences he described how, having a quarrel with the Count, he had used a pretext to get him to his apartment, then set upon him, and how, owing to an entirely unforeseen sequel, Yagerhorn had been left there to die instead of being released the following morning.

"If this be true," said the Empress coldly, "you are not quite the monster that you have been represented; yet you are bandit enough to have attacked an unsuspecting man, and the fact that your serf failed to carry out your orders in no way relieves you of the responsibility for Count Yagerhorn's death."

"Nay, your Majesty," Roger replied with sudden boldness. "That

257

I admit, and a bandit I may be; but, vast as the gulf is that lies between us, we have at least two things in common; and 'tis on this similarity of our natures that I rely in pleading for your clemency."

"Such insolence merits the knout," muttered the Empress and her thin mouth hardened. But Roger ignored the danger signal. He knew that it was now or never, and he hurried on:

"I beg you, Madame, hear what led me to this deed and tell me then if, placed in similar circumstances, you would not have done as I did."

She nodded. "Speak then. But if you fail to prove your words your punishment shall be the more severe."

Roger took a pace forward. One of his most fortunate gifts was the ability to put his thoughts with ease and grace into either writing or speech; and he was making his plea in French, the second language of himself and Catherine, which both of them spoke as fluently as their own.

"Gracious Majesty," he began. "The two things which we have in common are courage and a love of gallantry. The devastation that your eyes have wrought in innumerable hearts and your amiability to those who are fortunate enough to find favour with you, are too well-known for me to need to dwell upon them. As for your courage, all the world knows that no male ruler has ever taken braver decisions than yourself. Yet there is one example of it that I would recall, for it made me think you braver than any fabled knight or classic hero."

At last the Empress's glance softened a little, and she inquired: "What deed of ours is it that you have in mind?"

" 'Twas when the small-pox was raging in Petersburg, and even striking down people of your Majesty's court," replied Roger promptly. "Fearing that your little son, His Highness the Grand Duke, might fall a victim to the fell disease you determined rather on submitting him to the risks of inoculation, a precautionary treatment then entirely untried in Russia. You sent to England for Dr. Dimsdale, and refusing to allow him to experiment first, as he wished, on any of your Majesty's subjects, insisted on his inoculating you with the deadly virus in secret, before he did so to your son and others."

The Empress shrugged her plump shoulders, but she smiled.

"Only a sovereign unfitted to rule would submit a helpless child or a subject to a risk that they were unwilling to face themselves. But if this be courage and we have a natural leaning towards romance, tell us now how these qualities led you to your present pass?"

Without naming Natalia Andreovna, Roger told Catherine then of his love-affair in Stockholm, and of the way in which Yagerhorn had ambushed him. He stoutly maintained that his plan to be revenged had been fully justified, and claimed that he had proved his courage by spurning the thought of hiring ruffians to waylay his enemy in the street at night. Instead, although the Count was far more heavily built, he had armed himself with only a whip, faced him man to man, and overcome him.

When the tale was done the Empress regarded Roger thoughtfully for a moment, then she said: "We will allow that you had some provocation for your act and that you gave Count Yagerhorn the opportunity to defend himself with his superior strength, which was more than he had any right to expect. Yet the fact remains that you deprived him of his life. It is our pleasure that you should remain in the palace while we deliberate upon the matter further. In due course we will have conveyed to you our will."

Sinking again to one knee Roger threw in his last reserves. "May it please your Majesty. Should you decide that my fault merits a major penalty I pray you let me die like a gentleman rather than live like a slave; and should death be the portion you decree for me I have one boon to crave."

"What would you?" asked the Empress a trifle impatiently.

Roger rose to his feet and smiled. " 'Tis that, before I am led out to die, I may kiss the hand that sends me to my premature fate, in token of my respect for the august Princess who has done more for her people than any other ruler."

He had taken a terrible gamble in saying that he would prefer death to a long imprisonment, but it was the only means that enabled him to follow up with his theatrical request, which, if she agreed to it, would ensure him a further, eleventh-hour, chance to plead for mercy.

It was all or nothing now; but, as she signed to his guards to take him away, he felt sure that he saw her bridle slightly at the compliment, and she murmured: "Your request is granted."

Instead of turning to be marched out like a prisoner, he played the well-trained courtier, and made her three perfect bows while backing unerringly towards the doors. He was then taken down to the guardroom, given some supper and provided with a truckle-bed on which to spend the night.

The following day passed uneventfully. The guards treated him courteously and he had no reason for complaint, but with nothing to do he found it terribly difficult to stifle the anxiety he was feeling. He felt sure that he had made a good impression on the Empress, but she prided herself so greatly on her sense of justice that he did not believe for one moment that she would let him go scot-free. She had vowed that she would suppress crimes of violence in her capital, and there was no half-way house between imprisonment and death, so she well might take him up on his quixotic gesture.

When, at seven o'clock in the evening, two guards appeared to fetch him, his first sensation was one of relief, at the thought that, in a few moments now, he would know the worst. But as he accompanied them up the grand staircase it dawned upon him that the Empress would send for him again only to do him the favour he had asked in the event of her decreeing his death. His mouth suddenly grew dry, and strive as he would, he could not think of a single new argument which might incline her to mercy. He had had all day to do so, yet somehow, he had never thought that it would come to this, and had frittered the hours away in idle speculation.

While these thoughts were occupying his agitated mind he was taken down the opposite corridor to that which he had entered the previous night. There were no sable-cloaked officers, chamberlains and footmen on duty here. One of his companions knocked upon a door, and a sharp voice called *"Entrez."* Next moment he found himself ushered into a small salon, and seated in it was old black-eyed Katerina Ivanovna.

As he automatically made a leg to the skinny, sallow-featured old woman, she beckoned him forward to a chair opposite her and said; "Monsieur, Her Majesty was not altogether unimpressed by the figure you cut before her last night; but before she pronounces sentence upon you she desires to know if you are nought but an adventurer gifted with a silver tongue or if you are, as you appear to be, a somewhat more worthy subject for her benevolent consideration. She has charged me to develop your acquaintance with a view to reporting to her on this matter; and as I am entertaining a few friends to supper to-night I felt that the best means of executing my commission was to bid you join us."

With mingled surprise and relief Roger made the old witch another bow and declared himself to be enchanted by the honour. At that moment the entrance of an officer and two ladies gave him a brief respite, while he was introduced to them, to gather his wits and prepare himself for this new ordeal upon which his life and freedom hung. Then he set about charming old Katerina Ivanovna with a greater assiduity than he would have displayed had she been half a century younger and the loveliest young woman of the Court.

Within a dozen minutes they were a party of ten, then the door opened again, and without the least formality, the Empress walked in.

Instantly they fell silent; the men bowed deeply, the women curtseyed to the ground. As Katerina Ivanovna rose she exclaimed: "Oh, your Majesty! How gracious of you! What a joyous surprise! I had no idea that you intended to honour me to-night. Permit me to have the table re-set." And after curtseying again she glided off into another room.

The Empress accepted a glass of wine, and with a few brief sentences, put the company at their ease. Katerina Ivanovna returned, and, shortly afterwards, supper was announced. Fat little Catherine led the way alone and, with a glance, Katerina Ivanovna signed to Roger to give her his arm. As they brought up the rear she whispered: "There has been no time to change the general seating. I should have been at the head of the table and had placed you on my left, but now Her Majesty takes my place and you will be next to her. For good or ill your destiny now lies in your own hands."

As he took his seat the Empress greeted him civilly, and gave no sign that she regarded him as in any way different to the other guests.

To each in turn she asked some question calculated to lead to a general discussion and Roger was filled with admiration at the way in which she dominated the party yet made it pleasant for everyone present. It was soon clear to him that at this intimate gathering she did not wish to be treated as a sovereign, to whom people spoke only when they were addressed, but simply as a distinguished guest, to whom good manners dictate a certain deference without servility. She even permitted some of those present to rally her gently on her acknowledged idiosyncrasies and joined freely in the laughter.

Once Roger had gauged the atmosphere, he worked like a demon to make himself pleasant, and he was wise enough to give an almost equal share of his attention to anyone who happened to be holding the table as he did to Catherine when she was speaking. He knew that he was fighting now with his wits and ready laugh for his life and freedom, every bit as much as if he had been sword in hand opposed to a troop of enemy horsemen in a battle. When the dessert was put on the table, knowing the Empress's love for French culture, he led the conversation in that direction, and with becoming modesty, displayed his knowledge of it. He had always despised Rousseau as a windy visionary and adored the brilliant cynicism of Voltaire. As the Empress was also entirely of that mind she openly applauded his witticisms and beamed approval on him.

At ten o'clock she stood up to retire. Everyone rose with her, and to Roger's sudden consternation, she held out her hand for him to kiss.

White as a sheet he bowed over it and touched it with his lips. He *hoped* that she had done him this honour as a sign of forgiveness, but, knowing the cruelty, treachery, and cynicism that permeated the whole Russian court, he could not be certain that the same plump hand had not signed his death-warrant a few hours earlier, and that she thought it amusing to honour her promise to him in this way.

The incident brought him back with a horrid jerk to the realisation that for the past two hours he had not really been a welcome guest at a jolly supper-party, but a prisoner with one foot on the scaffold. It was all he could do to regain his composure sufficiently to bid a polite good-night to the other guests, who shortly afterwards took their leave.

Finding himself once more alone with Katerina Ivanovna, he said: "Madame, if I knew this definitely to be my last night on earth I could not conceivably have wished for a more pleasant one; and I am more grateful than I can say for your charming entertainment. May I now spare you the trouble of calling the guard and ask you to accept my word that I will find my own way back to the guardroom?"

She shook her bony old head. "Nay, you are in my charge now, Chevalier, and I wish to be able to converse with you at my pleasure. Come with me."

He followed her out into the corridor and along it for fifty paces, then she opened a door and showed him into a well-furnished bedroom. When he thanked her the only reply she made was to wish him

261

good-night, and after a formal curtsey to which he bowed gravely, she left him.

On finding himself alone his first thought was to escape. He had not been asked for his parole and this seemed a heaven-sent chance to do so. Running to the window he opened it and peered out. Below him was a broad paved terrace, that gave onto the gardens. It was a twenty-foot drop, but, undaunted by that, he looked swiftly round for means to get down to it. As he did so he caught the mutter of voices below him; two figures moved out of the shadows and began to pace up and down. He knew then that it was no good. His bonds might have been changed from iron to silk, but they were still there. It was only that a less obtrusive watch was being kept upon him, and even if he could overcome the two sentries on the terrace, he was alone and almost friendless in Russia. How could he possibly hope to remain uncaught long enough to get out of the country? Reluctantly he undressed himself and made the best of the comfortable bed.

Next morning a footman came to draw back his curtains, then brought him an appetising breakfast. Having eaten it he got up and dressed himself to be in readiness should he be sent for. At nine o'clock there came a knock on the door and a fat, serious-looking man presented himself, announcing in German that he was a doctor and had been ordered to ascertain the state of Roger's health.

At first Roger thought that there must be some mistake, and said so, but his visitor replied thickly: "If you are the Chevalier de Breuc there is no mistake. It is the usual procedure, and you will oblige me by undressing."

As it seemed most unlikely that convicted criminals had to undergo a medical examination before they were taken to execution, Roger could only assume that this was a regulation measure adopted with everyone who came to reside in the palace, as a precaution against infectious and contagious diseases being carried into it. In his own case it seemed a little belated, but he thought that was probably owing to the unorthodox means by which he had become a resident there.

When Roger had stripped as requested the doctor made a most careful examination of every part of his body, and at length, pronouncing himself satisfied, packed up his little black bag and departed.

Half an hour later the footman came in again, carrying a pile of books. After presenting Madame Katerina Ivanovna's compliments, he said that, as she had an exceptionally heavy day, she begged that Roger would entertain himself as well as he could with the books and excuse her until the evening.

Having no choice, Roger returned his thanks, browsed among the books, ate the good dinner that was sent to him, and spent a few hours dozing. Soon after seven o'clock the door opened and Katerina Ivanovna appeared framed in it. She did not enter the room but beckoned to him to join her outside.

When he did so she led him along several corridors, then down a long arched passageway with windows on either side of it through which the gardens could be seen dimly in the fast-failing light. He knew then that she was taking him across to the Empress's own private retreat, the Hermitage, and he assumed that he was on his way to learn his fate from Her Majesty's own lips.

On entering the smaller palace they went downstairs to the ground floor. Katerina Ivanovna then opened a door and took him into a long suite of private apartments consisting of two ante-rooms, a library, a reception-room, a dining-room and a bedroom; all of which had beautifully painted ceilings and were furnished with great splendour.

In one corner of the bedroom a spiral staircase, elaborately carved from rare woods, led up to a small circular opening in the high ceiling above. Pointing at the staircase Katerina Ivanovna said with her crooked smile: "In ten minutes' time you are to go up those stairs and perform the duties for which you have been selected."

"Duties!" repeated Roger. "To what duties do you refer, Madame?"

She gave him a pitying look. "I thought you keener-witted. These are the apartments of the official favourite. Those of Her Majesty are immediately overhead. I received orders to clear that fool Momonof out this morning."

Suddenly the old harridan sank to the floor in a flurry of black lace and, bowing her head before him, cried:

"Live long, Rojé Christorovitch! These rooms are yours! You are the favourite now! Live long; and while you share the Empress's bed forget not last night, and those who smoothed the path for you to become the most powerful man in All the Russias."

CHAPTER XVIII

HER MAJESTY'S PLEASURE

ROGER'S heart missed a beat and his mind baulked for a second, refusing to accept the extraordinary vision that Katerina Ivanovna's words had conjured up. It was fantastic, impossible; a dream from which he would soon wake with a start. It simply could not be true. The old witch was seeking to make a fool of him; or perhaps he had not heard her aright.

Then as he stared at her, still sunk in her curtsey at his feet, he knew that she was not making a mock of him, but had hailed him as the new Imperial consort in sober earnest.

Into his racing mind came all that Natalia Andreovna had told him of the making and unmaking of the favourites. When the Empress tired of one she never quarrelled with him or warned him that he was about to be dismissed. She began to look round for another; and shrewd Potemkin, to whom her mind was an open book on such matters, put a few likely young men in her way, taking care to select only those whom he felt had not sufficiently strong personalities to undermine his own position as her chief counsellor. When she found one of Potemkin's lusty young protégés pleasing to her, old Katerina Ivanovna was called in to give a party. Without knowing himself to be a candidate for the Empress's favour the young man was invited, and she attended as a private guest, so that she could talk to him informally without giving cause for gossip in her court. If, on closer acquaintance, she still found him to her liking, he was given a thorough medical examination. Then, without warning, the old favourite was presented with a big sum of money and told to travel, and the new one was installed in his place.

For many years past this had become an accepted ritual, and in a flash, Roger realised that he had been through it, with the only exception that, Potemkin being away at the wars, in this case the change of favourites was being made without his knowledge.

Raising Katerina Ivanovna to her feet, he said, a little breathlessly: "It is then to you, Madame, that I owe this sudden elevation?"

She leered at him. "I knew Her Majesty to be wearied of Momonof, and saw the moment that you were brought before her that she was taken with you. I have been her confidant for so long that I know her every mood. I had but to drop a word in her ear and arrange for suitable people to be at last night's supper party, and the result was a foregone conclusion."

As he did not reply, she went on: "For many years past the favourites have been no more than puppets dancing to Prince One-eye's tune. But unless I have lost the art of judging men you will prove different. Her Majesty still leans greatly on his advice, but there are times when she resents his dictatorial manner to the point of vowing that she will be rid of him. You are handsome enough to become another Lanskoi; but you can become greater than he. If you can establish yourself firmly with the Empress during Potemkin's absence, with my help it should not prove beyond you to unseat him on his return. Then you and I will rule Katinka and Russia between us. Now, what say you to my proposition?"

Roger had been thinking swiftly, and he was quick to realise that it would be madness to antagonise this evil, ambitious woman; so he replied: "I like it well, Madame, and I shall rely upon your guidance in all things."

"You are a youth of sense," she cackled. "We will talk more anon, but now I must leave you. Not more than five minutes remain for you to prepare yourself; then go you up the stairs to reap an Empire."

She curtseyed again, glided to the door and slipped through it with barely a rustle of her laces, leaving him to his wildly whirling thoughts.

The prospect she had offered him was so tremendous that he found it difficult to grasp. Potemkin's drunken, dissolute life had aged him shockingly, and everyone said that he was far from being the man he had been when he first became the Empress's lover. Roger had enormous confidence in his own abilities and believed that, if he could protect himself from assassination, and retain the goodwill of Katerina Ivanovna, between them they would prove more than a match for the one-eyed prince. She evidently believed that too, and she had far better grounds for forming an accurate judgment of the situation than he had. If the intrigue proved successful he would, within a few months, find himself virtually seated on the throne of the greatest Empire in the world.

In such a position his power would be almost limitless. He could change the face of Europe if he would. But better, he could serve his own country infinitely more effectively than his wildest imaginings had ever led him to hope, by making Russia the keystone in a Grand Alliance for the permanent preservation of the peace of Europe. That was the one certain way of saving Britain's substance from being wasted away by future wars. With Russia's might upon the land and England's on the seas, in firm alliance to curb the ambitions of other powers, young Mr. Pitt's great dream of peace and prosperity for all could be made to come true.

But there was a price to be paid for all this. His thoughts reverted to the stocky, elderly woman from whom his power would be derived. She was very far from being evil, and the scope of her mind was infinitely greater than that of any other living ruler. She was courteous, gentle and beneficent by nature. As a girl she had come to a country which was still considered to be outside Europe and peopled almost entirely by savages. In a quarter of a century she had brought it permanently within the family of nations which composed the civilised world, and launched vast educational schemes which had now brought a degree of literacy to the whole of her nobility and more prosperous subjects. She had subdued the wild tribes of Asia and established a *Pax Romana* among them. At her instigation costly missions of exploration, headed by able scientists, had been sent to China, Persia, and the Arctic. On learning that great tracts of her fertile lands were unpeopled, she had financed whole tribes of industrious Germans and Magyars to migrate and colonise them. Under her sway religious toleration had been established with a completeness unknown to any other country in the world. She had abolished torture and the terrible "crying of the word," which, before her time, had made every Russian go in constant fear that an enemy might denounce him for some crime he had not committed, and that, although innocent, the rack and thumb-screws would be applied with the object of wringing a confession from him. She had fought smallpox with inoculation even in the remote villages of the Steppes, and while other rules hypocritically endeavoured to ignore venereal disease she had established clinics where sufferers could be treated without the shame of having to acknowledge their ailment publicly...

She was great, brave, cultured and generous, and, if he would, he could take his stand beside her, help her further to improve the lot of her thirty million subjects, and guide her future foreign relations to a point where he could initiate the lifting of the scourge of war for ever from suffering humanity.

But there was a price to pay—a price to pay; and it was he who must pay it.

Suddenly, at the thought of that fat jelly-bag of a body pressed against his own, his healthy young flesh revolted. He could not do it—no, not even if it was to bring about the reign of Heaven on Earth.

Frantically now, he cast round for the means to escape. He felt sure that Katerina Ivanovna had not locked the door behind her, and it was unthinkable that guards would have been placed to keep the new favourite a prisoner in his own apartments. He was a free man again and could walk out when he wished; but he had neither money nor weapons, and he knew that it would be impossible for him to get very far without either. Unless he could hold up someone for their money, or had the means already, with which to bribe a nearby cottager to hide him for the next few days, the soldiers whom the Empress was certain to send in pursuit of him would run him down in no time.

The long suite of lofty rooms was hung with priceless tapestries and fine paintings; the chests, cabinets and tables furnishing them were of rich lacquer, rare marbles and ebony inlaid with ivory; a ton of precious embroidered silks draped the windows and fauteuils, the parquet floors were covered with carpets and rugs of the most costly close-woven designs. One tenth of their price would have kept him in affluence for a life-time; yet there seemed nothing there that he could seize upon which was readily convertible into cash.

As he moved round the foot of the big four-poster bed his eye suddenly fell on a small pile of luggage, topped by a long sword. Instantly he recognised them as his sword, his money-chest, his travelling trunks, and realised that they must have been brought that day from Schlüsselburg for him.

Running to them he snatched up the sword. He was just about to buckle it on when he heard a footfall at the top of the spiral staircase, and a soft voice called: "Chevalier, why do you tarry?"

The voice was that of the Empress. Roger hesitated only a moment. It was too late to fly now. If he attempted it he would be a prisoner again within five minutes, and she would send him back to Schlüsselburg. Worse, stung to the quick by the insult he had offered her, it would not be to the comfortable room he had occupied there, but to that ghastly dungeon.

"Pray pardon me, Madame," he called up. "I hesitated to join your Majesty only from bashfulness."

As he recrossed the room to mount the stairs his wits were working fast again. He thanked his stars now that she had called him when she had. It would have been madness to attempt to escape at the very moment she had given an order for him to present himself. He must choose a time when he could be reasonably certain of a few hours clear start before his absence was discovered. Perhaps later to-night.

But to-night, yes—to-night he would be. . . . He swallowed and, as he mounted the staircase, strove to force himself to face the facts. If he refused her she might yet have him executed for Yagerhorn's murder. One unpalatable amorous encounter seemed a small price to pay to gain the time to make a favourable bid for life and freedom. It looked as though he must screw himself up to go through with it. The pleasuring of her might not prove as nauseating as he expected. If so he might perhaps succeed in blindfolding his mind to it in future, and even yet sway the destinies of millions from a chair beside her throne.

She was standing at the top of the stairway dressed in a loose robe and underskirt of flowered silk. The robe was cut very full so as to conceal her heavy figure, and its sleeves were short, ending in wide-mouthed ruffles which enabled her to display her plump, and still pretty, forearms to advantage. On her hair was set a jaunty little lace cap. The only jewel she wore was a star with eight points, alternatively of gold and silver, which dangled from her neck on a black ribbon with a red stripe down its centre.

As she held out both her hands to him he took them at once and kissed them one after the other, declaring it impossible to express the depth of his feelings at the supreme honour that she intended him. He knew she would expect that; and if he was to play either for time or for the permanent power that she could bestow upon him, he must throw himself wholeheartedly into the part of a young man who was utterly amazed by the turn in his fortunes but overwhelmed with delight.

After accepting his protestations graciously, she said with commendable frankness that he might think it strange that a woman of her years still indulged in gallantry; but the ordering of a great Empire was a mighty and unceasing labour; she had found that the pleasures of love were the one thing which could take her mind off the innumerable problems she was constantly called on to face, and refresh her sufficiently to endure her toil yet another day.

On glancing round he saw that her apartments were arranged differently from those below. They were in a boudoir, handsomely furnished, but with a homely atmosphere, everything in it showing signs of constant use. Beyond it, through an open door, he could see the bedroom; a circular chamber with fluted pillars framing the painted panels of its walls, and in one segment of it, a big round bed, entirely draped in brocaded curtains which hung from a circular frame surmounted by a huge tuft of ostrich feathers.

Having made Roger sit down in a comfortable chair near the fire Catherine went over to a chiffonier, poured out a glass of wine and brought it back to him. The gesture was made so naturally that he felt no embarrassment at her waiting on him, and settling herself on the opposite side of the fire she at once began to tell him of her routine.

"I vow," she declared, dropping the royal 'we,' "that I am the hardest worked woman in my Empire. I rise at six, or often earlier; and, as I much dislike servants fussing about in my private apartments, I prepare my own breakfast in a kitchenette I have had fitted

267

up here. While my ladies dress me I have such documents as are awaiting my attention read aloud, and while my hair is being dressed I sign them. From eight till eleven I either preside at my council or work in my cabinet. From eleven to twelve I attend chapel; from twelve to half-past one I give audience to such of my ministers as request to see me. A half-hour generally suffices me for dinner and by two I am at work again on my correspondence. I count it a lucky day if I can get in more than an hour's walk or drive in the park before six, at which time I am due to appear in my theatre; and between the acts of whatever is performed I am beseiged by the ambassadors and others. Sundays and Saint's days are holidays for most people, but not for me; since I must then hold a Court, sup in public, and afterwards take a hand at cards, often with people for whom I do not particularly care, but feel that I should invite to join me from diplomacy. So you see I get little leisure, and after my normal working day of fourteen hours I feel well justified in supping with a friend in private."

Roger heartily agreed with her and added: "Before I left Paris, Madame, I was for some time confidential secretary to Monsieur le Marquis de Rochambeau, who advised Queen Marie Antoinette privately on Foreign Affairs. If I could lighten your burden a little by assisting you with your less important correspondence, it would give me the happiness of feeling that in some small measure I was repaying your graciousness to me."

"Indeed!" she exclaimed, her big blue eyes brightening. "Then, in acquiring a gallant with whom I can discuss foreign business, I have chosen better than I knew. But when we are alone together I wish you to call me Catherina Alexeyevna. Tell me, Roje Christorovitch, what think you of the new Triple Alliance that England, Prussia and the United Provinces have recently entered into?"

"That it appears to be aimed at my beloved France, but may not necessarily be so," he replied promptly. "I have an English godmother and on my visits to her have come to know something of the English. When I was last in London I discussed the matter with several gentlemen who are near to Mr. Pitt. 'Twas their opinion that he is a man of peace, and has entered into this Alliance only as a counterpoise to the Bourbon Family Compact; so that the likelihood of a new war may be rendered more remote."

"Think you so?" she said doubtfully. "Should you be right the fear of war suggests that the English are becoming weak and decadent. War in itself is a brutal business and begets much misery, yet only by experiencing it can nations maintain their full health and vigour. Long periods of peace have always been followed by a decline in national power."

With due deference Roger disagreed, instancing the *Pax Romana*, during which for four hundred years peace had been maintained among the nations of southern and western Europe, enabling them to develop their agriculture, arts and commerce to a degree that would otherwise have been quite impossible.

268

She laughed. "You prove my point, for afterwards came the warrior races, the Vandals, Goths, Vikings and Huns, and reduced all those nations who had forgotten how to defend themselves to a state of slavery."

He countered that by suggesting that if only the barbarous nations of the north had also been brought under the sway of Rome, they too would have developed peaceably, with greater ultimate benefit to themselves and others. He went on to urge that no permanent development of humanity as a whole was possible as long as strong nations preyed upon their weaker neighbours; and that small states had as good a right to enjoy their liberties as great ones.

"Monsieur Diderot held much the same language to me when he visited my Court," she remarked with a shake of her grey head, "and I said of him afterwards that, though he was a hundred years old in some respects in others he was no more than ten. You, too, are a child in these matters, Rojé Christorovitch, and my long experience of the ways of nations makes me think very differently. Such idealism is well enough to talk of in an idle hour, but my first interest must always be the security and wellbeing of my own people; and, as long as I live, they shall have their wars, that they may practise their valour and afterwards rest easy in the comforting knowledge of their own strength."

It had been far from Roger's expectations to gain so swiftly such a full and definite expression of the Empress's general convictions, which must certainly have an overriding influence on all her future policies. It was clear now that the chance of persuading her to join in a pact for the maintenance of a permanent peace was extremely remote; so he had his answer for Mr. Pitt, and there seemed no alternative but for the British Prime Minister to take such measures as he could to curb the ever-growing power of Russia. But as Roger thought of that, he also wondered with considerable misgivings if he would ever be in a position to pass on this extremely valuable information to Whitehall.

Meanwhile Catherine had risen and gone again to the chiffonier. From it she began to take several dishes, and as Roger hurried over to help her, he saw that they had been resting on a special arrangement of burners which had kept them hot during the past ten minutes' conversation. Together they carried the dishes and plates to a small table which was laid for two, then sat down to sup.

During the meal the Empress's active mind flitted from subject to subject with extraordinary agility and Roger had all his work cut out to keep up with her; but evidently she was pleased with him, as while they were eating their dessert, she congratulated him on his conversation, remarking that he had an exceptionally wide knowledge of affairs for so young a man.

For his part Roger found her easy, vivacious and extraordinarily interesting to talk to; and he caught himself thinking that, had she been nearer his own age he could easily have fallen in love with her.

But, as it was, a gulf of nearly forty years separated them, and each time he looked at her sagging, heavily-painted face, redeemed only by the marvellous blue eyes, he felt a shiver run down his spine.

Ever since a night five years earlier, when, as a boy of fifteen, he had been taken to a brothel in Le Havre and had run from it in disgust, he had had a horror of making love to any woman who did not attract him; and more recently, there had been numerous occasions on which he had felt sickened at the advances of voluptuous ladies past their prime. Only the memory of the dungeon at Schlüsselburg kept him from throwing down his napkin and rushing from the room. He knew that later, somehow or other, he would have to bring himself to caress her and, mentally, he shuddered at the thought; but she gave him little time to think of that, and for longish periods he forgot it altogether, only to recall it again with amazement at the fact that she had so bewitched him with her brilliant personality that he had actually been enjoying himself. Again it entered his mind that if he could only get through this first night with her he might yet endure the physical relationship for the sake of the great place in the world it would bring him.

When they rose from table she went to a secretaire and produced two parchments, which she handed to him, as she said:

"The one is your official pardon for the Yagerhorn affair. I cannot find it in myself to blame you for taking your revenge upon him, and, even had I not taken a liking to you, I should have let you off with a severe reprimand."

He gave a nervous laugh. "The night I was arrested I fully believed that I should end by paying for that business with my life. Doubtless I would have, too, had not you chanced to learn of my case, and believing me a monster, became curious as to my appearance."

"Nay, 'twas not chance," she said quickly, "for I should have learned of the matter in any event. I allow no person in my realm to be condemned to death without first having had full information of the circumstances laid before me; and in nine cases out of ten I commute the punishment to imprisonment. The other paper will compensate you somewhat for your fright. 'Tis the title-deed to an estate, carrying three hundred and fifty serfs, in the province of Tula."

As he began to stammer his thanks she took the black and red ribbon from round her neck, and reaching up, passed it over his head, exclaiming as the shining star fell on the lace frills of his shirt: "I make you, too, a Knight of my Order of St. Vladimir, for I would think but meanly of myself did I keep a friend long landless and undecorated in my company."

Roger felt horribly embarrassed by this generous payment in advance for a service that he was still uncertain that he could bring himself to render. But the volatile Empress did not notice his confusion, as she half turned away and, indicating a door partially concealed by a curtain, went on: "Now, before we give ourselves up to

270

the pleasures of the night, let us take a turn or two in the winter garden, for the good of our digestions."

Heaving an inaudible sigh of relief at this respite Roger accompanied her through the door, and on glancing round, was amazed to find himself in a veritable paradise. The place they had entered was a conservatory of such vast dimensions that he could not see its ends and could only vaguely discern its roof. There were no pots or wooden stages, and, except for being enclosed, it had all the appearance of a richly-stocked tropical garden in the open. Gravel walks wound between gay flower-borders and banks of flowering shrubs scented the air with a heady perfume; there were fountains, trees twenty feet in height, and open spaces with shaved grass lawns. Chains of fairy-lamps illuminated the whole, and as they moved, scores of parakeets and other brightly-coloured birds fluttered away to seek fresh cover among more distant foliage.

Catherine told him that she had built this wonder on a great row of arches in each of which big furnaces were kept going day and night; so that the temperature never altered, and even in the depths of the Russian winter it provided her with grapes, pineapples, hyacinths and roses.

But as they walked sedately between the palms and oleanders, her hand resting lightly on his arm, Roger's thoughts were whirling again. It suddenly struck him as grimly humorous that, within a fortnight, he should have been the recipient of two Orders of Chivalry for such fantastically divergent reasons. What would she do, he wondered, if he told her that in the filthy straw on the floor of a dungeon in her castle of Schlüsselburg he had buried the Star and yellow ribbon of a Swedish decoration, and how he had earned it. Send him to take what joy of it he could there for the rest of his life, seemed the almost certain answer. But the thought prompted him to express his admiration for the fearlessness she had shown when first attacked by Gustavus, and the way in which she had despatched the few troops that she could muster to oppose his greatly superior army on her frontiers.

She smiled at him. "The Romans never asked after the number of their enemies, but where they were, in order to fight them; and I am of their mind."

When he asked her if she thought that the Swedish army in Finland would disintegrate before winter, she replied with a chuckle. "I care not, now that its sting has been drawn from it. Realising his army to be a broken reed, the insolent Gustavus has abandoned it to its fate. My spies report that he fled from his camp by night, with a few intimates, a fortnight back. I fear that by now 'tis as good as certain that he has succeeded in eluding Admiral Greig's blockade; but his homecoming will be far from a triumph, and his position will soon be rendered desperate by a pretty little surprise I have in store for him."

In a low voice she went on to tell Roger of the secret clause she had inserted in the treaty of 1773, by which she had ceded Holstein

271

to the Danes, and how they had now agreed to honour their bond by launching a surprise attack on Sweden.

Already being aware of this deep secret his mind began to wander again to what lay ahead of him; but it was brought back with a jerk by her adding: "When Gustavus hears the news that a Danish army has invaded his western provinces from Norway he will naturally expect it to march direct on Stockholm, and devote all his energies to preparing the defences of his capital. But instead, 'tis the Danes' intention to overrun the south and seize undefended Gothenbörg."

As in a dream, Roger realised that, without effort on his part, he had come into possession of the Danish plan of campaign. If he could get it to Gustavus in time, counter-measures might be taken and the tables turned. In view of Catherine's statement before supper it had become more than ever important to aid Sweden in her fight against Russia, and thus delay further Muscovite penetration into Europe. But how could he conceivably escape from his present situation; let alone, as a fugitive pursued by the police of a bitterly insulted Empress, reach Stockholm?

No further time was given him even to consider means by which he might secure a flying start next day. They had returned to the hidden door leading into Catherine's boudoir. She pressed a spring and it swung open. Damp under the collar now, he followed her inside.

Giving him an arch glance from her big blue eyes, she said, "So far I have found your company most stimulating, dear Rojé Christorovitch. In one short evening I have come to know you well enough to look forward with most pleasurable anticipation to your giving me more intimate proof of your regard. I will leave you now, but I will not keep you waiting long. In five minutes you may rejoin me."

As she turned away towards the bedroom he swallowed hard, staggered, and clutched at the table.

Swinging round she looked at him in quick alarm, and cried: "What ails thee?"

" 'Tis nought, Catherina Alexeyevna," he stammered. "Nought but over-excitement. A glass of wine will put me right. I shall be myself again by the time you—you are ready to receive me."

Reassured she walked into her bedroom and closed the door behind her.

In an agony of indecision and distress he looked wildly round him. He knew now that he positively could not make love to that lecherous old woman who was undressing beyond the carved and gilded door. No, not for all the riches or power in the world. Not even to save Europe from a cataclysm. He had got to get away from her. But how? How? How?

His mind had gone blank and refused to work. Vaguely he looked at the rail that guarded the spiral staircase. He could dash down it. But if he did, what was he to do then? She would call him in another few minutes, and if he did not appear, she would send her guards after him. They would catch him before he had even got out of the palace, and, despite all her natural clemency, Messalina baulked of her pleasure would exact a dire vengeance. To break in upon her now and tell her to her aged, painted face, that he could not go through with it, would serve him little better. The cheated nymphomaniac would smother the kindly woman in her, and he would be dragged off to that ghastly dungeon at Schlüsselburg to repent his momentary assertion of his rights as a man during months of incarceration in a living tomb.

Suddenly his despairing glance fell upon the vinegar-bottle on the table. He loathed vinegar, and even a dash of it in a sauce was enough to make his mouth dry up and the perspiration break out on his forehead. Grabbing the bottle, he tilted it to his mouth. In two, frightful, choking gulps he swallowed its whole contents.

His eyes bulged from his head, his stomach heaved with nausea. Fighting it down he lurched to the door and threw it open. Catherine had just got into bed, and she drew aside the curtain to smile a welcome. Only a nightlight was now burning in the room but its steady glow was sufficient for her to see his condition.

Leaning against the doorpost for support, he gasped out: "Succour me I beg! I am faint, dizzy, near collapse! My stomach burns! I think I have been poisoned!"

In a moment she had thrown aside the bedclothes and came hurrying towards him.

Through her thin nightdress he glimpsed her squat repulsive body. Her legs and thighs were swollen to such a size that it seemed a miracle that her little feet could still carry her. As she reached him the sweat was pouring down his face and the tears streaming from his eyes. He retched, staggered out into the boudoir and collapsed upon a chair.

Seizing the silver soup-tureen she held it for him while he vomited. When he got back his breath he panted. "Your—your pardon, Madame. Someone must have known of your—your intent to honour me. And—and out of jealousy put poison in the claret you—you refused at supper —knowing that you never drink it. I—I beg you to allow me to retire— and to send your doctor to me."

Without a word she hurried back to her room and picking up a handbell rang it vigorously. As he was being sick again she returned with a chamber-robe now pulled over her nightdress, to hold his head, and, a moment later, two of her ladies-in-waiting ran in.

Concealing her annoyance, she now spoke kindly to him, smoothing his hair and soothing him like a mother, as she begged him not to distress himself on her account. With quiet efficiency she gave brief orders to her women. They assisted him down the staircase to his room, helped him to undress to his shirt, and tucked him up in bed.

They had hardly done so when the old German who had given him his medical examination arrived upon the scene. He looked at Roger's tongue, felt his pulse, gave him an emetic, and waited by the bedside until he was sick again. After examining the nauseous mess the doctor told the two women that they might return to Her Majesty and report that the patient was in no grave danger. He intended to give him a sleeping-draught and had good hopes that he would be recovered by the morning.

The ladies-in-waiting tiptoed away and, much against his will, Roger was compelled to swallow the draught. The doctor then lit a nightlight, blew out the candles that the women had lighted, and softly left the room.

Roger lay quiet for a few moments. He still felt shaken and queasy but he knew that he dare not remain inactive for very long, or the sleeping-draught might overcome him. His eleventh-hour inspiration to make himself ill had saved him from his terrible dilemma and given him a real chance to escape. It was only a little after ten and unlikely that anyone would come to inquire after him till six, so he reckoned that he had the best part of eight hours before him. His money, sword, pistols and travelling-clothes were there beside the bed. If he could succeed in getting out of the palace unchallenged he should be able to reach Oranienbaum well before dawn. There, his gold would enable him to bribe the captain of a coaster to take him along the south shore of the Gulf of Finland to Reval, without asking any awkward questions. At the bigger port there should be no difficulty in finding a neutral ship that would carry him to Sweden. By far the worst fence that he had to surmount was getting out of the palace undetected, as he had only the scantiest knowledge of its geography and not the faintest idea where the sentries would be stationed. But he was full of resolution now and, if caught, meant to attempt to fight his way out rather than tamely submit to capture.

His head buzzing with these new plans, he sat up. As he did so he suddenly saw that the door leading onto the corridor was slowly opening. A white-clad figure glided inside. The nightlight flickered as he moved and shimmered on the ash-blonde hair of Natalia Andreovna.

Closing the door carefully behind her, she ran across the room and, with a little gulp, flung herself full length on the bed beside him. Surprised, annoyed, and acutely worried by this new complication he put his arms round her without enthusiasm, and waited for her to speak.

After sobbing wildly for a few moments she began to choke out bitter reproaches. "Oh, Rojé Christorovitch, how could you! How could you bring yourself to do such a thing when you know how much I love you?"

"Do what?" he inquired tersely.

"Why pay court to that horrible old woman, and induce her to take you as her lover."

He was itching to be on his way, and the last thing he wanted was to be delayed by a lengthy explanation with Natalia. Yet, even as he sought for the quickest means of getting rid of her, it occurred to him that she might prove a most valuable ally in his escape. He had meant to go out by one of the windows, but it was certain that sentries would be patrolling the terrace and grounds. She would be able to tell him where they were stationed or, perhaps, better still, give him the pass-word for the night, so that he could walk confidently out of one of the doors.

"I learned of it but ten minutes back," Natalia went on tearfully. "All of us were still up at a table of cards when she rang her bell for the two ladies in immediate attendance. On their return they told us what had occurred, and they had your name from the Empress her-self. Oh, Rojé Christorovitch, I would have secured your freedom had you but been patient. Did I not vow that I would do so? How could you conceive so hideous an idea as to get someone to arrange for you to be brought before her, so that you might deliberately tempt her with your looks, merely to escape another week or so in prison?"

"I did no such thing," Roger assured her, now tightening his em-brace. "The thing was sprung upon me a few hours back without a word of warning. Even so I managed to evade her embrace. I. . . ."

Suddenly he paused. A footfall had sounded on the top step of the spiral stairs. Next moment there came the voice of the Empress. "To whom are you talking? Who is that with you down there?"

The footfalls came again, almost at a run. They were both staring up from under the canopy of the bed at the dimly-lit corner of the ceil-ing. Before they had time to move apart, the white blob of a face showed, peering down at them over the carved banister-rail.

With a cry of fear Natalia wriggled off the bed. Roger drew the sheets up round him. Like the knell of doom the Empress's footfalls echoed hollowly as she descended the remaining stairs. As she approached the bed Natalia floundered into a trembling curtsey.

"So!" said Catherine coldly. " 'Tis the Baroness Stroganof who thinks fit to pay midnight visits to the chamber in which her mistress lodges her own chosen friends."

She swung upon Roger. "And you, Chevalier! It seems that you have made a remarkably quick recovery, that you are well enough so soon to wanton with one of my ladies!"

Thrusting aside the clothes, Roger slipped out of the far side of the bed. Picking up his cloak, that was lying on a chair nearby, he drew it round him; then he came round the foot of the bed and bowed to her.

He had seen at once that the only course now was to make a clean breast of matters, so he said gravely: "Your Majesty has less cause than you can realise for anger. This is no spontaneous amour of the moment in which you have surprised us. I told you, Madame, of my love-affair in Sweden that led to Count Yagerhorn's attack on me. The Baroness Stroganof was the lady then concerned. I accompanied her to Russia and for the past two months we have been lovers here. 'Twas but natural that, hearing of my condition, the Baroness should come to see for herself how I fared."

The Empress looked down at Natalia and said coldly: "I recall now that 'twas you who first presented the Chevalier to me, at Count Orlof's reception. Is what he says the truth? Do you love him?"

"With all my heart, Madame," she whispered. "I had meant to seek a favourable opportunity of pleading with you to exercise your mercy, and give him his freedom."

The clothes that Roger had been wearing that evening were lying on a couch at the foot of the bed. Taking the two parchments from the pocket of the coat and picking up the star of St. Vladimir, he bowed again and offered them to Catherine, with the words:

"Here, Madame, is the title to the estate and the Order that you so generously gave me. Here, too, is the pardon which I fain would have kept. But I pray you take them all. I surrender my future into the keeping of God and your Majesty."

Catherine could have annulled all three by a word, but it was a splendid gesture, and she was not the woman to be outdone. With a regal sweep of her hand she cried: " 'Tis not our habit to give a thing one moment and take it back the next. Had the Baroness come to us with the truth she could have had your pardon. As for the other things we are not so poor that we cannot afford to pay well for a good evening's conversation. Keep them as mementoes of your visit to our Court."

As Roger went down on one knee she turned to Natalia.

"Rise child, and go to your room now. Your sovereign has loved enough to know the pains of it, and she still comes by lovers with too great an ease to wish to spoil your romance. You may tell your companions that they may aid your preparations; for 'tis our pleasure that you should be married to the Chevalier to-morrow morning."

Natalia and Roger came abruptly to their feet. She gave a cry of joy; he a gasp of dismay. But Catherine had not yet shot her final bolt. Her voice becoming a shade colder she went on:

"We have no desire to be reminded of this episode, so will dispense with the further attendance of either of you upon our person. 'Tis our will that after the ceremony you should depart forthwith, to take up your residence in any town of your choice—provided it be situated in Siberia."

CHAPTER XIX

LIKE A SHEEP TO THE SLAUGHTER

ROGER sat on the edge of the bed, a prey to the most shattering emotions. The Empress and Natalia had gone. He had joined his bride-to-be, with apparent sincerity, in rendering thanks for mercy to the arbitress of their fates because he had seen no other course to take. He supposed that, as a lady-in-waiting and the appointed lover of the Empress caught in one another's arms, they had got off very lightly by merely being sent to reside where they liked in Arctic Russia. And Catherine had no means of knowing that he had grown to hate Natalia

Andreovna, so her decree that they should marry had, in the circumstances, been a most humane and generous gesture.

Yet, for him, her orders amounted to a savage double sentence. The thought of Siberia was, in itself, bad enough. Its terrible desolation; the incredible cold which was said to hold all life there in its grip for eight months of every year; the miserable little towns composed solely of wooden buildings; the lack of cultured society; its uncouth, fur-clad, bear-like inhabitants; the vast distance that it lay from all the capitals of the civilised world. And, in his case, the hardship of exile to this remote and barren land was to be accentuated a hundred-fold by being permanently tied to a cruel and violent woman to whom he was hardly even physically attracted any longer.

Had he been himself, the moment the two women had left him he would have pulled on his clothes and made his bid to escape. As it was he was still feeling sick and giddy, and his mind was half-stunned by the succession of violent shocks that it had sustained. He lost several precious moments before he began to dress, wondering if he dared beg the Empress to rescind her order that he should marry Natalia, and he had only just finished dressing when the chance to get away was suddenly reft from him.

Old Katerina Ivanovna suddenly walked in, slammed the door behind her, then stood there for three whole minutes, cursing him for the idiotic way in which he had allowed an intrigue with a lady-in-waiting to ruin his golden prospects with the Empress.

He was too tired to attempt any explanation; and when the old harridan told him to leave his things where they were and come with her, he obediently followed her out into the corridor.

She led him past the entrance of the Court theatre and up some stairs to a landing on which two sentries were pacing to and fro. Opening a door, she led him into a comfortably furnished bedroom; then she said:

"You will sleep here. Your marriage will take place at Her Majesty's usual chapel-hour to-morrow, and she will honour you with her presence. On peril of your life you will say nothing to anyone of what has taken place to-night, or that you have been ordered into exile. The Empress is always most averse to any scandal in connection with her love-affairs, and has forbidden her ladies to mention the matter. The public ceremony is designed to counteract any rumours that she threw her cap at you and you threw it back at her. Had it been myself that you had so insulted I would have had you beaten with the *battagues* until your backbone was a pulp." Having delivered herself of these malicious sentiments, she left him.

Going to the window he saw that it looked out on a small interior courtyard to which there was no exit, and that it was a twenty-foot drop to the flagstones below. Even if he could have accomplished the descent without breaking his neck he now had neither his money nor his sword with him, so he was forced to abandon as hopeless any further thought of escape.

Wearily pulling off his clothes he tumbled into bed and lay there turning over wildly impossible schemes for evading the hateful marriage that had been arranged for him. After a while the sleeping-draught took effect and he fell into a troubled slumber, in which he dreamed that he had fallen through a hole in the ice of a frozen river, and that Natalia Andreovna was standing on the bank laughing at his futile efforts to save himself from drowning.

He was awakened by two footmen, one of whom drew back the curtains and began to tidy the room while the other brought him breakfast. He ate it in a half-dazed state while grimly going over in his mind the nerve-racking events of the preceding night. No sooner had he finished than the German doctor came in. Having examined Roger and pronounced him fit to resume his normal activities, he spent some time in questioning him as to what he had eaten the day before, in a fruitless effort to trace the cause of the attack. When he had gone the two footmen returned with Roger's baggage and offered to help him dress. Only then did he realise that he had been left to sleep late and that it was already half-past nine. A quarter of an hour later a barber arrived to do his hair, and on the completion of his toilette the two Chevalier guards who had escorted him from Schlüsselburg appeared.

Whether or not they knew of the great elevation that had been planned for him they said nothing of it; but they smilingly congratulated him on having received his pardon and on his forthcoming marriage. A tray with wine, vodka and pastries stuffed with caviare was then brought in and his visitors drank his health.

After two glasses of wine he felt somewhat better; but, rack his brains as he would, he could still think of no way to escape making the green-eyed Baroness Stroganof into Mrs. Roger Brook; and now there was no further time to do so, as one of his companions remarked that the hour had come for them to proceed to the chapel.

As they left the room Roger placed himself between them and they took him through the covered passage that led to the parent palace, then along several corridors till they reached a pair of doors that opened into the Imperial basilica.

A huge painting of God the Father occupied the whole ceiling and a row of gilt Ionic columns soared to it on either side, but an incongruous note was struck by the walls being covered with tawdry and ill-executed pictures of Russian saints. A gilt rail ran across its far end, in front of the great gilded doors of the sanctuary, and the body of the chapel was already filled with the Empress's brilliantly-clad household.

On Roger's entrance the ceremony opened with solemn vocal music, no other being permitted in the Greek church, but two double lines of richly-robed choristers made up amply for the deficiency. His companions conducted him to the rail and he had scarcely reached it when a stir behind him caused him to turn his head. Followed by half-a-dozen young women of her own age, Natalia Andreovna was advancing towards him. She was dressed in white brocade, the figuring of which was outlined in gold thread; on her head she wore a big hooped headdress sparkling with gold and jewels.

Despite all his bitter thoughts of her Roger felt his breath catch at the sight of her loveliness.

As he bowed to her the voices of the choristers swelled to a mighty pæan and the Empress entered. On reaching the rail she passed through it by a gate and took her place alone under a richly-decorated canopy to the south side of the holy doors. They swung open displaying the penetralia of the temple; a picture of the descent from the Cross and an altar covered with golden tissue. A number of venerable, long-bearded priests, wearing vestments and bun-like mitres that blazed with precious stones, then appeared. By the Greek ritual no one is allowed to sit in church, so there were no seats, even for the Empress; but as the ceremony proceeded, the congregation seemed in a state of almost constant genuflexion as it responded to the prayers and loud ejaculations of the priests.

Roger found himself dipping with the rest. Someone had given him a long candle to hold and produced a ring. Crowns were held over their heads; as in a dream he repeated a number of phrases after the most gorgeously-clad priest, was given a Bible to kiss and placed the ring on Natalia's finger.

He wondered if he was now really married to her or if he could regard this alien service as not binding upon him. But he recalled the Reverend William Tooke having told him how he had once stood sponsor at the christening of a Roman Catholic child, and feared that his having gone through this ceremony with apparent willingness must make it as legal as any other.

Nevertheless these thoughts gave him an idea, and while the chanting and genuflecting continued he swiftly developed it. At last the priests retired within the temple and the holy doors swung to behind them. As the Empress left her place Roger watched her anxiously. He had a boon to ask, but having observed the air of devout humility that she had affected during the service, he feared that she might take it ill if he threw himself on his knees before her while she was still in church.

When she walked past him with downcast eyes, a Chamberlain made a sign to him to follow her; so he gave his arm to Natalia Andreovna and they fell into step in the wake of the Sovereign, the rest of the congregation forming a procession behind them.

On leaving the chapel Catherine crossed the hall and entered a reception-room. At its far end there was a gilt armchair on a low dais. Seating herself upon it, she gave an affable smile to the advancing couple, and extended her hand for them to kiss. It was Roger's opportunity and, on rising from a deep obeisance, he said:

"I cannot thank your Majesty sufficiently for all you have done for us; yet I still have one favour that I would beg."

"You may proceed," she replied, non-committally.

" 'Tis in connection with my marriage," he told her. "Not being of the Greek Orthodox faith I must confess that as yet I do not feel properly wed. As I had the honour to tell your Majesty, I have an English godmother, and strange as it may seem for a Frenchman, I was baptised into the Church of England. Would your Majesty therefore graciously permit the Baroness and myself to go through a second ceremony to be performed by the Reverend Mr. Tooke, the Chaplain to the English Factory, before we set out on our journey?"

Catherine nodded. "Your devotion to your own communion is fully understandable. We will send for Mr. Tooke and you may arrange for him to remarry you in Petersburg to-morrow morning."

Heartened a little by the successful initiation of his new plan, and having secured a temporary postponement of his departure into exile, Roger bowed his thanks, and with Natalia, took his stand beside the Empress to receive the congratulations of the assembled company.

The first to approach was Natalia's crotchety old grandfather, the ex-Hetman Cyril Razumofsky, who, with numerous of her other relatives, had been hastily summoned from St. Petersburg. None of them appeared to think that there was anything queer about the wedding taking place without previous announcement, as it was carried out under the auspices of the Empress, and they were all accustomed to accept her sudden whims about such matters without question. They assumed that as Roger was the Imperial choice of a second husband for Natalia the match must obviously be a suitable one, and in consequence, treated him with the utmost politeness. It was from their conversation he gathered that the estate in the province of Tula was now supposed to be the Empress's wedding-gift, and that they believed him to be taking Natalia there for the honeymoon.

After half-an-hour spent in introductions and receiving compliments, a Chamberlain rapped three times with his staff on the parquet floor and the Empress led the way into an adjoining room where a wedding-breakfast had been prepared. She took her seat a little apart at the top of the table and the bridal pair were conducted to its bottom, so they were not embarrassed by having to make further conversation with her. At two o'clock she rose, and as she passed out she paused to say to Natalia:

"Remain with your friends as long as you wish, child. Since your husband desires a reformed ceremony, you can hardly consider yourself fully married as yet, and your departure for your honeymoon must be postponed until to-morrow. For to-night you had best occupy your old chamber. The breath of St. Nicholas be upon you."

When the Empress, her immediate entourage, and such court officials as had duties to perform, had left the room, the remainder of the company resumed their seats; fresh dishes were brought to the table and the wedding feast continued.

Between toasts and friendly badinage Roger sought to grasp the full implications of his position. For no particular reason Georgina's vision of their future came into his mind. On the last day of March she had seen a wedding-ring for one of them, but could not determine which. Well, there it was, shining on Natalia Andreovna's finger. He was married now, and his wife was very far from being the woman of his heart's desire. He did not see what he could have done to avoid going through the ceremony but on one thing he was determined; he was not going to allow himself to be packed off to Siberia without a struggle.

At half-past three they left the table; but only to return to the reception-room, where the company could move about with greater freedom while the footmen offered them more drinks and silver salvers loaded with a cold collation. By mid-day the news of the wedding had spread all over St. Petersburg and scores of people were driving out to Peterhof to pay their respects to the newly-married couple; so that, instead of there being any signs of the party breaking up, the big room was becoming ever more crowded.

It was close on five when Roger caught sight of the Reverend Mr. Tooke threading his way through the crowd. Greeting the clergyman eagerly, he presented him to Natalia, secured him a glass of wine, and as soon as he decently could, led him away into a corner.

"Tell me, I beg," said Roger, almost breathlessly. "Is a ceremony of marriage gone through in the Greek Church binding upon an English Protestant?"

"Why, yes; indeed it is, young Sir," replied Mr. Tooke, with a smile. "I am happy to relieve your anxieties on that score. But I received a message from Her Majesty that you had expressed a wish to have the benefit of the Protestant rites, and if you still desire it, I will willingly perform them for you."

"I thank you. I—er—shall be greatly your debtor, Sir," Roger muttered awkwardly. Then, after a quick look round, he added: "The truth is, this marriage was none of my seeking, and I am in grave trouble. Not only has the Empress decreed this union for me but she has ordered my wife and I to take up our residence in Siberia. That is not generally known, and the company here believe that after you have performed your kind offices for us to-morrow we shall be setting out on our honeymoon. I used my religious scruples to delay our departure and as an excuse to get a word with you. I beg you, Sir, to devise some means of helping me to escape."

Mr. Tooke's studious face had become very grave. "As to your marriage, there is nought to be done on that score; and whether I bless your union or not, you are already tied. In the other matter you have my profound sympathy; but, you will remember, when you first called upon me, I warned you that I could give you no assistance which might contravene the duty that I owe Her Majesty."

"Please!" Roger pleaded. "Even if you cannot square it with your conscience to give me your active help, I implore you, Sir, advise me as to if there are any steps which I can take that might lead to my evading this sentence of banishment."

"If Her Majesty has not set a period upon your exile it may not prove of long duration. Her clemency in such matters is well-known.

281

Even in the case of Elizaveta Romanovna Vorontzoff, who endeavoured to have her repudiated and imprisoned, so as to take her place as the wife of Peter the third, the Empress showed extraordinary leniency. No great time after the Czar's death she allowed her rival to return to court and marry Admiral Paliansky. So 'tis unlikely that your enforced absence will last more than a year or two."

"A year or two!" groaned Roger, who saw the one chance upon which he had been able to buoy up his hopes during the past few hours slipping away. "In my situation that is near as bad as a lifetime."

"You will not think so when you reach my age," the clergyman endeavoured to console him.

Roger knew that once he reached Siberia he would find few people who could even speak any language that he understood, and that the difficulties of making his way to a frontier without being stopped and sent back would be immense. He was convinced that his only hope of getting out of Russia with any speed lay in the next night and day, while he was still in the vicinity of the Gulf of Finland; and that Mr. Tooke, with his great knowledge of the country, must be able to suggest some means of escape if only he could be persuaded to do so.

Making a great effort to control his agitation, he said gravely: "I do not ask this for myself, Sir, but in the name of those I represent. I have news of great import which I must convey to certain people as a matter of the utmost urgency. I propose to use the excuse of going through a Protestant ceremony to wait upon you with my wife, at your church, at eleven o'clock to-morrow morning. You will then have an opportunity of passing a message to me. I beg you to reconsider the matter, and aid me if you can."

Without waiting for an answer he turned away to talk to some other guests. He felt very badly about having forced the friendly clergyman to choose between two loyalties, and he could be by no means certain that the choice would prove to his advantage; but he considered that his knowledge of the Danish plan of campaign justified his action.

By this time Roger was heartily sick of making smiling small talk to people, the great majority of whom he had never seen before and had not the slightest wish ever to see again; but, as the hero of the hour, he was the cynosure of all eyes and had to pretend that this was the happiest day of his life. Concealing his gloomy thoughts as best he could, he prayed for his ordeal to end, although he knew that it might continue for hours yet, as on their country estates the Russians often kept wedding festivities up for a week.

His forebodings that he would not escape being lionised until he could get to bed were made a certainty when, a little before six, an orchestra appeared and began to tune up. Evidently the Empress meant there to be no hint that the marriage had been anything but of her own contriving, and had sent the band to ensure that there should be no flagging of the entertainment owing to the delayed departure of the newly-wed couple. With jaws that ached from smiling, Roger duly opened the ball by leading Natalia Andreovna out for the first minuet and their gracefulness in the dance was much applauded.

Dancing continued till half-past ten, then Natalia's bridesmaids formed a bevy round her and prepared to escort her to her chamber. Among the guests there was much disappointment that the bride and bridegroom were not to be put to bed in public, as was the custom, and that they were thus deprived of the opportunity of making the bawdy jokes usual on such occasions; but the Empress's dictum, that Natalia must not consider herself fully a wife until after the Protestant ceremony which her husband had requested, was now known to all, so they could do no more than commiserate with her.

As Roger had not been alone with her for a single moment during all these hours they had had no opportunity of exchanging anything but the amiable civilities required by the occasion, and exhausted as he was by the events of the day, he was by no means sorry that he was to be spared an explanation with her that night. Having smilingly kissed her hand, forehead and cheeks he wished her good sleep, and with considerable relief, watched her being led away by her companions.

Throughout the whole afternoon and evening he had rarely been without a glass in his hand, and the drinkings of his health to which he had had to respond had been innumerable; so had it not been for his excellent head he would have been drunk already. As it was a little crowd of his newly acquired in-laws now gathered round him, and insisting that it would be against all custom for him to go to bed sober, plied him with further liquor.

Wishing to be rid of them as soon as possible he tossed off several brandies to Natalia's green eyes, then pretended a greater degree of drunkenness than he was actually feeling. Seeing his apparent state his two old acquaintances of the Chevalier guard presented themselves, and after many noisy good-nights had been said, escorted him to the room from which they had brought him nearly twelve hours earlier.

Alone at last, he sat with his head in his hands for a few minutes; then with an effort stood up, splashed his face with water from the jug, struggled out of his clothes and flung himself into bed. Fatigue even more than the amount he had drunk weighed upon his brain, and after a brief period of futile speculation as to whether or not Mr. Tooke would devise a means to pull him out of the frightful mess he was in, he fell asleep.

In the morning the two footmen called him at seven and brought his breakfast. When he had eaten it one of them told him that a carriage had been ordered for nine o'clock to take him into St. Petersburg; so he got up, dressed in his travelling-clothes, and unlocking his money chest, distributed all the cash he had about him. By the time he had finished repacking his other belongings it was close on nine; a knock came on the door, and in reply to his call of "Entrez!" the two Chevalier guards appeared.

Giving him a polite good-morning, they asked if they might have the pleasure of attending him to his second marriage ceremony.

Roger was somewhat surprised at their couching their proposal to accompany him in the form of a request, as he had a shrewd suspicion that the two young men were among the few people who knew that he had incurred the Empress's displeasure, and that she had ordered them to keep an eye on him. In any case he did not feel that he was in a position to refuse their offer, so he accepted with a good grace and went downstairs with them.

He had expected that he and Natalia would be sent in to St. Petersburg together, and that he would at last be called on to face a *tête-à-tête* with his wife; but it transpired that she was to follow him in a separate carriage with two of the ladies who had attended her the previous day. So Roger and his companions got into a four-horse barouche, and at a spanking pace set out to cover the sixteen miles to the capital.

Having as yet not the faintest idea as to the procedure adopted towards people exiled to Siberia, Roger thought this a good opportunity to secure some information on it, so he remarked:

"I little expected, gentlemen, when you brought me from the Fortress of Schlüsselburg four days ago, that I should leave the Peterhof in such pleasant circumstances. It seemed far more likely that I should leave it but to be conveyed back to my cell, or as a prisoner on his way to exile."

Having waited for their laugh, he went on: "Had the latter proved my fate I take it that you would hardly have been put to the inconvenience of escorting me further than Petersburg, and that there you would have handed me over to the police for transportation to Siberia."

They both looked at him in surprise, and the taller of the two answered. "You are mistaken, Sir. None but felons and people of the baser sort, sentenced to work in the mines, are transported thither by the police. Persons of quality are simply ordered by the Empress to take up their residence there in a specific place, or, more generally, in a town of their own choosing; they then make their own arrangements for the journey."

This was the best news Roger had had since his return from Finland. Apparently it meant that, if Mr. Tooke remained adamant in his refusal to help him, once he was clear of St. Petersburg he would be able to change his course and drive hell-for-leather for the Polish or Austrian frontier. Concealing his elation, he said:

"In that case what surety has Her Majesty that those she banishes will ever go to Siberia? It seems that, without her knowledge, they might quite well take another direction and go into comfortable retirement on some country estate."

The tall man shook his head. "For a Russian to even contemplate disobeying a direct order from Her Majesty is unthinkable."

"But in the case of a foreigner, such as myself," Roger hazarded.

"You would soon be brought to book," laughed his informant. "The chief of police in every town and district keeps a record of all persons entering or leaving the area for which he is responsible, and these reports are forwarded to the Residence. Were your name not found upon them as travelling in the right direction an inquiry would be set on foot, and 'tis no easy matter for persons of quality to hide themselves in Russia; so you would soon be located and arrested to suffer a severer penalty."

With that Roger had to be content for the time being, but he felt that his prospects of devising some means of getting out of the country were considerably brighter than he had thought them the previous day. He therefore led the talk into other channels, and a little before eleven, they arrived at the English Factory.

To his surprise a stream of people, mostly dressed in sober black, was crossing the main courtyard, and entering the church. A few equipages were setting down richly-clad Russians, some of whom he recognised as relatives of Natalia's to whom he had been introduced the day before, but the bulk of the little crowd had a curiously home-like, British look; and only then did he realise that it was Sunday morning. His recent experiences had made him lose count of the days, but evidently Mr. Tooke's usual congregation were assembling for the Sabbath service, so he assumed that his wedding-ceremony would not take place until after it.

The Reverend William was waiting in the porch to receive him, and Roger anxiously scanned his face, hoping for a sign that he had decided to help him in some way; but the clergyman's expression was blankly courteous as he asked Roger and his companions to go in and seat themselves in the front pew on the right. A few minutes after they had taken their places, Natalia Andreovna, dressed ready for a journey, arrived with her bridesmaids and they filed into the opposite pew. The service then commenced.

By contrast to that of the previous day it was the essence of simple, genuine worship, and it made Roger homesick to a degree that he found almost unbearable. The English voices, the hymns and psalms, all brought back to him with poignant clarity the services he had attended with such regularity during his boyhood in Lymington at the old parish church of St. Thomas á'Becket. When he closed his eyes in prayer he could so easily imagine himself back there again, but on opening them one sideways glance showed him Natalia's beautiful, wicked profile barely a yard away across the aisle. More than once he was seized with the impulse to spring to his feet and shout aloud that he would not marry her, but he knew that it was too late, the deed was already done.

Mr. Tooke preached upon resignation to the will of the Lord. Roger felt sure that the text had been chosen for his benefit, and that the good man was urging him both to make the best of the marriage into which he had entered so unwillingly and to accept with becoming humility the banishment decreed for him. It was certainly not a good

285

augury that Mr. Tooke had any intention of suggesting a means by which he could escape, and it plunged Roger into further depths of gloom.

At the conclusion of the service Mr. Tooke announced the marriage and that any of the congregation who wished to remain as witnesses to it were welcome to do so. Roger and Natalia then took their places and were united according to the rites of the Church of England; after which Mr. Tooke addressed them briefly in a low voice, in French.

He said that they had met and married in what was to Roger a land distant both in thought and customs from his own, and that in the course of time Natalia might be called on to follow her husband to a country which she would find strange and different from that of her birth. Moreover he believed there was some reason to suppose that their union had been brought about with little time for the deep consideration that such a step merited, and in unusual circumstances. But that they should never allow such extraneous matters to impair their acceptance of the cardinal fact that, for better or for worse, they had been joined together in the sight of God. Now that they were wed they must consider themselves as one, each giving way to the other's prejudices as often as they could bring themselves to do so, and abiding loyally by the solemn vows they had taken to love and cherish one another.

Natalia cried openly during this short address, and Roger was deeply moved. It brought home to him as nothing else yet had done the full implications of the step he had taken. That he had been forced to it now seemed beside the point, as was also the unlovely vicious streak in Natalia's nature. Apparently she could not help the delight which seized her at the thought or sight of physical brutality, and since their arrival in Russia she had given ample proof that she had conceived a deep passion for him. She was beautiful, rich, vivacious and unfailingly interesting to talk to. Most men, he knew, would consider themselves fortunate to have won such a bride.

Suddenly, he saw the whole issue in a new light. It was borne in upon him that no possible good could come of his continuing to regard his marriage as a trap into which he had fallen. He must accept it as the will of God and follow Mr. Tooke's wise counsel.

There and then he determined both to make every effort to eradicate Natalia's love of cruelty, and to treat her with all the generosity and kindness of which he was capable. Looking at her tear-stained but radiant face as they left the altar, he felt that if he acted on this new resolution, their strange marriage could yet be made a success and that he might come truly to love her.

Followed by their relations and friends they went to the vestry, and while everyone else was watching Natalia sign the register Mr. Tooke slipped a small, three-cornered note unobserved into Roger's hand. In view of the sermon on resignation to which he had just listened he was hard put to it to conceal his surprise, but the emotion was swiftly overcome by acute impatience to read it and learn if the clergyman had, after all, devised some means by which he might evade having to set out for Siberia.

His gloves were out of sight in the pocket of his travelling-coat, so exclaiming that he must have left them in the pew, he hurried back into the now empty church. Opening the note with trembling fingers, he read:

The brig White Rose out of Hull, Captain Tommy Bell, is lying at the timber-wharf and is due to sail for home a few days hence. I have spoken with Mr. Bell, who tells me that he could accommodate two passengers, and I have arranged with him to expect you aboard some time to-night.

Roger could have jumped for joy. Coming immediately after the familiar service, the English voices and the sight of the sturdy independent-looking congregation, the very words "White Rose—Hull—Tommy Bell" held a magic ring; they seemed to epitomize British courage, honesty and freedom, and at the same time to conjure up so many gentle decencies of life that he had found totally lacking in Russia.

Thrusting the note into an inner pocket, he hurried back to the vestry, to find that Mr. Tooke had just invited the company to adjourn to the parsonage and join him and his wife in a glass of wine. Upstairs in the pleasant drawing-room Roger paid his respects to Mrs. Tooke, and, a few minutes later, managed to get a word in private with her husband. Having thanked the clergyman from the bottom of his heart he spoke to him of Zaria and asked him to take charge of her when she came out of hospital. On Mr. Tooke agreeing, he wrote a brief note making the little serf over to him, and added to it a gold Imperial as a present for her. Then, happy in the thought that he had at one stroke made a useful gift to the man who had helped him and assured the girl a good home, he rejoined Natalia.

"We must not long delay our setting out, my love," she smiled, as he came up to her, "for we have far to go before night."

Some of her friends who were standing nearby then rallied him on his impatience to carry her off, and said that he might at least have allowed her one night in St. Petersburg.

Knowing the secret reason which lay behind their starting at once he laughed the matter off; but he still had no idea what arrangements had been made for their journey until, on going downstairs, he saw two heavy travelling-coaches drawn up outside.

The first was for the bridal pair and was almost as commodious as a caravan; its wide seats pulled down to form sleeping-bunks and in addition to a great pile of fur rugs it contained most of their personal belongings. In the second were to ride a maid for her and a valet for him; from its boot protruded the chimney of a small field-kitchen and a good part of its interior was occupied by cases containing food and wine.

The good-byes were said, they took their seats, and the two heavy coaches rumbled out of the yard. For the first time since their wedding, some twenty-six hours before, he was alone with his wife.

True to his decision taken in the church he put his arm round her, drew her head down onto his shoulder, and kissed her.

She nestled against him, and after a moment murmured:

"How prodigious strange it is that, whereas a week ago, I should never have dared to ask the consent of my family or the Empress to marry an untitled gentleman like yourself, we should now find ourselves wed by her decree. 'Tis hard that, having been generous enough to give you to me, she should have driven us away from most of the things that make life worth living. But we have one another, and our exile may not be of long duration; so, all things considered, we should count ourselves monstrous fortunate."

"If we are called upon to face hardship together no worse equipped than we are at present, we shall have little cause to grumble," he smiled. "However did you manage to arrange for us to journey into exile in such comfort ?"

Glancing up at him in surprise, she replied. "Wherever we were bound we could hardly travel with less than two coaches; and were you in truth taking me to honeymoon on your Tula estate the arrangements would not have differed. 'Twould have been all of eight hundred *versts*, and in Russia towns having inns of a good enough standard to accommodate persons of quality are often several days' journey apart; so even in the depths of winter one must be prepared to take most of one's meals on the roadside."

"Even so, seeing that, like myself, you were confined to the Peterhof until your going to church this morning, I marvel at your having succeeded in smoothing the first stage of our rough path so altogether admirably."

" 'Twas quite simple," she confessed. "In order to conform to the Empress's orders, I told my grandfather yesterday that you were averse to abiding for even a night in Petersburg, and I asked him to provide travelling coaches for us this morning. Then I sent my maid in with orders to pack such things as I might require for several months' absence and to make all other arrangements."

"Did you not tell even your grandfather that we had been ordered into exile?"

"Nay, I dared not. Had I done so he would have gone to the Empress and made a scene, which would have achieved nothing except to mar our prospects of an early reprieve. Clearly it is her wish that no one should learn of our disgrace until sufficient time has elapsed for it to be no longer connected with your brief stay at the Peterhof. When we have been at our destination long enough to expect to have news of me I intend to write to them, saying that the Empress banished us in a fit of temper brought about by an indiscretion of yours. I'll say that you were rash enough to demand that on marrying you, I should cease my attendance on her, and she retorted that since you were so greedy for my company you should take me to a place where you would have no other. She will, I am sure, appreciate the cleverness of such an explanation, and when my relatives then urge that you erred only through lack of knowledge of her Court she will pardon and recall us."

"All that you say seems to me the essence of wisdom," Roger agreed. "But in the meantime, whither are we bound?"

"Our first stage is to Tosno, a township some forty *versts* from Petersburg upon the Moscow road, which we should take were we going to Tula. But from Tosno we shall turn east, and by way of Vologda, Viatka and Perm, come to Ekaterinburg; the new city which has been founded by the orders of the Empress in the gap through Ural mountains. It is the gateway to Asiatic Russia, and residence there is accepted as exile in Siberia. Few people of our station go further east unless definitely ordered to do so, and the offspring of a considerable number of the nobility who settled there on being banished by the Empress Elizabeth now form a by no means uncultured society."

Roger gave her a gentle squeeze. "You have planned well, sweetheart; but I think I can offer you a brighter future. That is, if you are prepared to leave Russia?"

"Leave Russia!" she exclaimed. "But in our present situation that is impossible."

"On the contrary, my love, I have already arranged passages in a ship that is sailing from Petersburg in a few days' time. We have but to return there and go aboard in secret to-night."

She considered that for a moment, then she said: "I would not be averse to leaving Russia for a year or two; but I am greatly attached to my country and 'twould break my heart were I never to see it again. To do as you suggest would be such flagrant disobedience of the Empress's orders she might decree that I was never to return."

"Since she loves Russia so dearly herself I cannot think that she would be so harsh as to place a permanent ban on one of her subjects returning to the country of their birth. Particularly as you would be able to urge your marriage vows as your excuse for leaving without her consent. 'Tis a wife's duty to obey her husband and go with him wherever he chooses to take her."

"True, and Katinka is not by nature given to bearing malice for long. So be it then; we will return to Petersburg after dark. I have heard so much of the Court of Versailles and the fair land of France, that 'twill pleasure me greatly to see it all with you as my cicerone."

Her words gave Roger a nasty jolt. He had forgotten for the moment that in spite of the ceremony in the English church she still believed him to be a Frenchman. His mind had been so occupied with more urgent matters that he had entirely overlooked this complication, and he wondered anxiously what he had better do about it.

His first impulse was to tell her the truth, but on second thoughts he saw that to do so would be to invite a score of awkward questions. Knowing her passionate love for Russia he dared not admit that he had come there as a spy. She would realise at once that he had used her as his catspaw and the result would be disastrous. Worse, she might guess the unpalatable truth, that he had never really loved her, but became her lover only in order to ferret out Russia's secrets. Her love for her country might then prove stronger than her passion for himself and feeling herself utterly humiliated and outraged, the violence of her anger might even lead her to denounce him.

Swiftly he decided that he must leave that skeleton in its cupboard at least until he had her out of Russia, so he said: " 'Twill be the greatest joy to show you Paris and Versailles; but this is a British ship, so first we go to England. I also know that country well and have many friends there. London is near as gay as Paris and I'll be as proud as a peacock to show you off in its most fashionable salons."

They were now on the outskirts of St. Petersburg and as the coach rumbled on into the country he told her about life in the western capitals, and thoroughly enjoyed answering all her eager, excited questions.

At four o'clock they halted by the wayside and the servants cooked a meal for them. Then, while they ate it, Roger raised several points that had been troubling him considerably.

"Our ship," he said, "may not sail for two or three days. We shall remain concealed on board, of course; but what of your two servants and the coachmen? Can you rely on their discretion? What, too, of the coaches? Their premature return to your grandfather's stable is certain to arouse comment; moreover, if the progress of our journey is not reported by the police in the towns through which we are expected to pass, a hue-and-cry may start, and that might lead to a search for us in all the ships in port."

"The servants will say only what I tell them," she replied at once. "They are my serfs and brought up to die rather than disobey me. But the matter of the coaches presents a most tricky problem."

He smiled. "If you can trust your people, I think I have a way to prevent the suspicions of the police being aroused. After the coaches have taken us to the port we will send them off again to Ekaterinburg. Whenever they halt near a village or town the maid and valet can make purchases of poultry, eggs, fruit and so on, just as they would if we were still with them; but you must instruct them to say that what they buy is for us, and to keep the blinds of this coach down whenever it is driven through a street. The police, who seem to miss little in this country, will then believe us to be pursuing our journey as intended and duly report our progress."

"What a clever husband I have," she laughed. Then, when they had finished their meal she called the servants round her, gave them their orders, and made each of them kiss her *ikon* in token of obedience.

As soon as dusk had fallen the coaches were turned about and set out on their three-hour drive back to St. Petersburg. On reaching the outskirts of the city they took a circuitous route to avoid all the main streets, and soon after ten o'clock reached the timber-wharf without incident.

The *White Rose* out of Hull was lying there with only a mast-light burning. While the servants began to unload the baggage under Natalia's supervision Roger went aboard and introduced himself to Captain Tommy Bell. The Captain proved to be a jolly, red-faced, downright little Yorkshireman. He damned the Russians for a set of "scurvy cheating knaves," called Roger "lad" and told him to bring aboard "the Missis."

Within an hour they were installed with all their belongings in a clean roomy cabin under the poop, and for the next three days they did not leave it. On Wednesday, the 12th of September, the *White Rose* set sail for England, and Captain Bell took them down to a cubby hole normally used for confining drunken or mutinous seamen, where they remained hidden while the ship was cleared by the Customs off Cronstadt. By mid-day the formalities were completed, sail was set again, and they were able to come up on deck as the ship headed for the open waters of the Gulf.

It transpired that Tommy Bell had a great fund of racy stories, and as soon as he found that Natalia was not easily shocked he kept his passengers in fits of laughter at every meal, their gaiety being added to by her attempts to imitate his Yorkshire dialect.

They had left St. Petersburg with the chill of autumn already upon it, the first snow being expected in a few weeks, but the weather remained good and became somewhat warmer as the ship steadily ploughed her way south. She called at Reval, Libau and Dantzig, then on the morning of Wednesday, the 19th, dropped her anchor in the roads of Copenhagen.

Although Roger's honeymoon had been thrust upon him, he had to admit to himself that he had thoroughly enjoyed it. Captain Bell's unfailing good humour and Natalia's own happiness had both contributed to making things easy for him, and not a single incident had occurred to arouse the sadistic viciousness that he so hated in her.

But now he had to give his thoughts again to his own work. Had he been free to do so he would have gone straight from St. Petersburg to Stockholm in order to acquaint King Gustavus with the Danish plan of campaign. As it was he considered that he had been lucky in losing so comparatively little time; since, although he had overshot the mark by being carried so far south as the Danish capital, he felt sure that Mr. Hugh Elliot would find swift means to send a despatch to Stockholm. He must therefore see the British Minister as quickly as possible, and once this duty had been performed, he would be able to return with a clear conscience in the *White Rose* to England.

On learning that the ship was to lie for two nights off Copenhagen, he decided that it would be worth while to take Natalia ashore and put up at the Silver Hart, as it would both make a pleasant break in the voyage for her and enable them to enjoy themselves in the city more easily.

By two in the afternoon a hackney coach deposited them with their baggage at the inn. As soon as their things had been carried up to a room, he asked her if she would mind unpacking while he went out for an hour or so, as he wished to change some money and also to call on Baron le Houze, the French Minister, who was an old acquaintance of his.

She agreed without demur; so he ran downstairs, picked the carriage with the most promising-looking horse from a line of vehicles awaiting hire outside, and told its coachman to drive at top speed out to Christiansholm.

On arriving at Mr. Elliot's house, he learned, to his relief, that the Minister was at home and would see him at once. After greeting Roger as an old friend, Hugh Elliot asked him to sit down and tell him how he had enjoyed his trip to Russia.

Roger laughed. "Strap me, Sir! But I am monstrous lucky to have got back here alive. To be brief, I penetrated the Russian lines with news of import for King Gustavus, narrowly escaped being tried for murder, had to poison myself to avoid becoming the lover of the Empress, got married to Count Andrew Razumofsky's daughter, and was exiled to Siberia. I trust within the next two days to find an opportunity of entertaining you with a full account of these trifles; but at the moment I must beg leave to return as swiftly as possible to my inn. No doubt you are already aware that the Danes intend to attack Sweden. The purpose of this flying visit is to give you the essence of the Danish campaign, so that you may transmit it with all speed to Stockholm. Instead of advancing direct on the Swedish capital, as one would naturally expect them to do, they intend to overrun the south and capture Gothenbörg."

"Good God, man!" Hugh Elliot exclaimed, springing to his feet. "Are you sure of this?"

"Indeed I am. I had it from the Czarina Catherine's own lips."

"Then we are undone!" The Minister's face showed acute alarm, as he hurried on. "Prince Charles of Hesse-Cassel and the young Crown Prince of Denmark have been in Norway for weeks past raising an army there. They are said to have mustered twenty thousand men, and are expected to march against Stockholm any day now. But if they march south Gothenbörg will fall to them without a blow, and with it will founder all hope of Sweden proving the buckler of the Triple Alliance in the north."

"Why so, Sir?" asked Roger, utterly astounded.

"Because Gothenbörg is Sweden's greatest commercial city. Its loss will deprive Gustavus of more than half his supplies of war-like stores, and his credit will be ruined. Seeing his cause so utterly lost his discontented nobles will then declare openly against him and force him from the throne. His overthrow would so strengthen Russia, Austria, France and Spain that the security of every other country in Europe would be menaced.

Hugh Elliot paused for a second, then added with swift decision. "This Danish plan will render the King's position desperate, but speedy news of it may yet enable him to save himself. 'Tis imperative that you should leave instantly to carry a warning to Stockholm."

CHAPTER XX

FOR THE HONOUR OF ENGLAND

"HOLD fast, Sir!" Roger exclaimed. "I'd gladly oblige you, but to journey into Sweden at a moment's notice is more than I can undertake."

"Why so?" Elliot shot at him. "Despite your extraordinary experiences in Russia you have survived them looking monstrous fit. What is there to prevent you setting out immediately I have made the necessary arrangements?"

"The fact that I brought my wife out of Russia with me. She is awaiting my return at the Silver Hart; but we lie there for two nights only, then rejoin the ship that is carrying us to England."

"Then you must tell her that duty detains you here, and that you will follow her as soon as you are able."

"Nay, Sir. That is impossible. How can I send her, a Russian, who as yet can only speak a few words of English, alone to a strange land where she knows no one?"

"Then let her remain in Copenhagen. I will see to it that she is well cared for; you should be back here within a week."

Roger shook his head. "To require that I should desert her after being married less than a fortnight is asking too much. Besides, she knows nothing of my work. In fact I have not even broken it to her yet that I am an Englishman. How could I possibly explain my leaving her so suddenly?"

"That is deuced awkward," muttered the Minister. "But we will think of a way to get over it. I can only repeat that I consider it imperative that you should carry this warning to Stockholm with the least possible delay."

"Why myself and not another?"

"Because you alone can vouch for the truth of the news you bring, and convince Gustavus of his peril."

"I'd do it readily, Sir, but for the appalling complications arising from my marriage. My wife has as great a love for her country as we have for ours. Think of the state to which she would be reduced were I to confess that, having wooed and married her under the guise of a Frenchman, I am English, and all this time have been secretly a servant of the British crown."

Elliot shrugged his narrow shoulders. "I sympathise with your predicament, Mr. Brook; but, in any event, you will be compelled to reveal your nationality to her when you get her to England. And, since you have mentioned your love for your country, I must appeal to you on that."

He paused then went on very earnestly. "It is but fair that I should reveal to you the true state of affairs; and I vow it has near turned my hair grey with worry during recent weeks. Since your departure from Copenhagen the Government at home have at last seen the sense in my reiterated arguments, that the only way to prevent the Czarina Catherine from turning the Baltic into a Russian lake is for Britain to give active support to Gustavus in his war against her. This being agreed by the Cabinet, they have, through me, secretly promised him this help in the form of a Fleet to be sent to his assistance. That was months ago; yet, owing to dissensions in our parliament, and Mr. Fox's opposition, nothing has been done. I have had to sit here, watching the situation of the Swedes go from bad to worse, turning a deaf ear to their appeals and unable to lift a finger to aid them. If King Gustavus is finally overcome and compelled to abdicate, not only will our plan for maintaining Sweden as the outpost of the Triple Alliance in the north be brought to nought but it will leave an indelible stain on British honour. Gustavus is a man of great resolution and resource. Even at this eleventh-hour, if warned in time, he may devise a means of cheating his enemies. But you and I alone have the combined authority and knowledge to place new weapons in his hands. Now, Mr. Brook! Will you, or will you not, accompany me to Sweden?"

"Accompany you, Sir!" Roger repeated in surprise. " 'Tis the first that you have said of going thence yourself."

The tall Scotsman smiled at him. "I took the resolution only in these last few moments. But desperate situations require desperate remedies. Although I am accredited to the court of Denmark, I am also charged with a watching brief over British interests at the court of Sweden as long as the post there remains unoccupied. We are far from London and despite my appeals no guidance has been forthcoming from my Lord Carmarthen. The step I contemplate may mean the premature ending of my career, but since our Government hesitates to fulfil its obligations, 'tis all the more fitting that their representative should stand beside the King of Sweden in his hour of trial. If they repudiate me afterwards at least I'll have the satisfaction of having saved my own honour."

"Well said, Sir!" exclaimed Roger. "Then I'll go with you! Though God alone knows how I'll account for my projected absence to Mistress Brook. But stay! Since you are now resolved on going yourself, and will be able to acquaint the King with the Danish plan, surely 'tis no longer essential that I should quit my wife and thus embroil myself with her?"

"I fear it is," replied the Minister. "You seem to have overlooked the fact that I am accredited to both Courts. As His Majesty's representative here I cannot betray the Danish plans to Sweden, or vice versa. The retailing of the news you have brought is your affair and, officially, I must know nothing of it. My reason for going is to show Gustavus that Britain has not totally deserted him; and, if I can, concert means with him to persuade the Danes to cease hostilities."

"Surely that would be well-nigh impossible?"

"It certainly appears so; but at least I can make the attempt, and as I have a foot in both camps I am well placed to do so."

Roger saw that, having committed himself in a moment of enthusiasm for Hugh Elliot's fine integrity, he could not possibly back down now; but he was at his wit's end how to break the news to Natalia Andreovna. He had known all along that before they reached England he would have to disclose his real identity, but while they were cruising down the Baltic he had let sleeping dogs lie, in the belief that he would still have ample time after they left Copenhagen to consider how to do so with the least chance of disrupting their good relations.

But now he was called on to tell her as much of the truth as was essential without any preparation. Whatever he said must come as a grave shock to her, and to make matters worse, he would be unable to remain with her afterwards to soften the effects of the blow.

Elliot guessed from Roger's worried look what was passing in his mind, so he said quietly: "Why, instead of returning to have an explanation with your wife, do you not leave a letter for her. 'Tis not, I admit, the bravest course in such a situation, but as the proverb has it, 'discretion is oft the better part of valour'."

"I could do that," Roger murmured uneasily, "providing she gets the letter speedily. Otherwise she will begin to fear that some accident has befallen me."

"She shall have it within the hour, I promise you. Come, now. Sit down at my table and write it while I ride over to the Reventlows. You will remember spending a Sunday with them when you were here before. The Count owns a splendid sea-going yacht, and I feel sure that he will lend it to us for our journey. We'll make better time going by sea than over land to Stockholm. I shall also speak to the Countess of the straits in which duty compels you to leave Mrs. Brook, and I can vouch for it that your wife will be well taken care of."

"So be it," agreed Roger, sitting down. "To slide out thus from dancing to the music now the tune is called goes all against the grain; but as a man of your courage recommends it, that salves my conscience to some extent. 'Twill not quiet my anxieties during our absence, for I shall be fretting to know how my wife has sustained the impact of learning the deceit that I have practised upon her; but since our departure must be immediate 'tis perhaps better that I should leave without her reproaches and abuse ringing in my ears."

"You intend, then, to tell her that you are an Englishman?"

"Yes. It would but make matters worse to continue to hide under my French *nom-de-guerre* and pretend that I am deserting her on account of some business connected with that nation; for that, at no distant date, would prove one more deceit that I should be hard put to it to justify. I pray you tell the truth to Countess Reventlow, and tender my apologies to her for having accepted her hospitality under a false nationality.

The diplomat nodded. "I will take full responsibility for that, and am confident that she will not hold it against you. As for the rest, while we are in Sweden your wife will have time to calm her thoughts, and on your return she may prove much more amenable than had you thrown this bombshell into her lap yourself."

Comforted a little by this last suggestion Roger wryly smiled good-bye to his host and sat down to compose his letter. For some moments he chewed the end of the quill, made three false starts, and, finally, wrote as follows:

My dearest love,

I have to crave your forgiveness upon two matters which will, I fear, come as a severe shock to you; but I pray that you will do your best to give them your sympathetic understanding and accept my assurance that the duplicity which circumstances have forced me to practise in no way affects the depths of my feelings for you.

In the first place I must disclose that my real name is Roger Brook, and that I am the son of an English Admiral. Having acquired in my upbringing some knowledge of maritime matters I was requested, during my tour of the Northern capitals, to make an investigation into the sea-trade carried on by our commercial rivals, the French, in the Baltic ports, and to report upon it on my return.

The suggestion that I should combine the mission with what was originally intended to be a tour, undertaken solely for education and pleasure, arose from the fact that I had already spent some years in France, and that during the latter part of my sojourn in that country, it had often amused me to pass myself off as a Frenchman.

Obviously, to assume that role again opened to me better prospects of carrying out my mission than I should have otherwise enjoyed. In consequence, on my arrival in Copenhagen last April the British Minister here, Mr. Hugh Elliot, introduced me into Danish society as M. le Chevalier de Breuc, and I naturally journeyed on to Stockholm and Petersburg in that role.

I suppose that when I first fell in love with you I ought to have confided my secret to you; but as we then had no thought of marrying it did not seem essential to me that I should do so. Then, later, the circumstances of our marriage were so unusual that I was denied the opportunity of revealing the matter before the ceremony.

I intended, of course, to acquaint you with the facts before we reached England; but I was so very happy during our recent voyage, that a cowardly, and I trust, unjustified fear of marring our bliss by this disclosure caused me to postpone an explanation with you.

And now, with the utmost reluctance and distress, I must acquaint you with my second disclosure. On my reporting to Mr. Elliot, this afternoon, the results of my mission to date, he seized upon my coming to request that I would undertake another matter for him. 'Tis, in short, that I should set out instantly to carry a despatch for him to Stockholm.

None of his usual couriers are, at the moment, available; and he considers it essential that the document he wishes to send should go by the hand of someone in whom he can place implicit trust. Moreover, it is of the utmost urgency. Despite my pleas that it was unreasonable to ask me to interrupt our honeymoon, he insisted that I had been sent to him by Heaven in his extremity; so I could not find it in myself to refuse.

I shall be gone only the inside of a week, and during my absence Mr. Elliot is arranging for the Countess Reventlow to introduce you into Danish society and see that you lack for nothing. Meanwhile I send you the key of our money chest, and do assure you that I shall be thinking only of the moment when I can rejoin you.

I beg you, my dear love, to think of me with such forbearance and kindness as you can. And should the least doubt linger in your mind as to my complete devotion to you, I pray you to recall that it was at my own solicitation that we were remarried in the English church at Petersburg. The vows which I took there remain my most cherished memory, and you may rest assured of my intention to honour them for all my days.

Your greatly distressed but most loving husband.

ROGER BROOK.

Having finished the letter Roger read it through and was moderately pleased with it. He regretted having to tell her two new lies, but that was unavoidable, as the real truth involved Mr. Pitt and therefore had to remain secret. The cover-story that he had invented to explain his having masqueraded as a Frenchman was a partial admission that he was a secret agent; but the inference was that he had been concerned only in ferreting out the secrets of the French, and to that, he felt, Natalia Andreovna could take no serious exception.

After addressing the missive and sealing it with a wafer he remained sitting moodily at the desk for a further quarter of an hour; then Hugh Elliot came hurrying in.

"Cheer up, man!" he cried, giving Roger a friendly slap on the shoulder. "You are in nowhere near so serious a scrape as some in which it seems you got yourself while in Russia; and all goes excellently. I found the Reventlows at home, and on my telling the Count that I desired to get swiftly to Stockholm to see if I could not act as a mediator between the two warring nations he readily agreed to lend me his yacht."

"And the Countess?" Roger inquired.

"She is the sweetest creature, and I knew that we could count upon her. I said that for the negotiations I hope to set on foot 'twas essential that I should take with me a trustworthy companion to act as secretary or confidential messenger when the need arose. The moment I told her of my intention to tear you from your bride she volunteered at once to take her into her own home during your absence. She ordered her carriage and, having accompanied me back here, is now sitting in it

297

outside. You have but to give her your letter and she will drive with it into the city, to deliver it with her own hand and comfort Mrs. Brook when she learns its contents."

"I am indeed grateful," Roger said more cheerfully. Then he went out to renew his acquaintance with the Countess and thank her personally for her kindness.

Since there was nothing more that he could do about Natalia, he endeavoured to put her out of his mind while Hugh Elliot brought him up to date with events in Copenhagen. At four o'clock they sat down to dinner, and over it he gave the Minister a more detailed version of all that had befallen him in Stockholm and St. Petersburg. Then at five o'clock they prepared to set out for the harbour. Roger had come ashore wearing his sword, but otherwise he had only the clothes he stood up in, so his companion packed some extra shirts and stockings into his valise.

In the meantime Count Reventlow had sent a message to the captain of his yacht to collect his crew and prepare the ship for sea; so when the two Englishmen went aboard they found the long low craft all but ready to set sail. By seven o'clock the last hamper of fresh provisions had been stowed away and the anchor was weighed.

Soon after midnight they were challenged off the island of Bornholm by a warship of the Russo-Danish squadron, which was now operating in the Southern Baltic, again and next morning, as they headed north through Calmar Sound, by a Swedish frigate; but, in deference to Mr. Elliot's presence on board, the yacht was flying the British flag, so, as a neutral, she was allowed to pass on her way. The weather was cold but fine and the beautiful little ship scudded along at a fine pace, bringing them safely to Stockholm a little before mid-day on Friday, the 21st, only forty-one hours after she had left Copenhagen.

At such a time of crisis it seemed more probable that Gustavus would be with his army than at his palace out at Drottingsholm, so on landing, at Roger's suggestion, they went straight to the house of Prebendary Nordin, to ascertain the King's whereabouts.

They found the Prebendary at home and were shown up at once to the book-lined room in which Roger had had his fateful interview with the Swedish King. Nordin's surprise at seeing Mr. Elliot was only equalled by his joy. Rising from his desk he said with a grave smile:

"Your Excellency finds us in most dire straits; but even if you bring bad news it will be more than counterbalanced by the effect of your presence among us."

"I thank you, Sir," Elliot replied, "and only trust that your hope may be justified. Having formed the opinion that the only chance of saving Sweden is to arrange an immediate accommodation with the Danes I am come to offer my services as mediator should His Majesty be pleased to accept them."

"His Majesty has never doubted your Excellency's kind intentions towards us," said the Prebendary a shade uncomfortably. "But unfortunately your Government has so far shown no signs of implementing the promises you have made on its behalf. Therefore, 'tis only fair to tell you that, seeing his affairs in so critical a state, His Majesty has recently contemplated renewing his old friendship with France, and asking King Louis to endeavour to arrange an accommodation between him and his enemies."

" 'Tis for His Majesty to decide," replied Elliot quickly. "But were he to do that I fear he would have cause to rue it. This is no occasion to enter into the respective advantages which a lasting friendship with either country would offer His Majesty; but one factor is clear. Any delay in an attempt to open negotiations with the Danes must now spell his final ruin. There is no time to seek the good offices of the Court of Versailles, whereas I am on the spot, and if His Majesty is willing, could act immediately."

"Our plight is bad, but not yet desperate," countered Nordin.

"I fear you are mistaken, Sir," Roger cut in, and he then disclosed the Danish plan to swing south on Gothenbörg.

As the Prebendary listened his expression became one of the deepest gloom, and when Roger had done, he muttered: "Since the Danes announced their intention to honour their treaty with Russia we have taken such measures as we could. 'Tis believed that they mean to invade us by way of the Friedrikshald gap. Our fortress of Quistrum, there, should hold them for a time; but once it is passed the province of Nordmark will be open to them. It is natural to anticipate that they would advance due east upon the capital, and His Majesty intends to deploy such forces as he can muster in their path. As he has little but a rabble of armed peasants with which to oppose them our case even then would be bad enough. But if their objective is Gothenbörg our situation is indeed desperate; and nought but your Excellency's good offices, immediately applied, can save us."

The British Minister nodded. "With Sweden now so weak the Danes must know that they have victory in their grasp before the war's begun; so 'twill be no easy task to induce them to throw away its fruits and agree a settlement. I can but try, and pray that they may be delayed in launching their attack. Are there no troops at all between them and Gothenbörg?"

"None but a small garrison at Uddevalla. The country was almost denuded of troops for the Finnish campaign, and most of our best regiments are still moribund there under His Majesty's second brother, the Duke of Ostrogothia. Yet, such is the King's courage and resource that on his return he refused to be dismayed by our new danger. Lacking adequate regular troops to form another army he resorted to an extraordinary expedient. When his illustrious predecessor, Gustavus the First, was in a similar predicament he appealed to the Dalecarlians to rise and deliver Sweden from the Danish yoke, and these sturdy mine-workers achieved the seemingly impossible."

"Has His Majesty left Stockholm to do likewise, then?" asked Roger quickly.

The Prebendary nodded. "First, with his usual energy, he secured the adherence of the bourgeois in the capital. They were heartily sickened with the defection of the nobility and army, and the more readily pledged their loyalty to the King. In a short time we had raised three thousand burghers vowed to defend both their city and the throne. Having secured his rear from the risk of a *coup d'état* by the nobles, His Majesty hurried to the Dales and is touring the mines, making a series of those patriotic orations of which he is such a master. From such news as reaches us I gather that the results are fully justifying his exertions, and that he has now raised several thousand Dalecarlians with whom he hopes to check the enemy's advance on Stockholm."

"Alas!" said Hugh Elliot. "I fear that this last desperate effort must now be brought to nought. In a pitched battle fought on their own soil these hardy partisans might possibly have repulsed the enemy; but by selecting Gothenbörg instead of Stockholm for their objective the Danes will outflank His Majesty. Their forces will pass a hundred miles to the southward of him, and long before he can bring his rude army that distance through the mountains his richest city will have fallen to the enemy. I trust that you can inform me of His Majesty's whereabouts, for I feel the urge more strongly than ever to place myself at his disposal without delay."

"When I last heard he was at Falum; and he will, I know, bless your Excellency's coming, as an omen that he has not been totally abandoned to his fate by those powers who have given him firm assurances of their friendship. The journey is all of one hundred and forty miles, but I will despatch a courier at once to ride on ahead of you and arrange relays of horses for your carriage."

As he finished speaking Nordin left the room. When he returned some moments later he asked them to follow him, and led them across the landing to a dining-room where cold food had hastily been set out on the table. They knew that inns were very few and far between on the Swedish roads, and that it might be many hours before they got another decent meal, so they ate as heartily as they were able, while Nordin toyed with some fruit in gloomy silence.

It was nearly two o'clock when they went downstairs. Outside, a closed carriage with six horses and an escort of four Hussars was waiting for them. They got in and drew the fur rugs about them; as they waved good-bye to the harassed Prebendary the carriage clattered away down the cobbled street.

The journey was a nightmare that seemed never-ending. The horses moved at a fast trot, and sometimes even at a canter, along all the flattish portions of the road, falling into a walk only when they were breasting or descending a steep hill. As the first half of the way lay through Sweden's lowest lying province these easings of the pace were few and far between, so that all through the afternoon and evening the travellers had to support an almost constant rocking, as the stout springs of the carriage reacted to the bumps of the road taken in such swift succession.

300

The highway wound for the most part along the shores of a succession of lakes and through farm lands in which the corn had already been harvested; but as dusk fell they entered more desolate country in which hills became more frequent and habitations lay farther apart. With the advance of night the gradients grew steeper, and there came longer intervals during which the carriage ceased its violent swaying, so its occupants were able to snatch quite considerable periods of fitful sleep.

When dawn came, they were winding their way down towards another plain, and having crossed it they reached a lake, on the north shore of which lay Falun. At seven o'clock they entered the little town with the satisfaction of knowing that they had accomplished their long and wearisome journey in a bare seventeen hours. But, to their intense annoyance, they soon learned they had suffered to no purpose, as Gustavus had left the place three days before.

Having raised a company of volunteers the King had despatched them south-west to Annefors and ridden off himself ahead of them in that direction. After a meal and a change of horses Mr. Elliot and Roger followed, reaching the place at nightfall. But the King was still two days ahead of them, and reported to be fifty miles to the north-west at Malung.

Hugh Elliot, although trained for a soldier, had never been strong and was now suffering from a slight fever; so Roger insisted that they should pass the night where they were. On reaching Malung the following evening they learned that Gustavus had never been there at all, so next morning they decided to head for Charlottenburg, on the frontier, as the most likely place that he would choose for his headquarters in an attempt to intercept the Danes.

Their route now lay crosswise to the chains of lakes and mountains, necessitating many lengthy detours, so they did not reach the frontier town until the evening of the 27th. As Gustavus was not there, they pushed on further south next day, only to be met with the news that the Danes had opened hostilities on the 26th and were now pouring through the Friedrikshald gap, some thirty miles distant. Having come upon no indication that any Swedish forces had passed that way, they turned back and spent another night in Charlottenburg.

Fatigue, and the additional strain of knowing that the war he had sought to prevent was now in active progress, had increased Elliot's fever to such a degree that Roger refused to let him proceed further until they had something definite to go on. That night, the 29th, a courier informed them that Gustavus was at Carlstadt, on Lake Vener; but, just as they were about to set out in the morning an officer came riding up, and as they learned later, suspecting that they might be spies, swore to them that the King was further north at Edeback.

Wearily they recrossed the chains of mountains, only to find two days later that they had been deceived, and have it confirmed that Gustavus had made Carlstadt his headquarters. A road down a long winding valley led south directly to the lake; and, making a great effort to catch the King before he moved again, they reached the town at dawn on the 3rd of October. Gustavus's camp was just outside it, and after eleven gruelling days and nights, on driving up before a little group of tents they found that they had at last run him to earth.

On alighting and stretching his limbs Roger was quite shocked by the appearance of the camp. The brave show that Gustavus's quarters had made in Finland was entirely lacking. A bare dozen tents were perched upon a knoll, and round about it spread hundreds of wretched-looking bivouacs, among which groups of hairy men clad in jerkins of sober black or grey were eating a meal that appeared to be distinctly scanty.

The guards were few and the formalities of approaching Gustavus of the simplest. Two minutes after their arrival they were shown into his tent. At the sight of them he sprang to his feet and, extending both his hands to Hugh Elliot, cried:

"This is a surprise, indeed! But never was I more glad to see any man. Your Excellency's presence in our camp is worth an Army corps." Then he turned to Roger and added: "And you, Mr. Brook, bringer of good tidings. Are you come with Mr. Elliot to tell us that a British fleet is at last upon its way to our assistance?"

Gravely, and as gently as they could, they disabused him of his hopes and told him the bitter truth. For a moment he was silent, then he said: "I might have guessed it, when I learned last night that two days since the Danes had taken Uddevalla. The cowardly surrender of Quistrum by Colonel Tranfelt on the 29th left the whole southeast open to them; yet I supposed that they had sent a column to Uddevalla only to secure their flank. 'Tis clear now that the town fell to their main army in its advance on Gothenbörg. The city is Sweden's treasure-chest, and with it I'll lose my crown. So you find me, gentlemen, in much the same condition as your James the Second; and, like him, it seems that I'll be left no option but to spend my declining years as a pensioner of France."

Ill and exhausted as he was, Hugh Elliot rose magnificently to the occasion, and cried with superb self-confidence: "Give me your crown, Sire, and I will return it to you with new lustre."

"What mean you?" muttered the despondent King.

Drawing himself up, the soldier-diplomat answered: "I pray, Sire, that you will never find yourself compelled to leave your Kingdom against your inclination; but that should you be forced to it you would give the preference to Britain. In fact, I am come to propose that your Majesty should cease to rely further at any time on King Louis' empty protestations of friendship, and lean henceforth when you have need upon the support of Britain, Prussia and the United Provinces."

The King gave him a cynical glance. "I promised to do so months ago, but what have any of them done for me so far?"

"'Tis not what they have done, Sire, but what they are both capable of and pledged to do, that merits your Majesty's consideration. France is so enervated from internal unrest that she no longer has the power to help you, whereas the Triple Alliance grows stronger every day, and is actively concerned to aid your Majesty in your difficulties. Before I left Copenhagen I saw the Prussian Minister, Count Von Rhoda, and we were entirely of one mind. The Count declared to me his intention of proceeding to Berlin to urge his government to exert pressure on the Danish court to cease from its attack upon you. My own government is too far removed for me to take a similar step; but, pending the receipt of fresh despatches, I am willing to take it on myself to use the prestige of the British Crown in your Majesty's interest, should you so desire."

"What! You are prepared to exert pressure on the Danes to cease hostilities?" cried the King, joyfully.

"I can at least proceed to open negotiations with the Danish headquarters, should your Majesty give me your authority to do so."

"Go to it then, and may God prosper your endeavours; for 'tis clear now that an armistice alone will enable me to repair my shattered fortunes. You will be acting, too, in a just cause, since their attack upon me was made in most treacherous fashion. In all these years it was never once hinted that they had pledged themselves to aid Catherine should a war break out between Sweden and Russia. Still worse, His Danish Majesty's brother-in-law, Charles of Hesse-Cassel, who now commands their army, came into Sweden and made a tour of my Southern provinces as an honoured guest, while their forces were already being prepared in Norway for this invasion. For a Prince and a General to have thus come ahead and, while pretending friendship, acted the part of spy is infamous; and I pray you tell him so."

Hugh Elliot shook his head. "I fear, Sire, that such matters, however reprehensible, will carry little weight when it comes to their deciding whether or no to carry the conflict to a final issue. The critical factor lies in the degree of loyalty that the garrison of Gothenbörg may display to your Majesty; or rather the degree of resistance which the Danes expect to encounter from the city. If they believe that it can be had by a mere summons to surrender I doubt if aught that I can say will dissuade them from taking it, and your prestige among your own subjects will then be lost for good. But if the Danes think they will be put to a long and arduous siege they may be persuaded to give you an honourable accommodation rather than risk incurring the ill-will of Britain and Prussia."

"Your Excellency is right in that!" Gustavus's eyes suddenly showed their old fire. "While you proceed with these negotiations Gothenbörg must be held at all costs. I have taken up my quarters here in order that the constant sight of their King may hearten my loyal Dalesmen, but I have two good regiments billeted in the town, and I will despatch them instantly to reinforce Gothenbörg."

"'Tis all of a hundred and seventy miles, Sire," hazarded Roger. "And if the Danes captured Uddevalla three days ago their advance columns must already have penetrated as far as the outer defences of the city. I trust your Majesty has a reliable commander there, for if not he may be panicked into surrendering before the arrival of this help that you propose to send him."

Gustavus shot him a shrewd glance. "I fear that your apprehensions are well-grounded, Mr. Brook. Having no thought that the place was liable to attack, I left old General Duretz there with but a handful of troops; and he has never been accounted any hero."

"Then there is but one thing for it!" Hugh Elliot cried, his feverish eyes flashing. "Your Majesty must instantly to horse, ride south at breakneck speed and fling yourself into Gothenbörg; that by your example you may hearten the garrison and save both the city and your throne."

"One moment!" Roger intervened, with justifiable apprehension that Elliot's sense of the dramatic had carried him too far. "The south end of the lake is already known to be in enemy hands. His Majesty would have to run the gauntlet of their vedettes, and should he be captured. . . ."

But the impetuous Gustavus had already been fired by the soldier-diplomat's idea, and he retorted swiftly: "Better be captured in an attempt to save one's crown than sit still while 'tis torn from one's head. I pray your Excellency to proceed with all speed in your carriage down the western shore of the lake to Uddevalla, or wherever the Danish headquarters are to be found, and do your utmost to procure us a truce; while I get me by the eastern shore to Gothenbörg and take measures for the city's stout defence."

He paused for a moment, a sudden look of cunning masking his handsome face, then he went on: "But my Dalesmen must get no hint that I have left them, or they would become disgruntled and fast melt away to their homes. We will go into the town and there I will have it given out that I am suffering from a slight indisposition. That will cover my disappearance until sufficient store of provisions can be amassed to feed them on their march south. They can then be told that I am but a day ahead of them and impatient for them to rejoin me. The fewer people who know of our intent the less likelihood of betrayal; so I shall confide our plan only to General Armfeldt. I have here, too, so few officers that none can be spared to accompany me; but that has its compensations, in that their sudden disappearance will not arouse comment and, perhaps, be connected with my own."

Roger's levelheadedness again caused him to intervene. "May it please your Majesty to reconsider your last decision. 'Twould be the most terrible calamity if you went alone and some accident befell you by night upon the road."

The King gave him a friendly pat upon the arm. "Since you are so concerned for my safety, Chevalier, I would welcome your attendance on me, should you care to give it. Nay, more, on further thought I do request it; for once I am in Gothenbörg I may be beleaguered there, and in such a case you would be invaluable to me. It may be of the first importance that I should communicate with Mr. Elliot, and you, as a neutral, would be allowed free passage through the enemy lines."

"His Majesty is right, Mr. Brook," added Elliot. "The presence at his side of an English gentleman who can come and go freely between him and myself may prove the saving of us all."

But Roger had already bowed his acquiescence, and he said: "I will gladly accompany you, Sire. No man could witness a sovereign contemplating so valiant an endeavour without desiring to serve him. I am entirely at your Majesty's disposal."

"Come then!" cried the King. "Let us to the town. With so much that is fresh to think upon I had forgot my duties as a host. After your long night's journey you must both be in sore need of refreshment and rest. The former we can easily provide, but for the latter I fear you will have to go on short commons; as I intend to set out as soon as I have given Armfeldt his orders, and he has made arrangements for our departure."

The carriage which had brought Elliot and Roger from Stockholm was still outside, so the three of them got into it, drove into the little market-town and pulled up at the entrance to the Guildhouse, which had been taken over as Army headquarters.

There the King turned his guests over to Count Ugglas; one of his intimates, who owed his rise from a simple clerk in the Chancellery to the fact that on the day of Gustavus's *coup d'état*, forgetting the distance that separated them, his enthusiasm had led him to clasp the King in his arms and hail him as the saviour of Sweden. The Count himself put cold meat and wine before them, and, when they had eaten, took them to a room that he shared with another officer, where they lay down on the truckle beds. They had had a certain amount of sleep during the night, but they were none the less grateful for the rest and soon fell into a doze.

An hour passed, although it seemed to them that they had only just lain down, when Ugglas returned and roused them. He took them downstairs and out into a courtyard at the back of the building. Their carriage was waiting there with fresh horses and its blinds drawn down. As they got in they saw that Gustavus was already seated inside it, but he now wore no decorations and was dressed as a simple lieutenant of the Yemland Infantry. The moment they were seated the carriage moved off at a trot, and the King said:

"I regret, Mr. Elliot, that I should have to carry you some five miles out of your way, but I have already despatched my Guards and the Yemland regiment on their march to Gothenbörg, and this offered the most convenient means of passing through them undetected. I have arranged for horses to be awaiting Mr. Brook and myself just beyond the village of Skattkarr, and having seen us on our way you can then turn back."

As the carriage sped on they talked earnestly of the hazardous journey that the King was about to undertake, and the none too rosy prospects of the British Minister proving successful in his mission. Then the vehicle was brought to a halt, and they alighted on the outskirts of a pine wood, in the fringe of which two mounted men were holding six led horses.

" 'Tis my groom and body-servant," Gustavus explained to Roger. "They will accompany us part of the way, leading a pair apiece which we will take for remounts as required, and press on; leaving them to follow with the horses we have exhausted when they are somewhat rested."

The good-byes were brief but heartfelt on both sides and two minutes later the King's little cavalcade cantered away with Hugh Elliot waving them good luck from beside the carriage.

The first lap lay round the north-eastern corner of the lake to Christinehamn; a distance of some twenty-five miles from where the carriage had set them down. It was soon clear to Roger that Gustavus had no intention of sparing the horses, and after fifteen miles had been covered at a furious pace their first mounts were badly winded. Pulling up they changed to the two horses led by the groom, leaving him to rub down the whistling sweat-drenched creatures that they had ridden so hard.

They had left Carlstadt as the clocks were striking nine, and at a quarter past ten a bend in the road brought them in sight of Christinehamn. It was at that moment that the horse which had been ridden by the King's body-servant for the whole twenty-five miles, staggered, neighed loudly, and foundered.

Its rider was still clinging to the reins of his two led horses. Dismounting at once, Gustavus seized one of them and hoisted himself on to it. Roger swiftly followed suit, and, abandoning the horses they had ridden for the past ten miles, they sped on again through the township.

Roger realised then that Gustavus had had the foresight to save his two best mounts till last. Both were splendid animals of over sixteen hands and with powerful quarters. In spite of the distance they had already covered unmounted they still responded gamely to whip and spur, but another ten miles saw them flagging badly, and although the rough track along the lake-side still remained flat, their riders were compelled to walk them for a mile between each mile that they could cover at a trot.

Just before mid-day they espied a village in the distance which the King said was Otterbacken; adding that he counted on getting fresh horses there. With feverish impatience he lashed the poor brute he was riding into a canter and Roger, perforce, followed his example. When they drew rein in the village square both beasts stood head down and quivering, their forelegs apart, rasping pitifully and broken-winded.

Ignoring them, Gustavus, white-faced and trembling himself, staggered to the door of the post-house, beat with his crop upon the door and yelled for horses.

An ostler appeared in answer to the impatient summons and, not recognising the King, but scared by his cursing and galvanised into activity at the sight of some gold that Gustavus threw upon the cobbles, speedily furnished them with the two best mounts in the stable.

For another hour and a half they pressed on, now rocking in their saddles, so that when they reached the town of Mariestad at half-past one even Gustavus had to admit that the pace was proving too much for him, and that they must rest a while before proceeding further.

At the inn he curtly demanded refreshments, a bedroom to lie down in, and fresh horses to be ready for him at three o'clock. Again he was unrecognised, so after they had munched a piece of sausage and drunk a mug of beer apiece, they were shown up to a room with a big double bed. Flinging himself on it the King insisted that Roger should lie down beside him and for over an hour they relaxed their wearied limbs.

When they got up they found that it had begun to rain, but they put on their cloaks and a few minutes after three were on their way once more. The road now left the lake-side and ran up into the foot-hills of the mountains; so it was a quarter to five before they reached Skara and could change their mounts again at the post-house there.

From Skara the way descended sharply to the coastal plain, then ran through flattish country; but in spite of their rest they were no longer capable of maintaining the pace that they had made during the earlier stages of their journey. It was past six and twilight had fallen by the time they trotted into Vara.

They still had a third of their journey before them and were now soaked to the skin, so Roger no longer believed it possible that they could finish it without further rest and a change of clothes. Even allowing for the fact that he had slept only fitfully and in considerable discomfort the previous night, he was many years younger than the King and felt that his youth qualified him to sustain a greater effort. Yet he was already appallingly tired and sore, and he now feared that they would both fall off their horses from sheer exhaustion before they reached Gothenbörg.

At Vara a kindly postmaster, seeing their condition, pressed them to put up for the night at his house and, since they would not, insisted on producing a bottle of wine for them to drink. As wine was an expensive luxury rarely found in the Swedish countryside Gustavus was much touched, and without revealing his identity, vowed that if the business on which they were riding at such a pace proved successful he would secure a handsome promotion for their host in recompense for his generosity.

Much refreshed by the wine and a twenty-minute rest they set off again. Full darkness had now come, but the rain had ceased and the road ran flat and straight between dark forests with a ribbon of star-lit sky overhead, so they were little incommoded by it. There was only Alingsäs and one more wayside posting-house now between them and Gothenbörg.

Gustavus crouched over his horse's neck and rode on with such relentless determination that it seemed as if he was possessed of a demon. Roger was aching in every limb, but gritting his teeth, he continued to spur his mount into keeping neck to neck with that of the still resolute King. At half-past eight they breasted a slight rise and pulled up in front of the châlet where they expected to make their last change of horses.

To their consternation the postmaster told them that his stable was empty, as a troop of Danish cavalry had seized all his horses that afternoon.

The news could hardly have been worse since, not only were their mounts flagging sadly from the twenty-five miles that they had already covered, but it meant that the Danes had now infiltrated to the south-east of the great lake and at any moment the King and Roger might ride straight into a vedette of enemy skirmishers.

Nevertheless Gustavus would not be deterred from his purpose, so, flogging their tired mounts into a canter they clattered off down the far side of the slope.

The next twenty minutes were a nightmare. For alternate stretches they walked and trotted the poor beasts, alarmed at their ever increasing signs of exhaustion and rocking in their saddles from fatigue each time they managed to urge them into a trot. To the strain of keeping the horses moving was added a constant apprehension that they would encounter an enemy patrol.

Their only comfort was the rising of the moon, which now showed the track clearly for some way ahead, and twice they swiftly took cover in the woods on seeing little groups of horsemen in the distance.

At last, having walked their horses up a hill, they saw from its top their journey's end. Below them, no more than three miles distant, the spires and gables of Gothenbörg glinted in the moonlight, and beyond them shimmered the sea.

With a cry of joy Gustavus spurred his horse forward and in a stumbling canter it lopped down the easy gradient. Roger too, urged his mount into a last effort and the spurt carried them for half a mile down on to the flat.

Suddenly, the King's horse halted with a jerk which nearly threw him over its head, stood quivering for a moment, then collapsed; rolled over and lay still in the middle of the road.

Gustavus had had time to jump clear and stood by the dead animal, cursing furiously. Roger had overshot him by several yards. Pulling up, he dismounted, and now desperately anxious lest the King should yet be captured, cried:

"Take my mount, Sire! Your goal is but a few miles ahead. She'll carry you that far if you use her gently. Ride on, I beg, and I'll follow on foot."

With a word of thanks the King hurried to him, hauled himself into the saddle, and ambled off towards the city.

Heaving a sigh from weariness, Roger watched him cover the first quarter of a mile; then, although big clouds had just obscured the moon and a new downpour commenced, he sat down to rest on a bank by

the roadside. Now that he could no longer help Gustavus his task was done, and there was no particular urgency about his reaching the city. Even if a Danish patrol came upon him it was highly unlikely that they would interfere with a solitary English traveller.

For half an hour he remained sitting there in the pouring rain. He was very tired physically, but his brain was still so excited from the hazards of his mad ride that he felt no desire to sleep. As eleven o'clock chimed out from the bells of the city he judged that, unless the King had fallen foul of the enemy or his horse had foundered, he would now be at its gates.

He thought of the famous ride of Swift Nick, often wrongly attributed to Dick Turpin, in which the highwayman had ridden from Gad's Hill, via Gravesend ferry, Chelmsford, Cambridge and Huntingdon, to York; a distance of one hundred and ninety miles, in fifteen hours. King Gustavus and himself had covered a hundred and seventy miles in fourteen hours; but, whereas Swift Nick had used only one splendid bay mare, they had changed their mounts many times. Nevertheless Roger felt that their feat was one of which any King or subject might well be proud. Standing up he stretched his aching limbs, shook the raindrops from him, and began his trudge to Gothenbörg.

He met no one on the way and when, nearly an hour later, he arrived looking and feeling like a drowned rat, at the Gamla Port of the city, he found it closed against him.

His shouts brought a ready response from a group of sentinels up on the wall and one said to his companions in German with a laugh: "'Having had one fellow here to-night who claims to be the King, what will you wager me against this one telling us that he's the Crown Prince?"

On Roger giving his name and vowing that he had accompanied the King to within three miles of the city, their hilarity was suddenly stilled. It then transpired that Gustavus having arrived at the gate in a junior officer's uniform, and unattended by a single companion, they had refused to believe that he was their King, and had kept him outside as a butt for their jests for nearly an hour. He had only just been admitted and was still being questioned in the guardroom.

Roger's story tallying so completely with that which Gustavus had already given, he was let in without more ado, and he rejoined the furiously angry monarch just as he was being led under escort to the Guild House.

The rumour that a man who claimed to be the King had arrived had now spread through the city, and lights were appearing everywhere as people hurried from their beds to ascertain the truth. The prisoners and their guards had not proceeded far when a man ran out of the crowd, and throwing himself at Gustavus's feet, proclaimed that he was indeed their King, for he knew him well, and that by his timely arrival he had saved them all from destruction.

The joy of the people was then wonderful to behold. Cheering and shouting they crowded about Gustavus, striving to kiss his hands or

even touch his person; and, swiftly gaining the mastery over his outraged feelings, he smilingly adopted his favourite role of their father
and paladin. It was only with the greatest difficulty that he persuaded
the citizens to allow him to continue on his way; but, at length, hundreds of them waving torches formed into a great procession and led
him in triumph to the Governor's house.

Old General Duretz was both surprised and confounded by the
unexpected appearance of his sovereign; and, wringing his hands,
told him that he had been most ill-advised to come, as nothing could
save the city from capture.

"You mistake, General!" replied the King disdainfully. "I came
on purpose to save it. Now I require beds for myself and the gallant
gentleman who accompanied me. I will make my pleasure known to
you in the morning."

It then transpired that neither beds, plate, tables nor chairs
remained in the house, as the General had sent them all away the day
before to prevent them being pillaged by the Danes. At this an English
merchant who was standing among the crowd came forward and begged
the King to accept the use of his house, which chanced to be next
door; so Gustavus and Roger gratefully followed him to it and, flinging
themselves down on two piles of rugs before the fire, fell asleep from
sheer exhaustion.

The King's famous ride had taken place on the 3rd of October;
yet, in spite of that gruelling experience, he arose before dawn on the
4th and sent for the principal personages of the city, to whom he
announced his intention of defending it to the last extremity.

General Duretz fell on his knees before him and begged him not to
do so. In an effort to cover his own shame and partly, perhaps, from
an honest conviction, the Governor urged that the place was in no
state to resist. He said that by the previous evening it had been three-
parts surrounded and within a few hours would be so entirely, and that
he had received intelligence that by mid-day they would be sent a
summons to surrender. Should it be rejected a bloody assault would
follow and His Majesty's sacred person be exposed to grave danger.

Gustavus heard him out in silence, then said quietly: "Such being
your opinion, General, you will, of course, feel much obliged to me for
releasing you from the charge of this garrison. Retire, Sir, and follow
your baggage."

He then appointed Count John Sparr to be the new Governor,
and told the assembled magistrates and officers that if only they could
hold the city for a few days his army of Dalecarlians would have
time to come to their assistance; and of his hopes that if they could thus
rob the enemy of a major triumph, Britain and Prussia would actively
intervene before it was too late.

Charmed by his eloquence and animated by his courage, his listeners
pledged themselves to give him their utmost support and broke up
to set about the defence of the city in earnest.

The King then made a personal tour of the defences, and Roger, who accompanied him as one of his suite, soon saw that General Duretz had at least had some grounds for believing the place to be indefensible. Although the greatest fortress in Sweden it had been allowed to go to rack and ruin, the timbered platforms of the batteries having become so rotten that they would not bear the weight of a cannon.

It was already abundantly clear that Gustavus's momentous decision to throw himself into Gothenbörg had been fully justified, as, had he not done so, the city would certainly have been surrendered without firing a shot; but by the end of the tour of inspection Roger feared that the gallant gesture would have been made in vain if the Danes attacked the place with even moderate determination.

Nevertheless, as far as emergency measures could be taken they were now in full train, and the whole population was enthusiastically engaged in digging earthworks and dragging up great baulks of good timber to replace those that had rotted in the gun emplacements.

At mid-day, General Duretz's intelligence was proved correct by the arrival of a herald from Prince Charles of Hesse-Cassel, bearing a letter for the Governor which peremptorily demanded the surrender of Gothenbörg. To the herald's astonishment, he was taken, not to the Governor, but before the King, who promptly returned a defiant answer.

The die was now cast and an assault could be expected as soon as the Danish General had deployed his troops. In a private conversation with Roger that evening Gustavus admitted that in spite of the new heart he had put into the garrison he feared that the city could not possibly resist a serious attack, and that their one hope now lay in Mr. Elliot.

Nevertheless, they laboured on all through the next day improving the defences and, late that night, just as they were about to retire, Hugh Elliot joined them. He was looking very tired and ill, and his news was of the blackest. He had reached Uddevalla, where the Danish headquarters were established, late on the night of the 4th, but found that both Prince Charles and the young Crown Prince were absent, directing the movements of their troops. During the day he had despatched two letters to the Danish Commander-in-Chief, requesting that a truce should be called so that negotiations might be opened to prevent a general European conflagration. To both Prince Charles had disdained to reply.

"And so, Sire," the British Minister concluded. "Since I have failed you as a diplomat I am come to offer myself to your Majesty as a soldier. Having been trained in arms as a young man I have some knowledge of artillery; and if my country is dilatory in honouring its obligations, I can at least prove my belief that she will yet do so by acting as if Britain was at war with Denmark, and dying in our united cause."

Gustavus embraced him, vowing that no man could have done more, and that he accepted his offer with deep gratitude. After talking gloomily together for a little they then parted for the night.

311

Next morning Elliot, although still suffering from a fever, threw himself into the work of defence. There were several British ships in the harbour, and taking Roger to assist him, he mustered their crews and addressed them. He told the officers and men that Britain had pledged herself to assist Sweden in her war against an unjustified aggression, and asked them to join him in honouring their country's obligation by taking part in the defence of the city. To a man they agreed to do so, and as all the ships carried cannon there were many good gunners among them. Under his direction the British seamen cheerfully set about disembarking their pieces and manhandling them through the streets to the redoubts where they were most needed.

Yet, after seeing the miserable, makeshift state of the defences, Hugh Elliot confessed to Roger that he saw small hope of their holding the city in the face of a determined assault. All that he had seen during the morning had made him so pessimistic of Gustavus's chances of successfully giving battle to the Danes, and escaping being made their prisoner on the fall of the city, that at mid-day, when they rejoined the King, he told him that he had determined on writing yet a third letter to Prince Charles in an eleventh-hour attempt to induce the enemy to negotiate.

The letter was written and despatched to Uddevalla by a galloper early in the afternoon. After that they could only continue with their feverish preparations against attack and wait, with such fortitude as they could muster, for what the night might bring.

In the middle of the night the messenger returned with a despatch which stated that, while the Danish forces would continue their preparations for a mass assault on Gothenbörg, Prince Charles was prepared to give the British Minister an audience the following day.

The relief of Gustavus and his entourage was immense. Yet they recognized that their lives and safety still hung in the balance, and the outcome of the interview was awaited with feverish impatience.

Mr. Elliot departed for Uddevalla at dawn on the morning of the 7th, taking Roger with him to act as his confidential courier, but when Roger returned to Gothenbörg late that night he could only report that negotiations were proceeding. Between six a.m. and one p.m. he had covered the sixty miles with Hugh Elliot in his carriage, and between four in the afternoon and ten at night he had done the return trip on horseback, so he again slept the sleep of exhaustion.

At eight o'clock next morning he set out again, to see if he could secure more definite tidings which might lift the sense of doom from the anxious and breathless city; but when he reached Uddevalla Hugh Elliot had none to give him, so he slept there that night.

On the morning of the 9th there was a further conference, and after leaving it at mid-day the British Minister said to him with a wry smile: "Half-a-loaf is better than no bread. I have succeeded in inducing the Danes to grant King Gustavus an eight-day armistice. You have well earned the right to inform him of these good tidings, for what they are worth, so ride on ahead and tell him. I feel desperately ill, so shall follow more slowly in my carriage to give him full particulars."

Roger rode all out and reached Gothenbörg by five in the afternoon. Gustavus received his news with the utmost thankfulness, and asked him how he might reward him for bringing it. Roger then told him how he had been forced to abandon his Star and ribbon in a dungeon at Schlüsselburg; upon which the King promptly replied: "I will make you an Officer of the Order, for no man has better deserved it!" and presented him with his own Star, mounted in diamonds.

At ten o'clock Hugh Elliot arrived and gave the King details of his negotiations. On the carrying out of very modest stipulations the Danes were prepared to cease hostilities and evacuate their entire army to Norway.

Gustavus was utterly amazed and could scarcely find words to express his gratitude; but the diplomat warned him that nothing definite had been agreed, and that the Danes had only consented to abandon the conflict on the confirmation of certain eventualities. Tired out but in a far more optimistic frame of mind, Gustavus and his suite sought their beds.

Hugh Elliot and Roger were sharing a room in the English merchant's house, and when they reached it Roger said:

"Tell me, Sir! How did you achieve this miracle?"

The Minister sank upon the bed. His thin face was flushed and his eyes unnaturally bright, as he replied: "I can make no secret of it from you, since you are intimately involved. I could not find it in myself to stand by and witness this great city, with all its people, become the spoil and plaything of a brutal invader. Upon my own responsibility I took a high tone with the Danes and threatened them with the destruction of their whole kingdom did they not instantly desist from their invasion of Sweden, and withdraw."

"S'Death, you did!" gasped Roger. "And this still without orders from Whitehall?"

"I said that I had received fresh despatches, though 'twas not the truth," Hugh Elliot admitted with a feeble smile. "I wrote in my third letter to Prince Charles as follows: 'At this very moment war is perhaps declared against Denmark by Prussia and England, but if your Highness will consent to what I propose, I will immediately despatch couriers, if possible, to stop the invasion of Holstein by a Prussian army and the sailing of our fleet'. 'Twas that alone which gave him pause. Since then I have elaborated this supreme bluff and half-persuaded them to believe that they would do better to accept a present humiliation and eat humble-pie before Gustavus, than find themselves the victims of the wrath of two mighty powers which have already taken up arms to destroy them."

"You have all my admiration, yet I tremble for you," Roger exclaimed. "For if the bluff be called, what then? And how will you fare if our government at home repudiates the ultimatum that you have issued in its name?"

"As to myself, I care not," the ill man replied. "But by the honour of England and the saving of this brave Swedish King I set great store. And 'tis in this, my friend, that you also are concerned. The armistice that I have gained for Gustavus extends only for eight days from midnight to-night. If the Danes do not receive definite confirmation within a week that either a Prussian army is mobilising to invade Demark from the south, or that a British fleet is preparing to sail against them, they will know that I have lied, and the game will be up."

He paused for a moment, racked by a fit of coughing, then went on: "In the matter of the Prussians we can do nothing. Before I left Copenhagen Von Rhoda promised me that he would do his utmost to persuade King Frederick William to despatch troops to the Danish frontier. He will have the backing of Mr. Ewart, our Minister in Berlin, who played so great a part in founding the Triple Alliance, and of that good friend of ours, Prime Minister Von Hertzberg; but whether the King will agree to commit Prussia to war on Sweden's account no man can say. Therefore we must forget the Prussians and place our hopes only in what we may achieve ourselves. One final effort must be made to induce my Lord Carmarthen and Mr. Pitt to realise the imperative necessity of instantly publishing an order for the despatch of a fleet. You alone can tell them of our frightful situation at first hand. So at crack of dawn to-morrow you must go aboard the fastest British ship that is lying in the harbour here and get you off to England."

"But . . . " Roger began.

"I know!" The Minister waved his scarcely begun protest impatiently aside. "You are thinking again of that wife of yours in Copenhagen. Well, what of her? You told me yourself that you married her only because you were forced to it."

"Even so," Roger objected quickly. "I made my vows to her in an English church. She loves me, and I am determined to honour them to the best of my ability."

"Who seeks to prevent you? Not I." The diplomat shrugged wearily. "But she is safe and well cared for where she is. Surely you will not set her temporary inconvenience against a chance of saving ten thousand Swedish matrons and maids from being exposed to the licentious assaults of the brutal Danish soldiery?"

Roger thought miserably of Natalia Andreovna. She was now an exile. He had brought her out of Russia, and without a moment's notice, deserted her in Denmark. He had not even given her an opportunity, as yet, to ask him those questions about his family and status, to which she had every right to expect an answer. He had promised that he would rejoin her within a week, and seventeen days had already elapsed since he had abandoned her in the middle of their honeymoon. Now he was called upon to leave her marooned among strangers, with no further news of him than that he had sailed for England on urgent business, and would get back to her somehow, sometime, when his services were no longer required. To her it would appear abominably callous treatment, and few courses could be better calculated to disrupt the marriage that, once committed to it, he had determined to do his best to make a happy one.

Yet, what else could he do, other than agree to Hugh Elliot's request that he should set out for England in the morning? So much hung upon it. The fate of nations was involved; the lives and happiness of scores of thousands of people, and, above all, the honour of his country.

"So be it," he sighed. "I will write her another letter, explaining matters as well as I am able. May I rely upon you to ensure it being conveyed to her by a safe hand; and also to see that she does not lack for funds during my absence?"

"Indeed, I will; and I shall consider Mistress Brook to be my personal charge until your return. I, too, must pen a letter, for you to carry with you to my Lord Carmarthen. Let us set about it before I am quite overcome by this fever that assails me."

There was a table in the middle of the room with quills, ink and paper on it; so they sat down opposite one another and commenced their respective tasks.

As Roger began to write it struck him with grim humour that the excuse he had invented to cover his leaving Natalia had now become the truth; so there was little that he could say except that, Mr. Elliot still being without a trustworthy courier now required him to go to England. He sugared the bitter pill as best he could with endearments, perfectly truthful protestations that he was compelled to go entirely against his wish, and promised that he would rejoin her as fast as a ship could bring him back to Denmark.

When they had done they sealed and exchanged their letters, doused the candles, and pulling off their neckbands flopped still dressed upon their beds.

In the morning Roger took his leave of King Gustavus, who presented him with a miniature of himself set in brilliants, and assured him that he would always be an honoured guest at the Swedish court. Then he accompanied Hugh Elliot down to the docks.

He had come ashore from the *White Rose* wearing his sword, but his pistols and all his other baggage had been left behind with Natalia in Copenhagen; so, on the way to the harbour, he bought a few toilet articles and a couple of changes of linen.

Since speed was of the utmost importance Elliot chose for Roger's voyage a full-rigged ship, the *Bonny Bride* out of Leith. Her captain, Hamish McDougal, at first protested most strongly against his ship being commandeered, as he was already freighted with a cargo of goods for his home port. But the British Minister would take no denial, and the King's business taking precedence of all others Captain McDougal had to resign himself with such grace as he could muster to preparing to set sail for London.

In spite of the marital complications in which Elliot had landed him, Roger had conceived a great admiration for the diplomat, and the desperate days they had been through together had made them firm friends, so they took leave of one another with reluctance and genuine affection.

The bosun and his mates were sent ashore to collect the crew from the dockside dives, then they were despatched to recover the ship's cannon that had been landed three days before. A stock of fresh meat and vegetables was procured, and four hours after Roger had come on board the *Bonny Bride* put out to sea.

In a ship carrying so much sail Roger expected to reach London in from three to four days, but it was not to be. On passing out of the Skager Rack that night she was met by an ominous calm which lasted for some hours, then at four o'clock in the morning a tempest of extraordinary violence suddenly broke upon her.

For two days and nights Captain McDougal fought the storm with all the courage and tenacity for which his race are justly famous, but on the second night he lost his foremast, and after its upper part had been cut away, it was hurled back by a great wave end on against the ship's side, doing her considerable damage.

Roger was a moderately good sailor but not good enough to stand up to really bad weather, and for hours on end he was terribly ill, so knew little of what was happening.

On the third morning the storm eased somewhat and he came on deck. He knew that the foul weather must have delayed them but hoped that they might be running down the east coast of England and that after all these months he would be able to get a sight of his native land. To his disappointment he could see nothing but a waste of heaving grey-green waters, then, to his horror and dismay, Captain McDougal told him that they had been driven several hundred miles out of their course and were now somewhere off Norway.

Worse was to follow. At mid-day the Captain managed to get an observation and, finding their position to be approximately 62° N., 3° E., decided to put into Bergen, to have urgent repairs done before proceeding further. In vain Roger stressed the urgency of his mission, cursed, pleaded and finally threatened. Captain McDougal refused to risk his ship and crew by remaining at sea a moment longer than he had to, and would not even consider the suggestion of making for a port in the north of Scotland. Early the following morning, Sunday the 14th of October, the *Bonny Bride* limped into Bergen. Roger had hoped that he might find another ship there sailing in a day or two for a British port, but he was disappointed; and if he attempted the ghastly journey of three hundred miles over almost trackless mountains to Kristiania there was no guarantee that he would have better luck there; so he decided that it would be best to remain where he was for the five or six days which it was estimated the repairs would take.

Muffled in his cloak against the cold, he spent most of his time watching the shipwrights at work, in a fever of impatience for them to be done; but it took a full six working days to render the *Bonny Bride* sea-worthy, so it was not until Sunday the 21st that she put out from the bleak Norwegian port.

The weather was now moderately good, so they made an average passage and entered the estuary of the Thames late on the night of the 24th. At dawn on Tuesday morning Roger landed at Gravesend and took the first coach to London. On arriving there he went straight to Downing Street and sent his name up to the Prime Minister.

He was kept waiting for some twenty minutes, and during them he brooded miserably, as he had done almost uninterruptedly through his waking hours of the past ten days, on the possibly disastrous results of his belated arrival. The voyage that he had expected to make in four days had taken him fourteen. The armistice of eight days that Hugh Elliot had secured from the Danes had expired on the 17th and it was now the 25th. Unless some drastic measure had been taken since he left Gothenbörg the city was by now probably in ruins and Gustavus killed, captured or a fugitive King who had lost his throne.

It was Roger's first big failure; and although he knew that it had not occurred through any lack of diligence or foresight on his part, that did not alleviate his feeling that he had badly let down those friends in Sweden who had relied upon him.

At length a footman took him upstairs and showed him in to Mr. Pitt, who was still in his morning-robe drinking coffee. As was his custom Roger went straight to the point and, producing his letter, said:

" 'Tis from Mr. Hugh Elliot, Sir, and should have reached you ten days ago, but I was delayed by tempest. You will see that it is addressed to my Lord Carmarthen, but if I am not come too late, every moment may still be of vital importance, so I decided to bring it straight to you."

"You were right in that," said Mr. Pitt kindly, after a swift look at Roger's face. "Sit down and pour yourself a cup of coffee while I read it."

Roger did as he was bid, stealing an anxious glance now and then at the Prime Minister, whom he thought looked older and frailer than when he had last seen him. There also seemed to be a curious air of detached helplessness about his expression as he skimmed through the letter. Having finished it he tossed it aside as casually as if it had been a vulgar broadsheet, and remarked almost tonelessly: "I had news out of Denmark yesterday. The armistice has been prolonged for a further period of a month."

"Thank God!" Roger exclaimed. "Then I am not, after all, come too late!"

The Prime Minister shrugged his shoulders. "If it is of any comfort to you, Mr. Brook, you may rest assured that had you arrived ten days ago it could have made little difference."

"You mean, Sir, that you had despatched a fleet already?"

"Nay; and I have no intention of doing so."

"What say you!" cried Roger, springing to his feet. "But Britain's

317

word is pledged in this. And you, of all men, cannot play the shuffling politician now! You *must* send the aid that you have promised to King Gustavus."

"You use strong words, Mr. Brook," the Prime Minister frowned.

"No stronger than my feelings, Sir!" Roger rapped back. "And if excuse be needed 'tis that you have hitherto encouraged me to speak my mind to you."

"Aye; that is true," Pitt agreed more gently. "And on that score 'tis I who should ask your pardon. Yet what you propose cannot be done. Mr. Elliot has acted with a courage that does him credit, yet he has gone beyond his instructions and I cannot publicly endorse his statements. Neither can I despatch a fleet; for I no longer have the power to do so."

"In God's name why?" ejaculated Roger, staring at him in amazement. "Has, then, the government fallen overnight?"

Poor Billy Pitt shrugged wearily. "Nay; though in some ways I almost wish it had. I am but the First Minister of the crown, and I could never have held my place these past five years had it not been for His Majesty's constant encouragement and support. The Princes and the opposition would prove too much for me were I to attempt to introduce any controversial measure which they knew to be without the King's full knowledge and approval. So at this juncture it is unthinkable that I should take a step which might involve Britain in a war."

"Is the King dead then?"

"Nay; but three days ago His Majesty's doctors officially informed the Cabinet that he has become insane."

CHAPTER XXI

IN BAULK

" I HAVE, of course, known this for some time," Pitt went on sadly. "All through the summer His Majesty's health was in a low state, and a stay at Cheltenham did nothing to improve it. On his return to Windsor he was compelled to give up those long walks and rides which have always proved so exhausting to his suite, but which were such a feature of his life. In fits and starts he still attempts them; I think in an effort to escape his own thoughts, for the poor man is fully aware that he has become subject to fits of mental derangement. But they serve only to make his malady worse; on his return from these excursions he talks at an incredible speed and often with complete inconsequence. He is behaving very bravely about it. As late as last night he insisted on appearing at a levée at St. James's Palace, as he wrote me himself 'to stop further lies, and any fall in the stocks,' but his condition was pitiable, and 'twas plain to us all that we were in the presence of a madman."

"What you tell me, Sir, is truly terrible," Roger murmured. "Do His Majesty's physicians offer any explanation as to the cause of the disease?"

"None. 'Tis not hereditary in the family, or caused by any particular mental shock. But some of us who know him most intimately have formed the opinion that his brain has become overwrought from brooding on the conduct of his sons. The King has ever been a plain-living man with a particular horror of gambling and debauchery. It may well be that the scandalous excesses of the Prince of Wales and the Duke of York have upset the balance of their father's mind."

Roger sighed. "And should His Majesty not recover, I take it there is no escaping the Prince becoming our ruler. In such a case God help us all."

"Now that the Cabinet has been officially informed that the King is mad, we have no alternative but to consider some form of Regency. Whatever limits Parliament may see fit to impose upon the Regent's powers 'twould hardly be feasible for them to deny him the right to choose his own Ministers. It follows therefore that the present government will swiftly be replaced by the Prince's friends."

"With Mr. Fox as Prime Minister," added Roger bitterly.

Pitt laughed, not unkindly. "Mayhap; but it looks as if the unlucky star that has ever dogged poor Charles in his hopes of the Premiership is still in the ascendent. He is at present touring Italy with Mrs. Armistead, and by the time he is returned all may have been settled. Sheridan has stepped into his place as the Prince's chief confidant, and now heads the cabal which would so joyfully hound me from office."

"Oh, God, Sir! Can naught be done?" exclaimed Roger.

"Nay, nothing. Events must take their course. But you see how impossible it is, now that my enemies know me to hold no longer anything but the shadow of power, for me to commit Britain to a war. Tell me now briefly such other news as you may have, for I can give little time to anything except the present emergency."

Roger had taken the letter he had stolen from Alexis Orlof from the buckram lining of his coat-collar that morning, and he now produced it.

"I brought this out of Russia, Sir. Its meaning may at first appear obscure to you; but 'tis the written proof that the Czarina Catherine gave orders for the murder of her husband and, as such, I imagine it to be a document of considerable value."

The Prime Minister read it through, and asked curiously: "How did you come by this?"

"If you are pressed for time, Sir, 'tis too long a story to tell now; as would also be my impressions of the Russian Court, and my dealings with King Gustavus and Mr. Elliot."

"Then I will appoint a more suitable occasion " Pitt agreed. "As to this letter, pray do not think that I wish to belittle the risks you may have been put to in obtaining it. But I fear that it is more a thing of historic interest than political value. Its publication would be taken by the Empress as a deliberate attempt on our part to alienate the affection of her subjects. So we should never publish it unless our intention was to provoke a quarrel with Russia, and such a' contingency is remote. May I take it that when I can find the leisure to hear a full account of your travels, a message to my Lord Amesbury's will reach you?"

Roger stood up. "Yes, Sir. Lord Edward Fitz-Deverel most kindly affords me hospitality in his father's house when I am in London."

Having taken leave of the Prime Minister, Roger walked across the park to Arlington Street. He was greatly disturbed by what he had been told of the King's madness, both on account of the disastrous effect it must have on the nation and on his own affairs. It was good news that Hugh Elliot had succeeded in prolonging the armistice between the Danes and the Swedes for a further period of a month, but what was to happen at the end of that time if no fleet was sent and Mr. Pitt were out of office? Moreover, he had counted on a squadron being despatched at once in answer to Mr. Elliot's appeal, and had intended to sail with it himself to rejoin Natalia Andreovna. It was now five weeks since he had left her and, in spite of his letters, he feared that she must be thinking very badly of him.

At Amesbury House he found Droopy Ned just going to bed. It transpired that the eccentric young nobleman had been up all night owing to an experiment with one of his eastern drugs, which had made his mind so active that he had found it impossible to sleep; but the effects were now wearing off so he had intended to sleep through the day.

Having greeted Roger with delight he changed his intention, took another dose of the drug to keep himself awake, and ordered breakfast for them both.

From Droopy, Roger had no secrets, so over the meal he gave him an account of his adventures, including a perfectly frank statement as to how he had come to marry Natalia, and his present relations with her.

When the story was done, Droopy looked considerably perturbed. "Egad, my poor Roger," he exclaimed. "You have got yourself into a pretty pickle, to have taken such a vixen for a wife. Were I in your shoes I must confess I'd be much tempted to leave her where she is."

"How can I?" Roger shrugged. " 'Twas at my behest that she accompanied me out of Russia, and she dare not return there. In her strange way, I have not a doubt that she loves me; so I would think myself despicable did I abandon her for good."

"You are fixed in your determination to bring her to England, then?"

"Aye. I see naught else for it. She is a handsome baggage and of a pretty wit, so her appearance in society will make quite a stir and plenty of men will envy me. Do I but treat her fairly she may make me no worse a wife than one I might have taken to the altar out of a sudden passion, or married to please my parents."

"I scarce imagine this Russian Madame will do the last; and did your lady-mother know the truth of how you came to marry I vow she would be monstrous upset."

"You are right there, Droopy. But I have no intention of disclosing aught of this to her. Hugh Elliot I told because he was intimately concerned with my Russian mission; yourself because I count you my closest friend, and if things go ill between Natalia and myself I'll need someone to whom I can ease my mind. But to allow anyone else to suppose that I do not love her would place her in a false position; and I have vowed that I will make her happy if I can."

"Do your parents yet know the bare fact of your marriage?"

"Nay. I have been so fully occupied these two months past, that I have not writ them a single line since I left Petersburg to go into Finland. I dread having to tell them, too; for I fear they will be much distressed at my having married without their knowledge, and it will be hard to explain why I did not at least write to tell them of my intention. It would be far easier if I had Natalia with me, as I could then break the news in a letter from London asking their permission to take her down and present her to them. They are too generous not to receive her kindly, and by the time we arrived maybe the excitement of meeting her would cause them to forget my inconsiderate behaviour. As things are I have no excuse to write, so must hie me to Lymington, administer this shock, and be prepared to spend some miserable days in an atmosphere of restrained displeasure."

Droopy sat silent for a moment, a thoughtful look in his pale blue eyes, then he said: "I think you right, in that they would take it better if you could produce your wife within a day or two of having exploded this bombshell. You tell me that Mr. Pitt requires you to wait upon him again with full particulars of your mission. That is excuse enough for you to remain in London for the present. As soon as your business is completed you intend to set out for Denmark to fetch Mistress Brook home. Since the matter is near two months old already an extra week or two will make no difference; so why not shelve the problem of acquainting your parents with it until your return."

Roger grinned at him. "You were ever a sage counsellor, Ned, and I think your advice excellent. We will let sleeping dogs lie then, until I can produce my Russian bride."

They talked gloomily for a little about the King's illness, then Droopy began to yawn; so Roger left him and went up to the room that, since his return from France, his friend had insisted he should consider as his own.

There, he found a number of letters that had accumulated for him and, among them, two from Georgina.

The first was from Athens, where she and her father had spent the early summer. She said that the society of the city was provincial in the extreme, but that its surrounding scenery and ancient temples made it fascinating beyond anything of which she had ever dreamed. The classic names, Parnassus, Corinth, Eleusis, Delphi tumbled over each other in her vivid descriptions of snow-capped mountains, olive-green hillsides and wine-dark seas. She had done a lot of painting; but, she declared archly, a plaguey persistent string of gallants had prevented her giving as much time to it as she would have wished. She confessed that one or two were not altogether lacking in those accomplishments and parts calculated to appeal to a poor lonely young widow; and that one in particular, a Count Zorbâs, who had eyes as black as sloes and moustachios as fierce as a pair of upturned scimitars, had regarded her with such longing for a whole week, that she had felt compelled to take pity on him.

The second letter came from Constantinople which, she said, stank to high heaven of rotting fish and was pestiferous with hordes of flea-ridden pariah dogs that were purposely retained to act as scavengers in the streets. But again, the Golden Horn, the Mosques and the Dolma Baghtche Palace were sights which it was well worth sustaining much petty inconvenience to see. Of the Grand Signior, Abdul Achmed IV, she spoke as being one of the most enlightened Princes of his era, speaking French, Italian and Spanish fluently, and quite amazingly *au courant* with the latest intrigues at the courts of Versailles, St. James, Naples and Madrid. His greatest delight lay in intimate private parties consisting almost exclusively of cultured foreigners and at which the principal guests were the English and French Ambassadors, Sir Robert Ainslie and Roger's old friend the Comte de Choiseul-Gouffier. Although the Sultan was a strict follower of the Mohammedan faith in public he treated his Christian subjects with wide tolerance and was, in private, a great connoisseur of fine wines. In fact, he had once jestingly remarked that "If he were to become an infidel he should assuredly embrace the Roman Catholic communion, for that all the best European wines grew in their countries; and indeed that he had never heard of a good Protestant wine."

Georgina went on to say that she had visited several seraglios and found the females in them abysmally ignorant in all things with the single exception of the art of love; and that it was to believe in a myth to think that husbands could ensure fidelity in their wives by shutting them up in harems, for the inmates of these zenanas employed themselves in little except intriguing with the eunuchs, who were supposed to guard them, to admit personable young men in the guise of pedlars and barbers. On going abroad she had been compelled to adopt the veil as a necessary precaution against the coarse insults of the vulgar. but, she declared, with her eyes left free a woman could wreak as much or more havoc than with a bare face, had she a mind to it, and it was on these expeditions to the bazaars that the Turkish ladies acquired their gallants. Several wealthy Turks had offered her father sums of a flattering magnitude to buy her in marriage, and the elderly but gallant Capudan Pasha, who commanded the Turkish fleet in the war against the barbarous and rapacious Russians, had become so enamoured of her that, on his offer for her being refused he had, mercifully without success, attempted to have her kidnapped.

As Roger read the many pages of bold, vigorous scrawl, tears came into his eyes. He saw again as clearly as though they had parted only the day before, his dear. vital, beautiful Georgina. She was, he felt, a woman in a million, and that whatever other passions he might experience, he would never truly love any other. Yet he felt no twinge of jealousy at her relation of her amours, only a sense of gladness that she was so obviously enjoying her travels, which must be made doubly interesting from the companionship of her wise, broadminded and erudite father.

He had written to her from Copenhagen, Stockholm and during the early part of his stay in St. Petersburg; and he recalled now, with some misgiving, that he had regaled her with a humorous account of the early stages of his affair with Natalia Andreovna. A little grimly he wondered what she would have to say when she learned that he had married the young widow who had first put him on a run-away horse and then put her maid in her bed after giving him an assignation. He had an uncomfortable feeling that when they eventually met they would dislike one another intensely.

However, that evening he wrote once more to Natalia, telling her of the tempest that had kept him a prisoner in Bergen for a week, and that now he had got home he would be further delayed in returning to her, as he had been asked to carry new instructions to the British Minister in Copenhagen, and these might take ten days or so to prepare. Once again he ended with most abject apologies and protestations of his unwavering devotion.

For a week he hung about awaiting a summons from the Prime Minister. During it he got himself a new wardrobe and renewed many of the acquaintances he had made in London during the previous winter. He also frequently accompanied Droopy Ned to White's. This Tory stronghold was plunged in gloom, owing to the King's malady and the approaching fall of Mr. Pitt's administration, but Roger and Droopy now spent much of their time there exchanging rumours and speculating on the final outcome of the crisis.

He felt that at such a time it would ill become him to pester his harrassed patron for an interview, but he was very anxious to get his report off his chest, so that he might be on his way back to Denmark. In consequence, having received no message by Monday, the 2nd of November, he went to Downing Street and, instead of sending up his name, patiently waited in the hall for nearly two hours, in order that he might put himself in the Prime Minister's way when he left for the House.

Pitt was abrupt and awkward only with people he did not know and, on seeing Roger, he apologised for having forgotten all about him in the stress of affairs, and asked him to dine with him at Holwood the following Sunday.

On the previous occasion when Roger had ridden down into Kent it had been spring. Then, the gardens had been gay with almond blossom and daffodils; but this time he left London in a November fog. On arriving at Holwood he found that the company there suited these changed conditions. Instead of that gay rascal Sir James Harris, handsome Lord Carmarthen and forthright, dissolute Harry Dundas, his fellow-guests proved to be the Very Reverend Dr. Pretyman and Pitt's cousin William Grenville.

The churchman had been Pitt's tutor at Pembroke, and, owing to his early ascendency over a young mind of exceptional promise, he had remained one of the closest intimates and advisers of the brilliant statesman. It was, perhaps, his vast classical learning and austere rectitude that appealed to Pitt, but everyone else considered him priggish, lacking in imagination and coldly unsympathetic. Grenville was the same age as the Prime Minister and, from his virtuous disposition and great industry, seemed naturally designed to be his satellite; but his pride encased him in a freezing manner which was enhanced by his heavy features and stiff carriage.

Before dinner Roger learned the latest news of the King. On the first and third of the month he had gone out hunting, on the latter day dismounting to waggle the branch of an oak-tree in the belief that he was shaking hands with his friend the King of Prussia, and on both occasions had ridden himself into a state of exhaustion. Then, on the fifth, during a dinner-party at which both the Prince and the Duke had been present, he had suddenly become dangerous. Without the slightest provocation he had rushed upon his eldest son, seized him by the throat, pinned him against the wall and dared him to contradict the King of England. The Prince had burst into tears, the poor Queen became hysterical, and only with the greatest difficulty had the King been persuaded to retire to his room. The following night had witnessed a similar outburst and he had attacked his principal physician, Sir George Baker, who now reported that he feared for His Majesty's life.

The distress of Pitt and his friends was materially increased by the brutal conduct of the Prince of Wales towards his mother. He had taken over the direction of all affairs at Windsor with an abruptness that had caused her much pain; and, without having the decency to wait until it was known if his father had any chance of recovery, he had seized all his private papers.

The Duke of York's behaviour was even more unseemly as, surrounded each night at Brook's by a crowd of sycophants and office-seekers, he was giving imitations of the maniacal noises made by his father, which resembled the barking of a dog.

Roger had already heard of these shameful scenes in which the habitués of Brook's were giving vent to their hilarious joy at their prospects of becoming the rulers of the realm; but, on his expressing his disgust, the Prime Minister said gently:

"Speak not too harshly of the members of Brook's. There are many good fellows among them. I am a member myself, for that matter.

With his usual generosity Charles Fox put me up the very day I made my first speech in the House and, rather than repay so handsome a gesture by a slight, I have never resigned my membership."

They talked then of the future and Pitt announced quite calmly that he was preparing to resume his long-neglected practice at the Bar as a means of livelihood.

"But even in opposition your influence will be invaluable, Sir, in counteracting the evil, selfish policies of these rascals who will assume office," Roger expostulated. "Surely you will not be reduced to giving the greater part of your time to earning your own living?"

"I fear so," shrugged the Prime Minister. "Perhaps I should have feathered my nest while I had the chance. Less than a month ago I refused a gift of a hundred thousand pounds from the City, and during my administration I have used all the sinecures which fell vacant to pension men whom I felt deserved well of the nation, instead of taking any of them for myself. But I was prompted by the feeling that as long as my enemies could not accuse me of self-seeking, I was the better placed to conduct the country's business."

After dinner Roger gave an account of his travels, tactfully glossing over the more hectic of his adventures in deference to the presence of the prim churchman. When he had done the Prime Minister commended him kindly for his zeal, then went on to say:

"You need no longer concern yourself on Mr. Elliot's account. His colleague in Berlin, William Ewart, has succeeded in pulling King Gustavus's chestnuts out of the fire for him. Since last seeing you I have had a despatch to the effect that he has persuaded King Frederick Wilhelm of Prussia to issue a manifesto, stating that unless the Danes abandon their attack on Sweden he will despatch an army of sixteen thousand men to invade their province of Holstein."

Roger had been fretting badly about his inability to carry reassuring news to Hugh Elliot, so he was greatly relieved, and very pleased when Mr. Pitt continued: "As to yourself, you have more than justified my belief in your capabilities, and served us well by procuring such a definite statement of the Empress Catherine's views with regard to war. It seems that there is naught for it now but to curb her ambitions where e'er we may. But that is a task which I must leave to the opposition, for my days in office are clearly numbered."

"I take it, then, Sir, that you will not be able to employ me farther," Roger said, forgetful now of the horrors of the dungeon at Schlüsselburg, and made miserable at the thought of this premature close to his promising career.

"I fear that is so, Mr. Brook," Pitt replied. "I would have liked to send you into France, for things are in a pretty tumult there; and a well-informed account as to King Louis's prospects of holding his own against his rebellious subjects would be of value to us. But circumstances deny me the privilege of availing myself of your abilities; though I trust you will allow me to continue to count myself among your friends."

"Indeed, Sir, I shall be greatly honoured," Roger bowed. "In any case, though, I was about to ask your leave to make a flying visit to Denmark, before receiving your instructions about other business. A personal matter requires my attention there, and I shall now set off as soon as I can secure a passage. Will you, perchance, have any missive that you would care for me to convey to Mr. Elliot?"

"Nay. I am too fully occupied with other matters to write to him just now. But I would be obliged if you would wait upon my Lord Carmarthen, at the Foreign Office, before your departure, as his Lordship may well have a despatch that he would like you to transmit."

Roger naturally agreed and, soon after, took his leave.

On his ride back to London he was harassed by a new worry. Before he left on his Russian mission he had been adequately financed by the Foreign Office, and had also had the nine-hundred guineas from the sale of Georgina's tiara; but his various journeyings and cutting a figure in the Northern capitals for five months had consumed nearly all his resources. He had enough money to reach Copenhagen and in the little chest he had left with Natalia there had been the equivalent of a hundred and thirty pounds. But he had sent her the key of it with his first letter, and the odds were that she had spent most of it by now. In any case they would be lucky if they had fifty guineas between them by the time they got back to England.

He had counted on taking Natalia with him when he was next sent to a foreign court, but there were to be no more missions at His Majesty's expense; and, with Mr. Pitt out of office, he might even have difficulty in securing a grant from the secret service funds which would reimburse him for his outlay while in Russia. He had only the three hundred a year that his father allowed him, and at near twenty-one had not so much as a foot on any ladder which might lead him to a lucrative post. Suddenly, and quite unexpectedly, he found himself faced with the frightening problem of how, in such straightened circumstances, he could possibly support an expensive wife like Natalia.

Equally unexpectedly, eight days later, it was solved for him. The first passage that he could get for Copenhagen was in a ship sailing on the 19th, so on the 17th he called on Lord Carmarthen. When he had made his bow, the Foreign Secretary said at once:

"Ah! Mr. Brook. I had you in mind but a short while ago. Scarcely an hour since we received a bag from Mr. Elliot, and in it there was a packet for yourself. It cannot have been despatched yet, so I will have it sent for."

While the letter was being sought Lord Carmarthen gave him the latest news from Denmark. Between them Hugh Elliot and the Prussian envoy had browbeaten the Danes into agreeing to withdraw their forces from Swedish soil and to extending the armistice for six months, from the 13th of November.

"This is most excellent news," Roger smiled. "I take it, then, that your Lordship will require me to carry little except your congratulations to Mr. Elliot?"

The Marquess looked slightly uncomfortable. "You may tell him privately that both the Prime Minister and myself admire the part that he has played in this as a man. But we cannot publicly approve the language he has held towards the Danes. We had hoped to bring them also within the sphere of influence of the new alliance. By taking such a high tone with them he has jeopardised our prospects with them there, for the time being at least. Moreover, by exceeding his instructions, he might have left us facing two equally unpalatable alternatives; either to show most damaging weakness by repudiating him, or to accept the burden of an expensive and unpopular war."

"Indeed, my lord, Mr. Elliot did not exceed his instructions!" Roger exclaimed, springing to the defence of his friend. "For he told me himself that they were 'to prevent by every means any change in the relative situation of the Northern nations'. And 'tis due to his courage and audacity alone that the *status quo* has been maintained. Had you been with us in Sweden you would have had a better opportunity of realising that any but the strongest measures would have failed, and I take it ill that your lordship should now cavil at the conduct of a man who has so ably upheld the prestige of our country."

He might have received a sharp rebuke for his temerity, if, at that moment, a clerk had not entered with the letter for him. Having waited until the man had gone, Lord Carmarthen contented himself with remarking:

"While one may admire such vigorous personalities as those of Harris, Ewart and Elliot, when witnessing events from their comparatively limited horizons, the final judgment on their actions must be made at the centre of government; for from there alone can the whole scene be surveyed." Then he added a trifle coldly: "No doubt you are anxious to read your letter, so please do not hesitate to do so."

With a murmur of thanks Roger broke the seal and scanned the first page. He could hardly have been more disconcerted had the paper burst into flames in his hands. Hugh Elliot broke the news as gently as he could and frankly assumed the blame of having been the prime cause of it, but the fact remained that on the 15th of October Natalia Andreovna had suddenly disappeared.

Elliot said that he would have informed Roger sooner, but for the fact that he had only just had the news himself in a letter from the Countess Reventlow which had been following him from place to place in Sweden. The Countess related that Natalia had been much shaken on receiving Roger's first letter, and she had carried the deserted wife home with her, insisting that she should accept her hospitality until Roger's return. After a few days Natalia had appeared reconciled to her situation, and had proved an interesting, if somewhat temperamental, guest. On October the 12th she had received Roger's second letter, from Gothenbörg, which had caused her to give way to a fit of extreme rage. Next morning she had appeared pale but normal, then, three afternoons later, without saying a word to anyone about her intentions, she had driven into Copenhagen and vanished.

That her disappearance had been deliberate, and not the result of an accident or foul play, seemed proved beyond question by the fact that she had set off with a portmanteau which she had said contained a dress that she was taking into the town to have altered; yet, on the examination of her effects, it had transpired that not only were her travelling clothes missing but also all her jewels. So far no word had been received from her, and all efforts to trace her had proved unavailing.

Having read the letter through a second time more carefully Roger pulled himself together, informed Lord Carmarthen that the news he had received rendered it no longer necessary for him to go to Copenhagen, and bowed himself out.

Completely oblivious of a chill drizzle he walked across the parade ground at the back of the old Palace of Whitehall, endeavouring to analyse his feelings. He could not make up his mind whether he was glad or sorry about Natalia having in turn deserted him, and presumably for good. Ever since he had married her a conviction had steadily been growing in his mind that his honour was involved in making good his marriage-vows, and now events had deprived him of the chance of preserving his self-esteem by doing so. During their cruise down the Baltic he had come to feel a new affection for her and had begun to hope that they might find lasting happiness together.

On the other hand, once he had left the sphere of her personal magnetism, he had known within himself that his seeming contentment had been only a flash in the pan, brought about by the novelty of their regularised status and his own exhilaration at having escaped from Russia. Time could not really change Natalia's nature, and the ingrained brutality with which she treated servants would alone be enough to make life with her in England a constant anxiety. Last, but not least, he felt certain now that, in his changed circumstances, their marriage would have come to grief from his inability to provide her with at least some of the luxuries to which she had been accustomed ever since childhood.

That night he discussed the matter very fully with Droopy Ned. Over supper in a private room at the Cock Tavern they went into every aspect of it, and the foppish but shrewd Droopy expressed himself as frankly delighted. In his lazy drawl, he pointed out that whereas Natalia could not have divorced Roger for desertion, he could certainly divorce her. She would have to be traced and the business would take time and money, but within a year or so Roger would again be a free man, and he should thank his stars for such a merciful escape. By that time Roger had reached a state in which he did not need much convincing of this. They drank seven bottles of Claret between them and went home very drunk, arm-in-arm.

Relieved now from the unpalatable task of having to tell his parents anything about his marriage, Roger set out next day for Lymington. He found that his father was from home, having been appointed by their Lordships of the Admiralty as the head of a Special Commission to investigate conditions at the Nore. Roger's mother, was, as usual, delighted to see her tall, brown boy, and he told her as much as he thought fit and proper for her to know about his adventures.

During the next few days he talked with dozens of his old friends among the shop-people in the little town, and visited at several of the larger houses in the neighbourhood, to find that the country folk were every bit as much perturbed by the King's illness and the premature end it would bring to Mr. Pitt's administration, as were the citizens of London.

There could be no doubt that in the five years since the ending of the American war, the King had won the love and respect of the vast majority of his subjects; and everyone agreed that it was young Billy Pitt's genius that had revived Britain from near bankruptcy to her present prosperity.

"Farmer" George and his Minister were both honest, frugal, clean-living men, and a pattern to the nation; whereas the Prince and his clique of depraved, unprincipled hangers-on typified the worst possible elements of the decadent Whig oligarchy. The Nonconformists, although the traditional opponents of the Royal prerogative, had begun to offer up prayers for the King's recovery in their chapels, spontaneously, over a week before the Established Church had formulated a prayer for the general use of its clergy. Even in the depths of the country the Tory squires knew of the excesses at Carlton House and Brook's; and dread of what would happen to the country if the King's dissolute sons, and men like Fox and Sheridan, got control of it, was now casting a gloom over the minds of rich and poor alike.

After ten days, made restless by the constant flow of rumours, and finding himself unable to settle down to anything, Roger decided to return to London. A talk with Droopy soon put him *au courant* with the latest information.

On the 12th of November Pitt had proposed to the Prince that Parliament should be adjourned for a fortnight, and the Prince had agreed. On the 17th Pitt had asked leave to inform the Prince of the course he proposed to take on the re-assembling of Parliament, but an audience had been refused. On the 24th the Prince had at length inquired if Pitt had any proposals to make and the slighted Prime Minister had retaliated by sending a polite negative.

That same day Fox arrived back in London from Italy. The news of the King's affliction had reached him at Bologna and he had made the return trip in nine days, which was believed to be a record. To his fury he found that Sheridan was not only managing everything for the Prince but actually living in Mrs. Fitzherbert's house, as the bailiffs were in possession of his own. But, although ill from the strain of his journey, the corpulent and flamboyant statesman immediately threw himself into the battle to wrest power from the King's friends, with all his old genius for intrigue.

The struggle now centred round the question whether there were any hopes of the King's recovery or if he was permanently mad; as upon that hinged the form that the Regency should take. Dr. Warren, who was now the King's principal medical attendant, being a Whig and a strong supporter of the Prince, took the blackest view; and his bulletins were received with acclamation at Brook's, from which a virulent campaign of rumour was now launched to persuade the public that there was no chance of the King ever becoming sane again.

But Pitt was determined to protect the future rights of the helpless monarch by every means in his power, so he consulted his father's old friend Dr. Addington, and Addington advised the calling-in of the Reverend Dr. Willis, who, during twenty-eight years, had supervised some nine hundred cases of lunacy at a private asylum in Lincolnshire.

That the King still enjoyed periods of sanity was made clear when his new doctor was presented to him. On being informed that Willis was a clergyman he remarked that he could not approve a minister of the church taking to the practice of medicine. Willis replied that Christ went about healing the sick; to which the King promptly retorted: "Yes, but I never heard that he got seven hundred a year for doing so."

On the 29th the King was removed to Kew, and Willis reported that he did not consider the case by any means hopeless. But the King's recovery, all hope of which was still denied by his other doctors, could not be expected, even if it occurred at all, for some time to come; so the arrangements to introduce a Regency Bill had to go on.

On December the 5th Pitt moved for a Committee to examine the physicians, and twenty-one members of the House, selected from both parties, were appointed. As was to be expected, the evidence of Doctors Warren and Willis conflicted to such a degree that their statements had little influence on their hearers' previous beliefs and prejudices.

On the 10th the Prime Minister presented the medical evidence and moved for a Committee to investigate precedents. Immediately Fox was on his feet with vehement protest. He denounced the proposal as merely a pretext for delay. The heir-apparent was of mature age and capacity. He had as clear a right to exercise the sovereign power during the King's illness as he would have in case of death. Parliament's only business was to determine when he should assume the reins of government, and that should be settled with the least possible delay.

In his impatience to pull down the government Fox had overreached himself, and the cool, logical brain of Pitt instantly seized upon his enemy's error. Turning to his neighbour he whispered: "I'll *un-Whig* the gentleman for the rest of his life." Then he rose to his feet and tore the demagogue to shreds; asserting that he advocated a breach of the constitution by implying that the House had not even the right to debate the question.

From this a most extraordinary situation arose. The Whigs, who for well over a century had claimed to be the defenders of the people's liberties, gave their full backing to Fox in his attempt to re-assert the Divine Right of Hereditary Royalty; while the Tories, who had always sought to protect the Royal prerogative, had, over-night, become the champions of the duly elected representatives of the people in their established right to place a check upon the arbitrary powers of the sovereign.

On the 12th, Sheridan's venomous hatred of Pitt led him openly to threaten the Prime Minister with the possibly dire consequences to himself, should he persist in opposing the Prince's claims further. Three days later the Duke of York attempted to offset the menace by a tactful speech in the House of Lords, but the damage was done. Pitt had the sympathy of every decent man and woman in the country. Yet there could be no altering the course that events must take, and arrangements were made for the introduction of the Regency Bill early in the New Year.

On the 19th of December Roger returned to Lyminton to spend Christmas with his mother. He got in a few days shooting and attended a number of dances at the big houses round about—Pylewell, Priestlands and Vicars Hill—and also in the town Assembly Rooms. It was now well over two months since he had left Natalia, and already he had come to regard her as an episode of his past; so he entered on an amusing flirtation with another Christmas visitor to the district, Amanda Godfrey, the Titian-haired niece of old Sir Harry Burrard of Walhampton.

She was a lively and audacious young woman, who did not take much persuading to slip out of her uncle's house after everyone else was in bed, to keep assignations with her beau. On several nights they went for stolen walks together round the star-lit lakes in the grounds and through the still, frosty woods; but it was no more than a holiday romance, and by the middle of the first week of January Roger was back in London.

At the opening of the first session of Parliament for 1789, the most fateful year in modern history, the Regency Bill was the one question which occupied every member's mind; so the House sat impatiently through the preliminary business, the chief item of which was the election of a new Speaker, the holder of that office having died. Pitt's cousin, the heavy-featured but incorruptible William Grenville, was elected and, on January the 6th, the acrimonious discussions on the Bill were resumed.

Pitt's proposals were, in brief, that the Prince should be empowered to exercise the royal authority, but that the guardianship of the King and the regulation of the royal household should be committed to the Queen, with a Council to assist her. Further that the Prince-Regent should have no power to assign the King's property, grant any office beyond His Majesty's pleasure, or bestow any peerage, except on the King's children after they had attained their majority.

Thus, while bowing to the inevitable, the faithful Minister sought to ensure that the poor stricken monarch should remain in the care of those who loved him, that his property should be protected against the possibility of his recovery, and that his affliction should not provide

331

an opportunity for his unprincipled son to swamp the House of Lords with the worthless and rapacious crew that formed his following.

For days on end the Whigs screamed their rage at the prospect of so considerable a portion of the vast treasure they had hoped to loot being secured against them; but in vain. The Ministerial proposals were carried in both Houses, the Prince had no option but to consent to act as Regent on the terms submitted to him, and towards the end of January, preparations were made for the actual introduction of the Bill which would enable the Regent to replace Pitt's administration by one composed of Fox and his friends.

These were dark days for the nation but their gloom was lightened at intervals for Roger by several pleasurable episodes and minor pieces of good fortune.

On his return to London he found a notification from the Foreign Office that some packages were awaiting his collection. These turned out to have been forwarded by Hugh Elliot, and contained all the things that both Roger and Natalia had left behind when they had quitted Copenhagen. He was a little disconcerted at the sight of Natalia's furs and dresses, and he found that his money-chest was empty, but he was extremely glad to recover his own expensive wardrobe.

Then, having had no acknowledgment of an application which he had put in privately to Lord Carmarthen early in December, for the reimbursement of his expenses while abroad, he waited upon that nobleman personally. True to the policy of the British Government, which reserves all but minor rewards and honours for its paid official servants working under those who have the distribution of them, and expects its private citizens to give their services from patriotism alone, his lordship pointed out that Roger must have had a very interesting time and that, in any case, a considerable proportion of the money he had spent must have been on his own enjoyment. However, Roger succeeded in obtaining a draft on the Treasury for five hundred pounds and, although several hundreds out on the deal, considered himself lucky to have settled for that sum before the dissolution of the administration jeopardised his chances of getting anything at all.

In mid-January he received a letter from Hugh Elliot, reporting that he had now succeeded in tracing Natalia. She had gone to Stockholm and was living there again in the Russian Embassy with her father, Count Andrew Razumofsky. Having known that she dared not return to Russia, Roger was a little surprised that this solution to the problem had not occurred to him before. He was much relieved to think that she was safe and well cared for; as, although he knew perfectly well inside himself that she was much too tough to come to any serious harm, he had occasionally had fits of morbid depression in which he had imagined her in the most dire straits, or even taking her own life on account of his having deserted her. He was glad, too, to know her whereabouts as it would facilitate his proceedings against her for divorce, although these could not be instituted for some time to come.

Next, towards the end of the month, he had another letter from Georgina. It was written from the Principality of Monaco on his birth-day, the 8th, and was to wish him good luck on his coming of age. She was still enjoying the sunshine of the Mediterranean but now had a heartache to be back at her beloved Stillwaters to see its gardens blossom in the spring. Fortunately, she wrote, her father's business interests now demanded his return to England after his long absence, so they planned to get home towards the end of the first week in February.

At the prospect of seeing her again so soon Roger felt the first real thrill of pleasure that he had known for many weeks. It was not that he wanted to make love to her; it was a feeling that he could not possibly have described, but he knew that he felt more content and happy when he was with her than with any other person that he had ever known.

Lastly, on the 1st of February he was elected a member of White's. On his attaining his majority he had become eligible for membership, and Droopy Ned had put him up. As a young man of respectable, but not distinguished, parentage, he felt that it was a considerable honour to belong to the Club which was the stronghold of all the great Tory families in the land; and he derived a particular satisfaction in having, in this way, nailed his colours to the mast at the very hour when Pitt's government was about to fall, and so many friends and protégés of the Prime Minister were turning their coats in the hope of saving their places or gaining benefits from the other side.

For well over three months now he had been like a billiards ball in baulk; in the forefront of events but out of action and with his future entirely problematical. Suddenly he was brought into play again, and his affairs began to move with staggering swiftness.

CHAPTER XXII

THE FATE OF THE NATION

O N the 3rd of February, a Foreign Office messenger brought Roger two letters. Both were addressed in the writing of Hugh Elliot, and on opening the more bulky of the two he found it to be an appeal for help.

The diplomat wrote that, although he had browbeaten the Danes into withdrawing their army from Sweden in mid-November and agree-ing to prolong the armistice for six months, the Northern powers were still far from showing any inclination to accept a permanent settlement on the basis of *status quo ante bellum.*

Gustavus, now cock-a-hoop in the belief that he had the full weight of the Triple Alliance behind him, had become overbearing towards the Danes and twice committed flagrant breaches of the armistice; so, if the *status quo* was to be maintained, it might next be the Danes whom Britain would be called on to protect from aggression.

They had been deprived of all the initial advantages of their surprise invasion and Gustavus was no longer naked in the wind before them. With his usual amazing energy he had set his country on its feet again, and had now considerable forces at his command. Just before Christmas he had returned to his capital and performed miracles in repatriating and re-organising a large part of the army he had left in Finland. All the officers who had shown mutinous tendencies, and had not succeeded in escaping into Russia, had been seized, court-martialled and punished with the utmost savagery. New levies were being trained in every province and in the dockyards shipwrights were working night and day to get new war-keels off the stocks. By the early summer he would therefore be in a position to resume the war both in the North and in the South.

The Danes believed that the Czarina Catherine would be able to afford them little aid, owing to the terrible casualties that her armies had sustained in a series of bloody battles with the Turks. It was anticipated that she would be able to hold her own in Finland, but do little more.

Elliot then went on to say that he had received secret intelligence that the news of King George's madness had caused the Empress to reconsider her position. She had always loathed and feared Pitt, but now that his downfall was assured she believed that the time had come when she might detach the support of Britain from the Turks. She had, accordingly, instructed her Ambassador, Count Vorontzoff, to make overtures to Charles Fox, and Fox had promised that on coming to office he would reverse Britain's foreign policy in her interests.

Should that, said Elliot, prove to be the attitude of the new Government it would be his duty to act upon such fresh instructions as he received; but he pointed out that if the burden of Catherine's war against the Turks was eased she would be able to send a strong army into Finland which might well result in the Russians and Danes achieving their old ambition of dividing Sweden between them. And, however provocative and unreasonable Gustavus's conduct might be at the moment, the elimination of Sweden from the European family must, in the long run, prove a major disaster; for Catherine would, in due course, turn upon and destroy the Danes. Russia would then be the mistress of the whole of Northern Europe, with her frontiers facing Scotland across the North Sea, and in a position directly to menace Britain with fleets based on the Danish and Norwegian ports.

Elliot gave it as his opinion that the only method of forestalling such a disastrous possibility was to bang the heads of the Swedes and Danes together, and dragoon them both into making a definite peace which it would be hard for either to break without contumely. But this must be done promptly, before the position worsened, and, for the purpose he needed more urgently than ever a British fleet which both the Swedes and the Danes would fear might be used against either of them should they prove recalcitrant in coming to terms.

In conclusion, Elliot said, he had written repeatedly to Lord Carmarthen on these matters and received no satisfaction; as it seemed that everyone at home was so occupied with the Regency question that they had no thought to spare for any other. But Roger's unusual position gave him special facilities for obtaining easy access to Mr. Pitt. Would he therefore, as a matter of the greatest urgency, do what he could to obtain the Prime Minister's consideration and appropriate action with regard to these momentous questions which were still threatening the balance of power in Northern Europe?

Having digested the contents of this long despatch, Roger opened the second letter. Its envelope proved to be only a cover for another and, on seeing the spidery writing on the inner one, his heart missed a beat. It was addressed to him care of the British Minister in Copenhagen in the hand of Natalia Andreovna.

With his mouth dry and his palms suddenly moist he read what she had to say:

His first letter had been a great shock to her, as she could not understand why he had not entrusted her with the secret that he was an Englishman when they had become so devoted to one another on first arriving in St. Petersburg; but she had freely forgiven the deceit and waited patiently in Copenhagen for his return. Then, after a far longer absence than he had led her to expect, had come his second letter, saying that he must go to England without her. Gothenbörg being no great distance from Copenhagen there seemed no reason why he should not have crossed to the latter place, in order to pick her up and carry her to England with him. As he had not done so, she had formed the conclusion that it was his definite intention to abandon her, but that he had lacked the courage to say so outright.

On this, rather than face the humiliation of disclosing her sad state to the Countess Reventlow, she had decided to leave Copenhagen in secret and rejoin her father in Stockholm. She had been very miserable there, as apart from her grief at Roger's treatment of her, she was unable to avail herself of the distractions afforded by re-entering Swedish society. In spite of the fact that she was now English by marriage, the Swedes regarded her as an enemy and refused to receive her among them. Her situation had greatly worsened in the New Year as King Gustavus had, at last, succeeded in expelling her father from Sweden. She was allowed to remain there in strict retirement but only, as she understood it, because the King had learned that she was married to Roger, and had some special reason for not wishing to act discourteously towards him.

She pointed out that it was, in any case, impossible for her to return to Russia, and, having stressed her loneliness, she vowed that neither time nor separation had affected the love she felt for her dear husband. On re-reading his letters, as she had done many times, she felt that she had acted precipitately in coming to the conclusion that he intended to abandon her for good; and she now begged his pardon for having left Copenhagen without his permission. If he would forgive her she would joyfully return to her duty and live with him in England or any other country to which his affairs might take him. She was now certain that with him alone could she find lasting happiness; so would he, therefore, bearing in mind the deceit he had practised upon her, overlook her temporary lapse of faith in him, and either come to Stockholm to fetch her, or send her instructions as to the swiftest method of joining him in England.

When he had read the letter Roger felt as though he had been struck by a thunderbolt. For over two months he had believed that Natalia Andreovna had gone out of his life for good, but here she was back again, and now the onus was on him; for he must definitely decide whether to accept or reject her.

Technically he had not deserted her. By leaving her, but writing to say that he did so only on account of urgent business, and would rejoin her as soon as possible, he had followed a course in which any court of law would uphold a husband as fully justified. She, on the other hand, had deliberately deserted him, and, if he chose to take divorce proceedings, he had little doubt that he could be rid of her for good. But, seeing the way he had brought her out of Russia and the miserable state of exile to which she was now reduced, could he possibly square it with his conscience to do so?

As Droopy Ned had left London that morning to spend a long week-end in the country, Roger had no-one with whom he could talk over his frightful problem in the hope of clarifying his own mind; so he decided to shelve the matter for the moment and respond to Hugh Elliot's urgent appeal by trying to obtain an interview with Mr. Pitt.

In this, at least, he was lucky. On arriving at No. 10 he met the Prime Minister on his own front doorstep, just about to enter the house. Pitt answered his salutation, gave him a sharp glance and remarked. "What ails you. Mr. Brook? You look as though you had just seen a ghost."

"I'd not be far off the mark if I said I had, sir," Roger replied with a worried grin. Then, his quick mind seizing on a way in which he might turn the allusion to his advantage, he added, "The devil of it is that this ghost follows me about."

"Have you come to me to lay it, then?" Pitt smiled.

"I have, sir; if you can give me ten minutes of your time?"

"Next month I'll give you ten days if you wish; but come upstairs and, if you'll be brief, I'll hear what you have to say."

Up in his room Pitt poured two glasses of port, handed one to Roger, and said, "You really look as though you needed this. Drink it down; then tell me what it is that troubles you?"

"'Tis true, that I have just sustained something of a shock," Roger admitted. "But the ghost that haunts me, sir, is the state of things I left in Sweden."

"Oh that!" the Prime Minister exclaimed a little irritably; but Roger produced Hugh Elliot's letter and hurried on.

"I pray you read this, sir. I ask it on the count that however deplorable the state of our internal affairs at the moment we still cannot afford to ignore events that are taking place overseas, or we'll have cause to rue it."

Pitt shrugged, read the letter through, refolded it and handed it back. "I have already told you," he said firmly, "that in this matter I can do nothing."

"But you *can*, sir," Roger protested. "You are still the principal executive of the Crown, and there is nought to prevent you ordering a fleet to sea."

"I could, but I have no mind to commit my successor in office to a policy on which he has not been consulted and of which he would almost certainly disapprove."

Roger stared at the thin, tired face of the harassed statesman; then he suddenly burst out. "How can you put such scruples before the interests of the country? Do you but act now, while you still have the chance, you may yet preserve the independence of two Kingdoms. But if you do not, Catherine of Russia will sweep the board. You know as well as I, sir, that once you are gone that traitor Fox will sell us out to her."

"Charles Fox is no traitor," Pitt replied sharply. " 'Tis merely that his views as to the country's best interests differ from my own. I sent you to Russia to ascertain if a rapprochement with the Empress was possible. Her personal dislike of me may have been the stumbling block. If Fox can secure a permanent alliance with her he will, in that, have served his country better than myself."

"What! By gaining her fickle friendship at the price of the partitioning of Sweden, and later allowing her to gobble up Denmark? Nay, I'll not believe it!"

After pouring himself another glass of port, Pitt sipped it moodily, and said, "Such fears are based only on the beliefs of men like Elliot and Harris. My Lord Carmarthen thinks quite differently, and events may prove him right. In any case, as things are, it would be morally indefensible for me to commit Britain to a war."

"You do not have to do so," Roger cried, on a sudden inspiration. "Britain is at peace with both Sweden and Denmark. Why should you not despatch a squadron on a courtesy-visit to the capitals of both countries?"

Pitt gave him a sharp glance. " 'Tis unusual without an invitation, yet it might be done. But no! I dare not trust that hot-head Elliot."

"Had Mr. Elliot's head been colder Sweden might by this time have been divided between the Russians and the Danes," Roger retorted. "But if you fear that he may act rashly you could give instructions to the Admiral commanding the squadron that he is not to fire a shot without first receiving orders from home."

"Then 'twould be but a cardboard armada, and useless in a crisis."

"Nay, sir! The very fact of its appearance in the Baltic should be enough. Unless Britain takes some step Prussia will believe herself deserted, and refrain from pursuing the policy that was decided on last autumn. But if we show the flag, she will continue to play her part; and you may be sure that the Prussian General will have no orders that his artillery is not to use its cannon."

"Mr. Brook, Mr. Brook!" The Prime Minister shook his head in mock disapproval. "From whom did you learn to cultivate such ideas? Was it from our mutual friend the Abbé de Talleyrand-Périgord, or during your conversations with the Czarina Catherine; for they are positively Machiavellian."

Roger grinned at him. "What matter, sir, if by their acceptance the *status quo* in the North may be preserved and the Empress's nefarious schemes brought to naught."

"So be it, then. I confess that you have won me over to your project by providing a safeguard against our irrevocable commitment. I will see the First Lord and arrange with him the dispatch of a squadron. Do you wish to sail with it in order to witness the outcome of the matter?"

"May, I—er, leave that open," Roger hesitated a second. "My private affairs are in something of a tangle; but I should know how I am placed in a day or two."

"Just as you wish. 'Tis unlikely that a squadron could be got ready to proceed to sea until Monday, at the earliest. I trust that by then you will have laid the other ghost that worries you."

Roger thanked him, made his bow, and hurried downstairs. During the last few minutes, almost subconsciously, he had formed the resolution of going to Lymington to see his mother. It was just after mid-day, and, if he set out at once, he thought that he would be able to get there in time for a late supper.

At Amesbury House he borrowed Droopy's Ned curricle as the fastest vehicle available. By one o'clock he was being driven out of London, and soon after nine the last change of horses brought him to his home.

Lady Marie Brook accepted his unannounced arrival with her usual placidity, but one look at her boy's face was enough to tell her that he was in grave trouble of some kind. She made no comment while he ate a meal, then, when he had done, she said quietly: "Now come into the drawing-room and tell me all about it."

He smiled, kissed her, and followed her into the familiar green and white room, that always smelt so pleasantly of lavender and pot-pourri. After raking the log-fire into a blaze he settled himself opposite her and, with a few unimportant omissions to spare her sensibilities, told her the truth about his meeting and marrying Natalia Andreovna.

When he had done she sat silent for a moment, then she said: "And you have come to tell me that you are going back to Sweden to fetch her."

He nodded. "There seems naught else for it."

"Of course there is not, dear boy." She came over and kissed him. " 'Twould be idle to pretend that this is the sort of marriage that your father and I would have wished for you. But you are vowed to her, and your first decision to abide by your vows was clearly a proper one. From all you say it seems she had fair cause to believe you had abandoned her, so 'twas but natural that she should seek an asylum with her father. Now that she has explained her disappearance and appealed for your forgiveness, I think you in honour bound to rescue her from her present unhappy situation. Bring her to me as soon as you get back to England, and you may be sure that I will afford her a mother's welcome."

In his heart of hearts Roger had known from the moment he had read Natalia Andreovna's letter that he would have to go to her, and what his mother's reaction would be; but he was, nevertheless, greatly relieved now that the decision was definitely taken.

Saturday he spent with his mother, and to reassure him further she set cheerfully about re-arranging the furniture in some of the rooms in preparation for Natalia's reception. Early on Sunday he set out for London and, on his arrival, drove straight to the Admiralty. The duty-captain informed him that the squadron would be sailing from Chatham, probably on Tuesday morning, and added, to Roger's surprise and delight, that his father had been appointed to command it.

Roger spent the night at Amesbury House, packed the things he intended to take with him, and, in the morning, took the coach to Chatham. His father had, he found, been notified that he might be sailing as a passenger, and the ruddy-faced Admiral welcomed him joyfully. They dined together in the flagship and once more Roger gave particulars of the events which had preceded and followed his marriage.

The Admiral asked if Roger had yet told his mother and, on learning Lady Marie's attitude, he nodded. "She's right, of course. She always is. Well; she and I married because neither Jacobite prejudice on her side nor lack of fortune on mine—nor the swords of her brothers for that matter—were enough to keep us apart. But 'tis not every crazy, run-away match that turns out so well as did ours. Against that I've known couples who were pushed into marriage for family reasons come to dote on one another. 'Tis a pity she is six years older than yourself, but your travels have made you much older than most youngsters of your age; so if you start the right way you should be able to keep the breeches on your own bottom. Let's crack another bottle to your making a good Englishwoman of her."

The squadron was to consist of three line-of-battle ships, four frigates and two sloops. In the evening Admiral Brook assembled his captains and gave them their instructions. With the turning of the tide, in the early hours of the morning, the squadron weighed anchor. Off Sheerness a trader, just arriving from Gibraltar, met and passed them. Unknown to either, Roger and Georgina were for a few minutes within a quarter of a mile of one another; he outward bound she very nearly home.

On February 11th the squadron arrived off Copenhagen. For the last lap of the voyage a sloop had been sent on ahead with letters from the Foreign Secretary to Mr. Elliot and from Mr. Pitt to Count Bernstorff, the Danish Prime Minister; the latter asking permission for the British squadron to pay a goodwill visit to the Danish fleet. The permission was readily accorded, Hugh Elliot came abroad the flagship and silently wrung Roger's hand until it hurt; then they accompanied Admiral Brook ashore in his barge for the official reception by representatives of the Danish Court and Admiralty. There was a great banging of guns and unfurling of flags and, that night, a handsome banquet at which a number of British and Danish naval officers cemented their friendship by getting very drunk.

Next day Roger paid his respects to the Reventlows and thanked them for their kindness to Natalia; then, that evening, he transferred his baggage to one of his father's sloops, which was to take him on to Stockholm. She reached the Swedish capital late on the evening of the 16th. Although it was already dark, Roger decided to go ashore, but the formalities took much longer than he expected, and it was getting on for midnight before he found a night-hawk coachman who agreed to drive him out to the Russian Embassy.

On alighting, a sudden impulse came to him; instead of going to the front-door he walked round the side of the house to the postern-gate overlooked by Natalia's bedroom window. It seemed a long time since those summer-nights when, full of romantic ardour, he had slipped in through the door and climbed up to her balcony. Yagerhorn, who had waylaid him the last time he had stepped out into that lane, was now dead, and the clever, green-eyed Russian widow was now his wife. A light showed dimly behind Natalia's curtains. He caught himself wondering if she had been faithful to him during their five months separation, or if, since her return to Stockholm, other gallants had paid her midnight visits by way of the postern-door.

It suddenly occurred to him that she might have a lover with her now, or be expecting one. If so, and he caught her out, he would have an eleventh-hour chance to repudiate her and return to England a free man. For the best part of a fortnight he had again become reconciled to their marriage, and had, in some ways, been looking forward to rejoining her; so he was by no means certain that he really wanted to be free of her now. He felt too, that he was probably doing her an injustice in thinking that she might have someone with her, up there in her room. All the same, he pushed the postern-door gently; and it opened.

Loosening his sword in its scabbard, he stepped inside. Treading very softly he stole over to the verandah, gripped the well-remembered holds in the iron trellis-work, and hoisted himself up on to the balcony. For a moment he paused there, listening intently; then, hating himself

340

for playing the part of a spy in this private capacity, he pulled open the French window.

A startled exclamation came from beyond the curtains. Wrenching them back he stepped into the room. Natalia Andreovna was there sitting up in bed, but alone, reading a book.

"Rojé Christorovitch!" she cried, as the light fell on his face. "What a fright you gave me! But oh, how pleased I am to see you!"

He laughed; half from relief, half to cover his guilty confusion; then ran across the room and took her in his arms.

Their reunion, occurring in such a fashion, could hardly have been of a greater warmth; as it aroused in both potent memories of their first stolen meetings, and their passion seemed to render redundant all further explanations of their past doubts of one another.

In the morning Roger told her that he had been able to come on from Copenhagen in a British sloop-of-war only because he was charged with a letter for King Gustavus, and it was agreed that she should set about her packing while he delivered it. Natalia ordered her surprised maid to bring breakfast for herself and her husband, and when he had dressed he left by the front-door of the almost deserted Embassy.

A waterman took him across the sound to the palace of Drottings-holm, and in less than half an hour he was granted an audience by Gustavus, who received him with the greatest affability. The letter that Roger bore was from Mr. Pitt, and in similar terms to that addressed to Count Bernstorff, asking if the King was agreeable to a British squadron paying a goodwill-visit to the Swedish fleet. After reading it, Gustavus, who saw perfectly well what lay behind this excuse, expressed his delight at its contents.

They talked for a while of the vast improvements in the King's affairs since Roger had left Sweden, then of the situation in England. It transpired that Gustavus had received intelligence the night before by a fast courier from Berlin; so he was more up to date than Roger with events in London. The House of Commons had passed the final draft of the Regency Bill, so it only remained for the Lords to do so and, on that, the Prince of Wales, Fox, Sheridan and the rest, would become the masters of Britain's destinies.

Gustavus was as much perturbed as Roger by the change in the British Government, which, to the best of his belief, had by now taken place; but the optimistic and imaginative monarch was of the opinion that, nine-tenths of the country being behind Mr. Pitt, before many months had passed some form of revolution would take place.

Roger replied that he thought a revolution possible in a few years time, as a result of the change-over from the rule of a God-fearing King with the most simple tastes to that of a dissolute Regent, who, with his unprincipled friends, would play ducks and drakes with the nation's resources. But that if it came it would be similar in character to that which now seemed inevitable in France, and launched to bring about the downfall of the monarchy; so Mr. Pitt would certainly not be the man to lead it.

"I agree that a popular uprising against privilege, coupled with folly and extravagance, is very likely to prove the final result of the Regency," said Gustavus. "But such movements take time to ferment; and 'tis at least a possibility that the political wheel may bring Mr. Pitt to power again before then. Therefore I have it in mind to write a private letter to him, informing him of my plans for the coming summer to put a further check upon the Czarina Catherine's ambitions. It will take a few days of careful thought to prepare, but I should be obliged if you would remain in Stockholm until it is ready, and carry it back with you."

It was impossible to refuse the request, so Roger bowed his acceptance of the mission. Then he thanked the King for having allowed Natalia Andreovna to stay on in the Russian Embassy, after his expulsion of her father.

Gustavus gave him an amused look. " 'Twas a small matter and a pleasure to oblige so good a friend as yourself, Mr. Brook; but I am still of the opinion that one can derive more contentment from a pipe than from a woman; particularly when one is married to her and her bedroom is adjacent to a postern-door. However, that is your affair."

A trifle uneasily Roger recalled that he had never ascertained why that postern-door had been left open the night before; and he wondered now if, had he not put the candles out soon after his arrival in Natalia's room, on the stroke of midnight another gallant might not have shinned up the iron trellis-work to join her. But, recalling also his own amorous dalliance with Amanda Godfrey over Christmas, he felt that the right course was to banish all such speculations from his mind, and regard the interim in his marriage, between his leaving Natalia in Copenhagen and rejoining her in Stockholm, as though it had never occurred.

On Monday the 20th Roger received the despatch for Mr. Pitt from King Gustavus and took his final leave. Natalia, with a mountain of baggage that she had collected from the Russian Embassy, was already safely aboard the sloop, and that afternoon they set sail for Copenhagen, arriving at the Danish capital on the evening of the 23rd.

That night Roger presented his wife to his father, and the three of them supped together in the flagship. Natalia was on her best behaviour and the Admiral swiftly won her favour by the gallantry with which he treated her; so the meeting passed off very pleasantly. It was agreed that as Roger was the bearer of a Royal despatch he should take the sloop straight on to London; then, before they parted, the Admiral took him aside to tell him that he could well afford to increase his allowance to six hundred a year, and would be very happy to do so.

Natalia's father had given her five thousand roubles before leaving Stockholm, as well as turning over to her all the plate, china and linen that he had there, and Roger still had intact the five hundred pounds that he had recovered from Lord Carmarthen, so they now had ample resources to set up a home in reasonable comfort. Roger's earlier fears on that score being happily dissipated, they were able to spend many intriguing hours on the voyage home discussing their future plans; for, on leaving Copenhagen, the sloop was beset with contrary winds which, while of no great violence, considerably delayed her passage, and she did not arrive in the Thames until the morning of March the 1st.

By two o'clock, having left their baggage to follow them, Roger and Natalia reached Amesbury House. Droopy Ned was not at home, but his portly father, the Marquess, assured Roger that he was delighted to be the first person to welcome Natalia to London, and pressed them to stay at Arlington Street until they had made all arrangements for a home of their own.

When they had partaken of sherry and biscuits, Lord Amesbury said that perhaps they would like to go upstairs and rest for a while before joining the family for dinner, to which Roger replied:

"I was just about to ask if I might leave my wife in your Lordship's care until this evening; as I have a letter for Mr. Pitt and must ride down with it to Holwood."

"And why, pray, should you take it there?" the Marquess asked, with a lift of his bushy grey eyebrows.

" 'Tis from King Gustavus, my lord; so cannot be forwarded by the post, and brooks no delay."

"But, since 'tis the middle of the week, I should be mighty surprised if you find Mr. Pitt at his Kentish home."

Roger bowed. "Perhaps then, your lordship can inform me where I am more likely to come upon him; for I had imagined that he would retire there on vacating Downing Street."

"What say you?" exclaimed the burly old nobleman; then he suddenly burst out laughing and began to slap his thigh. "Egad! But this is rich! How it will make 'em laugh at White's. 'Tis clear that the news had not reached Copenhagen before you sailed from thence, and that you still know nothing of it."

"I've heard naught out of London since seeing King Gustavus on the 17th of February." Roger smiled. "But I pray you enlighten me, for it sounds as if the news were good."

"Aye, 'tis the best, lad! The best that England ever had! 'Twas on that very day that the leeches declared our good King sane again, and unlikely to suffer a relapse. Half those scallywags at Brook's are being dunned by the bailiffs, for the money they borrowed in anticipation of the loot that they'll now never get; while young Billy Pitt, from his championing the rights of the helpless King, is become the idol of the nation, and more firmly seated in the saddle than was even his great father after all his victories."

Roger jumped to his feet, his eyes shining. "Then the Regency Bill never went through—never became law?"

"Nay. Had it done so, and the Prince once assumed power, it might have proved plaguey difficult to wrest it from him again. But the country was saved from its impending fate by a matter of hours. The Bill passed the Commons, and was actually before the Lords; but b y

343

mid-February it was known that His Majesty had not suffered an attack for some time. On the 17th even the Whig doctors could no longer maintain their refusal to add their signatures to a bulletin declaring him convalescent; and on the 19th the Lord Chancellor adjourned the debate as no longer in the national interest."

Lord Amesbury stood up, clapped Roger heartily upon the shoulder, and added: "Now, lad! Get you along to Downing Street with that letter; and give my respects to the greatest Englishman of us all."

An hour later Roger was with the Prime Minister, who accepted his joyful congratulations in the placid manner that rarely left him. With his quiet smile, he said:

" 'Twas a devilish near thing, and a nerve-racking time for us all; but from Dr. Willis's being called into consultation I was always hopeful of His Majesty's eventual recovery. That it should have come about so quickly, is one of those things which gives us good cause to believe that God ever extends a protecting hand over Britain in her direst extremities. For myself, I now know more clearly than I did who are my true friends; for many that I thought so went over to the enemy. But I have been greatly touched by the support and loyalty of others; and I set a very high value, Mr. Brook, upon the attachment that you showed me."

Roger reddened with pleasure, and, producing King Gustavus's despatch, handed it over.

As he took it, and slit the top of the envelope with a paper knife, Pitt remarked: "Have you opened this? The seal appears to be damaged."

"Indeed no, Sir," Roger exclaimed, and looking over he saw that the big red seal bearing the Royal arms of Sweden was cracked across its lower segment.

"I trust no one else could have done so," the Prime Minister said after he had scanned the first page of the letter. "For this impetuous, intriguing King writes fiery stuff, and 'twould be highly embarrassing both for him and us had any unauthorised person seen it."

"It never left my person, Sir. I'll swear to that."

Pitt shrugged. "In that case think no more of it. The seal must have become cracked through some pressure that it met with through being carried in your pocket."

After a moment he laid the letter down, and went on. "For the time being we have done all that we can do in the North; and, in my opinion, for some months to come we shall have no further worries from that quarter. As I told you early in February, France has again become the centre of European interest. The people are becoming ever more insistent that a States-general should be summoned for the ventilation of well-founded grievances. King Louis's advisers are strongly opposed to surrendering to the public clamour; so if he is forced to give way it may mean the beginning of the end of the monarchy. Are you willing to return to France and ascertain for me what is likely to be the outcome of these bitter antagonisms, which now threaten to provoke a bloody revolution there?"

Roger hesitated only a second. "I would like to do so, Sir. But I am now married. Would there be any objection to me taking my wife with me?"

"None, as far as I am concerned. I trust you will be very happy. How much you decide to tell Mrs. Brook of your real business I must leave to you. But if she is a lady of your integrity and wit, she may prove of considerable assistance to you in your mission."

"I thank you, Sir." Roger bowed. "Naturally I shall be discreet on special matters, and with regard to those for whom I am acting. At your convenience I will wait upon you for further instructions."

Standing up he took his leave, very well pleased with himself. The past few months had brought him much closer to his kind but un-effusive master. He had done good work and gained much valuable experience in his northern travels. He had ample funds to go on with, and his future in this fascinating game of ferreting out the secrets that moved nations to war or peace was now assured. Moreover, he had permission to tell Natalia Andreovna enough about his work to prevent her becoming unhappy and suspicious on account of it; and he felt that the sharing of this new interest would create a strong bond between them.

He had just reached the door when the Prime Minister called him back with the remark: "By the by! Did you not tell me, Mr. Brook, just before I sent you to Russia, that you had been a member of the house-party at Stillwaters, during the week-end that Sir Humphrey Etheredge met his death?"

"Why, yes, Sir!" Roger replied in surprise.

Pitt nodded. "I thought as much. Since you have only just returned from abroad, it may be news to you that Lady Etheredge is now on trial for her husband's murder."

CHAPTER XXIII

THE SHADOW OF TYBURN TREE

I T was just four o'clock when Roger walked dazedly out of the door of No. 10. The Prime Minister had been most distressed on seeing the shock that his announcement had caused, but he could give Roger no detailed information. He explained that his mind was always so occupied with Parliamentary business that he had not the leisure to follow proceedings in the criminal courts; and would not even have heard of the matter, had not the fact that a celebrated beauty stood accused of murdering her husband caused an unusual stir in the fashionable world.

Pitt's brain, so agile in debate and so brilliant when required to provide a cold, logical analysis, seemed suddenly to become benumbed when called on to offer sympathy to a friend stricken by a personal tragedy. Awkwardly, he had protested that he would never have broken the news so abruptly had he known that Roger and Georgina were such close friends, then patted Roger's shoulder and offered him a glass of port. Roger had declined and hurried away, now seized with a terrible urge to know the worst.

On the corner of the street a row of sedan-chairs was plying for hire. It struck him that, if the chairmen could be induced to keep at a trot, this offered a swifter means of getting through the narrow, congested streets than taking a coach; so, picking the two most stal-wart-looking bearers, he promised them half-a-guinea if they could get him to Colonel Thursby's house in Bedford Square in a quarter of an hour.

Inspired by the high reward, they set off at a run, and as Roger was jogged along he endeavoured to fight down his terrible appre-hensions. If Georgina had been accused and brought to trial that could only be Sir Isaiah Etheredge's doing. Evidently, as Colonel Thursby had feared, the new Baronet bitterly resented being deprived of the bulk of his inheritance through Georgina's marriage-settlement, and was endeavouring to recover it by getting her out of the way. But what evidence could he possibly have?

Georgina and Roger himself were the only people who knew the real truth as to how Humphrey Etheredge had died. Colonel Thursby suspected it and so did Count Vorontzoff. It was certain that the former would never even have hinted at anything which might have brought his beloved daughter into such a ghastly situation; but the Russian Ambassador might have done so. Yet even he could provide no proof. He might have recanted his statement that the midnight message which had brought Sir Humphrey to Stillwaters in the dawn had been inspired by Georgina as an April Fool's Day joke, and thus thrown dis-credit on the rest of her story; but, apart from that, anything he might say could be based only on surmise.

As the sedan was carried across Oxford Street by the perspiring chairmen, Roger came to the conclusion that this terrible thing could have come about only through Sir Isaiah and Count Vorontzoff having plotted together to destroy Georgina. The vindictive Russian must have allowed his rancour at Georgina's treatment of him to overcome his apprehensions of Roger's threat to kill him if he talked. Roger bared his teeth in a mirthless grin, at the thought that Vorontzoff had made a mistake that was going to cost him his life. That would be no con-solation if Georgina lost hers; and Roger knew that he, too, might now soon end his days swinging from a rope on Tyburn Tree; but he was determined that, before he did so, he would send the Russian on into the valley of the shadows ahead of him.

At Colonel Thursby's house the chair pulled up with a jerk. Roger jumped out, paid the men their money, and hammered on the front door. The footman who answered it told him in a subdued voice that the Colonel was not at home, as he was attending her ladyship's trial at the Old Bailey; but that the court rose at four o'clock, so he should be back quite shortly.

Roger said that he would wait, and was shown into a small sitting-room on the ground-floor. Impatient as he was for news he did not like to discuss the matter with the man; but he suddenly thought of Jenny and, having ascertained that she was in the house, asked that she should be sent to him.

Two minutes later Georgina's faithful maid appeared; her pretty face was drawn and her eyes were red from weeping. At the sight of Roger she burst into a fresh fit of weeping and buried her face in her frilled apron. Roger quickly put an arm about her shoulders and gave her a friendly squeeze, as he said:

"Come, Jenny, m'dear. I know how you feel, but crying will not help her ladyship. I have been out of England these past three weeks and knew naught of this terrible business till half-an-hour ago. Tell me, I beg, how it all came about?"

"Oh, Mr. Brook, Mr. Brook," wailed Jenny. " 'Tis right glad I'd be to see you did I dare look you in the face. But should they take my sweet mistress away in the hangman's cart, 'twill be on account of my stupidity."

"Nay, Jenny, I'll not believe that," Roger said gently. "You were ever a good, loyal girl; and I'd go bail any day that you n'er did a thing that you thought might bring harm to her ladyship."

Her head still bowed, Jenny turned a little, grasped one of his lapels and clung to him pathetically. "Oh, bless you for them words, Mr. Roger, dear. You was ever a real gentleman—even when you were a little boy and me nought but nursery-maid to Miss Georgina. I'd have bit out my tongue before I'd have said it. I swear I would; but I'd not a notion they were setting a trap for me."

"But what did you say?" Roger pressed her. "And who set a trap for you?"

" 'Twas yesterday, the second day of the trial," she whimpered. "I was taken to the law-court and put into the box. I'd fain have gone the first day, to be near her ladyship; but they wouldn't let me. There she was, bless her heart, looking a little pale but as calm as though she was in her box at the opera; and when I curtsied to her she gave me a sweet smile. The Judge was in a red robe and all the lawyer-gentlemen were wearing wigs and gowns. One of them was a big red-faced man with bushy black eyebrows. After I'd kissed the Bible he asked me a lot of questions, and very nice to me he was, at first. He said that he expected that as a good maid I took pride in keeping her ladyship's things clean and tidy; and I said of course I did. He said he had no doubt that I could remember just how many dresses her ladyship had, and what colours they were, and I told him, yes, to that too.

"Then—then he asked me to describe her bedroom at Stillwaters. At that I looked across at her ladyship and she nodded to me, so I did as I was bid. After that the gentleman asked about her ladyship's cosmetics, and what brushes and things she kept on her dressing-table. 'Twas not for me to say I thought that no business of his; and after telling him that I kept all her pots and jars in a special cabinet, I gave him the particulars he wanted. He made me repeat them, then he asked about the ornaments on the mantelpiece and the chest-of-drawers. At length he came to her bedside-table, and wanted to know what was kept on that. I told him her candle and night-light, one or two books and a big cut-glass bottle of scent."

Roger stiffened, drew in a quick breath, and said: "Yes, go on, Jenny."

She began to sob again. "He—he made me repeat that. Then—then he went back to the dressing-table and asked me if I had ever seen that particular scent-bottle on it; and—and I had to admit that I hadn't. I—I knew that I'd said something I didn't ought by then. But he'd become fierce and hor-horrible. He banged his fist on the edge of the box where I was standing and glowered at me as—as if he meant to strip my soul bare. Suddenly he—he pulled the bottle out from under his gown and thrust it within an inch of my face. He—he—he made me swear it was that bottle and no—no other; and that I'd never seen it anywhere except—except beside her ladyship's bed."

The grim significance of poor Jenny's evidence was already clear to Roger. To account for the reek of scent from Sir Humphrey's clothes and the bottle being found at the foot of the bed, Georgina had led everyone to believe that he had knocked it off the dressing-table with his whip, then fallen in the pool that the liquid had made on the floor. But the place where he had collapsed was a good twelve feet from her bedside-table; so, if it had been knocked from there he could not possibly have rolled in the spilled scent. The inference was damnably plain. She *must* have thrown it at him.

* * * * *

Roger was still endeavouring to comfort Jenny when Colonel Thursby came in. He seemed to have aged ten years since Roger had last seen him. After the briefest greeting, the housekeeper was summoned to take charge of Jenny, and the two men went upstairs.

"I landed from Sweden only after mid-day, Sir," Roger said, as soon as they were alone, "and learned of this ghastly business less than an hour ago. 'Tis beyond words terrible."

The Colonel slumped into a chair. "It is indeed! This is the third day of the trial. The final speeches for the prosecution and the defence were made this afternoon, and no sane man could doubt that the balance of evidence is heavily against us. To-morrow morning the judge will sum up. Somehow I must bring myself to listen to the cold logic he will employ; then await the verdict. But I already know what it will be. And there is nothing more that I can do."

On learning that the situation was now so desperate, Roger's heart was gripped by a fresh horror. But it was clear that if anything could still be done to save Georgina it lay with him to do it; for the Colonel was at the end of his tether. Going over to a side-table, he poured out a wineglass full of brandy, brought it over to the distraught father, and said:

"All is not yet lost, Sir. Thank God I got back when I did. To-morrow morning we will ask the Court to hear fresh evidence. I will go into the box and declare that, hearing the noise of an altercation in Georgina's bedroom, I ran in, and, on seeing Sir Humphrey hit her with his whip, I struck him dead."

Colonel Thursby took a gulp of brandy, coughed, and shook his head. " 'Twould be useless, Roger. I've never doubted your willingness to shoulder the blame for what occurred; but to attempt to do so now would be only to sacrifice yourself without saving her."

"It has always been my belief that 'twas my blow upon his heart that killed him. I cannot stand by and let her—let her pay the awful penalty for my act."

"Nay. We must endeavour to put a check upon our natural feel ings and, however hard, try to regard the matter dispassionately." The Colonel closed his eyes wearily, then went on after a moment: "None of us know, and no one will ever know now, what actually caused his death. It may have been your blow; it may have been the scent-bottle that Georgina threw at him. Again, neither injury need necessarily have been sufficiently serious to prove fatal. It may be that exhaustion and rage had so wrought upon his brain that before he was struck by either fist or bottle he was already beyond escaping an apoplexy."

"I know it," moaned Roger. "I know it! But the fact that either or neither of us may be guilty of his death cannot, from what you say, save one of us from being brought to book now. And, if so, I am determined that it shall be myself."

"Were it possible for you to take her place I would be hard put to it to dissuade you from doing so," the Colonel sighed. "God knows, 'twould be a frightful choice of evils; only the fact that I love her better than aught else in the world would force me to countenance it. But you have yet to hear my point. No one but you, I and she are aware that you struck him, or even that you were with her when he died."

"Count Vorontzoff saw the weal that Sir Humphrey's lash left on my hand. He told Georgina so; and of his conviction that her husband died as the result of a brawl at which I was present."

"No matter. No one else appears to have noticed the mark, and it has long since disappeared. Vorontzoff has said nothing of it and there is not a shred of evidence against you. On the other hand, alas, it is now proven beyond doubt that Georgina threw the bottle. Had you afterwards run your sword through Humphrey Etheredge's body and left it there as a mark of your identity, 'twould still make no difference to the case that has been established against *her*. They could hang you with her, but 'twould not save her from—from the gallows."

Roger mopped his face. "I—I see your reasoning, Sir. Yet I cannot let her face this—this dread ordeal alone."

" 'Tis her wish, my boy; and you would but add to her burden did you do otherwise. Each time I have been to see her, knowing so well what your attitude would be, she has thanked God that you were still abroad and so could not be called upon to give evidence. At her most earnest request I have done everything possible to prevent your being associated with the case. Your name has scarce been mentioned in it, and then only on a par with those of Charles Fox, Lord Edward Fitz-Deverel, and others who were of the house-party. If you are determined upon it 'tis still within your power to commit suicide. For that is what a confession from you would now amount to. But 'tis idle to imagine that such an act would benefit Georgina. In fact it would deprive her of her one consolation; the thought that you have been spared from sharing her fate."

"Then, since I cannot save her, I must submit to her wish in this," Roger muttered. "Yet I cannot sit here idle and let events take their course. There must be *something* we can do. I pray you tell me how this frightful thing came about?"

The older man sipped his brandy. "We had no inkling of what was afoot until we returned from abroad. Had Jenny or my man Thomas remained at home 'tis certain that they would have written to give us warning that an inquiry was being made; but both of them accompanied us on our travels. Stillwaters was left in the care of the steward, Tobias Wenlock, an old servant of the Etheredge family. I kept him informed of addresses which would find us, in case of fire or any other calamity; but he remained silent on this matter; being, as I have since learnt, under pressure from Sir Isaiah."

"I guessed this to be his work," murmured Roger.

The Colonel nodded. "It seems that directly he learned of Humphrey's death he returned hot-foot from Jamaica, and went down to Stillwaters to ascertain particulars of his nephew's sudden demise. The coroner's report can have told him nothing, but, as transpired in court on Monday, the doctor gave him details of the bruise over the heart, the cut on the temple and the scent-splashed clothing. On this Sir Isaiah applied for an order to exhume the body and, as next of kin, obtained it. The bruise, of course, was no longer discernable; and later it was accounted for by the very explanation I had given myself, or near enough to it; for it transpired that Humphrey had been kicked in the chest the day before he died, just before mounting that brute of a horse that he took to Goodwood. But at the new post-mortem it was found that the bone beneath the cut on Humphrey's temple had been fractured.

"The servants at Stillwaters were then questioned and Georgina's room examined. The housemaid who cleaned the room gave evidence on Monday that, on the first occasion she did so after Humphrey's death, she found no trace of hair or blood on the bed-posts or nearby furniture, which would suggest that his head had come into violent contact with anything as he fell. And, in fact, while a man might stun himself and suffer an abrasion of the skin by his head striking a piece of wood a glancing blow, 'tis difficult to believe that on falling limp he would actually crack his skull in such a manner.

"After the housemaid, John Gower, one of the footmen who carried Humphrey's body from the room, gave evidence. On picking up the feet of the corpse he had noticed the scent-bottle lying just beneath the valance at the foot of the bed. It was this emerging at the man's first questioning by Sir Isaiah that must have made him believe that he was getting near the truth, and had enough evidence to bring a case. Every witness had confirmed the almost overpowering reek of scent in the room, so that must have come to Sir Isaiah's notice early in his inquiry.

"When he had dredged every source at Stillwaters he called on all the members of the house-party; and I fear that George Selwyn said much more than he need have done. 'Twas certainly not from any malice against Georgina, but from his absorbing interest in all forms of death. In the box on Monday he gave his evidence with reluctance, but he substantiated many points; particularly the fact that it was Humphrey's head and shoulders which were drenched with scent, so he could hardly have become so soused through falling in a puddle of it; and he corroborated the statement of Vorontzoff as to the exact position in which the bottle was found."

"What attitude has the Russian taken in all this?" Roger asked, with an edge upon his tone.

"He has proved no friend to us," replied the Colonel. "Of that I am convinced. On Tuesday morning, having waived his status as Ambassador, he gave evidence. He stood by his original story, that the note he sent to Humphrey at Goodwood was inspired by Georgina's desire to make her husband an April Fool, and not knowing Georgina as well as you and I, everyone appears to believe him. In all other matters his conduct has been most correct. He has confirmed various pieces of evidence where he could hardly do anything else, but has refrained from mentioning you or otherwise blackening the picture, as he could have done had he chosen to infer all that he either knows or suspects. Yet, from various facts which have emerged in the evidence of others, I am convinced that, privately, he must have given Sir Isaiah a number of pointers towards Georgina's guilt that her accuser would otherwise have missed."

"I threatened to kill him," Roger announced, "if he let his tongue run away with him. So it seems that despite my absence abroad he is still anxious to give me no open proof that he has taken this opportunity to be revenged upon Georgina."

"If the worst befalls, 'twill not be on account of anything that he has said, but owing to the cross examination of poor Jenny. 'Twas her evidence, that in her knowledge the scent-bottle had never been kept anywhere but beside Georgina's bed, which makes it beyond doubt that she must have thrown it."

"Could it not have been pleaded that she did so in self-defence?"

"We considered such a course," said the Colonel, "and I put a hypothetical case to Counsel, but he advised against it. Had Georgina done so in defending herself against anyone but her husband she would have been accounted justified. But this was no case of a woman defending her honour; and in English law a wife is still her husband's chattel. Whether a wife be good or bad he is within his rights to give her a beating at any time he may feel so inclined. Had Humphrey threatened to kill her, that would have been different; but there is not the faintest suggestion that, at any time, he had meditated an attempt upon her life. The legal view is that no husband would be safe were a wife permitted to retaliate for a beating by snatching up some possibly lethal weapon; and that for a wife to kill her husband so, is one of the most heinous forms of murder."

* * * * *

For another hour they talked round and round the ghastly *impasse* from which it seemed there was no way to rescue the woman for whom they both felt so deeply. Then Roger said: "I see only one line as yet untried. From all you tell me no suggestion has so far been put forward that Sir Humphrey Etheredge had gone insane some time before he died. If it could be shown that Georgina believed him mad, and feared that he meant to kill her, she would have been justified in taking any steps she could to save herself."

"That means she would have to confess to having thrown the bottle and having consistently perjured herself these past three days."

"I know it. But if we succeed in making our case we can save her from the ultimate penalty. The charge would still be nothing less than manslaughter and perjury, but she would get off with transportation for life."

"Bless you, my boy!" the Colonel started up, clutching at this straw. "I would go with her, wherever she was sent. Anything would be better than what she faces now—anything!"

"But we need time for this," Roger hurried on. "We'll have to rake up all the excesses of Sir Humphrey's past and brief Counsel on entirely new lines. In fact, it virtually means asking for the case to be retried."

Colonel Thursby sank back with a groan. "Nay. I fear that after all 'tis useless. The judge would never grant an adjournment at this stage, unless we could produce at least some evidence in support of our new line of defence. Could we but bring a doctor into court to-morrow morning to swear that he had noticed signs of insanity in Humphrey, we should be given time to collect proof that he was really mad. But we cannot. Neither, were we granted the time, could we collect the proof. If drinking like a fish and reckless riding are to be accounted signs of lunacy, then half the squires in England would be chained to the walls of Bedlam."

"In Sir Humphrey's case 'twas not excessive drinking and hard riding alone," Roger persisted. "Towards the end his mind was definitely affected. He had a mania that Georgina was making a fool of him, and when he burst into her room he acted like a madman. I'll swear to that."

"You cannot, without revealing your presence there."

"I'll do so then. I would venture anything on a chance that Georgina's sentence may be transportation rather than a hanging."

The Colonel wrung his hands. "Oh, Roger, my boy, I know you would; and all my instincts urge me to let you make the attempt. But 'tis now that I must strive to keep a level head for both of us. Do you not see that even if the judge granted an adjournment, at the end of it we'd still have no solid evidence that we could bring to establish Humphrey's madness. Then, when the case reopened, your part in this affiair would be uncovered by the prosecution. You would find yourself in the dock beside Georgina. As two lovers accused of doing her husband to death between you, what chance would either of you stand?"

"None, I fear," agreed Roger miserably.

For a few moments they sat silent, then he burst out: "Yet, by hook or by crook, an adjournment we must get. Even in a week much could be done. We could find ways and means to throw discredit on the prosecution's witnesses. We could create a belief that Georgina went in terror of her husband, even if we have to bribe fresh witnesses of our own to say so. We could engage new Counsel to present the defence from a different angle. But all these things need time—time— time!"

" 'Tis the same thought that has haunted me these past three weeks," sighed the Colonel. "Yet, had I had longer, I know not what more I could have done; or even now if these measures you propose would prove effective. They sound so simple, but I fear you would find them far from easy of accomplishment."

Roger suddenly snapped his fingers. "I have it! I will go to the Prime Minister. As the King's first representative he must surely have the power to order the adjournment of a trial for a week."

Colonel Thursby did not seek to dissuade him. His own belief was, that although the Royal prerogative enabled the King to pardon a convicted person, if he wished, not even he had the right to stay the course of British justice once it was set in motion. Yet the Colonel, worn out as he was himself, could still sympathise with Roger's terrible urge to take some form of action, and thought it better that he should set out on a futile errand than remain inactive at the mercy of his heartrending thoughts.

Grabbing his hat and cloak, Roger promised that he would come back as soon as he could, and ran downstairs. As there was no hackney coach in sight, he dashed round to the mews at the back of the house, shouted for his old friend Tomkins, the Colonel's coachman, and told him to harness a pair of horses to a carriage. By half-past six he was back in Downing Street.

His luck was in to the extent that the Prime Minister had just finished dinner and was about to go across to the House, so consented to give him a few minutes before leaving, but there it ended. Pitt was gentle but adamant.

He said that if Roger was dissatisfied with the course that the case had taken, that alone, as a member of the public, gave him no right whatever to intervene. If he had private knowledge of the circumstances in which Sir Humphrey Etheredge had met his death, then it was his duty to disclose it. As far as he, the Prime Minister was concerned, even with the best will in the world, he could not instruct a judge to adjourn a case upon which he was already sitting. The only means by which an adjournment could be secured was by an application to submit fresh evidence before the judge ordered the jury to find a verdict.

"Fresh evidence!" "Time!" "Fresh evidence!" "Time!" were the words that hammered like the loud ticking of a clock in Roger's overwrought brain. How, without worsening Georgina's desperate position, by making it public that she had had a lover with her in her bedroom who had helped to bring about her husband's death, could he produce the one and secure the other?

Suddenly he saw that there was only one person in the world who, if he chose, could stave off the apparent inevitability of the judge donning the black cap and pronouncing the death sentence on Georgina the following morning. It was Vorontzoff. His enemy had been the first to arrive in the room and find Georgina kneeling by her dead husband's body. If he could be cajoled, bribed or bullied into retracting the evidence he had already given, and making a fresh statement, the situation might yet be saved.

For a further ten minutes Roger talked to Pitt, asking his advice on the legal aspects of certain courses which might be pursued. With some reluctance Pitt agreed that one of them was worth attempting; then he added:

"To approve what you have in mind is not consonant with my status as a barrister-at-law, and even less so with my functions as a Minister of the Crown. Yet, from what you tell me, I realise that you are driven to this extremity out of an attachment which combines the highest feelings of a brother, friend and lover. In such a case I cannot find it in myself to put a restraint upon you. Officially, I must know nothing of this matter, but as a friend I hope that you will succeed in your unorthodox endeavour to unveil the truth and establish Lady Etheredge's innocence."

*   *   *   *   *

Side by side they went downstairs to their respective carriages. Britain's great Prime Minister, sitting stiff-necked and unbending, as usual, drove the short distance to the House of Commons; while Roger directed Colonel Thursby's coachman to Amesbury House.

For the past three hours he had not given a single thought to Natalia Andreovna. Now, as he walked up the steps of the mansion it struck him that on this, their first night in England, he would have once more to plead urgent business as an excuse for leaving her. But he was not called upon to do so.

On entering the drawing-room, where several members of the family and their friends staying in the house were assembled round a dish of after-dinner tea, the old Marquess told him that when they had finished dinner, as he had not returned, Natalia had expressed a wish to take a drive round Piccadilly and the Parks to see them for the first time in the evening light. She had excused herself from accepting an offer that one of them should accompany her, on the plea that Roger would be disappointed if, during her first outing in London, anyone but himself showed her the sights. So, in order to indulge this whimsy of his foreign guest, the Marquess had sent for his second coachman, who spoke a little French, and told him to take her for an hour's drive round the town.

Roger's mind was too occupied with Georgina to give the matter anything but the scantiest thought. He inquired if Droopy Ned was at home and, on learning that he had not yet come in, excused himself and hurried up to his room.

There, he collected one of his pistols, loaded it, thrust it into the inner pocket of his coat, and, running down to the courtyard, told old Tomkins to drive him to Woronzow House in St. John's Wood.

It was now close on a quarter to eight and an unusually warm evening for early spring, but dusk was already obscuring the vistas as he drove up the splendid new thoroughfare of Portland Place and out into the country. For the best part of a mile the way lay through farm lands, then they turned off the Hampstead Road and entered the shadows of a woodland glade.

During the drive Roger had had time to think out his plan of campaign. He felt certain that if he drove up to the front door of the Embassy, and sent in his name, Vorontzoff would refuse to see him alone, from fear that he meditated an assault. The proposition that he meant to put to the Ambassador was not, as he had led Pitt to suppose, that he should reveal certain facts that he had so far suppressed out of malice, but that he should go into court next morning and tell a lie to save Georgina's life.

Roger had argued to himself that Vorontzoff was as much responsible for Sir Humphrey Etheredge's death as either he or Georgina, in fact, more so; for had the Russian not sent his midnight messenger to Goodwood it would never have occurred. Therefore he must be persuaded that in common decency it was for him to avert the penalty from falling on another. If entreaties, and appeals to any sense of chivalry he might have, were not enough, Roger meant to threaten

355

him and, as he had disclosed to Pitt, in the last extremity, force him to sign a statement at the point of a pistol.

But any such conversation could not possibly be held in the presence of witnesses; and Roger did not wish his visit to the house to be known even to the Embassy servants, if it could possibly be avoided. So, when the carriage drew level with the end of the Embassy garden, he told Tomkins to pull up, and wait there until his return.

Leaving the road he walked round the corner of a wall that enclosed the garden from the wood, and along it for some twenty paces until he came to a wrought-iron gate. He had thought that he would have to climb the wall, but he was saved the trouble, as the gate proved to be unlocked. Having peered through it to make certain that no one was about, he slipped inside.

*   *   *   *   *

The house, a large, rambling, two-storied building, was about a hundred yards away, and almost concealed from where Roger stood by a belt of trees, beyond which lay an irregularly-shaped lawn with big ornamental trees growing round its edges. In the failing light the young spring green, which was just beginning to sprout from the earlier trees and bushes, was hardly apparent; but it served to thicken a little the cover afforded by the winter foliage.

Moving cautiously from tree to tree Roger made his way round the west side of the lawn towards the main block of the building. As he got nearer he could see that the ground-floor windows, three of which had lights shining from them, were raised a few feet above a low gravel terrace, on which stood two carved stone seats. The main block had two big bow-windows, each of which supported a separate balcony for the room above, and between them was a doorway with a flight of iron steps leading down to the garden.

Having reached the side of the house, which consisted of a slightly lower wing, he began to tiptoe along the terrace. Just before he came to the first of the lighted windows he crouched down, so as to bring his head below the level of the sill; then he lifted it and risked a quick peep inside. It was a dining-room, and two footmen were in there laying the table for supper. Crouching again, he tiptoed on.

Suddenly a bang and a rattle in his rear, caused him to start and quickly flatten himself against the wall; but it was only one of the footmen in the room he had just passed, closing the window and drawing the curtains for the night.

Creeping another few steps he arrived at the first of the big bow-windows. This too, had a light coming from it but not so brightly as from the other. Lifting his head again he peeped in through its lower left-hand corner. The room was a handsomely-furnished study and in it, with his back half-turned to Roger, a wigless man was sitting writing at a desk by the light of a solitary two-branched candelabra. It gave the only light in the room, and so accounted for its dimness, but light enough for Roger to identify the writer. That broad, muscular frame and bull-like neck could belong only to Vorontzoff.

Roger saw that of the three windows that formed the bay those at each side were both open at the top; so he had only to ease up the lower sash of the one nearest him to crawl inside. But the noise he would make in doing so was certain to attract Vorontzoff's attention; and the Russian might shout for help, or if he were armed, become master of the situation before his visitor could cover him with a pistol.

To see the Russian sitting there with his back turned, and only some panes of glass in between them, was, for Roger, tantalising in the extreme. At first sight it had seemed such a piece of good fortune that the mildness of the weather had led to several ground-floor windows being open; so it was doubly aggravating now to realise that he could not take advantage of that without giving his enemy the advantage over him.

It occurred to him that he could smash one of the window panes, thrust his pistol through it pointed at Vorontzoff's back, and threaten to shoot him if he called for help; then make him come to the window, raise its lower sash and admit his visitor himself. But there was a danger attached to such a proceeding. One of the servants might hear the smashing of the glass, and come running to see if his master had met with an accident. On consideration that seemed unlikely, so Roger decided to risk it. But, just as he was about to pull out his pistol, he saw the door of the room opening, and was forced to duck out of sight.

A moment later he stole a cautious glance. A footman stood framed in the doorway and was just ending a sentence in Russian. Vorontzoff replied abruptly in the same language, and stood up.

Roger gave them another thirty seconds, then peeped again. The footman was lighting the candles in the chandelier and Vorontzoff was on the far side of the room putting on his wig in front of a gilt-framed wall-mirror. After a slightly longer interval Roger snatched another look. Vorontzoff was just going out of the door and the footman was walking towards the window. Scared that the man would see him, Roger dropped down on his knees and crouched almost flat, to get below the angle of the man's glance if he looked out.

The shadows were thickening now and the heavy foliage of a big magnolia *grandiflora*, climbing up the side of the house, helped to obscure the place where Roger was kneeling. The footman shut one of the windows but ignored the other, then pulled the heavy curtains, cutting off any further chance of Roger seeing into the room.

He got to his feet and stood there listening intently for a moment. He could hear the man's footfalls as they crossed the parquet of the floor, then they faded away. Roger had no idea if Vorontzoff had come back into the room or not, but he felt that it was now or never.

Gripping the lower framework of the window which was still open at the top, he eased it up. It ran smoothly on its weights making little noise. When he had it open a couple of feet he put his hands on the sill.

kicked himself off the ground and, as quietly as possible, wriggled inside. Between the window and the fall of the curtain there was a space about a foot wide, and ample in which to stand up. Getting cautiously to his feet he listened again.

For half a minute he could hear nothing but the beating of his own heart, then he caught Vorontzoff's voice, distant but clear, speaking in French.

"This way, Madame. In my room we shall be able to talk at our ease."

A woman murmured something that Roger did not catch. There came the noise of footsteps on the parquet and people settling themselves in chairs, then Vorontzoff spoke again:

"His Excellency wrote to warn me that there was a prospect of my being able to welcome you here either this month or next. But there seemed some little doubt then whether you would be able to make the journey. I am delighted that you managed to do so, as I feel certain that you will be of the very greatest assistance to me in London."

"I am, I believe, exceptionally well placed to be so," replied the woman, with a little laugh; and Roger stiffened where he stood, for the voice was that of Natalia Andreovna.

*   *   *   *   *

"I gather that you are married to a young man in the service of the British Foreign Office?" Vorontzoff remarked, continuing the conversation in French; and Roger blessed the custom of educated Russians of rarely using their own language, except when addressing servants.

"Yes, Monsieur," replied Natalia. " 'Tis too long a story to tell in detail now. This is my first night in London, and I succeeded in slipping away from the mansion where he lodged me only on the pretext of wishing to see the city at sunset by myself. I will give you simply the bare outline.

"I believed my husband to be a Frenchman when he married me at the order of the Empress, in Petersburg, towards the beginning of last September; but a fortnight later he left me at a moment's notice, marooned in Copenhagen, on the plea of urgent business. 'Twas on doing so that he disclosed in a letter that he was really an Englishman; and that gave me furiously to think. While we were in Stockholm, where we first met, and later in Russia, his curiosity on the subjects of Her Majesty's Court and our foreign policy had been insatiable. Naturally I wondered if he had been making use of me to gain information, so I determined to wait and find out. Then, early in October I had a letter despatched by him from Gothenbörg. In it he told me that he would not be able to rejoin me for some time. To begin with I had been much attracted to him physically, but the attraction was wearing thin, as these things do, and there was a certain softness about his nature which at times repelled me; so I decided to wait no longer, but rejoin my father."

So *that* was the truth of the matter, thought Roger grimly. Her feelings for him had been on a par with his for her, all the time. What a fool he had been to go out to Stockholm and fetch her, when by leaving her there he might have been rid of her for good.

Vorontzoff had interrupted her to say: "Pardon me, Madame, but am I not right in supposing that your return to your father was dictated, partly at least, by the fact that you could not go back to Russia, owing to your having incurred the Empress's displeasure?"

" 'Tis true, your Excellency," Natalia admitted, "and as I have a great love for our country I took it hard. 'Twas in the hope that I might earn reinstatement in Her Majesty's good graces, that I suggested to my father making a rapprochement with my husband for the purpose of gaining possession of his secrets."

Roger had guessed as much already from this secret visit of Natalia's to the Russian Embassy; and he smiled to himself at the thought that pure chance should disclose her intention to him before she had even had an opportunity to begin her nefarious operations. But from this comforting belief he was rudely awakened, for she went on quietly:

"I have already accomplished a *coup* of which I am not a little proud. Before leaving Sweden King Gustavus entrusted my husband with a letter to Mr. Pitt . . ."

Roger's heart missed a beat. In his mind he saw again Pitt looking at the cracked seal of the letter. If a copy of it fell into Vorontzoff's hands that would be a major calamity. If Natalia had one it was essential that he should see what happened to it, so that he could retrieve it at the earliest possible opportunity. Very gingerly he moved a few feet to the right until he was behind two of the curtains where they overlapped. Raising his hand he drew the under one gently aside until there was a chink between them through which he could see a narrow strip of the room.

Meanwhile Natalia was still speaking. "In it, the ambitious Swede gives details of the campaign he intends to wage against us this coming summer; he also makes various proposals by which the expansion of Russia might be checked. On our voyage here, one night when my husband was half-asleep, I succeeded in getting it from the pocket of his coat. I pretended a faintness from lack of air, and told him that I meant to walk for a while on deck; but I took the letter to another cabin and made a copy of it. I have it here, and to give it to your Excellency without delay was my reason for risking this visit to you so soon after my arrival. But now I must get back. I have already been away over long. To avert suspicion I had to support being driven for an hour round the parks before I dared propose to Lord Amesbury's coachman that he should drive me out here to see my country's Embassy."

As she finished speaking Roger had just managed to part the curtains. He could not see Natalia, but he was in time to see her hand stretch out and lay the packet on Vorontzoff's desk.

"You have done well, Madame," the Ambassador purred, as he picked it up. "But tell me, this husband of yours, Mr. Brook. Is he not a tall, slim young man of handsome countenance with brown hair and very deep blue eyes?"

"Why yes!" Natalia replied. "Does your Excellency then know him?"

Roger had adjusted the crack between the curtains a fraction, so that he could now see Vorontzoff. The Ambassador had slit open the cover of the packet and taken out the sheets of paper it contained. It was clear that next moment he would begin to read them. Roger had been praying that before he did so Natalia would go, as he would then be able to hold up the Russian, get the letter from him, and afterwards proceed to the original purpose of this clandestine visit. But his hopes were clearly doomed to disappointment. At all costs Vorontzoff must be prevented from reading even a part of King Gustavus's letter and, somehow, Natalia must be got out of the house before she had a chance to give any information about its contents.

"Aye," murmured the Ambassador. " 'Tis the same man without a doubt. I won three hundred guineas from him at cards, nigh on a year ago."

"Indeed you did; and I took your Excellency for a ride in a wheel-barrow," said Roger quietly, as he stepped from behind the curtains, pistol in hand.

"Rojé Christorovitch!" exclaimed Natalia, springing to her feet. "So you—you followed me here?"

"Nay, Madame," he replied coldly. "Our meeting is entirely fortuitous, but none the less fortunate."

Although he spoke to her his eyes were on Vorontzoff. Levelling his pistol at the Ambassador's heart, he said:

"Your Excellency will oblige me by laying those sheets of paper down on this side of your desk and stepping back four paces. They are an illegal copy of a secret document addressed to the British Prime Minister. It is my duty to prevent you from reading them. If you refuse I intend to shoot you and, despite your status as Ambassador, I shall be upheld by my Government in having taken the only course possible in the circumstances. I mean what I say, and I will give you only five seconds to decide."

As Roger began to count, Vorontzoff's brown face went whitish round the mouth and eyes. He had not forgotten their old quarrel and the ruthless way in which Roger had threatened him in the ice-house. He had not the faintest idea that for the next twenty-four hours Roger actually set more value on his life and well-being than on his own; and his guilty conscience caused him to believe that the young Englishman had found out about the part he had played in giving Sir Isaiah Etheredge pointers which would assist in Georgina's conviction, so meant to take this opportunity to kill him.

The Russian was no coward, but he thought he knew death when he saw it approaching. As Roger counted three he shrugged his broad shoulders, refolded the sheets of paper and, leaning forward, laid them down on the far side of his desk.

From that instant everything seemed to move with startling suddenness.

*   *   *   *   *

Roger stepped forward to pick them up, but with a swish of her silken skirts, Natalia Andreovna ran in and snatched them from under his hand.

As he turned his pistol on her and demanded that she give them up, Vorontzoff grabbed a heavy paper-weight up from his desk and flung it at him.

The missile caught him on the ear, knocking him off his balance and half-stunning him for a moment. Before Vorontzoff could get round his desk to hurl himself on him, Roger had recovered sufficiently to jump back a pace and level the pistol at his head.

The Ambassador stopped dead in his tracks; but Natalia, the papers still clutched in her hand, was now running towards the door. Roger hesitated only an instant. He must catch her and get them back before she had a chance to secrete them somewhere about the house.

Thrusting Vorontzoff aside, he pelted after her, shouting: "Stop, damn you! Stop, or I'll shoot you." But she already had the door open and, ignoring his cries, dashed out into the hall.

The two footmen on duty were standing at its far end near the door of the vestibule. As she raced towards the stairs she screamed something at them in Russian. Instantly they sprang to life and ran at Roger.

Natalia was half-way up the semi-circular staircase when the three men met in a rush at the bottom. Roger had uncocked his pistol as he ran and, reversing it, now gripped it by the barrel like a club. His first blow with it caught one of the Russians on the side of the head and knocked him senseless. But the other grabbed him round the waist in a bear-like hug.

For a moment they swayed there, then Roger brought the metal-shod butt of his pistol down with all his force on the top of the man's white wig. With a groan he relaxed his hold and slid to the ground senseless.

Natalia was now up on the landing. Turning, Roger took the stairs three at a time in pursuit of her. Suddenly he heard Vorontzoff yelling in his rear: "Halt or I'll kill you! Stay where you are or you're a dead man!"

Roger had reached the curve of the stairs and had only to glance sideways to see the Ambassador ten feet below, now armed with a brace of pistols, both of which were pointing up at him. Ignoring the threat he leapt up another three stairs. There was a loud report and he was thrown sideways by a bullet smashing into the back of his left shoulder.

Swaying violently he mounted the last six stairs, just in time to see

Natalia dive through a doorway on the opposite side of the landing. The door slammed behind her, momentarily drowning the shouts of Vorontzoff and half a dozen servants who had come running into the hall at the sound of the pistol-shot.

Dashing across the landing, Roger flung himself against the door through which Natalia had disappeared. At the impact the wound he had received gave him a frightful twinge but the door yielded slightly, so he knew that she must be holding it shut by leaning against it. Stepping back a few paces he ran at it, bringing up his right foot so that it should strike the door flat, like a battering-ram.

The door gaped open eighteen inches and, thrown off her balance, Natalia fell to the floor on its far side with a scream. Before she could get to her feet, Roger had forced his way through and grasped her by the wrist of the hand that held the papers.

Struggling up she clenched her other fist and hit him with it in the face with all her strength. The blow landed on his right eye. For a second he saw stars and whorls of red fire. As he staggered back she tore her wrist from his grip and ran across the room to the window.

With a shake of his head, Roger recovered from the blow and went after her. In the darkness he collided with the end post of a bed and half-stunned himself. The check gave Natalia time to open the window. Darting through it she ran out on to the balcony and began to shout: "Here! Here! Count Vorontzoff! I have the letter! I'll throw it to you!"

Vorontzoff was no longer in the room below, as she thought, but crossing the landing as fast as his legs would carry him, followed hot-foot by his servants. Roger sprang across to the window and out on to the balcony. At the sound of his trampling feet Natalia turned and faced him. In a last effort to prevent his snatching the letter she held it high above her head and leaned right back over the ornamental iron balcony railing.

Roger stretched out his hand to grab her, but it met empty air. To avoid his grasp she jerked violently backwards. The rusty iron railing gave way under the shock and she went hurtling head over heels down to the terrace.

For a second Roger swayed above the abyss, within an ace of pitching after her. No sooner had he regained his balance than he heard the sound of his pursuers crashing through the room behind him. Desperately he cast round for a way of escape. To his right he suddenly caught a faint glint of the first starlight on the big, shiny leaves of the magnolia tree.

To gain the few moments needed to scramble out on to it he had, somehow, to give a temporary check to the pursuit. Turning, he re-cocked his pistol and fired it blind through the open window into the darkness of the room. Then, thrusting the still-smoking weapon back into his pocket he knelt down, seized a stout branch of the magnolia and swung himself off the balcony.

The branch bent and nearly gave under his weight; but before it could snap he managed to get a hold on the thick, twisted trunk that was set firmly against the wall. Each time he had to take a part of his weight on his left shoulder it pained him so greatly that he felt as though his arm was being torn from its socket. Gritting his teeth against the pain he managed to slither down, hand over hand, to the terrace.

White-faced and trembling, he looked round for Natalia. After a second he saw her. She had fallen upon one of the stone seats and hung, face down, doubled up across its back.

Hurrying over to her, he lifted her up and supported her against the back of the seat. Every breath of wind had been driven out of her body. She could not speak but in the starlight her green eyes glared defiance and hatred at him. The copy of the letter was still clenched in her right hand. Between agonised gasps for breath she made a last feeble effort to prevent his getting it; but he tore it from her and pushed it into his pocket.

Suddenly, as he strove to keep her from slipping to the ground, she was sick and vomited all over his feet. By this time Vorontzoff and his men had come out on to the balcony, and were peering down over the broken ironwork to see what was going on in the semi-darkness below them. The Ambassador levelled his second pistol and pulled the trigger; there was a crash, a spurt of flame and the bullet whistled past Roger's head.

A moment later, above the cursing of the men up on the balcony, he caught the sound of hurried footsteps on the gravel some fifty paces to his right. He guessed at once that the shouting and the shooting had reached the ears of the outdoor servants and that they were running from the stables. In another minute his retreat would be cut off. If he was to save the letter he had not a second to lose.

As he straightened himself Natalia broke from his grasp, turned, spat in his face, and staggered away up the iron garden steps to the house. That she had survived her fall of fifteen feet on to a stone seat appeared a miracle, but as she had fallen on her stomach, it seemed that she had not sustained any permanent injury.

As she stumbled away from him, Roger swung round, jumped off the terrace and ran across the lawn. Shouts, curses and the sound of pounding feet followed him, but fear of capture lent speed to his long legs. Outpacing the stable-hands he reached the iron gate with a good lead, wrenched it open and staggered through the fringe of wood to the road. Flinging himself into the waiting carriage he shouted to Tomkins to drive like hell back to Bedford Square.

* * * * *

While the carriage bowled along Roger tried to examine his wound; but as it was at the back of his left shoulder it was almost impossible for him to do so. It was very painful and he thought that the bullet had smashed his shoulder blade. He had lost a lot of blood and felt faint and dizzy.

His physical distress was only dominated by his mental agitation. The all-important project which had inspired his clandestine visit to the Russian Embassy had, as yet, not even been broached. Natalia's unexpected appearance there had prevented him from saying a single word to Vorontzoff about Georgina. Still worse, the ensuing fracas had now entirely shattered any prospect of a calm, straightforward conversation with the Russian, in which he might have been argued into assuming a share of the responsibility for Sir Humphrey Etheredge's death and coming to Georgina's rescue. And her only hope of escaping the rope lay in Vorontzoff being persuaded or forced into agreeing to do so before morning.

By the time the carriage had covered a mile Roger's brain had cleared a little, and he saw that the first thing he must do was to get his wound attended to; otherwise he would lose so much blood that he would be rendered *hors de combat*, and incapable of making any eleventh hour effort at all on Georgina's behalf.

When, some seventeen months earlier, he had fought his duel with George Gunston in St. John's Wood, they had had their hurts attended to by a Doctor Dillon. He was an Irishman and a drunkard, but he was a clever surgeon and knew how to hold his tongue; which was important in such matters, as duelling was strictly illegal. Roger remembered that Dillon lived in a cottage just off the Edgware Road, so he told Tomkins to drive there.

He had been in the precincts of the Russian Embassy for little more than half-an-hour, so it was still only a few minutes past nine when the carriage drew up outside Dillon's cottage. To his intense annoyance the Doctor was out, but his wife said that he was only round at the local tavern, and she would go and fetch him.

Roger made himself as comfortable as he could in the parlour and waited there with such patience as he could muster for a quarter of an hour. Then Mrs. Dillon returned to say that her husband had gone off with two friends to have a night-cap in some other haunt; but she felt sure that he would be back in an hour or so, and, in the meantime, if Roger would let her, she would dress his wound herself.

She was a hard-faced looking woman, and Roger recalled having heard it said that before her marriage she had first been a nurse, then a midwife who at times resorted to certain dubious practices; but if that was so it detracted nothing from her possible competence, so he agreed to submit himself to her ministrations.

After cutting away his coat and shirt she examined the wound by the light of a candle and said that she did not think that the bone was broken, but the ball might have lodged beneath it. Then she bathed the ugly gash, dressed it, and revived him after the ordeal by giving him a cup of hot, strong tea well laced with gin.

Roger knew that if there was a bullet in the wound he ought to have it removed as soon as possible, otherwise complications might set in; so, anxious as he was to be on his way, he must stay where he was till the Doctor returned, as Dillon was the only surgeon he knew who would undertake such a job without asking awkward questions.

It was past eleven when the Irishman came in, and when he did he was three-parts drunk, but he set to work with cheerful unconcern on Roger. The probing for the bullet was excruciatingly painful, but it proved to be there, and, after Dillon had fished it out, the cauterizing of the wound was equally agonising. For over half-an-hour Roger groaned and cursed while rivulets of sweat ran down his face, and several times he felt near to fainting. At last the gruelling business was over, his injured shoulder properly bandaged and his arm strapped firmly to his side; but, even then, the Doctor would not hear of his getting to his feet until he had had at least an hour to recover.

Having already been deprived of the opportunity of attempting anything further that evening, Roger did not feel that the loss of an extra hour round midnight would now make any material difference. While waiting for the doctor he had had ample time to review the situation, and he had come to the conclusion that it would be futile for him to try to see Vorontzoff again.

In the first place, after what had already occurred, the Ambassador would be extremely incensed against him and, in the second, he was now in no shape for further heroics. Therefore, he must get somebody else to go and talk to the Russian on the lines that he had meant to adopt himself; and the most suitable person for this delicate mission was clearly Droopy Ned.

Droopy had been at Stillwaters over the fatal weekend. He already knew most of the facts and could be told the rest, as he was entirely to be trusted. He was shrewd, diplomatic, and a person of sufficient prestige to secure an interview with Vorontzoff at any time, if he requested it on the plea of urgent business. The only possible alternative was Colonel Thursby, and Roger ruled him out as already so exhausted and overwrought by his daughter's impending fate, as temporarily to be lacking in the agility of mind and force of will necessary to bring Vorontzoff to heel.

Dr. Dillon insisted on seeing Roger home, so at one o'clock in the morning, they walked down the garden-path, got into the waiting carriage and told the patient Tomkins to drive to Arlington Street.

The moon was up, and five minutes later, as the carriage turned out of the Edgware Road into Oxford Street, they could see on the west side of the corner the three stout posts and their cross-beams that formed the gallows, standing out clearly against the night sky.

"Look at old Tyburn Tree," remarked the jovial Irishman. "I've seen many a good hanging yonder, and may the blessed St. Brigit preserve me to see many more."

Roger shuddered, but did not reply. Already the very sight of the gibbet had conjured up an awful vision in his mind. He could see his dear, beautiful Georgina hanging there; her head lolling limply on one shoulder, her dark curls hanging in disorder over her purple face; her flashing eyes dull and lifeless as they protruded blindly from their sockets, and her laughter-loving lips horribly swollen about a gaping, sagging jaw.

He knew that unless he could do something within the next few hours that nightmare vision would become an actual fact, and that, even if he gave his own life uselessly, no course must be left untried which might avert that grim reality.

At Amesbury House he shook hands with old Tomkins, asked him to take Dr. Dillon home on his way back to Bedford Square, and gave him a handsome tip. Then, bidding good-night to the Doctor he pulled the bell beside the big carved door.

The night-footman let him in and told him that Lord Edward had come home an hour before and gone straight to bed. Roger went up to Droopy's room and found him in bed, lying on his back and snoring loudly. All attempts to rouse him failed, so, much perturbed, Roger went downstairs and sent the footman to rout out Droopy's valet.

When the valet appeared he said that his master had been much worried by the course that Lady Etheredge's trial had taken. He had been present at each session and given evidence himself on Tuesday. After the adjournment which had taken place on the previous afternoon, he had gone to Lincoln's Inn to consult the Counsel who were defending her ladyship, in the hope that a conversation with them would produce some hopeful aspect of the case. He had returned greatly depressed at half-past seven, and on learning that Roger had arrived in London, went out again to try to find him at White's Club, Colonel Thursby's, and various other places to which he might have gone. He had been back twice after that to see if Roger had come in, and on his final return at midnight, had told his man that "he meant to sleep this night if he died of it"; then he had taken a large dose of one of his Eastern drugs and allowed himself to be put to bed.

Droopy's deep concern for Georgina was, Roger realised, mainly inspired by his friend's knowledge of his own attachment to her. He had obviously felt himself to be *in loco parentis*, even to the point of interviewing Counsel; but, as matters stood at the moment, that made it all the more exasperating that, only an hour before, he should have thrown his hand in and sought refuge from further anxiety in impenetrable oblivion.

Too late, Roger saw that if only he had not been in such a hurry to dash off to Mr. Pitt that afternoon the Marquess would have told him about Georgina's trial and Droopy's pre-occupation with it. Then, if he had waited until Droopy had come in they could have put their heads together, and things might have been in far better shape. As it was he could only ask the valet to come upstairs and help him to undress; then, when he had been propped up in bed, issue an imperative order that in no circumstances was he to be called later than six o'clock.

In spite of a distinct feverishness and the gnawing pain in his left shoulder, mental exhaustion carried him off to sleep quite quickly.

Yet when Droopy's man came to rouse him he felt that barely ten minutes could have elapsed since he had closed his eyes.

On looking in the mirror he saw that he had a black eye where Natalia had struck him, and he wondered if, apart from a black, blue and aching tummy, she was by now well on the way to recovery from the effects of her nasty fall. Then his mind snapped back to Georgina, and the fact that this was the fateful day upon which it must be decided whether her generous youth and vital loveliness was to be preserved as a joy to all who knew her, or soon be transmuted into a lump of senseless, ugly clay.

* * * * *

It took three-quarters of an hour for Droopy's man to get Roger into his clothes, adjust the sling round his arm, and make him as presentable as possible. Immediately this painful process had been accomplished, they hurried downstairs. Droopy still lay like a log and, for over an hour, defied all efforts to wake him.

They shook and slapped him; put an ice-compress on his head and poured the most fiery liquor they could find down his throat. The valet tickled the soles of his master's feet and Roger stuck pins in his arms, but still he lay impervious to this violent treatment, except for an occasional jerk, or a snort through his fleshy nose.

It was not until eight o'clock, after Roger had ordered a hip-bath to be brought in and filled with cold water, and had Droopy's limp form plunged into it, that he at last showed signs of returning consciousness. Then it took them another quarter of an hour of slapping his face, holding smelling-salts under his nose, and pouring black coffee into him to restore him to his full senses.

He took this arbitrary treatment with perfect good temper and only protested mildly that he was well-acquainted with the properties of the drug he had taken; and, that had he been left alone, he would in any case, have woken round about eight o'clock and been at the Old Bailey soon after nine to hear the judge's summing-up.

When he was stretched comfortably on his gilt day-bed with Roger seated beside him, the valet brought them up breakfast. Only then did Roger realise that he had not eaten since breakfasting with Natalia Andreovna in the sloop that had brought them home from Stockholm. Relays of food were sent for, Droopy cut the eggs, sausages, mushrooms and ham into mouthfuls, and between them, the now one-handed Roger spoke rapidly and forcefully of Georgina's frightful situation.

By a quarter to nine they had fully agreed on the only course of action which might still possibly save her, and leaving Droopy to complete his dressing as swiftly as he could, Roger hurried downstairs, got into a coach that he had already ordered, and drove to the Old Bailey.

The trial of a lady of fashion on a charge of murder had aroused great interest, so ghouls from the social world had vied with all the enthusiastic amateurs of crime in London to get places in the portion of the Court reserved for the public. As the Court was already sitting when Roger arrived he would have stood no chance at all of getting in, had it not been for his intimacy with Colonel Thursby. By bribery accompanied by alternate smiles and menaces he eventually succeeded in being conducted through the press to a seat beside the Colonel at the solicitors' table.

Georgina, dressed entirely in black and looking very pale but quite calm, and still strikingly lovely, was seated in the dock. The stir caused by Roger's entrance caused her to look round. The second her glance fell on him her eyebrows went up and her mouth opened as though she was about to emit a piercing scream. With an obvious effort she stifled it in her throat but made a swift gesture with her hands as if to say: "Go away! Please! Please! I beg you to go away from here."

He gave her a reassuring smile, sat down and looked round the Court. It was packed to capacity with row upon row of hard, avid, gloating faces. Few but those of the lawyers, the court officials and the double row of "twelve good men and true," in their jury-box, showed any trace of solemn decency.

The place had a dank, chill atmosphere, which was calculated to make a stranger to it shiver even on a summer's day. The floor was dirty and there was a subtly unpleasant smell which conjured up the thoughts of gaol-fever. Roger did not wonder that the judge held in his hand a paper-frilled posy of sweet-smelling flowers, and that learned Counsel occasionally sniffed at oranges stuffed with cloves.

The judge, an elderly, red-faced man, was addressing the jury almost tonelessly; yet, obviously, he felt that this was no clear-cut case of crude murder arising out of a proven hate or desire for gain, since he was taking great pains to present an unbiased analysis of the evidence that had been given by both sides.

Roger soon realised that had he not had such difficulty in getting into the Court he would have been in time to hear the opening of the day's proceedings, as it was apparent that the judge had only just started his summing-up. What length of time could be hoped for before he completed it, was the question which now agitated Roger's mind.

His final plan before going to sleep had been that Droopy should set off for the Russian Embassy soon after seven, so that he would have a full hour in which to argue with Vorontzoff and, if he was successful, be able to bring the Ambassador to the Old Bailey by the time the Court opened at nine. But Droopy's addiction to strange drugs had ruined all hope of that.

Now, even in his racing curricle, he could not have got out to Woronzow House before nine; he might be kept waiting anything up to a quarter of an hour before Vorontzoff was ready to see him, and it was hardly likely that it would take less than half an hour to induce the

Russian entirely to reverse his attitude towards Georgina; then they had to get from St. John's Wood to the Old Bailey, so, at the very best, it could not be hoped that they would appear there before ten.

If the judge was still summing up all would be well. Georgina's Counsel would be able to request permission to submit new evidence; but if the jury had been sent to consider their verdict the judge might rule that, since Vorontzoff had already given his evidence and the defence had had ample time to recall him if they wished, the minds of the jury must not now be influenced further in either direction.

What was to happen then? Or if Vorontzoff proved adamant and Droopy arrived alone to say that he had failed to secure the Russian's co-operation?

From time to time Georgina turned to look at Roger. Each time their glances met her black eyes said: "What stroke of ill-fortune has enabled you to appear here at this last moment? I beg you to remain silent! Say nothing! Say nothing!"

And Roger's solitary blue one, for the other was now almost closed in a great purple bruise, replied: "Courage, Georgina, courage! All is not yet lost. But if we have to swing, we'll swing together!"

Ten o'clock came and the judge was still talking. Roger had his watch out lying in front of him on the table. Every other moment he glanced at it and the long hand seemed to leap from minute to minute; five past, ten past, a quarter past, twenty past, twenty-five past. Still the judge was speaking, yet still the faces that Roger was so desperately anxious to see failed to appear among the crowd that packed the doorway.

At half-past Colonel Thursby leaned over and whispered in Roger's ear: "I think he is near through; and I doubt if our agony will be greatly prolonged by the jury."

Roger knew that he referred to the general tendency that the summing-up had taken. The judge had been scrupulously fair, but the dominant motif of his instruction to the jury was that—if they reached the conclusion that the cut-glass scent-bottle could have struck Sir Humphrey Etheredge upon the head only through the agency of the prisoner's hand, and that she had thrown it at him with deliberate intent to cause him an injury, then her act had resulted in wilful murder, and they would have no alternative but to return a verdict of "Guilty."

In his hour-and-a-half's review of the evidence those questions had been answered beyond further dispute, so it now seemed certain that the jury would be absent only for a few minutes before returning such a verdict. That was the thought in the Colonel's mind, and Roger would have given a very great deal to be able to give him some comfort, by telling him that he had dispatched Droopy Ned on an attempt to induce Vorontzoff to appear in court and make a fresh statement. But he dared not raise the distraught father's hopes, because he was far from certain that Droopy would succeed in his mission; as, however justifiable in this particular case, it would prove no easy matter to persuade the Russian to come into court and bear false witness. All Roger could do was to write a note and pass it across to Georgina's leading counsel.

At twenty-five to eleven the judge concluded his address, and he was just about to instruct the jury to retire to consider their verdict when Georgina's counsel rose with the note in his hand, and said:

"My lord. I crave your indulgence to produce a new witness. My excuse for not putting him in the box at an earlier stage of the trial is that he returned from abroad only yesterday. But he is a Mr. Roger Brook, whom your lordship will recall as having already been named in this case among the members of the house-party that has been the subject of this inquiry. I therefore submit that his testimony may prove highly relevant, and pray that your lordship will be pleased to hear him."

Georgina had come to her feet with a half-strangled cry. Leaning out of the dock she wrung her hands towards the judge and gasped imploringly: "I *beg* you, Sir, not to hear this gentleman! He can know nothing of the matter! Nothing!"

There was an excited rustle among the crowd, then the judge waved her sternly back to her seat and said quietly to counsel: "You may swear your witness."

* * * * *

As Georgina sank back on to her chair and burst into a flood of tears, Roger stepped up into the witness-box and was duly sworn. Then counsel for the defence asked him to tell the court anything that he could relating to Sir Humphrey Etheredge's death.

It was now a quarter to eleven. Roger's hopes that Droopy would arrive with Vorontzoff were fast diminishing. But as long as Droopy did not appear alone, to announce failure, there was still a chance that the two of them might make a belated appearance. So Roger meant to gain a little more time by giving irrelevant evidence to start with.

He thought that he might be able to keep it up for about a quarter of an hour, but by eleven o'clock Droopy would have had nearly an hour and a half in which to plead with and threaten the Russian, and if by eleven they were not in court, it could only be because Vorontzoff had proved adamant, and Droopy was too distressed at his failure to come and admit it.

In that case Roger had determined to make a clean breast of the whole affair, in the slender hope that the jury might disagree as to whether Georgina throwing the scent-bottle or his striking Sir Humphrey over the heart had been the real cause of death. Owing to the ensuing doubts as to which of them had inflicted the fatal injury they might get off with transportation for life, if not they would die as they had ived and go bravely side by side in the death-cart to Tyburn.

To begin with he spoke of his first meeting with Georgina. Of her lonely childhood and unhappy upbringing from the fact that all her neighbours in the county had ostracised her on account of her gipsy blood. The judge heard him patiently at first and then began to fiddle restlessly with his nosegay. Roger saw that he must soon come to more cogent matters, and was preparing to start on the story of the fatal week-end when there was a sudden stir in the doorway of the court.

With his heart in his mouth Roger stopped speaking and stared in that direction. To his bitter disappointment it was only a messenger, but the message was for him, and an usher brought it over to the witness-box.

Having asked the judge's permission he read it. The folded paper bore a scrawl by Droopy Ned which ran:

"When I reached the Russian Embassy I learned that Vorontzoff had already gone out, to spend the day at Richmond. I have gone after him."

Roger drew his hand across his eyes. This was too terrible. Everything still hung in the balance. Droopy might yet succeed in bringing the Russian to the Old Bailey, but, perhaps not for another hour or so. On the other hand Vorontzoff might refuse to come, so it was impossible to tell the judge that another witness was still being sought for. There was only one thing to do. Somehow he must spin out his evidence without finally committing himself until the very last possible moment.

It was eleven o'clock as he resumed his tale. He spoke of Georgina's unfailing generosity and of her kindness to her servants; then when he saw that the judge was getting restless again he brought in her strange gift of second sight, and managed to intrigue the court for some minutes by giving examples of it.

Where the minutes had flown during the judge's summing up they now seemed to drag interminably, and Roger had never realised before how many words had to be spoken to fill sixty seconds.

For some twelve minutes the judge listened to him without comment, then he suddenly coughed, and said: "None of this is relevant. The witness must confine himself to facts affecting the case."

Roger murmured an apology and was forced to start on the house-party at Stillwaters. On coming into court that morning he had felt ghastly. The torn muscles of his shoulder throbbed and nagged, seeming to thrust their pain down into his backbone and chest. His swollen eye felt as big as a cricket ball, and his head ached intolerably. But now, in the intensity of his effort to hold the interest of the court he forgot all his pains and injuries. He was a natural orator and an excellent raconteur, and as he described the house and guests it was clear that everyone in court was following the picture that he drew with the closest attention.

But by half-past eleven there was no more that he could say without getting to the meat of the matter. For a few minutes he attempted to hold his audience with an account of witty remarks that Fox and Selwyn had made over dinner, but the judge rapped sharply on his desk and said sternly:

"This is *not* material evidence. The witness is wasting the time of the court. He must come to the point or stand down."

Roger again apologised, then started to tell how they had played cards after dinner. But under the judge's disapproving stare began to falter, and it was still only twenty-five to twelve. He knew that he had reached the last extremity.

* * * * *

But there was just one more thing that he could try. He broke off what he was saying and asked the judge's permission to send a written note up to him. Consent was given and paper brought to him. On it he wrote:

My Lord,
I tender my humblest apologies, but I have been talking of irrelevant matters with the object of gaining time. A friend of mine is urgently seeking another witness who, if he will, can I believe, give fresh evidence which would prove the prisoner's innocence. I can make no promise that this witness will ever come into Court; but I beg you most earnestly to allow me to continue to occupy the witness-stand without further admonition until the Court adjourns for dinner. Should the witness not appear I then solemnly undertake to disclose all I know regarding Sir Humphrey Etheredge's death.

The note was passed up to the judge. Having read it he looked first at Georgina, then at Roger, and said:

" 'Tis obvious to us all that the witness is suffering considerable pain from his injuries. The time being twenty minutes to twelve, in order to afford him a respite, the court will adjourn for dinner twenty minutes earlier than usual. But I warn the witness that when he returns to the stand on our reopening the proceedings at one o'clock I will listen to nothing further from him except relevant facts."

As the judge rose Roger sighed his thanks and staggered half-fainting from the box.

A few minutes later he left a message with the porter on the door, to be given to Droopy in the event of his arrival, then he accompanied Colonel Thursby and his lawyers to a tavern across the street. After swallowing three gills of neat rum in quick succession he felt slightly better. He realised that he had performed a great feat in just talking out the time of the court and then securing an adjournment; but he also knew that his victory was only a temporary one. If Droopy and Vorontzoff did not appear by one o'clock the game was up.

But he was not doomed to be the victim of that consuming anxiety for much longer. Shortly after mid-day they did appear, and the Russian's demeanour was cold but courteous.

When the court reassembled, Georgina's counsel asked leave to place the Russian Ambassador in the box at once, as his evidence would render further testimony by Roger unnecessary.

Vorontzoff told the court through an interpreter that his second appearance there was occasioned by the fact that, as a foreigner, he had little knowledge of the workings of British justice. When he had given his evidence before he had been under the impression that although Lady Etheredge denied throwing the scent-bottle, if it was proved that she had, she would still be able to enter a plea of having done so in self-defence, and so secure her acquittal.

He went on smoothly to the effect that he had since been too occupied with his own affairs to follow the case, and it was only that morning, when Lord Edward Fitz-Deverel had come to him at Richmond, that he had realised that Lady Etheredge was in serious danger of being condemned to death for her act. This had caused him to take an entirely new view of his own responsibility in the matter.

He then confessed that previously he had omitted a part of the evidence he could have given, from a natural reluctance to disclose the fact that he had been spying on Lady Etheredge on the morning of her husband's death. Intrigued to learn the result of his own letter to Sir Humphrey he had risen early. He had heard the Baronet arrive and followed him to Lady Etheredge's room. The door having been left ajar he had peeped through the crack and actually witnessed the altercation. Sir Humphrey had raised his whip to strike his wife and, as he struck, she had thrown the scent-bottle at him. She had fainted as a result of the blow, but, although the bottle had caught him on the head, it had not even knocked him down. He had appeared a little stunned for a moment, then walked over to her washstand and bathed the cut on his temple. Therefore he obviously could not have died from the crack on the head, but must have been seized by an apoplexy a few moments later. Not wishing to be seen, Vorontzoff had then stolen away. He concluded his evidence by saying that had Lady Etheredge seen what he had, she would no doubt have told the truth about throwing the bottle, but her swoon had prevented her from knowing the comparatively harmless effect it had had, and finding her husband in a fit on the floor when she came to, she had obviously thought that to have been the result of her own act.

Roger sighed with relief. The Russian had told the story, almost word for word as he had briefed Droopy to give it to him.

The judge then instructed the jury that they should return a verdict of "Not Guilty."

A quarter of an hour later Georgina, Roger, Droopy Ned and Colonel Thursby were in the latter's coach heading westward. Georgina was holding Roger's hand and she squeezed it tenderly as she said:

"My dear, my sweet, my perfect knight. I can scarce yet believe it true. But tell us, I beg, how you worked this wondrous miracle?"

He laughed. "Did you not see Droopy hand Vorontzoff a piece of yellowed parchment as they left the court? 'Twas the Russian's fee for bearing false witness."

"I saw him do so," said the Colonel. "What was it, Roger?"

" 'Twas a letter that I stole whilst in Russia, Sir; the only evidence in the world that the Czarina Catherine murdered her husband. The Prime Minister said that it was useless to him as it could never be published, so last night I got it back from him to use as a bargaining-counter with Vorontzoff. Thank God he considered it his duty to buy it; for I was damnably afraid that he would be of the same mind as Mr. Pitt. And, had he been so, Georgina and I would have danced our last dance together on empty air."

"May it please God to spare you both for many years of joyous dancing yet," said the Colonel, with tears in his eyes.

"Or years of married bliss, for that matter," added Droopy Ned.

"Natalia!" exclaimed Roger, recalling for the first time in many hours that he had a wife.

Droopy shook his head. "Vorontzoff asked me to break it to you. As a result of her fall your wife died of an internal hæmorrhage in the early hours of the morning. He said, too, that since she lived as a Russian, and died as a Russian, he hoped you would agree to his sending her body back to Russia for burial."

"So you were married, Roger," Georgina whispered. "That was the wedding-ring that I saw in the glass. Then the whole of my prophecy came true."

"But he is married no longer," persisted Droopy mischievously.

Roger and Georgina looked at one another; then they both smiled and slowly shook their heads.

"Nay," she said with a little sob, and she squeezed Roger's hand until it hurt. "We'll not risk marriage; but in this life, and in all our lives to come, we will remain for ever friends."

*This book
designed by William B. Taylor
is a production of
Heron Books, London*

*Printed in England by
Hazell Watson and Viney Limited
Aylesbury, Bucks*